READER'S DIGEST
CONDENSED BOOKS

www.readersdigest.co.uk

The Reader's Digest Association
Limited 11 Westferry Circus
Canary Wharf London E14 4HE

For information as to ownership of
copyright in the material of this
book, and acknowledgments, see
last page.

Printed in France
ISBN 0 276 42739 4

READER'S DIGEST CONDENSED BOOKS

*Selected and edited
by Reader's Digest*

CONDENSED BOOKS DIVISION

THE READER'S DIGEST ASSOCIATION LIMITED, LONDON

CONTENTS

PUBLISHED BY MACMILLAN

PUBLISHED BY FOURTH ESTATE

THE ANALYST

John Katzenbach

The arrival of a threatening letter signed 'Rumplestiltskin' sends chills down Dr Starks's spine. Who *is* the mystery writer hell-bent on revenging a mistake that Starks supposedly made years ago? The analyst has just two weeks to find out. If he fails, he's told he must either kill himself or watch the destruction of his family. A tense page-turner about a man trapped in a nightmarish battle to outwit his tormentor.

PUBLISHED BY BANTAM PRESS

UNSCATHED

Major Phil Ashby

Throughout his young life, and especially during a distinguished career in the Royal Marines, Phil Ashby had tested his courage and resourcefulness to the limit. So a posting to Makeni in war-torn Sierra Leone, to assist a UN peace-keeping mission, seemed relatively straightforward. It wasn't. Before long Ashby and his colleagues found themselves under attack from hostile and ruthless rebels. A remarkable story of a real-life hero.

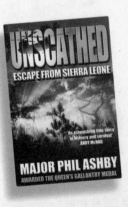

PUBLISHED BY MACMILLAN

HORNET

FLIGHT

KEN FOLLETT

In the summer of 1941 the war is not going well for the Allied Forces. The Germans seem to be able to anticipate the RAF's bombing missions, and MI6 intelligence analyst Hermia Mount suspects that the Germans may have perfected a radar system, but the evidence eludes her.

Then, from across the North Sea, from Nazi-occupied Denmark, comes a surprising message . . .

PROLOGUE

A man with a wooden leg walked along a hospital corridor.

He was a short, vigorous type with an athletic build, thirty years old, dressed in a charcoal-grey suit and black toecapped shoes. He walked briskly, but you could tell he was lame by the slight irregularity in his step: tap-*tap*, tap-*tap*. His face was fixed in a grim expression, as if he were suppressing some profound emotion.

He reached the end of the corridor and stopped at the nurse's desk. 'Flight Lieutenant Hoare?' he said.

The nurse looked up from a register. 'Last bed on the left.'

He turned on his heel and strode along the aisle to the end of the ward. In a chair beside the bed, a figure in a brown dressing gown sat with his back to the room, looking out of the window, smoking.

The visitor hesitated. 'Bart?'

The man in the chair stood up and turned round. There was a bandage on his head and his left arm was in a sling, but he was smiling. He was a younger, taller version of the visitor. 'Hello, Digby.'

Digby put his arms round his brother and hugged him hard. 'I thought you were dead,' he said. Then he began to cry.

'I WAS FLYING A WHITLEY,' Bart said. The Armstrong Whitworth Whitley was a cumbersome, long-tailed bomber. In the spring of 1941, Bomber Command had 100 of them, out of a total strength of 700 aircraft. 'A Messerschmitt fired on us and we took several hits,' Bart continued. 'But he must have run out of fuel, because he peeled off without finishing us. I thought it was my lucky day. Then we started to lose altitude. I realised the Messerschmitt must have damaged both engines and we'd have to ditch in the North Sea.'

Digby sat on the hospital bed, dry-eyed now, watching his brother's face, seeing the 1,000-yard stare as Bart remembered.

'I told the crew to jettison the rear hatch then get into ditching position, braced against the bulkhead,' Bart said. The Whitley had a crew of five, Digby recalled. 'When we reached zero altitude I opened the throttles, but the aircraft refused to level out, and we hit the water with a terrific smash. I was knocked out.'

They were half-brothers, eight years apart. Digby's mother had died when he was thirteen, and his father married a widow with a boy of her own. From the start, Digby had looked after his little brother. Both had been mad about planes and dreamed of being pilots. Digby lost his right leg in a motorcycle accident, studied engineering, and went into aircraft design, but Bart had lived the dream.

'When I came to, I could smell smoke. The aircraft was floating and the starboard wing was on fire. The night was dark as the grave, but I could see by the light of the flames. I crawled along the fuselage and found the dinghy pack. I bunged it through the hatch and jumped.'

His voice was low. 'I was wearing a life jacket and I came to the surface like a cork. Luckily, the dinghy pack was right in front of me. I pulled the string and it inflated. But I didn't have the strength to heave myself out of the water. I couldn't understand it—didn't realise I had a dislocated shoulder, a broken wrist and three cracked ribs. Eventually Jones and Croft appeared. They'd held on to the tail until it went down. Neither could swim, but they managed to scramble into the dinghy and pull me in. I never saw Pickering. I assume he's at the bottom of the sea.'

'What about the fifth man?' Digby asked.

'John Rowley was alive. We heard him call out. I was in a bit of a daze, but Jones and Croft tried to row towards the voice.' He shook his head. 'You can't imagine how difficult it was. The swell must have been three or four feet, the flames were dying down so we couldn't see much, and the wind was howling. Jones yelled and Rowley would shout back, then the dinghy would go up one side of a wave and down the other and spin round, so that when he called out again his voice seemed to come from a completely different direction. It became weaker as the cold got to him. Eventually he went quiet.'

Digby found he was holding his breath, as if the mere sound of breathing would be an intrusion on such a dreadful memory.

'We were found soon after dawn, by a destroyer on U-boat patrol.' Bart looked out of the window, blind to the green Hertfordshire landscape, seeing a different scene. 'Bloody lucky, really,' he said.

They sat in silence for a while, then Bart said, 'Was the raid a success? No one will tell me how many came home.'

'Disastrous,' Digby said.

'What about my squadron?'

'Sergeant Jenkins and his crew got back safely. So did Pilot Officer Arasaratnam. And Sergeant Riley's aircraft made it back.'

'What about the rest?' said Bart.

Digby just shook his head.

'But there were six aircraft from my squadron on that raid!' Bart protested.

'I know. As well as you, two more were shot down. No survivors.'

'So Creighton-Smith is dead. And Billy Shaw. And . . . oh God.' He turned away.

'I'm sorry.'

Bart's mood changed from despair to anger. 'It's not enough to be sorry,' he said. 'We're being sent out there to die! For heaven's sake, Digby, you're part of the government.'

'I work for the Prime Minister, yes.' Winston Churchill liked to bring people from private industry into the government and Digby, a successful aircraft designer, was one of his trouble-shooters.

'Then this is your fault as much as anyone's. You shouldn't be wasting your time visiting the sick. Go and do something about it.'

'I am doing something,' Digby said calmly. 'I've been given the task of finding out why this is happening. We lost fifty per cent of the aircraft on that raid.'

'Bloody treachery at the top, I suspect. Or some fool air marshal is boasting in his club about tomorrow's raid, and a Nazi barman is taking notes behind the beer pumps.'

'That's one possibility.'

'I'm sorry,' Bart said. 'It's not your fault. I'm just blowing my top.'

'Seriously, have you any idea why so many are being shot down? You've flown more than a dozen missions. What's your hunch?'

'I wasn't just sounding off about spies,' Bart said. 'When we get to Germany, they're ready for us. *They know we're coming.*'

'What makes you say that?'

'Their fighters are in the air, waiting for us. You know how difficult it is for defensive forces to time that right. The fighter squadron has to be scrambled at the right moment, they must navigate from their airfield to the area where they think we might be, then they have to find us in the moonlight. The whole process takes so much time that we should be able to drop our ordnance and get clear before they catch us. But it isn't happening that way.'

Digby nodded. Bart's experience matched that of other pilots he had questioned.

'I get the feeling the Luftwaffe can follow us through cloud,' Bart continued. 'Might they have some kind of equipment on board that enables them to locate us even when we're not visible?'

Digby shook his head. 'We're working hard to invent that kind of device, and I'm sure the enemy are too, but we're a long way from success, and we're pretty sure they're well behind us.' Digby stood up. 'I have to get back to Whitehall.' He squeezed Bart's uninjured shoulder. 'Sit still and get well.'

'They say I'll be flying again in a few weeks.'

'I can't say I'm glad.'

As Digby turned to go, Bart said, 'On a raid like this one, the cost to us of replacing lost aircraft must be more than the cost to the enemy of repairing the damage done by our bombs.'

'Undoubtedly.'

'Then why do we do it? What's the point of bombing?'

'What else can we do?' Digby said. 'The Nazis control Europe: Austria, Czechoslovakia, Holland, Belgium, France, Denmark, Norway. Italy is an ally, Spain is sympathetic, Sweden is neutral, and they have a pact with the Soviet Union. We have no military forces on the Continent. We have no other way of fighting back.'

Bart nodded. 'So we're all you've got.'

'Exactly,' Digby said. 'If the bombing stops, the war is over—and Hitler has won.'

THE PRIME MINISTER was watching *The Maltese Falcon* in a private cinema at Admiralty House. It had fifty or sixty plush seats and was usually used to show film of bombing raids and to screen propaganda pieces before they were shown to the public. Late at night, when he was too worried and tense to sleep, Churchill would sit in one of the large VIP seats in the front row with a glass of brandy and lose himself in the latest enchantment from Hollywood.

As Digby walked in, the air was thick with cigar smoke. Churchill pointed to a seat. Digby sat down and watched the last few minutes of the movie. As the credits appeared over the statuette of a black falcon, Digby told his boss that the Luftwaffe appeared to have advance notice of when Bomber Command was coming.

When Digby had finished, Churchill stared at the screen for a few minutes. He said, 'What does the RAF think?'

'They blame poor formation flying. In theory, if the bombers fly in close formation, their armament should cover the entire sky, so any enemy fighter that appears should be shot down immediately.'

'And what do you say to that?'

'Rubbish. Formation flying has never worked. Some new factor has entered the equation. My brother blames spies.'

'All the spies we've caught have been amateurish, but that's why they were caught, of course. It may be that the competent ones have slipped through the net.'

'Perhaps the Germans have made a technical breakthrough.'

'The Secret Intelligence Service tell me the enemy are far behind us in the development of radar.'

'Do you trust their judgment?'

'No.' The ceiling lights came on. Churchill was in evening dress. His face was lined with weariness. He took a folded sheet of flimsy paper from his waistcoat pocket and handed it to Digby. 'Here's a clue,' he said.

Digby studied the sheet. It appeared to be a decrypt of a Luftwaffe radio signal, in German and English. It said that the Luftwaffe's strategy of dark night-fighting had scored a great triumph, thanks to Freya's information. 'Freya' was not a word in either language. 'What does this mean?' Digby said.

'That's what I want you to find out.' Churchill stood up and shrugged into his coat. 'Walk back with me.'

They passed through the building, emerged on the parade ground and went through a gate in the barbed-wire fence to the street. London was blacked out, but the moon gave enough light for them to find their way.

They walked along Horse Guards Parade to 1 Storey's Gate. A bomb had damaged the rear of 10 Downing Street, so Churchill was living at the nearby annexe over the Cabinet War Rooms. The entrance was protected by a bombproof wall.

'It can't go on,' said Churchill. 'At this rate, Bomber Command will be finished by Christmas. I need to know who or what Freya is.'

'I'll find out.'

'Do so with the utmost dispatch.'

'Yes, sir.'

'Good night,' said the Prime Minister, and he went inside.

ONE

O n the last day of May, 1941, a strange vehicle was seen on the streets of Morlunde, a city on the west coast of Denmark.

It was a Nimbus motorcycle with a sidecar. That in itself was an unusual sight, because there was no petrol for anyone except doctors and the police and, of course, the German troops occupying the country. But the petrol engine in this Nimbus had been replaced by a steam engine. The seat had been removed from the sidecar to make room for a boiler, firebox and chimney-stack. The substitute engine was low in power, and the bike had a top speed of about twenty-two miles per hour.

In the saddle was Harald Olufsen, a tall youth of eighteen, with clear skin and fair hair brushed back from a high forehead. He looked like a Viking in a school blazer. He had saved for a year to buy the Nimbus, then, the day after he got it, the Germans had imposed petrol restrictions. Harald had been furious. What right did they have? But he had been brought up to act rather than complain.

It had taken him another year to modify the bike, working during school holidays, fitting it in with preparing for his university entrance exams. Today, home from his boarding school for the Whitsun holiday break, he had spent the morning memorising physics equations and the afternoon attaching a sprocket from a rusted lawn mower to the back wheel. Now, with the motorcycle working perfectly, he was heading for a bar to hear some jazz.

Harald loved jazz. The American musicians were the best, of course, but even their Danish imitators were worth listening to. You could sometimes hear good jazz in Morlunde. It was an international port, visited by sailors from all over the world.

But when Harald drove up to the Club Hot, in the dockland district, its door was closed and its windows shuttered. He was mystified. It was eight o'clock on a Saturday evening, and this was one of the most popular spots in town. It should be swinging. As he sat staring at the silent building, a passer-by stopped and looked at his vehicle. 'What's that contraption?'

'A Nimbus with a steam engine. Do you know anything about this club?'

'I own it. What does the bike use for fuel?'

14

'Anything that burns. I use peat.' He pointed to the pile in the back of the sidecar.

'*Peat?*' The man laughed.

'Why are the doors shut?'

'The Nazis closed me down for employing Negro musicians.'

Harald had never seen a coloured musician in the flesh, but he knew from records that they were the best. 'The Nazis are ignorant swine,' he said angrily. His evening had been ruined.

The club owner looked up and down the street to make sure no one had heard. The occupying power ruled Denmark with a light hand, but, even so, few people openly insulted the Nazis. However, there was no one else in sight. He returned his gaze to Harald. 'I'm hoping they'll let me open again in a few weeks. But I'll have to promise to employ white musicians.'

Harald opened the tap that admitted steam into the engine. 'Jazz without Negroes?' He shook his head in disgust. 'It's like banning French cooks from restaurants.' He took his foot off the brake and the bike moved slowly away. He steered for the harbour.

His father was pastor of the church on Sande, a small island a couple of miles offshore. The ferry that shuttled to and from the island was in dock and he drove straight onto it. It was crowded with people, most of whom he knew. A well-dressed couple he did not recognise were probably going to dine at the island's hotel restaurant.

At the last minute a German-built Ford sedan drove on. Harald knew the car: it belonged to Axel Flemming, owner of the island's hotel. The Flemmings were hostile to Harald's family. Axel Flemming felt he was the natural leader of the island community, a role which Pastor Olufsen believed to be his own. Harald wondered how Flemming had managed to get petrol for his car.

The sea was choppy and there were dark clouds in the sky. A storm was coming in. Harald took out a newspaper he had picked up in town. Entitled *Reality*, it was an illegal publication, printed in defiance of the occupying power. The Danish police had not suppressed it and, in Copenhagen, people read it openly. Here they were more discreet, and Harald folded it to hide the masthead while he read about the shortage of butter. Denmark produced millions of pounds of butter every year, but almost all of it was now sent to Germany, and Danes had trouble getting any. It was the kind of story that never appeared in the censored legitimate press.

The flat shape of the island came closer. It was twelve miles long and a mile wide, with a village at each end. Fishermen's cottages, and the church with its parsonage, constituted the older village at the south end. Also at that end, a school of navigation, long disused, had been taken over by the Germans and turned into a military base. The hotel and the larger homes were at the north end. The island was mostly sand dunes and scrub, but all along the seaward side was a magnificent ten-mile hard-sand beach.

Harald felt a few drops of rain as the ferry approached its dock at the north end of the island. The hotel's horse-drawn taxi was waiting for the well-dressed couple. Harald decided to cross the island and drive home along the beach. He was halfway from the dock to the hotel when he ran out of steam. He was using the bike's petrol tank as a water reserve, and he realised now that it was not big enough. He would have to get a five-gallon oil drum and put it in the sidecar. Meanwhile, he needed water to get him home.

There was only one house within sight, and unfortunately it was Axel Flemming's. Despite their rivalry, the Olufsens and the Flemmings were on speaking terms: the Flemming family came to church every Sunday. All the same, Harald did not relish the thought of asking the antagonistic Flemmings for help. Rather than knock at the front door, he went round the side of the house. A manservant was putting the Ford in the garage. 'Hello, Gunnar,' said Harald. 'Can I have some water?'

The man was friendly. 'Help yourself. There's a tap in the yard.'

Harald found a bucket beside the tap and filled it. He went back to the motorcycle and poured the water into the tank. It looked as if he might manage to avoid meeting any of the family. But when he returned the bucket to the yard, Peter Flemming was there.

A tall, haughty man of thirty, in a well-cut tweed suit, Peter was Axel's son. Before the families had quarrelled, he had been friends with Harald's brother, Arne. Peter now lived in Copenhagen but had come home for the holiday weekend, Harald assumed.

Peter was reading *Reality*. He looked up from the paper to see Harald. 'What are you doing here?' he said.

'Hello, Peter, I came to get some water.'

'I suppose this rag is yours?'

Harald touched his pocket and realised that the newspaper must have fallen out when he reached down for the bucket.

Peter saw the movement and understood its meaning. 'Are you aware that you could go to jail for having it in your possession?'

The talk of jail was not just an empty threat: Peter was a police detective. Harald said, 'Everyone reads it in the city.'

'This is not Copenhagen,' Peter intoned solemnly.

Harald knew that Peter would love the chance to disgrace an Olufsen. Yet he was hesitating. Harald thought he knew why. 'You'll look a fool if you arrest a schoolboy on Sande for doing something half the population does openly.'

Peter was visibly torn between the desire to humiliate Harald and the fear of being laughed at. 'No one is entitled to break the law.'

'Whose law—ours, or the Germans'?'

'The law is the law.'

Harald felt more confident. Peter wouldn't be arguing if he intended to make an arrest. 'You only say that because your father makes so much money giving Nazis a good time at his hotel.'

That hit home. The hotel was popular with German officers. 'While your father gives inflammatory sermons,' Peter angrily retorted. It was true: the pastor had preached against the Nazis, his theme being 'Jesus was a Jew'. Peter continued, 'Does he realise how much trouble will be caused if he stirs people up?'

'I'm sure he does. The founder of the Christian religion was something of a troublemaker himself.'

'Don't talk to me about religion. I have to keep order here on earth.'

'To hell with order, we've been invaded!' Harald's frustration boiled over. 'What right have the Nazis got to tell us what to do? We should kick the whole evil pack of them out of our country!'

'You mustn't hate the Germans, they're our friends,' Peter said.

'I don't hate Germans. I've got German cousins.' The pastor's sister had married a successful young Hamburg dentist. 'They've suffered more from the Nazis than we have,' Harald added. Uncle Joachim was Jewish and, although he was a baptised Christian and an elder of his church, the Nazis had ruled that he could only treat Jews, thereby ruining his practice. A year ago he had been arrested and sent to a special prison, in the Bavarian town of Dachau.

'People bring trouble on themselves,' Peter said. 'Your father should never have allowed his sister to marry a Jew.' Throwing the newspaper to the ground, he went into the house and slammed the door. Harald bent and picked up the newspaper.

It started to rain heavily as he headed back towards the road. When he returned to his bike, Harald found that the fire under the boiler had gone out. He tried to relight it, but after twenty minutes bent over the firebox in the rain, he gave up. He would have to walk home.

He pushed the bike half a mile to the hotel and left it in the car park, then set off along the beach. At this time of year, the

Scandinavian evenings lasted until eleven o'clock, but tonight clouds darkened the sky and the rain further reduced visibility. Before long, Harald's clothes were so soaked that he could have swum home without getting any wetter.

He was strong and as fit as a greyhound, but two hours later he was tired, cold and miserable when he came up to the fence round the German base and realised he would have to walk three miles round it in order to reach his home a few hundred yards away.

If the tide had been out, he would have continued along the beach for, although that stretch of sand was officially off limits, the guards would not be able to see him. However, the tide was in, and the fence reached into the water. It crossed his mind to swim the last stretch, but he dismissed the idea. It would be dangerous to swim in this weather when he was already exhausted. But he could climb the fence.

A quarter-moon showed fitfully through racing clouds, shedding an uncertain light over the drenched landscape. Harald saw a wire fence six feet high with two strands of barbed wire at the top. Fifty yards inland, it passed through a copse of scrubby trees. That would be the place to get over.

He knew what lay beyond the fence. Last summer he had worked as a labourer on the building site, not knowing that it was destined to be a military base. The builders had told everyone it was to be a new coastguard station. Then, when the buildings were up, all the Danes had been sent away and the Germans had been brought in to install the equipment. But Harald knew the layout. The disused navigation school had been refurbished, and two new buildings had been put up on either side of it. The buildings were set back from the beach, and much of the ground at this end of the site was covered with low bushes that would help conceal him. He would just have to keep an eye out for patrolling guards.

He found the copse, climbed the fence, eased himself gingerly over the barbed wire, and jumped down softly on the wet dunes. He headed across the base, moving as fast as he dared, staying close to the bushes. He passed a tall structure, and recognised it, in the dimness, as a searchlight tower. The whole area could be lit up in an emergency, but otherwise the base was blacked out.

He passed through a stand of conifers and went down into a dip. As he came to the bottom, a structure loomed. Coming closer, he saw a curved concrete wall as high as his head. Above the wall something moved, and he heard a hum, like an electric motor. This had not been built while he was working here. He tried to make out the details. Above the circular wall was a huge square grid of metal or wire like an oversize mattress, twelve feet on a side. It was rotating like a merry-go-round, completing a revolution every few seconds.

Harald was fascinated. It was a machine he had never seen before, and the engineer in him was spellbound. What did it do? Why did it revolve? The sound told him only that the motor turned the thing. He felt sure it was not a gun, at least not the conventional kind, for there was no barrel. His best guess was that it was something to do with radio.

Nearby, someone coughed.

Harald reacted instinctively. He jumped, got his arms over the edge of the wall, and hauled himself up, easing himself down on the inside. After a tense moment, his feet touched a concrete floor. A sentry was passing by, he presumed. Harald flattened himself against the inside of the wall, waiting for a flashlight beam to betray him.

But no light shone on him. He waited to be sure. He thought he could see heavy cables coming from the lower edge of the grid and disappearing into the far side of the pit. This had to be a means of sending radio signals or receiving them, he thought.

When a few minutes had passed, he clambered to the top of the wall and tried to see through the rain. No sentry was visible. He slid down the wall and set off across the dunes.

In a dark moment, when the moon was obscured by cloud, he walked smack into a wooden wall. Shocked and scared, he let out a muffled curse. A second later, he realised he had run into a derelict boathouse once used by the navigation school. He walked on until he reached the far fence. Scrambling over it, he headed for home.

He came first to the church. Light glowed from the row of square windows in its seaward wall. Surprised that anyone should be in the building on a Saturday night, he looked inside. The church was long and low-roofed. Rows of seats faced a wooden lectern. There was no altar. The walls were bare except for some framed texts.

Danes were undogmatic about religion, and most of the nation subscribed to Evangelical Lutheranism. However, 100 years ago, the fishing folk of Sande had been converted to a harsher creed. For the last thirty years Harald's father had kept their faith alight, setting an example of uncompromising puritanism in his own life, stiffening the resolve of his congregation in weekly brimstone sermons. Despite this blazing conviction, his son was not a believer. Harald went to services whenever he was at home, not wanting to hurt his father's feelings, but in his heart he dissented.

Now, as he looked through the window, he heard music. His brother Arne was at the piano, playing a jazz tune. Harald smiled. Arne was home for the holiday. He was amusing and sophisticated, and he would enliven the long weekend at the parsonage.

Harald went inside. Without looking round, Arne changed the music seamlessly to a hymn tune. Harald grinned. Arne had heard the door open and thought their father might be coming in. The pastor disapproved of jazz and would not permit it to be played in his church. 'It's only me,' Harald said.

Arne turned round. He was wearing his brown army uniform. At twenty-eight, he was ten years older than Harald. He was a flying instructor with the Army Aviation Troops, based at the flying school near Copenhagen. The Germans had halted all Danish military activity and the aircraft were grounded most of the time.

'Seeing you out of the corner of my eye, I thought you were the old man.' Arne looked Harald up and down fondly. 'You look more and more like him.'

It was true. Arne had their mother's dark hair and hazel eyes. Harald was fair, like their father, and had also inherited the penetrating blue-eyed stare with which the pastor intimidated his flock.

'I've got something to play you,' Harald said. Arne got off the stool and Harald sat at the piano. 'I learned this from a record someone brought to school. You know Mads Kirke?'

'Cousin of my colleague Poul.'

'Right. He discovered this American pianist called Clarence Pine Top Smith.' Harald hesitated. 'What's the old man doing?'

'Writing tomorrow's sermon.'

'Good.' The piano could not be heard from the parsonage, fifty yards away. Harald began to play *Pine Top's Boogie-Woogie*, and the room filled with the sexy harmonies of the American South. He could not sit still to play, so he stood up, bending his long frame over the keyboard. He banged out the last chord and said in English, 'That's what I'm talkin' about!' just as Pine Top did on the record.

Arne laughed. 'Not bad! Come outside. I want to smoke.'

They stood outside the church door, sheltered from the rain by a little porch. On the far side of a patch of sandy ground they could see the dark shape of the parsonage. Light shone through the window set into the kitchen door. Arne took out his cigarettes.

'Have you heard from Hermia?' Harald asked him. Arne was engaged to an English girl whom he had not seen for more than a year, since the Germans had occupied Denmark.

'I tried to write to her. I found the British Consulate's address in Gothenburg.' Danes were allowed to send letters to Sweden, which was neutral. 'I thought I'd been clever not mentioning the consulate on the envelope, but the censors aren't so easily fooled. My commanding officer brought the letter back to me and said if I ever tried anything like that again I'd be court-martialled.'

Harald liked Hermia. She had been a little scary on first acquaintance, with her dramatic dark looks and her direct manner; but she had endeared herself to Harald by treating him like a man, not just someone's kid brother. 'Do you still want to marry her?'

'Yes, if she's alive. She might have been killed by a bomb in London.'

'It must be hard, not knowing.'

Arne nodded, then said, 'How about you? Any action?'

Harald shrugged. 'Girls my age aren't interested in schoolboys.' He said it lightly, but he was hiding real resentment. He had suffered a couple of wounding rejections.

'I suppose they want to date a guy who can spend some money on them.' Arne threw away the stub of his cigarette. 'Let's go and talk to the old man.'

'Before we go in . . .'

'What?'

'How are things in the army?'

'Grim. We can't defend our country, and most of the time I'm not allowed to fly. The Nazis have won everything. There's no opposition left but the British, and they're hanging on by a thread.'

'Surely someone must be starting a Resistance movement?'

Arne shrugged. 'If they were, and I knew about it, I couldn't tell you, could I?' Then, before Harald could say more, Arne dashed through the rain towards the light shining from the kitchen.

TWO

Hermia Mount looked at her lunch—charred sausages, runny mashed potato and overcooked cabbage—and she thought with longing of a bar on the Copenhagen waterfront that served three kinds of herring with salad, pickles, warm bread and lager.

She had been brought up in Denmark. Her father had been a British diplomat who had spent most of his career in Scandinavian countries. Hermia had worked in the British Embassy in Copenhagen, first as a secretary, later as assistant to a naval attaché who was with MI6, the secret intelligence service. When her father died, and her mother returned to London, Hermia stayed on, partly because of her job, but mainly because she was engaged to a Danish pilot, Arne Olufsen.

Then, on April 9, 1940, Hitler invaded Denmark. Four anxious days later, Hermia and a group of British officials had left in a special diplomatic train for London.

Now, at the age of thirty, Hermia was in charge of MI6's Denmark desk. Along with most of the service, she had been evacuated from its London headquarters to Bletchley Park, a large country house on the edge of a village fifty miles north of the capital. A hastily erected Nissen hut served as the canteen. Hermia was glad to be escaping the bombs, but she wished that they could also have evacuated one of London's charming little French restaurants. She forked a little mash into her mouth and forced herself to swallow.

Glancing up, she saw a man of about her own age coming towards her, carrying a cup of tea, walking with a noticeable limp. 'May I join you?' he said cheerfully, and sat opposite her without waiting for an answer. 'I'm Digby Hoare. I know who you are.'

She raised an eyebrow and said, 'Make yourself at home.'

The irony in her voice had no impact. He just said, 'Thanks.'

She had seen him around once or twice. He was no matinée idol, with his unruly dark hair, but he had nice blue eyes and his features were pleasantly craggy in a Humphrey Bogart way. She asked him, 'What department are you with?'

'I work in London actually.'

That was not an answer to her question, she noted. She pushed her plate aside.

He said, 'You don't like the food?'

'Do you?'

'I'll tell you something. I've debriefed pilots who have been shot down over France and made their way home. We think we're experiencing austerity, but the Frogs are actually starving to death. After hearing those stories, everything tastes good to me.'

'Austerity is no excuse for vile cooking,' Hermia said.

He grinned. 'They told me you were a bit waspish.'

'What else did they tell you?'

'That you're bilingual in English and Danish—which is why you're head of the Denmark desk, I presume.'

'No. The war is the reason for that. Before, no woman ever rose above the level of secretary in MI6. We didn't have analytical minds, you see. But since war broke out, our brains have undergone a remarkable change, and we have become capable of work that previously could only be accomplished by the masculine mentality.'

He took her sarcasm with easy good humour. 'I've noticed that, too,' he said. 'Wonders never cease.'

'Why have you been checking up on me?'

'Two reasons. First, because you're beautiful.'

He had succeeded in surprising her. Men did not often say she was beautiful. Handsome, perhaps; striking, sometimes; imposing, often. Her face was a long oval, but with severe dark hair, hooded eyes, and a nose too big to be pretty. 'What's the other reason?'

He glanced sideways. Two older women were sharing their table, and although they were chatting to one another, they were probably also half listening to Digby and Hermia. 'I'll tell you in a minute,' he said. 'Would you like to go out with me?'

'Certainly not.'

For a moment he seemed nonplussed. Then his grin returned, and he said, 'Don't sugar the pill, give it to me straight.'

She could not help smiling. 'I'm engaged.'

'Oh, who's the lucky fellow?'

'A pilot in the Danish army.'

The two ladies left the table, and Digby's voice became quiet but urgent. 'Take a look at this, please.' He drew from his pocket a sheet of paper and handed it to her. It was a decrypt of an enemy radio signal. 'You speak German as well as Danish?'

She nodded. 'In Denmark, all schoolchildren learn German, and English and Latin as well.' She studied the signal for a moment. 'Information from Freya?'

'That's what's puzzling us. It's not a word in German. I thought it might mean something in a Scandinavian language.'

'It does, in a way,' she said. 'Freya is a Norse goddess—in fact she's the Viking Venus, the goddess of love.'

'Ah!' Digby looked thoughtful. 'Well, that's something, but it doesn't get us far.'

'What's this all about?'

'We're losing too many bombers.'

Hermia frowned. 'I read about the last big raid in the newspapers—they said it was a great success.'

Digby just looked at her.

'Oh, I see,' she said. 'You don't tell the newspapers the truth. How many aircraft did we lose?'

'Fifty per cent.'

'Dear God.' Hermia looked away. 'If this goes on . . .'

'Exactly.'

She looked again at the decrypt. 'Is Freya a spy?'

'It's my job to find out. Tell me more about the goddess.'

Hermia dug back into her memory. She had learned the Norse myths at school. 'Freya has a precious gold necklace. It's guarded by the watchman of the gods . . . Heimdal, I think his name is.'

'A watchman. That makes sense.'

'Freya could be a spy with access to air-raid information.'

'She could also be a machine for detecting approaching aircraft before they come within sight,' Digby said.

'I've heard of such machines, but I've no idea how they work.'

'Three possible ways: infrared, lidar and radar. Infrared detectors would pick up the rays emitted by a hot aircraft engine, or possibly its exhaust. Lidar is a system of optical pulses sent out by the detection apparatus and reflected back off the aircraft. Radar is the same thing with radio pulses.'

'I've just remembered something else. Heimdal can see for a hundred miles by day or night.'

'That makes it sound more like a machine.' Digby finished his tea and stood up. 'Let me know if you have any more thoughts.'

'Of course. Where do I find you?'

'Number 10, Downing Street.'

'Oh!' She was impressed. 'Goodbye.'

'Goodbye.'

She sat there for a few moments, watching him walk away. It had been an interesting conversation. Digby Hoare was very high-powered: the Prime Minister himself must be worried about the loss of bombers. Was the use of the code name 'Freya' mere coincidence, or was there a Scandinavian connection?

She scraped her uneaten lunch into the pigbin and stepped out of the wooden hut. The wide green lawn, with its cedar trees and swan pond, had been disfigured by huts thrown up in haste to accommodate the hundreds of staff from London. She crossed the park to the house, an ornate Victorian mansion built of red brick.

Hermia passed through the grand porch and made her way to her office in the old servants' quarters, a tiny L-shaped space. On her desk she found a package from Copenhagen.

After Hitler's invasion of Poland, she had laid the foundations of a small spy network in Denmark. Its leader was her fiancé's friend, Poul Kirke. He had put together a group of young men who believed that their small country was going to be overrun by its larger neighbour, and the only way to fight for freedom was to cooperate with the British. The group, who called themselves the Nightwatchmen, passed military information to British Intelligence.

The package on her desk contained a batch of reports, already decrypted for her by the code room, on German military dispositions in Denmark. Also in the package was a copy of an underground newspaper called *Reality*. The package had been smuggled out of Denmark to a go-between in Sweden, who passed it to the MI6 man at the British Legation in Stockholm. With the package was a note from the go-between saying he had also passed a copy of *Reality* to the Reuters wire service in Stockholm. Hermia frowned. She did not like her agents mixing espionage with other work that could attract the attention of the authorities.

Thinking about the Nightwatchmen reminded her painfully of her fiancé. Arne was not one of the group. His character was all wrong. She loved him for his careless *joie de vivre*. But a happy-go-lucky man with no head for mundane details was not the type for secret work. She admitted to herself that she was not sure he had the courage. He was a daredevil on the ski slopes—they had met on a Norwegian mountain—but she wondered how he would face the subtle terrors of undercover operations.

Falling in love with him had been like skiing downhill, Hermia thought: a little push to get started, a sudden increase in speed, and then, before she was quite ready, the exhilarating feeling of hurtling downhill at a breakneck pace, completely unable to stop.

She had considered trying to send Arne a message via the Nightwatchmen. Poul Kirke worked at the flying school, and if Arne was still there they must see one another every day. It would have been shamefully unprofessional to use the spy network for a personal communication, but that was not what stopped her. It was the danger to Arne that held her back. Secret messages could fall into enemy hands. Hermia's inquiry about him could turn into his death warrant. So she sat at her desk with acid anxiety burning inside her.

She composed a message to the Swedish go-between, telling him to keep out of the propaganda war and stick to his job as courier. Then she typed a report to her boss containing all the military information in the package, with carbon copies to other departments.

JANSBORG SKOLE was 300 years old, and proud of it. Originally the school had consisted of a church and one house where the boys ate, slept and had lessons. Now it was a complex of old and new red-brick buildings.

Harald Olufsen was walking from the refectory to the gym. As he passed the headmaster's house, the head's wife came out and smiled at him. 'Good morning, Mia,' he said politely. The head was always called Heis, the Ancient Greek word for the number one, so his wife was Mia, the feminine form of the same word. The school had stopped teaching Greek five years ago, but tradition died hard.

Harald's next lesson should have been maths, but today there was a visitor, an old boy of the school who now represented his home town in the Rigsdag, the nation's parliament. The school was to hear him speak in the gym. Harald would have preferred to do maths.

He had been thrilled to discover that the inventor of quantum physics was a Danish scientist, Niels Bohr. Bohr's interpretation of the periodic table of the elements, explaining chemical reactions by the atomic structure of the elements involved, seemed to Harald a fundamental and deeply satisfying account of what the universe was made of. He worshipped Bohr and had applied to study physics at the University of Copenhagen, where Bohr taught.

Education cost money. Since Harald's father had entered a profession that would keep him poor all his life, Harald's grandfather provided for his grandsons. His legacy had paid for Arne and Harald to go to Jansborg Skole and would finance Harald's time at university.

Harald entered the gym. The younger boys had put out benches in neat rows. Harald sat at the back, next to Josef Duchwitz. Josef was very small, and his surname sounded like the English word 'duck', so he had been nicknamed Anaticula, the Latin word for a duckling. Over the years it had got shortened to Tik. The two boys had very different backgrounds—Tik was from a wealthy Jewish family—yet they had been close friends all through school. A few moments later Mads Kirke sat next to Harald. Mads came from a distinguished military family. His cousin Poul was a pilot with Arne at the flying school. The three friends were science students.

Heis came in with the visitor, and all the boys stood up politely. Tall, thin and mild-mannered, Heis seemed apologetic about being in authority. He was liked rather than feared. When they had sat down again, Heis introduced the parliamentary deputy, Svend Agger, who talked about the German occupation.

Harald remembered the day it had begun, fourteen months ago.

He had been woken up in the middle of the night by aircraft roaring overhead. The Germans landed in Denmark the next morning, but the school was in a village outside Copenhagen, and it was a year before they saw the occupying forces. There had never been any bombing or even gunfire.

Denmark had surrendered to Germany within twenty-four hours. 'Subsequent events have shown the wisdom of that decision,' said the speaker. 'Our king continues on his throne.' Mads Kirke grunted disgustedly. Harald shared his annoyance. King Christian X rode out on horseback most days, showing himself to the people of Copenhagen, but it seemed an empty gesture.

'The German presence has been, on the whole, benign,' the speaker concluded. 'Denmark has proved that a partial loss of independence need not lead to undue hardship and strife. The lesson, for boys such as yourselves, is that there may be more honour in obedience than in ill-considered rebellion.' He sat down.

Heis clapped politely, and the boys followed suit. 'Well, boys,' he said, 'any questions for our guest?'

Mads was on his feet in an instant. 'Sir, Norway was invaded on the same day as Denmark, but the Norwegians fought the Germans for two months. Doesn't that make us cowards?' There was a rumble of agreement from the boys.

'A naive view,' Agger said. His dismissive tone angered Harald. 'Norway is a land of mountains and fiords. Denmark is a flat country with a good road system—impossible to defend against a large motorised army. To put up a fight would have caused unnecessary bloodshed, and the end result would have been no different.'

Mads said, 'Except that we would have been able to walk round with our heads held high.' The boys clapped.

'Now, now, Kirke,' said Heis mildly. 'I know you feel strongly about this, but there's no need for discourtesy.' He looked round the room and said, 'Would any boy like to ask Mr Agger about his everyday work as a member of the Rigsdag?'

Tik stood up. 'Don't you feel like a puppet?' he said. 'After all, it's the Germans who really rule us. You're just pretending.'

'Our nation continues to be governed by our Danish parliament,' Agger replied. 'We have our own police and armed forces.'

'But the minute the Rigsdag does something the Germans disapprove of, it will be closed down, and the police and the military will be disarmed,' Tik argued. 'So you're acting in a farce.'

'Remember your manners, please, Duchwitz,' Heis said.

'That's all right,' said Agger. 'I like a lively discussion. Duchwitz should compare our circumstances with those prevailing in France. Because of our policy of cooperating with the Germans, life is a great deal better, for ordinary Danish people, than it might be.'

Harald had had enough. He stood up. 'And what if the Nazis come for Duchwitz? Will you advise friendly cooperation then?'

'And why should they come for Duchwitz?'

'The same reason they came for my uncle in Hamburg—he's a Jew.'

Agger showed irritation for the first time. 'The Germans have demonstrated complete tolerance towards Danish Jews.'

'So far,' Harald argued. 'But what if they change their minds? Shall we stand aside while they seize Tik? Or should we be organising a Resistance movement in preparation for that day?'

'Your best plan is to make sure you are never faced with such a decision, by cooperating with the occupying power.'

'But what if that doesn't work? There won't be time for debate when they bang on Tik's door in the middle of the night.'

For a moment, Heis looked ready to reprimand Harald for rudeness, but in the end he answered mildly, 'You've made an interesting point. We've had a good discussion. Let's thank our guest for coming to visit us.' He began to lead a round of applause.

Harald stopped him. 'Make him answer the question!' he shouted. 'Should we have a Resistance movement, or will we let the Nazis do anything they like?'

The room went quiet. 'I think you'd better leave us,' Heis said.

Boiling with frustration, Harald stood up. All the boys watched him as he went out and slammed the door.

PETER FLEMMING'S ALARM CLOCK went off at half past five in the morning. He silenced it and turned on the light. Inge was lying on her back, eyes open, looking at the ceiling expressionlessly.

He got up, went into the kitchen of their Copenhagen apartment and put a pot of oatmeal on the cooker, then laid a tray. He buttered a slice of rye bread and made ersatz coffee.

He felt optimistic, and after a moment he recalled why. Yesterday there had been a break in the case he was working on. He was a detective inspector in the security department, whose job was to keep tabs on union organisers, Communists, foreigners and other potential troublemakers. His boss was Superintendent Frederik Juel, clever but lazy. He was fond of the Latin proverb *Quieta non movere*: Let sleeping dogs lie.

In the past fourteen months their work had expanded, as opponents of German rule had been added to the department's watch list. So far the only outward sign of resistance had been the appearance of underground newspapers such as *Reality*. Juel believed they were harmless, if not actually beneficial as a safety valve, and refused to pursue the publishers. This attitude infuriated Peter. Leaving criminals at large to continue their offences drove him mad. Juel's liaison with the occupying power was General Walter Braun. Braun did not like Juel's attitude, but had not pushed the matter to a confrontation.

Last night Peter had learned that copies of *Reality* were being smuggled to Sweden. Until now, he had abided by his boss's hands-off rule, but he hoped Juel's complacency would be shaken by the news that the papers were finding their way out of Denmark. A Swedish detective, who was a personal friend of Peter's, had called to say he thought the papers were being carried on a Lufthansa flight from Berlin to Stockholm that stopped at Copenhagen. That was the breakthrough that accounted for Peter's earlier optimism.

When the oatmeal was ready, he took the tray into the bedroom. He helped Inge sit upright, then began to feed her with a spoon.

A year ago Peter and Inge had been driving to the beach when a young man in a new sports car had crashed into them. Peter had broken both his legs, but had recovered rapidly. Inge had smashed her skull, and she would never be the same.

The other driver, Finn Jonk, had been thrown clear and landed in a bush, unharmed. He had no driving licence—it had been taken from him by the courts after a previous accident—and he had been drunk. The Jonk family had hired a top lawyer, who had succeeded in delaying the trial for a year, so Finn had not been punished for destroying Inge's mind. The personal tragedy, for Inge and Peter, was also an example of the disgraceful way crimes could go unpunished in a modern society.

When Inge had eaten her breakfast, Peter took her to the toilet, then bathed her. Finally he dressed her. He helped her into a cheerful yellow cotton dress. When he had brushed her hair, they both looked at her reflection in the mirror. She was a pretty, pale blonde, and before the accident she had had a flirtatious smile and a coy way of fluttering her eyelashes. Now her face was blank.

Peter's father had tried to persuade him to put Inge into a nursing home. Peter could not afford the fees, but Axel was willing to pay. However, Peter felt it was his duty to take care of his wife. If he shirked his duty, he would lose his self-respect.

29

He took Inge to the living room and sat her by the window. He left the radio playing, returning to the bathroom to shave.

The face in his shaving mirror was well-proportioned. Since the accident he had noticed a few grey hairs in his red morning stubble, and there were lines of weariness round the orange-brown eyes.

When he had shaved he dressed and strapped on his holster with his Walther 7.65mm pistol. Then he stood in the kitchen and ate three slices of dry bread, saving the scarce butter for Inge.

The nurse who took care of Inge was supposed to come at eight o'clock, but she did not arrive until eight fifteen, which meant that Peter was late leaving the apartment. He jumped on a tram heading for the city centre and got off outside the Politigaarden, the building that housed police headquarters. In his section, he was greeted by Detective Constable Tilde Jespersen. The young widow of a policeman, she was as tough and smart as any cop in the department. She was rather attractive, with blue eyes and fair curly hair and a small, curvy figure. 'Tram delayed?' she said sympathetically.

'No. Inge's nurse turned up late. Anything happening?'

'General Braun is with Juel. They want to see you.'

That was bad luck: a visit from Braun on the day Peter was late. He headed for Juel's office.

Juel spoke German as a courtesy to Braun. 'Where have you been, Flemming?' he said to Peter. 'We are waiting.'

'I apologise,' Peter replied in the same language. He did not give the reason for his lateness: excuses were undignified.

General Braun wore an immaculate field service uniform, complete with high boots and holstered pistol. 'Take a look at this, Mr Flemming,' he said. He had spread several newspapers on Juel's desk, all folded open to an account of the butter shortage in Denmark. The newspapers were the *Toronto Globe*, the *Washington Post* and the *Los Angeles Times*. Also on the desk was *Reality*, which contained the original story the others had copied.

Juel said, 'We know most of the people who produce these home-made newspapers. We could pick them all up. But I'd rather leave them alone and keep an eye on them. Then, if they do something serious like blow up a bridge, we'll know who to arrest.'

Braun said, 'That might have been acceptable when their activities were confined to Denmark. But this story has gone all over the world! Berlin is furious.'

Peter was gratified. 'I'm already working on this,' he said. 'All these newspapers got the story from Reuters, which picked it up in

Stockholm. I believe that *Reality* is being smuggled to Sweden.'

'Good work!' said Braun. 'But how is it smuggled out?'

Peter hesitated. He had wanted confirmation before revealing what he suspected. However, Braun was in front of him, champing at the bit. 'I've had a tip. A detective friend in Stockholm has been discreetly asking questions at the wire service office. He thinks the newspaper comes on the Lufthansa flight that stops here.'

Braun nodded excitedly. 'So if we search every boarding passenger we should find the latest edition. Does the flight go today?'

'Yes, in a few hours,' he said.

'Then let's get moving!'

'May I make a suggestion, General? We must avoid forewarning our culprit. Let's assemble a team of detectives and German officers, but keep them at headquarters until the last minute. Allow the passengers to assemble for the flight. I'll go alone to Kastrup aerodrome to make arrangements quietly. When the passengers have checked their baggage, and they're about to board, it will be too late for anyone to slip away unnoticed—then we can pounce.'

Braun smiled knowingly. 'You're afraid that a lot of Germans marching around would give the game away.'

'Not at all, sir,' Peter said with a straight face. When the occupiers made fun of themselves, it was not wise to join in. 'It will be important for you and your men to accompany us in case there is any need to question German citizens.'

Braun's face stiffened. 'Quite so,' he said. He went to the door. 'Call me when your team is ready to depart.' He left.

'Good detective work tracing the smuggling route,' Juel said. 'But it would have been tactful to tell me before you told Braun.'

'I'm sorry, sir,' Peter said.

'All right,' Juel said. 'Put together a squad, then go to the aerodrome and phone me when the passengers are ready to board.'

Peter left Juel's room and returned to Tilde's desk. 'There's a raid on at the aerodrome this morning,' he told her. 'I'll take Bent Conrad, Peder Dresler and Knut Ellegard. And I'd like you to come along, too, in case there are female suspects to be searched.'

'Of course.'

Peter went to the door. 'I'm going ahead to Kastrup.'

He took one of the department's unmarked black Buicks out of the city and across a bridge to the island of Amager. Kastrup aerodrome was a scatter of low buildings on one side of a single runway. Peter parked outside the office of Christian Varde, the aerodrome controller. Inside, he showed his police badge. 'There will be a special security check on the flight to Stockholm today,' he told Varde. 'It has been authorised by General Braun. Do not forewarn anyone. Do you have a list of passengers expected to board the flight here?'

Varde gave Peter a sheet of paper. There were four names: two Danish men, a Danish woman, and a German man.

'Call the pilot and say that no one will be permitted to disembark at Kastrup today,' Peter said.

'Very good.'

'Where are the passengers now?'

'They should be checking in.'

'Do not load their baggage onto the aircraft until it has been searched. Is anything else loaded on the plane?'

'Coffee and sandwiches for the flight. And the fuel, of course.'

'The food and drink must be examined. One of my men will observe the refuelling.'

'Fine.' Varde went out to send the message to the pilot.

After the passengers had been checked in, Peter went to a payphone, called Juel, and told him all was ready for the raid.

He checked his watch. The flight was due now. He looked out of the window and saw the Junkers Ju-52 trimotor touch down and taxi to the terminal. The door opened, and the crew threw down the chocks that secured the wheels when the aircraft was parked.

There was a German colonel, two Danish businessmen and a white-haired lady due to board. They were waiting in Varde's office.

Juel and Braun arrived with the four detectives Peter had chosen. Tilde searched the lady in another room, while the three male suspects removed their outer clothing. Braun patted down the colonel, and Sergeant Conrad did the Danes. Nothing was found.

The passengers were allowed to go to the departure lounge, but not to board the aircraft. Their luggage was lined up outside the terminal. Bent Conrad got the keys from the passengers and Peter searched the bags himself with Juel and Braun looking on. There were no newspapers nor anything suspicious.

Taking a penknife from his pocket, Peter slit the silk lining of the old lady's expensive luggage and ran his hand beneath it. To his dismay, nothing was hidden there. He did the same to the businessmen's leather suitcases. Frustrated, he cut the stitching on the colonel's canvas duffle bag and felt inside. There was nothing. He looked up to see Juel, Braun, and the detectives staring at him.

Juel said languidly, 'Perhaps your information was wrong.'

But Peter was not finished yet. 'Let me see the food.'

A trolley bearing a tray of sandwiches and several coffeepots was wheeled out for Peter's inspection. He opened each pot and poured the coffee out. He poked about among the sandwiches. To his horror, there was nothing.

'Begin refuelling,' he said. 'I'll watch.'

A tanker was driven out to the Junkers. Fuel was pumped into the tanks of the aircraft, then the caps were closed.

'Let the passengers board,' Peter said, feeling humiliated as he returned to the departure lounge.

Juel, Braun and the detectives waited with Peter as the four angry passengers boarded. Varde tried to look as if nothing out of the ordinary had happened. The chocks were removed from the wheels by the ground crew and thrown on board, then the door was closed.

As the aircraft moved off its stand, Peter was struck by inspiration. 'Stop the plane,' he said to Varde.

Varde turned to General Braun. 'Sir, my passengers . . .'

'Stop the plane!' Peter repeated.

Varde continued to look pleadingly at Braun. After a moment, Braun nodded. 'Do as he says.'

Varde picked up a phone.

Juel said, 'Flemming, this had better be good.'

The aircraft rolled onto the runway, turned a full circle, and came back to its stand. The door opened, and the chocks were thrown down to the ground crew.

Peter led the detectives out onto the apron. Two men in overalls were wedging the chocks in front of the main wheels. Peter addressed one of them. 'Hand me that chock.'

The man looked scared, but did as he was told. The chock was a simple triangle of wood about a foot high—dirty, heavy and solid.

'And the other one,' Peter said.

The mechanic picked up the other and handed it over. It looked the same, but felt lighter. Peter found that one face was a sliding lid. He opened it. A package was inside, wrapped in oilcloth.

The mechanic turned and ran.

'Stop him!' Peter cried, but it was unnecessary. Tilde let him pass, then stuck out a foot and tripped him. He went flying.

One of the detectives jumped on him, hauled him to his feet, and twisted his arm behind his back.

'Arrest the other mechanic. He must have known what was going on,' Peter said, unwrapping the oilcloth. Inside were two copies of

33

Reality. He handed them to Juel, staring at him expectantly.

Juel said reluctantly, 'Well done, Flemming.'

Peter smiled. 'Just doing my job, sir.' He nodded at Tilde. 'Take both mechanics to headquarters for questioning.'

Also in the package was a sheaf of papers, covered with typed characters in five-letter groups that made no sense. Then enlightenment dawned. The papers bore a message in code.

Peter handed the papers to Braun. 'I think we have uncovered a spy ring, General,' he said.

 **THREE**

On Saturday, an old-fashioned carriage drawn by two horses and driven by a coachman picked up Harald Olufsen and Tik Duchwitz at the railway station in Tik's home village of Kirstenslot.

They drove from the station through a village with a tavern. At the edge of the village they turned off the road. At the far end of a half-mile drive Harald saw a fairytale castle with battlements and turrets.

Harald was intimidated. He had known the Duchwitz family were wealthy—Tik's father was a banker—but he was not prepared for this. He wondered if he would know the right way to behave.

The carriage dropped them at the cathedral-like front entrance. Harald walked in, carrying his small suitcase. The marbled hall was crammed with antique furniture, statues and paintings. Tik led him up a grand staircase into a bedroom. 'This is my room,' he said. There were no paintings here, just the stuff an eighteen-year-old collected: a football, a picture of Marlene Dietrich looking sultry, a clarinet, and a framed advertisement for a Lancia Aprilia sports car.

Harald picked up a framed photo. It showed Tik about four years ago with a girl about the same age. 'Who's the girlfriend?'

'My twin sister, Karen.'

'Oh.' She was taller than Tik in the picture. 'Obviously not an identical twin, she's too good-looking. Where does she go to school?'

'The Danish Royal Ballet.' Tik opened a door to a second, smaller bedroom. Harald followed him. 'You'll be in here, if it's all right.'

'Great,' said Harald, dropping his case on the bed.

'You could have a grander room, but you'd be miles away. Come and say hello to my mother.'

Harald followed Tik along the first-floor corridor. Tik tapped on a door. 'Are you receiving gentlemen callers, Mother?'

A voice replied, 'Come in, Josef.'

Harald followed Tik into Mrs Duchwitz's boudoir. Tik's mother looked like him. She was short, and she had the same dark eyes. She was about forty, but her black hair was already going grey.

Tik presented Harald, who shook her hand with a little bow. Mrs Duchwitz made them sit down and asked them about school. She was amiable and easy to talk to.

After a while she said, 'Go along and get ready for dinner, now.' The boys returned to Tik's room. Harald said anxiously, 'You don't wear anything special for dinner, do you?'

'Your school blazer and tie are fine.' It was all Harald had. He had no other clothes, apart from sweaters for the winter and shorts for the summer. 'Would you like to bath first?'

'Sure.'

After his bath, Harald put on his shirt and school trousers and went into Tik's room to comb his hair in the mirror over the dressing table. While he was doing this, a girl walked in without knocking. 'Hello,' she said. 'You must be Harald.'

It was the girl in the photograph. She had white skin and green eyes, and her curly hair was coppery red. She wore a long, dark green dress. She glided across the room with the easy strength of an athlete. She said, 'Well? Are you Harald?'

He managed to speak. 'Yes, I am. He felt very conscious of his bare feet. 'You're Tik's sister.'

'Tik?'

'That's what we call Josef at school.'

'Well, I'm Karen, and I don't have a nickname.'

Tik emerged from the bathroom wrapped in a towel. 'Have you no regard for a gentleman's privacy?' he said.

'No, I don't,' she retorted. 'I want a cocktail, and they won't serve them until there's at least one male in the room. How are you, anyway, you black-eyed dwarf?'

'I'm fine, though I'll be finer when the exams are over.'

'What will you do if you fail?'

'I'll work at the bank. Father will probably make me start at the bottom, filling the inkwells of the junior clerks.'

Harald said to Karen, 'He won't fail the exams.'

She replied, 'I suppose you're clever, like Josef.'

Tik said, 'Much cleverer, actually.'

Harald could not honestly deny it. Feeling bashful, he asked, 'What's it like at ballet school?'

'A cross between serving in the army and being in jail.'

Harald stared at Karen. He did not know whether to regard her as one of the boys or one of the gods. She bantered with her brother like a kid. Nevertheless she was extraordinarily graceful. He thought she was the most beautiful girl he had ever met.

'You'd better put some shoes on,' Tik said to Harald.

Harald retreated to his room and finished dressing. When he returned, Tik was looking spiffy in a black jacket and plain dark tie. Harald felt very much the schoolboy in his blazer.

Karen led the way downstairs. They entered a room with several large sofas, a grand piano, and an elderly dog on a rug in front of the fireplace. A young woman in a black dress and white apron asked Harald what he would like to drink. 'Whatever Josef is having,' he replied. There was no alcohol at the parsonage and he wasn't sure what a cocktail was.

He bent down and patted the dog, a red setter with a sprinkling of grey in its gingery fur. It opened an eye and wagged its tail.

Karen said, 'That's Thor.'

At that moment Tik's father came in, and he looked so like the dog that Harald almost laughed. A tall, thin man, his curly red hair was turning grey. Harald stood up and shook hands.

'I'm so glad to meet you,' Mr Duchwitz said. 'Josef is always talking about you. How are things at school, after your anti-Nazi outburst?'

'I wasn't punished, oddly enough,' Harald answered. 'But Heis just gave me a lecture about how much more effectively I would have made my point if I had kept my temper.'

'Setting an example himself by not being angry with you,' Mr Duchwitz said with a smile.

Harald had a question for Mr Duchwitz. 'Sir, aren't you worried about what the Nazis might do to you? We know how badly Jews are treated in Germany and Poland.'

'I do worry. But Denmark is not Germany, and the Germans seem to regard us as Danes first and Jews second.'

'So far, anyway,' Tik put in.

'It's not as if we're shopkeepers,' Karen said. 'What are they going to do to the family that owns the largest bank in Denmark?'

Harald thought that was stupid. 'The Nazis can do anything they like, you should know that by now,' he said scornfully.

'Oh, should I?' Karen said coldly and he knew he had offended her.

At that moment Mrs Duchwitz joined them, and they talked about the Danish Royal Ballet's current production, *Les Sylphides*.

'I love the music,' Harald said. He had heard it on the radio.

'Have you seen the ballet?' Mrs Duchwitz asked him.

'No. To be honest, I've never been to the theatre,' he confessed.

'Then Karen must take you,' Mrs Duchwitz said.

'Mother, I'm terribly busy,' Karen protested. 'I'm understudying a principal role!'

Harald felt hurt by her rejection, but guessed he was being punished for speaking dismissively to her about the Nazis.

The maid announced that dinner was ready. They sat at a long table in the dining room and had vegetable soup and lamb chops. There was plenty of food, despite rationing, and Mrs Duchwitz explained that much of what they ate came from the estate.

Throughout the meal, Karen said nothing directly to Harald. He was dismayed. She was the most enchanting girl he had ever met, and he had already got on the wrong side of her.

Afterwards, they returned to the drawing room. Karen went out onto the terrace for a cigarette. Harald was awestruck at the sophistication of a girl who drank cocktails *and* smoked.

When she came back in, Mr Duchwitz sat at the piano. Mrs Duchwitz stood behind him. 'Beethoven?' he said, and she nodded. He played a few notes and she began to sing a song in German. Harald was impressed, and at the end he applauded.

Tik said, 'Sing another one, Mother.'

'All right,' she said. 'But then you have to play something.'

When Tik fetched his clarinet, he played a simple Mozart lullaby. Mr Duchwitz played a Chopin waltz, from *Les Sylphides*, and Karen kicked off her shoes and showed them one of the dances she was understudying. Then they all looked at Harald.

He realised he was supposed to perform something. 'I'm not very good at classical music,' he said.

'Rubbish,' Tik said. 'You play the piano in your father's church, you told me.'

Harald sat at the piano. He really could not inflict Lutheran hymns on a cultured Jewish family. He began to play *Pine Top's Boogie-Woogie*. His left hand began the insistently rhythmic bass pattern, and the right hand played the blues discords. After a few moments he lost his self-consciousness and called out in English, 'Everybody, boogie-woogie!' at the high points just like Pine Top.

When he finished, Mr Duchwitz wore the pained expression of a man who has accidentally swallowed something rotten. Even Tik looked embarrassed. Mrs Duchwitz said, 'Well, I must say, I don't think anything quite like that has ever been heard in this room.'

Harald realised he had made a mistake. The highbrow Duchwitz family were cultured, but that did not make them open-minded. 'Oh dear,' he said. 'I see that was not the right sort of thing.'

'Indeed not,' said Mr Duchwitz.

From behind the sofa, Karen caught Harald's eye. To his surprise and delight, she gave him a broad wink.

ON SUNDAY MORNING, Harald woke up thinking about Karen. He hoped to see her, but she did not appear at breakfast. Afterwards, Tik and Harald went for a walk round the estate.

Near the end of the long drive was a ruined monastery. They explored the cloisters, where the monks had walked. Their cells were now used as storerooms for garden equipment. 'Some of this stuff hasn't been looked at for decades,' Tik said, poking at a rusty wheel.

They entered the disused church, now a junk room. A thin, black and white cat stared at them, then escaped through a glassless window. Harald lifted a canvas sheet to reveal a gleaming Rolls-Royce sedan mounted on blocks. 'Your father's?' he asked.

'Yes—put away until petrol goes on sale again.'

There was a scarred workbench with a collection of tools, presumably to maintain the car. In the corner was a washbasin with a tap. Against the wall were stacks of boxes that contained old toys.

In the far corner was a single-engined aeroplane with no wings.

Harald looked at it with interest. 'What's this?'

'A Hornet Moth, made by de Havilland, the English company. Father bought it years ago. We had great rides when it was new.'

Harald touched the great propeller, at least six feet long. The mathematically precise curves made it a work of art in his eyes. The aircraft leaned slightly to one side, and he saw the undercarriage was damaged. The fuselage was made of some kind of fabric with small rips and wrinkles in places. It was painted light blue, but the paint-work was dull, dusty and streaked with oil. It did have wings, he now saw—biplane wings, painted silver—but they were hinged, and had been swung round to point backwards.

He looked through the side window into the cabin. There were two seats side by side, and a wooden instrument panel with an assortment of dials. The controls appeared simple. In the middle was a Y-shaped joystick that could be operated from either seat.

'Did you ever fly it yourself?' Harald asked Tik.

'No, but Karen took lessons. Come on, let's go.'

Harald imagined himself soaring over the castle like a giant bird, with the roar of the engine in his ears. He could have spent another hour looking at the aircraft, but Tik was impatient.

From the back of the monastery, they followed a track through a wood. Attached to Kirstenslot was a large farm. 'It's been rented to the Nielsen family since before I was born,' Tik said. On the dirt road leading to the farmhouse they came across a tractor, and a young man in overalls peering at the engine.

Tik shook hands with him. 'Hello, Frederik, what's wrong?'

'Engine died on me in the middle of the road.'

'My friend Harald here is a wizard with all kinds of engines.'

'I wouldn't mind if he'd take a look.'

The tractor was an up-to-date model with a diesel engine. Harald bent down to study it. 'What happens when you turn her over?'

'I'll show you.' Frederik pulled a handle. The motor whined, but the engine would not catch. 'I think she needs a new fuel pump. We can't get spare parts for any of our machines.'

Harald frowned sceptically. He could smell fuel which suggested to him that the pump was working, but the diesel was not reaching the cylinders. Looking more closely, he saw that diesel was leaking from the release valve. He reached in and wiggled the nut. The entire valve assembly came away. 'There's the problem,' he said. 'The screw thread inside this nut has worn down and it's letting fuel escape. Have you got a piece of wire?'

Frederik reached into his pockets. 'I've got a stout bit of string.'

'That will do temporarily.' Harald put the valve back in position and tied it to the fuel filter outlet pipe. 'Try the starter now.'

Frederik pulled the handle, and the engine started. 'Well, I'm damned,' he said. 'You've mended it.'

'When you get a chance, replace the string with wire,' Harald said. 'Then you won't need a spare part.'

'Well, thanks.' Fred climbed on his tractor and drove off.

'That was impressive,' Tik said.

Harald shrugged. For as long as he could remember, he had been able to fix machines.

They returned to the castle. In the front courtyard Harald was surprised to see Poul Kirke, the cousin of their classmate Mads and friend of Harald's brother Arne. Poul was wearing shorts, and a bicycle was propped against the brick portico. Harald had met Poul several times, and now he stopped to talk while Tik went inside.

'Are you working here?' Poul asked Harald.

'No, visiting. School isn't over yet.'

'The farm hires students for the harvest, I know. What are you planning to do this summer?'

'I'm not sure. Last year I worked as a labourer on the site of a new German base on Sande.'

Poul seemed interested. 'Oh? What sort of base?'

'Some kind of radio station, I think. They fired all the Danes before they installed the equipment.' Harald was about to ask what Poul was doing at Kirstenslot when the answer became obvious. Karen came round the side of the castle, looking ravishing in khaki shorts and pushing a bicycle.

'Good morning, Harald,' she said. She went up to Poul and kissed him. 'Hi,' she said.

Harald was dismayed. He had been counting on an hour with Karen at the lunch table. But she was off on a bicycle ride with Poul, who was obviously her boyfriend.

Poul held Karen's hands. 'Are you ready to go?'

'All set.'

They climbed on their bikes and Harald watched them set off side by side down the half-mile drive in the sunshine.

HERMIA MOUNT was about to get the sack. Two Danes working for MI6 had been arrested at Kastrup aerodrome. They were now in custody and undoubtedly being interrogated. It was a bad blow to the Nightwatchmen network.

Hermia had worked for the British civil service for a decade, and she knew its ways. Her boss, Herbert Woodie, was a peacetime MI6 man, a long-serving bureaucrat. He needed someone to blame in the department, and Hermia was a suitable candidate. Woodie had never been comfortable working with a woman, and he would be happy to see her replaced by a man.

But there was no one else in MI6 who had her ground-level knowledge of Denmark. Furthermore, the visit of Digby Hoare had given an urgency to her work. The Germans' aircraft detection system could be the weapon that would win the war. The more she thought about it, the more likely it seemed that the key to the problem could lie in Denmark. The Danish west coast seemed the ideal location for a warning station designed to detect bombers approaching Germany. She had to keep her job. And that meant outwitting her boss.

'This is bad news,' Woodie said as she stood in front of his desk.

'There's always danger when an operative is interrogated,' Hermia said. 'However, in this case I feel the risk is slight.'

Woodie grunted. 'We may need to set up an inquiry.'

Her heart sank. An inquiry meant he would have to come up with a scapegoat. 'The two men arrested don't have any secrets to betray,' she said. 'They were ground crew at the aerodrome. One of the Nightwatchmen would give them papers to be smuggled out, and they would stow the contraband in a hollow wheel chock.'

'Who passed them the papers?'

'Matthies Hertz, an army lieutenant. He's gone into hiding. And the ground crew don't know anyone else in the network.'

'But how did the Danish police get to them in the first place?'

'I think the problem is at the Swedish end.'

'Ah.' Woodie brightened. Sweden, being a neutral country, was not under his control. 'Take a seat, Miss Mount.'

'Thank you,' Hermia said. 'The Swedish go-between has been passing illegal newspapers to Reuters in Stockholm, and this may have alerted the Germans. You have always had a strict rule that our agents avoid ancillary activities such as propaganda work.' This was flattery: she had never heard Woodie say any such thing.

However, he nodded sagely. 'Indeed.'

'I reminded them of this, but the damage had been done,' Hermia said. 'Shall I do you a memo, mentioning your rule and quoting my signal reminding the Swedish office of the rule?'

'Good idea.'

'We'll need a new way of getting information out of Denmark.'

Woodie had no idea how to organise an alternative smuggling operation. 'Ah, that's a problem,' he said with a touch of panic.

'Fortunately, we have a fall-back option, using the boat train that crosses from Elsinore in Denmark to Helsingborg in Sweden. I could say in my memo that you've authorised me to action that.'

'Fine.'

She hesitated. 'And . . . the inquiry?'

'You know, I'm not sure that will be necessary. Your memo should serve to answer any questions.'

She concealed her relief. She was not going to be fired after all. 'Very good, sir.'

'What are the rest of your Nightwatchmen up to?'

'I'm about to ask them to keep their eyes open for any indications that the Germans have developed long-distance aircraft detection.'

'Don't do that! If the enemy finds out we're asking that question, he'll guess we've got it!'

'But, sir—what if he does have it?'

'He doesn't. You can rest assured.'

'The gentleman who came here from Downing Street last week seemed to think otherwise.'

'In strict confidence, an MI6 committee looked into the whole radar question quite recently, and concluded that it would be another eighteen months before the enemy developed such a system.'

She smiled. 'That's so reassuring,' she lied. 'I expect you were on the committee yourself, sir?'

Woodie nodded. 'In fact I chaired it.'

'Thank you for setting my mind at rest. I'll get on with that memo.'

Hermia walked back to her office. She had saved her job, and she had found out the name of the long-distance aircraft detection system—radar—but it was clear Woodie would not let her investigate whether the Germans had such a system in Denmark.

She could investigate enemy radar without Woodie's permission, of course. However, she did not know what to tell her Nightwatchmen. What should they be looking for, and where? She needed more information before she could brief Poul Kirke. And Woodie was not going to give it to her.

She sat down at her desk, picked up the phone, and said, 'Please connect me with 10 Downing Street.'

SHE MET DIGBY HOARE in Trafalgar Square. She stood at the foot of Nelson's Column and watched him cross the road from Whitehall. They shook hands, then walked towards Soho.

She had thought they were going for a drink in a pub, but Digby led her to a small French restaurant. The tables either side of them were empty, so they could talk without being overheard.

As soon as they had ordered, she said, 'I want to use my agents in Denmark to find out whether the Germans have radar.'

He looked at her through narrowed eyes. 'The question is more complicated than that. It's now beyond doubt that they have radar, as we do. But theirs is more effective than ours—devastatingly so.'

'Oh.' She was taken aback. 'Woodie told me . . . never mind.'

'We're desperate to find out why their system is so good.'

'All right.' She rapidly readjusted her ideas in the light of this new information. 'Just the same, it seems likely that some of this machinery is in Denmark.'

'It would seem to be a logical place—and the code name "Freya" suggests Scandinavia.'

'So what should my people be looking for?'

'That's difficult.' He frowned. 'We don't know what their machinery looks like—that's the point, isn't it?'

'I presume it gives out radio waves. And the signals must travel a good distance otherwise the warning wouldn't be early enough.'

'Yes,' Digby said. 'It would be useless unless the signals travelled at least, say, fifty miles. Probably more.'

'Could we listen for them?'

He raised his eyebrows in surprise. 'Yes, with a radio receiver. Clever notion—I don't know why no one else thought of it.'

'Can the signals be distinguished from other transmissions?'

He nodded. 'You'd be listening for a series of very rapid pulses. You'd hear it as a continuous musical note. It would be quite different from the dots and dashes of military traffic.'

'Could you put together a radio receiver for picking up such signals?'

He looked thoughtful. 'It's got to be portable, presumably.'

'It should pack into a suitcase and work off a battery, so it can be used anywhere.'

'It might be possible. There's a team of boffins in Welwyn who do this stuff all day. They could probably cobble something together.'

Their food came. Hermia had ordered a seafood fricassee. The dish contained sliced eel and winkles, and was fresh and well seasoned, and she tucked in with relish.

Now and again she caught Digby's eye, and he always had the same look, a mixture of adoration and lust. It alarmed her. If he fell in love with her, it could only lead to trouble and heartbreak. But it was pleasing, as well as embarrassing, to have a man so obviously desire her. At one point she felt herself flush, and she put her hand to her throat to hide her blushes. She deliberately turned her thoughts to Arne which made her feel cooler towards Digby.

When they finished their meal, they left the restaurant and found that it was dark, although there was a full moon. As they were crossing St James's Park the moon went behind a cloud, and Digby turned and kissed her. She could not help admiring the swift sureness of his moves. His lips were on hers before she could turn away. She knew she should be indignant, but to her consternation she found herself responding. She suddenly remembered what it was like to feel a man's body and hot skin.

They kissed hungrily for a minute, then his hand went to her breast, and that broke the spell. How could she enjoy kissing Digby when she loved Arne? She put a resisting hand on Digby's chest. 'No more,' she said firmly.

THERE HAD BEEN about 200 Danish ships at sea on April 9, 1940, when Hitler invaded Denmark. All that day, Danish-language broadcasts by the BBC had appealed to sailors to head for Allied ports rather than return home to a conquered land. About 5,000 men accepted the offer of refuge. Most sought harbour on the east coast of England and continued to sail throughout the war.

Hermia decided to go to the fishing town of Stokeby. She had visited the place twice previously to talk to the Danes there. On this occasion she told Herbert Woodie that her mission was to check her somewhat out-of-date plans of the main Danish ports and make any alterations necessary. He believed her.

She had a different story for Digby Hoare. Two days after she had met him in London, Digby came to Bletchley with a radio receiver neatly packed into a tan leather suitcase. He showed her how to use the equipment.

Her original plan had been to attempt to smuggle the radio receiver to the Nightwatchmen, but she had since thought of something simpler. The signals from the radar apparatus could probably be picked up at sea just as easily as on land. She told Digby she was going to pass the suitcase to the captain of a fishing boat and teach him how to use it. Digby approved. That plan might well have worked, but in truth she did not want to hand such an important job over to someone else. So she intended to go herself.

She took a train on Friday afternoon, dressed for the sea in trousers, boots and a loose sweater. She arrived in Stokeby at eight o'clock and went from the railway station to the dock. There she learned that a Danish captain she had met on her last visit here, was due to sail the North Sea in the morning in his vessel. Hermia explained that she needed to get close to the Danish coast in an attempt to listen to a German wireless transmission. The captain did not question her story and agreed to take her as a passenger.

The next morning Hermia and four crew members boarded the *Morganmand*. Dawn was breaking as the little vessel threaded its way through the defensive minefield at the mouth of the harbour.

The weather was fine, but they encountered a swell of five or six feet as soon as they left the shelter of the land.

When the boat approached its nearest point to Denmark—about

seventy-five miles offshore—Hermia took her suitcase receiver on deck. After connecting the battery to the radio, she was relieved to see the dials flicker. She fixed the aerial to the mast with a length of wire, let the set warm up, then put on the headphones.

Hermia roamed up and down the wireless frequencies. At the first pass, she heard nothing that might have been radar. She repeated the exercise more slowly, making sure she missed nothing. For the next two hours, she continued to scan the frequencies. The likeliest place for a radar station was at the southern end of Denmark's coast, near the border with Germany.

Finally, as she scanned through the frequencies once again she thought she heard a musical note. She reversed the knob and went down, searching for the spot. She got a lot of static, then the note again—a machine-like tone about an octave above middle C. The wavelength was 2.4 metres. She made a note in the little book Digby had tucked into the suitcase.

Now she had to determine the direction. Incorporated into the receiver was a dial graduated from one to 360 with a needle pointing to the source of the signal. Digby had emphasised that the dial had to be aligned precisely with the centre line of the boat. Then the direction of the signal could be calculated from the heading of the boat and the needle on the dial.

A crew member established their heading and position. Hermia wrote down those numbers, then took another reading of the odd sound so that she could triangulate the source of the broadcast.

After getting another update on the boat's heading and position, Hermia went into the wheelhouse and found a large-scale chart. She marked the two positions she had noted and drew lines for the bearing of the signal from each position. The lines intersected off the coast, near the island of Sande.

'Good Lord,' she said. 'That's where my fiancé comes from.'

'Sande?' the captain said. 'I know it—I went to watch the racing car speed trials there a few years back.'

A few minutes later, she took another heading. The signal was weak now, but the third line on the map made a triangle with the other two, and the island of Sande lay mainly within that triangle.

Hermia was jubilant. Her guess had been right. The signal she had been expecting was coming from the most logical place.

Now she needed to send Poul Kirke, or one of his team, to Sande to look around. As soon as she returned to Bletchley she would send a coded message. She could hardly wait to tell Digby.

FOUR

Harald Olufsen thought the Tiger Moth was the most beautiful machine he had ever seen. It looked like a butterfly poised for flight, its upper and lower wings spread wide, its toy-car wheels resting lightly on the grass. A sprightly, gleaming cousin to the dilapidated Hornet Moth he had seen at Kirstenslot, it had two open cockpits behind the single engine in the nose, which drove the big cream-painted propeller. The two aircraft were also mechanically similar.

'You'll notice that the wings are flat underneath but curved above,' said Arne. 'When the aircraft is moving, the air over the wings is forced to move faster than the air passing underneath.' He gave an engaging grin. 'For reasons I've never understood, this lifts the aircraft off the ground.'

'It creates a pressure difference,' Harald said.

The senior class at Jansborg Skole were spending the day at the Army Aviation School at Vodal. They were being shown round by Arne and Poul Kirke. It was a recruiting exercise by the army, who were having trouble persuading bright young men to join an air force that had nothing to do.

The fifteen boys had toured the air base and sat through a lecture. Now they were eager for the individual flying lesson that had been promised to each of them as the climax of the day. Five Tiger Moths were lined up on the grass. Danish military aircraft had been grounded since the beginning of the occupation, but special permission had been granted for today's exercise.

Poul Kirke took over. 'I want you to look into the cockpit, one at a time,' he said. 'Stand on the black walkway on the lower wing. Don't step anywhere else or your foot will go through the fabric.'

Tik Duchwitz went first. Poul said, 'On the left side you see a silver throttle lever, which controls speed, and a green trim lever, which applies a spring loading to the elevator control. If the trim is correctly set when cruising, the aircraft should fly level when you take your hand off the stick.'

Harald went last. He could not help being interested, despite his resentment at the smoothly arrogant way Poul had swept Karen Duchwitz off on her bicycle.

As he stepped down, Poul said, 'So, what do you think?'

Harald shrugged. 'It seems straightforward.'

'Then you can go first,' Poul said with a grin.

The others laughed, but Harald was pleased. They went to the hangar and put on flying suits. Helmets and goggles were also given out. To Harald's annoyance, Poul made a point of helping him.

'Last time we met was at Kirstenslot,' Poul said as he adjusted Harald's goggles.

Harald nodded curtly, not wishing to be reminded. He could not help wondering exactly what Poul's relationship with Karen was.

When they were ready, the first five students returned to the field, each with a pilot. Harald would have liked to go up with his brother, but once again Poul chose Harald.

An airman in oily overalls was refuelling the aircraft. 'First, the preflight inspection,' Poul said. He kicked the tyres and wiggled the ailerons. 'You mentioned that you had worked on the new German base at Sande,' he said casually.

'Yes.'

'What sort of work?'

'Just general labouring—digging holes, mixing concrete.'

Poul moved to the back of the aircraft and checked the elevator. 'You said last time that you think the place is a radio station of some kind. How do you know?'

'I've seen the equipment.'

Poul looked at him sharply, and Harald realised this was no casual enquiry. 'Is it visible from outside?'

'No. The place is fenced and guarded, and the radio equipment is screened by trees, but one night I was in a hurry to get home so I took a short cut across the base. I saw a large aerial, maybe twelve feet square, on a rotating base.'

The airman finished refuelling the aircraft and interrupted the conversation. 'Ready when you are, sir.'

Poul said to Harold, 'Ready to fly?'

'Front or back?'

'The trainee always sits in the back.'

Harald climbed into the narrow cockpit and sat down.

Poul leaned in to adjust Harald's safety harness. 'These aircraft were designed for training, so they have dual controls,' he said. 'While I'm flying, rest your hands and feet lightly on the controls and feel how I'm moving them. I'll tell you when to take over.'

'How will we talk?'

Poul pointed to a Y-shaped rubber pipe like a doctor's stethoscope.

'This works like the speaking tube on a ship.' He showed Harald how to fix the ends to earpieces in his helmet.

Poul climbed into the front seat.

After the airman primed the engine, he swung the propeller, stepping back immediately afterwards. The engine fired and the propeller turned. There was a roar, and the little aircraft trembled. Harald had a sudden vivid sense of how light and frail it was, and remembered that it was made, not of metal, but of wood and linen.

Once the engine note rose, the airman removed the wheel chocks. Suddenly, the throttle lever beneath Harald's hand moved forward, the engine roared louder, and the Tiger Moth taxied eagerly along the runway. After a few seconds, the control stick eased away from Harald's knees. The little aircaft gathered speed, rattling and shaking over the grass. Harald's blood thrilled with excitement. Then the stick eased back, the aircraft seemed to jump from the ground, and they were airborne.

It was exhilarating. They climbed steadily. To one side, Harald could see a small village. Poul banked right. Feeling himself tipped sideways, Harald fought the panicky notion that he was going to fall out of the cockpit. To calm himself, he looked at the instruments. The rev counter showed 2,000rpm, and their speed was sixty miles per hour. They were at an altitude of 1,000 feet. The needle on the turn-and-slip indicator pointed straight up.

The aircraft straightened out and levelled off. The throttle lever moved back, the engine note dipped, and the revs slipped back to 1,900. Poul said, 'Are you holding the stick?'

'Yes.'

'Check the line of the horizon. It probably goes through my head. When I release the controls, I want you to simply keep the wings level and the horizon in the same place relative to my ears.'

Feeling nervous, Harald said, 'OK.'

'You have control.'

Harald felt the aircraft come alive in his hands. The line of the horizon fell to Poul's shoulders, showing that the nose had lifted, and he realised that a barely conscious fear of diving to the ground was making him pull back on the stick. He pushed it forward and the horizon line rose to Poul's ears.

The aircraft lurched sideways and banked. Harald felt they were about to fall out of the sky. 'What was that?' he cried.

'Just a gust of wind. Correct for it, but not too much.'

Fighting back panic, Harald moved the stick against the direction of bank. Then he saw that he was climbing again, and brought the nose down.

'That's good,' Poul said. 'Now press lightly on the rudder pedals with both feet, then look at the turn-and-slip indicator.'

Harald wanted to say, How can I do that and fly the aircraft at the same time? He forced himself to take his eyes off the horizon for a second and look at the instrument panel.

'When I take my feet off the rudder, the nose will yaw left and right with the turbulence. In case you're not sure, check the indicator. When the aircraft yaws left, the needle will move to the right, telling you to press down with your right foot to correct.'

'All right.'

Harald felt no sideways movement, but a few moments later, when he managed to steal a glance at the dial, he saw he was yawing left. He pressed down on the rudder pedal with his right foot. Slowly, the pointer edged back to the central position. He looked up and saw that he was diving slightly. He pulled the stick back.

Poul said, 'Now let's try a turn. Ease the stick to the left.'

Harald did so. The aircraft banked left and he again experienced the sickening feeling that he was going to fall out. But the aircraft began to swing round to the left and Harald felt a surge of excitement as he realised he was actually steering the Tiger Moth.

The angle of bank seemed dangerously steep to Harald, but he held the turn, keeping the nose up. He had turned through three-quarters of a circle before Poul at last said, 'Straighten up.'

Harald eased the stick right and the aircraft straightened.

'Can you see the airfield?'

At first Harald could not. He had no idea what the air base would look like from above.

Poul helped him out. 'A row of long white buildings beside a bright green field. Look to the left of the propeller.'

'I see it.'

'Head that way, keeping the airfield on the left of our nose.'

Until now, Harald had not thought about the course they were following. It had been all he could manage to keep the aircraft steady.

'You're climbing,' Poul said. 'Throttle back an inch and bring us down to a thousand feet as we approach the buildings.'

Harald throttled back and eased the stick forward.

'That's it. But keep heading for the runway.'

Harald saw that he was headed for the hangars. He put the aircraft into a shallow turn, correcting with the rudder, then lined it up with the runway. But now he could see that he was too high.

'I'll take over from here,' Poul said. He closed the throttle, and the aircraft glided gradually to the runway. A few seconds before touch-down, he eased the stick back. At last there was a bump as the wheels touched the ground.

Poul turned off the runway and taxied towards their parking space. He shut down the engine and climbed out. Harald pushed back his goggles, took off his helmet, fumbled with his safety harness, and stepped out of his seat.

'You did very well,' Poul said. 'Showed quite a talent for it, in fact.'

'I'm sorry I couldn't bring it in to the runway.'

'I doubt if any of the other boys will even be allowed to try. Let's go and get changed.'

When Harald had got out of his flying suit, Poul said, 'Come to my office for a minute.' Harald went with him to a small room with a filing cabinet, a desk and a couple of chairs.

'Would you mind making a drawing of that radio equipment you were describing to me earlier?' Poul's tone was casual.

Harald had wondered if the topic would come up again. 'Sure.'

'Sit at the desk. There's a box of pencils and some paper in the drawer. I'll come back in fifteen minutes.'

Poul left and Harald began to draw. He cast his mind back to that rainy night. He was no artist but he could render machinery accurately. When he had finished, he turned the paper over and made a plan of the island of Sande, showing the position of the base.

Poul came back, studied the drawings intently, then said, 'This is excellent—thank you.'

'You're welcome.'

Poul opened the filing cabinet. The files were labelled with names, presumably of pupils. He selected a file marked 'Andersen, H.C.'. Hans Christian Andersen was Denmark's most famous writer, and Harald guessed the file might be a hiding place. Sure enough, Poul put the drawings in the folder and returned the file to its place.

'Let's go back to the others,' he said. He went to the door. 'Making drawings of German military installations is a crime. It would be best not to mention this to anyone—not even Arne.'

Harald nodded. 'I'll agree to that—on one condition. That you tell me something honestly.'

Poul shrugged. 'All right, I'll try.'

'There is a Resistance movement, isn't there?'

'Yes,' Poul said, looking serious. 'And now you're in it.'

TILDE JESPERSEN WORE a flowery perfume that wafted across the table and teased Peter Flemming's nostrils. He imagined how the fragrance would rise from her skin as he slipped off her blouse.

'What are you thinking about?' she said.

He was tempted to tell her. Then he thought of his wife. He took his marital vows seriously. Other people might think he had a good excuse for breaking them, but he set himself higher standards.

So he said, 'I was thinking about you tripping up the runaway mechanic at the aerodrome. You showed great presence of mind.'

'I didn't even think about it, just stuck out my foot.'

'You have good instincts. I was never in favour of women police officers, but no one could deny you're a first-class cop. The great thing about you, Tilde—you never try to get men to do your work by playing the helpless female.'

He intended his remark as a compliment, but she did not look pleased. 'I never ask for help at all,' she said crisply.

The waiter came. They ordered soft cheese and cucumbers on their smorrebrod. They handed their ration cards to the waiter.

Tilde said, 'Any progress in the spy case?'

'Not really. The two men we arrested at the aerodrome were sent to Hamburg for what the Gestapo calls "deep interrogation", and they gave the name of their contact. But he has disappeared.'

'A dead end, then.'

'Yes.' The phrase made him think of another dead end he had run into. 'Do you know any Jews?'

She looked surprised. 'One or two, I should think. Why?'

'I'm making a list.'

'A list of Jews? Why?'

'The usual reason. It's my job to keep tabs on troublemakers.'

'And Jews are troublemakers?'

'The Germans think so. Now, it's easy to identify new Jewish immigrants. They dress funny, they speak with a peculiar accent, and most of them live in the same few Copenhagen streets. But there are thousands of Jews whose families have been Danish for centuries. *They* look and talk the same as everyone else. If Jewish groups start to organise resistance to the Germans, we'll need to know where to look for suspects. So I'm making a list.'

'How? You can't just go around asking people.'

'I have two junior detectives going through the phone book, making notes of Jewish-sounding names. What I'd really like to do is raid the synagogue. They probably have a membership list.'

She was looking disapproving, but she said, 'Why don't you?'

'Juel won't allow it.'

'I think he's right. What if the Nazis decide to round up all the Jews and send them to those concentration camps they have in Germany? They'll use your list!'

'There's always a risk that information will be misused.'

'So wouldn't it be better not to make the damn list?'

How could she be so stupid? It maddened him to be opposed by someone he thought of as a comrade in the war against lawbreakers. 'No!' he shouted. 'If we thought that way, we wouldn't have a security department. So, you'd refuse to work on this with me?'

'I'm a police officer, and you're my boss. I'll do what you say.'

'Do you mean it?'

'Look, if you wanted to make a complete list of witches in Denmark, I'd tell you I didn't think witches were criminals or subversives—but I'd help you make the list.'

Their food arrived. There was an awkward silence as they began to eat. After a few minutes, Tilde said, 'How are things at home?'

'Inge is the same,' he said.

'No improvement?'

'When the brain is damaged that badly, it doesn't mend.'

'It must be hard for you.'

'I'm fortunate to have a generous father. I couldn't afford a nurse on police wages—Inge would have to go into an asylum.'

Tilde gave him a look that was hard to read. It was almost as if she felt the asylum might not be a bad solution.

After lunch they returned to the Politigaarden. As they entered the building, they were hailed by Frederik Juel. 'Come with me, Flemming,' he said. 'We've been summoned by General Braun.'

It was a short walk from the Politigaarden to the town square, where the Germans had taken over a building called the Dagmarhus. They were shown to Walter Braun's office, a corner room furnished with an antique desk and a leather couch. Braun wore his pistol even here, Peter noted, as if to say that although he had a cosy office, nevertheless he meant business.

Braun looked pleased with himself. 'Our people have decoded the message you found in the hollow aeroplane chock,' he said.

'Very impressive,' Juel murmured.

Braun opened a file on his desk. 'It comes from a group calling themselves the Nightwatchmen. Does that mean anything to you?'

'I'll check the files, but I'm pretty sure we haven't come across this name before,' Peter said. 'What's the content of the message?'

'Details of our military dispositions in Denmark. Locations of anti-aircraft batteries in and around Copenhagen,' Braun said. 'German naval vessels in the harbour last month. Regiments stationed in Arhus and Morlunde. Can you find these people?'

'I certainly hope so.'

Braun's focus of attention had switched entirely to Peter, as if Juel were not there. 'Do you think the same people are putting out the illegal newspapers?'

'We keep an eye on the underground editors. If they were making observations of German military dispositions, we'd have noticed. I believe this is a new organisation we haven't encountered.'

'Then how will you catch them?'

'There is one group of potential subversives whom we have never properly investigated—the Jews.'

Peter heard a sharp intake of breath from Juel.

Braun said, 'You had better take a look at them.'

'It's not always easy to know who Jews are, in this country.'

'Then go to the synagogue!'

'Good idea,' Peter said. 'They may have a membership list.'

Juel gave Peter a thunderous look, but said nothing.

BACK AT HEADQUARTERS, Peter swiftly assembled his team, choosing the same detectives he had used at Kastrup: Conrad, Dresler, Ellegard, and Tilde Jespersen. They drove to the yellow-brick synagogue. Peter stationed Ellegard at the gate.

An elderly man in a yarmulke appeared from the Jewish old people's home next door. 'May I help you?' he said politely.

'We're police officers,' Peter said. 'Do you have the keys to the synagogue?'

The man's face took on a look of fear. 'Yes.'

'Let us in.'

The man took a bunch of keys from his pocket and opened a door. Most of the building was taken up by the main hall, a richly decorated room with gilded Egyptian columns.

Peter said to the man, 'Show me your membership list.'

'Membership? What do you mean?'

'You must have the names and addresses of your congregation.'

'No—all Jews are welcome.'

Peter's instinct told him the man was telling the truth, but he told Dresler and Conrad to search the place anyway. They returned in a few minutes from opposite ends of the building empty-handed.

Peter supposed it was possible the synagogue had no register of members. More likely, they used to have one but destroyed it the day the Germans invaded. 'You must write to your people sometimes, asking them to donate to charities, telling them of events.'

'We put up a notice,' the rabbi said, 'in the community centre.'

'Ah,' said Peter with a satisfied smile. 'The community centre.'

It was about a mile away in a large building. A young man with a disdainful air was in charge of the office. He said they had no list of names and addresses, but the detectives searched the place anyway.

The young man's name was Ingemar Gammel, and something about him made Peter thoughtful. He sat at a desk and looked on coolly while his office was ransacked.

'I think this is what we're looking for, boss,' said Conrad, passing Peter a black ring binder.

Peter looked inside and saw page after page of names and addresses. 'Well done,' he said. He flicked through the pages, looking for anything odd or familiar, but nothing caught his eye.

Gammel's jacket hung from a hook behind the door. In the inside pocket Peter found a slim diary. He opened it.

The entries looked normal: lunch dates, Mother's birthday, phone Jorgen about Wilder. 'Who is Jorgen?' Peter asked.

Gammel said, 'My cousin, Jorgen Lumpe. We exchange books.'

'And Wilder?'

'Thornton Wilder, an American writer.'

Peter turned to the back of the diary. He found a list of names and addresses, some with phone numbers. He picked a name at random. 'Hilde Bjergager—who is she?'

'A lady friend,' Gammel answered coolly.

Peter tried another. 'Bertil Bruun?'

Gammel remained unflustered. 'We play tennis.'

'Poul Kirke?'

'Old friend.'

'Preben Klausen.'

'Picture dealer.'

For the first time, Gammel showed a hint of emotion, but it was relief, rather than guilt. Did he think he had got away with something? What was the significance of the picture dealer? Or was the previous name the important one? 'Poul Kirke is an old friend?'

'We were at university together.' Gammel's voice was even, but there was just the suggestion of fear in his eyes.

Peter looked again at the diary. Beside the phone number was a capital 'N'. 'What does this mean—the letter N?' Peter said.

'Naestved. It's his number at Naestved.'

'What's his other number?'

'He doesn't have another.'

'So why do you need the annotation?'

'To tell you the truth, I don't remember,' Gammel said irritably.

It might have been true. On the other hand, 'N' might stand for Nightwatchman. 'What does he do for a living?' Peter said.

'He's an army pilot.'

'Ah.' Peter had speculated that the Nightwatchmen might be army people because of their observations of military details. 'Which base?'

'Vodal.'

'I thought you said he was at Naestved.'

'It's nearby.'

'It's twenty miles away,' Peter said to Conrad. 'Arrest him.'

THE SEARCH of Ingemar Gammel's apartment was disappointing. Peter found nothing of interest: no code book, no subversive literature, no weapons. He concluded that Gammel must be a minor figure in the spy ring, one whose role was simply to make observations and report them to a central contact. That key man would compile the messages and send them to England. But who was the pivotal figure? Peter hoped it might be Poul Kirke.

The flying school where Poul Kirke was stationed was fifty miles away. They went in two cars, black police Buicks. Peter thought the army might put obstacles in his way, so he had asked General Braun to detail a German officer to impose authority if necessary, and a Major Schwarz from his staff was in the lead car.

Vodal was a grass airfield with a scatter of low buildings. Half a dozen Tiger Moths were parked in a line. As Peter got out of the car, he saw Arne Olufsen, his boyhood rival from Sande, saunter across the car park in his smart brown army uniform.

The sour taste of resentment came into Peter's mouth. Peter and Arne had been friends, all through childhood, until their families had quarrelled twelve years ago. Alex Flemming, Peter's father, had been convicted of tax fraud and Pastor Olufson had publicly expelled him from the congregation for a week. This humiliation had been much worse for Axel than the fine with which the court had punished him. Peter had sworn then that if any member of the Olufsen family ever transgressed there would be no mercy.

He hardly dared hope that Arne was involved in the spy ring. That would be sweet revenge.

Arne caught his eye. 'Peter!' He looked surprised.

'Is this where you work?' Peter said.

'When there's any work to do.' Arne was as debonair and relaxed as ever. If he had anything to feel guilty about, he was concealing it well. 'More to the point, what are *you* doing here?' Arne glanced at the German major. 'A dangerous outbreak of littering?'

Peter did not find Arne's raillery funny. 'Routine investigation,' he replied. 'Where will I find your commanding officer?'

Arne pointed to a low building. 'Base headquarters. You need Squadron Leader Renthe.'

Peter left him and went into the building. Renthe was a lanky man with a bristly moustache. Peter introduced himself. 'I'm here to interview one of your men, Flight Lieutenant Poul Kirke.'

The squadron leader said, 'What's the problem?'

Peter told a polite lie. 'He's been dealing in stolen property.'

'When military personnel are suspected of crimes, we prefer to investigate the matter ourselves.'

'Of course you do.' He moved a hand in the direction of Schwarz. 'However our German friends want the police to deal with it, so your *preferences* are irrelevant. Is Kirke on the base?'

'He happens to be flying.'

'I thought your planes were grounded.'

'As a rule, yes, but there are exceptions. We're expecting a visit from a Luftwaffe group tomorrow and they want to be taken up in our training aircraft, so we have permission to do test flights today. Kirke should land in a few minutes.'

'I'll search his quarters meanwhile. Where does he bed down?'

Renthe hesitated. 'Dormitory A, at the far end of the runway.'

'Does he have an office, or a locker?'

'He has a small office three doors along this corridor.'

'I'll start there. Tilde, come with me. Conrad, go out to the airfield to meet Kirke when he comes back. Dresler and Ellegard, search Dormitory A. Squadron leader, thank you for your help.'

Peter and Tilde went along the corridor to a door marked CHIEF FLYING INSTRUCTOR. A desk and a filing cabinet were squeezed into a small room. Peter and Tilde began to search the filing cabinet.

After fifteen minutes, Tilde made a surprised noise and said, 'This is odd.' She handed him a sheet of paper. It bore a careful sketch of a large square aerial on a stand, surrounded by a wall.

Tilde looked over his shoulder. 'What do you think it can be?'

'I've never seen anything like it. Anything else in the file?'

'No.' She showed him a folder marked 'Andersen, H.C.'.

Peter grunted. 'Hans Christian Andersen—that's suspicious in itself.' He turned the sheet over to a sketch of an island whose long, thin shape was as familiar to Peter as the map of Denmark itself. 'This is Sande, where my father lives,' he said. Looking more closely, he saw that the map showed the new German base.

'Bang,' Peter said softly.

Tilde's blue eyes were shining. 'We've caught a spy.'

'Not yet,' Peter said. 'But we're about to.'

They went outside and walked to the airfield. Standing beside Conrad, near where the planes were parked, he pointed to an incoming aircraft and said, 'I think this must be our man.'

It was a Tiger Moth. As it descended for landing, Peter reflected that there was no doubt Poul Kirke was a spy. The evidence in the filing cabinet would be enough to hang him. But before that happened, Peter had a lot of questions to ask.

One of the police Buicks arrived on the runway in a tearing hurry. It skidded to a stop, and Dresler jumped out, excitedly waving a bright yellow book. 'This is his code book!' he said.

Peter threw him a nervous look. He did not want a kerfuffle that might forewarn Poul Kirke. Glancing around, he realised the group at the edge of the runway appeared somewhat out of place: himself in a dark suit, Schwarz in German uniform, a woman, and now a man jumping out of a car. They looked like a reception committee.

Peter looked at the aircraft now taxiing towards the parking area. He could see Kirke in the open cockpit but could not read the man's expression behind the goggles and helmet. However, there was no room to misinterpret what happened next. The engine suddenly roared louder as the throttle was opened wide. The aircraft swung round. 'Damn, he's going to run for it!' Peter cried.

The plane picked up speed and came directly at them.

Peter drew his pistol. He wanted to take Kirke alive, and interrogate him, but he would rather have him dead than let him get away.

The aircraft's tail came up off the ground, bringing Kirke's head and shoulders into view. Peter took aim at the helmet and pulled the trigger, emptying the seven-shot magazine of the Walther PPK. He saw with disappointment that he had shot too high, for a series of small holes appeared in the fuel tank over the pilot's head, and petrol was spurting into the cockpit, but the aircraft did not falter.

The others threw themselves flat.

As the spinning propeller approached him at sixty miles per hour, Peter flung himself to the ground. The lower wing passed within inches of his head. He looked up. The aircraft was climbing. The bullets seemed to have had no effect. Peter had failed.

Then there was the whoosh of a sudden fire, and a single big flame rose from the cockpit. It spread with ghastly speed all over the head and shoulders of the pilot, whose clothing must have been soaked with petrol. The aircraft continued to climb. Then Kirke's body slumped, apparently pushing the control stick forward, and the Tiger Moth turned nose-down and dived the short distance to earth, plunging like an arrow into the ground.

Tilde was shaking. 'My God, how dreadful—the poor man.'

Peter put his arms round her. 'Yes,' he said. 'And the worst of it is, now he can't answer questions.'

 **FIVE**

The sign outside the building read DANISH INSTITUTE OF FOLK SONG AND COUNTRY DANCING, but that was just to fool the authorities. Down the steps and inside the windowless basement, there was a jazz club.

On the tiny stage, a young woman sat at the piano, crooning ballads into a microphone. Perhaps it was jazz, but it was not the music Harald was passionate about. He was waiting for Memphis Johnny Madison, who was coloured, even though he had lived most of his life in Copenhagen and had probably never seen Memphis.

It was two in the morning. Earlier this evening, after lights out at school, Harald, Mads and Tik had put their clothes back on, sneaked out of the dormitory building, and caught the last train into the city. It was risky—they would be in deep trouble if they were found out—but it would be worth it to see Memphis Johnny.

The aquavit Harald was drinking was making him even more euphoric. In the back of his mind was the thrilling memory that he was now in the Resistance. After Poul had admitted that there was a secret organisation, Harald had said he would do anything else he could to help. Poul had promised to use him as one of his observers. He still had the sour taste of jealousy in the pit of his stomach every time he thought about Poul dating Karen Duchwitz. But he suppressed the feeling for the sake of the Resistance.

The club manager picked up the microphone and announced Memphis Johnny Madison, and there was a burst of applause.

Johnny walked onstage, sat at the piano, and leaned towards the microphone. He said, 'I'd like to open with a composition by the great boogie-woogie pianist, Clarence Pine Top Smith.'

There was applause, and Harald shouted, 'Play it, Johnny!'

Some kind of disturbance broke out near the door, but Harald took no notice. Johnny played four bars of introduction then stopped abruptly when a German officer walked onstage.

Harald looked around, bewildered, as the officer snatched the microphone from Johnny. 'Entertainers of inferior race are not permitted. This club is closed.'

'No!' cried Harald. 'You can't do that, you Nazi peasant!' Fortunately, his voice was drowned in the general hubbub of protest.

'Let's get out before you make any more errors of etiquette,' said Tik. He took Harald's arm and the three young men made their way upstairs to the street. 'We might as well go to the railway station and wait for the first train home,' Tik said. Their plan was to be in bed, pretending to sleep, before anyone at school got up.

They headed for the town centre. At the main intersections, the Germans had erected octagonal concrete guard posts, with room in the middle for a soldier to stand, visible from the chest up. They were not manned at night. Harald was still furious about the closure of the club, and he was further enraged by these ugly symbols of Nazi domination. Passing one, he gave it a futile kick.

'They say the sentries at these posts wear lederhosen, because no one can see their legs,' Mads said. Harald and Tik laughed.

A moment later, they passed a pile of rubble outside a shop that had been newly refitted. Harald leaned across the rubbish and picked up a paint can. There was a little black paint left in the bottom. From among the bits of timber on the pile, Harald selected a wooden slat. He walked back to the guard post, knelt in front of it with the paint and stick. He heard Tik say something in a warning voice, but ignored him. With great care, he wrote on the wall: THIS NAZI HAS NO TROUSERS ON.

Harald stepped back to admire his work. The letters were large. Later this morning, thousands of Copenhageners on their way to work would see the joke and smile.

'What do you think of that?' he said. He looked around. Tik and

Mads were nowhere to be seen, but two uniformed Danish police-men stood immediately behind him.

'Very amusing,' said one of them. 'You're under arrest.'

HARALD SPENT the rest of the night at the Politigaarden, in the drunk tank. He was too disgusted with himself to contemplate sleep. As the hours went by, he developed a headache and a raging thirst. But he was more concerned about being interrogated about the Resistance. What if he were turned over to the Gestapo and tor-tured? He did not know how much pain he could stand. Eventually he might betray Poul Kirke, and all for a stupid joke! He could not believe how childish he had been. He was bitterly ashamed.

At eight o'clock in the morning he was taken from the cell to an interview room. A sergeant sat at a table, reading a typed report. 'A Jansborg schoolboy, eh?' he said. 'You ought to know better, lad. Where did you get the liquor?'

'At a jazz club, sir.'

'Do you often get drunk?'

'No, sir. First time.'

'And then you saw the guard post, and you happened to come across a can of paint . . .'

'I'm very sorry.'

The cop grinned suddenly. 'Well, don't be too sorry. I thought it was pretty funny, myself. No trousers!' He laughed.

Harald was bewildered. 'What's going to happen to me?'

'Nothing. We're the police, not the joke patrol.' The sergeant dropped the report in a wastepaper basket. 'Go back to school.'

'Thank you!' Harald could hardly believe his luck. He wondered if he could sneak back into school unnoticed.

The sergeant stood up. 'A word of advice. Keep off the booze.'

'I will,' Harald said fervently.

The sergeant opened the door, and Harald suffered a dreadful shock. Standing outside was Peter Flemming.

The sergeant said, 'Can I help you, Inspector?'

Peter ignored him and spoke to Harald. 'Well, well,' he said. 'I wondered, when I saw the name on the overnight arrest list. Could Harald Olufsen, graffiti writer and drunk, be Harald Olufsen, son of the pastor of Sande? Lo and behold, they are one and the same.' He turned to the sergeant. 'All right, I'll deal with it now.'

The sergeant hesitated. 'There are to be no charges, sir, the super-intendent has decided.'

'We'll see about that.'

Harald felt he could weep. 'What are you going to do?'

Peter smiled. 'I think I'll take you back to school.'

THEY ENTERED the Jansborg Skole grounds in a police car driven by a uniformed officer, with Harald in the back like a prisoner. The car drove up to the main office. Peter showed his police badge to the school secretary, and he and Harald were taken to Heis's study.

Jerking a thumb at Harald, Peter said, 'Is this one of yours?'

The gentle Heis flinched. 'Olufsen is a pupil here, yes.'

'He was arrested for defacing a German military installation.'

Heis looked mortified. 'I'm very sorry to hear that.'

'Frankly, we'd rather not prosecute a schoolboy for a prank.'

'Well, I'm glad that—'

'On the other hand, our German friends will want to know that the perpetrator has been dealt with firmly.'

'Of course, of course.'

Peter went on, 'The outcome depends on you. If we let him go, will you expel him from school?'

Harald saw what Peter was up to. He just wanted to be sure that Harald's transgression became public knowledge. He was only interested in embarrassing the Olufsen family.

Heis said, 'Expulsion seems a bit harsh—'

'Not as harsh as a prosecution and possible jail sentence.'

'No, indeed. It's almost the end of the academic year. He wouldn't miss much schooling if he were expelled now.'

'But it will satisfy the Germans,' Peter said. 'If you can assure me that he will be expelled, I can release him from custody. Otherwise, I'll have to take him back to the Politigaarden.'

Heis threw a guilty look at Harald. 'It does seem as if the school has no real choice in the matter, doesn't it?'

'Yes, sir,' Harald said.

Heis looked at Peter. 'Very well, then. I will expel him.'

Peter gave a satisfied smile. 'I'm glad we've resolved this so sensibly.' He shook hands with Heis and went out.

Harald felt all his muscles relax. He had got away with it. There would be hell to pay at home, of course, but the important thing was that his foolishness had not compromised the Resistance.

Heis said, 'A dreadful thing has happened, Olufsen.'

'I know I've done wrong—'

'No, not that. I think you know Mads Kirke's cousin, Poul.

Yesterday he was in a plane crash at the flying school.'

'My God! I was flying with him a few days ago!'

Heis hesitated. 'I am sorry to have to tell you that he is dead.'

'DEAD?' SAID HERBERT WOODIE. 'How can he be dead?'

'They're saying he crashed his Tiger Moth,' Hermia replied. She was angry and distraught. They were in Woodie's office at Bletchley Park, with Digby Hoare. 'The message came this morning from Jens Toksvig, one of Poul's helpers,' Hermia went on. 'He said the crash was being passed off as an accident, but Poul was trying to escape from the police and they shot at the aircraft.'

'The poor man,' said Digby.

'The message came in this morning. I was about to come and tell you, Mr Woodie, when you sent for me,' Hermia said.

'So where does that leave us?' Woodie asked Hermia.

'According to Jens, the Nightwatchmen have decided to lie low for a while and see how far the police carry their investigation. So, to answer your question, it leaves us without any sources of information in Denmark.'

'Makes us appear damned incompetent,' Woodie said.

'Never mind that,' Digby said. 'The Nazis have found a war-winning weapon. We thought we were years ahead with radar—now we learn that they have it too, and theirs is better than ours! I don't care how you appear. We need to find out more.'

Woodie looked outraged but said nothing. Hermia asked, 'What about other sources of intelligence?'

'We're trying them all. And we've picked up one more clue: the word *himmelbett* has appeared in Luftwaffe decrypts.'

Woodie said, '*Himmelbett?* What does it signify?'

'It's their word for a four-poster bed,' Hermia told him.

'Makes no sense,' Woodie said grumpily, as if it were her fault.

She asked Digby, 'Any context?'

'Not really. It seems that their radar operates in a *himmelbett*. We can't figure it out.'

Hermia reached a decision. 'I'll have to go to Denmark myself. I know the ground better than anyone else in MI6. And I speak the language like a native.'

'Don't be ridiculous,' Woodie said. 'We don't send women on missions like that.'

Digby said, 'Yes, we do.' He turned to Hermia. 'You'll leave for Stockholm tonight. I'll come with you.'

THE FOLLOWING DAY Hermia and Digby were walking through the Stadhuset, Stockholm's famous City Hall, looking at wall mosaics, pretending to be tourists. In reality, they were here for a rendezvous.

After a few minutes they left the Stadhuset, crossed an arcade and stepped into a garden overlooking Lake Malaren. Turning to look up at the 300-foot tower that rose over the red-brick building, Hermia checked that their shadow was with them.

A bored-looking man in a grey suit made little effort to conceal his presence. As Digby and Hermia had pulled away from the British Legation, in a chauffeur-driven limousine, he had followed in a black Mercedes 230. When they stopped outside the Stadhuset, the man in the grey suit had followed them inside.

According to the British air attaché, a group of German agents kept all British citizens in Sweden under constant surveillance. They could be shaken off, but it was unwise. Men who evaded surveillance had been arrested and accused of espionage.

Hermia had to escape without the shadow realising it.

Following a prearranged plan, Hermia and Digby wandered across the garden to look at the cenotaph of the city's founder, Birger Jarl. Concealed from view on the far side of the cenotaph was a Swedish woman of the same height and build as Hermia, with similar dark hair.

Hermia suffered an instant of fear. From this moment on, she would be on the wrong side of the law, for the first time in her life.

'Quickly,' the woman said in English.

Hermia slipped off her light raincoat and red beret, and the other woman put them on. Hermia took from her pocket a dull brown scarf and tied it round her head, partly concealing her face.

The Swedish woman took Digby's arm, and the two of them sauntered back into the garden in full view. Hermia waited a few moments, then moved out from behind the cenotaph. She saw Digby and the decoy heading for the gate at the far end. The shadow was following them. The plan was working.

Digby and the woman went straight to a Volvo, got in, and drove away. The tail followed in the Mercedes. They would lead him all the way back to the Legation, and he would report that the two visitors from Britain had spent the afternoon as innocent tourists.

Hermia headed for the centre of the city, walking fast.

Everything had happened with bewildering rapidity in the last twenty-four hours. Hermia had been given only a few minutes to throw a few clothes into a suitcase, then she and Digby had been driven to Dundee, Scotland. This morning at dawn an RAF crew had flown them to Stockholm, a three-hour journey. They had had lunch at the British Legation then put into operation the plan they had devised in the car between Bletchley and Dundee.

As Sweden was neutral, it was possible to phone people in Denmark from here. Hermia was going to try to call her fiancé. At the Danish end, calls were monitored, so she would have to be extraordinarily careful to mount a deception that would sound innocent to an eavesdropper yet bring Arne into the Resistance.

In 1939, when she had set up the Nightwatchmen, she excluded Arne because of his careless nature. He was too open and friendly for clandestine work. She had been unwilling to put him in danger, but now she was desperate. She had no one else.

She turned into a busy street and entered the railway station. There would be nothing unusual about a woman who spoke hesitant Swedish with a Danish accent going there to phone home.

The Germans could not possibly eavesdrop on every phone call. However, they were more likely to pay attention to international calls, and to calls to military bases, so Hermia would have to communicate in hints and double talk.

She stood in line at the phone bureau. When she got to the counter, she told the clerk that she wanted to make a call to Arne Olufsen, and gave the number of the flying school.

She waited apprehensively while the operator tried to get Arne on the line. It would be strange to talk to him after more than a year. The mission was the important thing, but she could not help fretting about how Arne would feel about her. Perhaps he no longer loved her. What if he were cold to her? It would break her heart.

She was called to a booth. She picked up the phone. 'Hello?'

Arne said, 'Who is it?'

She had forgotten his voice. It was low and warm and sounded as if it might break into laughter at any minute. She had planned her first sentence, but for a moment she could not speak at all.

'Hello?' he said. 'Is anyone there?'

She swallowed and found her voice. 'Hello, Toothbrush, this is your black cat.' She called him toothbrush because that was what his moustache felt like when he kissed her. Her nickname came from the colour of her hair.

It was his turn to be dumbstruck. There was a silence.

Hermia said, 'How are you?'

'I'm OK,' he said at last. 'My God, is it really you?'

'Yes.' Suddenly she could not stand any more small talk. Abruptly she said, 'Do you still love me?'

He did not answer immediately. That made her think his feelings had changed.

'I love you,' he said. 'I've missed you terribly.'

She closed her eyes. Feeling dizzy, she leaned against the wall.

'I love you, too,' she said.

'How are you? Where are you calling from?'

She pulled herself together. 'I'm not far away.'

He noticed her guarded manner. 'OK, I understand.'

She had prepared the next part. 'Do you remember the castle?'

'You mean the ruins?' he said. 'How could I forget?'

'Could you meet me there?'

'It's a long way—'

'It's really very important.'

'I'll ask for leave, but if it's a problem I'll just go AWOL—'

'Don't do that. When's your next day off?'

'Saturday.'

The operator came on the line to tell them they had ten seconds.

Hastily, Hermia said, 'I'll be there on Saturday. If you don't make it, I'll come back every day for as long as I can.'

'I'll do the same.'

'Be careful. I love you.'

'I love you—'

The line went dead. Hermia kept the receiver pressed to her ear, as if she could hold on to him a little longer that way. She paid at the counter then went out, dazed with happiness. He still loved her. In two days' time she would see him.

The ruined castle to which they had referred was Hammershus, on the Danish holiday island of Bornholm, in the Baltic Sea. They had spent a week on the island in 1939, and had made love among the ruins one warm summer evening.

Arne would have to take the ferry from Copenhagen, a trip of seven or eight hours, or fly, which took about an hour. The island was 100 miles from mainland Denmark, but only twenty miles from the south coast of Sweden. Hermia would have to find a fishing boat to take her across that short stretch of water illegally. But it was the danger to Arne, not herself, that she kept thinking about. He was going to meet secretly with an agent of the British secret service. She would ask him to become a spy.

If he were caught, the punishment would be death.

ON THE SECOND DAY after his arrest, Harald returned home.

Heis had allowed him to stay at school another two days to take his exams. He would be permitted to graduate, though not to attend the ceremony. But the important thing was that his university place was safe. He would study physics under Niels Bohr.

During those two days he had learned, from Mads Kirke, that the death of Poul had not been a straightforward crash. The army was refusing to reveal details, but other pilots had told the family that the police had been on the base and shots had been fired. Harald was sure that Poul had been killed because of his Resistance work.

Nevertheless, he was more afraid of his father than of the police as he made his way home. It was a tediously familiar journey across Denmark from Jansborg in the east, to Sande, off the west coast. The journey took the whole day, but he wished it could be longer.

When at last Harald arrived at the parsonage, late in the evening, his mother was alone. He put down his suitcase and kissed her.

'Your father is out,' she said. 'Ove Borking is sick.' Ove was an elderly fisherman.

His mother looked solemn and tearful. Harald said, 'I'm sorry to have caused you distress, Mother.'

'Your father is mortified. Why did you do it?'

He had no answer.

She made him a ham sandwich for his supper. They stayed up until midnight, then his mother said, 'Your father could be out all night. You'd better go to bed.'

He lay awake for a long time. He asked himself why he was scared. His father's wrath was formidable, but Harald was not easily intimidated. Rather the reverse: he was inclined to resent authority and defy it out of sheer rebelliousness. At dawn Harald drifted into sleep.

An hour later, the door burst open, and the pastor stood beside the bed, fully dressed. 'How could you do it?' he shouted.

Harald sat up, blinking.

'What were you thinking of? What possessed you?'

Harald did not want to cower in his bed like a child. He threw off the sheet and stood up. Because the weather was warm, he had slept in his undershorts. 'Cover yourself, boy,' his father said. 'You're practically naked.'

'If underwear offends you, don't enter bedrooms without knocking.'

'Don't tell me to knock on doors in my own house! How could you bring such disgrace upon yourself, your family and your school?'

Harald pulled on his trousers and turned to face his father.

'Well?' the pastor raged. 'Are you going to answer me?'

'I'm sorry. I thought you were asking rhetorical questions.'

His father was infuriated. 'Don't try to use your education to fence with me—I went to Jansborg, too.'

'I'm not fencing. I'm asking whether there's any chance you'll listen to anything I say.'

The pastor raised his hand as if to strike Harald, then dropped it. 'Well, I'm listening. What have you got to say for yourself?'

'I'm sorry I daubed the guard post, because it was an empty gesture, a childish act of defiance.'

'At the least!'

'I'm sorry to have brought disgrace on the school. I'm sorry I got drunk, because it made me feel dreadful the next morning. Most of all, I'm sorry to have caused my mother distress.'

'And your father?'

Harald shook his head. 'You're upset because your pride has been hurt, but I'm not sure you're worried about me at all.'

'Pride?' his father roared. 'What has pride to do with anything? I've tried to bring up my sons to be decent, god-fearing men—and you've let me down. You were *arrested*. No member of this family has ever been to jail for any reason. You've dragged us into the gutter. What is to be done with you?'

'I've only missed a few days of school. I can do the preliminary reading for my university course here at home.'

'No,' his father said. 'You're not getting off so lightly.'

Harald had a dreadful foreboding. 'What do you mean?'

'You're not going to university. I'm not going to send you to Copenhagen to pollute your soul with strong drink and jazz music.'

'But they've given me a place.'

'They haven't given you any money, though.'

'Grandfather bequeathed money for my education,' Harald said.

'But he left it to me to dispense. And I'm not going to give it to you to spend in nightclubs.'

Harald was stunned. It was the only punishment that could really hurt him. 'You've always told me that education was important.'

'Education is not the same as godliness. Get dressed. Put on your school clothes and a clean shirt. You're going to work.'

THEY RODE THE FAMILY'S HORSE, Major, the length of the island. He was a broad-backed Irish gelding strong enough to carry them both. When they reached the dock, they waited for the ferry, then crossed to the mainland and rode up the hill to Esbjerg town square. The stores were not yet open, but the pastor knocked at the door of the haberdashery. It was opened by the owner, Otto Sejr, a deacon of the Sande church. He seemed to be expecting them.

They stepped inside and Harald looked around. Glass cases displayed balls of coloured wool. The shelves were stacked with lengths of wool cloth and cotton and a few silks. There was a dusty smell of mothballs and lavender, like an old lady's wardrobe.

What was he doing here?

His father answered the question. 'Brother Sejr has kindly agreed to give you a job. He needs an assistant.'

Harald stared at his father, speechless.

Sejr was a small man, bald with a moustache. Harald had known him all his life. He was pompous, mean and sly. He wagged a fat finger and said, 'Work hard, pay attention, and be obedient, and you may learn a valuable trade, young Harald.'

The pastor shook hands with Sejr and thanked him, then said to Harald in parting, 'You'll come straight home when you finish work. I'll see you tonight.' When Harald said nothing he went out.

'Right,' said Sejr. 'There's just time to sweep the floor before we open. You'll find a broom in the cupboard.'

Harald began his task. Seeing him brush one-handed, Sejr snapped, 'Put both hands on that broom, boy!'

Harald obeyed.

At nine o'clock Sejr put the OPEN sign in the door. 'When I want you to deal with a customer, I'll say, "Forward," and you step forward,' he said. 'But watch me with one or two customers first.'

Harald watched Sejr sell six needles on a card to an old woman. Next was a smartly dressed woman of about forty who bought two yards of black braid. Then it was Harald's turn to serve. The third customer was a thin-lipped woman who asked for a reel of white cotton.

Sejr snapped, 'On your left, top drawer.'

Harald found the cotton. The price was marked in pencil on the wooden end of the reel. He took the money and made change.

The morning wore on with painful slowness. Sejr checked stock, wrote orders, and dealt with phone calls; but Harald was expected to stand waiting for the next person to come through the door. It left him plenty of time to ponder. Was he really going to spend his life selling reels of cotton to housewives? It was unthinkable.

By midmorning, he had decided he could not even spend the summer working here. By lunchtime he knew he was not going to last the day. As Sejr flipped the CLOSED sign, Harald said, 'I'm going for a walk.'

'You've only got an hour,' Sejr said.

Harald opened the door, walked down the hill and got on the ferry. He crossed to Sande and walked along the beach towards the parsonage. He felt a strange, tight sensation in his chest when he looked at the miles of damp sand and the endless sea. He almost felt like crying, and after a while he realised why.

He was going to leave this place today.

The rationale came after the realisation. He did not have to do the job selected for him—but he could not continue to live in the house after defying his father. He would have to go. As he strode along the sand, he realised he could no longer trust his father to have his best interests at heart. He had to look after himself now.

When he reached the parsonage, the horse was not in the paddock. He went in by the kitchen door. His mother looked frightened when she saw him. He kissed her but gave her no explanation.

He went to his room and packed his case as if he were going to school. His mother came to the bedroom door and stood watching him, her face lined and sad. She said, 'Where will you go?'

'I don't know.'

He thought of his brother. He went into his father's study, picked up the phone, and placed a call to the flying school. When Arne came on the line, Harald told him what had happened.

'The old man overplayed his hand,' Arne commented. 'Where will you go now?'

Harald had a flash of inspiration. 'Kirstenslot. Tik Duchwitz's place. But don't tell Father. I don't want him coming after me.'

'Old man Duchwitz might tell him.'

That was a good point, Harald reflected. Tik's respectable father would have little sympathy for a runaway. 'I'll sleep in the old monastery,' he said. 'Tik's father won't even know I'm there.'

'How will you eat?'

'I may be able to get a job on the farm.'

'Well, phone if you need anything. Good luck, kid.'

As Harald hung up, his father walked in. 'Why aren't you at the shop?'

'I don't believe it's my destiny to be a haberdasher.'

'You don't know what your destiny is.'

'Perhaps not.' Harald left the room. He went outside to the workshop, lit the boiler of his motorcycle, and stacked peat in the sidecar.

He returned to the house and picked up his suitcase.

His father waylaid him. 'Where do you think you're going?'

'I'd rather not say.'

'I forbid you to leave.'

'Father, you're doing your best to sabotage my education. I'm afraid you've forfeited the right to tell me what to do.'

The pastor looked mortally wounded. Harald felt regret like a sudden pain. It gave him no satisfaction to see his father's distress, but he was afraid that if he showed remorse he would lose his strength of purpose, and allow himself to be bullied into staying.

So he turned away and walked outside. He strapped his suitcase to the back of the bike and drove it out of the workshop. His mother came running across the yard. She was crying.

'Your father loves you, Harald. Do you understand that?'

'Yes, Mother, I think I do.'

'Let me know you're all right.' She kissed him. 'Promise.'

'I promise.' He drove away.

SIX

Peter Flemming undressed his wife. She stood passively in front of the mirror as he undid the hooks and eyes of her dress.

Inge was as lovely today as she had been on their honeymoon night. But then she had been smiling, her expression showing eagerness and a trace of apprehension. Today her face was blank.

He hung her dress up, then took off her brassiere. He made her sit on the dressing-table stool, then removed her shoes, her garter belt and her stockings. He drew a white nightdress embroidered with flowers over her head. The flower pattern suited her, and she looked pretty. He thought he saw a faint smile touch her lips.

He took her to the bathroom then put her to bed. He put on pyjamas, but did not feel sleepy, so he decided to return to the living room and smoke a cigarette. Inge lay still with her eyes open.

In the living room, he found his cigarettes then, on impulse, took a bottle of aquavit from a cupboard and poured some into a glass. Sipping his drink and smoking, he thought about the past week.

He had caught two spies, but Poul Kirke had died before he could reveal who his collaborators were or where his orders came from, and Ingemar Gammel's 'deep interrogation' by the Gestapo had revealed nothing further.

Peter had questioned Poul's commanding officer, his parents, his friends, and even his cousin, Mads, and had got nothing from them. He had detectives tailing Arne Olufsen. But Arne had spent the week blamelessly going about his duties. After a brilliant start, the case seemed to have dead-ended. Peter was wondering where to go next with the investigation when there was a knock at the door.

He glanced at the clock on the mantelpiece. It was ten thirty, an unusual time for an unexpected visit. He stepped into the hallway and opened the door. Tilde Jesperson stood there.

'There's been a development,' she said.

'Come in. You'll have to excuse my appearance.'

She glanced at his pyjamas and grinned as she walked into the living room. 'Elephants,' she said. 'I wouldn't have guessed.'

He felt embarrassed and wished he had put on a robe.

Tilde sat down. 'Where's Inge?'

'In bed. Would you like some aquavit?'

'Thank you.'

He got a fresh glass and poured for both of them.

She said, 'Arne Olufsen is in Copenhagen. He's bought a ticket for tomorrow's ferry to Bornholm.'

Peter froze with his glass halfway to his lips. 'Bornholm?' he said softly. The Danish holiday island was tantalisingly close to the Swedish coast. Could this be the break he was waiting for?

'Of course, he might simply be due for a vacation,' Tilde said.

'Quite so. On the other hand, he may be planning to escape to Sweden.' Peter swallowed his drink. 'Who's with him now?'

'Dresler. He relieved me fifteen minutes ago.'

Peter forced himself to be sceptical. It was too easy, in an investigation, to let wishful thinking mislead you. 'Why would Olufsen want to leave the country?'

'Maybe he's just noticed the surveillance. Alternatively, he might be going to Bornholm to spy. Or perhaps it's a rendezvous. The death of Kirke probably broke their line of communication.'

'I'm not convinced, but there's only one way to find out. Tell Dresler to get on the ferry with him.'

'Olufsen has a bicycle. Shall I tell Dresler to take one?'

'Yes. Then book us both on tomorrow's plane. We'll get there first.'

Tilde stood up. 'Right.'

Peter did not want her to go. The aquavit was warm in his belly, and he was enjoying having an attractive woman to talk to. He followed her into the hallway. 'I'll see you at the airport,' she said.

'Yes.' He put his hand on the doorknob. 'Tilde . . .'

She looked at him with a neutral expression. 'Yes?'

'Thanks for this. Good work.'

'Sleep well.' She touched his cheek, but did not move away.

He leaned forward, and suddenly he was kissing her.

She kissed him back with fierce passion. He was surprised, and after a moment of shock, he responded.

He saw a movement out of the corner of his eye. He broke the kiss and turned his head. Inge stood in the bedroom doorway. Her face wore its perpetual blank expression, but she was looking straight at them. Peter heard himself make a sound like a sob.

Tilde slipped from his embrace. She opened the apartment door and stepped outside. The door slammed shut.

THE FLIGHT FROM COPENHAGEN to Bornholm departed at 9.00am and took an hour. The plane landed at an airstrip a mile or so outside Bornholm's main town, Ronne. Peter and Tilde were met by the local police chief, who gave them the loan of a car.

The town was a sleepy place, with more horses than cars. In the afternoon Peter and Tilde drove down to the harbour to meet the ferry. Neither mentioned last night's kiss, but Peter was intensely aware of Tilde's physical presence. At the same time, he kept remembering Inge in the bedroom doorway, her expressionless face a more agonising reproach than any explicit accusation.

The ferry docked and the passengers disembarked.

'There,' said Tilde, pointing.

Peter saw Arne Olufsen, wearing his army uniform, pushing his bicycle. 'But where's Dresler?'

'Four people behind.'

'I see him.' Peter put on sunglasses, then started the car.

Arne cycled up the cobbled street, Dresler did the same, and Peter and Tilde followed. A few miles out of town they were the only people on the road, and Peter was obliged to fall behind and drop out of sight for fear of being noticed. After a few minutes, he speeded up until he caught sight of Dresler, then slowed again.

'This is impossible,' Tilde said. 'He's bound to spot us.'

Peter nodded. She was right, but now a new thought occurred to him. 'And when he does, his reaction will be highly revealing.'

She gave him an inquiring look, but he did not explain.

He increased speed. Rounding a bend, he saw Dresler at the side of the road and, 100 yards ahead, Arne sitting on a wall, smoking. Peter continued another mile, then reversed down a farm track.

A few minutes later, Arne cycled past, followed by Dresler. Peter pulled onto the road again. Three miles further on, they came to a crossroads. Dresler had stopped there and was looking perplexed. The daylight was fading and there was no sign of Arne.

Dresler came up to the car window. 'I'm sorry, boss. He put on a burst of speed and got ahead of me. I lost sight of him.'

Tilde said, 'Maybe he planned it. He obviously knows the road.'

'This is good news,' Peter said.

Tilde was bewildered. 'What do you mean?'

'If an innocent man thinks he's being followed, what does he do? He stops, turns round, and says, "Why are you following me?" Only a guilty man deliberately shakes off a surveillance team. Don't you see? This means we were right: Arne Olufsen is a spy.'

HARALD'S LIFE was in ruins. All his plans were cancelled and he had no future. Yet, instead of agonising over his fate, he was looking forward to seeing Karen Duchwitz again.

Denmark was a small, pretty country, but at twenty miles per hour Harald's peat-burning motorcycle took a day and a half to get across its width. He arrived at Kirstenslot late on Saturday afternoon. Although he was impatient to see Karen, he did not go immediately to the castle. He passed through the village and found the farm he had visited with Tik.

He parked the bike and found the farmer at the rear of the farmhouse, smoking a pipe. 'Good evening, Mr Nielsen,' he said.

'Hello,' Nielsen said guardedly. 'What can I do for you?'

'My name is Harald Olufsen. I need a job, and Josef Duchwitz told me you hire summer labourers.'

'Times are hard, son. The Germans buy what I produce at a price decided by them. There's no cash to pay casual workers.'

'I'll work for food,' Harald said desperately.

Neilsen gave him a penetrating look. 'You sound as if you're in some kind of trouble. But I can't hire you on those terms. Sorry, son. Come on, I'll see you off the premises.'

The farmer probably thought he was desperate enough to steal, Harald thought. The two of them walked to the front yard.

'What's that?' said Nielsen when he saw the bike, with its boiler gently puffing steam.

'It's an ordinary motorcycle, but I've rigged it to run on peat.'

'It looks ready to blow up any minute!'

'It's perfectly safe,' Harald said indignantly. 'I know about engines. In fact I mended one of your tractors, a few weeks ago.'

Nielsen frowned. 'What do you mean?'

'I was staying at Kirstenslot for the weekend. Josef and I came across one of your men, trying to start a tractor.'

'I heard about that. So you're the lad. Maybe I can hire you. A mechanic is a different matter. I've got half a dozen machines lying idle for lack of spares. Do you think you could make them work?'

'Yes.' This was no time for modesty, Harald decided.

'All right.' Nielsen looked at the motorcycle. 'If you can do this, maybe you can repair my seed drill. I'll give you a trial.'

'Thank you, Mr Nielsen!'

'Come on Monday morning at six o'clock. We farmers start early.'

'I'll be here.' Harald drove off before Nielsen could change his mind. As soon as he was out of earshot, he let out a triumphant yell. He had a job—and he had done it himself! He was on his own, but he was young and strong and smart. He would be all right.

Daylight was fading as he drove back through the village. He almost failed to see a man in police uniform who stepped into the road and waved him down. He braked hard at the last minute. He recognised the policeman as Per Hansen, the local Nazi.

'What the hell is this?' The man pointed to the bike.

'It's a Nimbus motorcycle, converted to steam power.'

'It looks dangerous to me.'

'I assure you, officer, it's perfectly safe. Are you making official inquiries, or just indulging your curiosity?'

'Never mind the cheek, lad. Have I seen you before?'

Harald told himself not to get on the wrong side of the law again. 'My name is Harald Olufsen.'

'You're a friend of the Jews at the castle?'

Harald lost his temper. 'It's none of your damn business who my friends are.'

'Oho! Is it not?' Hansen looked satisfied, as if he had the result he wanted. 'I shall keep a close eye on you. Off you go, now.'

Harald pulled away. He cursed his short temper. He had made an enemy of the local policeman, just because of a throwaway remark about Jews. When would he learn to keep out of trouble?

A quarter of a mile from Kirstenslot, he turned onto the track that led through the wood to the monastery. He stopped the bike at the front of the church, then walked through the cloisters and entered the church by a side door. In the evening light that came through the high windows, he made out the Rolls-Royce under its tarpaulin and the Hornet Moth biplane with its folded wings. He opened the large main door, drove his bike in and closed the door.

He recalled that Karen liked to smoke a cigarette on the terrace after dinner. He decided to go and look out for her. Next to the workbench and tool rack was a sink with a cold-water tap. He got cleaned up as best he could and put on the spare shirt from his bag.

An arrow-straight drive half a mile long led from the main gates to the castle, but it was too exposed, and Harald took a roundabout route through the wood. Studying the house from the shelter of a cedar tree, he was able to identify the dining room and saw the flicker of candles. He guessed the family was having dinner and decided to risk a closer look. After crossing the lawn, he crept to the dining-room window. Dinner was over, and a maid was clearing the table.

A voice behind him said, 'What do you think you're doing?'

He spun round. Karen was walking along the terrace, her skin luminous in the evening light. She wore a blue-green silk dress.

'Hush!' he said. 'It's Harald Olufsen. I was here two weeks ago.'

'Oh—the boogie-woogie boy! What are you doing skulking on the terrace?' Karen sat on a low wall and lit a cigarette.

He sat facing her. 'I quarrelled with my father and left home.'

'Why did you come here?'

'I've got a job with Farmer Nielsen, repairing his machines.'

'You are enterprising. Where are you living?'

'Um . . . in the old monastery.'

'Presumptuous, too. I assume you brought blankets and things.'

'Actually, no.'

'It may be chilly at night.'

'I'll survive.'

'Hmm.' She sat in silence for a while, watching darkness fall like a mist over the garden. Eventually she threw her cigarette into a flowerbed and stood up. 'Well, good luck.' She went into the house.

That was abrupt, Harald thought. He felt deflated. He could have talked to her all night, but she had got bored with him in five minutes. He remembered that she had made him feel both welcomed and rejected during his weekend visit. Perhaps it was a game she played.

He walked back to the monastery. The night air was already cooling. The church had a tiled floor that looked cold. He wished he had thought to bring a blanket from home. In the starlight that came through the windows he looked around for a bed. The east end of the church had a curved wall that had once enclosed an altar. A broad ledge was incorporated into the wall. It looked more like a bed than anything else he could see, and he lay down.

He thought about Karen. He imagined her fondly touching his hair, brushing his lips with hers, putting her arms round him.

He was cold. He got up. Maybe he could sleep in the Rolls-Royce. He was fumbling with the canvas cover, when he heard footsteps. He froze. A moment later, the beam of an electric torch swept past the window. He heard a voice. 'Harald?'

His heart leapt with pleasure. 'Karen!'

Her beam found him. She entered the church, and he saw that she was carrying a bundle. 'I brought you some blankets.'

He smiled. 'I was just thinking of sleeping in the car,' he said.

'You're too tall.'

When he unfolded the blankets he found something inside.

'I thought you might be hungry,' she explained. In the light of her torch he saw half a loaf of bread, a small basket of strawberries, and a length of sausage. There was also a flask of coffee.

He fell on the food, trying not to eat like a starved jackal. He heard a mew, and a cat came into the circle of light. It was the black and white tom he had seen the first time he entered the church. He dropped a piece of sausage on the ground. The cat sniffed it, then began to eat it. 'What's the cat called?' Harald asked Karen.

'I don't think it has a name. It's a stray.'

At the back of its head it had a tuft of hair like a pyramid. 'I'll call him Pine Top,' Harald said. 'After my favourite pianist.'

'Good name.'

Harald ate everything. 'Boy, that was great. Thank you.'

'I should have brought more. When was the last time you ate?'

'Yesterday.'

'How did you get here?'

'Motorcycle.' He pointed to where he had parked the bike. 'But it's slow, because it runs on peat, so I took two days to get here.'

'You're a determined character, Harald Olufsen. In fact, I've never met anyone quite like you.'

'Well, to tell the truth, I feel the same about you.'

'Oh, come on. The world is full of spoilt rich girls who want to be ballet dancers, but how many people have crossed Denmark on a peat-burning motorcycle?'

He laughed. They were quiet for a minute. 'I was sorry about Poul,'

Harald said eventually. 'It must have been a terrible shock for you.'

'It was completely devastating. I cried all day.'

'Were you very close?'

'We only had three dates, and I wasn't in love with him, but all the same it was dreadful.' Tears came to her eyes.

Harald was shamefully pleased to learn that she had not been in love with Poul. 'Do you know how it happened?'

'No—the army has been ridiculously secretive about it. They just say he crashed his plane, and the details are classified.'

'Perhaps they're covering something up.'

'Such as what?' she said sharply.

Harald realised he could not tell her what he thought without revealing his own connection to the Resistance. 'Their own incompetence? Perhaps the aircraft wasn't properly serviced.'

'They couldn't use the excuse of military secrecy to hide something like that. I don't believe our officers would be so dishonourable,' she said stiffly.

Harald realised he had offended her. 'I expect you're right,' he said. That was insincere, but he did not want to quarrel with her.

'I must get back before they lock up.' Karen's voice was cold.

'Thanks for the food and blankets—you're an angel of mercy.'

'Not my usual role,' she said, softening a little. 'Good night.'

HERMIA SLEPT BADLY. She woke up to find herself on a narrow bed in a lodging-house on the island of Bornholm. She felt nervous now that she was in occupied territory, carrying forged papers.

Back in Stockholm, she and Digby had again deceived their German followers with substitutes, and taken a train to the south coast. In the tiny fishing village of Kalvsby they had found a boatman willing to take her across the twenty miles of sea to Bornholm. She had said goodbye to Digby and climbed aboard. He was going to London for a day to report to Churchill, but he would be waiting for her on the jetty in Kalvsby when she returned—if she returned.

The fisherman had put her and her bicycle ashore on a lonely beach at dawn yesterday, promising to return in four days. She had cycled to Hammershus, the ruined castle, and waited for Arne all day.

He had not come.

She told herself not to be surprised. She guessed he had not been able to catch the evening ferry from Copenhagen. He had probably taken the Saturday-morning boat and arrived on Bornholm too late to reach Hammershus before dark. He would find somewhere to spend the night and come to the rendezvous first thing in the morning.

Late in the day, she had given up on Arne and cycled to the nearest village. She found a place to stay without difficulty.

She decided to have breakfast this morning before cycling back to Hammershus. She got dressed and went downstairs, feeling nervous as she walked into the dining room. It was more than a year since she had been in the habit of speaking Danish.

There was one other guest in the room, a middle-aged man with a friendly smile who said, 'Good morning, I'm Sven Fromer.'

Hermia forced herself to relax. 'Agnes Ricks,' she said, using the name on her false papers. 'It's a beautiful day.' She helped herself to porridge, poured cold milk over it, and began to eat. The tension she felt made it difficult for her to swallow.

Sven smiled at her and said, 'English style.'

She stared at him, appalled. How had he found her out so fast? 'What do you mean?'

'The way you eat porridge.'

He had his milk in a glass, and took sips from it in between mouthfuls of porridge. That was how Danes ate porridge, she knew perfectly well. She cursed her carelessness. 'I prefer it this way,' she said. 'The milk cools the porridge and you can eat it faster.'

'A girl in a hurry,' he said. 'Where are you from?'

'Copenhagen.'

'Me, too.'

'Are you on holiday?'

'Unfortunately not. I'm a surveyor. However, the job is done, and I don't have to be home until tomorrow, so I'm going to spend today driving around and catch the overnight ferry this evening. I'd be happy to take you around.'

'I'm engaged to be married,' Hermia said firmly.

He smiled ruefully. 'I'd still be glad of your company.'

'Please don't be offended, but I want to be alone.'

'I quite understand. I hope you don't mind my asking.'

She gave him her most charming smile. 'I'm flattered.'

Another guest came in, a man dressed in a suit. He spoke Danish with a German accent. 'Good morning. I am Helmut Mueller.'

Hermia's heart raced. 'Good morning,' she said. 'Agnes Ricks.'

Mueller turned expectantly to Sven, who stood up, pointedly ignoring the newcomer, and stalked out of the room.

Mueller sat down, looking hurt. Hermia tried to behave normally. 'Where are you from, Herr Mueller?'

'I was born in Luebeck.'

'You speak our language well.'

'When I was a boy, my family came here for holidays.'

Hermia stood up. 'I hope you have a pleasant day.'

'Thank you. I wish you the same.'

She left the room, wondering if she had been too nice. Over-friendliness might arouse suspicion as easily as hostility. But he had shown no sign of mistrust.

As she was leaving on her bicycle, she saw Sven putting his luggage in his car, a slope-backed Volvo. The rear seat had been removed to make room for his surveying equipment.

'I apologise for creating a scene,' he said. 'I didn't wish to be rude to you. I come from a military family. It's difficult for me to accept that we surrendered so quickly. We should have fought. We should be fighting now!' He made a gesture of frustration.

She touched his arm. 'You have nothing to apologise for.' She rode off.

HAMMERSHUS was on the northern tip of Bornholm. The old castle stood on a hill that looked across the sea to Sweden. Hermia wheeled her bicycle up the rocky slope. She was early, and the place was deserted. What would it be like if Arne did turn up today, she wondered. He had said he still loved her—but he had not seen her for more than a year. Would he find her the same, or changed? She began to feel nervous.

She walked to the seaward side, leaned her bike against a low stone wall and looked down at the beach far below.

A familiar voice said, 'Hello, Hermia.'

She whirled round and saw Arne walking towards her, smiling, his arms spread wide. He had been waiting behind a tower. She ran into his arms and hugged him hard enough to hurt them both.

He kissed her cheeks. She held his face in both hands. She nuzzled his neck, breathing in the smell of him, army soap and brilliantine and aeroplane fuel.

She was overwhelmed by emotion as their tender kisses turned searching, their gentle caresses became demanding. When her knees felt weak she sank to the grass, pulling him down with her. She fumbled with the buttons of his trousers. He pushed up the skirt of her dress. They were in full view of any early tourists coming to see the ruins, she knew, but she could not hold back. She clung to him, hungry for the touch of his body. A node of intense pleasure began small and hot, like a distant star, and grew steadily, seeming to possess more and more of her body, until it exploded.

They lay still for a while. Then a shadow fell on them. It was only a cloud passing over the sun, but it reminded her that someone could come along at any time. 'One more kiss. Then we'd better get up,' she murmured.

'OK.' He kissed her softly, then stood up.

She got to her feet and brushed grass off her dress. She leaned on the wall, looking at the sea, and Arne put his arm round her. It was hard to wrench her mind back to war, deception and secrecy.

'I'm working for British Intelligence,' she said abruptly.

He nodded. 'I was afraid of that. You're in even more danger than if you had come here just to see me.'

'Now you're at risk, too, just because you're with me.'

She had to tell him everything. She was going to ask him to risk his life, and he needed to know why. She told him about the Nightwatchmen, the devastating rate of bomber losses, the radar installation on his home island of Sande, and the involvement of Poul. As she talked, his face changed. The merriment went from his eyes, and his perennial smile was replaced by a look of anxiety. She wondered whether he would accept the mission.

If he were a coward, surely he would not have chosen to fly the flimsy wood-and-linen machines of the Army Invasion Troops? On the other hand, being a pilot was part of his dashing image. And he often put pleasure before work. It was one of the reasons she loved him: she was too serious and he made her enjoy herself.

'I've come to ask you to do what Poul would have done, if he had lived: go to Sande, get into the base, and examine the radar installation. We need photographs, good ones.' She leaned across to her bicycle, opened the saddlebag and took out a small 35mm camera. 'When we understand their radar system, we will be able to devise ways to defeat it, and that will save the lives of thousands of airmen. But if you're caught, you'll be executed for spying.'

Arne nodded, looking solemn, but he did not take the camera. 'Poul was the head of your Nightwatchmen.'

She nodded.

'I suppose most of our friends were in it.'

'Better that you don't know—'

'Just about everyone except me.'

She nodded. She feared what was coming.

'You think I'm a coward.'

'It didn't seem like your kind of thing—'

'Because I like parties, and I make jokes, you thought I didn't have the guts for secret work.'

She nodded miserably.

'In that case, I'll have to prove you wrong.' He took the camera.

She did not know whether to be happy or sad. 'Thank you,' she said. 'You'll be careful, won't you?'

'Yes, but there's a problem. I was followed to Bornholm.'

This was something she had not anticipated. 'Are you sure?'

'Yes. I noticed a couple of people hanging around the base, a man and a woman. She was on the train to Copenhagen with me, and he was on the ferry. When I got here, he followed me on a bicycle, and there was a car behind. I shook them off outside Ronne.'

'They must suspect you of working with Poul. Who do you think they are?'

'The Danish police, acting under orders from the Germans.'

'Now that you've given them the slip, they undoubtedly feel you're guilty. They'll be watching the ferry port and the aerodrome. We'll have to smuggle you to Copenhagen somehow.'

'And then where would I go? I can't return to the flying school— it's the first place they'd look.'

'You'll have to stay with one of the Nightwatchmen, Jens Toksvig, in Copenhagen. I'll give you the address. He won't turn you away. How long will it take you to get to Sande?'

'First I'll talk to my brother, Harald. He worked as a labourer on the base, so he can give me the layout. Then you have to allow a day to get to Jutland, because the trains are always delayed. I could get there late on Tuesday, sneak into the base on Wednesday, and return to Copenhagen on Thursday. How do I get in touch with you?'

'Come back next Friday. I'll meet you right here. We'll cross to Sweden with the fisherman who brought me. We'll get you false papers at the British Legation and fly you to England. If this works out, we could be together again, and free, in a week's time.'

He smiled. 'It seems too much to hope for.'

While they had been talking, the first few tourists had arrived. 'Let's get out of here,' Hermia said. 'Did you come on a bicycle?'

'It's behind that tower.'

Arne fetched his bike and they left the castle. Hermia considered the problem of escape as they freewheeled down the hillside. Could she devise a disguise for Arne? She had no wigs or costumes, nor any make-up other than the lipstick and powder she used herself.

At the foot of the hill she spotted her fellow guest at the boarding house, Sven Fromer, getting out of his Volvo. She hoped to ride past without his noticing her but he waved and stood beside the path. It would have been rude to ignore him, so she stopped.

'We meet again,' he said. 'This must be your fiancé.'

She was not in any danger from Sven, she told herself. He was anti-German. 'This is Oluf Arnesen,' she said, reversing Arne's name. 'Oluf, meet Sven Fromer. We're staying at the same place.'

The men shook hands. 'Have you been here long?' Arne said.

'A week. I leave tonight.'

Hermia was struck by a thought. 'Sven,' she said. 'This morning you told me we should be fighting the Germans. If I gave you a chance to help the British, would you take a risk?'

He stared at her. 'But how . . . Do you mean that you—'

'Would you be willing? You'll have to trust me. Yes or no?'

'Yes,' he said. 'What do you want me to do?'

'Could a man hide in the back of your car?'

'Sure. I could conceal him behind my equipment.'

'Would you be willing to smuggle him on the ferry tonight?'

Sven looked at his car, then at Arne. 'You?'

Arne nodded.

Sven smiled. 'Hell, yes,' he said.

 **SEVEN**

Harald's first day working at the Nielsen farm was more successful than he had dared to hope. Old Nielsen had a small workshop with enough equipment to enable Harald to repair just about anything. He had patched the water pump on a steam plough, welded a hinge on a caterpillar track, and found the short circuit that caused the farmhouse lights to fuse every night. He felt weary but pleased with himself as he walked back to the old monastery.

When he entered the ruined building, he was astonished to find his brother in the church, staring at the derelict aircraft. 'A Hornet Moth,' Arne said. 'The gentleman's aerial carriage.'

'It's a wreck,' Harald said.

'Not really. The undercarriage is a bit bent.'

Arne looked terrible. Instead of his army uniform, he wore what seemed to be somebody else's old clothes, a worn tweed jacket and faded trousers. He had shaved off his moustache. He held a small 35mm camera. There was a strained expression on his face.

'What happened to you?' Harald said anxiously.

'I'm in trouble. I'm a wanted man. Every policeman in Denmark has my description, and there are posters of me all over Copenhagen. I was chased by a cop along the Stroget and barely got away.'

'Are you in the Resistance?'

Arne shrugged, then said, 'Yes.'

Harald was thrilled. He sat on the ledge he used as a bed, and Arne sat next to him. 'So you were working with Poul Kirke?'

'No. I was left out at first, but now they're desperate, so I'm in it. I have to take photos of machinery at the Sande military base.'

Harald nodded. 'I drew a sketch of it for Poul.'

'Even you were in it before me,' Arne said bitterly.

'Poul told me not to tell you. I could redraw my sketches although they were only from memory.'

Arne shook his head. 'They need accurate photos. I came to ask you if there's a way to sneak inside.'

'There's a place where the fence is concealed by trees, but how are you going to get to Sande if the police are looking for you?'

'I've changed my appearance.'

'Not much. What papers are you carrying?'

'Only my own—how would I get any others?'

'So if you're stopped by the police, it will take them about ten seconds to establish that you're the man they're all looking for.'

'It has to be done. This equipment enables the Germans to detect bombers when they're still miles away—in time to scramble their fighters. The RAF is desperate to figure out how they're doing it. It's worth risking my life.'

'If you're caught, you won't be able to pass the information on to the British.' Harald took a deep breath. 'Why don't I go?'

'I knew you were going to say that.'

'No one's looking for me. I know the site. And I've already been over the fence—I took a short cut one night.'

'The police may have found your sketch when they came for Poul, and they will probably have improved their security as a result. Getting over the fence may not be as easy as it was.'

'I still have a better chance than you. Give me the camera.'

Before Arne could reply, Karen came in. She walked softly and appeared without warning, so Arne had no chance to hide.

'Who are you?' Karen said. 'Oh! Hello, Arne.' Harald guessed they must have met when she was dating Poul. 'You've shaved off your moustache—I suppose that's because of all the posters I saw in Copenhagen today. Why are you an outlaw?'

Arne hesitated, then said, 'I can't tell you.'

Karen's agile mind raced ahead. 'My God, you're in the Resistance! Was Poul in it too? Is that why he died?'

Arne nodded. 'He didn't crash his aircraft. He was trying to escape from the police, and they shot him.'

'Poor Poul. So you've taken up where he left off. But now the police are onto you. Someone must be sheltering you—probably Jens Toksvig, he was Poul's closest friend after you.'

Arne shrugged and nodded.

'But you can't move around without risking arrest, so . . .' She looked at Harald, and her voice went quiet. 'You're in it now, Harald.' She looked concerned, as if she were afraid for him.

He was pleased that she cared. 'Well, am I in it?' he asked Arne.

Arne sighed and gave him the camera.

HARALD ARRIVED IN MORLUNDE late the following day. He left his bike in a car park next to the ferry dock, feeling it would be too conspicuous on Sande. He was in time for the last ferry of the day.

When the boat docked, a handful of people got off. To Harald's surprise, a Danish policeman and a German soldier stood at the head of the gangway. Harald's heartbeat seemed to falter. He hesitated, unsure whether to board. Had they simply stepped up security round the base, as Arne had forecast, or were they looking for Arne himself? Would they know Harald was his brother?

He considered his options. There were other ways of getting to Sande. He might be able to steal a small boat. However, if he were seen beaching it on Sande he would be sure to be questioned.

He might do better to act innocent. He boarded the ferry.

The policeman asked him, 'What is your reason for wanting to travel to Sande?'

'I live there,' he said. 'With my parents.'

The policeman looked at his face. 'I don't remember seeing you before, and I've been doing this for four days.'

'I've been away at school. It's the end of term.'

The officer grunted, apparently satisfied. He checked Harald's identity card and showed it to the soldier, who let Harald on board.

At midnight the boat left the dock. There was no moon. In the starlight, the flat island of Sande was a dark swell like another wave on the horizon. Harald had wondered when he left on Friday if he would ever see the place again. Now he was back as a spy, with a mission to photograph the Nazis' secret weapon. He vaguely recalled thinking what a thrill it would be to become part of the Resistance. In reality it was no fun at all. He was sick with fear.

He felt worse as he disembarked on the quay, made his way to the beach, and began to tramp south. It was near dawn when he came within sight of the base. He could just make out the fence posts. If he could see, so could the guards, he realised. He dropped to his knees and began to crawl forward.

A minute later he was glad of his caution. He spotted two guards patrolling inside the fence, side by side, with a dog. He dropped flat. The two men did not seem especially alert. The one holding the dog was talking animatedly while the other smoked.

As the guards approached, the dog sniffed the air and barked uncertainly. It could probably smell Harald. The guard holding the lead told the animal to shut up, then continued talking. The dog barked again, and the other guard turned on a powerful flashlight. The beam played along the dunes but passed over Harald.

The guards walked on, and the dog became quiet again.

Harald lay still until they were out of sight. Then he approached the section of the fence that was concealed by vegetation. He crawled through the bushes, climbed the fence, stepped over the barbed wire, and jumped down the other side.

He walked quickly, looking around constantly. He passed the searchlight tower, and then he descended a gentle slope and entered a stand of conifers which concealed the secret radio equipment.

He could see clearly the circular wall and the big rectangular grid rising from its hollow core, the aerial slowly rotating. He heard again the low hum of the electric motor. On either side of the structure he could make out two smaller shapes, and he saw that they were miniature versions of the big rotating aerial.

So there were three machines. He wondered why. Might that somehow explain the superiority of German radar? Looking more closely at the smaller aerials, he thought they were constructed differently. It seemed to him they might tilt as well as rotate.

The first time he was here, he had jumped over the circular wall, after hearing a guard cough nearby. He felt sure there must be an easier way in. He walked round the circle, and came across a door. It was not locked, and he passed through.

He looked up at the revolving grid. It must pick up radio beams reflected off the aircraft, he guessed. The aerial must act like a lens, focusing the signals received. The cable protruding from the base carried the data back to the buildings, where, presumably, monitors displayed the results, and operators alerted the Luftwaffe.

He looked up. The sky was turning from black to grey. At this time of year, dawn broke before three o'clock. In another hour, the sun would rise. He took the camera out of his satchel and moved quietly around inside the wall, figuring out the best angles for photographs that would reveal every detail of the machinery.

He and Arne had agreed that he would take the shots at about a quarter to five. As soon as he had taken them, it would be full daylight. His departure would be a lot more dangerous than his arrival.

He considered which way to go. To the south, towards his parents' home, the fence was only a couple of hundred yards away, but the route lay across open dunes. Going north, retracing his steps under cover of bushes, would take longer but might be safer.

At last it was time to take the pictures. In the clear morning light, he could see every rivet and terminal of the complex piece of machinery in front of him. He photographed the revolving base of the apparatus, the cables, and the grid of the aerial.

Next he had to shoot pictures of the two smaller aerials. He cracked the door. All was still. There was no sign of life.

Snapping photographs, he wondered how the three devices working together could increase the kill rate of Luftwaffe fighters. Perhaps the large aerial gave advance warning of a bomber's approach and the smaller one tracked the bomber within German airspace. Could the third aerial be used by the Luftwaffe to track *their own aircraft*? It seemed crazy, but as he stepped back to photograph the three aerials together, showing their placement relative to one another, he realised it made perfect sense. If a Luftwaffe controller knew the positions of the bomber and the fighter, he could direct the fighter by radio until it made contact with the bomber. After that, it was like shooting fish in a barrel.

That thought made Harald realise how exposed he was: standing in full daylight, in the middle of a military base, photographing top-secret equipment. Panic surged through his veins like poison.

He started walking quickly away. Forgetting his resolution to take the longer but safer route north, he headed south across the dunes. In that direction, the fence was visible just beyond the old boathouse he had bumped into last time. As he approached it, a dog barked.

He looked around but saw no soldiers and no dog. Then he realised the sound came from the boathouse. The soldiers must be using it as a kennel. A second dog joined in the barking, then the noise became hysterically loud. Harald broke into a run.

He reached the fence, climbed it like a monkey and vaulted over the barbed wire. He came down hard, then scrambled to his feet. No soldiers were in view. He turned and ran. He left footprints in the hard sand, but when he reached the dunes, he left no visible trace.

Breathing hard, he headed for the parsonage. The kitchen door was open. His parents were always up early. He stepped inside. His mother was at the stove, wearing a dressing gown, making tea. When she saw him she gave a cry of shock. 'Harald!'

He kissed her cheek and hugged her. 'Is my father at home?'

'In the church.'

By now, guards would have gone to find out what had disturbed the dogs. If they were thorough, they might check nearby houses and look for a fugitive in sheds and barns.

'Mother,' he said, 'if the soldiers come here, will you tell them I've been in bed all night?'

'Whatever has happened?' she said fearfully.

'I'll explain later. Tell them I'm still asleep—will you?'

'All right.'

He left the kitchen and went upstairs to his bedroom. He shed his clothes quickly, put on his pyjamas and got into bed.

He heard his father's voice. 'What's he doing here?'

His mother replied, 'Hiding from the soldiers.'

'For goodness' sake, what has the boy got himself into now?'

'I don't know, but—'

His mother was interrupted by a loud knocking. A young man said in German, 'Good morning. We're looking for someone. Have you seen a stranger in the last few hours?'

'No, nobody at all.' Harald's mother's voice was nervous.

'Is there anyone else here?'

Harald's mother replied, 'My son. He's still asleep.'

'I need to search the house.' The voice was polite.

'I'll show you around,' said the pastor.

Harald heard booted footsteps on the tiled floors downstairs. Then the boots came upstairs. They entered his parents' bedroom, then Arne's old room. Finally the handle of Harald's door turned.

He closed his eyes, making his breathing slow and even.

The German voice said quietly, 'Your son.'

'Yes,' Harald's father said.

There was a pause. 'Has he been here all night?'

Harald held his breath. He had never known his father to tell even a white lie. Then he heard, 'Yes. All night.'

He was flabbergasted. His father had lied for him. The hard-hearted, stiff-necked, self-righteous old tyrant had broken his own rules. He was human after all. Harald felt tears behind his eyes.

The boots receded down the stairs. Harald heard the soldier taking his leave. He got out of bed and went to the top of the stairs.

'You can come down now,' his father said. 'He's gone.'

He went down the stairs. His father looked solemn. 'Thank you for that, Father,' Harald said.

'I committed a sin,' his father said. Harald thought he was going to be angry. Then the old face softened. 'However, I believe in a for-giving God.' His father drew Harald to him. He closed his eyes, struggling to contain a profound emotion. When he spoke, his words came out in a murmur of anguish. 'I thought they would kill you,' he said. 'My dear son, I thought they would kill you.'

ARNE OLUFSEN HAD slipped through Peter Flemming's fingers.

Peter brooded over this as he boiled an egg for Inge's breakfast. After Arne shook off the surveillance on Bornholm, Peter had believed Arne was not cunning enough to get off the island unob-served—and he had been wrong. He did not know how Arne had managed it, but there was no doubt he had returned to Copenhagen, for a policeman had spotted him in the city centre. The patrolman had given chase, but Arne had outrun him—and vanished again.

Arne had not returned to barracks, nor was he with his parents on Sande, so he had to be hiding out at the home of a fellow spy. But they would all be lying low. However, one person who probably knew most of the spies was Karen Duchwitz. She had been Poul's girl-friend, and her brother was at school with Poul's cousin. She was not a spy, Peter felt sure, so she had no reason to lie low. She might lead Peter to Arne.

It was a long shot, but it was all he had.

He took the soft-boiled egg into the bedroom. He sat Inge up and gave her a spoonful of egg. He got the feeling she did not much like it. She pushed it out of her mouth, like a baby. The egg ran down her chin and onto the bodice of her nightdress.

Peter stared in despair. Inge had made a mess of herself several times in the past week or two. This was a new development. She had always been so fastidious. He put the dish down and went to the phone. He dialled the hotel on Sande and asked for his father, who was always at work early. When he got through, he said, 'You were right. It's time to put Inge in a home.'

PETER FLEMMING STUDIED THE Royal Theatre, a domed nineteenth-century building of yellow stone. He and Tilde were sitting on the verandah of the Hôtel d'Angleterre. They had a good view across the Kongens Nytorv, the largest square in Copenhagen. Inside the theatre, the students of the ballet school were watching a dress rehearsal of *Les Sylphides*, the current production.

Peter glanced down at the photograph in his hand. He had taken it from Poul Kirke's bedroom. It showed Poul sitting on a bicycle with Karen perched on the crossbar. They were both wearing shorts. They looked such a happy couple, full of energy and fun, that for a moment Peter felt sad that Poul had died. He had to remind himself that Poul had chosen to be a spy and to flout the law.

'Here she comes,' said Tilde.

Peter looked across the square and saw a group of young people emerging from the theatre. He picked out Karen immediately. She was wearing a straw boater at a jaunty angle and a yellow summer dress with a flared skirt. She crossed the square and turned into the main drag, the Stroget. Peter stood up and hurried after her. Tilde followed at a distance, by prearrangement.

At the end of the Stroget, Karen walked past the Tivoli Garden and approached Vesterport, a suburban railway station from which she could catch a train to her home village of Kirstenslot.

This was no good. Clearly she was not going to lead him to one of the circle. He would have to force the situation.

Peter caught up with her at the entrance to the station. 'Excuse me,' he said. 'I must speak to you.'

She gave him a level look and kept walking. 'What is it?'

'Could we talk just for a minute?' He pretended to be nervous. 'I'm taking a terrible risk just speaking to you.'

'What's this about?' She stopped and glanced around.

'It's about Arne Olufsen. Aren't you a friend of his?'

'No. I've met him. I used to go out with a friend of his, but I don't really know him. Why are you asking me?'

'Could you get a message to him?'

She hesitated. 'Possibly,' she said.

'I'm with the police.'

She took a frightened step back.

'It's all right, I'm on your side. I'm nothing to do with the security department, I do road accidents. But our office is next to theirs, and sometimes I hear what's going on.'

'What have you heard?'

'Arne is in great danger. The security department know where he's hiding. They're going to arrest him tonight.'

'Oh, no!'

Peter noted that she did not ask what the security department was, nor what crime Arne was supposed to have committed, and she showed no surprise about his being in hiding. She must therefore know what Arne was up to, he concluded with a sense of triumph. 'Please try to get a warning to him.'

'I don't think I can—'

'I can't risk being seen with you. I have to go. I'm sorry. Do your best.' He turned and walked rapidly away.

As he left the station, he passed Tilde, who was pretending to read a timetable. Across the street, a man was unloading crates from a wagon. Peter stepped behind the cart, took off his trilby hat, and replaced it with a peaked cap. He knew from experience that this simple switch effected a remarkable change in his appearance. Concealed by the wagon, he watched the station entrance. Karen came out. Tilde was a few paces behind her. Peter followed Tilde.

They turned a corner and on the next block, Karen turned into the main post office. Tilde followed her in.

She was going to make a phone call, Peter thought. He ran to the staff entrance and hammered on the door. He showed his police badge to the manager. 'A woman in a yellow dress just entered the post office,' Peter told him. 'I need to know what she does.'

'Come with me.' The manager hurried along a corridor and opened a door. 'I think I see her. Curly red hair and a straw hat?'

'That's the one. What is she doing?'

'Looking in the telephone directory.'

'If she makes a phone call, I need to listen. It's important.'

'But she's putting the phone book down. She's not coming to the counter . . . She's leaving!'

Peter cursed with frustration and ran for the exit. He cracked the door and peeped out. He saw Karen crossing the road. He waited until Tilde emerged, following Karen. Then he tagged along.

Karen knew the name of someone who could get in touch with Arne. She had looked the name up in the phone book, but she had not phoned the person. If she had not wanted the phone number, she must have been looking for the address. And now, if Peter's luck was in, she was heading for that address.

He let Karen get out of sight but kept Tilde in view. They crossed the small island of Christiansborg and followed the waterfront. Karen headed for Nyboder, a neighbourhood of small houses originally built as cheap accommodation for sailors.

They entered a street called St Paul's Gade. Peter could see Karen in the distance, looking at a row of yellow houses with red roofs, apparently searching for a number. He had a strong, exciting feeling of being close to his quarry.

She knocked on a door.

As Peter caught up with Tilde, Karen stepped inside and the door closed. It was number 53, Peter noted.

Peter looked up and down the street. On the opposite side was a corner shop. 'Let's go over there,' he said. They crossed the road and stood looking in the window. Peter lit a cigarette.

The door opened, and Karen came out. She walked away alone.

'What do we do now?' Tilde asked.

Peter thought fast. Suppose Arne was inside the house. Then Peter needed to summon reinforcements, bust into the house and arrest him and anyone with him. On the other hand, Arne might be somewhere else, and Karen could be on her way there—in which case Peter needed to follow her.

He made a decision. 'We'll split up,' he told Tilde. 'You follow Karen. I'll call headquarters and raid that house.'

'OK.' Tilde hurried after Karen.

Peter went into the shop and asked a grey-haired woman in an apron if he could use the phone. He called the Politigaarden, and hurried back outside. He had been less than a minute. If anyone had left the house during that time they should be visible on the street. He saw an old man walking a dog and a group of boys playing football. There was no sign of Arne. He crossed the street.

The door of number 53 opened. Arne stepped out of the house. He had shaved off his moustache and covered his black hair with a workman's cap, but Peter recognised him immediately.

Arne walked towards Peter. As they came closer, Arne avoided his eye, walking on the inside of the pavement, near the houses, in the manner of a fugitive. Peter walked on the kerb side. When they were ten yards apart, Arne glanced at Peter's face. Peter saw a puzzled frown, recognition, then Arne stopped, momentarily frozen.

'You're under arrest,' Peter said. He drew his gun. 'Lie on the ground face down with your hands behind your back.'

For a moment the familiar careless grin flickered across Arne's face. He said in a challenging tone, 'Are you ready to shoot me?'

'If necessary,' Peter said. He levelled the gun threateningly.

Arne smiled enigmatically, then turned and ran.

Peter held his gun arm straight, and sighted along the barrel. He aimed at Arne's legs and pulled the trigger. Arne kept running.

Peter fired again repeatedly. After the fourth shot, Arne staggered. Peter fired again, and Arne hit the ground with a thud.

Peter ran forward. The figure on the ground lay still. Peter knelt beside it. Arne opened his eyes. His face was white with pain. 'You stupid pig, you should have killed me,' he said.

HARALD STEERED THE BIKE through Copenhagen's Nyboder district in the morning sunshine. He was about to hand the film over to Arne, who was hiding out at Jens Toksvig's house.

After his escape from the guards on Sande, Harald had spent the day with his parents and slept in his old bed that night. Early the next morning his mother woke him, fed him breakfast, and pleaded with him to tell her where he was living. Weakened by her affection and his father's mellowing, he had told her he was staying in Kirstenslot. However, he had not mentioned the disused church, for fear she would worry about him sleeping rough, and he had left her with the impression he was a guest at the big house. Then he had set out to drive across Denmark from west to east.

He easily found St Paul's Gade, a narrow street of small houses. Harald parked the bike outside 53 and knocked.

It was answered by a policeman with a grey moustache.

For a moment, Harald was struck dumb. Where was Arne?

'What is it, lad?' the policeman said impatiently.

Harald was inspired. Displaying a panic that was all too real, he said, 'The doctor must come right away, she's having the baby!'

The policeman smiled. 'There's no doctor here.'

'But there must be!'

'Calm down, son. What address have you got?'

'Dr Thorsen, 53 Fischer's Gade.'

'Right number, wrong street. This is St Paul's Gade. Fischer's Gade is one block south.'

'Thank you!' Harald jumped onto the bike and pulled away. Very clever, he thought, but what do I do now?

HERMIA SPENT ALL Friday morning in the beautiful ruin of Hammershus castle, waiting for Arne to arrive with the film.

It was now even more important than it had been five days ago, when she had sent him on the mission. In the interim, the world had changed. The Nazis had invaded the Soviet Union. Intelligence estimates put the size of the invading army at 3 million men. Their total air superiority was devastating the Red Army.

Digby had told Hermia that Stalin had asked Churchill to step up the bombing campaign against Germany, hoping that it would force Hitler to bring aircraft home to defend the Fatherland.

Churchill had ordered a bombing raid, committing 500 of Bomber Command's planes, over half of England's entire strength, in an attempt to draw Luftwaffe strength away from the Russian front and give the Soviet soldiers a chance to fight back. That raid was now eleven days away, scheduled for July 8, the next full moon.

Digby had also talked to his brother, Bart, who was back on active service and certain to be piloting one of the bombers.

The raid would be a suicide mission, and Bomber Command would be fatally weakened, unless they developed ways to evade German radar in the next few days. And that depended on Arne.

Hermia had persuaded her Swedish fisherman to bring her across the water again. At dawn she had splashed through the shallows, carrying her bike, onto the beach below Hammershus. Then she had climbed the steep hill to the castle.

But Arne did not show up during the morning. This made Hermia anxious, but she assumed he had taken the morning sailing and would arrive that evening. Last time she had sat tight and waited for him. Now she decided to cycle to Ronne.

She felt nervous as she passed from the lonely country roads into the little town. When the ferry docked, she stood on the harbour with a small group of people waiting to meet passengers. As they disembarked she scrutinised every face. Arne was not on the boat.

She fretted over what to do next. There were a hundred possible explanations for his non-appearance, ranging from the trivial to the tragic. Had he lost his nerve and abandoned the mission? He might be dead. But it was most likely he had been held up by a delayed train. Unfortunately, he had no way of letting her know. But she might be able to contact him. She had told him to hide out at Jens Toksvig's house. Jens had a phone, and Hermia knew the number.

She went to a nearby hotel and placed the call.

The phone was picked up, and a man's voice said, 'Hello?'

It was not Arne. The voice was that of an older man, and Jens was twenty-nine. She said, 'Let me speak to Jens Toksvig, please.'

'Who is calling?'

She was not going to give her real name. 'It's Hilde.'

'May I have your second name, please?'

This was ominous. She decided to try to bully him. 'Look, I don't know who you are, but just put Jens on the phone, will you?'

It did not work. 'I must have your surname.'

'Who are you?'

There was a pause. 'Sergeant Egill of the Copenhagen police.'

Hermia hung up. She was shocked and frightened. Arne had taken refuge in Jens's house, and now the house was under police guard. It could only mean that they had found out that Arne was hiding there. They must have arrested Jens and Arne. Hermia fought back tears. She walked out of the hotel and looked across the harbour towards Copenhagen, a hundred miles away.

There was no way she was going to meet up with her fisherman and return to Sweden empty-handed. She would be letting down Digby Hoare, Winston Churchill and thousands of British airmen.

The ferry's horn sounded the all-aboard with a noise like a bereaved giant. Hermia jumped on her bicycle and cycled to the dock. She bought a ticket and hurried on board. She had to go to Copenhagen and find out what had happened to Arne. She had to get his film, if he had taken any pictures. When she had done that, she would worry about how to get the film to England.

HARALD HAD SPENT the day brooding over his plight. The presence of police at Arne's hide-out almost certainly meant that Arne had been found out. If by some miracle he had evaded arrest, the only place he might be hiding was the old monastery at Kirstenslot, so Harald had driven there and checked. He found the place empty.

He sat on the floor of the church, alternately grieving at his brother's fate and trying to figure out what he should do next. If he were to finish the job Arne had started, he had to get the film to London. Arne must have had a plan for this, but Harald did not know what it was and could not think of a way to find out.

He wondered where Arne was now. Probably in a cell in the Politigaarden in Copenhagen, being interrogated. Would Arne talk? Not at first, Harald felt sure. Arne would not crumble immediately. But would he have the strength to hold out?.

That evening, Harald told Karen the whole story, about getting into the base on Sande, then hiding in his parents' house.

'You've got such nerve!' she exclaimed. He was pleased by her admiration.

When he related how a police sergeant had answered the door of Jens Toksvig's house, she interrupted him, 'I got a warning. A stranger came up to me at the railway station and told me the police knew where Arne was. This man was a cop himself, in the traffic department, but he happened to have overheard something, and he wanted to let us know because he was sympathetic.'

'Didn't you warn Arne?'

'Yes, I did! I went to Jens's house. I told Arne what had happened. He told me to leave first, and said he was going to get out immediately after me, but obviously he left it too late.'

'Or your warning was a ruse,' Harald mused. 'Maybe your policeman was lying. Suppose he wasn't sympathetic at all. He might have followed you to Jens's place and arrested Arne when you left.'

'That's ridiculous—policemen don't do things like that!'

Harald realised once again he had run up against Karen's faith in the goodwill of those around her. 'What did the man look like?'

'Tall, handsome, heavy, red hair, nice suit.'

'A kind of oatmeal tweed?'

'Yes.'

That settled it. 'He's Peter Flemming. He is more of a spy than a policeman. I know his family, back on Sande.'

'I don't believe you! You've got too much imagination.'

He did not want to argue with her. It pierced his heart to know that his brother was in custody. Harald wondered grievingly if he would ever see Arne again. But there were more lives at stake. 'Arne won't be able to get this film to England.'

'How was he going to do it?'

'I don't know, he didn't tell me.'

They were silent for a while. Harald felt depressed. Had he risked his life for nothing? 'Have you heard any news?' he asked.

'Finland declared war on the Soviet Union. So did Hungary.'

'Vultures scenting death,' Harald said bitterly.

'It's maddening to be sitting here while the Nazis are conquering the world,' Karen said. 'I wish there was something we could do.'

Harald touched the film canister in his trouser pocket. 'This would make a difference, if I could get it to London.'

Karen glanced at the Hornet Moth. 'It's a pity that won't fly.'

Harald looked at the damaged undercarriage. 'I might be able to repair it. But I've only had one lesson, I couldn't pilot it.'

Karen looked thoughtful. 'No,' she said slowly. 'But I could.'

ARNE OLUFSEN PROVED surprisingly resistant to interrogation.

Peter Flemming questioned him on the day of his arrest, and on the following day, but he revealed no secrets.

He had no more luck with Jens Toksvig, but he felt sure Arne was the prime suspect. He knew Poul Kirke, he was familiar with Sande, he had an English fiancée, he had gone to Bornholm, which was so close to Sweden, and he had shaken off his police tail.

Peter had to break Arne. He wanted to know how the spy ring worked, who else was in it, what means they used to communicate with England. He planned the third interrogation very carefully.

At four o'clock on Sunday morning he burst into Arne's cell with two uniformed policemen. Shining a torch in his eyes, they pulled him out of bed and marched him to the interrogation room.

Peter sat on the only chair in the room, behind a cheap table, and lit a cigarette. Arne looked pale and frightened in his prison pyjamas. His left leg was bandaged and strapped, but he could stand—Peter's two bullets had not broken any bones.

Peter said, 'Your friend Poul Kirke was a spy.'

'I didn't know that,' Arne said.

'Why did you go to Bornholm?'

'For a little holiday.'

'Why would an innocent man on holiday evade police?'

'He might dislike being followed around by a lot of flatfoots.' Arne had more spirit than Peter had expected. 'As it happens, I didn't notice them. If I evaded surveillance, I did it unintentionally.'

'Rubbish. You deliberately shook off your tail. I know. I was part of the surveillance team. Whom did you meet on Bornholm?'

'No one.'

'When you came back to Copenhagen, you went into hiding.'

'Hiding? I was staying with a friend.'

'Jens Toksvig—another spy.'

'He didn't tell me that.'

Peter was dismayed that Arne was sticking to his story. 'So you had no idea the police were searching for you?'

'No.'

Peter let the sarcasm sound in his voice. 'You didn't happen to see any of the one thousand posters of your face that have been put up around the city? You shaved off your moustache.'

'Someone told me I looked like Hitler.'

Tilde came in with a tray. The smell of hot toast made Peter's mouth water. He trusted it was having the same effect on Arne. Tilde poured tea. She asked Arne, 'Would you like some?'

He nodded.

Peter said, 'No.'

Tilde shrugged. She brought in another chair and sat down. Peter ate some buttered toast, taking his time. When he had finished eating, he resumed the questioning. 'In Poul Kirke's office, I found a sketch of a military installation on Sande. If he had not been killed, he would have sent it to the British.'

'He might have had an innocent explanation for it, had he not been shot by a trigger-happy fool.'

'Did you make those drawings?'

'Certainly not.'

'Four nights ago, there was a security alert at the base on Sande. Something disturbed the guard dogs. The sentries saw someone with a camera running across the dunes in the direction of your father's church.' Peter watched Arne's face. So far, Arne did not look surprised. 'Was that you running across the dunes?'

'No.'

Peter continued, 'Your parents' home was searched.' He saw a flicker of fear in Arne's eyes. He had not known about this. 'The guards found a young man asleep in bed, but the pastor said it was his son. Was that you?'

'No. I haven't been home since Whitsun.'

'Yesterday morning, a young man called at Jens Toksvig's house. One of our officers answered the door. The boy pretended to have come to the wrong address, looking for a doctor, and our man was gullible enough to believe him. But it was a lie. The young man was your brother, wasn't he?'

'I'm quite sure he was not,' Arne said, but he looked frightened.

'Harald was bringing you something—perhaps photographs of the military installation on Sande.'

'No.'

'That evening, a woman in Bornholm, who called herself Hilde, telephoned Jens Toksvig's house. Could she have been your fiancée, Hermia Mount?'

'She's in England.'

'You are mistaken. According to Swedish immigration authorities, she flew to Stockholm ten days ago, and has not departed.'

Arne feigned surprise, but the act was unconvincing. 'I know nothing of that,' he said. 'I haven't heard from her for more than a year.'

If that had been true, Arne would have been astonished and shocked to learn that she had been in Sweden and possibly Denmark. He was definitely lying now.

Tilde poured some tea into a mug and gave it to Arne without consulting Peter. Peter said nothing; this was all part of the prearranged scenario. Arne took the mug and drank thirstily.

Tilde spoke in a kindly voice. 'Arne, you're in over your head. This isn't just about you any more. You've involved your parents, your fiancée and your young brother. Harald is in deep trouble. If this goes on, he'll end up hanged as a spy—and it will be your fault. We can make a deal with you. Tell us everything, and you and Harald will escape the death penalty. You don't have to take my word for that—General Braun will be here in a minute, and he will guarantee that. But first you have to tell us where Harald is.'

'Go to hell,' Arne said quietly.

Peter sprang to his feet. 'You're the one who's going to hell!' he shouted. 'Don't you understand what's happening to you?'

Tilde got to her feet and left quietly.

'If you don't talk to us, you'll be turned over to the Gestapo,' Peter went on angrily. '*They* won't give you tea and ask polite questions. They'll pull out your fingernails, and light matches under the soles of your feet. They'll strip you naked and beat you with hammers. You'll beg them to let you die, but they won't—not until you talk. And you will talk. In the end, *everyone talks*.'

White-faced, Arne said quietly, 'I know.'

Peter was taken aback by the poise and resignation behind the fear. What did it mean?

The door opened and General Braun came in, the picture of cold efficiency in his crisp uniform with his holstered pistol. 'Is this the man to be sent to Germany?'

Arne moved fast, despite his injury.

Peter was looking the other way, towards Braun, and he saw only a blur as Arne reached for the tray. The earthenware teapot flew through the air and struck the side of Peter's head, splashing tea over his face. When he had dashed the liquid from his eyes he saw Arne charge into Braun, knocking him over. Arne unbuttoned the general's holster, snatched out the pistol, swinging it towards Peter.

Peter froze. The gun was a 9mm Luger. Was it loaded? Or did Braun wear it just for show?

Tilde stepped inside the open door, saying, 'What—?'

'Stay still!' Arne barked.

Peter asked himself urgently how familiar Arne was with weapons. He was a military officer, but in the air force he might not have had much practice. As if to answer the unspoken question, Arne switched off the safety catch.

The door was still open and Peter could see the two uniformed policemen who had escorted Arne from his cell.

None of the four policemen was carrying a gun. They did not bring weapons into the cell area. It was a strict regulation imposed to prevent prisoners doing exactly what Arne had just done. But Braun did not consider himself subject to the regulations. Now Arne had them all at his mercy.

Peter said, 'You can't get away. This is the largest police station in Denmark. There are dozens of armed police outside.'

'I know,' Arne said.

There was that ominous note of resignation again.

Suddenly Peter knew what was going to happen next. Arne feared he was going to betray his friends—perhaps even his brother—and the only way to be completely safe was to be dead. But Peter wanted Arne to reveal his secrets. He could not let Arne die.

Despite the gun pointed straight at him, Peter dashed at Arne.

Arne did not shoot him. He jerked back the gun and pressed its nose into the soft skin under his own chin. The gun barked once.

Peter struck it from Arne's hand, but he was too late. A gush of blood sprayed from Arne's head. Arne still had the ironic smile he had worn as he put the gun to his throat. After a moment, he fell sideways. His body hit the floor with a lifeless thud and he lay still.

 EIGHT

When Harald woke up, he knew that something wonderful had happened, but for a moment he could not recall what it was. He lay on the ledge in the apse of the church, with Karen's blanket around him and Pine Top the cat curled up against his chest, and waited for his memory to work. It all came back in a rush: Karen had agreed to fly him to England in the Hornet Moth.

The danger was that they might both be caught, arrested, and killed. What made him happy, despite that, was that he would be spending hours alone with Karen. Not that he thought anything romantic would happen. He realised she was out of his league. Even if he was never going to kiss her, he was thrilled at the thought that they would be together. But the whole plan depended on whether he could repair the Hornet Moth. He got up, washed at the cold tap, pulled on his clothes and began to inspect the aircraft.

Just then, Karen arrived. 'I've been thinking about mending this thing,' she said. 'I'm not sure it can be done.'

'We'll see.' Harald began to study the Hornet Moth with an engineer's eye. 'I think I could refit the wings,' he said, looking at the hinges by which they were attached to the fuselage.

'That's easy. It only takes a few minutes.' She touched the nearer wing. 'The fabric is in a bad state though.'

'It's only superficial damage,' Harald said. 'Does it matter?'

'Yes. The rips in the fabric might interfere with the airflow over the wings.'

'So we'll patch them. I'm more worried about the undercarriage.'

Harald knelt down to look more closely at the damaged landing gear. The solid steel stub axle appeared to have two prongs that fitted into a V-shaped strut. Both arms of the V-strut had creased and buckled at their weakest point. They looked as if they would easily break. A third strut appeared undamaged. Nevertheless the undercarriage was too weak for a landing.

'I did that,' Karen said. 'I landed in a crosswind and swerved sideways. The wing tip hit the ground.'

It sounded terrifying. 'Were you scared?'

'No, I just felt a fool, but my instructor said it's not uncommon in a Hornet Moth.'

'Why was it never repaired?'

'Because we don't have the facilities here.' She waved at the workbench and the tool rack. 'We have no welding gear. Then Daddy lost interest in learning to fly the plane. So the work never got done.'

That was discouraging, Harald thought. How was he going to do metalwork? He walked to the tail and examined the wing that had hit the ground. 'It doesn't seem to be fractured,' he said. 'I can easily repair the tip. Well, let's see what else is wrong.' He moved to the nose, opened the left cowling, and studied the engine.

'It's a four-cylinder in-line layout,' Karen said.

'Yes, but it seems to be upside-down.'

'By comparison with a car engine, yes. The crankshaft is at the top.

That's to raise the level of the propeller for ground clearance.'

Harald was surprised by her expertise. He had never met a girl who knew what a crankshaft was.

He moved to the other side and opened the right cowling. All the fuel and oil hoses seemed to be firmly attached. He unscrewed the oil cap and checked the dipstick. There was still a little oil in the tank. 'It looks OK,' he said. 'Let's see if it starts.'

'You can sit inside while I swing the propeller.'

'Won't the battery be flat after all these years?'

'There's no battery. The electricity comes from two magnetos which are driven by the engine itself. I'll show you what to do.'

Karen opened the cabin door, then let out a squeal and fell back into Harald's arms. It was the first time he had touched her body, and an electric thrill went through him. He hastily set her upright and detached himself. 'Are you all right?' he said. 'What happened?

'Mice.'

He opened the door again. Two mice jumped through the gap to the floor. Karen made a disgusted noise.

There were holes in the cloth upholstery of one seat, and he guessed they had nested in the stuffing. 'That problem is quickly solved,' he said. He made a kissing sound with his lips, and Pine Top appeared, hoping for food. Harald put the cat into the cabin.

Pine Top suddenly became energised. He leapt onto the seat and investigated the holes in the upholstery. There he found a baby mouse, and began to eat it with delicacy.

On the luggage shelf, Harald noticed two small manuals, one for the Hornet Moth and one for the Gipsy Major engine that powered it. He was delighted. He showed them to Karen.

'But what about the mice?' she said. 'I hate them.'

'I'll leave the cabin doors open, so Pine Top can get in and out. He'll keep them away.' Harald opened the Hornet Moth manual.

'What's he doing now?'

'Oh, he's eating the babies. Look at these great diagrams!'

'Harald!' she yelled. 'That's disgusting! Go and stop him!'

'What's the alternative? We have to get rid of the nest.'

'It's so cruel!'

'They're *mice*, for heaven's sake,' Harald said.

'Can't you see that I hate it! You're just a stupid engineer who thinks about how things work and never about how people feel.'

Now he was wounded. 'That's not true.'

'It is,' she said, and she stamped off.

Harald was astonished. Did she really believe he was a stupid engineer who never thought about how people felt?

He thought of following her and decided not to. He might as well try to start the engine. The instructions were in the manual. He leaned into the cabin and turned the petrol control knob on. He followed the directions for flooding the carburettor. He had no way of telling whether what he was doing was having any effect. For all he knew, the tank was dry. He set the throttle in a slightly open position, then flipped a switch that operated the twin magnetos.

He felt dejected now that Karen had gone. Why was he so clumsy with her? He was desperately keen to be friendly and charming and do whatever it took to please her, but he could not figure out what she wanted. Why could girls not be more like engines?

Harald stood at the front and grasped one of the blades of the propeller. He turned it. It gave a sharp click then stopped. He turned it again. It clicked again. The third time, he gave it a vigorous heave, hoping the engine would fire, but it remained silent.

Karen came in. 'Won't it start?' she said.

He looked at her in surprise. He had not expected to see her again today. 'Too early to say. I've only just begun.'

She seemed contrite. 'I'm sorry I stormed off.'

'That's all right,' he said.

'I know it's foolish to think about baby mice when men like Poul are losing their lives.'

That was how Harald saw it, but he did not say so. 'Pine Top's gone anyway.'

'I'm not surprised the engine won't start,' she said. 'It hasn't been turned over for at least three years.'

'Water may have condensed inside the fuel tank. But oil floats, so the fuel will lie on top. We might be able to drain the water off.'

'Let's turn off the switches, for safety,' Karen said. 'I'll do it.'

Harald learned from the manual that there was a panel on the underside of the fuselage that gave access to the fuel drain plug. He took a screwdriver from the tool rack then lay on the floor and wriggled under the aircraft to unscrew the panel.

When the panel came off, Karen handed him an adjustable spanner. The drain plug was awkwardly placed, being slightly to one side of the access hole. When his hand was in the gap, he could no longer see the drain plug, so he had to work blind.

He turned the plug slowly but, when it opened, freezing liquid spurted onto his hand. He withdrew his hand quickly, banging his numbed fingers on the edge of the access hole and, to his intense irritation, he dropped the plug. Fuel poured from the drain. He and Karen quickly wriggled out of the way of the gush, but there was nothing they could do except watch.

Harald cursed. 'Now we've got no fuel,' he said bitterly.

'We could siphon some out of the Rolls-Royce,' Karen said.

'That's not aeroplane fuel.'

'The Hornet Moth runs on car petrol.'

'Does it? I didn't realise that.' Harald perked up again. After he had retrieved the drain plug he found a funnel and a clean bucket, while Karen used a pair of heavy pliers to cut a length off a garden hose. They pulled the cover off the Rolls-Royce. Karen undid the fuel cap and fed the hose into the tank.

Harald said, 'Shall I do that?'

'No,' she said. 'My turn.'

Karen put the end of the hose between her lips and sucked. When the petrol came into her mouth she quickly directed the hose into the bucket, grimacing and spitting. Harald watched the grotesque expressions on her face. Miraculously, she was no less beautiful when she was screwing up her eyes and pursing her lips. She caught his gaze and said, 'What are you staring at?'

He laughed and said, 'You, of course—you're so pretty when you're spitting.' He realised immediately that he had revealed more of his feelings than he wanted to, but she just laughed.

They emptied the tank of the car. There was only a gallon or so of petrol in the bucket, Harald guessed, but it was plenty for testing the engine. He carried the bucket over to the Hornet Moth. Karen held the funnel while Harald poured the petrol into the tank.

'I don't know where we're going to get any more,' Karen said. We certainly can't buy it.'

'How much do we need?'

'The tank takes thirty-five gallons. But that's another problem. The Hornet Moth's range is six hundred miles in ideal conditions.'

'And it's about that distance to Britain.'

'So if we have strong head winds, which is not unlikely . . .'

'We'll come down in the North Sea. One problem at a time,' said Harald. 'We haven't started the engine yet.'

Karen knew what to do. 'I'll flood the carburettor,' she said.

Harald turned on the fuel.

Karen worked the priming mechanism until fuel dribbled on the floor, then called, 'Mags on.'

Harald switched on the magnetos and opened the throttle.

Karen grasped the propellor and pulled it down. Again there was a sharp click. 'Hear that?' she said. 'It's the impulse starter. That's how you know it's working.' She swung the propellor a second time, then a third. Finally, she gave it a heave and stepped back.

The engine gave a shocking bark, then it died.

Harald cheered.

Karen said, 'What are you so pleased about?'

'It fired! There can't be much wrong. Try again.'

She swung the propellor again, but with the same result.

He turned the switches off. 'The fuel is flowing freely now. It sounds as if the problem is with the ignition. We need some tools.'

'There's a tool kit.' Karen reached into the cabin and took out a canvas bag with leather straps.

Harald took a spark plug spanner out of the bag and started to check all the plugs. When he had finished he removed the Bakelite caps over the contact breakers and checked the points.

'We've done all the obvious things,' he said. 'If it doesn't start now, we've got serious trouble.'

Karen primed the engine again then turned the propeller three times. Harald opened the cabin door and threw the magneto switches. Karen gave the propeller a final heave and stepped back.

The engine turned over and roared to life.

Harald whooped with triumph, but he could hardly hear his own voice over the noise. The sound of the engine bounced off the walls and made a deafening racket.

Karen came up to him, her hair blowing wildly in the slip-stream from the propeller. In his exuberance, Harald hugged her. 'We did it!' he yelled. She hugged him back, to his intense pleasure, then stepped away. 'Turn it off, before someone hears!' she shouted.

Harald remembered that this was not a game, and that the purpose of repairing the aircraft was to fly a dangerous secret mission. He switched off the magnetos. The engine stopped.

When the noise died away, the inside of the church should have been silent, but it was not. A strange sound came from outside.

Harald stood on a box to look out of one of the high windows. Karen jumped up beside him.

A troop of about thirty soldiers in German uniform were marching up the drive towards the castle.

At first he assumed they were coming for him, but he quickly saw that they were in no shape for a manhunt. Most of them appeared to be unarmed. They had a heavy wagon drawn by four weary horses, loaded with what looked like camping gear.

'What the hell is this?' Harald said in dismay.

'I don't know,' Karen said. 'I'd better go and find out.'

HERMIA HAD LIVED more years in Denmark than England, but suddenly it was a foreign country. The familiar streets of Copenhagen had a hostile air. She hurried like a fugitive down streets she had walked as a child, innocent and carefree. She was exhausted from her overnight ferry trip, and racked with worry about Arne.

The home of Jens Toksvig in St Paul's Gade was one of a row. Number 53 appeared empty.

Hermia went to one of the neighbour's houses and knocked. An older woman came to the door. Looking at the little suitcase Hermia was carrying, she said, 'I never buy anything on the doorstep.'

Hermia smiled. 'I've been told that number 53 might be available to rent.'

The neighbour's attitude changed. 'Oh?' she said with interest. 'Looking for a place to live, are you?'

'Yes. I'm getting married.'

'That's nice. It would be a relief to have a respectable family next door, after the goings-on. It was a nest of Communist spies.'

'No, really?'

'They were arrested last Wednesday, the whole pack of them.'

Hermia felt a chill of fear. 'Goodness! How many?'

'I couldn't say exactly. There was the tenant, Mr Toksvig, who I wouldn't have taken for a wrongdoer; then lately an airman was living there, a nice-looking boy, though he never said much; but there were all sorts in and out of the place, mostly military types.'

'And they were arrested on Wednesday?'

'There was a shooting, on that very pavement. A plain-clothes policeman shot one of the Communists.'

Hermia gasped. She was so afraid of what she might learn that she could hardly speak. 'Who was shot?'

'I didn't actually see it myself,' the woman said. 'It wasn't Mr Toksvig himself, that I can say for sure, because Mrs Eriksen in the shop saw it, and she said it was a man she didn't know.'

'Was he . . . killed?'

'Oh, no. Mrs Eriksen thought he was wounded in the leg. He cried out when the ambulance men lifted him onto the stretcher.'

Hermia seemed to feel the pain of the bullet wound herself. She was breathless and dizzy. 'I must be going,' she said. 'What a dreadful thing to happen.' She turned away.

'I should think the place will be to rent, before too long.'

Hermia walked away, paying no attention. She turned corners at random. She had to find out what had happened to Arne and where he was now. But first she needed somewhere to spend the night.

She got a room at a cheap hotel near the waterfront. She spent most of the night awake, wondering if Arne had been the man shot in St Paul's Gade. If so, how badly was he hurt? Whom could she ask? She knew many of his friends, but the ones who were likely to know what had happened were dead, or in custody, or in hiding.

In the early hours of the morning, it occurred to her that there was one person who was almost certain to know if Arne had been arrested: his commanding officer.

At first light she went to the railway station and caught a train to Vodal. When she got to the flying school she asked to see the base commander at the headquarters building. 'Tell him I'm a friend of Arne Olufsen's.'

She knew she was taking a risk. She had met Squadron Leader Renthe before, but she had no idea what his politics were. If he happened to be pro-Nazi, he might phone the police and report an Englishwoman asking questions. But he was fond of Arne, so she was hoping that for his sake Renthe would not betray her.

She was admitted immediately and Renthe recognised her. 'You're Arne's fiancée!' he said. 'I thought you'd gone to England.' He hurried to close the door—a good sign, she thought.

'I'm trying to find out where Arne is. He may be in trouble.'

'It's worse than that,' said Renthe. 'You'd better sit down.'

Hermia sat down. 'What's happened?'

'He was arrested last Wednesday. He was shot and wounded trying to escape from the police.'

'How is he?'

Renthe hesitated. In a low voice he said slowly, 'I'm dreadfully sorry to have to tell you that Arne is dead.'

She cried out in anguish. In her heart she had known this might be so, but the possibility had been too dreadful to think about. Now she felt as if she had been struck by a train.

'He died in police custody,' Renthe said.

'What? Did they torture him?'

'I don't think so. It seems that, in order to avoid revealing information, he took his own life.'

'Oh God!' Renthe looked blurred, and Hermia realised she was seeing him through tears, which were streaming down her cheeks.

Renthe said, 'I've got to phone Arne's parents and tell them.'

Thinking of them drew Hermia's thoughts away from her own loss, and she felt a surge of compassion. They would be distraught. 'How dreadful to be the bearer of such news,' she said.

'Indeed. Their first-born son.'

That made her think of the other son, Harald. He was more serious, with little of Arne's easy charm, but likable in his own way. Arne had said he would talk to Harald about ways to sneak into the base on Sande. How much did Harald know? Was he involved?

'What else did the police tell you?' she asked Renthe.

'They would say only that he had died while giving information, and that "No other person is thought to have been involved," which is their euphemism for suicide. But a friend at the Politigaarden told me Arne did it to avoid being turned over to the Gestapo.'

'Did they find anything in his possession, such as photographs?'

Renthe stiffened. 'My friend didn't say so, and it's dangerous for you and me to even discuss such a possibility. Miss Mount, please remember that as an officer I have sworn loyalty to the King, whose orders to me are to cooperate with the occupying power. Whatever my personal opinions might be, I can't countenance espionage— and, if I thought someone was involved in such activity, it would be my duty to report the facts.'

Hermia nodded. It was a clear warning. 'I appreciate your frankness, Squadron Leader.' She stood up.

Renthe came round his desk and put his hands on her shoulders. 'Please accept my deepest sympathy.'

'Thank you,' she said, and she left.

As soon as she was out of the building, the tears came again. Somehow she made her way back to the railway station.

The mission that had killed Poul and Arne was not done. She still had nine days to get photos of the radar equipment on Sande before the next full moon. But now she had an additional motive: revenge. Completion of the task would be the most painful retribution she could inflict on the men who had driven Arne to his death. And she found a new asset to help her. She no longer cared for her own safety.

Arne's brother, Harald, might know if Arne had returned to Sande before the police got to him, and if Arne had photos in his possession when he was arrested. Hermia thought she knew where to find Harald. Surely he would go to Sande for Arne's funeral.

NINE

The German army had a million horses. Most divisions included a veterinary company, dedicated to healing sick and wounded beasts, finding fodder, and catching runaways. One such company had now been billeted on Kirstenslot.

It was the worst possible stroke of luck for Harald. The officers were living in the castle, and about 100 men were bedded down in the monastery. The cloisters, adjacent to the church where Harald had his hide-out, had been turned into a horse hospital.

The army had been persuaded not to use the church itself. Karen had pleaded with her father to negotiate this, saying she did not want the soldiers to damage the childhood treasures stored there. Mr Duchwitz had pointed out to the commanding officer, Captain Kleiss, that the junk in the church left little usable room anyway. Kleiss had agreed to its remaining locked up.

On top of all the difficulties Harald faced repairing the Hornet Moth, he now had to do everything under the noses of the soldiers.

He was undoing the nuts that held the buckled wishbone axle. His plan was to detach the damaged section, then sneak past the soldiers and go to Farmer Nielsen's workshop. If Nielsen would let him, he would repair it there. As he worked, Harald kept glancing up at the windows. But no one came, and after a few minutes Harald had the V-shaped strut in his hand.

He stood on a box to look through a window. The eastern end of the church was obscured by a chestnut tree. There seemed to be no one in the vicinity. Harald pushed the strut through the window, and dropped it on the ground outside, then jumped after it.

Beyond the tree, he could see the lawn in front of the castle. The soldiers had pitched four tents and parked their vehicles there: Jeeps, horseboxes and a fuel tanker. A few men were passing from one tent to another, but most of the company were away on missions. Harald picked up the strut and walked quickly into the wood. As he turned the corner of the church, he saw Captain Kleiss.

The captain was a big man with an aggressive air. He was talking to a sergeant. They both turned and looked at Harald.

Harald suffered the nausea of fear. Was he to be caught so early? He wanted to turn back, then realised that would be incriminating.

All he could do was try to bluff it out. He tried to hold the strut in a casual way, as he might carry a tennis racket.

Kleiss addressed him in German. 'Who are you?'

He swallowed, trying to remain calm. 'Harald Olufsen.'

'And what's that you've got?'

'This?' Harald could hear his own heartbeat. 'It's, um . . . part of the mower assembly from a reaping machine.'

Kleiss said, 'What's wrong with the machine?'

'Er, it ran over a boulder and buckled the frame.'

Kleiss took the strut from him. Harald hoped he did not know what he was looking at. Harald stopped breathing, waiting for Kleiss's verdict. At last the man spoke. 'All right. On your way.'

Harald walked into the woods. When he was out of sight, he stopped and leaned against a tree. That had been an awful moment.

He pulled himself together and walked on. As he approached the farm, he wondered how angry old Nielsen was that he had left after working only one day.

He found Nielsen in the farmyard staring truculently at a tractor with steam pouring from its engine. Nielsen gave him a hostile glare. 'What do you want, runaway?'

'I'm sorry I left without explanation,' Harald said. 'I was called home to my parents' place quite suddenly, and I didn't have time to speak to you before I left.'

'I can't afford to pay unreliable workers.'

'I'm not asking you to pay me.'

'What do you want then?'

'I'd like to use your workshop to repair a part from my bike.'

Nielsen looked at him. 'You've got a nerve, lad.'

I know that, Harald thought. 'It's really important. Perhaps you could do that instead of paying me for the day I worked.'

'Perhaps I could.' Nielsen's parsimony got the better of him. 'If you fix this tractor first.'

Harald did not want to waste time on Nielsen's tractor when he had such a short time to fix the Hornet Moth. But it was only a boiling radiator. 'All right,' Harald said.

Nielsen stomped off, leaving Harald to repair the radiator. When, at last, he'd finished, he went into the workshop.

He needed some thin sheet steel to reinforce the fractured part of the axle strut. There were four metal shelves on the wall. Harald took everything off the top shelf and rearranged the items on the three lower shelves. Then he lifted the top shelf down. Using metal shears, he cut four strips to use as splints. He hammered one strip into a curve to fit over the oval tube of the strut. He did the same with the other three strips. Then he welded them into place.

He looked at his work. 'Unsightly but effective,' he said aloud.

Tramping back through the woods to the castle, Harald could hear the sounds of the army camp. It was now early evening, and the soldiers had returned from their day's duties.

He approached the monastery from the back and walked round to the side of the church. He found a log, rolled it under one of the windows, stood on it and looked into the church. He passed the strut through the glassless window, then he wriggled through.

A voice said, 'Hello!'

His heart stopped, then he saw Karen. She was partly concealed by the aircraft, working on the wing with the damaged tip. Harald picked up the strut and went to show it to her.

Then a voice said in German, 'I thought this place was empty!'

Harald turned. A young private was looking through the window.

Harald stared at him aghast, cursing his luck. 'It's a storeroom.'

The soldier wriggled through the window and dropped to the floor. He said in Danish, 'I am Leo.'

Harald tried to smile. 'I'm Harald, nice to meet you.'

He glanced back at the aircraft. Karen had vanished. The soldier seemed curious rather than suspicious. The Hornet Moth was covered from propeller to cabin, and the wings were folded back, but the fuselage was visible. How observant was Leo?

Luckily, the soldier seemed more interested in the Rolls-Royce. 'Nice car,' he said. 'Is it yours?'

'Unfortunately not,' said Harald. 'The motorcycle is mine.' He held up the axle strut from the Hornet Moth. 'This is for my sidecar. I'm trying to fix it up.'

'Ah!' Leo showed no sign of scepticism. 'I'd help you, but I don't know anything about machinery. Horseflesh is my speciality.'

'Of course,' Harald said.

A shrill whistle sounded. 'Supper time,' Leo said. 'It was a pleasure talking to you. I look forward to seeing you again.' He stood on the box and pulled himself through the window.

Karen emerged from behind the tail of the Hornet Moth, looking shaken. 'That was a nasty moment.'

'He just wanted to talk.'

'God preserve us from friendly Germans,' she said with a smile.

Harald loved it when she smiled. It was like the sun coming up. He turned to the wing she had been working on.

'I'm gluing patches of linen over the damaged areas,' Karen explained. 'I'll paint over them to make them airtight.'

'Where did you get material, the glue, and the paint?'

'From the theatre. I fluttered my eyelashes at a set builder.'

'Good for you.' He was jealous of the set builder. 'What do you do at the theatre all day, anyway?' he asked.

'I'm understudying the lead role in *Les Sylphides*.'

'Will you get to dance it onstage?'

'No. There are two casts, so both the other dancers would have to fall ill.' She returned her attention to the wing. 'We're making progress. Once I finish the work on the fabric and you bolt the axle strut back on, the airframe will be complete.' She looked at her watch. 'I'd better show up at the house for dinner, but I'll come back as soon as I can.' She washed her hands at the sink.

Harald watched her. He was always sorry when she left. He thought he would like to be with her all day, every day. He guessed that was the feeling that made people get married. Did he want to marry Karen? He had no doubt. He tried to imagine the two of them after ten years of marriage, fed up with one another and bored, but it was impossible. Karen would never be boring.

She dried her hands. 'What are you so thoughtful about?'

He felt himself blush. 'Wondering what the future holds.'

She gave him a startlingly direct look. 'A long flight across the North Sea. Six hundred miles without landfall. So we'd better be sure this old kite can make it.' She went to the window and stood on the box, pulled herself up, then dropped out of sight.

He turned his attention back to the Hornet Moth to reattach the strut. He found the nuts and bolts where he had left them. He knelt by the wheel, fitted the strut in place, and began to attach the bolts that held it to the fuselage and the wheel mounting. Just as he was finishing, Karen came back, much sooner than expected.

He smiled, pleased at her early return, then saw that she looked distraught. 'What's happened?' he said.

'Your mother telephoned.'

Harald was angry. 'Damn, I shouldn't have told her where I was going. Who did she speak to?'

'My father. He told her you weren't here, and she seems to have believed him. But there's bad news. It's about Arne.'

Harald realised guiltily that in the last few days he hadn't thought much about Arne, languishing in jail. 'What's happened?'

'He is . . . he's dead.'

At first Harald could not take it in. 'Dead? How could that be?'

'The police say he took his own life.'

'Suicide? Why would he do that?'

'To avoid interrogation by the Gestapo, Arne's commanding officer told your mother.'

'To avoid . . .' Harald saw immediately what that meant. 'He was afraid he wouldn't be able to withstand the torture. He killed himself to protect me.' Harald suddenly needed Karen to confirm his inference. He took her by the shoulders. 'I'm right, am I not?' he shouted. 'That must be it! He did it for me!'

'I think you're right,' she whispered.

In an instant Harald's anger was transformed into grief. Tears flooded his eyes, and his body shook with sobs. 'Oh God,' he said, and he covered his face with his hands. 'Oh, this is awful.'

He felt Karen's arms enfold him. Gently, she drew his head down to her shoulder. His tears soaked into her hair.

'Poor Arne,' Harald said, his voice choked by sorrow.

'I'm sorry,' Karen murmured. 'My darling, I'm so sorry.'

IN THE MIDDLE OF THE Politigaarden was a spacious circular courtyard open to the sunshine. It was ringed by an arcade with classical double pillars in a perfect repeating pattern. Peter Flemming and Tilde Jespersen stood in the middle of the arcade, smoking cigarettes. Tilde wore a sleeveless blouse that showed the smooth skin of her arms. 'The Gestapo have finished with Jens Toksvig,' Peter told her.

'And?'

'He has told them everything he knows. He is one of the Nightwatchmen, he passed information to Poul Kirke, and he agreed to shelter Arne Olufsen. He said that Arne's brother, Harald, was planning to sneak into the military base on Sande to take pictures of the military installation. Arne was waiting at Jens's house for Harald to deliver the film. Jens also said that this project was organised by Arne's fiancée, who is with MI6 in England.'

Tilde drew in smoke. 'Arne killed himself to protect someone,' she said. 'I assume that person has the film.'

'His brother Harald either has it or has passed it to someone else. Either way, we have to talk to him.'

'Where is he?'

'At the parsonage on Sande, I assume. It's the only home he's got. I'm catching a train in an hour. I'd like you to come with me.'

Her clear blue eyes gave him an appraising look. 'Of course, if you want my help.'

'And I'd like you to meet my parents.'

'Where would I stay?'

'I know a small hotel in Morlunde that I think would suit you.' His father owned a hotel, of course, but that was too close to home. If Tilde stayed there, everyone on Sande would know.

Tilde seemed to hesitate. 'What about Inge?'

'I'll get the nursing agency to provide twenty-four-hour cover.'

'I see.' She looked across the courtyard, considering.

He said, 'Don't you want to spend some time together?'

She smiled. 'Of course I do. I'd better go and pack a case.'

PETER AND TILDE boarded the first ferry of the morning at Morlunde. A policeman and a German soldier asked for their identity cards. Peter guessed it was a new security precaution brought in by the Germans. He showed his police badge and asked them to write down the names of everyone visiting the island over the next few days. It would be interesting to see who came to Arne's funeral.

On the other side of the channel, the hotel's horse-drawn taxi took them to the parsonage. When they arrived, Peter noticed that the door to the little church stood open, and he heard a piano. They dismounted from the buggy and entered the church. At the far end of the room, the pastor was playing a slow hymn in a minor key.

'Pastor!' Peter said loudly.

The pastor finished the line, then let the music hang in the air for a moment. Finally he turned round. 'Young Peter,' he said flatly.

'I'm looking for Harald,' Peter said.

'I didn't imagine this was a condolence call.'

'Is he here?'

'Is this an official inquiry?'

'Why do you ask? Is he in the house?'

'No. He's not on the island. I don't know where he went. Go away.'

'Your elder son killed himself because he had been caught spying,' Peter said. He heard Tilde gasp and realised he had shocked her by his cruelty, but he pressed on. 'Your younger son may be guilty of similar crimes. You're in no position to act high and mighty with the police.'

The pastor's normally proud face looked hurt and vulnerable. 'I've told you I don't know where Harald is,' he said dully. 'Do you have any other questions?'

'What are you hiding?'

The pastor sighed. 'You're one of my flock, and if you come to me for spiritual help I won't turn you away. But I will not speak to you for any other reason. You're arrogant and cruel, and as near worthless as one of God's creatures can be. Get out of my house.'

Peter did not want to submit to being thrown out, but he knew he had been defeated. After a moment he led Tilde outside. 'I told you he was hard,' he said.

She seemed shaken. 'I think the man is in pain.'

'No doubt. But was he telling the truth?' he asked her.

'Obviously Harald has gone into hiding—which almost certainly means that he has the film.'

'So we have to find him. Let's try the mother.'

They went to the house. Peter tapped on the kitchen door and went in without waiting for an answer, as was usual on the island. Mrs Olufsen was sitting at the kitchen table, looking at her hands.

'Mrs Olufsen?' Peter said.

She turned her face to him. Her eyes were red and her cheeks were drawn. 'Hello, Peter,' she said expressionlessly.

He decided to take a softer approach. 'I'm sorry about Arne.'

She nodded vaguely.

'This is my friend Tilde. We work together.'

'Pleased to meet you.'

They sat at the table. 'When is the funeral?' Peter asked.

'Tomorrow.'

'We saw the pastor in the church,' Peter said.

'His heart is broken. He doesn't show it to the world, though.'

'I understand. Harald must be dreadfully upset, too.'

She glanced at him and looked quickly down at her hands again. It was the briefest of looks, but Peter read fear and deceit in it. She muttered, 'We haven't spoken to Harald.'

'Why is that?'

'We don't know where he is.'

Peter couldn't tell if she was lying from moment to moment, but he felt sure of her intention to deceive. It angered him, and he raised his voice. 'You'd be well advised to cooperate with us!'

Tilde put a restraining hand on his arm. 'Mrs Olufsen, I'm sorry to have to tell you that Harald may have been involved in the same illegal activities as Arne. The longer he goes on, the worse trouble he'll be in when we finally catch up with him. If you would help us find him, you'd be doing the best thing for him.'

'I don't know where he is,' the woman repeated, but less firmly.

Peter sensed weakness. He stood up and leaned across the kitchen table, pushing his face into hers. 'I saw Arne die,' he said. 'I saw your son put the gun to his throat and pull the trigger.'

Mrs Olufsen's eyes widened in horror. She cried out with grief.

Tilde said, 'Peter, no—'

He ignored her. 'Your elder son was a spy and a criminal, and he met a violent end. Do you want the same to happen to Harald?'

'No,' she whispered. 'No.'

'Then tell me where he is!'

The kitchen door burst open and the pastor came in. 'You filth.'

Peter straightened up. 'I'm entitled to question—'

'Get out of my house.'

Tilde said, 'Let's go, Peter.'

'I still want to know—'

'Now!' the pastor roared. He advanced round the table.

Peter backed away. He knew he should not allow himself to be shouted down. But he found himself reversing to the door. Tilde opened it and they went out.

The hotel's buggy was waiting. 'To my father's house,' Peter said as they got in.

As they were driven away, Peter tried to put the humiliating scene out of his mind. 'Harald must be living somewhere,' he said.

'Obviously.' Tilde's tone was curt, and he guessed she was distressed by what she had just witnessed.

'He's not at school and he's not at home, and he has no relations except for some cousins in Hamburg.'

'So what's our next move?'

'I think he's staying with friends—don't you?'

'Makes sense.'

She would not look at him. He sighed. 'This is what you do,' he said in a tone of command. 'Call the Politigaarden. Send Conrad to Jansborg Skole. Get a list of the home addresses of all the boys in Harald's class. Then have someone to call at each house, ask a few questions, snoop around a bit. Use local police where necessary.'

'Very well.'

'If he's not staying with friends, he must be hiding out with another member of the spy ring. We're going to stay for the funeral and see who shows up. One of them must know where Harald is.'

The buggy slowed as it approached Axel Flemming's house. Tilde said, 'Do you mind if I go back to the hotel?'

His parents were expecting them for lunch, but Peter could see that

Tilde was not in the mood. 'All right.' He tapped the driver on the shoulder. 'Go to the ferry dock.'

They drove in silence for a while. As the horse stopped at the quay, Tilde said, 'I think I should return to Copenhagen. I didn't like what just happened.'

'We had to do it! It was our duty to try to make those people tell what they knew.'

'Duty isn't everything.'

'That's just playing with words. Duty is what you have to do. You can't make exceptions. That's what's wrong with the world.'

The ferry was in dock. Tilde got down from the buggy. 'It's just life, Peter, that's all.'

'It's why we have crime! Wouldn't you rather live in a world where everyone did their duty? If all crimes were punished and no excuses accepted, there would be a lot less for the police to do!'

'Is that really what you want?'

'Yes—and if I ever get to be chief of police, that's what it will be like. What's wrong with that?'

She nodded, but did not answer his question. 'Goodbye, Peter.'

As she walked away he shouted after her, 'Well? What's wrong with it?' But she boarded the ferry without turning round.

TEN

Harald stood outside the kitchen door of the castle in the grey gleam of dawn. It was half past three. In his hand he held an empty four-gallon oil can. The tank of the Hornet Moth would take thirty-five gallons of petrol, just under nine canfuls. There was no legitimate way to get petrol, so Harald had to steal it.

The door opened quietly and Karen stepped out, accompanied by Thor, the old red setter. She wore a chunky green sweater and old brown corduroys, but she looked wonderful. She called me darling, he said to himself, hugging the memory. She called me darling.

She smiled brilliantly, dazzling him. 'Good morning!'

Her voice seemed dangerously loud. Harald put a finger on his lips for quiet. It would be safer to remain silent. There was nothing to discuss: they had made their plan last night.

He led the way into the woods. When they drew level with the soldiers' tents, they peeked cautiously from the bushes. A single man stood guard outside the mess tent, yawning.

The veterinary company's fuel supply came from a small petrol tanker that was parked 100 yards from the tents, alongside the drive that led to the castle. Harald had already observed that the tanker had a hand pump, and there was no locking mechanism. The hose was on the drive side, for convenience. The bulk of the truck shielded anyone using it from view by the encampment.

Everything was as expected, but Harald hesitated. It seemed madness to steal petrol from under the noses of the soldiers. But it was dangerous to think too much. Fear could paralyse. Without further reflection he left Karen and the dog behind, and walked across the damp grass to the tanker.

He took the nozzle from its hook and fed it into his can. It filled quickly. Harald screwed on the cap and hurried back to the trees. Leaving Karen on guard, he cut through the woods to the monastery. He had already opened the big church door so that he could slip in and out. It would have been too awkward and time-consuming to pass the heavy can through the high window. He stepped inside and emptied the can into the aircraft's tank, then went back out.

While he was filling the can for the second time, the sentry decided to make a patrol.

Harald could not see the man but knew something was wrong when Karen whistled. He looked up to see her emerging from the wood with Thor. He dropped to his knees to look out from under the tanker. He saw the soldier's boots approaching across the lawn.

Karen met up with the sentry while he was still fifty yards from the tanker. She took out cigarettes. Would the sentry be friendly, and smoke with a pretty girl, or would he continue his patrol? Harald held his breath. The sentry took a cigarette, and they lit up.

He saw Karen point to a tree stump a little way off, and then lead the soldier to it. She sat down, placing herself so that he had to sit with his back to the tanker if he wanted to be next to her. She patted the surface beside her to encourage him. Sure enough, he sat down.

Harald resumed pumping. He filled the can and hurried into the woods. When he returned, Karen and the sentry were in the same positions. Would the sentry keep chatting?

He took the third canful to the church. According to the manual, the Hornet Moth should fly 632 miles on a full tank. That figure assumed no wind. The distance to the English coast was about 600 miles. The margin of safety was nowhere near enough. He would take a full can of petrol in the cabin, he decided. That would add seventy miles to the Hornet Moth's range, assuming he could figure out a way to top up the tank in flight.

Harald's arms were aching by the time he emptied the fourth canful into the aircraft. He carried the fifth and sixth canfuls, and felt he was two-thirds of the way to the English coast. Karen and the sentry were still talking.

Returning to the church with the seventh can, he was seen.

As he approached the church door, a soldier in underwear emerged from the cloisters. Harald froze. The soldier, half asleep, walked to a bush and began to urinate. Harald saw that it was Leo, the young private who had been so friendly three days ago.

Leo caught his eye and looked guilty. 'Sorry,' he mumbled.

Harald guessed that it was against the rules to pee in the bushes. The soldiers had dug a latrine behind the monastery, but it was a long walk. Harald tried to smile reassuringly. 'Don't worry,' he said in German. He could hear the tremor of fear in his own voice.

Leo did not seem to notice it. He frowned. 'What's in the can?'

'Water, for my motorcycle.'

'Oh.' Leo nodded, and stumbled away.

As he approached the tanker for the eighth time, he saw Karen walking away from the treestump. She gave the sentry a friendly wave. However, the man was walking away from the tanker, towards the mess tent, so Harald felt able to carry on, and he refilled the can.

Harald carried it into the woods and hurried on. He poured the eighth canful into the aircraft's tank and returned for the ninth. The sentry was nowhere to be seen, and Karen gave him the thumbs-up sign to indicate that he could go ahead. He filled the can and returned to the church. As he had calculated, this brought the level to the brim. But he needed an extra canful to carry in the cabin.

He returned for the last time. After Harald had filled the can, Karen walked with him back towards the monastery. As they were about to leave the shelter of the woods, Harald was shocked to see Per Hansen, the village policeman, standing outside the church.

What was he doing here? Harald put a restraining hand on Karen's arm, but he was too late to stop Thor, who ran barking from the woods towards Hansen. Hansen's hand went to his gun.

Karen whispered, 'I'll deal with him.' She went forward and whistled to the dog. 'Come here, Thor.'

Hansen said, 'You should keep that dog under control. If it attacks a member of the police force it might be shot.'

'Don't be ridiculous,' Karen said. 'He barks at intruders. What are you doing, snooping around my garden at the crack of dawn?'

'I'm on official business, young lady, so mind your manners.'

'Official business?' she said sceptically. 'What business?'

'I'm looking for someone called Harald Olufsen.'

Harald cursed. He had not been expecting this.

Karen was shocked, but she managed to cover up. 'Never heard of him.'

'He's a schoolfriend of your brother's. He's been to the castle.'

'Oh? What does he look like?'

'Male, eighteen years old, six foot one, fair hair and blue eyes, probably wearing a blue school blazer.'

'He sounds terribly attractive, but I don't recall him.'

'He's been here,' Hansen said. 'I've seen him myself.'

'I must have missed him. What's his crime?'

'I don't—I can't say. I mean, it's a routine inquiry.'

Hansen obviously did not know what the crime was, Harald thought. He must be asking on behalf of some other policeman—Peter Flemming, presumably.

Karen was saying, 'Well, there's no one here now apart from a hundred soldiers.'

'Last time I saw Olufsen, he had a dangerous-looking motorcycle.'

'Oh, *that* boy,' Karen said, pretending to remember. 'He was expelled from school. Daddy won't let him come here any more.'

'No? Well, I think I'll have a word with your father anyway.'

'As you please. Come on, Thor!' Karen walked away.

She approached the church, turned to check that Hansen was not watching her, then slipped through the door. Hansen walked up the drive to the castle, eventually disappearing from view, presumably heading for the castle's kitchen door.

Harald hurried into the church and put the last can of petrol down on the tiled floor. Karen closed the door, turned the key in the lock and turned to Harald. 'You must be exhausted.'

He was. But he was ecstatically happy. 'You were wonderful!' he said. 'Flirting with the sentry as if he were the most eligible bachelor in Denmark. And you completely fooled Hansen.'

'Not difficult, that.'

Harald picked up the can again and put it in the cabin of the aircraft. He closed the door and turned round to see Karen, grinning broadly. 'We did it,' she said.

'We did.'

She looked at him expectantly. It was almost as if she wanted him to kiss her. He closed his eyes and leaned forward. Her lips were soft and warm. He opened his eyes and was startled to see that she was looking at him, with bright merriment in her eyes.

'What are you thinking?' she said.

'Do you really like me?'

'Of course I do, stupid.'

'I like you, too.'

'Good.'

He hesitated, then said, 'As a matter of fact, I love you.'

'I know,' she said, and she kissed him again.

WALKING THROUGH the centre of Morlunde, in the bright light of a summer morning, Hermia Mount felt conspicuous. People in this small town might recognise her from the times when, two years before, Arne had brought her to his parents' home on Sande.

This morning she was going there again. She made her way to the harbour, carrying her small suitcase, and boarded the ferry. At the top of the gangway stood a German soldier and a Danish police-man. She showed her papers in the name of Agnes Ricks. The policeman studied her identity card. 'You're a long way from Copenhagen, Miss Ricks,' he said.

She had prepared her cover story. 'I'm here for the funeral of a relative.' She was not sure when Arne's interment was scheduled, but there was nothing suspicious about a family member arriving a day or two early, especially given the hazards of wartime travel.

'That would be the Olufsen funeral.'

'Yes.' Hot tears came into her eyes. 'I'm a second cousin.'

The officer said, 'My condolences. You're in plenty of time.'

'Am I? I couldn't get through on the telephone to check.'

'I believe the service is at three o'clock this afternoon.'

'Thank you.'

Hermia went forward and leaned on the rail. As the ferry chugged out of the harbour, she looked across the water to the flat, featureless island. She longed to go to the service, but she knew it was impossi-ble. Too many people would see and recognise her.

When she disembarked onto the quay at Sande she walked to the hotel beach. A few people were splashing in the waves or picnicking on the sand. Hermia found a sheltered dip in the dunes.

She waited there until half past four. The parsonage was ten miles away, a brisk walk of two and a half hours, so she would arrive at seven. She felt sure all the guests would have left by then.

Hermia walked along the beach. At last she saw the outlines of the low church and the parsonage. As she came nearer, she saw the fresh grave in the cemetery. She crossed the churchyard and stood by the grave of her fiancé. Grief took hold of her, and she began to shake with sobs. Then she knelt down and touched the piled-up earth.

When she stood up, she saw the tall figure of Arne's father, standing a few yards off. 'Hermia,' he said. 'God bless you.'

'Thank you, Pastor.' She wanted to hug him, but he was not a hugging man, so she shook his hand.

'You arrived too late for the funeral.'

'That was intentional. I can't afford to be seen.'

'You'd better come into the house.'

Hermia followed him to the kitchen door. Mrs Olufsen was sitting at the table in a black dress. When she saw Hermia she burst into tears.

Hermia hugged her, but her compassion was distracted. The person she wanted was not in the room. As soon as she decently could, she said, 'I was hoping to see Harald.'

'He's not here,' said Mrs Olufsen.

'Didn't he come to the funeral? Where is he?'

'We don't know,' said the pastor. 'He and I had harsh words, and he left in anger. Five days later he returned and there was a reconciliation. He told his mother he was going to stay at the home of a friend, but when we telephoned, they said he was not there.'

'Do you think he is still angry with you?'

'No. Well, perhaps he is, but that's not why he disappeared. My neighbour, Axel Flemming, has a son in the Copenhagen police.'

'I remember,' Hermia said. 'Peter Flemming.'

Mrs Olufsen put in, 'He had the nerve to come to the funeral.'

The pastor went on, 'Peter claims that Arne was a spy for the British, and Harald is continuing his work.'

'Ah.'

'You don't seem surprised.'

'I won't lie to you,' Hermia said. 'I asked Arne to take photos of the base on the island. He may have enlisted Harald's help. But Arne was arrested before he could give me the film.'

Mrs Olufsen cried, 'How could you? Arne is dead because of that! We lost our son and you lost your fiancé! How could you?'

'I'm sorry,' Hermia whispered.

The pastor said, 'There's a war, Lisbeth. Many young men have died fighting the Nazis. It's not Hermia's fault.'

Mrs Olufsen nodded. 'I know. I'm just so scared.' She told Hermia about Harald's visit the week before, and how, just minutes after he had arrived, a soldier from the base had come looking for him.

Hermia's spirits lifted. Maybe Harald had managed to sneak onto the base to take the photos. 'I have to see if Harald has the film,' she said. 'I have to find him. Where did Harald say he was going?'

Mrs Olufsen answered, 'Kirstenslot. It's a castle outside Copenhagen, the home of the Duchwitz family. The son, Josef, is at school with Harald. We telephoned to tell Harald about Arne, but Josef's father said he wasn't there.'

'Maybe he's in the vicinity though. I think I should go to Kirstenslot. Perhaps someone there will know where he's gone.'

'You've missed the last train,' the pastor said. 'You'd better stay the night. I'll take you to the ferry first thing in the morning.'

Hermia's voice dropped to a whisper. 'How can you be so kind? Arne died because of me.'

'The Lord giveth, and the Lord hath taken away,' said the pastor. 'Blessed be the name of the Lord.'

THE HORNET MOTH was ready to fly. Harald looked at it proudly. He had devised a method of refuelling in flight, knocking out a cabin window and passing a hose through it and into the petrol filler pipe. His final task had been to unfold the wings, fixing them in flying position with the simple steel pins provided. Now the aircraft filled the width of the church. They would go tonight.

His stomach clenched with anxiety when he thought of it. An aircraft such as this should always hug the coast, so that it could glide to land in case of trouble. But Harald and Karen would be many miles out to sea, well away from German-occupied Europe. If anything went wrong, they would have nowhere to go.

Harald was still worrying when Karen slipped in through the window, carrying a basket.

She looked at the Hornet Moth and said, 'Wow.'

He was pleased to have impressed her. 'Pretty, isn't it?'

She was solemn. 'We're ready, aren't we? When shall we go?'

'Tonight, of course.'

'Oh my God.'

'Waiting just increases the chance that we'll be found out.'

'I know, but I didn't think it would come so quickly.' She took a package out of her basket and handed it to him. 'I brought you some cold beef.' She fed him every night.

'Thanks,' he said. 'We ought to take some biscuits and bottles of water with us.'

'I'll get some from the kitchen. Do we have any maps?'

'No. I assumed we would just fly west until we see land, and that will be England.'

She shook her head. 'It's quite difficult to know where you are in the air. I used to get lost just flying around here. Suppose we get blown off course? We could come down in France by mistake.'

'I didn't think of that.'

'The only way to check your position is to compare the terrain below you with a map. I'll see what we've got in the house.' She slipped out through the window again carrying the empty basket.

After half an hour, Karen came back. She dropped her basket on the floor. 'We can't go tonight.'

Harald felt cheated. 'Why not?' he said.

'I'm dancing tomorrow.'

'Dancing? How can you put that before our mission?'

'I told you I've been understudying the lead role. Half the company have gone down with a gastric illness. There are two casts, but the leads in both are ill, so I've been called in. I'll be on the main stage at the Royal Danish Theatre. And the King will be there!'

'I can't believe you're saying this.'

'I reserved a ticket for you at the box office.'

'I'm not going.'

'Don't be so grumpy. We can fly tomorrow night, after I dance. The ballet isn't on again for another week, and one of the other two is sure to be better by then.'

'I don't care about the damn ballet! We'll be in deadly danger here for an extra twenty-four hours.'

'No one knows about the plane. Why on earth would they find out tomorrow?'

'It's possible.'

'Oh, don't be so childish, anything's *possible*. I might die in this plane. While I'm drowning in the North Sea or freezing to death, I'd like to be able to think that before I died, I achieved my life's ambition, and danced wonderfully on the stage of the Royal Danish Theatre in front of the King. Can't you understand that?'

'No, I can't!'

'Then you can go to hell.' She went out through the window.

Harald stared after her, thunderstruck. A minute passed before he moved. Then he looked inside the basket she had brought. There were two bottles of water, a packet of crackers, a flashlight and an old school atlas. He picked up the book and opened it. On the end-paper was written, in a girlish hand: 'Karen Duchwitz, Class 3.'

PETER FLEMMING STOOD on the quay at Morlunde. He had been disappointed that Harald had not shown up yesterday for his brother's funeral. He had carefully scrutinised all the mourners. Most were islanders whom Peter had known since childhood. He had ticked their names on the list given to him by the policeman on the ferry. And he noticed one name not ticked: Miss Agnes Ricks.

Returning to the ferry dock, he had asked the policeman if Agnes Ricks had gone back to the mainland. 'Not yet,' the man had said.

Peter was intrigued. Who was Miss Ricks and what was she doing? Instinct told him she had some connection with Arne Olufsen.

He was too conspicuous loitering at the quay on Sande, so he crossed to the mainland and made himself unobtrusive at the large harbour there. Miss Ricks did not appear. The ferry docked for the last time until morning, and Peter retired to a nearby hotel.

In the morning he went to meet the first ferry from Sande. A handful of passengers disembarked. Peter noticed a tall woman wearing sunglasses and a headscarf. As she came closer, he realised he had met her back in 1939. He saw black hair escaping from under the scarf, but it was the curved nose that gave her away.

She was Hermia Mount, Arne Olufsen's fiancée.

'You bitch, I've got you,' he said with profound satisfaction.

Anxious that she might recognise him, he put on heavy-rimmed glasses and pulled his hat forward to cover his red hair. He followed her to the station, where she bought a ticket to Copenhagen.

They boarded an old, slow, coal-burning train that meandered east across Denmark. Peter sat in a first-class carriage, fidgeting impatiently. Hermia was in the next carriage, in a third-class seat.

It was midafternoon when the train pulled into Nyborg, on the central island of Fyn. From here they had to transfer to a ferry to Zealand, where they would board another train to Copenhagen.

While waiting for the ferry, Peter phoned Tilde at the Politigaarden.

'Was Harald at the funeral?' she said immediately.

'No. I checked out the mourners. No clues there. What about you?'

'I spent yesterday on the phone to local police stations all over the country. I've got men checking on each of Harald's classmates. I haven't found Harald, but I've got a clue. Two weeks ago he visited Kirstenslot, the home of the Duchwitz family.'

'Jews?' Peter asked.

'Yes. The local policeman met him. He says Harald had a steam-driven motorcycle. But he swears Harald is not there now.'

'Make doubly sure. Go there yourself.'

'I was planning to,' Tilde said.

'There's one more lead I'm following up, a Miss Agnes Ricks. She's Hermia Mount, Arne Olufsen's fiancée.'

'The English girl?'

'Yes,' Peter said. 'She's on her way to Copenhagen now, and I'm following her.'

'Isn't there a chance she'll recognise you? In case she tries to give you the slip, why don't I meet the train?'

'I'd rather you go to Kirstenslot.'

'Maybe I can do both,' Tilde said. 'Where are you?'

'Nyborg.'

'You're at least two hours away. I can drive out to Kirstenslot, snoop around for an hour and still meet you.'

'Good.' He changed the subject. 'You walked off the job.'

'It wasn't a normal job, though, was it? You took me because you wanted to sleep with me.'

Peter ground his teeth. 'You disliked the way I interrogated the Olufsens. That's not a reason for a police officer to run away.'

'It would be all right if you had been tough just for the sake of getting the job done. But you liked what you were doing. You tortured the pastor and bullied his wife and you enjoyed it. I can't get into bed with a man like that.'

Peter hung up.

 **ELEVEN**

When Harald cooled down, he saw that Karen's decision to postpone their flight was not completely mad. He put himself in her place by imagining that he had been offered the chance to perform an experiment with the physicist Niels Bohr. He might have delayed the escape to England for such an opportunity. Perhaps he and Bohr together would change man's understanding of the universe. If he were going to die, he would like to know he had done something like that.

Nevertheless he spent a tense day. He checked everything on the Hornet Moth twice. He studied the instrument panel, familiarising himself with the gauges. The panel was not illuminated, for the aircraft was not designed to be used at night, so they would have to shine the torch on the dials to read the instruments. He practised folding and unfolding the wings. He put on clean clothes.

He was lying on his ledge bed, stroking Pine Top, the cat, when someone rattled the big church door. Harald sat upright, listening.

He heard the voice of Per Hansen. 'I told you it was locked.'

A woman replied, 'All the more reason to look inside.'

The voice was authoritative. Obviously she was with the police. Harald cursed. She would be more thorough than Hansen. It would not take her long to find a way into the church.

Harald's usual exit window was just round the corner from the main door. But there were windows all round the curved chancel, and he made his escape through one of those. He flattened himself against the church wall and listened. Hansen said, 'Mrs Jespersen, if we stand on that log, we could get through the window.'

'No doubt that's why the log is there,' the woman said.

Harald heard a thud as Hansen hit the tiled floor of the church. A lighter thud followed a few seconds afterwards. Harald crept around the church, stood on the log, and peeped through the window.

Mrs Jespersen was dressed in a blouse and skirt with a blue beret over her blonde curls. She looked at the bike. 'Well, here's the motorcycle you told me about. I see the steam engine. Ingenious.'

'He must have left it here.' Hansen sounded defensive.

'Perhaps.' She moved to the car. 'Very nice.'

'It belongs to the Jew.'

She crossed the room and picked up Harald's discarded shirt. Then she moved to the ledge and picked up his neatly folded blanket. 'Someone's living here,' she said.

'Perhaps it's a vagrant.'

'And perhaps it's Harald Olufsen.' She turned to the Hornet Moth. 'What have we here?' Harald watched in despair.

Hansen said, 'Duchwitz used to have a plane. He hasn't flown it in years, though.'

'It's not in bad condition.' She opened the cabin door. Reaching inside, she moved the control stick, looking at the tailplane at the same time, seeing the elevator move. 'The controls seem to work.' She peered at the fuel gauge. 'The tank is full.' Looking around the cabin, she added, 'And there's two bottles of water and a packet of biscuits, plus an atlas—with no dust on any of them.' She withdrew her head. 'Harald is planning to fly.'

'Well, I'm damned,' said Hansen.

Mrs Jespersen became very brisk. 'I have to go into Copenhagen. Inspector Flemming, who's in charge of this case, is coming in by train. Given the way the railways are nowadays, he could arrive any time in the next twelve hours. When he does, we'll come back. We'll arrest Harald, if he's here, and set a trap for him if he's not.'

'What do you want me to do?'

'Stay here. Find a vantage point in the woods, and watch the church. If Harald appears, phone the Politigaarden.'

'Aren't you going to send someone to help me?'

'No. If Harald sees you, he won't panic—you're just the village policeman. But a couple of strange cops might spook him. I don't want him to run away. But, if he tries to fly that plane, stop him. Shoot him, if you have to—just don't let him take off.'

Harald found her matter-of-fact tone terrifying. She had just told Hansen to shoot him if necessary. Until this moment, Harald had not confronted the possibility that the police might simply kill him.

'You can open this door to save me from scrambling through the window again,' Mrs Jespersen said. 'Lock it up when I've gone, so that Harald won't suspect anything.

Harald stood behind a tree and watched as Mrs Jespersen walked to her car, a black Buick. She shook hands with Hansen, got into the car and drove away. Hansen headed back to the church.

Harald leaned against the trunk of the tree, thinking. Karen had promised to come to the church as soon as she got home from the ballet. If she did that she might find the police waiting for her. Harald had to warn her somehow. He decided the simplest thing would be to go to the theatre.

Unexpectedly, Hansen came round the corner of the church. He saw Harald and stopped dead. They were both astonished. Harald had thought Hansen had gone back into the church to lock up.

Hansen reached for his gun. Without thought for the consequences, Harald rushed at Hansen. As Hansen drew his gun from the holster, Harald cannoned into him. Hansen was thrown back and hit the church wall, but he did not lose his grip on the gun.

He raised the gun to point it. Harald drew back his fist and hit him on the point of the chin. Hansen's head hit the brickwork with a sound like the crack of a rifle, then he slumped to the ground.

Dreadfully afraid the man was dead, Harald knelt beside the

unconscious body and saw that Hansen was breathing. Thank God, he thought. It was horrifying to think he might have killed someone.

The fight had lasted only seconds, but had it been observed? He looked across the park to the soldiers' encampment. No one was looking Harald's way. He stuffed Hansen's gun into his pocket, then lifted the limp body. Slinging it over his shoulder, he staggered round the church to the main door, which was still open.

Harald put Hansen down, then closed the church door. He got a ball of stout cord from the workbench and tied Hansen's feet together and his hands behind his back. He picked up his discarded shirt and stuffed half of it into Hansen's mouth, tying string round the man's head so that the gag would not fall out. He put Hansen in the boot of the Rolls-Royce and closed the lid. Not knowing what to do with the pistol in his pocket, he put it on the floor of the Hornet Moth.

He looked at his watch. He still had time to get to the city and warn Karen. He lit the boiler on his motorcycle. He might well be seen driving out of the church, but there was no time for caution. When the engine had a head of steam he opened the door and left.

He drove into the city and parked at the side of the Royal Theatre. A red carpet led up to the entrance, and he recalled that the King was attending this performance. A crowd of well-dressed people stood on the steps with drinks, and Harald gathered that he had arrived during the interval.

He went to the stage door. The entrance was guarded by a commissionaire. 'I need to speak to Karen Duchwitz,' Harald said.

'Out of the question,' the commissionaire told him. 'She's about to go onstage. You'll have to wait until afterwards.'

Harald remembered that Karen had left a ticket for him at the box office. He decided he would watch her dance.

He went into the marble foyer, got his ticket, and entered the auditorium. He had never been in a theatre before, and he gazed in wonder at the rising tiers of the circle and the rows of red plush seats. He found his place in the fourth row and sat down.

He picked up a programme that had been left on the seat beside him and looked for Karen's name. She was not on the cast list, but a slip of paper which fell out of the booklet said that the prima ballerina was indisposed and her place would be taken by Karen Duchwitz. It also revealed that the lone male dancer in the ballet would also be played by an understudy, Jan Anders.

He was startled to see Mr and Mrs Duchwitz seated two rows in front of him. He should have known they would not miss their daughter's big moment. He worried that they would see him. Then he realised that it no longer mattered. Now that the police had found his hiding place, he did not need to keep it secret any more.

He touched the roll of film in his pocket and wondered if there was any chance he and Karen could still escape in the Hornet Moth. A lot depended on Peter Flemming's train. If it came in early, Flemming and Mrs Jespersen would be back at Kirstenslot before Harald and Karen. On the other hand, with Hansen out of the way, if Flemming's train did not get in until the early hours of the morning, there was a chance they could take off.

When everyone was seated, the King came into the royal box, and the audience stood up. King Christian X's downturned moustache gave him a grim expression that was appropriate to the monarch of an occupied country. He was in evening dress.

When the King sat, the audience followed suit, and the lights went down. The curtain rose on twenty or more women and one man in a circle. The music played a slow, descending phrase, and the dancers moved. All the girls were in white dresses with tight bodices that left their shoulders bare. The circle widened, leaving four people, motionless upstage. A woman lay on the ground as if asleep.

She moved, and Harald recognised Karen's red hair. She glided to the centre of the stage, dancing on the tips of her toes, seeming to float, and the company formed patterns around her. The audience was still, captivated by her. Harald's heart filled with pride.

The dance closed with the slow phrase that had opened it. The ensemble dispersed and re-formed. Karen began a solo dance, and Harald was astonished at how she could perform some vigorous step then come to an abrupt stop in a perfectly graceful pose, as if she had no inertia. She seemed to flout the laws of physics.

Harald became nervous when Karen began a dance with the male dancer. Harald thought he seemed uncertain, and remembered that he too, was an understudy. Karen had made every move seem effortless, but tension gave the boy's dancing a sense of risk. He kept lifting her dramatically high in the air. Harald feared for her safety, but again and again she came down with ease and grace.

Then, during the last dance, disaster struck.

The man lifted Karen again, holding her in the air with one hand in the small of her back. Her legs curved forward with pointed toes, and her arms reached backwards over her head. Then he slipped, and he fell flat on his back. Karen tumbled to the stage beside him.

The audience gasped with horror. The other dancers rushed to the two fallen figures as the curtain came down.

Harald realised he was standing up.

He saw Mr and Mrs Duchwitz get to their feet and push urgently along the row of seats. They were obviously intending to go backstage. Harald decided to do the same. He reached the aisle at the same time as the Duchwitzes. 'I'm coming with you,' he said.

'Who are you?' said Karen's father.

Her mother answered the question. 'It's Josef's friend Harald, you've met him before, Karen is sweet on him, let him come.'

Mr Duchwitz grunted assent. Harald had no idea how Mrs Duchwitz knew that Karen was 'sweet' on him, but he was relieved to be accepted as part of the family.

The Duchwitzes hurried to the stage door, and Harald followed. An usher took them to Karen's dressing room.

She was sitting with her right arm in a sling. She looked stunningly beautiful in the white gown. The company doctor was kneeling in front of her, wrapping a bandage round her right ankle.

Mrs Duchwitz rushed to Karen, saying, 'My poor baby!'

'Oh, I'm all right,' she said, though she looked pale.

Mr Duchwitz spoke to the doctor. 'How is she?'

'She's fine,' the man said. 'She's sprained her wrist and her ankle. They'll be painful for a few days, but she'll get over it.'

Harald was relieved that her injuries were not serious, but his immediate thought was: Can she fly?

The doctor stood up. 'I'd better go and see Jan Anders. He didn't fall as hard as you, but I'm a bit worried about his elbow. You'll dance as wonderfully as ever, don't you worry.' He left.

Karen said, 'Poor Jan, he can't stop crying.'

'It was his fault—he dropped you!' Harald said indignantly.

'I know, that's why he's upset.'

Mr Duchwitz looked at Harald. 'What are you doing here?'

His wife answered. 'Harald has been living at Kirstenslot.'

Karen was shocked. 'Mother, how did you know?'

'Do you think nobody noticed how the leftovers disappeared from the kitchen every night? We mothers aren't stupid.'

'Good God,' Mr Duchwitz said. 'Where does he sleep?'

'In the disused church, I expect,' his wife replied. 'That would be why Karen was so keen to keep it locked.'

Mr Duchwitz was looking angry but, before he could explode, the King walked in.

Karen tried to stand up, but he stopped her. 'My dear girl, how do you feel? No permanent damage, I gather?'

'It hurts, Your Majesty, but that's what the doctor said.'

'You danced divinely, you know.'

'Thank you, sir.'

The King turned to Karen's parents. 'Hello, Duchwitz. It's good to see you again. Your daughter is marvellously talented.'

'Thank you, Your Majesty. You remember my wife, Hanna.'

'Of course.' The King shook her hand. 'This is very worrying for a mother, Mrs Duchwitz, but I'm sure Karen will be all right.'

'Yes, Your Majesty. The young heal fast.'

'Indeed they do! Now, then, let's have a look at the poor fellow who dropped her.' The King moved to the door and went out.

'Well!' said Mrs Duchwitz. 'How very charming!'

Mr Duchwitz said, 'I suppose we'd better get Karen home.'

Karen said, 'Do you mind if I have a word alone with Harald?'

Her father looked irritated, but her mother said, 'All right. Just be quick.' They left the room and Mrs Duchwitz closed the door.

'Are you really all right?' Harald asked Karen.

'I will be when you've kissed me.'

He knelt beside her chair and kissed her lips. Then, unable to resist the temptation, he kissed her bare shoulders and her throat.

'Oh, my goodness, stop,' she said.

The colour had returned to her face, and she was breathless. Harald was amazed to think his kisses had done that.

'We have to talk,' she said.

'I know. Are you fit to fly the Hornet Moth?'

'No, it hurts too much. I can't even open a door. I can hardly walk, so I couldn't possibly operate the rudder with my feet.'

Harald buried his face in his hands. 'Then it's all over.'

'We'll just have to wait a few days until I feel better.'

'There's something I haven't told you. Hansen came again tonight. This time he was with a woman detective, Mrs Jespersen. She went into the church and figured out everything. She guessed that I'm living there and planning to escape in the aircraft.'

'Oh no! What did she do?'

'Went to fetch her boss, who happens to be Peter Flemming. She left Hansen on guard and told him to shoot me if I try to take off.'

'What are you going to do?'

'I knocked Hansen out and tied him up,' Harald said.

'Oh my God! Where is he now?'

'In the boot of your father's car.'

She found that funny. 'You fiend!'

'I thought, if we got back to Kirstenslot tonight before Peter and Mrs Jespersen, we could still take off. But now that you can't fly . . .'

'We could still do it!' Karen said. 'You can be the pilot.'

'I can't—I've only had one lesson!'

'I'll talk you through everything. And I could operate the control stick with my left hand some of the time.'

'Do you really mean it?'

'Yes!'

Harald nodded. 'All right. That's what we'll do. Just pray for Peter's train to be late.'

HERMIA HAD SPOTTED Peter Flemming on the ferry.

She saw him leaning on the rail, looking at the sea, and recalled a man with a ginger moustache and a smart tweed suit on the platform at Morlunde. He looked familiar. The hat and the glasses put her off for a while, but eventually her memory dredged him up.

Peter Flemming. She had met him with Arne in happier days. The two had been boyhood friends, she recalled, then had fought when their families quarrelled. Now Peter was a cop. She realised that he must be following her, and she felt a chill of fear. But why had Peter not arrested her? Hermia was a British spy. What was he up to? Perhaps, like her, Peter was looking for Harald.

When the ferry docked, Peter followed her onto the Copenhagen train. As soon as the train got going, she walked along the corridor and spotted him in a first-class compartment.

She returned to her seat, worried. This was a very bad development. She must not lead Peter to Harald. She had to throw him off. She had plenty of time to think about how. The train was delayed repeatedly, and got into Copenhagen at ten o'clock in the evening.

As she left the train, she glanced back along the platform and saw Peter stepping down from the first-class carriage.

She walked at a normal pace out of the station. The Tivoli Garden was a few steps away. She bought a ticket at the main entrance. The paths wound charmingly between flowerbeds, but the lights in the trees had been switched off, and she managed to lose Peter. She made for a side exit, then looked back. He was not behind her.

Hermia headed for the suburban railway station and bought a ticket for Kirstenslot. She felt exhilarated. She had shaken Peter off. There was no one on the platform but a woman in a blue beret.

HARALD APPROACHED the church cautiously.

There had been a shower, and the grass was wet. A light breeze blew the clouds along and a three-quarter moon shone brightly.

There were no lights in the cloisters. It was after midnight, and the soldiers were in bed, all but the sentry. Harald stood on the log and peeped over the windowsill. He could see only the dim outlines of the car and the aircraft. There could be someone in there, lying in wait.

He heard a muffled grunt and a thud. He guessed it was Hansen, struggling with his bonds. Harald slipped through the window and padded across the floor to the aircraft. He got the flashlight out of the cabin and shone it around the church. There was no one here.

He opened the boot of the car. Hansen was still tied and gagged. Harald checked the knots, then closed the boot again.

He heard a loud whisper, 'Harald! Is that you?' He shone the torch on the window and saw Karen looking through.

She had been brought home in an ambulance. Her parents had ridden with her. Before they parted, at the theatre, she had promised to slip out of the house as soon as she could.

He opened the big church door for her. Karen limped in wearing a fur coat and carrying a blanket. 'How do you feel?' he asked.

'I hurt like hell, but I'll live.'

He looked at her coat. 'Are you cold?'

'Not yet, but I will be at five thousand feet over the North Sea. The blanket is for you.'

He took the blanket from her. 'Are you ready to do this?'

'Yes.'

He kissed her softly and held her good hand. 'I love you.'

'I love you, too.'

'Do you?' he said. 'You've never said that before.'

'I know. I'm telling you now, in case I don't survive this trip. You're the best man I've ever met, by a factor of ten. You're brainy, but you never put people down. You're gentle and kind, but you've got enough courage for an army. You're even nice-looking, in a funny way. What more could I want?'

'Some girls like a man to be well dressed.'

'Good point. We can fix that, though.'

'I'd like to tell you why I love you, but the police could get here any minute.'

'I know why, it's because I'm wonderful.'

Harald opened the cabin door and tossed the blanket in. 'We'd better get you on board now.'

'OK.'

He picked her up and eased her into the passenger seat on the right-hand side of the cabin.

'What's this on the floor?' she said, reaching down.

'Hansen's gun. I didn't know what to do with it.' He closed the door. 'Are you OK?'

She slid the window open. 'I'm fine. The best place to take off will be along the drive. The wind is blowing towards the castle, so you're going to have to push the aircraft all the way to the door of the castle, then turn it round to take off into the wind.'

'OK.' He opened the church door. There was a rope tied to the undercarriage which, Harald surmised, was used to pull the aircraft. He grasped the rope and heaved. The Hornet Moth was heavier than he had thought. As well as its engine, it was carrying thirty-nine gallons of petrol plus Karen. With considerable effort he pulled it out of the church into the park and got it as far as the drive.

The moon came from behind a cloud. The park was lit up almost like day. The aircraft was in full view of anyone who looked in the right direction. Harald had to work fast. He undid the catch holding the left wing against the fuselage and swung the wing into position. It took him three or four minutes. He looked at the soldiers' encampment. The sentry had seen him and was walking over.

He went through the same procedure with the right wing. By the time he had finished, the sentry was standing behind him, watching. It was friendly Leo. 'What are you doing?' he said curiously.

Harald had a story ready. 'We're going to take a photograph. Mr Duchwitz wants to sell the aircraft because he can't get fuel for it.'

'Photography? At night?'

'It's a moonlight shot, with the castle in the background.

'Does my captain know?'

'Oh, yes, Mr Duchwitz spoke to Captain Kleiss.'

'Oh, good,' Leo said, then he frowned. 'It's strange that the captain didn't tell me about it, though.'

'He probably didn't think it was important.' Harald leaned on the tailplane, pushing hard. Seeing him struggle to move the tail, Leo helped him. Together they swung the back round in a quarter-circle so that the aircraft was facing along the drive.

Leo said, 'I'd better check with the captain.'

Harald knew that the officers slept in the castle. 'Well, if you've got to go all that way, you could help me move this crate.'

With the two of them pushing, the plane moved more easily.

THE LAST TRAIN pulled into Kirstenslot station after midnight.

One other person got off the train with Hermia. It was the woman in the blue beret. Hermia suffered a moment of fear. Could this woman be following her, having taken over from Peter Flemming? She would have to check. Outside the station, Hermia stopped and pretended to search for something in her suitcase. If the woman were tailing her, she too would have to find a pretext for waiting.

The woman came out of the station and walked briskly to a black Buick, parked nearby. Someone was at the wheel, smoking. Hermia could not see the face, just the glow of the cigarette. The woman got in. The car started up and pulled away.

False alarm, Hermia thought with relief. She started walking.

HARALD AND LEO pushed the Hornet Moth along the drive, past the petrol tanker, all the way to the front of the castle, then turned it into the wind. Leo ran inside to wake Captain Kleiss.

Harald had only a minute or two.

He took the flashlight from his pocket, switched it on, and opened the cowling on the left side of the fuselage. 'Fuel on?' he called.

'Fuel on,' Karen called back.

Harald worked the lever of one of the two fuel pumps to flood the carburettor. He closed the cowling. 'Throttle set, mags on?'

'Mags on.'

He stood in front of the aircraft and swung the propeller. Imitating what he had seen Karen do, he turned it a second time, then a third. Finally he gave it a vigorous heave and stepped back.

Nothing happened. He cursed.

He repeated the procedure. Something was wrong. Before, when he turned the propeller, something had happened that was not happening now. In a blinding flash of recollection he realised what was missing. There was no click when he turned the propeller. He ran to Karen's open window. 'The impulse starter isn't working!'

'Magneto jam,' she said calmly. 'Open the right cowling. You'll see the impulse starter between the magneto and the engine. Give it a sharp tap with a stone or something. That usually does the trick.'

He opened the cowling. The impulse starter was a flat metal cylinder. He scanned the ground at his feet. There were no stones. 'Give me something from the tool kit,' he said to Karen.

She handed him a spanner. He tapped the impulse starter.

A voice behind him called, 'Stop that right now.'

He turned to see Captain Kleiss striding towards him, with Leo close behind. Kleiss was not armed, but Leo had a rifle.

Harald stuffed the spanner into his pocket, closed the cowling, and moved to the nose of the plane.

'Stand away from that aircraft!' Kleiss shouted.

Suddenly Karen's voice rang out. 'Stop right where you are or I'll shoot you dead!'

Harald saw her arm sticking out of the window pointing Hansen's pistol at Kleiss. Kleiss stopped, and so did Leo.

'Drop the rifle on the ground, Leo,' said Karen.

Leo dropped his weapon.

Harald reached for the propellor and swung it. It turned with a loud, deeply satisfying click.

PETER FLEMMING DROVE to the castle ahead of Hermia, with Tilde in the seat beside him. He said, 'About what happened on Sande—'

'Please don't speak of it.'

He suppressed his anger. 'What, never?'

'Never,' Tilde said. 'I'm sorry, Peter. I made a mistake. Let's just be friends and colleagues.'

'To hell with that,' he said, and turned into the castle grounds.

On the right of the drive was the ruined monastery. 'That's odd,' Tilde said. 'The church doors are open.'

Flemming stopped the Buick and turned off the engine. 'Let's have a look.' He took a flashlight out of the glove box.

They went into the church. Peter heard a muffled grunt followed by a thud. It seemed to come from the Rolls-Royce in the middle of the room. He opened the boot and shone his torch on a policeman, bound and gagged. 'Is this your man Hansen?'

Tilde said, 'The aeroplane isn't here! It's gone!'

At that moment, they heard an aircraft engine start.

THE HORNET MOTH roared into life, as if eager to go.

Harald walked to where Kleiss and Leo stood. He picked up the rifle, opened the left door, and threw the rifle behind the seats.

As he climbed in, a sudden movement made him glance past Karen out of the far window. He saw Kleiss throw himself forward, towards the aircraft. There was a deafening bang as Karen fired Hansen's pistol, but her shot missed him. Kleiss rolled under the fuselage, came up the other side, and jumped onto the wing.

Harald tried to slam the door, but Kleiss was in the way. The captain grabbed Harald by the lapels and tried to pull him out of his seat. Karen was holding the pistol in her left hand and could not turn round in the cramped cabin to get a shot at Kleiss. Harald pulled the spanner from his pocket and lashed out with all his might. The tool hit Kleiss under the eye. He cried out and fell back.

Harald slammed the door as Karen thrust the throttle lever all the way forward. The Hornet Moth bumped over the grass.

He reached for the control column in the centre, but Karen said, 'Leave the stick to me—I can do it left-handed.'

As the aircraft began to pick up speed it veered right. 'Use the rudder pedals!' Karen shouted. 'Keep it in a straight line!'

Harald pushed the left pedal down. Nothing happened, so he pressed it with all his might. The aircraft swung way over to the left, crossed the drive and plunged into the grass on the other side.

She yelled, 'There's a lag, you have to anticipate.'

He pushed with his right foot to bring the aircraft back, then as soon as it began to turn, he corrected with his left foot. As it came back to the drive he managed to line it up. The aircraft accelerated.

At the far end of the drive, a car's headlights came on.

PETER FLEMMING FLOORED the accelerator. Just as Tilde was opening the passenger door to get in, the car jerked away. She let go of the door with a cry and fell back. Peter hoped she had broken her neck.

He steered along the drive, letting the passenger door flap. In his headlights he saw a small biplane rolling down the drive, coming straight at him. Harald Olufsen was in that plane, he felt sure. He was going to stop Harald, even if it killed them both.

'DO YOU SEE THAT CAR?' Harald shouted.

'Yes—is he trying to ram us?'

'Yes.' He concentrated on keeping the aircraft on a straight course with the rudder pedals. 'Can we take off in time to fly over him?'

'I'm not sure—get ready to turn if I say.'

The car was dangerously close. Harald could see they were not going to lift over it. Karen yelled, 'Turn!'

He pressed the left pedal. The aircraft swung off the drive sharply—too sharply. He corrected quickly. Out of the corner of his eye, he saw the car turn the same way, still aiming to ram the Hornet Moth. But the aircraft had a rudder, whereas the car was steered by its wheels, and this made a difference on the wet grass. As soon as the Buick hit the grass it went into a skid. Harald glimpsed Peter Flemming behind the wheel, fighting for control.

The aircraft wobbled and straightened out. Then Harald saw that he was about to crash into the petrol tanker. He stamped on the left pedal, and the right wing tip missed the truck by inches.

Peter was not so lucky. Glancing back, Harald saw the Buick, out of control, smash into the tanker at top speed. There was an explosion, and both car and truck burst into flames.

'Steer the aircraft!' Karen yelled. 'We're about to take off!'

Harald saw that he was heading for the mess tent. He pressed the right pedal to miss it. When they were on a straight course he saw a woman in a blue beret kneel down, pull a gun from her shoulder bag, and aim at the aircraft.

It was Mrs Jesperson. There was nothing he could do. He was heading straight for her, and if he turned to one side, he would merely present her with a better target. He gritted his teeth.

Then he saw a second woman running across the grass, carrying a suitcase. 'Hermia!' he shouted in astonishment as he recognised her. She hit Mrs Jespersen over the head with her case. The detective fell sideways and dropped her gun. Hermia hit her again.

Then the aircraft passed over them and Harald realised it had left the ground. Looking up, he saw that it was about to crash into the bell tower of the church.

TWELVE

Karen thrust the control column sharply to the left. The Hornet Moth banked as it climbed, but Harald could see that the turn was not sharp enough. 'Left rudder!' Karen screamed.

He jammed his left foot on the pedal. The aircraft came round with excruciating slowness. He braced himself for the crash.

The wing tip missed the tower by inches. 'Oh my God,' he said.

The gusty wind made the aircraft buck like a pony, but as they gained height, the aircraft steadied.

Harald looked down. Flames still flickered in the petrol tanker, and by their light he could see the soldiers emerging from the monastery in their nightwear. Captain Kleiss was waving his arms and shouting orders. Mrs Jesperson lay still, apparently out cold. Hermia Mount was nowhere to be seen.

Karen pointed to a dial on the instrument panel. 'Keep an eye on this,' she said. 'It's the turn-and-slip indicator. Use the rudder to hold the needle, at the twelve o'clock position.'

They continued to climb, and the castle shrank behind them.

'Fasten your lap strap,' Karen said.

Harald fastened his belt. He allowed himself to feel triumphant. 'I thought I was going to die,' he said.

'So did I—several times!'

He touched her cheek. 'How do you feel?'

'A bit feverish. I'll be all right,' she said. 'I'd like to get above this cloud. What's our altitude?'

Harald shone the torch on the altimeter. 'Four thousand seven hundred feet.'

'So this cloud is at about five thousand.'

A few moments later the aircraft was engulfed by what looked like smoke, and Harald realised they had entered the cloud.

After a couple of minutes, they emerged from the cloud, and Karen eased the stick forward. She said, 'Take the stick. See if you can fly straight and level. All right, you have control.'

He grasped the stick in his right hand. 'I have control,' he said, but he did not feel it. The Hornet Moth had a life of its own, turning and dipping with air turbulence, and he had to concentrate hard to keep the wings level and the nose in the same position.

The cloud below them was not continuous, and they were able to see through gaps to the moonlit earth below. Soon they were flying over the sea. Karen said, 'Check the altimeter.'

He looked down at the instrument panel and saw that they had reached 7,000 feet. 'How did that happen?' he said.

'You're holding the nose too high. Unconsciously, you're afraid of hitting the ground, so you keep trying to climb. Dip the nose.'

He pushed the stick forward. As the nose came down, he saw another aircraft with crosses on its wings. He felt sick with fear.

Karen saw it at the same time. 'Hell,' she said. 'The Luftwaffe.'

'I see it,' Harald said. It was to their left and down, a quarter of a mile or so away, and climbing towards them.

She took the stick and put the nose down. 'I have control.'

The Hornet Moth went into a dive.

Harald recognised the other aircraft as a Messerschmitt Bf110, a twin-engined night fighter with cannons and machine guns. He said, 'What are we going to do?'

'Try to get back into that cloud layer before he gets within range. I shouldn't have let you climb so high.'

The Hornet Moth was diving steeply. Harald glanced at the air-speed indicator and saw that they had reached 130 knots. It felt like the downhill stretch of a roller coaster.

The other aircraft came rapidly closer. It was much faster than the Moth. There was a flash and a rattle of gunfire. To Harald's horror he saw a jagged rip appear in the fabric of the lower left wing. Karen shoved the stick over and the Hornet Moth banked. Suddenly, they were plunged into cloud. The gunfire stopped.

Karen pulled back on the stick and brought them out of the dive. Harald shone the torch on the altimeter and watched the needle steady at just above 5,000 feet. The air speed returned gradually to the normal cruising speed of eighty knots.

She banked the aircraft again, changing direction, so that the fighter would not be able to overtake them simply by following their previous course. 'Bring the revs down to about sixteen hundred,' she said. 'We'll get just below this cloud.'

Harald found the lever in the dark and drew it back.

'Was it just luck that the fighter turned up?' Karen said. 'Maybe they can see us with their radio beams.'

Harald frowned. 'I doubt it. Metal interferes with radio waves, but I don't think wood or linen does. A big aluminium bomber would reflect the beams back to their aerials, but our engine is probably too small to show up on their detectors.'

'I hope you're right,' she said. 'If not, we're dead.'

They came out below the cloud. 'Keep looking around,' Karen said. 'If we see him again, we have to go up fast.'

Harald did as she said, but there was not much to see. A mile ahead, the moon was shining through a gap in the clouds, and Harald could make out the irregular geometry of fields and woodland. They must be over the large central island of Fyn, he thought.

The Messerschmitt appeared ahead.

It dropped out of the cloud a quarter of a mile in front of them, heading away. 'Full power!' Karen shouted, but Harald had already done it. She jerked back on the stick to lift the nose.

'Maybe he won't even see us,' Harald said, but his hopes were immediately dashed as the fighter went into a steep turn.

The Hornet Moth rose towards the cloud. The fighter came round in a wide circle and pitched up to follow their climb.

The Hornet Moth climbed through the cloud. When the moon-light began to illuminate the swirling mist around them, Harald realised they were near the top of the cloud layer. 'Throttle back,'

Karen said. 'We'll have to stay in the cloud as long as we can.'

Just then the Messerschmitt appeared only yards away.

It was slightly lower and to the right, heading across their path. For a split second, Harald saw the terrified face of the German pilot, his mouth opening in a shout of horror. They were all an inch from death. The fighter's wing passed under the Hornet Moth, missing the undercarriage by a hair.

Harald trod on the left rudder pedal and Karen jerked back on the control stick, but the fighter was already gone from view.

Karen said, 'My God, that was close.'

Harald stared into the swirling cloud, expecting the Messerschmitt to appear. Karen said, 'I think he was as scared as us.'

'What do you think he'll do?'

'Fly above and below the cloud for a while, hoping we'll pop out. With luck, our courses will diverge, and we'll lose him.'

Harald checked the compass. 'We're going north.'

'I went off-heading in all that dodging about,' she said as she banked left. When the compass read two-fifty, she straightened.

They came out of the cloud. They both scanned the sky in all directions, but there were no other aircraft.

They flew on. The engine gave a reassuringly constant roar.

'I feel so tired,' Karen said.

'It's not surprising. Let me take control. Rest for a while.'

'Keep an eye on the dials,' Karen warned Harald. 'Watch the oil pressure, the fuel gauge, the altimeter, and the air speed indicator.'

'OK.' He forced himself to look at the dashboard every minute or two, and found, contrary to what his instincts told him, that the aircraft did not fall out of the sky when he did so. The moon was low on the horizon. A minute later they passed over the Morlunde coast.

'We're leaving the land behind,' he said.

She made no reply, and he saw that her eyes were closed.

He glanced back at the coastline disappearing behind him in the moonlight. 'I wonder if we'll ever see Denmark again,' he said.

THE SKY WAS CLEAR of cloud, and Harald could see stars. He was grateful for them, as they were the only way he could tell up from down. The engine gave a reassuringly constant roar. He flew at 5,000 feet and eighty knots.

He took his hand off the control stick and touched Karen's face. Her cheek was burning. He trimmed the aircraft to fly straight and level, then took a bottle of mineral water from the locker under the dashboard. He poured some on his hand, then dabbed her forehead to cool her. She was breathing normally, though her breath was hot on his hand. She seemed to be in a feverish sleep.

When he returned his attention to the outside world, he saw that dawn was breaking. He checked his watch: it was just after three o'clock in the morning. He must be halfway to England.

By the faint light, he saw cloud ahead. There seemed to be no top or bottom to it, so he flew into it. There was also rain, and the water stayed on the windscreen. Unlike a car, the Hornet Moth had no windscreen wipers. To get above the weather, he began climbing. The temperature dropped, and cold air came in through the window he had smashed out for his improvised fuel line. At 10,000 feet, he was about to level off when the engine misfired.

He felt as if his heart had stopped. He was about 200 miles from land in any direction. If the engine failed now, he would come down in the sea. 'Karen!' he shouted. 'Wake up!' She slept on. He took his hand off the stick and shook her shoulder. '*Karen!*'

Her eyes opened. She appeared better for her sleep, calmer and less flushed, but a look of fear came over her face as soon as she heard the engine. 'What's happening?'

'I don't know!'

'Where are we?'

'Miles from anywhere.'

'What's our altitude?' Karen said.

'Ten thousand feet.'

'Is the throttle fully open?'

'Yes, I was climbing.'

'That's the problem. Bring it back halfway.'

He pulled the throttle back.

Karen said, 'When the throttle is on full, the engine draws air from outside, rather than from within the engine compartment, so it's cold enough at this altitude to form ice in the carburettor.'

'What can we do?'

'Descend.' She pushed the stick forward. 'As we go down, the air temperature should rise, and the ice will melt—eventually.'

'If it doesn't . . .'

'Look for a ship. If we splash down near one, we may be rescued.'

With the engine misfiring, they had little thrust and lost altitude rapidly. Harald watched the altimeter. They came down to 1,000 feet, then 500. The sea looked black and cold. Harald scanned the horizon, but there was no ship in sight.

Karen said, 'See if you can give me a few more revs, so we don't splash down too hard.'

Harald pushed the throttle forward. The engine note rose. It missed, fired, and missed again. 'I don't think—'

Then the engine seemed to catch. It roared steadily for several seconds, then it misfired again. Finally, it burst into a steady roar. The aircraft began to climb. The revs rose to nineteen hundred.

'The ice melted!' Karen said.

Harald kissed her.

'That was nice,' she said.

'If we survive this, I'm going to kiss you every day for the rest of my life,' he said happily.

'Really?' she said. 'The rest of your life could be a long time.'

'I hope so.'

She looked pleased. Then she said, 'We should check the fuel.'

Harald looked at the gauge. 'The tank is almost dry.'

She looked at her watch. 'We've been in the air five and a half hours, so we're probably still half an hour from land.'

'That's all right. I can top up the tank.' He unbuckled his lap strap and knelt on his seat. The petrol can stood behind the seats. Beside it was a funnel and one end of a length of garden hose. Harald had passed the hose through the broken window, lashing the other end to the petrol inlet in the side of the fuselage. But now he could see the outside end of the hose flapping in the slip-stream. He cursed.

Karen said, 'What's the matter?'

'The hose has worked loose in flight. I didn't tie it tight enough. I've got to put the hose into the filler neck. And it can't be done from in here.'

'You can't go outside!'

'What will it do to the aircraft if I open the door?'

'It's like a giant air brake. It will slow us down and turn us left.'

'Can you cope with that?'

'I can maintain air speed by putting the nose down. I suppose I could press down on the right rudder pedal with my left foot.'

'Let's try it.'

Karen put the aircraft into a gentle dive, then put her left foot on the right rudder pedal. 'OK.'

Harald opened the door. Kneeling on the seat, he put his head out of the door. He could see the end of the hose flapping round the petrol access cover. He stretched out his right arm and grasped the hose. Now he had to feed it into the tank. He could see the open access panel. He got the hose positioned roughly over the panel, but the length of rubber in his hand flopped around with the movement of the aircraft, and he could not get the end into the pipe. It was like trying to thread a needle in a hurricane.

Karen tapped his shoulder.

He drew his hand back into the cabin and closed the door.

'We're losing altitude,' she said. 'We need to climb.'

'I can't do it this way,' Harald told her. 'I can't get the hose into the pipe. I need to be able to hold the other end of the tube.'

'How?'

He thought. 'Maybe I can put one foot out of the door.'

'Oh God.'

'Let me know when we've gained enough altitude.'

After a couple of minutes she said, 'OK.' Harald unlatched the door and pushed it open. He unbuckled his lap strap.

Karen said, 'Be careful.'

With his left knee on the seat, he put his right foot out onto the wing. Holding the lap strap with his left hand, he leaned out and grasped the hose. He ran his hand along its length until he held the tip. Then he leaned out further to put the end into the pipe.

The Hornet Moth hit an air pocket. The aircraft bucked in the air. Harald lost his balance and thought he was going to fall off the wing. He jerked hard on the hose and his lap strap at the same time, trying to stay upright. The other end of the hose, inside the cabin, broke free of the string holding it. As it came loose, Harald involuntarily let go of it. The slip-stream whisked it away.

Shaking with fear, he eased back into the cabin, closing the door.

'What happened?' she said. 'I couldn't see!'

'I dropped the hose.'

'Oh, no.'

He checked the fuel gauge. 'We're running on empty. I'll have to stand on the wing and pour the petrol directly from the can. It will take two hands—I can't hold a four-gallon can with one hand.'

'But you won't be able to hold on.'

'You'll have to hold my belt with your left hand.'

'Then I won't be able to move the control stick.'

'We'll just have to hope you don't need to.' He looked around. There was no land in sight. Then the engine missed.

'We're out of fuel,' Karen said.

The engine caught again, but he knew she was right. 'Let's do it,' he said.

She trimmed the aircraft. Harald unscrewed the cap of the four-gallon can, and the cabin filled with the unpleasant smell of petrol.

Karen took hold of his belt. 'I've got you tight. Don't worry.'

He opened the door and put his right foot out. He moved the can to the seat. He put his left foot out, so that he was standing on the wing and leaning inside the cabin. He was absolutely terrified.

He lifted the can and stood upright on the wing. He made the mistake of looking beyond the edge of the wing to the sea below. His stomach lurched with nausea. He almost dropped the can. He closed his eyes, and got himself under control. He opened his eyes, resolving not to look down. He leaned over the petrol inlet. His belt tightened over his stomach as Karen took the strain. He tilted the can and began to pour. The aircraft's movement made it hard to pour straight. The petrol seemed to flow as slowly as honey.

At last the can was empty. He dropped it into the air and gratefully grabbed the door frame with his left hand. He eased himself back into the cabin and closed the door.

'Look,' said Karen, pointing ahead.

In the far distance, on the horizon, was a dark shape. It was land.

'Hallelujah,' he said.

'Just pray that it's England,' Karen said.

Eventually the dark shape turned green and became a landscape. Then it resolved into a town with a harbour, and an expanse of fields.

Harald checked the gauge. 'We're going to have to land soon.'

'But we need to know whether we're in enemy territory.'

Harald glanced up through the roof and saw two aircraft. 'We're about to find out,' he said. 'Look up.'

They both stared at the two small aircraft, which were rapidly approaching from the south. As they came closer, Harald stared at their wings, trying to make out the markings. Would they turn out to be German crosses? Had all this been for nothing? At last Harald saw that they were Spitfires with RAF roundels.

He let out a whoop of triumph. 'We made it!'

As the aircraft came closer, Karen said, 'I hope they don't think we're enemy spies and shoot us down.'

It was dreadfully possible. 'Flag of truce,' Harald said. He pulled off his shirt and pushed it out of the broken window.

It seemed to do the trick. One of the Spitfires moved in front of the Hornet Moth and waggled its wings.

Karen said, 'That means "Follow me." But I haven't got enough fuel.' She looked at the landscape below. 'I'll come down in that field.' She put the nose down and turned. The Spitfires circled, but maintained their altitude, as if to see what would happen next.

Karen came down to 1,000 feet and flew downwind past the field she had chosen. She turned into the wind for landing.

When they were twenty feet above the grass, Karen said, 'Throttle all the way back, please.' Harald pulled the lever back. There was a bump as the wheels made contact with the earth.

As the aircraft came to a halt, a young man on a bicycle was staring at them open-mouthed, from a pathway a few yards away.

'Hello there!' Harald said in English. 'What is this place?'

The young man looked at him as if he had come from outer space. 'Well,' he said at last, 'it's not the bloody airport.'

EPILOGUE

Twenty-four hours after Harald and Karen landed in England, the photos Harald had taken at the radar station on Sande had been printed, enlarged, and pinned up on one wall of a big room in a grand building in Westminster. In the room were three men in RAF uniforms, examining the pictures and talking in low, urgent voices.

Digby Hoare ushered Harald and Karen into the room. A tall man with a grey moustache turned round and said, 'Hello, Digby.'

'Good morning, Andrew,' Digby said. 'This is Air Vice-Marshal Sir Andrew Hogg. Sir Andrew, may I present Miss Duchwitz and Mr Olufsen.'

Hogg shook Karen's left hand, as her right was still in a sling. 'You're an exceptionally brave woman,' he said. 'An experienced pilot would hesitate to cross the North Sea in a Hornet Moth.'

'I had no idea how dangerous it was when I set off,' she replied.

Hogg turned to Harald. 'Digby and I are old friends. He's given me a full report on your debriefing, and frankly I can't tell you how important this information is. But I want you to go over again your theory about how these three pieces of apparatus work together.'

Harald pointed to the general shot he had taken of the three structures. 'The large aerial rotates steadily, constantly scanning the skies. But the smaller ones tilt up and down and side to side, and it seemed to me they must be tracking aircraft. So I guessed that the large machine gives long-range warning of the approach of bombers. Of the smaller machines, one tracks a single bomber, and the other tracks the fighter sent up to attack it. That way, a controller could direct a fighter to the bomber with great accuracy.'

Hogg turned to his colleagues. 'I believe he's right. What do you think?'

One of them said, 'I'd still like to know the meaning of *himmelbett*.'

Harald said, 'That's German for one of those beds . . .'

'A four-poster bed, we call it in English,' Hogg told him. 'We've heard that the radar equipment operates in a *himmelbett*, but we don't know what that means.'

'Oh!' said Harald. 'I've been wondering how they would organise things. This explains it.'

The room went quiet. 'Does it?' said Hogg.

'Well, if you were in charge of German air defence, it would make sense to divide your borders up into blocks of airspace, and assign a set of three machines to each block . . . or *himmelbett*.'

'You might be right,' Hogg said thoughtfully. 'That would give them an almost impenetrable defence.'

'If the bombers fly side by side, yes,' said Harald. 'But if you made your RAF pilots fly in line, and sent them through one single *himmelbett*, the Luftwaffe would be able to track only one bomber, and the others would have a better chance of getting through.'

Hogg stared at him for a long moment.

'Like a stream of bombers,' Harald said, not sure they understood. 'Do you see what I mean?'

'Oh, yes,' said Hogg at last. 'I see exactly what you mean.'

THE FOLLOWING MORNING, Digby drove Harald and Karen out of London to a country house that had been commandeered by the air force as officers' quarters. They were each given a small room with a bed, then Digby introduced them to his brother, Bartlett.

In the afternoon they all went with Bart to the nearby RAF station where his squadron was based. They attended a briefing where the commanding officer explained the new formation the pilots would use for that night's raid on Hamburg—the bomber stream.

The same scene was repeated, with different targets, on airfields up and down eastern England. Digby told Harald that more than 600 bombers would take part in tonight's raid.

The moon rose a few minutes after six o'clock, and the twin engines of the Wellingtons began to roar at eight. On the big blackboard in the operations room, takeoff times were noted beside the code letter for each aircraft. Bart was piloting G for George.

As night fell, the wireless operators reported in from the bombers. Their positions were marked on a big map.

The lead aircraft, C for Charlie, reported that it was under attack from a fighter, then its transmissions stopped. A for Able approached the city, reported heavy flak, and dropped incendiaries to light the target for the bombers following.

When they began to drop their bombs, an officer came over to Digby and said that they had lost radio contact with Bart's aircraft. Digby buried his face in his hands.

One by one, the bombers called in to report that they were heading back—all but C for Charlie and G for George.

Digby made a phone call to London, then said to Harald, 'The bomber stream worked. They're estimating a lower level of losses than we've had for a year.'

In the early hours, the bombers began to come back in. Digby went outside, and Karen and Harald joined him, watching the big aircraft land and disgorge their crews. They were all back but Charlie and George. Bart Hoare never did come home.

HARALD UNDRESSED and put on the pyjamas Digby had loaned him. He should have been jubilant. He had survived an incredibly danger-ous flight, given crucial intelligence to the British, and seen the infor-mation save the lives of hundreds of airmen. But the loss of Bart, and the grief on Digby's face, reminded Harald of Arne, who had given his life for this, and Poul Kirke, and the other Danes who had been arrested and would almost certainly be executed for their parts in the triumph, and all he could feel was sadness.

After a while Karen came in. Her face was solemn. She climbed into bed next to him, and he held her warm body in his arms. She began to cry. He did not ask why. He felt sure she had been having the same thoughts as he. She cried herself to sleep in his arms.

He drifted into a doze. When he opened his eyes again, the sun was shining through the thin curtains. He gazed in wonderment at the girl in his arms. He felt as if his heart would burst with love.

Eventually she opened her eyes. She smiled at him and said, 'Hello, my darling.' Then she kissed him.

THREE DAYS LATER, Hermia Mount appeared.

Harald and Karen walked into a pub near the Palace of Westminster, expecting to meet Digby, and there she was, sitting at a table with a gin and tonic in front of her.

'But how did you get home?' Harald asked her. 'Last time we saw you, you were hitting Detective Constable Jespersen over the head with your suitcase.'

'There was so much confusion at Kirstenslot that I was able to slip away before anyone noticed me,' Hermia said. 'I walked into Copenhagen under cover of darkness. Then I came out the way I had gone in: Copenhagen to Bornholm by ferry, then a fishing boat across to Sweden, and a plane from Stockholm.'

Karen said, 'I'm sure it wasn't as easy as you make it sound.'

Hermia shrugged. 'It was nothing compared with your ordeal.'

'I'm very proud of you all,' said Digby, though Harald thought, by the fond look on his face, that he was especially proud of Hermia.

Digby looked at his watch. 'And now we have an appointment with Winston Churchill.'

They met the Prime Minister in the underground complex known as the Cabinet War Rooms.

'So you're the lass who flew the North Sea in a Tiger Moth,' Churchill said to Karen, shaking her left hand.

'A Hornet Moth,' she corrected him. The Tiger Moth was an open aircraft. 'We might have frozen to death in a Tiger Moth.'

'Ah, yes, of course.' He turned to Harald. 'And you're the lad who invented the bomber stream.'

'One of those ideas that came out of a discussion,' he said with some embarrassment.

'That's not the way I heard the story, but your modesty does you credit.' Churchill turned to Hermia. 'And you organised the whole thing. Madam, you're worth two men.'

'Thank you, sir,' she said.

'With your help, we have forced Hitler to withdraw hundreds of fighter aircraft from the Russian Front and bring them back to defend the Fatherland. And, partly thanks to that success, it may interest you to know that I have today signed a co-belligerency pact with the Union of Soviet Socialist Republics. Britain no longer stands alone. We have as an ally one of the world's greatest powers. Russia may be bowed, but she is by no means beaten.'

'My God,' said Hermia.

'And what are you two young people thinking of doing next?' Churchill asked.

'I'd like to join the RAF,' Harald said immediately. 'Learn to fly properly. Then help to free my country.'

Churchill turned to Karen. 'And you?'

'Something similar. I'm sure they won't let me be a pilot, even though I can fly much better than Harald. But I'd like to join the women's air force, if there is one.'

'Well,' said Churchill, 'we have an alternative to suggest.'

'We want you both to go back to Denmark,' Hermia said.

It was the one thing Harald had not been expecting.

Hermia went on, 'First, we'd send you on a six-month training course. You'd learn radio operation, the use of codes, handling firearms, and so on. You'd parachute into Denmark with false papers. Your task would be to start a new Resistance movement.'

Harald's heart beat faster. It was a remarkably important job. 'I kind of had my heart set on flying,' he said. But the new idea sounded even more exciting—though dangerous.

Churchill intervened. 'I've got thousands of young men who want to fly. But so far we haven't found anyone who could do what we're asking of you two. You're unique. You're Danish. You know the country, you speak the language. And you have proved yourselves quite extraordinarily courageous and resourceful. Let me put it this way: If you don't do it, it won't be done.'

It was hard to resist the force of Churchill's will—and Harald did not really want to. He was being offered the chance to do what he had longed for, and he was thrilled at the prospect. He looked at Karen. 'What do you think?'

'We'd be together,' she said, as if that was the most important thing for her.

'Then you'll go?' said Hermia.

'Yes,' said Harald.

'Yes,' said Karen.

'Good,' said the Prime Minister. 'Then that's settled.'

THE DANISH RESISTANCE became one of the most successful underground movements in Europe. It provided a continuous flow of military intelligence to the Allies, undertook thousands of acts of sabotage against the occupying forces, and provided secret routes by which almost all Denmark's Jews escaped from the Nazis.

KEN FOLLETT

Writing exclusively for Condensed Books, best-selling novelist Ken Follett explains where he gained the inspiration for *Hornet Flight*, and the lengths to which he went in the name of research.

'I was reading *Between Silk and Cyanide*, the wartime memoirs of Leo Marks, when I came across the true story that forms the basis of *Hornet Flight*.

'Two young Danish pilots wanted to escape from German-occupied Denmark in 1941. They found a derelict Hornet Moth biplane in a barn, repaired and fuelled it under the noses of the occupying forces, and flew it across the North Sea to England. The day I read this I happened to be having lunch with my American publisher, Phyllis Grann, and I told her the story, whereupon she said: "That's your next book."

'Of course, I had to learn a great deal about Denmark and the Danish Resistance, but I realised immediately that the most challenging parts of the book would be the flying scenes that must inevitably form its climax.

'In fact, I soon realised I would have to learn to fly!

'I couldn't find anyone who would give me lessons in a Hornet Moth, but there was a 1941 Tiger Moth, mechanically similar, available at Sywell Aerodrome in Northamptonshire, and a plucky young woman called Rachel Lloyd who was willing to attempt to teach me to fly it. I had no idea, previously, how very difficult it is to pilot those old biplanes. It feels like riding an unbroken horse.

'Frankly, I never really mastered it, and the one time I landed the plane myself we came down with a terrible bump, and Rachel had to sit down for a while and recover with a hot cup of tea. Even that was inspiring, though, and in the book I made my hero, Harald Olufsen, a highly inexperienced amateur, and gave him all the problems I'd had myself.'

YEAR OF
WONDERS

GERALDINE BROOKS

O let it be enough what thou hast done,

When spotted deaths ran arm'd through every street,

With poison'd darts, which not the good could shun,

The speedy could outfly, or valiant meet.

The living few, and frequent funerals then,

Proclaim'd thy wrath on this forsaken place:

And now those few who are return'd agen

Thy searching judgments to their dwellings trace.

From *Annus Mirabilis, The Year of Wonders*
John Dryden

1

LEAF-FALL, 1666

I used to love this season. The wood stacked by the door, the tang of its sap still speaking of forest. The hay made, all golden in the low afternoon light. The rumble of the apples tumbling into the cellar bins. Smells and sights and sounds that said this year it would be all right: there'd be food and warmth for the babies by the time the snows came. I used to love to walk in the apple orchard at this time of the year, to feel the soft give of fallen fruit underfoot. Thick, sweet scents of rotting apple and wet wood. This year, the hay stooks are few and the woodpile scant, and neither matters much to me.

They brought the apples yesterday, late pickings, a cartload for the rectory cellar. I saw brown spots on more than a few, but we were lucky to get as good as we got. There are so few people to do the picking. So few people to do anything. And those of us who are left walk around as if we're half asleep. We are all so tired.

I took an apple that was crisp and good and sliced it, thin as paper, and carried it into that dim room where he sits, still and silent. His hand is on the Bible, but he never opens it. Not any more. I asked him if he'd like me to read it to him. He turned his head to look at me, and I started. It was the first time he'd looked at me in days. I'd forgotten what his eyes could do—what they could make us do—when he stared down from the pulpit and held us, one by one, in his gaze. His eyes are the same, but his face has altered so, drawn and haggard, each line etched deep. When he came here, less than three years since, the whole village made a jest of his youthful looks. If they saw him now, they would not laugh, even if they could remember how to do so.

'You cannot read, Anna.'

'To be sure, I can, Rector. Mrs Mompellion taught me.'

He turned away as I mentioned her, but his voice, when he spoke again, was composed. 'Did she so? Perhaps one day I'll hear you. But not today, thank you, Anna. Not today. That will be all.'

In the kitchen, I chose a couple of the spotted apples and walked out to the stables. The courtyard hadn't been swept in a sennight. I had to hitch up my skirt to keep it off the muck. Before I was halfway across, I could hear the thud of his horse's rump as he turned and strutted in his stall, gouging clefts into the floor. There's no one strong or skilled enough now to handle him.

The stableboy was lying on the floor of the tack room. He jumped when he saw me. I was set to scold him about the filth outside, but his poor face, so pinched and exhausted, made me swallow the words.

As I opened the stable door, the horse stopped his pawing and blinked in the unfamiliar sunlight. I don't know when a brush was last laid on him, yet his coat still gleamed like bronze where the light touched it. When Mr Mompellion had arrived here on this horse, the talk had been that such a fine stallion was no fit steed for a priest. And people liked not to hear the rector call him Anteros, after one of the old Puritans told them it was the name of a pagan idol.

I stood with my back pressed against the stall, talking gently to the horse. 'I'm so sorry you're cramped up in here all day. I brought you a small something.' Slowly, I reached into the pocket of my pinafore and held out an apple. I kept prattling softly. 'You like apples. I know you do. Go on, then, have it.' He pawed the ground again, but with less conviction. Slowly, his nostrils flaring, he stretched his broad neck towards me and took the apple in a single bite. Well, I thought, it's easier to bring a small comfort to that poor beast than it is to his master.

When I came back into the house, I could hear the rector out of his chair, pacing. Up and back he walked, up and back, up and back. When I went to fetch his plate, the apple slices were all there, untouched, turning brown. Tomorrow, I'll start to work with the cider press. He'll take a drink without noticing sometimes, even when I can't get him to eat anything. And it's no use letting a cellar full of fruit go bad. If there's one thing I can't stand any more, it's the scent of a rotting apple.

AT DAY'S END, when I leave the rectory for home, I prefer to walk through the orchard on the hill rather than go by the road and risk meeting people. After all we've been through, it's just not possible to pass with a polite, 'Good night t'ye.' And yet I haven't the strength for more. Sometimes, in the orchard of a summer night, if I close my eyes, I can hear the voices of children, their whispers, laughter and running feet. Come this time of year, it's Sam that I think of—strong Sam Frith grabbing me round the waist and lifting me into the low branch of a gnarly old tree. I was just fifteen. 'Marry me,' he said. And why wouldn't I? My father's croft was a joyless place. My father loved a pot better than he loved his children. To my stepmother, Aphra, I was a pair of hands before I was a person, someone to toil after her babies. Yet it was her words that swayed my father to give his assent. In his eyes I was a child still, too young to be handfasted. 'Open your eyes, husband, and look at her,' said Aphra. 'You're the only man in the village who doesn't. Better she be wedded early than bedded untimely.'

Sam Frith was a miner with his own good lead seam to work. He had a fine small cottage and no children from a first wife who'd died. He gave me two sons in three years. Three good years. It was not a time when we were raised up thinking to be happy. The Puritans had the running of this village then. It was their sermons we grew up listening to in a church bare of adornment, their notions of what was heathenish that quieted the church bells, took the ale from the tavern, the lace from the dresses and the laughter out of the public lanes. So the happiness I got from my sons, and from the life that Sam provided, burst on me as sudden as the first spring thaw.

When it all turned to hardship and bleakness again, I was not surprised. I went calmly to the door that terrible night and stood with the baby in my arms, watching the torches bobbing and smoking and the men with their faces all black, jostling and shuffling. They pushed the biggest one, Sam's friend, out in front. I was looking down so that I wouldn't have to look into his face. There was a mush of rotten apple on his boot.

They were four days digging out Sam's body. They took it straight to the sexton's instead of bringing it home to me. They tried to keep me from it, but I wouldn't be kept. I would do that last thing for him. She knew. 'Tell them to let her go to him,' Elinor Mompellion said to the rector in that gentle voice of hers. Once she spoke, it was over. She so rarely asked anything of him. And once Michael Mompellion nodded, those big men moved aside and let me through.

There wasn't much there that was him. But what there was, I tended. That was two years ago. I've tended many bodies since. But Sam's was the first. I bathed him with the gentle soap he liked, because he said it smelt of the children. Poor slow Sam. He never quite realised that it was the children who smelt of the soap. I washed them in it every night before he came home. I made it with heather blooms. The one I made for him was almost all grit and lye, to scrape that paste of sweat and soil from his skin. He would bury his tired face in the babies' hair and breathe the fresh scent of them. It was the closest he got to the airy hillsides. Down in the mine at daybreak, out again after sundown. A life in the dark. And a death there, too.

And now it is Elinor Mompellion's Michael who sits all day in the dark, with the shutters closed. And I try to serve him, although sometimes I feel that I'm tending just another in that long procession of dead. But I do it. I do it for her. I tell myself I do it for her. Why else would I do it, after all?

I OPEN THE DOOR to my cottage these evenings on a silence so thick it falls upon me like a blanket. This moment is the loneliest of my day. Sometimes I mutter my thoughts aloud like a madwoman when the need for a human voice becomes too strong. I mislike this, for I fear the line between myself and madness is as fine as a cobweb, and I have seen what it means when a soul crosses over into that dim and wretched place.

When I have a tallow stub, I read until it gutters. Mrs Mompellion allowed me to take the stubs from the rectory, and although there are few nowadays, I would not manage without. For the hour in which I lose myself in someone else's thoughts is the greatest relief I can find from the burden of my own memories. The volumes, too, I bring from the rectory, as Mrs Mompellion bade me borrow any book I chose. When the light is gone, the nights are long, for I sleep badly, my arms reaching in slumber for my babies' small, warm bodies, jolting suddenly awake when I do not find them.

Mornings are kinder to me than evenings, full as they are of birds' songs and fowls' clucking and the ordinary promise that comes with any sunrise. I keep a cow now, a boon that I was not in purse to have in the days when Jamie or Tom could have benefited from the milk. I found her last winter, wandering in the middle of the road. I drove her inside my neighbours' empty cottage and fitted it up as her boose, fattening her through the cold months with their oats—abundant food of which the dead had no need. She had her calf alone there, without complaint. He is sleek now, and his mother's brown eyes regard me with a kindly patience. I love to lean my head against her warm flank as the steaming milk foams into my bucket. I carry it to the rectory to make a posset or churn sweet butter or skim the cream to serve with blackberries—whatever I think will best tempt Mr Mompellion.

Bucket in hand, I leave the cottage by the front door, for in the mornings I feel more able to meet whomever might be abroad. Our village is a thin thread of dwellings, unspooling east and west of the church and set on the steep flank of the White Peak. The main road, now grassed over, frays here and there into narrower paths that lead to the mill, to Bradford Hall, the larger farms and the lonelier crofts. Behind the cottages on either side of the road lie tilled fields and grazing commons, but these end in a sudden rise or fall of ground: the looming Edge to the north of us, its sheer stone face marking the beginning of the moors, and to the south, the swift, deep dip of the Dale.

I made my way to the rectory gate without meeting a soul. So my guard was down and I was unready to face the person who, in all the world, I least wished to see. I had entered the gate and had my back to the house, refastening the latch, when I heard the rustle of silk behind me. I turned suddenly, slopping milk from my bucket as I did so. Elizabeth Bradford scowled as a droplet landed on her gown. 'Clumsy!' she hissed. And so I re-encountered her much as I had last seen her more than one year earlier: sour-faced and spoiled.

Typically, she did not even bother with a greeting. 'Where is Mompellion?' she demanded. 'I have been rapping upon that door for a good quarter-hour. Surely he cannot be so early abroad?'

I made my voice unctuously polite. 'Miss Bradford,' I said, ignoring her question, 'it is a great surprise, and an honour unlooked for, to see you in our village. You left us in such haste, and so long since, that we had despaired of ever more being graced by your presence.'

Elizabeth Bradford's pride was so overweening and her understanding so limited that she heard only the words and missed the tone. 'Indeed.' She nodded. 'My parents were aware that our departure would leave an unfillable gap here. They have always felt their obligations most keenly. It was that sense of obligation that caused them to remove us all from Bradford Hall, to preserve the health of our family so that we could continue to fulfil our responsibilities. Surely Mompellion read my father's letter to the parish?'

'He did,' I replied. I did not add that he had used it as an occasion to preach one of the most incendiary sermons we ever had from him.

'So, where is he?' she asked. 'My business is urgent.'

'Miss Bradford, the rector sees no one at present. The late events in this place, and his own grievous loss, have left him exhausted and unequal to shouldering the burdens of the parish.'

'Well, that may be, in so far as the normal run of parishioners is concerned. But he does not know that my family is returned here. Be so good as to inform him that I require to speak with him at once.'

I saw no purpose in further discourse with this woman and so I swept by her and walked ahead to open the rectory's great door. She pinched her face at this, and I could see she had expected me to pass to the kitchen garth and then come and let her in with accustomed ceremony. Well, times had changed, and the sooner she accustomed herself to the inconveniences of the new era the better.

She pushed past me and found her own way to the parlour. I saw the surprise in her face as she registered the bareness of the room, stripped as it was of all its former comforts.

Upstairs, I took a minute to compose myself before I knocked on the door. I did not want to say, or look, more than I should when I announced to the rector his caller.

'Come,' he said. He was standing by the window when I entered, and the shutters, for once, were opened. His back was to me. 'Elinor would be sorry to see what has become of her garden.'

'I expect she would understand why it is so,' I said, bending to set out the dishes from his tray. 'And even if we had hands enough to pull the weeds and prune the dead wood, it would not be her garden. We would lack her eye. What made it her garden was the way she could look at a handful of seeds in winter and imagine how they would be, months later, sunlit and in flower.'

When I straightened, he had turned and was staring at me. 'You *knew* her!' He said it as if it had only just come to him.

To cover my confusion, I blurted out what I had hoped to convey with care. 'Miss Bradford is in the parlour. The family is returned to the Hall. She says she needs to speak with you urgently.'

What happened next astonished me. He laughed. A rich, amused laugh the like of which I hadn't heard for so long I'd forgotten the sound of it.

'I know. I saw her. Banging on my door like a siege engine.'

'What answer should I give her, Rector?'

'Tell her to go to Hell.'

When he saw my face, he laughed again. Wiping a tear of mirth from his eyes, he struggled for composure. 'No, I see. You can barely be expected to carry such a message. Put it into whatever words you like, but convey to Miss Bradford that I will not see her.'

It was as if there were two of me, walking down those stairs. One of them was the timid girl who had worked for the Bradfords in a state of dread, fearing their harsh words. The other was Anna Frith, a woman who had faced more terrors than many warriors. Elizabeth Bradford was a coward. She was the daughter of cowards. As I entered the parlour and faced her thunderous countenance, I knew I had nothing more to fear from her.

'I am sorry, Miss Bradford, but the rector is unable to see you at present.' I kept my voice as level as I could, but as her jaw worked in that angry face I found myself thinking of my cow worrying at her cud. It was all I could do then to keep my composure and continue. 'He is, as I said, not currently performing any pastoral duties, nor does he go into society or receive any person.'

'How dare you smirk at me, you insolent slattern!' she cried. 'He will not refuse me, he dare not. Out of my way!' She moved for the door, but I blocked her path. We stared at each other for a long moment. 'Oh, very well,' she said, picking up her gloves from the mantel. I stood aside then, meaning to show her to the front door, but she pushed past me and was upon the steps to Mr Mompellion's room when the rector himself appeared on the landing.

'Miss Bradford,' he said, 'do me the kindness of remaining where you are.' His voice was low but its tone stopped her. 'I would be obliged if you would refrain from insulting members of my household whilst they are carrying out my instructions. Please be good enough to allow Mrs Frith to show you to the door.'

'You can't do this!' Miss Bradford replied. 'My mother has need of you—'

'My dear Miss Bradford,' he interrupted coldly. 'There were many people here with needs this past year, needs that you and your family were in a position to have satisfied. And yet you were not here. Kindly ask your mother to advance the same tolerance for my absence now that your family arrogated for so long in regard to its own.'

Suddenly, surprisingly, she began to cry. 'My mother is very ill. She fears she will die of it. The surgeon swore it was a tumour but there is no question now . . . Please, Reverend Mompellion, she speaks of nothing but seeing you. That is why we are come back here, that you may console her and help her to face her death.'

He was silent for a long moment, and his face, when he spoke, was sad. But his voice was rough. 'If your mother seeks me out to give her absolution like a papist, then she has made a long journey to no end. Let her speak direct to God to ask forgiveness. But I fear she may find Him a poor listener, as many of us here have done.' And with that he turned and climbed the stairs to his room, closing the door behind him.

Elizabeth Bradford threw out a hand to steady herself and gripped the banister. Her shoulders shook with sobs that she struggled to suppress. Instinctively, I went to her. Despite my aversion for her, and her contempt for me, she folded up into my arms like a child.

I shepherded her to the kitchen and eased her down upon the bench. I offered her a mug of water and she drank it thirstily.

'I said the family was back, but in truth it is just my mother and me and our servants. My father will have none of her since he learned the truth of her condition. My mother has no tumour. But what she has, at her age, may kill her just the same. And my father says he cares not. He is saying the most terrible things . . . He has called his own wife whore . . .' And there she stopped herself. She had said more than she intended. Rising suddenly from the bench, she squared her shoulders and handed me the empty mug without a thank you. 'I can find my own way out,' she said, brushing past me. I did not follow her, but I knew she was gone by the slam of the great oaken door.

It was only with her going that I gave myself pause to be astonished by what Mr Mompellion had said to her. His mind had become even darker than I had thought. I quietly climbed the stairs to his room, and knocked gently. When he did not answer I opened the door. He was seated with his head in his hands. The Bible was beside him, unopened. I had a sudden memory of him, sitting just so, with Elinor seated beside him, her gentle voice reading from the Psalms. Without asking his leave, I picked up the Bible and turned to a passage I knew well:

'Bless the Lord, O my soul, and forget not all His benefits:
who forgiveth all thine iniquities,
who healeth all thy diseases,
who redeemeth thy life from destruction . . .'

He rose from his chair and took the book from my hand. 'Very well read, Anna. I see my Elinor may add a credential as a fine teacher to her catalogue of excellent qualities. But why did you not choose this one?' He flipped a few pages, and began to declaim:

'Thy wife shall be as a fruitful vine by the sides of thine house;
thy children like olive plants round about thy table . . .'

He raised his eyes and glared at me. Then slowly, deliberately, he opened his hand. The book slipped from his fingers. I leapt forward to catch it, but he grabbed my arm, and the Bible hit the floor with a dull thump.

We stood there, face to face, his hand tightening on my forearm until I thought he might break it. 'Rector,' I said, struggling to control my voice. At that, he dropped my arm as if it were a burning brand. The pressure of his grip had left a welt, throbbing. I could feel the tears welling in my eyes, and I turned away so that he would not see them. I did not ask his leave to go.

2

SPRING, 1665

The winter that followed Sam's death in the mine was the hardest I had ever known. So the following spring, when George Viccars came banging on my door looking for lodging, I thought God had sent him. Later, there were those who would say it had been the Devil.

Little Jamie came running to tell me, tripping over his feet and his words. 'There a man, Mummy. There a man at the door.'

George Viccars swept his hat from his head as I came from the garth, and kept his gaze on the floor, respectfully.

'If you please, Mistress Frith, they told me at the rectory you might have a room to let.'

He was a journeyman tailor, he said, and his own good, plain clothes told me that he was a competent one. He had just secured a post with my neighbour, Alexander Hadfield. Though he'd been on the road all the way from Canterbury, he was clean and neat, and he seemed a modest, quiet-spoken man. Still, when he told me he would pay sixpence a week for the attic space in my eaves, I'd have taken him if he was loud as a drunkard and muddy as a sow. I sorely missed the income from Sam's mine, for I was still nursing Tom, and my small earnings from the flock were only a little augmented by my mornings' work at the rectory and occasional service at the Hall. Mr Viccars's sixpence would mean a lot in our cottage. But by the end of the week, it was me who was ready to pay him. George Viccars brought laughter back into the house. And later, when I could think at all, I was glad I could think about those spring and summer days when Jamie was laughing.

The young Martin girl minded the baby and Jamie for me while I worked. She was a decent girl and watchful with the children but Puritan in her ways, thinking that laughter is ungodly. Jamie misliked her sternness and was always so glad when he saw me coming home that he'd rush to the door and grab me round the knees. But the day after Mr Viccars arrived, Jamie wasn't at the door. I could hear his high little laugh, and I remember wondering what had come over Jane Martin that she'd actually brought herself to play with him. When I got to the door, Jane was stirring the soup with her usual thin-lipped glare. It was Mr Viccars who was on the floor, on all fours, with Jamie on his back, riding round the room, squealing with delight.

'Jamie! Get off poor Mr Viccars!' I exclaimed.

Mr Viccars just threw back his blond head and neighed. 'I'm his horse, Mrs Frith. He's a fine rider, and rarely beats me with the whip.'

The day after that, I came home and found the two of them slinging oat sacks from the chairs to make a hiding house. I tried to let Mr Viccars know how much I valued his kindness, but he brushed my thanks away. 'Ah, he's a fine boy. His father must have been proud of him.'

The neighbouring towns at that time had no tailor, so Mr Hadfield had work to spare for his new assistant. Mr Viccars would sit by the fire and sew late into the evening. Sometimes I would set myself some chore near the hearth to keep him company, and he would reward me with tales of the places he'd sojourned. Mr Viccars knew the great cities of London and York, the bustling port life of Plymouth, and the pilgrim trade at Canterbury. I was pleased to hear his stories of these places and, as spring softened into summer, we became easy with each other.

These were a kind of evening I'd never had with Sam, who looked to me for all his information of the tiny world for which he cared. He was content to sit, exhausted, his big frame spilling from the chair that seemed small when he was in it. I would prattle of what I'd heard and he would let the words wash over him. Sam's world was a dark, damp maze of rakes and scrins thirty feet under the ground. He knew how to crack limestone with water and fire; he knew the going rate for a dish of lead; he knew who had nicked whose claim up along the Edge. In as much as he knew what love meant, he knew he loved me, and all the more so when I gave him the boys. His whole life was confined by these things.

Mr Viccars seemed never to have been confined. When he entered our cottage, he brought the wide world with him. He had been born a Peakrill lad but had been sent off to Plymouth to take up tailoring, and in that port town had seen silk traders who traversed the Orient and had befriended lace makers from among our enemies the Dutch. He had gone to London at the end of his apprenticeship, for the restoration of King Charles had created prosperity among all manner of trades. There, he had enjoyed much work sewing liveries for courtiers' servants. But the city had tired him.

'London is for the very young and the very rich,' he said. 'Others cannot long thrive there.'

I smiled and said that since he had yet to pass his middle twenties he seemed young enough to me to withstand late nights in alehouses.

'Maybe so, Mistress,' he replied. 'But I grew tired of seeing no further than the blackened wall at the opposite side of the street and hearing nothing but carriage wheels. I longed for space and good air. In London the coal fires send soot and sulphur everywhere.'

Mr Hadfield had ordered a box of cloth from London and, when it arrived, many in the village were interested to see what manner of colour and figure might now be worn in town. Because the parcel arrived damp, having travelled the last of its journey in an open cart unprotected from rain, Mr Hadfield asked Mr Viccars to see to its drying. He contrived lines in the garth of our cottage and slung the fabrics out to air, thus giving everyone ample chance to look and comment. Jamie made a game of it, of course, running between the flapping fabrics, pretending he was a knight at a joust.

Mr Viccars was so well fixed with orders that I was surprised when, a few days after the fabrics arrived, I returned from my work to find a dress of fine-spun wool lying on the pallet in my room. It was a golden green, of modest style, but well cut and trimmed in Genoa lace. I'd never had so fine a thing—even for my handfast I'd worn the borrowed dress of a friend. And since Sam had died I'd been in the one shapeless smock of rough black serge. I held the soft gown up to me and walked by the window, trying to glimpse my reflection. It was in the glass I saw Mr Viccars standing behind me, and I dropped the dress, embarrassed to be caught preening. But he was smiling his big open smile, and he looked down deferentially when he grasped my mortified state.

'Forgive me, but I thought of you directly I sighted that cloth, for the green is exactly the colour of your eyes.'

I felt my face flush. 'Good sir, you are kind, but I cannot accept this dress from you. You are here as my lodger, and glad I am to have such a one as you. But you must know that to be man and woman under one roof is a perilous matter. I fear that we approach too near to terms of friendship . . .'

'I would we may,' he interrupted quietly, his expression now serious and his eyes on mine. At that I blushed again and knew not how to answer him. His face also was rather flushed, and I wondered if he, too, was blushing. But as he took a step towards me, he staggered a little and flung a hand against the wall to steady himself. He raised his hands to his brow as if it pained him. 'Have the dress in any wise,' he said quietly. 'For I mean only to thank you for keeping a comfortable house and welcoming a stranger.'

'Sir, I thank you, but I cannot think it right,' I said.

'Seek advice on the morrow at the rectory,' he said. 'Surely if your pastor sees no harm in it, there may be found none?'

I saw some wisdom in what he proposed and assented to it. If not the rector—I knew that Mrs Mompellion would advise me. And there was still, I was surprised to discover, woman enough alive within me to want to wear that dress.

'Will you not at least try it upon yourself? If you learn on the morrow that you mayn't accept this gift in all propriety, at least you will have rewarded my pains by letting me see how I have done.'

I stood there in the doorway, and my curiosity to have the dress upon my body overbore my sense of what was fit to do. I waved Mr Viccars down the stairs to await me and shrugged myself out of my rough tunic. For the first time in months, I noticed how dingy were the linens I wore beneath. It seemed improper to put the new dress over these unclean things, so I slipped them off as well and stood for a moment, regarding my body. Hard work and a lean winter had robbed me of the softness left after Tom's birth. Sam had liked me fleshy. I wondered what Mr Viccars liked. The thought stirred me, so that my skin flushed and my throat tightened. I gathered up the green dress. It slid softly over my bare flesh. My body felt alive as it hadn't in a long time, and I knew that the feel of the dress was only part of the reason. As I moved, the skirt swayed, and I felt an urge to move with it, to dance again like a girl.

Mr Viccars had his back to me, warming his hands at the fire. When he heard my tread on the stair, he turned and caught his breath, and his face brightened in a smile of appreciation. He clapped his hands and held them wide. 'Mistress, I would make you a dozen such gowns to display your beauty!' Then the playful tone left his voice and it dropped, becoming husky. 'I would you might think me worthy to provide for you in all matters.' He crossed the room and placed his hands on my waist, drew me gently towards him, and kissed me.

I will not say I know what would have happened then if his skin, when it brushed mine, had not been so hot that I pulled back. 'But you are fevered!' I exclaimed, laying a hand on his forehead.

'It is true,' he said, releasing me and rubbing at his temples. 'All this day I have felt a grudging of ague, and now it rises and my head pounds, and I feel a dreadful ache probing at my bones.'

'Get you to your bed,' I said gently. 'I will give you a cooling draught to take up with you. We will speak again of these things on the morrow, when you are restored.'

I DO NOT KNOW how Mr Viccars slept that night, but I rested ill, confused by a tumble of thoughts and reawakened feelings. I lay a long time in the dark, listening to the babies breathe beside me. My hand reached in the darkness and closed round Tom's tiny, budlike fist. I loved the touch of my children's little hands, yet there was another kind of touch for which my body hungered.

In the morning, I rose before cockcrow to accomplish my chores before Mr Viccars descended from his garret. I left the children in their sleepy tangle, tiny Tom curled up like a nut in its shell, Jamie's slender arms flung across the pallet. Their heads, covered in their father's fine, fair down, gleamed bright in the dimness. My heavy, dark hair could not have been more unlike their pale curls, but their small faces were said to favour my own looks more than their father's. I put my face to their necks and breathed the yeasty scent of them.

Downstairs, I relaid the fire and went out to the well to draw the day's water, setting a big kettle to heat and drawing a basinful to wash myself as soon as the chill had gone from it. Drawing more, I scrubbed the gritstone flags, and while they dried I took my broth and bread out into the brightening garth, watching the sky's edge turn rosy. It was a morning fit for the contemplation of new beginnings, and as I watched a whinchat trailing a worm to feed his young, I wondered if I, too, should look for a helper in the rearing of my boys.

Sam had left me the cottage and the sheepfold, but they nicked his stowe the day they brought his body out of the mine. I told them that they need not wait to nick it again, for three weeks, six weeks, or nine, I could neither shore the fallen walls nor was I in purse to have another do it. Jonas Howe has the seam now, and being a good man, and a friend of Sam's, he feels he has choused me, though it can hardly be a swindle when the law here makes it plain that those who cannot pull a dish of lead from a mine within three nicks may not keep it. He said he would make miners of my boys alongside his own when they were of age. Though I thanked him for his promise, I firmly hoped not to see them in that rodent life, gnawing at rock, fearing flood and fire and crushing fall. But the tailoring trade was another business, and I would be pleased to have them learn it. Beside, George Viccars was a good man with a quick understanding. I enjoyed his company. Certainly, I had not shrunk from his touch. I had married Sam for less cause. But I was not fifteen any more, and choices no longer had that same clear, bright edge to them.

When I'd broken my fast I searched the bushes for a brace of eggs for Mr Viccars and another for Jamie. My fowl are unruly and never will lay in their roost. Then I returned inside to knead the dough for the morrow's bread and covered it to rise in a bowl near the fire. I returned upstairs to set Tom to my breast so that Jane Martin would find him with full belly when she arrived shortly to watch over him.

I was at the rectory well before seven, yet Elinor Mompellion was already in her garden where she loved to work.

At five and twenty, Elinor Mompellion had the fragile beauty of a child. She was all pale and pearly, her hair a fine, fair nimbus round skin so sheer you could see the veins at her temples. Her eyes were a white-washed blue like a winter sky. But the frail body was paired with a sinewy mind, capable of violent enthusiasms and possessed of a driving energy. Something in her could not, or would not, see the distinctions the world made between weak and strong, women and men, labourer and lord.

That morning I found her on her knees, deadheading the midsummer daisies. 'Good morning, Anna,' she said as she saw me. 'Did you know that the tea made of this unassuming little flower serves to cool a fever?' Mrs Mompellion never let a minute pass without trying to better me, and for the most part I was a willing pupil, ready to take what she gave.

I had always loved high language. My chief joy as a child had been to go to church, not because I was uncommonly good, but because I longed to listen to the fine words of the prayers. Every Sunday I set myself to learn bright snatches of the liturgy. Sometimes, if I could escape from under my stepmother's eye, I would linger in the church-yard, trying to copy the letters inscribed upon the tombstones. When

I knew the names of the dead, I could match the shapes engraved there with the sounds I reasoned they must stand for. I used a sharpened stick for my pen and a patch of smoothed earth as my tablet.

Once, my father, carting firewood to the rectory, came upon me so. I started when I saw him, so that the stick snapped in my hand. Josiah Bont was a man of few words, and those mostly curses. I cringed from him that day, waiting for his fist to fall. He was a big man, ever quick with a blow—and yet he did not strike me for shirking my chores, but only looked down at the letters I had attempted, rubbed a grimy fist across his stubbled chin, and walked on.

Later I learned that my father had been crowing about me at the Miner's Tavern that day, saying that he wished he had the means to have me schooled. It was an easy boast, for there were no schools, even for boys, in villages such as ours. But this news warmed me, for I had never had a word of praise from my father's lips, and to learn that he thought me clever made me begin to think that I might be so. After this, I became more open and would go about my work muttering snatches of Psalms, meaning purely to pleasure my ear but earning an undeserved name for religious devotion. It was such a reputation that led to my recommendation for employment at the rectory, and thus opened the door to the real learning I craved.

Within a year of her coming, Elinor Mompellion had taught me my letters so well that, though my hand remained unlovely, I could read with only some small difficulties from almost any volume in her library. She would come by my cottage most afternoons, while Tom slept, and set me a lesson to work upon while she went on the remainder of her pastoral visits. She would call in again on her way home to see how I had managed. Often, I would stop in the midst of our lessons and laugh for the sheer joy of it. And she would smile with me, for as I loved to learn, so she loved to teach.

Sometimes, I would feel guilt in my pleasure, for I believed I gained this attention because of her failure to conceive a child. When she and Michael Mompellion arrived here, so young and newly wedded, the village watched and waited. Months passed, and then seasons, but Mrs Mompellion's waist stayed slim as a girl's. The whole parish benefited from her barrenness, as she mothered the children who weren't mothered enough in their own crowded crofts, counselled the troubled and visited the sick, making herself indispensable to all kinds and classes of people.

But of her herb knowledge I wanted none; it is one thing for a pastor's wife to have such learning and another for a widow woman of my sort. I knew how easy it is for widow to be turned witch in the common mind, and the first cause generally is that she meddles in medicinals. We had had a witch scare in the village when I was but a girl, and the one who had stood accused, Mem Gowdie, was the woman to whom all looked for remedies and help with confinements. It had been a year of scant harvest, and many women miscarried. When one strange pair of twins was stillborn, fused together at the breastbone, many had muttered of Devilment, and their eyes turned to Widow Gowdie, clamouring upon her as a witch. Mr Stanley, our Puritan pastor, tested the accusations, taking Mem Gowdie with him into a field and spending many hours there, dealing with her solemnly. Afterwards, he declared her innocent as to that evil and upbraided those who had accused her.

Though none now dared whisper witch against old Mem, there were some who looked aslant at her young niece, Anys, who assisted at confinements and in the growing and drying and mixing of her brews. My stepmother was one of these. Aphra harboured a wealth of superstitions and approached Anys with a mixture of fear and awe, and perhaps some envy. I had been at my father's croft when Anys had come with a salve for the sticky-eye, which all the young ones were catching at the time. I had been surprised to see Aphra hiding a scissors, spread open like a cross, under a bit of blanket upon the chair upon which she invited Anys to sit. I chided her for it, after Anys was gone. But she waved off my disapproval.

'Say what you will, Anna. That girl walks with too much pride in her step for a poor orphan. She carries herself like one who knows more than we do.' Well, I said, and so she did. Was she not skilled in physic, and weren't we all better off on account of it?

Aphra made a face. 'You've seen the way the men sniff round her. Call it physic all you like, but I think she's brewing up more than cordials in that croft of her'n.' I pointed out that when a young woman was as fine figured and fair of face as Anys, men hardly had to be bewitched into interest in her. Aphra scowled at this, and I felt I probed near the place where her ill will to Anys resided.

Aphra had settled for marriage with my dissolute father when she had passed six and twenty years with no better man making her an offer. They did well enough together since neither expected much. But I think that in her heart Aphra had never ceased to pine for the power a woman like Anys might wield. It was true that Anys cared not for conventions, yet there were others less upright who did not draw such disapproval. Aphra's superstitious mutterings found many willing ears amongst the villagers, and I worried for Anys on account of it.

I let Mrs Mompellion wax on about the efficacy of rue and camomile and busied myself rooting out the thistleweeds. Presently, I went to the kitchen to begin the day's real labour and in the scrubbing of deal and sanding of pewter consumed the morning hours. There are some who imagine that the work of a housemaid is dull drudgery, but I have never found it so. At the rectory and at Bradford Hall, I found enjoyment in tending fine things. Sometimes, as I polished the Mompellions' damascene chest, I would study its delicate inlays and wonder about the faraway craftsman who had fashioned it. Mr Viccars had a rich fabric he called damask, and I fell to wondering if it had made the same long journey from desert to this damp mountainside. Thinking of Mr Viccars broke my reverie and reminded me that I had not raised the problem of the dress with Mrs Mompellion. But then I noticed it was nigh to noon and knew that Tom would be mewling for his milk. So I left the rectory in haste, thinking that the matter of the dress could be raised with Mrs Mompellion at some later time.

When I arrived at the cottage, the quiet inside was of the old kind in the days before Mr Viccars joined our household. There was no laughter from within, and in the kitchen I found Jane Martin distracting Tom with a finger of arrowroot and water, while Jamie, all subdued, played alone by the hearth. Mr Viccars's sewing corner was as I'd left it that morning, with threads and patterns piled neat and untouched from the night before. The eggs I'd left for him lay still in their whisket. Tom, seeing me, squirmed in Jane Martin's arms and I reached for him and set him to nurse before I enquired about Mr Viccars.

'Indeed, I have not seen him,' she said. 'I believed him to be gone out early to the Hadfields'.'

'But his breakfast is uneaten,' I replied.

Jane Martin shrugged. She had made it plain by her manner that she misliked the presence of a male lodger in the house.

'He a bed, Mummy,' said Jamie forlornly. 'I goed up to find him but he yelled me, "Go 'way."'

Mr Viccars must be ill indeed, I reasoned. I drew a pitcher of fresh water, cut a slice of bread, and climbed to Mr Viccars's garret. I could hear the moans as soon as I set a foot on the attic ladder. Alarmed, I failed to knock, simply opening the hatch into the low-ceilinged space.

I almost dropped the pitcher in my shock. George Viccars lay with his head pushed to the side by a large lump, a great, yellow-purple knob of pulsing flesh. His face, half turned away from me because of the excrescence, was flushed scarlet. His blond hair was a dark, wet mess upon his head, and his pillow was drenched with sweat. There was a sweet, pungent smell in the garret. A smell like rotting apples.

'Please, water,' he whispered. I held the cup to his parched mouth, and he drank greedily. I poured, and poured again until the pitcher was drained. 'Thank you,' he gasped. 'And now I pray you be gone from here lest this foul contagion touch you.'

'Nay,' I said, 'I must see you comfortable.'

'Mistress, none may do that now except the priest. Pray fetch Mompellion, if he will dare to come to me.'

'Say not so!' I scolded him. 'This fever will break, and you will be well enough presently.'

'Nay, Mistress, I know the signs of this wretched illness. Just get you gone from here, for the love of your babes.'

I did go at that, but only to my own room to fetch my blanket and pillow—the one to warm his shivers and the other to replace the drenched thing beneath his head. He moaned as I re-entered the garret. As I attempted to lift him to place the pillow, he cried out, for the pain from that massive boil was intense. Then the purple thing burst open, slitting like a pea pod and issuing forth creamy pus. The sickly smell of apples was gone, replaced by a stench of week-old fish. I gagged as I made haste to swab the mess from the poor man's face and shoulder and stanch his seeping wound.

'For the love of God, Anna'—he was straining his hoarse throat—'Get you gone from here! You can't help me! Look to yourself!'

I feared this agitation would kill him in his weakened state, and so I picked up the ruined bedding and left him. Downstairs, two horrified faces greeted me, Jamie's wide-eyed with incomprehension and Jane's pale with dread. She had shed her pinafore in preparation to leave us for the day, and her hand was upon the door bar as I appeared.

'I pray you, stay with the children while I fetch the rector, for I fear Mr Viccars's state is grave,' I said and swept by her, dumping the bedding in the door yard as I went.

I was running, my eyes fixed on the path, so I did not see the rector astride Anteros, on his way from an errand in nearby Hathersage. But he saw me, turned and wheeled that great horse, and cantered to my side.

'Good heavens, Anna, whatever is amiss?' he cried, sliding from the saddle and offering a hand to steady me as I gasped to catch my breath. Through ragged gulps, I conveyed the gravity of Mr Viccars's condition. 'Indeed, I am sorry for it,' the rector said, his face clouded with concern. Without wasting any more words, he handed me up onto the horse and remounted.

It is so vivid to me, the man he was that day. I can recall how naturally he took charge, calming me and then poor Mr Viccars; how he stayed at his bedside all through that afternoon and again the next. Mr Viccars muttered and raved, cursed, and cried out in pain. Much of what he said was incomprehensible. But from time to time he would cease tossing on the pallet and open his eyes wide, rasping 'Burn it all! Burn it all! For the love of God, burn it!' By the second night, he had ceased his thrashing and simply lay staring, locked in a silent struggle. His mouth was all crusted with sordes, and hourly I would dribble a little water on his lips and wipe them; he would look at me, his brow creasing as he tried to express his thanks. The night wore on, and Mr Mompellion would not leave him, even when, towards morning, Mr Viccars passed into a fitful kind of sleep, his breath shallow and uneven.

He died clutching the bedsheet. Gently, I untangled each hand, straightening his long, limp fingers, and tears spilled from my eyes. I told myself I was crying for the waste of it: that those skilful fingers would never fashion another lovely thing. In truth, I think I was crying for a different kind of waste, wondering why I had waited until so near this death to feel the touch of those hands.

I folded them on George Viccars's breast, and Mr Mompellion laid his own hand atop them, offering a final prayer. There was not much between Mr Mompellion and Mr Viccars in age, for the reverend was but eight and twenty. And yet the rector's face was scored with furrows at the brow and crow's-feet beside the deep-set grey eyes—the marks of a mobile face that has frowned much in contemplation and laughed much in company.

He turned his eyes on me then, and thanked me for my assistance through the night.

'It is a hard thing,' I said, 'for a man to die amongst strangers, with no family to mourn him.'

'Death is always hard, and untimely death harder than most. But I think George Viccars passed his last weeks happily in your family. You should console yourself in the joy that you and your sons were able to give to him, and the mercy that you, especially, have shown.'

3

The sexton came early for George Viccars's body. Since there were no kin, his funeral rites would be simple and swift. 'Sooner the better, eh, Mistress,' the old man said as he hauled the corpse to his cart.

Mr Mompellion had bidden me not to come to the rectory that morning. 'Rest instead,' he said, pausing at the doorway in the early light. Anteros had been tethered all night in the garth and had trod the soil into craters. I nodded, but anticipated little rest. I had been commanded to serve at dinner at the Hall that afternoon, and before that I would have to scour the house from bottom to top and then figure on the disposition of Mr Viccars's effects.

As if he'd caught my thought, the rector paused as he raised his foot to the stirrup. 'You would do well to follow Mr Viccars's instructions as to his things,' he said. 'He said to burn everything, and that may be good advice.'

I was still on my hands and knees in the attic, scrubbing the worn floorboards, when the first of Mr Viccars's customers came rapping on the door. Before I opened it, I knew the caller was Anys Gowdie. Anys was so skilled with plants that she knew how to extract their fragrant oils, and these she wore on her person so that a light, pleasant scent always preceded her. I had always had admiration for Anys. She was quick of mind and swift of tongue, and few women would do without her in the birthing room. She brought a calm kindness with her there, and had a deft-handedness in difficult deliveries.

She had come looking for Mr Viccars, to collect a dress he had made for her. When I told her what had befallen him, her face clouded with sorrow. Then she upbraided me. 'Why did you not call on my aunt and me, instead of Mompellion? A good infusion would have served George better than the mutterings of a priest.'

I was used to being shocked by Anys, but this time she outdid herself. The first shock was her frank blasphemy. The second was the familiarity with which she referred to Mr Viccars, whom I had never yet called by his first name. On what terms had they been that she should call him so? My suspicions were heightened when, after rummaging through the whisket in which he kept his work, we found the dress he had made for her. For all the years of my childhood, when the Puritans held sway here, we wore for our outer garments only what they called the sad colours—black or brown. Since the return of the King, brighter hues had crept back, but long habit still constrained the choices of most of us. Not Anys. She had bespoke a gown of vivid scarlet. I had never seen Mr Viccars at work on it, and I wondered if he had contrived to keep it from me. The gown was finished but for the hem. When she held the dress up, I imagined her, tall and splendid, her honey-gold hair tumbling loose, her amber eyes half closed, and Mr Viccars kneeling at her feet, letting his long fingers drift from the hem to caress her ankle, skilled hands on fragrant skin . . . Within seconds, I was flushed as scarlet as that damnable dress.

'Mr Viccars told me to burn his work for fear of spreading his contagion,' I said, swallowing hard to ease the tightness in my throat.

'You shall do no such thing!' she exclaimed, and I foresaw in her dismay the difficulty I would have with all his clients. Anyone who had placed a deposit on work from Mr Viccars would want whatever of that work he had accomplished, and I had no right to withhold it from them. Anys Gowdie left with her gown folded under her arm, and as the news of Mr Viccars's death spread, I was interrupted again and again by his clients claiming pieces of his work. All I could do was to pass on what he had said in his delirium. Not a one of them consented to having his or her garment consigned to the fire. In the end, I burned only his own clothes. And then, finally, I found the will to toss the green dress he had made for me into the grate.

IT WAS A LONG WALK, and all uphill, to Bradford Hall, and I was as tired as I've ever been as I set out that afternoon for my employment there. And yet I did not go direct, but headed towards the Gowdie cottage. I could not get Anys's 'George', or her scarlet gown, out of my mind. Now that Mr Viccars was dead, it hardly mattered whom he might have tumbled. And yet I had a mind to know how matters had stood between him and Anys Gowdie.

The Gowdies' cottage was set off at the eastern edge of town, after the smithy, a lonely dwelling set into the side of the hill, at the edge of the Riley farm. It was a tiny, ill-built place, just one room propped upon another. The cottage announced itself by smell long before you could catch sight of it. Sometimes sweet, sometimes astringent, the scents of herbal brews and cordials wafted powerfully from its precincts. Inside, the light was always dim, to protect the virtue of the drying plants. At this time of year, when the

Gowdies were cutting their summer herbs, the bunches hung from the low beams in such profusion that you had to bend almost double when you entered the door.

There was no answer when I knocked upon the door, so I walked round to the stone wall that sheltered the Gowdies' physic garden.

Anys was digging as she knelt amidst a clump of glossy green stems. She rose as I came down the straw-strewn path, dusting the soil from her hands. 'Come inside and take a drink with me,' she said.

We entered the cottage, and she set a bunch of roots upon a bench and washed her hands in a bucket. 'Be kind enough to sit, Anna,' she said. She shooed a grey gib-cat off a rickety chair and pulled up a stool for herself. I was grateful to have found Anys alone. I would have been ill-set to raise the matter on my mind if her aunt were sitting at our elbow. As it was, I hardly knew how to begin upon such a delicate subject. Although we were of an age, Anys and I had not grown up together. She had been raised in a village closer to the Dark Peak, and had been sent to her aunt after her mother died when she was ten years old.

She handed me a glass of strong-smelling brew and poured herself one. 'Nettle beer. It will strengthen your blood,' Anys said. 'All women should drink it daily.'

The flavour, as I sipped, was mild and not unpleasant, while the effect on my tired body was refreshing. I held the cup to my lips longer than I needed, so as to postpone launching myself upon my awkward subject. I need not have troubled.

'I suppose you need to know whether I lay with George,' Anys declared. The cup trembled in my hand, and the nettle beer sloshed onto the swept-earth floor. Anys gave a short laugh. 'Of course I did.' Her eyes as she regarded me were lit with amusement. But it was naught more to either of us than a meal to a hungry traveller.'

She leaned forward to stir some leaves steeping in a big black kettle near the fire. 'His intentions to you were otherwise. If that's what's worrying you, set your mind easy. He wanted you to wife, Anna Frith, and I told him he'd do well with you, if he could talk you round to it. For I see that you've changed somewhat since Sam Frith passed. I think you like to go and come without a man's say-so. I told him your boys were his best chance to win you. For, unlike me, you have them to look to, so you can never live just for yourself.'

I imagined them lying together discussing such things. 'But why,' I blurted, 'if you were on such terms, did you not marry him yourself?'

'Oh, Anna, Anna!' She shook her head and smiled as one does at a slow-witted child. Then, sensing my vexation, she stopped smiling and looked at me with seriousness. 'Why would I marry? I'm not made to be any man's chattel. I have my work, which I love. I have my home—it is not much, I grant, yet sufficient for my shelter. But more than these, I have something very few women can claim: my freedom. I will not lightly surrender it.'

She rose then to be about her work, and so I left her, more confused than when I'd arrived. She was a rare creature, Anys Gowdie, and I had to own that I admired her for listening to her heart rather than having her life ruled by others' conventions. I, meanwhile, was on my way to be ruled for the afternoon by people I loathed.

I trudged on towards Bradford Hall, passing through the edge of the Riley woods. The sun was bright that day, and shadows from the trees fell in bands across the path. I began skirting the golden fields of the Riley farm. They had been all day scything there—twenty men for twenty acres. The Hancocks, who farmed the Riley land, had six strong sons and so needed less help than others at their harvest. Mrs Hancock and her daughters-in-law wearily followed behind their husbands, tying up the loose stalks into sheaves.

Lib Hancock, the eldest brother's wife, had been a friend to me since childhood, and as she straightened for a moment to ease her back, she perceived that it was I, walking at the field's edge. She waved, then turned for a word to her mother-in-law before leaving her work and crossing the field towards me.

'Sit with me for a short while, Anna!' she called. 'For I need a rest.'

I was in no hurry to get to the Bradfords', so I walked with her to a grassy bank. She dropped down on it gratefully and closed her eyes.

'A sorry business about your lodger,' she said. 'He seemed a good man.'

'He was that,' I said. 'He was uncommonly kind to my boys.'

'My mother-in-law had him in mind for Nell,' Lib said. Nell, the only girl in the Hancock family, was so strictly kept by her brothers that we often jested that she'd never get wedded, since no man could venture near enough to see what she looked like.

Knowing what I now knew, I laughed despite my sadness. 'Was any woman in this village *not* considering the bedding of that man?'

Lib and I had ever exchanged girlish confidences. It was this habit, I suppose, that led me into the account I made her then, a bawdy confession of my own lust, which I had the right to confide to her, and then that which I did not: the news I'd just learned of Anys's sport with my lodger.

'Now, Lib,' I said at last, rising to continue on my way, 'mind you do not prate my news all around the Hancock house this night.'

She laughed at that. 'As if I'd be talking of tumblings in front of Mother Hancock and that houseful of men! The only mating fit for remark at the Hancock table is when the tups get put to the ewes!' We both laughed then, kissed each other and parted to our diverse toils.

At the edge of the field, the hedgerows were deep green in their glossy leaves and the blackberries beginning to plump and redden. Fat lambs grazed, their fleeces gilded by sunlight. But for all its loveliness, the last half-mile of this walk was always unpleasant to me. I disliked all of the Bradford family, and I especially feared the colonel. And I misliked myself for giving way to that fear.

Colonel Henry Bradford was said to have been an intelligent soldier who had led his men with uncommon valour. But there was no sign of wise leadership in the way he conducted his household. He took perverse amusement in belittling his wife, the daughter of a wealthy but ill-connected family. She had become brittle and cowed after long years of such treatment. She fretted constantly over where next her husband would find fault, and kept her staff on edge, always reordering the household routine. The Bradfords' son was a rake-shamed drunken fanfaroon who stayed mostly in London. On the rare occasions he was at the Hall, I endeavoured to stay out of his sight. Miss Bradford was, as I have said, a proud and sour young woman, whose only goodness came from a real solicitude for her unhappy mother. When her father was away, she seemed able to soothe her mother's fretfulness, and one could work there without fear. But when the colonel returned, everyone, from Mrs Bradford and her daughter down to the lowliest scullery maid, tensed like a cur waiting for the boot.

Since Bradford Hall had a moderately large staff, I was required to serve at table only for parties of some size or importance. The Hall had a great room that looked very well when arranged for dining. The dark oak table was polished to a rich, black gleam. Silver shone in the low light and the canary, glowing in large goblets, warmed even the cold faces of the Bradfords. No one, of course, ever thought to tell me who the guests were, and so I was pleased to see the friendly faces of the Mompellions among the dozen at that afternoon's dinner.

The colonel's pride was gratified by the presence of Elinor Mompellion at his table, who looked exquisite in a simple gown of creamy silk. But more than her delicate beauty, Colonel Bradford appreciated her substantial connections. She had been a member of one of the oldest and most extensively landed families in the shire. It was noised about that in choosing Mompellion she had spurned another suitor who might have made her a duchess.

As I dipped to take away her soup plate, Elinor Mompellion, seated to the colonel's left, placed a hand lightly on the forearm of the London gentleman to her left, interrupting the flow of his prattle. She turned to me with a grave smile. 'I hope you are feeling quite well after your dreadful night, Anna.'

I heard the hiss of the colonel's indrawn breath. I kept my eyes on the dishes in my hand, afraid to glance in his direction. 'Quite, thank you, ma'am,' I murmured and slid on to clear the next plate. I feared if I gave her a second's chance she would continue to converse with me.

At the Hall, I had learned to keep my mind on my duties and let the talk wash over me. At that large table, most people exchanged empty pleasantries with those seated next to them, and the result was a low buzz of mingled voices. When I left the room with the meat platters, that was the state of things. But by the time I returned, carrying desserts, candles had been lit against the gathering dark and only the young Londoner next to Mrs Mompellion was speaking. He was a style of gentleman we did not much see in our village, his periwig so elaborate that his white-powdered face seemed lost beneath its tumbling curls. He looked grave, and as he spoke, his hands fluttered from lace cuffs like white moths, throwing long shadows across the table. The faces turned towards him were pale and alarmed.

'You have never seen anything like it on the roads. Innumerable men on horseback, wagons bulging with baggage. Everyone capable of leaving the city is doing so or plans to do it. The poor meantimes are pitching tents out on Hampstead Heath. One walks, if one must walk, in the very centre of the roadway to avoid the contagion seeping from dwellings. People go through the streets like drunkards, weaving from this side to that to avoid passing too close to each other. And yet one cannot take a hackney-coach, for the last person inside may have breathed contagion.' He dropped his voice then and looked all around, seeming to enjoy the attention his words were garnering. 'There is talk that the King plans to remove his court to Oxford. For myself, I saw no reason to tarry. The city is emptying so fast that there is little worthwhile society to be had, for wealth and connection are no shield against Plague.'

The word dropped like an anvil among the tinkling silverware. I stood stock-still until I was sure of my balance and tried to steady my breath. There are many fevers that can kill a man other than the Plague. And George Viccars hadn't been near London in more than a year. So how could he have been touched by the city's pestilence?

Colonel Bradford cleared his throat. 'Come now, Robert! Do not alarm the ladies. They will shun your company for fear of infection!'

'Do not joke, sir, for on the turnpike north of London, I encountered an angry mob, brandishing pitchforks, denying entry to their village inn to any who were travelling from London. It was a low place, in any wise, nowhere I would have sought shelter even on the filthiest of nights, so I rode onwards unmolested. But before long, to be a Londoner will not be a credential worth owning to. Many of us will invent rusticated histories for ourselves, mind me well.'

'Well, good thing you got out, eh?' said the colonel. 'Clean air up here, no putrid fevers.'

Down the table, I noticed the Mompellions exchanging meaning looks. Trying to still my shaking hands, I set down the dessert I carried and stepped back into the shadows against the wall.

'It's hard to believe,' the young man continued, 'but some few are staying in town who have the easy means to go. Lord Radisson has been bruiting it about that he feels it his duty to stay and "set an example". Example of what? A wretched death, I warrant.'

'Think of what you are saying,' Mr Mompellion interrupted. His voice—rich, loud, grave—cut off the Bradfords' airy laughter. 'If all who have the means run each time the Plague appears, then its seeds will go with them and be sown far and wide throughout the land until the clean places are infected. If God saw fit to send this scourge, I believe it would be His will that one face it where one was, with courage, and thus contain its evil.'

'Oh?' said the colonel superciliously. 'And if God sends a lion to rip your flesh, will you stand steadfastly then, too? I think not. I think you will run from the danger, as any sensible man would.'

'Your analogy is excellent, sir,' said Mr Mompellion. 'For I will certainly stand and face the lion if, by running, I would cause the beast to follow me, and thus draw him closer to the dwelling places of innocents who demand my protection.'

At the mention of innocents, Jamie's little face flashed before me. What if the young Londoner were correct? Jamie had lived in George Viccars's pocket. All that day before the illness first rose in him, Jamie had been climbing on his back, prancing by his side.

The young man broke the silence that greeted Mr Mompellion's speech. 'Bravely stated, sir. But those who know this disease best—the physicians and the barber-surgeons—have been the fleetest of foot in leaving town. Which leads me to conclude that they have written us a clear prescription: the best physic against the Plague is to run away from it. And I intend to follow that prescription religiously.'

'You say "religiously" but I think your choice of word is poor,' said Mr Mompellion. 'For if one speaks "religiously" then one must recall that God has the power to keep you safe in peril, or to bring peril to overtake you, no matter how far or fast you run.'

'Indeed, sir. And many who believed that now are rotting corpses passing through the streets in cartloads, on their way to the great pits.'

Miss Bradford raised a hand to her brow, feigning a faintness that her avid eyes belied. The young man turned to her, reading her desire for morbid detail, and continued, 'I have had it from one whose man had need to go there in search of a kinsman. He reported that the corpses are tipped in, afforded no more respect than one would give a dead dog. A layer of bodies, a few spades of soil and then more bodies tumbled in atop.' He turned pointedly towards the rector.

'And do you know who were the fastest to follow the physicians out of the city, sir? Why, it were the Anglican ministers. There's many a London pulpit being filled by a Nonconformist on account of it.'

Michael Mompellion looked down then and studied his hands. 'If what you say is true, sir, then my brothers in faith are the lesser men, and I am indeed sorry for it.' He sighed and looked at his wife. 'Perhaps they might believe that God now is preaching to the city, and what needs add their small utterance to the thunder of His voice?'

THERE WAS A FULL MOON that night, which was fortunate, for otherwise I'm sure I would have fallen into a ditch as I stumbled home, almost running despite my exhaustion. I could barely speak to the Martin girl as she roused herself from her fireside slumber. I threw off my cloak and rushed up the stairs. A square of silvery light bathed the two little bodies. Both breathed easily. Jamie had an arm round his brother. I stretched out a hand to his forehead terrified of what I might feel. My fingers brushed his soft skin. It was blessedly cool.

'Thank you,' I said. 'Oh, thank you, God.'

THE WEEKS THAT FOLLOWED George Viccars's death ushered in the loveliest September weather I ever recall. The sky was clear blue almost every day, and the air remained warm and dry. I was so relieved that Jamie and Tom were not ill, I lived in those days as at a fair. Jamie himself was downcast, having lost his dear friend Mr Viccars, who had become an indispensable companion. His death left an emptiness I resolved to fill, taking time to make our simple chores into something of a game.

In the afternoons, when I went to check the flock, I would take Jamie and Tom with me, and we would dawdle along our way, stopping to find what story each clump of stones or hollow tree might yield us.

Our flock is small, just one and twenty ewes. My rule has been to make mutton of any who proves an inept mother, and the result is an easy lambing when the weather is with us. We had had a good lambing in the spring, so the last thing I was looking for that day was a ewe in labour. But we found her, lying on her side, panting and straining in the shade of a rowan. I unslung Tom and laid him on a patch of clover. Jamie stood behind me as I knelt down and ran my hands inside the ewe. I could feel a nose and one hoof, but I could barely get all my fingers in to grasp it.

'Mummy, may I help?' said Jamie, and looking at his tiny fingers I said yes, sitting him down in front of me. He slid his hands easily into the ewe's slippery wetness and exclaimed as he felt the knobbly knees of her backward baby. I braced against the ewe with my heels and together we tugged, he gripping the knees while I strained at the hoofs. Suddenly a bundle of wet wool flew out with a big, sucking slosh, and the two of us fell backwards on the grass. It was a fine lamb, small but strong. The young ewe set straight to work cleaning the caul from its face. The lamb rewarded her with an enormous sneeze. We laughed, Jamie's eyes round and proud and happy.

We left them, and wandered into the copse where the stream runs, to wash the blood and muck from our hands and clothes. Because the day was warm, I stripped Jamie down to his skin and let him splash naked while I rinsed his smock and my pinafore and flung them over a bush to dry. I unpinned my whisk, untied my cap and pulled off my hose. My skirt tucked up, I found a flat rock and sat down to feed Tom, letting the rills run over my toes. I leaned back against the stream's bank and closed my eyes.

I must have dozed for a moment, or otherwise I surely would have heard the tread of boots coming through the trees. As it was, he was almost upon me when I opened my eyes and met his, lifted from the open book he carried. I jumped up, fumbling and tugging at my bodice. Tom howled indignantly at the interruption to his feeding.

The rector smiled. 'He is quite just to protest. Do not discompose yourself, Anna. I'm sorry to have startled you, but I was so lost in my book that I was not aware there was anyone else in the copse.'

I was too mortified by the rector's sudden appearance to make any civil reply. To my further astonishment, he sat down upon a neighbouring rock and pulled off his own boots so that his feet, too, could dandle in the rills.

Tom continued to cry loudly. Mr Mompellion looked at him, squirming in my arms, and then reached across to take him from me. Surprised, I gave him over, and was even more surprised at the practised way that Mr Mompellion held him against his shoulder, firmly patting him on the back. Tom stopped crying and let forth a huge, wet belch. The rector laughed. 'I learned from caring for my little sisters that one who is neither mother nor wet nurse must hold a babe so, upright, so that it ceases to search for the teat.' I must have looked amazed at this, for Mr Mompellion laughed again. 'You must not think that a minister's life is lived entirely among lofty words spoken from high pulpits.' He inclined his head to where Jamie, downstream from us, was engrossed in building his stick dams across the stream. 'We all begin as naked children, playing in the mud.'

At that, he handed Tom back to me, rose, and made his way towards Jamie. Halfway there, he set his foot on a moss-slicked stone. His arms circled as he tried to regain his balance, and Jamie jumped up in the water, laughing with the uncouth mirth of a three-year-old. I glared at Jamie, but Mr Mompellion laughed with him, splashing the few yards left between them with his hands outstretched to grab my squealing little boy and toss him high into the air. The two of them played so for a time, and then Mr Mompellion turned back towards me and settled himself once more on the bank near us. He sighed, and closed his eyes again, his lips curved in a smile.

'I pity those who live in towns and do not learn to love all this— the scent of wet weeds and the ordinary miracles of creation. It was of these I was reading when I interrupted you. Would you like to hear some words from my text?' I nodded, and he reached for his book. 'These are the writings of Augustine of Hippo, a monk who grew great in his theology long ago on Africa's Barbary Coast. Here he asks himself what we mean when we talk of miracles.'

I can recall only snatches of what he read. But I do remember how his voice seemed to blend with the cadences of the stream. 'Consider changes of day and night . . . the fall of leaves and their return to the trees the following spring, the infinite power in seeds . . . then give me a man who sees and experiences these things for the first time . . . he is amazed and overwhelmed at these miracles.'

I was sorry when he ceased reading, and would have asked him to go on, if I had not been struck silent by awe of him. For though I worked every day in his house, it was only with his wife that I had easy communication. He must have taken my silence for boredom, for he stood up and reached for his boots, saying that he had imposed upon me quite enough and must be about his business.

At that, I did find a small voice in which to thank him for his consideration in sharing these great thoughts with me. 'For it is wonderful to me that such a lofty thinker should have so close a communion with the ordinary things of the soil and of the seasons.'

He smiled. 'Mrs Mompellion has spoken to me of your understanding. She believes it is superior, and I see it may be so.' He took his leave then and turned back towards the rectory. I lingered there with the children for a while, thinking what a strange thing it was to have such a man, so open and so kindly, in our pulpit.

At last, I called to Jamie and we, too, set our feet on the path for home. All along the way, Jamie kept darting off to pluck the blowzy, late-blooming dog roses. When we neared the cottage, he made me wait by the door while he ran inside. 'Close your eyes, Mummy,' he cried. Obediently, I waited, my face buried in my hands. I heard him thump up the stairs, and then I heard the upstairs casement open.

'All right, Mummy. Now! Look up!' I tilted my face and opened my eyes to find myself in a velvet rain of rose petals. The soft, sweet-scented shower brushed my cheeks. I pulled off my cap and shook out my long dark hair and let the petals land in its tangles. Little Tom gurgled with joy, his fat fists batting at the bright cascade of pink and creamy yellow. Jamie leaned out over the sill above me, shaking the last few petals from a corner of sheet.

This, I thought, smiling up at him, this moment is my miracle.

4

Thus we passed the wondrous days of our reprieve, and I busied myself in preparation for winter. There were apple ladders poking through the trees and tripods going up all round, waiting for a day cool enough for the hog butchering. Though we had no swine of our own, I always helped my neighbours the Hadfields in return for a portion of bacon. Alexander Hadfield was a fastidious man who preferred cutting cloth to hacking at flesh and bone. So Mary's eldest by her first husband would do the slaughter and the butchery. Jonathan Cooper was a big lad like his late father and made short work of it, while his little brother Edward ran about with Jamie, finding ways to shirk the small chores we laid on them. Every time we sent them to fetch a bavin to keep the cauldron boiling, the two of them would disappear behind the woodpile, howling with delight over some new game they'd invented. Finally, Mary went to see what mischief they'd devised. She came back with one hand holding Edward by the ear and the other extended in front of her, dangling something glossy and black, tied to a string. As she drew closer I could see it was a dead rat, a sorry little corpse with blood about its muzzle. Behind her, Jamie walked sheepishly, dragging another such. Mary flung the one she carried into the fire, and at her prompting, Jamie did the same.

'Can you believe it, Anna? They were playing with these pests as if they were poppets. The woodpile's full of them. All dead, thanks be for small mercies.' Since we couldn't halt our work, Mary called Alexander to deal with the rat fall, and the two of us shared a quiet laugh as her man, too nice to give a hand with the hog butchery, dispatched bloody rodent corpses instead. The sight of him at his task eased our load a little as we toiled on, competing against the fading light to get the fat rendered and the sides salted. It was hateful work, but I kept my mind fixed on the smell of the bacon sizzling in my skimmer and thought how Jamie would enjoy it a few weeks hence.

WHEN AT LAST the skies clouded it was almost a relief. The misty rains seemed restful to the eyes, rinsing the landscape. But the damp after the heat brought fleas beyond any infestation I remember. It is odd how biting pests will find one person flavoursome and another not to their liking. In my house, the fleas feasted on my tender children. I burned all our bedstraw before I went to see the Gowdies for a balm. I was hoping to find Anys by herself again, for I longed to talk more with her. And so I was disappointed when it was old Mem who met me on the step.

'I could have saved you the walk, Anna, as I'm on my way to the Hadfields. Young Edward Cooper is burning up with fever, so I'm bringing him a draught.' I turned to walk back with her, fretful at this news.

When we got to the cottage, a strange pied horse was tethered to the post by the watering trough. Mary met us at the door, flustered with anxiety and embarrassment. 'Thank you indeed for coming, Mem, but Mr Hadfield sent to Bakewell for the barber-surgeon, and he is with Edward now.'

Mem made a sour face. She thought no more of barber-surgeons than they were wont to think of women such as she. Bowing coldly, Mem turned and walked away. But I was curious, so I lingered until Mary signalled me to follow her. The barber-surgeon had asked to have the child brought downstairs. Mr Hadfield had cleared his tailor's bench and little Edward was laid naked upon it. The poor little soul was covered in squirming leeches, their sucking parts embedded in his tender arms and neck. It was fortunate that Edward was too far gone in his delirium to understand what had befallen him. Mary clasped the child's limp hand. Mr Hadfield nodded deferentially at the surgeon's every utterance.

'He is a small child, so we need not draw overmuch to restore the balance of his humours,' the surgeon said. When time had elapsed to his satisfaction, he called for vinegar and applied it to the engorged creatures so that they twitched all the harder, their jaws relaxing as they sought to escape the irritant. With a series of deft tugs, he pinched them off, a spurt of blood following, which he stanched with scraps of linen. He rinsed each leech in a cup of water and dropped it into a leather pouch. 'If the child is not improved by nightfall, you must purge and fast him. I will give you a tincture that will open his bowels.' The man was packing his bag as Mary and her husband thanked him. I followed him into the street and, when the Hadfields were out of hearing, made bold with the question that was tormenting me.

'If you please, sir—the child's fever—could it be the Plague?'

The man waved a gloved hand dismissively. 'No chance of it. The Plague, by God's grace, has not been in our shire these score years. And the child has no Plague tokens on his body. It is a putrid fever merely, and if the parents follow my instructions, he will live.'

His foot was in the stirrup, such was his impatience to be gone. The saddle leather creaked as he settled his ample rump. 'But, sir,' I continued, 'if there has been no Plague here these twenty years, then perhaps you have seen no cases against which to judge the child's condition.'

'Ignorant woman!' he said. 'Are you saying I don't know my profession?'

'Are lumps at the neck not Plague tokens?' I cried.

He pulled up sharply and looked me in the face for the first time. 'Where have you seen these things?' he demanded.

'On the body of my lodger, buried at last full moon,' I replied.

'And you bide near the Hadfields?'

'The next door.'

'Then God save you and this village,' he said. 'And tell your neighbours to call upon me no more.' Then he was off, heading down the road at such a gallop that he almost collided with Martin Miller's haywain as it turned the sharp bend by the Miner's Tavern.

LITTLE EDWARD COOPER was dead before sunset. His brother lay ill a day later, and Alexander Hadfield but two days after that. At the end of a sennight, Mary Hadfield was widow for a second time, and her sons lay in the churchyard beside their dead father. I was not there to see them buried, for by then I had mourning of my own to do.

My Tom died as babies do, gently and without complaint. The fever rose in him suddenly, before noon, while I was working at the rectory. Jane Martin sent for me, and took Jamie to her mother's house. Tom cried for a while, when he tried to suckle and couldn't find the strength for it. Then he just lay in my arms, staring at me and whimpering now and then. Soon, his stare became distant, and finally he closed his eyes and panted. I sat by the hearth and held him, amazed at how his body had grown, spilling out of my arms now, when once he'd fitted into the crook of my elbow. 'Soon you will be with your father,' I whispered. 'You'll be so comfortable in his strong arms.'

Lib Hancock came, saying words of comfort that blurred into nonsense in my head. In the afternoon, Elinor Mompellion came to take her place.

She knelt beside us, enfolding us in her arms. She shared my grieving with me, and so calmed my weeping and my rage. Afterwards, she drew a chair to the window and read to me from Our Lord's words of love for little children until the light became too dim. I believe she would have stayed all night had I not told her that I would take Tom up to my bed.

I crooned to him as I climbed the stairs and laid him down upon our pallet. He lay just as I placed him, his arms splayed limply. I lay down beside him and drew him close. For a time his little pulse beat fast, his tiny heart pounding. But towards midnight the rhythms became broken and weak and finally fluttered and faded away. I told him I loved him and would never forget him, and then I wept until, for the last time, I fell asleep with my baby in my arms.

When I woke, the light was streaming through the window. The bed was wet, and there was a wild voice howling. Tom's little body had leaked its life's blood from his throat and bowels. My own gown was drenched where I'd clutched him to me. I gathered him up off the gory pallet and ran into the street. My neighbours were all standing there, their faces turned to me, full of grief and fear. Some had tears in their eyes. But the howling voice was mine.

WHEN I WAS A CHILD, my father would talk sometimes of his boyhood as a prentice seaman. Usually, he told us these tales when we had misbehaved, to scare us. He spoke of the lash and said the cruellest of the boatswains would lay on the whip so that the blows fell time and again on the same place.

The Plague is cruel in the same way. Its blows fall and fall again upon raw sorrow, so that before you have mourned one person you love, another is ill in your arms. Jamie was crying for his brother when his tears turned into the fevered whimpering of the ill. My merry little boy loved his life, and fought hard to hold on to it.

Elinor Mompellion was at my side from the first, and her gentle voice is what I remember best from those woeful days and nights. 'Anna, I must tell you that my Michael suspected Plague from the moment he attended Mr Viccars's sickbed. You know that he was a student at the University at Cambridge, and he sent at once to his friends, asking them to enquire of the great physicians who are teachers there, to find out what could be known of the latest preventives and remedies. He has had an answer back from a dear friend, who declares that the learned doctors place great faith in these new means of combatting the Plague.' And so it was that on the best authority, and with the best of intentions, my poor boy suffered through some treatments that in the end maybe only prolonged his pain.

Where Mr Viccars's sore had erupted near his neck, Jamie's rose in his armpit, and he cried piteously from the agony of it, holding his slender little arm far out so as not to hurt himself by the pressure of his own flesh. Mr Mompellion's friend had written out a receipt from the College of Physicians, and with Mrs Mompellion's help I tried this. It called for the roasting in embers of a great onion, hollowed out and filled with a fig, chopped rue and a dram of Venice treacle. Mem Gowdie had both the dried figs and the treacle, which is honey mixed with a great number of rare ingredients.

I roasted those onions, one after the other, even though their pressure on the swollen place made my child scream with pain. It is the hardest thing in the world to inflict hurt on your own child, even if you believe you act for his salvation. I cried as I bound on the hated poultices, then I held him and rocked him and comforted him as best I could, distracting him with all his favourite songs and stories, as many as I could rack my brain to invent.

In the morning, Anys Gowdie brought a cooling salve, fragrant of mint, and asked me if she might apply it to the child. She sat upon the floor with her back to the wall and her knees raised and laid his little body along her thighs, so that his head rested on her knees and his feet at her hips. She brought her hands in long, tender strokes across his brow and down body and limbs. As she stroked him, she sang softly: 'Two angels came from the East. One brought fire, one brought frost. Out, fire! In, frost! By all the Mothers' gentle ghosts.'

Jamie had been restless and whimpering, but he grew quiet under her touch, and soon fell into a blessed sleep. When I lifted him from her lap and laid him upon the pallet, his skin had lost its livid colour and felt cool to my touch. I thanked her from my heart for the relief she had brought him. She took my outstretched hand.

'You are a good mother, Anna Frith. Your arms will not be empty for ever. Remember that when the way looks bleak.'

Anys, I now see, knew well enough that her care would bring my boy but a brief respite. Hour by hour, as the good effects of the draught and the salve wore off, the fever rose again, and by afternoon he had become delirious. 'Mummy, Tom's calling you!' he whispered urgently in his tiny, cracked voice.

'I'm here, my darling. Tell Tommy I'm right here,' I told him, trying to keep the tears out of my voice.

Elinor Mompellion brought me food, though I could eat none of it. She sat by me and held my hand and whispered whatever words she thought I could bear to hear. I learned only later that when she left after long hours with me she would go next door to Mary Hadfield, whose mother, having come to comfort her in her great loss, now lay ill herself. And thence across the street to the Sydells, who had three lying sick, and from there on to the Hawksworths' where Jane, who was pregnant, lay ill alongside her husband, Michael.

Jamie suffered for five days before God finally saw fit to take him. The day of his death, strange circles bloomed on him: vivid crimson welts rising just beneath the topmost layer of his skin. As the hours passed, these turned violet and then purple-black, hardening into crusts. It seemed as if his flesh was dying while he yet breathed. Both of the Mompellions came when word reached them that these new Plague tokens had appeared. Jamie lay on a makeshift pallet before the hearth, where I had lit a low fire against the evening chill. I sat at the head of the pallet, pillowing Jamie's head in my lap and stroking his brow. The reverend knelt down upon the hard gritstone floor and commenced to pray. His wife slid silently from the chair and knelt beside him. I heard the words as if they came from far away.

'Omnipotent God, and most merciful Father, bow down Thine ear at our request. We cry unto Thee for mercy. Call home Thine Angel of Wrath and let not this child perish under the heavy stroke of this dreadful Plague . . .' The fire in the hearth threw a warm glow on the kneeling pair, their heads, dark and fair, bent close together. It was only at the end of the prayer that Elinor Mompellion raised her eyes and looked at me. I shook my head as the tears ran down my face, and she knew her husband's pleas had been in vain.

I cannot recount the days that followed. I know I fought the sexton when he came to take Jamie's body away, crying out in my disordered state and trying to claw off the linen piece wound round him because I feared he could not breathe through it. I know I walked to the church many times. I saw Jamie laid in the ground there beside Tom, and then Mary Hadfield's mother, and three of the Sydell children and Jane Hawksworth's husband and after that her son, born too soon and dead a day later. I stood with Lib Hancock while her husband was buried, and the two of us clung to each other in our grief. But I cannot tell you what was said, in the church or at the graveside, save for the line 'In the midst of life, we are in Death.'

Within a day or two, I found a way to trudge once again through my work, though I could not tell you a single task I did during that fortnight as the days and nights slid by. It was as if a deep fog had settled on me and everything around me, and I groped my way from one chore to the next without seeing anything clearly.

I believe I might have gone on so, given up to grief and confusion, if it had not been for a hirsel from my flock losing itself upon the moors. It was the third sennight after Jamie's death. I had been negligent of the sheep, and some of them had moved off on their own, searching for better grass. The sky was pewter that afternoon, and the air had the metallic taste of an early snowfall, so I had no choice but to seek them out, even though the effort of placing one foot before the other on the uphill walk seemed beyond me. I was following what I hoped was the trail of their scat along a clough at the edge of the moors, when I heard a horrible yelling coming from near a mine that had flooded some half-dozen years earlier.

There were ten or twelve people in a rough circle, jostling and staggering, their voices slurring as if they'd come straight from the Miner's Tavern. Lib Hancock was among them, stumbling from the effects of drink, which I knew she was not used to. In the centre, upon the ground, was Mem Gowdie, her frail old arms bound before her with a length of rope. Brad Hamilton knelt across her chest as his daughter, Faith, grasped a fistful of the old woman's hair and raked at her cheek with a hawthorn prick. 'I'll have it yet, witch!' she cried. 'Your blood will drive this sickness from my mother's body.' In the circle, Hamilton's oldest boy, Jude, held his mother in his arms. Rubbing her hand over Mem's bleeding cheek, Faith stood up and smeared the blood on her mother's neck, where the Plague sore rose throbbing.

I was running towards them, sliding down the steep side of the clough, when Mary Hadfield broke from the throng and flung herself down beside poor Mem, pushing her face within inches of the old woman's. 'You killed my family, hag!' Mem writhed, trying to shake her head in denial. 'I heard you curse us for bringing the physician to Edward! I heard you as you left my door! Your malice has brought Plague on my man and my mother and my boys!'

'Mary Hadfield!' I yelled, struggling to be heard over the drunken din. A few faces turned round as I pushed my way, panting, into the circle. 'Mem Gowdie did no such thing! Why are you saying this? I was on your very doorstep with her when that quack physician was in your house. She left your door with her lips sealed.'

'Why do you defend her, Anna Frith? Do not your own babies lie rotting in the ground from her cursing? You should be helping us here. Get you gone if you have nowt to do but hinder.'

'Let's swim her!' yelled an ale-soused voice. 'Then we'll see if she's witch or no!'

'Aye!' yelled another, and soon they were dragging Mem towards the adit of the flooded mine.

'You throw her down there, and you'll be murderers!' I yelled, trying to get in front of Brad Hamilton. When I grabbed his arm I saw that his face was distorted by drink and grief, and then I remembered he'd buried his son John that day. He flung me aside, and I missed my footing and fell hard, my head hitting stone. When I tried to raise it, the earth spun and turned dark.

When I came to myself, Mary Hadfield was wailing, 'She's sinking!

She's sinking! She's no witch! God forgive us, we've killed her!' She was tugging first one of the men and then the other, trying to pull them to the adit. I struggled to my feet and peered down into the dark, but I could see nothing but the distorted reflection of my own bloodied, anguished face peering back from the surface of the water. When I saw that no one was going to do anything, I pushed them aside and flung myself over the lip of the adit, feeling for the first stemple. But as I put my boot upon it, the rotted wood crumbled and fell away, and I dangled for a moment over the pit before someone, I did not see who, reached out an arm and pulled me back.

It was Anys Gowdie. Breathing hard from running uphill from the village, she wasted no words. Someone clearly had brought news to her of what was afoot, for she had a fresh rope tied ready round her waist. She slung it over the old turn-tree and secured it to the stowes, then she slid straight down into that slimy dark. The others had fallen back from her, but now they surged forward, peering down into the mine. I, too, strained to see into the adit. I could just make out Anys's hair, bright against the black water. There was a great deal of splashing, and then she began to climb, the limp body of her aunt lashed to her back. Luckily, many of the stemples were still sound, and as she neared the top, Mary Hadfield and I reached down to grasp her arms and pull her up the last few feet.

Mary and I laid Mem upon the ground and Anys knelt beside her and pressed on her chest. Dark water spewed from her mouth. The old woman wasn't breathing. 'She's dead!' wailed Mary, and that disordered group took up the keening. Paying them no mind, Anys covered her aunt's mouth with her own, and breathed into it. After the third breath, Anys paused. Mem Gowdie's chest rose by itself. She sputtered, groaned and opened her eyes. The relief I felt lasted only an instant, for Lib, in a crazed voice, began crying: 'Anys Gowdie's raised the dead! It's her that's the witch! Seize her!'

'Lib!' I cried, rising dizzily up off the ground beside Mem and grasping her by both arms. 'Don't be a fool! Who amongst us here hasn't put their mouth to a lamb born unbreathing?'

'Shut *your* mouth, Anna Frith!' Lib Hancock yelled, throwing off my hands and at the same time stepping towards me, bringing her face inches from mine. 'For you yourself told me that this witch consorted with the Devil's spawn who brought the Plague here! Viccars was a manwitch and she was his vessel!'

'Lib!' I shouted. 'Don't speak so of the blameless dead! Is not poor Mr Viccars in his grave as surely as your dear husband?'

Her eyes, glazed and strange, regarded me with hatred. Cries of 'whore' and 'jade' and 'fornicator' were coming now from every twisted mouth, as the mob surged at Anys where she knelt beside her aunt, leaping upon her and clawing at her flesh. Only Mary Hadfield stood back, her face stricken. I pushed Lib out of my way and tried to get to Anys. Anys was strong and fought them, and I tried to help her, grasping at one and then another, trying to pull them off her until my head began again to spin. Then Urith Gordon screamed.

'I can't see my reflection in her eyes! Sign of a witch! Sign of a witch! She witched my husband into lying with her!' At that, John Gordon began laying into Anys like a man possessed. I grabbed at his arm, trying to pull him back from her, but I knew my strength was insufficient to his frenzy. *Must get Mompellion* was my last thought; as I turned to run, someone struck me a blow that sent me sprawling.

I groaned and tried again to rise, but my limbs would not obey me. I saw the noose go round Anys's neck and knew they planned to hang her with her own rope, using the stowes as the scaffold.

Anys Gowdie ceased her struggling and drew herself up to her full, impressive height. A wind had whipped up from the north. Her cap had fallen off and the tendrils of her wet hair fell about her like strange golden snakes. A trickle of bright blood ran from her mouth.

'Yes,' she said, 'I am the Devil's creature, and, mark me, he will be revenged for my life!' The men who held her stepped back, making the sign of the cross and the other, older sign, against strong magic.

'Anys!' I groaned. 'Don't say these things! You know they are not so!'

She looked at me where I lay on the ground and gave a ghostly smile. But in her eyes I read judgment: my loose tongue had helped to betray her. She looked away and stared around her at her persecutors. The sun, slipping below the horizon, found a narrow slit in the louring clouds. Through it, sudden and swift, beamed a lonely finger of light. It sped over the hillsides, touching each tree and stone until it reached Anys and lit her up as if she were on fire. Her amber eyes glinted yellow as a cat's.

'I have lain with him. Yes! I have lain with the Devil, and he is mighty and cold to the touch. But I have not lain with him alone! No! I tell you, I have seen your wives lie with him! Yours, Brad Hamilton, and yours, John Gordon, and yours, Martin Highfield!'

The women moaned or screamed their outrage, but their men were transfixed by Anys and did not look at them.

'We rejoice to do it, all of us together and without shame, many times, one after another. He is as a stallion amongst geldings compared to you.' Here she fixed her glare on the men she had named, and laughed. The men bellowed like oxen then and tugged as one upon the rope. It snapped tight and silenced her laughter. Her long legs kicked as they pushed her into the adit.

They were still kicking when John Gordon let go of the rope and looked wildly around for his wife. She saw his crazed eyes and began to run. John Gordon reached her and brought her down with a blow. He grasped her hair and rolled her over. 'Is it true?' he yelled, and smashed his fist into her face. Blood streamed from her nose.

Michael Mompellion's fierce voice came thundering down the clough. 'What in the name of God have you done here?'

John Gordon's arm dropped to his side. He turned to stare at the rector who plunged Anteros down the steep slope, sending the stones flying from beneath his hoofs. Mary Hadfield, cowering behind him in the saddle, had clearly had the wit to go and fetch him here. He bore down first upon Brad Hamilton, who was closest to the stowes. Hamilton raised both arms as if to defend himself, but Anteros reared like a battle charger, driving him back. The rector turned the horse and slid from the saddle. He pulled a knife from his belt. Reaching up, he cradled Anys in one arm, slashing the rope with the other. Her beautiful face was purple and bloated, with the tongue hanging out like a cur's. He drew his cloak up so that it covered her.

Someone—I think it was Martin Highfield—was still drunk or crazed enough to try to defend what had been done.

'She . . . she confessed it,' he slurred. 'She lay with the Devil . . .'

Mompellion raised his voice to a roar. 'Oh, yes, the Devil has been here this night! But not in Anys Gowdie! Ignorant wretches! She fought you with the only weapon she had to hand—your own ugly thoughts and evil doubting of one another! Fall on your knees, now!'

And they did, dropping as one to the ground. 'Pray to God that in His infinite mercy He will save your miserable souls.' He drew a breath then and sighed. When he spoke again, the rage was gone from his voice. 'Have we not suffering enough in this village? Is there not Death enough here for you all that you bring the crime of murder amongst us as well? Gird yourselves, and pray that God does not exact from you the price that this day's deeds deserve.'

At once, the voices began: some in slurred murmurs, some crying out upon the Lord, others weeping and beating their breasts. At that time, you see, we all of us believed that God listened to such prayers.

5

The snow that blew in on that night's wind blanketed the village and brought a deep silence upon us. People crept through the white streets, hunched and muffled in their shawls as if in hiding. Witch's blood did nothing to aid Grace Hamilton, who died of Plague that week, leaving her children Jude and Faith sickening. I was blurred and vacant from the blow to my head and slept for a whole day and night before I was steady enough to resume the search for my lost sheep. By the time I found the poor beasts, huddled together in the lee of a rock, the snow had covered them and froze them near solid. My flock was reduced by a third.

Michael Mompellion held a funeral for Anys but Mem Gowdie was not there. She had got the coughing sickness from her near drowning and lay insensible in the rectory, where Elinor Mompellion had insisted she be brought. Together, we tended her. She had asked, when she was still able to speak, for a comfrey salve on her wounded face. We bound it there with fresh linen, but the bandage would hardly stay upon her sunken cheek. Her skin bloomed purple and yellow with bruises from the blows she had received.

She died just five days after Anys. With them went the main part of the physic we relied upon, along with the best chance our women had of living through their confinements with healthy infants in their arms.

The Justice of the Peace from Bakewell refused to come near our village or accept from us any persons for arrest, saying that no gaol in the parish would consent to hold them until the next assizes. Instead, those few from the mob who were not struck down with the Plague skulked amongst us, gaunt and haunted and awaiting God's judgment. By the following Sunday a mere five of the dozen who had been at the clough that night were well enough to put on the penitents' garb and go barefoot to church to make their prayers for forgiveness.

When Sunday morning dawned, we all trudged thither, the snow crunching beneath our feet. John Gordon was one of those who slipped into the corner of contrition, meeting no one's eyes but bending solicitously over Urith, who clung to his arm. Lib Hancock, too, was there. She walked past me as I stood in my pew, and did not meet my eyes.

Pale and hushed, we took our appointed places, the grieving and the guilty. We were, in this village, some three hundred and three score souls. Less the babes, the frail elderly, those few who must labour even on the Lord's Day, and the handful of Quakers and Nonconformists, the number who gathered each week in our church was a firm two hundred and one score worshippers. Since our places were set from long tradition, an absence was as obvious as a missing tooth. That Sunday, the growing roll of dead and ailing left many empty spaces.

Michael Mompellion did not use his pulpit as I had expected. All week he had been taut as a bowstring, as if struggling to contain a terrible rage. One night, late in the week, as I was making my way bent double under a load of hay for the sheep, I caught sight of him in the orchard with a stooped figure beside him. It was bitter cold and it was strange to me that the rector should choose such a night for an outdoor audience. But then I recognised the figure at his side and understood why he would not want to announce such a meeting.

Mr Mompellion was conferring with Thomas Stanley, the Puritan who had quit our parish on Saint Bartholomew's Day, in the Year of Our Lord 1662. Parson Stanley had told us then that he could not in conscience accept the order to use the Book of Common Prayer, and that he was but one of hundreds of priests who were resigning his pulpit on that day. Not long after his protest, a law was passed saying that dissenting clergy should keep at least five miles from their old parishes, so that they might not stir up differences. Accordingly, Mr Stanley left the village, and we were without a resident priest for almost two years, until the Mompellions came. By then, Mr Stanley's wife had died, leaving him alone among strangers. It was not in the Mompellions' nature to turn the old man away from the place and people he best knew. I do not know what words were said, but one day he was amongst us again, having slipped quietly back into a croft on the high farm of the Billings, a Nonconformist family. By the time the Plague arrived here, he had been returned for almost a year, an old man who kept his own counsel and stayed well clear of village affairs.

But now, it seemed, Mr Mompellion had sought out Mr Stanley. It was not until Sunday that I was able to know why. Mr Mompellion climbed the pulpit steps, and instead of the frown that had creased his brow all week, his face looked serene. And so he launched into the sermon that sealed our fates, and yet he was more than halfway into it before we saw where he was leading us.

'"Greater love no man hath than this, that he lay down his life for a friend."' He said the familiar words and then dropped his head, letting the fragment of text hover in a silence so lengthy that I worried he had forgot what next he purposed to say. But when he looked up, his face was alight and wreathed in such a smile that the church felt suddenly warmer. His words flowed then, as he spoke with passion about God's love and reminded us of how that love had fallen, in our time, upon each of us. He intoxicated us with his words, taking each of us to that place where we kept our sweetest memories.

Finally, he approached his point. Were we not bound to return this love to our fellow humans? Even to lay down our own lives, if God asked it of us? 'Dear brothers and sisters,' he said, 'we know God sometimes has spoken to His people in a terrible voice, by visiting dread things upon them. Of these things, Plague is one of the most terrible. Yet God has singled us out, alone amongst all the villages in our shire, to receive this Plague. It is a trial for us, I am sure of it. He is giving us an opportunity that He offers to very few upon this Earth. Here, we poor souls of this village may emulate Our Blessed Lord. Who would not seize such a chance? Dear friends, I believe we must accept this gift. It is a casket of gold! Let us plunge in our hands to the elbows and carry away these riches!'

He dropped his voice. 'There are some who would say that God sends us this thing not in love, but in rage. They will say Plague is here because we have earned it in our sinning. But I do not think God sends us this Plague in anger. Oh, yes, surely we have sinned in our lives, each one of us, and many times. There is none here who has not fallen. But God does not send this Plague as punishment for our sins. No!' His eyes travelled across the congregation, searching out the miners, and addressing himself to them, particularly. 'Like the ore that must be melted all to liquid to find the pure metal, so must we be rendered in the fiery furnace of this disease.' Five pews in front of me, I saw the white head of Alun Houghton, Barmester to our miners, coming slowly erect on his massive shoulders as the rector's words penetrated his understanding. The rector stretched out his hand towards him. 'Therefore, let us not flinch, let us not fail! Let us choose *not* the dull lustre of our base state when God would have us shine!'

'Amen!' Houghton's gravelly voice rumbled. A scattering of 'Amens' followed from the other miners.

'Friends,' he said, 'some of us have the means to flee. Some of us have relatives nearby who would gladly shelter us. Some few of us have means to go far from here—anywhere we choose.'

The Bradfords shifted in the foremost pew.

'But how would we repay the kindness of those who received us, if we carried the seeds of the Plague to them? What burden would we bear if, because of us, hundreds die who might have lived? No! Let us accept this Cross. Let us carry it in God's Holy Name!' The rector's voice had been gaining in power till it rang like a bell. But now he dropped back into a tone of intimacy. 'Dear friends, here we are, and here we *must* stay. Let the boundaries of this village become our whole world. Let none enter and none leave while this Plague lasts.'

He turned then to the particulars of his scheme for our voluntary besiegement, to which it seemed he had already given much thought. He said he had written to the earl at Chatsworth House not so many miles distant, setting out his proposal and asking aid. The earl had undertaken that if we sealed ourselves off he would provision us from his own purse with our basic needs in food, fuel and medicines. These would be left at the Boundary Stone at the southeastern edge of the village. Those who wished to purchase other items would leave payment either in a shallow spring-fed well to the north of Wright's Wood, where the flow of water would carry away any Plague seeds, or in holes gouged into the Boundary Stone that would be kept filled with vinegar, which was said to kill cóntagion.

He looked down and wiped his hand across his brow. The church was still. We were all concentrated on the pulpit and the tall man who stood there, his head bent as if gathering the strength to go on. 'Stay here,' he said at last, 'upon that piece of Earth whose golden grain and gleaming ore has ever nourished you. Stay here, and the Lord's love will be here for us. Stay here, my dearest friends. And I promise you this: while I am spared no one in this village will face their death alone.'

He advised us then to reflect and pray and said that shortly he would ask us for our decision. He came down from the pulpit and went amongst us with Elinor beside him, speaking to any who would have words with him. Some families stayed in their pews, their heads bent in prayerful reflection. Others wandered restlessly, forming into clusters here and there, seeking advice from friends. It was only then that I noticed that Thomas Stanley had entered the church and taken a place in the last pew. Now, he came forward, speaking softly to those who had been, or secretly still were, of a precisian leaning. Quietly, the old man was making clear his support of the younger.

I saw to my shame that my father and Aphra were among a small group whose gestures and head-shakes indicated that they did not agree with the rector's scheme. Mr Mompellion moved towards these unconvinced, and before long, Mr Stanley joined them. My father and his wife had drawn a little away, and I came near to them to try to overhear what they were saying to each other.

'Think of our bread, husband! If we take to the road, who will feed us? Like as not, we will starve. Here, he says we will have it surely.'

'Aye, "he says". Well, *I* say that you cannot eat "he says". Oh, aye, I'm sure he and his lady wife will get their bread from the earl, but when have the likes of them ever given a ha'penny for the likes of us?'

'Husband, where are your wits? It's not love of us will keep them to their word, but love of their own fine skins. It's a surety that the earl wants his estate kept free from Plague, and how better to do that than give us cause to bide here? A few penn'orth of bread each day would look like a good bargain to him, I'll be bound.' She was a shrewd woman, my stepmother, in spite of her superstitious fancies.

She saw me then and seemed about to beckon me over to help her plead her case. But I wanted no part in any person's decision other than my own, and I turned my face away.

When the Mompellions came to where I stood, Elinor Mompellion held out both her hands and took mine tenderly as the rector spoke to me. 'And you, Anna?' he said. 'Tell us you will stay with us, for without you, Mrs Mompellion and I would be ill set. Indeed, I do not know what we would do without you.'

I had made my decision. Still, I could not command my voice to give him a reply. When I nodded, Elinor Mompellion embraced me and held me to her for a long moment. The rector moved on, whispering quietly to Mary Hadfield, who was weeping and wringing her hands. By the time he mounted the steps again and faced us, he and Mr Stanley between them had shored up every doubter. All of us in the church that day gave our oath to God that we would stay, and not flee, whatever might befall us.

All of us, that is, except the Bradfords. They had slipped out of the church unnoticed and were already at the Hall, packing for their flight to Oxfordshire.

I LEFT THE CHURCH borne aloft by a strange bliss. We all partook of it: the faces that had been gaunt and careworn now seemed warm and alive, and we smiled as we caught one another's eyes, aware of the common grace our decision had brought us. And so I was not prepared for the harried look of Maggie Cantwell, the Bradfords' cook, pacing by my gate. As a consequence of her employment, Maggie had not been in church that morning. She still had on her large white pinafore, and her face was ruddy with exertion.

'Anna, they have turned me off! Eighteen years, and ordered out on a second's notice! I have come to ask your help to gather my few possessions, for the Bradfords mean to leave this hour, and they have told us all that after their departure the Hall will be locked and none of us may enter. It has been our home for all these years, and they put us out without a way to earn our bread!' She had been wringing a corner of her pinafore in her fleshy hands, and now she raised it to her cheek to catch her tears.

'Come, Maggie, we don't have time for this now,' I said. 'I will fetch a handcart and we will go directly for your things.' And so we set off, Maggie, who was above forty years old and stout from the enjoyment of her own fine cooking, labouring for breath as we toiled through the snowdrifts back up the hill to the Hall.

'There I was,' she panted, 'basting the joint for the Sunday dinner, when they storm in from church, early like, and I'm thinking there'll be what for if the meal's not on the table when the colonel looks for it, and I'm rushing meself and worrying at Brand, me pantry boy, when in comes the colonel hisself, who never set foot in the kitchen until this very day, and it's turned off we all are, and no thank you or how'll ye do, just put the food on the table and clear out.'

The Hall hummed like a struck hive. Horses stamped in the drive as maids and footmen staggered in and out, bent under the weight of boxes. We entered through the kitchen and could hear the scurrying feet above us, punctuated by the voices of the Bradford ladies giving their commands. Not wanting to be noticed by the Bradfords, I crept behind Maggie up the narrow backstairs to the little attic she shared with the maidservants. There were three cots crammed in the tiny space, and by one of them crouched a pale, wide-eyed girl named Jenny, who was trying to tie her few small possessions into a bundle and fumbling the knot in her hurry.

'Lordy, Cook, she says we are to be out of here this hour, yet she gives us no time to tend to our own going. I'm off my feet fetching and carting her things. They are taking none of us, not even Jane, who has been with Mrs Bradford since a girl. Jane cried and begged her, but she said that all of us have been too much about the village and might already have Plague in us, so they just mean to leave us here to die, and in the streets, for none of us has a place to go to!'

'No one is going to die in the streets,' I said as calmly as I could.

Maggie had a small oak coffer wedged beneath her bed, but her girth was such that she couldn't bend down low enough to get it. I dragged at it while she folded her quilt. Such, with a small sack of clothing, was the sum of her life's goods. We managed to work the coffer down the narrow stairs. In the kitchen, she paused, her eyes filling again. She ran her big red hands over the scored and scorched deal table. 'My life, this is,' she said. 'I know every mark on this and how it came there. And now I'm to turn me back and walk away with nothing.' Her head drooped and a tear splashed onto the table.

Just then, there was a commotion from the courtyard. I glanced out of the kitchen door in time to see Michael Mompellion pulling up Anteros in a scatter of stones. He was off the horse and upon the steps before the startled groom had gathered up his dropped reins.

He did not wait to be announced. 'Colonel Bradford!' His voice in the entrance hall was so loud that all the clatter quieted at once. The dustsheets were already upon the large furnishings in the Hall. I crept behind a shrouded settle, and from the cover of a fold of sheet I could see the colonel appear at the door to his library. He had a volume in one hand and a letter in the other. Miss Bradford and her mother appeared at the top of the stairs, hesitating there, as if unsure of the etiquette of this encounter.

'Rector Mompellion?' said the colonel. 'You should not have troubled yourself to ride here in such haste to fare us well, I had planned to make my adieus to you and your fair wife in this letter.'

He extended his hand with the letter. Mompellion took it absently but didn't look at it. 'I do not want your goodbyes. I am here to urge you to reconsider your departure. Your family is first here. The villagers look to you. If you quail, how may I ask them to be brave?'

'I do *not* quail!' the colonel replied coldly. 'I am merely doing what any man of means and sense must do: safeguarding what is mine.'

Mompellion took a step towards him, his broad hands outstretched. 'But think of those you are putting at risk . . .'

The colonel stepped back, keeping his distance from the rector. His voice became a slow, soft drawl. 'We have had this conversation, sir, here in this very Hall, albeit in a hypothetical context. Well, now the hypothesis is proven, and I mean to do as I said I would. I said then, and I say now, that my life and the lives of my family are of more consequence to me than some possible risk to strangers.'

The rector was not to be gainsaid. 'If the plight of strangers cannot move you, think of the good you might yet do here, among the villagers that know you and look to you.' He moved towards the colonel and clutched him by the arm. 'I could learn much from your counsel as to how best to go on as events unfold here. And while I am pledged to do my utmost to bring these people comfort, from you and your wife, and from Miss Bradford, the smallest gesture would mean so much more.'

On the landing, Elizabeth Bradford stifled a snort. Her father glanced up at her, his eyes sharing her amusement. 'How flattering!' he exclaimed with a sneer. 'Dear sir, I did not raise my daughter to have her play wet nurse to a rabble. And if I desired to succour the afflicted I would have joined you in Holy Orders.'

Mompellion dropped the colonel's arm as if it were something foul. 'One does not have to be a priest to be a man!' he cried.

The rector turned and strode towards the hearth. He held the colonel's letter still but seemed to have forgotten that he did so. It crumpled under his hand as he leaned against the mantel. From where I crouched, I could glimpse his face. He breathed in, deeply, and as he breathed out it seemed that he willed away the deep lines drawn all about his brow and jaw. His expression was calm when he turned his back to the hearth and again faced the colonel.

'If you must send your wife and daughter away, then I pray you, stay here yourself and do your duty.'

'Do not presume to tell me my duty! I do not tell you yours, although you would do well to look to that delicate bride of yours.'

Mompellion coloured at this. 'My wife, sir, I will admit I implored to leave this place when I first suspected what now we know in fact. But she refused, saying that her duty was to stay, and now she says I must rejoice in it, for I could hardly ask of others what I had not lain upon the nearest to me.'

'So. Your wife, it seems, is expert at making poor choices. She certainly has had some practice.'

The insult was so broad that I had to swallow a gasp. Mompellion's fists clenched, but he managed to maintain his level tone. 'You may be right. But I believe that the choice you make today is wrong. If you do this, your family's name will be a hissing in the laneways and the cottages. The people will not forgive you for abandoning them.'

'And you think I care for the opinion of a few sweaty miners and their snotty-nosed brats?'

Mompellion drew a sharp breath at that and took a step forward.

The colonel raised his hand in a conciliating gesture. 'Look, man, do not think I disparage your efforts this day. I do not say that you do ill in making your congregation feel righteous in staying here. On the contrary, I think it was well done of you. They may as well have some comfort, since they have no choice.'

Since they have no choice. I felt myself tumbling from the high plain onto which Mr Mompellion's sermon that morning had lofted me. What choice had we, after all? Perhaps, if my children yet lived, there might have been some decision to make; perhaps I would have been driven to consider a desperate flight to some uncertain destination. But I doubted it. For as Aphra had said to my father, it is not easy to surrender the safety of a roof and the certainty of bread for the perils of an open road. And, as it was, with my boys lying in the churchyard, I had no reason to leave. The Plague had taken from me the greatest part of what I had to lose; what was left of my life seemed, at that moment, barely worth saving. So I deserved no great credit for swearing I would stay. I would stay because I had small will to live—and nowhere else to go.

The colonel had turned away from the rector, back towards his library, and now he let his eyes travel over his bookshelves with feigned indifference as he continued to speak. 'But I, as you yourself so astutely perceived, do have a choice. And I propose to exercise it. Now, if you will excuse me, I have a great many other choices to make in consequence, such as whether to pack the Dryden or the Milton. Perhaps the Milton? Dryden's rhymes grow rather tedious, do you not think?'

'Colonel Bradford!' Mompellion's voice rang through the Hall. 'If you do not value these people, there is one who does. And be sure, He is the one to whom you will have to answer. I do not lightly speak of God's judgment, but on you I say the vials of His wrath will be opened, and a terrible vengeance poured down! Fear it, Colonel Bradford! Fear a far worse punishment than Plague!'

And at that, he turned, strode back into the courtyard, leapt upon Anteros and cantered away.

THERE WAS NO HISSING in the street as the Bradfords' carriage passed out of the village. Men doffed their caps and women curtsied, just as we had always done. With the exception of the coachman, who was to be turned off when they reached Oxford, the Bradfords had not retained a single one of their servants.

There were tearful scenes at the last when those who had nowhere to go fell on their knees by the Bradford carriage, grabbing at the hems of the ladies' travelling mantles and kissing the toe of the colonel's boot. Mrs Bradford and her daughter seemed to relent, and enquired of the colonel whether their maids might not take shelter in the stables or the well house, but Colonel Bradford refused them even that.

By nightfall, all the Bradfords' servants had been taken in by one or other village family—all but Maggie and Brand, the pantry boy, who both came from Bakewell and, not being bound by what we now called the Sunday Oath, decided to journey on there and see if their kin would take them in. The rector had charged them with carrying letters he had written to the surrounding villages, so that everyone would know how we purposed to go on. And that was almost all they carried. After all the rush to gather her coffer, Maggie decided to leave it behind lest her kin in Bakewell fear that Plague seeds were secreted within it. Maggie and Brand left on foot, the stout woman on the arm of the slender boy, and I suspect not a few in the village envied them as they turned and waved at the Boundary Stone.

And so the rest of us set about learning to live in the wide green prison of our own election. The weather warmed that week, and the snow melted into slush. Generally, the day after such a thaw would have brought a clatter of traffic to the streets, as carters held back by the snow made up on late deliveries and travellers took to the roadway. But this time the thaw brought no such busy movement, and the consequences of our oath began to come clear to us.

It was perhaps only a half-dozen times a year that I ventured beyond the limits in which we had now confined ourselves. And yet I found myself walking that Monday morning in the direction of the Boundary Stone, which sat at the edge of a high meadow. A path, well worn from traffic, plunged down the hill to the village of Stoney Middleton. I stood and looked longingly at that forbidden path. At the stone, the mason, Martin Milne, was drilling holes for the conducting of our strange new way of commerce. It was a still morning and the ringing of sledge on graver carried all the way back to the village. Several folk, drawn by the sound, came to watch the work. Down the dell we could see the carter waiting, his mule grazing. He would not approach until he received the signal. Mr Mompellion, too, was there, and when the holes were sufficiently deep he filled each with vinegar and placed coins inside. That first delivery was of standard stuffs: flour and salt and such staple goods. The next would add those items especially requested by villagers and written down by the rector upon a list to be placed beside the stone. There was also a list that named those who had died, for the nearby villages held many who were friends and kin and ached for news of how we did. There were three names on that first day's list: Martha Bandy, the innkeeper's daughter, and Jude and Faith Hamilton, the latest of the Gowdies' tormentors to be placed along-side them in the ground.

When all was accomplished, Mr Mompellion waved to the carter and we all backed off to a safe distance as the man led his mule up the slope. He unloaded as swiftly as he might, took the money and the lists, and then waved back to us. 'Our prayers and our blessings be upon all of ye!' he shouted. 'God have mercy on your goodness!' And then he turned the mule's head down the slope and mounted. We stood and watched as the beast trod a careful path out to where the spur dipped suddenly. The clink of harness grew fainter, until the beast reached the place where the way flattens and becomes easy. There, he picked up his pace and trotted on, until the buildings of Stoney Middleton hid him from our sight.

Beside me, Michael Mompellion sighed. Then, noticing that we all looked downcast, he rallied himself, smiled, and raised his voice so that all might hear. 'You see? That man gave us his blessing and you may be sure that like prayers are on the lips of all those in our sur-rounding towns. You are becoming a byword for goodness, dear friends! And with all these prayers, surely God will hear, and grant us His mercy!' The faces that turned to him looked serious. For all of us had had the time to reflect on the gravity of our decision, and knew what it might bode for us. Mr Mompellion was quite aware of this. As we made our way back along the path to the village, to the tasks that beckoned us, he moved from one small group of persons to the next, offering words of support. Most seemed to pick up their spirits a little as they spoke with him.

And so we reached the village's main street. I was due to begin my morning's work at the rectory, so I walked on with Mr Mompellion. He had retreated into his own thoughts, and so I kept my peace.

Elinor Mompellion greeted us at the door, her shawl upon her, anxious to be out. She had, she said, been waiting for me, because she had a task that would require my help. She took my arm impa-tiently and almost pushed me down the path before the rector could gather himself to ask where we were going.

'Randoll Daniel was here this morning,' she said. 'His wife is in labour and, with the Gowdies gone, he knew not where to look for help. I told him we would be there directly.'

I turned pale at this. My own mother died in her childbed when I was four years old. The baby lay crosswise and she laboured four days as Mem Gowdie tried in vain to alter its position. In the end, with my mother unconscious from exhaustion, my father had ridden to Sheffield and returned at last with a barber-surgeon he'd shipped with as a boy. The man used a thatcher's hook. My father had taken so much grog that he did not have the wit to keep me from the room. I ran in there as my mother came to herself, bellowing. Mem grabbed me up and carried me away. But not before I saw the tiny, torn-off arm of my stillborn sister.

I started to tell Mrs Mompellion that I could not go with her, that I knew nothing of midwifery, but she cut me off. 'However little you know, it's more than I do, who never has laboured myself nor even birthed any livestock. But you have, Anna. You will know what to do, and I will assist you as best I can.'

'Mrs Mompellion! Giving birth is one thing! Midwifing is another. And neither is a lamb a living human soul. You do not know what you are asking me. Poor Mary Daniel deserves better than us!'

'That is no doubt true, Anna, but we are all she has. So we will do the best we can by her.' She patted the whisket at her side. 'I have here some poppy if her pain is great.'

I shook my head at that. 'Mrs Mompellion, I do not think we should give her poppy, for labour is not called labour by chance. A woman must do much real work to get her baby born. We would be sore pressed if she were fallen into a poppy stupor.'

'See, Anna! You have already helped me, and Mrs Daniel. You know more than you think you do.' We were approaching the Daniels' cottage. Randoll Daniel opened the door before we had even knocked upon it. Mary was sitting on a pallet, her back braced against the wall and her knees drawn up to her chest. She was quiet, but from the beads of sweat on her brow and the veins roping in her neck I perceived that we had found her in the midst of a strong surge.

Randoll had closed the shutters and laid a good fire, the day being chill, and Mrs Mompellion asked him to set some water to heat on it. I hoped that in the dim light Mary would not see that my hands were trembling, but as I approached her she closed her eyes. Elinor Mompellion did note my fear, and she laid a reassuring hand on my shoulder as I knelt down and lifted the sheet from Mary's knees.

Mary Daniel was a small, vigorous woman of about twenty, and her flesh felt firm and healthful under my hands. Mrs Mompellion held a candle for me, but it was by feel, not sight, that I was working. The news my fingers brought me was bad. The part of the baby presenting itself for birth was not hard skull but soft flesh, and I knew not at first if I felt a buttock or a back or part of a face. I spoke softly to Mary, encouraging her to walk, if she could. I thought if we could get her moving, then the baby might move, too, into a better lie. We walked up and down that little room, Mrs Mompellion the prop for her right side, while I took the left.

Time passed. An hour, maybe two or three. In that dim room the only time that mattered was measured in Mary's ever-increasing intervals of pain. At last the womb stood wide. There was no doubt now: the baby lay crosswise. A black panic started to rise in me.

But then a strange thing happened. It was as if truculent Anys was beside me, whispering impatiently in my ear. 'That man was a ship's barber; he pulled teeth and amputated limbs. He knew nothing of women's bodies. But you *do* know. You can do this, Anna.'

Gently then, I explored the tiny body of that unborn baby, fingering the knobs and curves to see if I could make sense of them. I found something that felt like a foot. If I could manipulate the feet, surely the buttocks would slip into place, and on buttocks one could get a good grip. Confident now that what I had under my hand was a toe, I pulled. The baby moved, a little. Slowly, working with the surges of Mary's body, I eased and tugged, eased and tugged. Mary stood up well to the pain that came at her now unrelentingly. Then the pace changed, and everything became urgent. Mary writhed and yelled. I yelled back at her, urging her to push harder, desperate when she surrendered just short of the ultimate effort, and I felt the baby slip back again. Finally, in a slick of blood, there he was—a small, slippery boy. And a moment later, he was yelling, too.

Randoll burst in when he heard his lusty son, and his hand fluttered from the damp head of the babe to his wife's flushed cheek and back again, as if he didn't know which he most wanted to touch. Elinor threw open the shutters and it was only as the fading light entered the room that I saw we hadn't cut the navel-cord. We sent Randoll for a knife and a piece of thread. Mrs Mompellion made the cut and bound it up. I looked at her, all dishevelled, spattered with blood, and imagined myself looking worse. We laughed. And, for an hour, in that season of death, we celebrated a life.

But even in the midst of that joy, I knew that I would have to leave the babe nursing at his mother's breast and return to my own cottage, silent and empty, where the only sound that would greet me would be the phantom echoes of my own boys' infant cries. And so, before we took our leave of the Daniels, I found the phial of poppy in Mrs Mompellion's whisket. I closed my hand upon it, stealthy as a practised thief, and plunged it, deep, into the sleeve of my dress.

6

Maggie Cantwell came back to us in a handcart. It was a chill morning, and a fog hung low in the valley, so it was difficult to descry exactly what was in the cart edging its slow way up the hill, with a slight figure behind, bent double, toiling under the load.

Jakob Merrill, the widower who lived nearest the Boundary Stone, ran out of his dwelling to wave the carter away, thinking he was some pedlar who had blundered towards us ignorant of the perils of this place. But the boy trudged on, and eventually Jakob saw that the bundle in the cart was a human form. It was hard to make out the features of the carter, for he was spattered from head to foot with the brown debris of rotten fruit. But as he toiled closer, Jakob recognised him as young Brand, the pantry boy from Bradford Hall.

When he reached the stone, Brand's legs folded under him. Jakob dispatched his boy, Seth, to carry the news to the rector, while he set a cauldron of water to heat and told his daughter to bring cloths so Brand could clean himself. I was at the rectory when the child arrived with the news. As I helped the rector with his hat and coat, I asked if I might ride with him to see if I could comfort poor Maggie.

When we drew up, Maggie still lay in the cart, it being beyond Jakob Merrill's strength to remove her. He had thrown a blanket across her, to give her warmth, but when he removed it, my first thought was that it had but covered a corpse, so blue was she with the cold. The small cart was insufficient to contain her big body, so her beefy calves and heavy arms spilled out over the sides. But it was her face that was most shocking.

While the left side, under the mess of fruit pulp, looked as vivid as ever, the right was a blur, the eye all but closed and seeping, the cheek drooped and the mouth a drooling sneer. Maggie turned her head to take us in with her one good eye, and when she recognised me she moaned and reached for me with a flailing left arm. I clasped her hand and told her all would be well, although I knew that very likely it would not.

Mr Mompellion went to work with Jakob Merrill to get poor Maggie from the cart into the cottage. Jakob gripped her fleshy legs while the rector wrapped his arms round her chest. As they heaved

Maggie into the croft Mr Mompellion spoke soothingly to her, trying to blunt the indignity. Inside, young Brand, clean now, sat wrapped in a rough blanket before the fire. Jakob Merrill's daughter, Charity, handed him a mug of mutton broth, and he gripped it tightly with both hands. Charity held up a blanket for a screen as I stripped off Maggie's befouled garments and bathed her, while Mr Mompellion crouched beside Brand and enquired gently as to what had happened.

It seemed they had had an uneventful journey through Stoney Middleton; the people there, while keeping a distance, had called out their good wishes as they passed through, and had left a parcel of oatcake and a flask of ale for them at the milestone. Farther along the road, a farmer had allowed them to sleep the night amongst his cows in their warm shippon. The trouble had come when they arrived at Bakewell. It was market day, nigh on noon, and the streets were crowded. Suddenly, someone recognised Maggie and raised a shout: 'A woman from the Plague village! Beware! Beware!'

Brand shuddered then. 'Lord forgive me, I ran off and left her. I been gone out from Bakewell since I was a small boy, and I be changed so much that no one now would know me. So I thought if I were not with Maggie, I might get to my kin in safety.' But Brand had not gone far when his own goodness drew him back.

'I could hear the yelling, and I needed to know if she were safe. She'd been good to me in that hard house. So I crept back and came up behind a vegetable-seller's stall. Then I seen what were happening. They'd taken all the bad apples cast into the pig trough and were hurling them at Maggie, yelling: "Out! Out! Out!" And believe me, she were trying to get out of there as fast as she might, but you know she don't move swift, and she were getting confused and staggering first one way, then t'other. I went to her and grabbed her arm, and we made a run for it as they kept pelting us. And that's when she were planet-struck. She just gave way, folded up in the middle of the roadway, like her right leg were made of string. And that set the mob into an even bigger to-do. One or two of the children started hurling stones, and I thought if they all took that up it'd be the finish of us.

'You're not going to like it too well, Rector Mompellion, when I tell what I did then. I stole the barrow from the nearest stall and somehow I found the strength to pile her in it. The barrow man cursed me to Hell, but he didn't give chase. Perhaps he reckoned I'd Plagued the cart by touching it. We been on the way here ever since. Scared to stop, I was, lessen another mob formed to get us.' He shivered then in his exhaustion and began to sob.

Michael Mompellion reached an arm round the boy's heaving shoulders and held him tightly. 'You did very well, Brand, even to taking the cart. Set your heart at rest over it. You could have run and sought your own safety, and yet your loyal heart taught you to do otherwise.' He sighed. 'This Plague will make heroes of us all, whether we will or no. But you are the first of them.'

Charity had brought a mug of the mutton broth for Maggie, and the two of us tried to prop her up and spoon a little into the good side of her mouth. But it proved futile; her tongue, it seemed, could not lift itself to steer the liquid down her throat. Broth came dribbling out and down her chin. A fat tear formed itself in her good eye and ran down to join the drool on her chin. Poor Maggie! Food had been her livelihood and her life. What would become of her if she couldn't eat?

'God damn the Bradfords!' The words slipped out of my mouth before I knew I'd uttered them. Rector Mompellion looked at me, but not with the rebuke I'd expected.

'Don't trouble yourself, Anna,' he said. 'I believe He already has.'

THE CARE OF MAGGIE CANTWELL seemed too big a burden for Jakob Merrill, struggling as he was to rear a girl of ten and a boy not yet six. But he did say he would give Brand a roof until the youth was able to find a better. I said I would have Maggie at my cottage if I could bespeak some suitable conveyance. We aimed to leave her at the Merrills' till the next morning, so that she could benefit from a full night's rest and warmth.

As Mr Mompellion mounted Anteros to return to the rectory, I set off to the Miner's Tavern, to see if their horse-trap might be had for the next day. It was so cold on the walk that my breath formed little clouds before my face, and I found myself trotting to warm my blood. The Miner's Tavern is an important gathering place, for as well as sheltering those who like a pot, it also hosts the gatherings of the Body of the Mine and the miners' Barmote Court, where all matters vital to the delving and marketing of our ore are decided.

The tavern has both a large court and a taproom. On such a bitter day it was to the taproom that I hurried. Inside, a good fire toasted the air. There was a fair crowd for a weekday morning, my father amongst them. It appeared that he had been at the pot for some time.

'Here, daughter, you look cold. Let me buy you an ale to put colour in your cheeks. Ale's the warmest lining of a naked man's coat, eh?'

I shook my head, saying I yet had much work to do at the rectory.

'Ahh, God's blood, girl! It's your father who invites you. And you can take back some wisdom to that prating priest. You tell him there's more good in a cask of ale than in the four Gospels.'

Why I said this next I do not know. My life with my father should have taught me better than to upbraid him before his friends. But my mind, as I have said, was brimful of Scripture, and some lines from Ephesians seemed to issue of their own accord in response to his blasphemy. '"Let no corrupt communication proceed out of your mouth, but that which is good to the use of edifying."'

The men around him had had a good guffaw at his utterance, but at my stony response, they turned their laughter on him.

'Eh, Joss Bont, your whelp knows how to nip!' said one, and when I saw the look on my father's face I wanted to hush them all. His colour had risen and his mouth had turned from grin to snarl.

'Don't think you're too good now, with your fancy quothings, just o' cause that priest and his missus make much o'ye,' and at that he grabbed me by the shoulders and forced me to kneel in front of him. 'See? I said you'd learn at me knee, and you'll damn well do as I tell ye. Someone fetch me a branks to muzzle this scold!'

The fear rose in me. I saw my mother's face framed in the iron bars, her desperate eyes, the inhuman sounds that came from her throat as the iron bit pressed against her tongue. He had clapped the branks on her after she cursed him in public for his drunkenness. The sight of her with her head in that fearful cage had terrified me, tiny child that I was, and I'd run off and hidden myself. When my father had drunk himself into insensibility, some kindly person cut the leather strap that bound the thing to her jaws. By then her tongue was raw, and it swelled so that it was days before she got her speech back.

The pressure of my father's hands weighed on my shoulders, but somehow I felt as if they were at my neck, choking me. The back of my throat tightened, and I wanted to retch. There was a gob of spittle forming in my mouth, and my impulse was to heave it all over him. But I knew him well enough to reason that if I did so in the sight of his tavern friends, he would beat me senseless. When I was a child, Aphra stood by and allowed it to happen, time after time. She would raise her voice only if he struck me on the face, 'For we'll never marry her off if you mar her there.'

Years later, when Sam Frith had taken me out of that unhappy croft, his hands, caressing me, found the knobbly place near my right shoulder where the bones had knit awry. I made the mistake of confiding to him how my father, in a drunken rage, had flung me against the wall when I was about six years old. Sam made me tell him then of all the other beatings, and as I went on, he grew rigid with rage. When I had recounted the last of it, he had gone directly to my father. 'This is from a child who was too small to do it for herself,' he said, and he placed his big fist in my father's face, knocking him flat.

But I had no Sam now. I felt a sudden hot gush down my thigh. Fear had made my body betray me, just as when I was a child. I crumpled at my father's feet and, in a tiny voice, begged his pardon. He laughed, his pride saved by my humiliation. The pressure of his hands eased, and he landed the toe of his boot into my side, just hard enough to push me over into my own puddle. I pulled off my pinafore and sopped up as much as I could, and then I rushed from the room, too abashed to seek out the innkeeper to arrange for his trap. I ran to my home, weeping and shaking, and as soon as I had the door closed behind me, I stripped every soiled garment and scrubbed myself roughly. I was still tearful and trembling when little Seth arrived at my door to fetch me back to Maggie.

As soon as I saw her, the contemplation of her predicament shamed me out of my self-pity. Maggie Cantwell would need no cart in the morning. While I was at the Tavern, she had been struck by another spasm that had turned her good side useless. She lay now in a deep, unnatural sleep from which no word or touch could rouse her. I reached for her hand, where it lay on the coverlet, twisted and shapeless, as if it had been boned. Maggie Cantwell was gone before midnight.

THE DAY AFTER ELINOR Mompellion and I delivered the Daniels' baby, I had repented of my theft and taken the phial of poppy to the rectory, meaning to slip it back into Mrs Mompellion's whisket before its loss was noticed. But every time I had the opportunity, I lacked the will. In the end, I brought it home again and placed it guiltily in a pipkin. On the night that Maggie Cantwell died I stared at the small plug of tawny resin and wondered what dose it would take to secure a few sweet dreams. I pinched off a sticky morsel of the stuff and put it to my mouth, only to wince at the bitterness. In the end, I cut the plug in half, formed a piece into a lozenge and coated it with honey. I swallowed the whole with a swill of ale. Then I stoked the fire and sat staring into its meagre wedge of light.

I drifted into a place where the sun so dazzled that I had to close my eyes. Somewhere, an owl hooted, and the note seemed to be pulled and stretched, like the call of a hunter's horn, and then a score of horns, sounding in harmony. The sun glinted off the serried instruments and I could see the notes of music, molten, dripping like golden rain. Where they touched the ground, walls rose, and soaring arches, building a city of shining towers. I saw myself drifting through the winding streets. My children gambolled on either side of me, merry little figures, clinging to my hands. On the high, white walls the sun blazed, beating and throbbing like the blows of a bell-clapper.

I woke to the slow tolling of our church bell, ringing once again for the dead. A pale finger of winter light streamed through a frosty pane and full into my face, which lay pressed against the gritstone floor. I'd lain all night just as I'd landed when I slid from the stool. My bones, aching from the cold, were so stiff I could barely ease myself upright and my mouth was dry as ashes. I crept round, making up the fire with the slow, crabbed gestures of a crone.

But my mind was more serene than it had been since that warm day when I had sat nursing Tom with my toes in the brook and Jamie laughing beside me. By the slant of the light, I could tell I'd slept ten hours—the first unbroken sleep I could remember in an age.

I washed my face and raked the tangles from my hair. I could not do much about the rumpled state of my tunic, but I pinned on a clean whisk. I hoped that the cold air would put some roses into my cheeks by the time I reached the rectory. As I stepped out into the street, I was clinging to the last wisps of my drugged serenity, but I had not gone but six steps when I dropped again into the dark place of our new reality.

Sally Maston, my neighbour's girl of but five years, was standing in the doorway of her cottage, wide-eyed and silent. The front of her flimsy nightdress bloomed like a rose from the blood of her burst Plague sore. I ran to her and gathered her up into my arms.

'There, there,' I cried. 'Where is your mummy?'

She gave no answer but fell limp against me. I carried her through the doorway and back into the dim cottage. The fire had guttered in the night, and the room was frigid. Sally's mother lay upon a pallet, pale and cold and many hours dead. Her father sprawled on the floor beside his wife, one hand twined in hers where it had fallen off the pallet. He was fevered and struggling for breath. In a wooden crib by the hearth, a baby mewled faintly.

Could a day contain two occasions of such utter misery? That day did, and more than two. Before sunset, no fewer than four families were visited by deaths that reached across generations, snatching children and parents with the same hand. The Mompellions reeled from one grievous scene to the next. While the rector prayed with the dying, wrote out wills and consoled where he could, I helped Mrs Mompellion with tending and feeding and finding kinfolk willing to care for the newly orphaned or soon to be so—no easy matter, especially if the child was already sick.

My work that day was to make the Maston children as comfortable as I might. Their mother's body I readied for the sexton. For the father I could do little. He lay insensible, barely breathing. When old Jon Millstone arrived with his cart and found that the man was not yet dead, I heard him cursing under his breath.

I must have looked sternly at him, for he swept his soiled cap from his head and wiped a hand across his brow. 'Ah, forgive me, Mistress, but these times, they do make monsters of us all. It's just that I'm so very tired, I cannot bear the thought of harnessing the horse twice when once might've served.' I bade him sit then and went to my cottage for a mug of broth, for the old man was working far beyond his strength. By the time I returned, had warmed the broth, and he had sipped it down, there were two corpses for his cart after all.

I listened to him go and settled to what would surely be a desolate night: the infant barely clinging to life, Sally restless in her fever. In the early evening, Mrs Mompellion appeared at the door, her face pale. 'Anna,' she said. 'I am just come from the Hancock farm. Swithin, the youngest son, is dead, and Lib lies very grave. I know she was dear to you once. If you wish, I will bide here while you go to her.'

I would not have left the children's side for any less cause. But the rift with Lib was like an ache, and I longed to ease it. By the time I toiled to the Hancock farm, my oldest friend was too far gone for speech. I sat with her and stroked her face, willing her to waken that I might say something to mend the breach between us. Even such small relief was not granted to me.

It was very late when I returned to relieve Mrs Mompellion at the Maston cottage. It snowed not long after, a wild snow that blew hard against the cottage and chinked every crevice in the stone. I built up the fire and laid every piece of cloth I could find upon the children.

The storm swiftly spent its fury. The wind dropped not long after midnight, and the baby died in the silence that followed. Little Sally lasted into the following afternoon but passed with the fading of the light. I bathed her thin body, wrapped her in clean linen, and left her, lying alone, until Jon Millstone found the time to take her. 'Sorry, little one,' I whispered. 'But I must save my strength for the living.'

And so I trudged home in the near dark, stopping at the sheepfold to fling some hay to my diminished flock. I did not bother to eat. Instead, I poured boiling water over the remaining poppy resin, stirring in honey to mask the bitterness, and carried the mug up to my bed. In my dreams that night, the mountains breathed like sleeping beasts, and a winged horse flew me over shimmering deserts of golden glass, through fields of falling stars.

Once again, I awoke in the morning blissfully rested. But I was plunged back into hard reality when I remembered that I had no further means to secure such oblivion. I lay in my warm bed, staring up at the beams of my own ceiling, and thought of my last visit to the Gowdies. Surely there must have been some poppy fruits hanging among the bunches of drying herbs? Perhaps there were already carefully prepared tinctures, put up in cupboards? Or resin in phials such as I had stolen from Mrs Mompellion? I determined to go there and see for myself.

The snow gleamed on the windward side of rocks and trees. My hens huddled in a corner of the garth, their feathers fluffed against the cold. I grabbed up some handfuls of hay and stuffed them into my boots to keep my feet dry and warm on the long, damp walk. The sky hung low, deep grey and threatening further snowfall. I trudged on, picking my way across frozen turves and trying to avoid the thawing mud. Then I noticed something amiss. By this hour, the oily black smoke of the Talbot smithy should have been pouring from the new-fired forge and drifting, in that still, cold air, into the valley. But the forge itself was cold, and the Talbot cottage silent. Heavily, I set my feet on the track up to the smith's house, knowing well enough what I would find when I got there.

Kate Talbot opened the door, her fist pressed into the small of her aching back. She was round-bellied with her first child, due at Shrovetide. As I had expected, the smell of rotten apples filled the house. But there was another smell, also: the odour of burnt meat left to rot. Richard Talbot, the strongest man in our village, lay whimpering upon his bed like an infant, the flesh of his groin singed black. The place where the iron had seared was laid open to the muscle, seeping pus and green with putrefaction.

Kate saw me staring at this terrible wound and wrung her hands. 'He demanded I do it,' she said in a hoarse whisper. 'Two nights ago, he bade me fire up the forge and heat the poker till it glowed red. I could not bring myself to lay it on him, so he grabbed it from my hand, feeble as he was, and buried the brand in his own flesh. Afterwards, he lay in a cold sweat trembling for an hour. He said if we burned the Plague sore away then the disease would surely follow. But he has only worsened since.'

I muttered some empty words of comfort, knowing that Richard Talbot would be dead of the rot, if not the Plague, before nightfall, and looked around for tasks. The room was chill, for Kate said her back pain was so sharp that she had not been able to bring in more than one log at a time, and the fire had burned to embers. I went out to haul in a bushel-skep of wood, and as I re-entered the room I saw Kate bending over Richard, closing her hand on a small triangle of parchment she'd laid near his wound. As quick as she was, I saw plainly what she tried to hide. It was a spell, inscribed thus:

ABRACADABRA
BRACADABR
RACADAB
ACADA
CAD
A

'Kate Talbot!' I chided. 'Surely you know better than these wicked follies!' Her face fell, and the tears started. 'No,' I said, regretting my harshness and reaching out to embrace her. 'I'm sorry I spoke so. I know you turn to this because you do not know what else to do.'

'Oh, Anna,' she sobbed. 'I do not, in my heart, believe in it, and yet I bought this charm because that which I do believe has failed me. Our prayers bring no relief. So the voice of the Devil whispers to me, "If God will not help you," he says, "mayhap I might . . ."'

At first, she would not say how she had come by the charm, for the charlatan who had choused her out of a shilling for it had told her that a death curse would come upon her if she told. But I pressed her, trying to make her see that it was a malign trick to take her money. Finally, she swallowed hard.

'No, Anna, it were no trick. Wicked, yes, but magic, in truth. For the charm were given me by the ghost of Anys Gowdie.'

'Nonsense!' I blurted. But she was pale as the drifting snow outside. More gently, I pressed her: 'Why say you so?'

'I heard her voice in the wind last night when I went out to fetch in a log. She said to place a shilling on the lintel and in the morning a potent charm would lie there in its stead.'

'Kate,' I said gently. 'Anys Gowdie is dead and gone. And if she were alive she would not come with worthless charms, for her cures were practical things, made of common weeds and worts. Throw that paper away, Kate, and put aside these foolish, poisonous thoughts. For I am sure we will find that someone of this village—corrupt and greedy, but very much alive—was the voice you heard.'

Reluctantly, she opened her hand and let the parchment flutter down onto the bavins. As I blew on the embers, a flame leapt up and seized it. 'Take your ease now,' I said. 'With rest you might find the world a small bit brighter.'

Having done what I could, I continued on my own errand. A stiff wind had blown up. At the Gowdies' cottage, the snow lay in drifts, knee-deep. At the door, I paused, fighting down the guilt I felt at invading the property of the dead. As I stood there, trying to find courage, snowmelt dripped down the thatch and landed upon my neck. I began to wrestle with the damp-swollen door, but my cold hands were clumsy. I pushed until the door budged enough to admit me, and sidled into the dark.

The wind whipped round the house, its sighs like a hundred voices. I felt myself trembling and told myself it was the cold and damp, merely. I needed to kindle a fire for light as well as warmth. Since the Gowdies were too poor for glazing, the cottage had but a wind-eye up under the eaves, and this they had stuffed with rushes since the first cool days of leaf-fall. It was so dim in the soot-stained room that I had to feel all round the hearth for the flint and tinder. When I found them, my hands shook so that I could not strike a spark.

A sudden light blazed behind me. 'Stand back from the hearth, Anna.'

I jumped up, caught my foot in a loose hearthstone, and slipped onto the earthen floor. Terrified, I raised my head and turned, blinded by the light emanating from the ghost of Anys Gowdie. She hovered in the air above me, white-gowned and brilliant.

'Are you all right?' Elinor Mompellion asked, climbing down the loft ladder with a candle held high in front of her.

Shock and relief descended upon me at once, and with such force that I burst into tears.

'Have you injured yourself?' Mrs Mompellion said, bending over me, her face, in the circle of candle glow, creased with concern.

'No, no,' I said, struggling for command of myself. 'I landed hard on my wrist, merely. I—I did not expect to find anyone else here.'

'It seems we shared the same idea,' she said, and I, in my confusion, thought she meant that she had come searching for the poppy also. But she continued: 'I came here late yesterday, for it is evident to me that we must take stock of such remedies as the Gowdies may have left here. The key to defeating this Plague must lie in such plants as can be used to nourish those who remain in health. We must strengthen our bodies that we may continue to resist contagion.' She had taken my place at the hearth now, and had kindled a promising flame. 'I became so engrossed in sorting the plants that I barely noticed the light fading, and by the time I thought to set out for home, it had begun to snow. I decided to sleep the night here rather than toil to the rectory in such weather. Mr Mompellion, I knew, would reason I was needed at someone's sickbed. And indeed, I slept so well that I believe I would be sleeping still if your struggles with the door had not waked me. And now we must set to work, for Anna, there are riches here indeed!' She launched then on a catalogue of what she had so far identified and the virtues of the tonics we could make.

As I listened to her plans, I felt the wretchedness of my own selfish scheme for escape into a false oblivion.

'Mrs Mompellion, I—'

'Elinor,' she said. 'You and I cannot work on such terms as we now are and continue with the old forms. You must call me Elinor.'

'Elinor . . . I have something to confess to you. I came here not seeking herbs to help others. Only myself.'

'Ah, yes,' she said, quietly. 'You came for these.' From the ceiling rafter, she reached up and unstrung a bunch of pregnant seedpods. 'The Greeks called them the Poppies of Lethe. Lethe—the Greeks' river of forgetfulness. Once the souls of the dead tasted its waters they forgot their past lives. It is natural to want to forget, when every day is a brimful of sadness. But those souls also forgot those they had loved. You do not want that, surely? You must cherish your memories of your babes, Anna, until you see them again in Heaven.'

'I took the poppy from your whisket at the Daniels' cottage.'

'I know it,' she said. 'And did it bring you sweet dreams?'

'Yes,' I whispered. 'The sweetest I have ever known.'

She nodded, her fine hair lit like a halo in the firelight. 'Yes,' she said. 'I remember well.'

'You?' I said, startled. 'You have used this thing?'

'Yes, Anna, even I. For there was a time when I had much that I, too, wanted to forget.' She stood up, reached into a pipkin in the corner and measured a quantity of crumbled camomile into a pot. The kettle in the hearth had begun to steam. From it, she poured water to make a pungent tea. 'Do you remember on the way to the Daniels', Anna, that I said to you that I had never birthed a child?'

I nodded dumbly. I could not think where this was leading.

'I did not say I had never been *with* child.'

I must have looked confused at this, for I had worked for Mrs Mompellion, laundering her linens, since the day she arrived in our village, a new bride. If she had been with child I would have known it.

She reached out a hand and turned my face to look full into hers. 'Anna, the child I carried was not Mr Mompellion's.' She read the shock in my face, and her hand sought mine. 'It is a story full of pain, but I tell it to you because I want you to know me. I have already asked much of you, Anna, and before this terrible time passes I may ask a great deal more. I want you to know who it is that lays these burdens upon you.'

She turned her face to the fire then, and as she spoke we looked at the flames. The story she unfolded began on a vast Derbyshire estate. She had been the only daughter of a gentleman of great wealth. She was indulged—spoiled, she said—especially after her mother died. Her father and her older brother had been loving but often absent, entrusting her care to a governess who was more learned than wise.

Elinor's childhood was filled with pleasure and with the acquisition of knowledge. 'Any fancy I had to know a thing—Greek or Latin, history, music, art—all I had to do was express a wish, and these treasures would be laid out before me. And I learned these things. But of life, Anna, and of human nature I did not learn.' Her father thought to keep her sheltered from the world, and so she did not leave the estate nor enter into any but a most restricted society. She had been fourteen when a neighbour, Charles, a young man of twenty and the heir to a dukedom, had begun pursuit of her.

'I was thrilled with this young man's attentions. He flattered me, he made me laugh, he interrogated everyone in the household about what I liked and did not like and cut the cloth of his behaviour to suit that intelligence. When my father returned from an absence and found that the two of us had been riding out alone almost daily, he told me that it must cease at once. He told me that I was far too young for any such intense friendships. But my father did not tell me that he had grave doubts about Charles's character.'

Elinor, who loved her father, had obeyed his wishes at first. But when his affairs took him from the estate again a month later, the young man renewed his pursuit. 'He begged me to elope with him, and promised to make it up with my father, who would not stand against the match once he saw the brilliance of my new state. My governess uncovered the scheme and could have thwarted it. But Charles charmed her, and bribed her into silence. With her help, we stole away at dead of night. We planned, as I thought, to make for the Fleet, where marriages could be bought without licence. But I had never seen London, and so when Charles proposed that we first try this or that entertainment or excursion, I did not hesitate to say, yes, yes, let us do it all.

'You will have guessed,' Elinor said in a small voice, 'that the union was consummated before it was consecrated. And then it became clear to me that he did not intend to have it consecrated at all. But, Anna, I was so lost in the fires of my own lusts that I did not greatly care.' She went on to tell how she and Charles had lived together for more than a fortnight until, one evening, he simply failed to return to the inn where they were hiding. He had abandoned her.

'There were days when I would not let myself believe it. I told myself that he had fallen ill. It was some time before I faced the fact of my ruin and called upon those who still loved me.' Her father and brother, who had been searching for her, came swiftly. They carried her home, where the matter was to have been hushed up. But she was with child.

She was weeping now, but she dashed the tears away with the heel of her hand and went on. 'I was desperate, and I was deranged,' she said. 'I violated my own body with a fire iron.'

I drew a ragged breath at this and hid my face in my hands. I could not bear to imagine such suffering.

'My father engaged the best physician, and my life was saved. But not my womb, Anna. They gave me poppy at first for the pain, and then I think to keep me quiet. And I might still be wandering, lost in those empty dreams, if it were not for Michael.'

And so I learned that Michael Mompellion was not, as I had always thought, the scion of a distinguished clerical family. His father had been a cleric, but a curate merely. Michael was but a small boy at the outbreak of the civil war. His father, instead of leading people to their prayers, had led them to war on behalf of the Parliament. At first his troop did well, but after the King escaped, the war went ill for him. The Cavaliers routed the forces in his parish and plundered his own dwelling. Michael's father was mortally wounded.

As a result, the family was destitute, and Michael had to be sent into a situation where he could be provided for. He was placed into service with the steward of Elinor's family estate. His childhood learning came at the elbow of the farrier, the gamekeeper and the tenant farmers. He grew up ploughing ground, breaking colts and shoeing mares, learning every detail of the estate's complexity.

'Before long, he was offering suggestions for its better management. His intelligence caught the attention of my father, who undertook Michael's education. He went to the best of schools, where he excelled, and then to Cambridge. When he came home, he found me, frail from my long illness. They would carry me out to the garden each day, and I would sit there, lost in grief and remorse. Michael offered me his friendship, Anna. And, later, his love.'

She was smiling slightly now. 'He brought the brightness back into my dim world. He understood suffering, having felt it in his own life. He taught me how futile it is to wallow in regret for that which cannot be changed and how atonement might be made for the gravest sins. Even mine.'

Gradually, with his encouragement, she regained some physical strength. Mental peace followed more slowly. 'At first, I borrowed his brightness and used it to see my way, and then, gradually, the light in my own mind rekindled itself.' They were wed soon after he took Orders. 'To the world at large, it seemed that I stooped to marry him,' she said. 'But the sacrifice in the match was all on the side of my dear Michael. More sacrifice than anyone could imagine.'

We sat for a while, staring into the fire, until a log suddenly shifted and sent a scatter of sparks onto the earth floor. Elinor stood up then, and smoothed her pinafore. 'And now, my dear Anna, now that you know everything, will you still work with me?'

I was too stunned by all I had heard to say anything, so I simply rose from my stool, grasped her hands, and kissed them. How little we know, I thought, of the people we live amongst. Many things about the rector now seemed clearer to me—his physical strength, his easiness with all trades and classes of people. So, too, did Elinor's kindness and her unwillingness to judge the faults in others.

Elinor embraced me, and I felt certain at that moment I would do anything for this woman, anything she asked of me. 'Good,' she said, drawing away, 'for there is much to do. Look at this.' She reached into the pocket of her pinafore and pulled out a folded parchment. 'I have made a list of all who have succumbed so far to the Plague and have laid it down upon a map of the dwellings in this place. From this I believe we can grasp how this pestilence spreads, and to whom.'

There it was, our Plague-scoured village, with the names of all its three hundred and three score sorry souls written on the map. Under the names of near fifty, Elinor had drawn a black line.

'Look at the victims. What is the first thing you notice?' I stared at the map dumbly. 'Can you not see? The Plague does not distinguish between man and woman. But it *does* make a distinction—it selects the young over the old. Almost half of the dead here were not yet sixteen years of age. The rest are persons in their prime. None, as yet, have been silver-hairs. Why, Anna? Why? Here is what I think. I think the old have lived long because they are good fighters of sickness, veterans in the war against disease. So, what must we do? We must arm the children, make them stronger. We have been trying, in vain, to cure the sick. Of all those who have the Plague, only one— old Margaret Blackwell—has lasted more than a week with it.'

Margaret, the cooper Blackwell's wife, had sickened at the same time as the Sydells, and though she still ailed, it did seem she was destined to live. Some doubted that she had Plague at all. But I had seen the swelling in her groin and tended her when it burst. Margaret might be our first survivor.

'What we must do,' Elinor continued, 'here in this sorry little cottage, is find all the herbs of a strength-giving virtue and combine them in a tonic to fortify the healthy.'

And so for the rest of that day, we pored through the books that Elinor had carried from the rectory, looking first for the names of plants said to be strengthening for any of the many body parts the Plague seemed to attack. It was tedious going, for the books were in Latin or Greek, which Elinor had to translate for me. Eventually, we discovered that the best of them was a volume by one Avicenna, a Mussulman doctor who, many years since, had set down all his learning in a vast canon. When we had the names of the plants, we went through the herb bunches, trying to match the descriptions in the books with the drying leaves and roots before us. By afternoon, we had assembled the weapons for our armoury. Nettle for the blood, starwort and violet leaves for the lungs, silverweed to cool a fever, cress for the stomach, dandelion for the liver and vervain for the throat. We gathered all the bunches we could carry into a sack to take to the rectory kitchen.

I was about to extinguish the fire in the grate when Elinor reached out and stayed my hand. 'What about these, Anna?' She held out the poppies. 'What shall we do with them?'

'Surely, we need these for the succour of the afflicted,' I said, though my thoughts sped to my own needs rather than those of the dying.

'The Gowdies were sensible of the risk posed by this thing, Anna.

They have enough here to relieve only a handful of grave cases. How should we choose who should suffer and who should be soothed?'

Without speaking, I reached for the bunch. I made to throw it on the fire, but did not have the will to open my hand. It held my only chance of exit from our village and its agonies. But then I saw that this was not true. There was our work. I had found that it was possible to lose myself in it. From this study might come much good. But surely I could not attempt it without clarity of mind. I grasped the bunch then and flung it on the fire. The pods hissed, then burst, their showers of tiny seeds falling invisible among the ashes.

7

As we approached the rectory, we saw Michael Mompellion in the churchyard, his coat off, the sleeves of his white shirt rolled up, his hair damp from sweat. He was digging graves. Three long holes lay open around him, and he was at work on the fourth.

Elinor hurried to him, reaching up to wipe his brow. He waved away her hand. His face was grey with exhaustion. She begged him to stop and rest, but he shook his head. 'I cannot stop. We need six graves this day, one of them for poor Jon Millstone.' Our aged sexton had died that morning. The rector had found him, sprawled half in, half out of the grave he had been digging. 'His heart gave out. He was too old for the labour that of late has been laid upon him.'

Looking at Mr Mompellion I worried that he, too, might drop. He had not slept the previous night but gone from one deathbed to the next. His pledge that none should die alone had become a heavy burden. It was clear he could not survive if now he attempted the sexton's work as well.

'Sir, this is not seemly work for you,' I said. 'Let me fetch one of the men from the Miner's Tavern to do it.'

'And who will come, Anna? The miners are ill set trying to pull ore enough from their claims to keep their mines from being nicked. The farmers are become too few to gather in the grain or milk their kine. How can I lay this work upon them?'

And so he worked on, until the light failed. And then he sent word to the various houses that they might bring their dead for burial. It was a sorry procession. No one troubled with coffins; families simply carried or dragged their loved ones to their graves. Mr Mompellion prayed over each one by candlelight and then helped in piling the soil back into the graves. While he toiled in the churchyard, pleas came from two more families that he attend them in their extremity. When he came in, Elinor carried the heated water for his toilet and fetched him fresh linens while I prepared a nourishing meal. He ate quickly and then put on his coat and rode off to keep his word.

'He cannot go on like this,' I said as the sound of hoofbeats faded.

'I know it,' Elinor replied. 'His body is strong, but I fear the strength of his will far exceeds it. It can drive him to do what any normal man cannot do, for better and for worse. Believe me, I have seen this.'

THE RECTOR GOT little sleep that night, and the next day brought no respite. In the morning I went with him to the Merrill farm, where Jakob lay dying. Brand, who had lived with the Merrills since his return with Maggie Cantwell, had taken Seth to the sheepfold, to do some necessary chores but also to get the little boy out of sight of his father's agony. Charity had fallen asleep on her pallet in the corner. As I patted out oatcakes for the children's supper, the rector spoke with Jakob Merrill, asking him gently if there was aught he wished to say before he became too ill to think clearly.

Merrill's face was florid with fever and he got each breath by terrible effort. 'Rector Mompellion, I know it is unseemly to fear death, but I do fear it. I fear it, for my children's sake. I don't want Charity married off hastily as her mother was to me . . . And little Seth . . . I would not see him in the poorhouse, but who will care for him here? Charity is a capable girl, but a ten-year-old cannot be expected to raise a brother and run a farm . . .'

Mr Mompellion laid his hand tenderly upon Jakob Merrill's face. 'Hush now, for I hear your concerns. But do you not see that God has already made provision for your children? He sent young Brand to you, and you took him into your home in his need. Do you not see God's hand at work there? I do, Jakob. For now, in *your* need, Brand is here for you: a good young man who has shown much character and has no place of his own in the world. Make him part of your family, Jakob, so that he might stay on here as he is, and so you will give to Charity and Seth an older brother to care for them.'

Jakob Merrill's hand tightened on the rector's, and his brow unknotted. He asked the rector then to help him to make a last will to bind such an arrangement, and the rector pulled out the parchment he always carried upon his person, as he often was asked to write wills these days. It took much time, for Jakob Merrill was failing fast and had difficulty marshalling his thoughts, but the rector's patience seemed limitless. He called me over to witness Jakob Merrill put his mark: a faint and wobbly cross. It was only when I took up the parchment to blot it and set it away that I saw the telltales of the rector's exhausted mind.

'In the name of God, amen. I'—here Mr Mompellion, in a moment of mental darkness, had written his own name instead of Jakob Merrill's and then had scored it out before inscribing the name of the farmer—'Jakob Merrill in the county of Derby, yeoman, on this'—here the rector's mind had failed him again, for he had left the date blank, probably because he wasn't able to recall it—'being sick and weak but in good memory, do make this my last Will and Testament. I give all my estate, house, land, goods and chattels to my son Seth, my daughter Charity, and to Brand Rigney, formerly servant of Bradford Hall, whom I do assign as my heir equally with mine own natural children in the hope that he will dwell with them as a brother and be guardian over them.'

I did not say anything to the rector about the missing date, for it was not for me to be reading Jakob Merrill's private will. As I set the document in the tin box that Merrill had pointed to, I saw that Charity was stirring in her corner. So I warmed the child some caudle, instructed her how to complete the making of the stew I had begun, and set out with the rector.

Elinor met us, her face creased with concern. Two more bodies awaited their graves. Mr Mompellion sighed, shrugged off his coat and went straight to the churchyard.

I let go of my pride then, and took my courage into my hands instead. Without telling Elinor what I proposed, I trudged out to my father's croft, hoping to find him sober. Happily, Aphra and her children remained in health, although, as always, the little ones looked thin, and I noticed that Steven, their eldest boy, had an angry welt across his cheek. I did not need to ask how it had come there.

I carried some of the herbs we had prepared and showed Aphra how to make them up into the tonic that Elinor and I had devised. My father, who had not yet risen from his pallet, stirred himself as we talked and rose, cursing his aching head.

Speaking with a respectful deference I did not feel, I explained the plight at the rectory, and beseeched his help. As I had expected, he cursed and said he had more than enough work to lay his hand to, and that it would do my 'prating priest' a power of good to get his white hands dirty. So I offered him his choice of my lambs for that Sunday's dinner and another at the new moon. These were generous terms, and though my father cursed and haggled, he and I eventually came to an agreement. And so I bought Mr Mompellion a respite from the graveyard.

THE WEEKS OF THAT COLD season wore me to a wraith. There were demands upon me every minute. I snatched at sleep as I could, at the bedside of the dying or upon a stool in the rectory kitchen. Yuletide passed and we barely marked it. At Shrovetide, I delivered Kate Talbot a healthy baby girl, and I hoped it might ease her grief over the loss of her husband. A week later, I midwifed Lottie Mowbray, a poor and simple woman who delivered her baby with the least complaint or difficulty I had yet encountered.

Every day we had occasion to bless the Earl of Chatsworth, who continued to provision us as he had pledged to do. Every day, the carters came with their loads to the Boundary Stone, or to the little spring we had come to call Mompellion's Well. People like Kate Talbot, who had lived by her husband's skilled work, or Lottie and her husband, Tom, who struggled to eke an existence even in good times, would have starved without the earl's provisioning. But from the Bradfords, safe in their Oxfordshire haven, from whom we might have expected to receive some token of concern, we had neither alms nor kindly word.

At the rectory, the kitchen had begun to look like an alchemist's den. Chopped leaves bled green onto my well-scrubbed table, turning the wood a grassy colour. Elinor wore her eyes red trying to glean more from diverse books. But chiefly we learned by doing, trying one way and then another to extract a plant's virtues. Some leaves we seeped in oil, some in spirit, some in water, to see which medium would yield the best results. With boiling water and our store of dried herbs, we made teas. Some we evaporated until they were potent decoctions; when they were too bitter we dribbled honey to turn them into syrups. Then I chopped again, bundles of roots wrested out of the frosty ground. When I judged the plant had given up its virtue I plunged my hands into the silky pulp and kneaded in a piece of beeswax until I had a drawing salve to smooth on angry Plague sores. We saw our work as having two natures: the one, to ease the suffering of the afflicted, and the other, more important but less certain in its outcome, to bolster up the defences of the well.

Elinor and I distributed our preparations, but we knew it might be many weeks before we could hope to see some abatement in the death roll. As the days lengthened, we spent much time at the Gowdies', trying to understand the layout of the physic garden and what was sown there, studying the packets of saved seeds, readying the soil to assure the continued supply of our strengthening herbs.

Only on Sunday did we cease from the constant round of gathering and gardening, making and visiting. And it was on Sunday, in church, that our failure to arrest the Plague's ravages was apparent in the emptying pews and missing faces. There were also, I should say, some few new faces. For Mr Stanley had commenced to attend Mr Mompellion's services ever since the Sunday Oath, and now the Billings family and some other Nonconformists had come as well. They did not join in all the hymns, nor did they follow the words of the Book of Common Prayer, but that they gathered with us at all was a wonder, and I was not the only one who seemed glad of it.

It was on the first Sunday in March that Mr Mompellion closed the church. He stood in the pulpit that morning, his knuckles white on the oak, straining to support himself. Elinor had insisted that I share her pew, since I was, she said, now a part of the rectory family. So I was close enough to see the exhausted tremor in his body and the lines etched in his face as he struggled to command his voice.

'My dear friends,' he said. 'God has tried us sorely these months. You have met His test with courage, and you will be rewarded for it. I had dared to hope, we all had hoped, that the test would not be so long nor so hard. But who can presume to read the mind of God? Who can understand the intricacy of His great design?'

He paused and looked down, trying to gather his strength. 'My dear friends, God sets us a new test, perhaps the hardest we have yet faced. For soon the weather here will warm, and this Plague—we know from past accounts—thrives upon warmth. We can pray that it has spent its fury here, but we cannot count upon it. My beloved friends, worse times may be coming to us.'

There were moans as he spoke. Someone started weeping. As he said he must close the church, Mr Mompellion wept, too, his exhaustion making his tears invincible. 'Do not despair!' he said, struggling to smile. 'For a church is not a building, merely! We shall have our church, but in the midst of God's own creation. We will meet and pray together under the ceiling of Heaven, in Cucklett Delf. In the Delf, friends, we may stand at a safe distance from one another, so that the ill do not infect the well.'

His face became more haggard as he came to the hardest part of his message. 'Beloved, as well as our church, we must close our churchyard, for it has become impossible to bury our dead in a timely way, and with the coming of the warm weather, what is now unseemly will become unsafe. Beloved, we must shoulder the grim task of burying our own dead in whatever near ground we can . . .'

There were howls now and terrified shouts of 'No!'

He raised his hands, calling for quiet. 'Beloved, I know you fear that God will not find those who are laid down to rest outside of hallowed ground. But I say to you, you have hallowed all the ground of this village by your sacrifice in this place! God *will* find you!'

The strain was too much for him then. He lowered his hands to grasp the pulpit railing but missed his grip. There was no more strength left in him. He slid to the floor in a faint.

Elinor and I hastened to him, as the congregation erupted in cries and weeping. Brand rushed to Mr Mompellion's aid, and he supported the dazed rector down the steps of the pulpit and towards the church door.

With Brand's help Michael Mompellion staggered to the rectory. Inside the house, we saw that we would not easily get him up the stairs, so Elinor and I ran up to the bedchamber and brought down some quilts to make a pallet in the parlour. After Brand had helped him down upon it, the rector rolled over and gave himself up, at last, to the sleep of the exhausted.

THE NEXT AFTERNOON he roused himself to attend two deathbeds, but Elinor and I conspired to keep from him another piece of news that bore more nearly on the living. With so much death around us, it was hard to give any mind to the future. But there was one child's future that had been weighing on my thoughts, that of a nine-year-old girl named Merry Wickford.

George and Cleath Wickford, a young Quaker couple with three children, had settled in an abandoned croft on the outskirts of the village some five years earlier after their queer faith had caused them to be driven from their tenant farm in the lowlands. They lived very poor till one summer night almost a year since. George Wickford, up late and pacing because he could not sleep for worry, saw a great burning drake streaking across the heavens. The lore in these parts is that a burning drake in the night sky marks out the lie of a lead seam below, so Wickford did not even wait till dawn to hie himself to where he thought the drake's path had passed across the moors. By morning he had dug out his cross in the turf to mark his claim and had cut his seven timbers for the stowe. The law holds that any man might claim himself a lead mine just so, no matter whose is the land it lies upon. He has nine weeks then to show the Barmester a dish of ore, and after, none may take his mine from him while he can keep it yielding.

George Wickford and his Cleath and their three young ones had delved tirelessly at the claim they named Burning Drake. The other miners laughed at him, for there was nothing in the lay of the land to give sign of lead beneath. But Wickford had the last laugh, for well within the Barmester's nine weeks he had his required dish of lead— and plenty more. What he had claimed turned out to be a pipe vein: a rich, mineral-lined cavern left behind from some long-ago underground stream. Wickford was considered a fellow blessed by fate.

That was before the Plague struck. George Wickford had been among the first felled by the disease. Then it took his elder son, a lad of twelve years. Cleath and her two younger children had struggled on at the delvings, but then the boy sickened and the mother failed to pull the required dish of ore from her mine in three weeks. David Burton, a neighbouring miner, placed the first nick upon the spindle of her stowe. There was talk of the rights and wrongs of this in the village, and more talk at the end of the sixth week, when David Burton placed his second nick on the day Cleath Wickford laid her other son into his grave. They said the shock of it hastened her own death, for the Plague took her faster than we had seen it dispatch any person. She buried her boy in the morning, and by nightfall she was dead, her corpse covered in the rosy rings of Plague tokens.

That left only the girl, the child whose name, Merry, now seemed a cruel joke. She was left in dreadful circumstances, for George Wickford had little but the mine, and young Merry seemed set to lose it in a sennight if someone did not bring out a dish of lead for her. I badgered every miner I knew, asking if one of them wouldn't do this kindness for an orphan. But the men felt that their loyalty had to lie with David Burton, who was one of their own. And so the end of the ninth week drew closer and finally just one more day stood between Merry and a bleak future in a poorhouse.

I suppose I should have known better than to raise this case with Elinor. Or say, rather, that I should not have been surprised by the proposal that followed. 'You know about the mines, Anna. You and I together shall get this dish out for the child.'

This suggestion landed on my ears even more unwelcome than her proposal that I midwife Mary Daniel. I had been afraid of the mines long before they claimed my Sam. I am not a creature for dim, slimy, airless places. But Elinor had that determined look upon her face that I now recognised too well. And I knew we were headed to the Wickford mine whether I would or no.

We set off early, for the mine was a long walk from the village. I heard Elinor speaking to Mr Mompellion in the library, telling him that we were going out in search of herbs. As she came from the room, I noticed that her skin was flushed. She saw me gazing at her, and her hand fluttered to her throat.

'Well, and so we shall, Anna, take satchels to gather likely plants on our way. For you know very well,' she added, 'that if he winds our true enterprise this day, he will insist on trying to do the labour himself, which would likely be the finish of him.'

We made our way first to the Wickford croft to tell the child Merry what we proposed. As we climbed the muddy track to her dwelling, she flew out of her door, her little face lit with joy, and it struck me what an odd time we now lived in, that a child of such tender years should be left all alone. Somehow, she was managing to thrive. She was a glowing child, even now, pink-cheeked and dimpled, with a tumble of dark curls that bounced as she skipped around us. On the table inside the croft I saw the remains of that morning's breakfast: a pipkin of lard, an eggshell, from which she'd sucked the contents raw, and an onion, with bites out of it that she'd eaten like an apple. Uncouth, perhaps, but sustaining.

As we entered the tiny, earth-floored croft, she made haste to clear the table and asked us, most politely, to sit. I felt a stab that I had not made more of an effort to know her parents. They must have been fine people to impart such manners to their child.

Elinor's thoughts had been tending along a similar vein. 'Your mother would be very proud of you, Merry, to see how bravely and how well you are managing here.'

'Think thou so?' she said earnestly. 'I thank thee for saying it. I feel that Mother watches me still, and Father, and my brothers, too, and my life here feels less lonely for it. I thank ye both for visiting me, for it is hard for me to face the loss of my family's mine alone.'

'We intend that you will not have to face any such thing,' I blurted, suddenly glad that Elinor had convinced me to do this.

Merry's gratitude turned to delight as we explained that we had not come to visit, merely, but to try to save her mine. Plucky little person, she then insisted on coming to do her share.

'You may help us, Merry,' I said, 'as you helped your parents. You shall have much to do in sorting the bouse and washing the ore. We will rely on you to send word down to us when we have achieved a dish. And mind, it must be a good dish, for David Burton will hold the Barmester to an exact measure.' Merry nodded, knowing well the dimensions of the Barmester's great dish. But Elinor looked puzzled, having never seen the thing, so I explained how it was sized to hold as much ore as an average man is capable to lift up off the ground.

The child looked troubled still, protesting that she had been down in the mine before and wished to guide us. We gently told her that we needed her above, in case aught went awry and we did not return to the surface by afternoon. Then, and only then, Elinor cautioned, was she to run to the rectory and tell Mr Mompellion what we were about.

When Sam died I had wrapped his tools in a piece of oiled cloth and set them away, meaning one day to give them to a needy miner. At the time the Wickfords found their seam, my mind was so much upon my own trials that I had forgot all about my intentions. Now, unwrapping the tools, I felt their heft in my hands. I thought of the hard muscles of Sam's huge arms and wondered how I would wield these things. From amongst the tools I picked out the three essentials of the lead miner: straight pick, short hammer and wedge.

Merry's family, in their thrift, had used a single tool, its tine balanced by a hammer end, and used it as either pick or sledge. This tool, lighter but less effective, would be what Elinor would work with. I asked Merry to look out the leathers her father and brother had worn against the mine's wet. Elinor was slight enough to fit into the breeches and jerkin that the elder boy had worn. I took George Wickford's leathers and, with a pair of wool-shears, cut about a third of the length off the legs to fit my stature. Then I plunged a few holes in the waist and ran a rope through to keep the trews upon me. The jerkin flapped loose, but to that I paid no mind. We took the hats, also: sturdy leather hats with ample brims to hold the tallow candles that would light our way through the dark.

And so we set off to the adit, with Merry leading the way. My feet felt like lead as I trudged along, imagining the day ahead of us. Just the fear of being in an airless place made me gasp as if I were already down the mine rather than in the open, heather-scented air.

Wickford had made his shaft well—wedging great slabs of grey limestone carefully into the walls and hewing sturdy boughs to make sound stemples. But the shaft ran with damp, as most mines do, and mosses and ferns bloomed in the crevices. I could not see how deep the shaft sank, but I knew that the longer I lingered there, the harder it would be to plunge ahead, and so I slung myself over and felt for the first stemple.

As it happened, the shaft was about six fathoms deep, and there it veered off from the eye above. Wickford had wrought out six or seven yards sideways before the shaft sank downwards once again so the bucket of bouse could be wound up in easier stages to reach daylight. Once away from the eye, the darkness was complete, so I stopped there to light my candle, dribbling tallow into the brim of my hat to fix it in place. The light leapt and trembled as I inched on and down. Merry had said I would find the cave mouth at the base of this second shaft, and so it was. The floor sloped sharply and was slick with mud, and in minutes I had lost my footing and landed hard. The air was already still and stale, just a few feet in from the shaft, and as I sat there in the cold muck I could feel the sweat break out upon me, and began to gasp in rapid, shallow breaths as I felt blackness closing in on me. But Elinor was behind me now and I felt her hand easing me up and onwards.

'It is all right, Anna,' she whispered. 'You *can* breathe. There *is* air. You must not let your fears be your master.' In a few moments my head cleared and I struggled to my feet and was able to go on. And so we inched and slithered, sometimes on two feet but stooped, other places dropping to hands and knees, and sometimes skidding on our bellies.

The flickering light showed walls that had been picked and cleft, and we followed the line of the delvings. When we got to the last pick-stroke, Elinor and I unslung our tools and set to work, and the effort of landing the blows drove my fears from my mind. I have worked hard all my life, but this labour—this tearing of rock from rock—was the hardest thing I had ever set my hand to. Within a half-hour, my arms were trembling. For Elinor it must have been much worse. I could see how soon the strain of it began to cost her, as she paused longer and longer between each stroke. At one point, she struck her thumb with the hammer and cried out. She tied a bit of rag round the wound and went back to her toil. She swung slowly on, her mud-streaked face set hard as the stone.

For myself, the greatest effort was to manage my terrors. I tried to concentrate only on the work and not on the walls of slimy darkness, nor on the choke-damp air, nor on the weight of the soil and rock piled heavy above me. Each time the pick landed I felt the jarring all through my bones. The cold numbed my fingers so that instead of gaining skill with practice, my hands fumbled more and more. As the hours passed I felt like weeping with pain and frustration, for as hard as we plied the picks, the pile of bouse beside us grew only by inches.

It was Elinor who voiced it before I had heart to do so. For all her effort, she had managed to loose a pitiful few pieces of stone. She sat back on her heels and let the pick clang heavily on the rock beside her. 'At this rate, we will not draw a dish by day's end,' she whispered.

'I know it,' I said, flexing my numb fingers. 'We were fools to think we could learn skills in a day that strong men toil for years to master.'

'I cannot face the child,' Elinor said. 'I cannot bear to see the disappointment in her.'

I said nothing and gathered my tools. Silently, we made our way back through the tunnel. My arms were so tired I could barely clutch the stemples, and as I gulped gratefully at the cool air, I told myself that in our exhausted state we would never have succeeded, even if I had confided to Elinor what more I knew.

It was Merry's face that undid me. Her look was so hopeful as we climbed out of the tunnel. And then, when she saw the miserable amount of bouse we brought up, her bright smile disappeared and her lip trembled. Yet she did not cry, but schooled her small voice and thanked us for our efforts. My cowardice shamed me.

'There is one other way to get the ore out,' I blurted. 'Sam used it when his seam vanished into toadstone. But it cost him his life in the end.' I told Elinor all I had heard of the way fire and water could be harnessed to do the work of many miners' hands.

Elinor leaned back against the stowes. 'Anna, these days, all our lives hang by a thread. If we are spared today, we may be felled by Plague on the morrow. I say we should take this risk . . . if you are willing.'

Merry looked concerned. Miners' children are quick to learn what miners fear. And there are so many fears that go with fire-setting. The smoke, added to the choke-damp, can steal the last breathable air out of the cavern. The cracking can free hidden water, letting in a torrent that floods the mine. Or, as happened with my Sam, the very bones and sinews of the Earth can break under the strain, and the ground above can come piling down to bury you.

I gathered the greenwood as fast as I could. Dry tinder was more difficult to come by, since it had lately rained, so Merry ran back to her croft to fetch kindling from her hearth. When we climbed back down the shaft, Merry let down a leather bucket of stream water.

I ran my hands then along the rockface, feeling for cracks and working with the wedge to widen them. When I had a large enough line in the rock, I showed Elinor how to hammer the greenwood boughs deep into every crevice. Then I laid the dry tinder for the fire all along the rockface. 'You must go back above now,' I said then to Elinor. 'I'll tug on the rope to summon you if we have any success.'

'Oh, no, Anna. I'll not leave you down here alone,' she said.

I spoke sharply. 'Elinor! We don't have time for this. Do you not have the wit to see that if this goes awry you'll do me more good outside, digging, than in here, smothering companionably?'

My words did their work. 'As you say,' she replied and began the long crawl out. I worked quickly to light the wood before it became too damp to catch, but my hands shook.

I'd rather die from Plague, I thought, than end my life down here in the dark. But then the fire flared, and it was dark no longer. The greenwood began to heat. The sap hissed, and then came the first report as the expanding pressure cracked a rock. It was so hard to wait, as the smoke filled the air and choked me. I held a wet rag over my mouth and crouched, trembling, forcing myself not to make the next move before the time was ripe. If the rock was not sufficiently heated, the entire effort would be wasted and our day's work lost. Finally, as my chest began to feel as if it would explode, I blindly reached for the bucket. I hurled icy water against hot rock. There was a sizzle, and steam, and a sound like a dozen muskets firing. And then the sheets of ore began to fall.

I stumbled to get out of the path of it, blinded by the smoke and coughing so that I thought my throat would tear. A shard struck me on the shoulder and then a heavier slab landed on my back, slapping me face down into the mud. I writhed to get out from under it, pushing myself up on forearms weak from the morning's delving.

Stop now! I prayed. *Oh, please, stop!* But the cracking did not stop, and with each crack came a new rain of rock. My arms flailed wildly, my fingers scrabbling on the hard stone. But the load pressed and pressed and pinned me still at last.

And so, I thought, it ends here after all. Dead in the dark like Sam. I felt the weight of the hillside shifting as rock slid against rock and earth oozed into every newly opened crevice. Wet mud pressed into my mouth. Blood hammered in my ears, louder than the crash of rock.

And then an odd thing. The panic drained away from me, and my mind filled with images of my boys, vivid as in life. I stopped fighting for movement and exhaled the breath I had been hoarding. There was no air now to give me another. I relaxed my cheek into the rocks that would be my cairn and my tombstone.

It's all right, after all. I can bear this ending. A dark rim formed round the picture of my boys, and I willed it back. Not yet. Let me see them a few moments more. But the blackness feathered inwards and their faces dimmed. With the darkness came blissful silence: a sudden stop to the beating of blood and the great roaring of rock.

I SUPPOSE that I would be dead if Elinor had gone back up the shaft as I had bidden her, and if Merry had not disobeyed the both of us. Elinor had crouched by a column of rock just a hundred yards from where I did the fire-setting. Merry had lowered herself to the cave entrance just off the shaft. Both of them, when they heard the great crashing, had rushed to save me. I came to myself still buried to my neck but with my face freed by their frantic scrabbling.

The silence that had closed in upon me had been real: the roaring *had* stopped, and with it the rock fall. As the smoke lessened, the three of us were able to see what had been done: my work had loosed a pile of the gleaming cubes of ore that would give Merry Wickford her dish of lead today, and many more days if she needed. Elinor and Merry heaved the rock off me, slab by slab, and with their help, I crawled painfully to the shaft and toiled my way to the surface.

I do not know how I stumbled back down to the village. I ached all over, and each step brought a fresh spasm. But we made what haste we could, racing against the fading light. Elinor supported me with one arm and with the other held the end of the sacking on which she and Merry dragged the ore. We went straight to the cottage of the Barmester, Alun Houghton.

If old Alun was shocked by the sight of us—mud-bedaubed, rock-grazed, smoke-blackened and sodden—he recovered himself quickly and executed his office, summoning David Burton and as many of the elected men of the Body of the Mine as could be gathered to the Miner's Tavern to bear witness. While the miners assembled, Elinor sent word to the rectory.

It was not very many moments before I heard the sound of Anteros's high-stepping hoofs. Elinor had set me down before Alun Houghton's hearth and was bathing my grazes with warmed water. She had not troubled with her own toilet, and so when the rector entered the cottage, she rose to greet him just as she was. She had lost her hat during my rescue, and she stood now bareheaded, her fine hair falling about her face in hard brown strands.

The rector stood, arrested, just inside the doorway. There was silence for a long moment, then he gave a great laugh and clapped his hands together. When he asked for a full account of our day's work, his voice brimmed with pride.

The rector accompanied us to the Miner's Tavern. I was relieved at it, for I knew not how Elinor Mompellion's reputation would weather this day's doings, falling as they did so far outside what is considered fit for a woman, much less a gentlewoman. But the men, scattered round the courtyard, stood up from their benches as they saw us. 'A cheer for the new miners!' called a voice, and almost to a man they gave us their huzzas. Only David Burton was silent. The Barmester hung up his great brass measuring dish—as long as a tall man's leg and as wide as a well-muscled thigh—and Merry came forward, struggling to drag the laden sack. The Barmester helped her up onto a table, so that she could reach the dish. Carefully, she piled up the ore until the dish was full, and at that, the company cheered again.

'Friends,' said Alun Houghton, 'young Merry Wickford retains the rights over Burning Drake vein. It is hers until her stowes be thrice nicked.' Then he stared round the room from under his impressive, bushy eyebrows. 'And think long and hard about cutting any nicks on this child's stowes, within our code tho' it may well be.'

That night I had to sleep by lying on my grazed face, since my back was abloom with a great bruise where the rock slab had caught me. Still, I slept better that night than I had since the nights of the poppy dreams. There had been so much futile effort expended since the coming of the Plague, so many lives that could not be saved and hurts that could not be healed. For one time, at least, in that hard season, I had the satisfaction of having done a thing that had come out right.

 8

In the days that followed, I tasted what life would be like if I survived to old age. For many days, my healing body ached at every move. To reach a crock on a high shelf was a vast effort; to draw a pail of water an agony. So I was uncommonly glad, one morning as I went out to battle with the well bucket, to mark my father approaching, for I could not think he would grudge me a hand. He was staggering, but not, this day, from drink. It was the weight of what he carried that unbalanced him—a large sack that clanked as he walked.

I gave him a good day and he raised his head and hailed me in turn. As he set down the sack, I heard the clang of metal plate. 'Eh, girl, and it *is* a good day, for Widow Brown has paid me in pewter for the graves of her man and boy. I suppose I should thank ye, for learning me the lesson that there's a profit in the hole-digging trade, these days.'

I did not know how to make an answer to that, and so I asked his help to draw water, which he did, though not without pausing to note that my bruised face 'looked worse than a cow pat'. When he hefted his sack and went on, I stood and stared after his retreating back, wondering what ill thing my good intentions had hatched.

All that week I began to notice that neighbours would break off their conversations when I drew near them, and gradually I became aware that they were speaking of my father, and sourly.

He had set himself up as gravedigger to the desperate. From those too ill or weak to bury their dead, he demanded a high fee. He would take whatever in the house or field had most value, be it a barrel of herring, a gravid sow or a brass candlestick. He ended every day in the Miner's Tavern, drinking until he could barely stagger home. When I suggested that he do this work, I had expected that he would take some pains about his person, so as not to expose Aphra and his children to the Plague seeds he might carry from the corpses. But day by day I saw him come and go in the same earth-crusted breeches, and I wondered that even he could be so uncaring.

When I encountered Aphra at the Boundary Stone, I begged her to insist that he take more care, but she laughed, saying that my father now was a good provider for the first time, and she was not about to scold him over it.

Though Mr Mompellion's strength had come back to him in some measure since his collapse in the church, he now knew he could not do the sexton's work as well as his own. So my father had no check on his increasing greed.

On Sundays, we gathered now at Cucklett Delf as the rector had bidden us. When I stood in the sloping basin with the rowan boughs arching above me, I saw the great wisdom in what he had wrought by moving us all there. For there we were not haunted by the missing faces. We placed ourselves so that some three yards separated each family group, believing this to be sufficient to avoid the passing of infection. The rector had chosen for his pulpit a massive rock of limestone. From there, he tried to find sweet words to salve our sorrows, and their music mingled with the tinkling of the nearby brook.

My father did not come to the Delf, not the first Sunday nor any following. In normal times he would have been paraded to the village green and set in the stocks for such behaviour. But none now had the strength or will to pursue such things. As the weeks passed his wickedness only grew. He had become so fond of his afternoons at the alepot that he let it be known that he would not bury anyone past noon. In his callousness, he would knock upon the doors of the ailing, saying if they wanted a grave he would dig it then and there or not at all. And so a person who yet lived would lie in his sickbed and listen to the rise and fall of my father's spud. I think that his heartless behaviour hastened more than one person into the ground.

And then he finally committed an act so vile that our diminished and exhausted population was spurred at last to action. Christopher Unwin, the last surviving son of a family that had numbered twelve before the Plague, had lain nine days in his sickbed, much longer than most survive when once afflicted. I had visited him several times, as had the Mompellions. We had begun to pray that he, like Margaret Blackwell, might live through it.

And then, one morning, just after I had carried in the brawn and oatcake for the Mompellions' breakfast, I found Randoll Daniel pacing in the kitchen garth. My first thought was that Mary or the babe had sickened, and my heart sank at it.

'No, by God's grace,' Randoll said, 'they are both well. It is my friend Christopher Unwin I am come about. He feels himself to be failing. He asked me to hasten here to fetch the rector.'

'Thank you, Randoll. I will tell Mr Mompellion.'

The rector had scarce begun his meal, and so I thought to save the news until he had done with it. But Elinor had heard voices in the garth, and summoned me to learn Randoll's business. I had no choice then but to tell it. The rector pushed his plate of uneaten food away, and rose wearily from the table. Elinor made to rise, too, but she looked even paler than usual that morning, so I suggested that I go with Mr Mompellion while she stayed behind to tend our herbals.

As we walked together to the Unwins' house, the rector asked me whom I had visited the previous day and how they fared. In the passing weeks, I had lost my shyness in his presence, and now could talk to him without reserve. He told me of those that he had seen, and gave a sigh. 'How strange it is, Anna. Yesterday I have filed in my mind as a good day. It was filled with mortal illness and grieving, yet it is a good day, for no one died upon it. We are brought to a sorry state, that we measure what is good by such a shortened yardstick.'

We had reached the Unwin gate. The family had prospered from its lead seam, and their house had grown, through well-built additions, into one of the finest in the village. The rector let himself in at the front door and called up to Christopher, where he lay alone in the room he had lately shared with his wife and infant son. The young man answered in a weak voice.

While I fetched a mug from the dresser to pour some cordials for the sick man, Mr Mompellion went on ahead of me to the upstairs bedchamber. When I entered a few moments later, the rector was standing at the window, staring out into the Unwins' field. When he turned, I saw that his brow was knotted and his scowl fierce.

'How long has he been at this?' he demanded of Christopher, who sat propped against a bolster, looking less grave than I had expected.

'Since shortly after sunup. I awoke to the sound of his spud.'

I coloured then, and walked to the window. As I had expected, my father was standing waist-deep in the half-dug pit. I felt sure then that it was my father's digging that had caused the young man to believe his state worsened, for he looked to me much improved. His expression was alert and his skin colour good, and I could see no signs of Plague upon him.

'I will go and speak with my father,' I said to the rector. 'I shall send him away directly, for I do not think the young master will have need of such services, on this or any other approaching day.'

'No, Anna. You stay here and attend to Mr Unwin. Leave me to deal with Josiah Bont.'

I did not protest, but felt much relieved. I was bathing Christopher Unwin's face with lavender water when the sounds of raised voices came ringing up from the field. My father was cursing Michael Mompellion in the foulest language, unwilling to hear that the young man was far from needing the grave he had dug. The rector was not standing mute, but answering my father in the kind of coarse language I had never heard from him.

My father bellowed that since he had laboured, he intended to be paid, 'Whether Unwin's arse feels the dirt this day or no.'

I went to the window then and saw him, his chest pushed out, almost touching the rector's chest, as they stood face to face at the lip of the grave. He made as if to head for the house—thinking, I expect, to claim his loot—but the rector put out a hand and seized him. My father tried to throw off the grip, and I saw the surprise register on his face when he found he wasn't able. His fist rose and Mr Mompellion waited just long enough for the whole force of my father's bulk to be committed to the punch, and at the last instant stepped deftly to the side. My father stumbled, and as his head went down, the rector landed a swift blow to the back of his neck, and shoved him, hard. For an instant my father teetered at the grave's edge, his hands flailing wildly. And then he toppled, landing with a wet slurp in the mud below. I saw the rector peering into the hole, probably assuring himself that my father wasn't badly hurt. As the rector turned towards the house, I backed away from the window, for I suspected that he would not want to know that this scene had a witness.

I went to the kitchen then to make a meal, for Christopher felt the stirrings of some appetite. When I returned, he ate like the healthy young man he soon would be, while the rector jested with him on how the two of them that morning had choused more than the Reaper.

THE NEXT DAY I rose just before dawn, ill rested, and went to the well to draw water. It was one of those rare days in early April when Nature lets us taste the coming spring. It was so mild that I lingered in the garth, breathing the soft scents of the slowly warming earth. The sky was beautiful, covered in a tumble of tufted clouds. As I watched, the rays of the rising sun lit the edge of each cloud, turning it silver. Then the light changed again, and the silvery grey turned deep rose-red. I thought absently about bringing the sheep into the fold before the gathering of the storm that this lovely sky foretold.

My reverie was broken by a bellowing. A figure from a nightmare hove into view. His skull was cleft across the crown, and his hair was matted into curtains of dried blood. He was covered in dirt and clay, naked save for the remnants of a winding sheet that trailed behind him. The figure cried out again, and it was my father's name he called. My first thought was that one of my father's graves had spewed forth a ghostly sleeper awakened for revenge. As the thought formed, I threw it off as impossible. And with that shred of sense came the knowledge that the figure in the torn shroud was Christopher Unwin.

My neighbours, those few gaunt survivors, had come out of their cottages in response to Christopher's cries. There was horror in their faces. I ran to him then and begged him to come inside where I could tend his hurts. 'Nay, Mistress, I will not, for what hurts me most is beyond your tending.' I tried to take his arm, but he threw me off, steadying himself, instead, against the gritstone wall.

'Your father tried to kill me in my sleep this night. I woke in my bed to see his spud bearing down upon me. And when I woke again,

I was in my grave! That spawn of Satan had laid me there, though I was yet quick as you are. Lucky for me, in his laziness he scattered just a crust of earth to hide me and not enough to smother me entire. Still, I had to scramble like a mole to get free. I tell you, it's him that will eat dirt this day and never see the light of morn again!'

'Aye!' yelled a voice. 'Aye! It's past time that villain was dealt with!' The crowd was thickening as yarn gathers on a spindle. Someone had brought out a cloak to throw round Christopher. 'I thank you,' he said, his voice issuing from soil- and blood-caked lips. 'That swine not only tried to rob me of my life—he stole the very clothes I lay in.'

I felt like stone as I stood and watched them, ten or twelve now, hurrying off in the direction of my father's croft. I did not move to warn him, or to fetch Mr Mompellion, or to do anything at all to save him. I stood there and all I could think of was the sting of his fist and the stink of his breath. I stood there until the mob turned up the hill and out of my sight. And then I went inside and prepared for the labours of my day.

THE STORM THAT HAD threatened at morning blew in by early afternoon. The snow came from the northeast, advancing across the far valley in columns of white outlined against the black clouds behind. I stood on the hill in the apple orchard, transfixed by the spectacle.

I was there when they came for me, a band of miners, led by Alun Houghton, marching up the hill through the trees as they had the night Sam died. They wanted me, he said, to bear witness at the Barmote Court to what I had seen at the Unwin house. 'And to speak, if you will, in defence of your father.'

'I do not wish to go, Barmester.' After Alan Houghton's gravelly voice, my words seemed weightless, carried away by the wind. 'There is nothing that I wish to say. Anything I have seen, others have seen also. Please do not ask this of me.'

But Houghton pressed me and would not be satisfied. So, as the snowy fury descended, I made my way with those men who would decide my father's fate in no less apt a place than the Miner's Tavern.

They gathered in the courtyard of the tavern. There were two long tables in the yard, and a gallery ran all around, one floor above. Some of the miners were up on the gallery, whether to take shelter from the snow or to keep a distance from their fellows I cannot say. When the Barmester's party entered, some six or seven drew close to the railing and peered down. The men at the tables huddled under their cloaks as the snow dropped upon us. Every expression was grim. I looked around for Aphra but did not find her, and wondered if she had been too cowed to come among these angry, sullen men. The snow seemed to muffle everything, even the booming voice of Alun Houghton, who had taken his place at the end of the larger table.

'Josiah Bont!'

My father, his hands bound in front of him, stood at the far end of the table, held fast by two miners. When he made no response to the Barmester, Henry Swope, the larger of the two miners, brought his hand down hard on the back of my father's head.

'Ye'll answer "Present" to t' Barmester!'

'Present,' said my father in a surly murmur.

'Josiah Bont, thou well knowest the crimes that have brought thee to this place. Thou art not a miner, and in normal times this court would have no dealings with such as thee. But we are all that is left of justice in this place, and justice we will do. Ye all assembled here must also know that attempted murder is beyond the scope of this Barmote Court. So we do not bring Josiah Bont here to answer to this. But the following we do ask him to answer:

'The first item: that on the third day of April in the Year of Our Lord 1666, thou art accused of entering the house of Christopher Unwin, miner, from whence thou didst take a silver ewer. What sayest thee?'

My father was silent, his head sunk on his chest. Swope roughly pulled my father's head up and hissed at him, 'Look 'e at yon Barmester, Joss Bont, and pronounce 'e aye or nay before I thump 'e.'

My father's voice was barely audible. 'Aye,' he said at last.

'The second item: that on the same day and from the same house thou art accused of taking a silver salt dish. What sayest thee?'

'Aye.'

'The third item: that on the same day and from the person of Christopher Unwin thou didst take one nightshirt of cambric. What sayest thee?'

Even my father seemed shamed by this last. His head dropped again, and his 'Aye' fell muffled into his breast.

'Josiah Bont, since thou dost own these crimes, we find thee guilty. Shall anyone speak for this man before I proclaim his penalty?'

Every eye turned to me then, where I stood by the wall to the right of Alun Houghton. Every eye, including my father's. His glare was hard and prideful at first. But as I gazed back at him in silence, the look changed to one of surprise, then confusion, and at last, as it came upon him that I would not speak, his whole face sagged. There was rage there, but also a sad understanding. I looked away, for that hint of his grief was more than I could bear. Oh, I knew I would pay for my silence. But I could not speak for him. Or, rather, would not.

There was a shuffling and mumbling as the men perceived that I remained mute. Alun Houghton raised a hand for silence.

'Josiah Bont, thou shouldst surely know that theft has ever been a sore matter to miners, who toil far from their dwellings and must leave their hard-got ore in places lonely and unwatched. And so our code has penalty enough to deter greedy hands. The court does hereby impose upon thee the age-old remedy: thou shalt be taken from here to the Unwin mine and impaled to its stowes by a knife through the hands.' Houghton shook his massive head. 'So there you have it,' he said, his voice no longer the formal boom of the Barmester but only that of a sad old man.

The light was fading as they led my father away. Later, I learned that he whimpered when he saw the blackened stowes rising from the snowy crust upon the moors, that he begged in vain for mercy and howled like a trapped animal when the dagger cleft his flesh.

The tradition is that once the knife is placed, the convicted man is left, unguarded. It is understood that before very long someone from his kin will come to free him. I believed that Aphra would do it.

That night, the snow turned to rain. By morning it was peeling the soil from the hillsides and filling the streams until they broke over their banks. All the next day, water landed on my windows as if hurled from a bucket that never emptied. To open the door was to admit the deluge; to step outside was to be drenched. So no one went anywhere except of dire need.

I believe my father died waiting for Aphra, expecting her until his last instant. Otherwise he surely would have taken the wolf's choice: torn his own hands, letting the blade slice through flesh and sinew to buy his liberty, and his life. But Aphra did not come. She could not. Three of her four children had sickened with Plague that day. Her youngest, Faith, a girl of three years, was the only one not stricken. And so she chose not to leave her children in that lonely croft while the rain soaked the thatch and the fire waned and they cried for comfort, not to make the long, soaking trek up to the moors to the man she blamed for bringing the infection upon them.

No one came near her all through that day or the next. I did not go, and for that I will for ever reproach myself. Because out of our negligence and her loneliness came much rage. Much rage and some madness—and a surfeit of grief. For Aphra, and for all of us.

THE RAIN EASED late on the second night, and by morning it had been replaced by a stiff wind. And so my father was three days dead before I learned what had become of him. Aphra appeared at my door that morning, earth clinging to her hands and falling from her smock. She carried her little girl, Faith, clutched to her waist.

'Tell me he is here, Anna,' she said, and at first I had no idea what she was speaking about. The expression on my face answered her question. She gave a great wail and dropped to the floor, beating her fists on the hearth. 'He's still there then! The Devil take you, Anna! You left him there to die!' The child, terrified, began wailing as well.

My bowels had turned to water at the implication of her words. In my heart, I hoped my father might have freed himself and just run off. It was the sort of thing he was capable of doing.

It was some time before I made enough sense out of her confused keenings to understand that her boys were all dead. She had buried them that morning. She had dug the grave big enough and laid them side by side, hand in hand. I thought that the last thing she need face after burying her boys was dealing with the matter of my father. If he were dead up there these three days, it would be a grisly business. I said I would send Brand or another of the young men up to the Unwin mine, but this suggestion only set her keening afresh.

'They all hate him! I'll not have them near him! You hate him, too. You needn't pretend otherwise. Just let me go and give him his due.'

In her anguished state, I could not gainsay her, so I resolved to go with her. But I made her leave the child with Mary Hadfield, so that the little one would be spared whatever we might find.

Alas, I didn't comprehend how great a horror, or perhaps I would have spared myself. The wild creatures had had ample time to do their work, so what was left on the stowes was more like a clumsily butchered beef than the mortal remains of a man.

Approaching that ruined body was one of the hardest things I have done in my life. I checked when I saw it and thought to turn back. But Aphra marched on. She walked straight up to the stowes and tugged at the dagger that held what was left of my father. It was driven hard into the wood. Only when she planted a boot on the upright and threw her weight against it did the knife slide free. She began to wield it on my father's hair, shearing off large locks and plunging them into her pocket. Then she tore off a piece of my father's jerkin to wrap the blade and tucked the dagger into her girdle.

We had brought neither pick nor shovel with us, and the ground up there was so hard, even after such a soaking, that I would have been ill set in any wise to dig a decent hole. Still, I dreaded carrying this remnant of a corpse any distance. I feared that Aphra would want to bury him near her boys. But she said she would rather lay him right there, at the Unwin mine, so that Christopher Unwin would ever be reminded of the cost of his justice. So I spent the next hour gathering stones to raise a cairn. When it was high enough, Aphra searched for sticks, then shredded pieces from the hem of her placket to bind them. I thought she meant to form a cross, but when she was done I saw that she had fashioned a figure that looked like a manikin. This she laid atop the cairn. I commenced to say the Lord's Prayer, and I thought she was saying it with me in a low murmur. But when I said amen, her muttering continued, and the sign she made at the end of it did not resemble the sign of the cross.

THAT AFTERNOON, I cried for my father. I had gone into the rectory kitchen to make a dish of vervain tea for Elinor, and as I stood there, waiting for the water to boil, the tears welled up and flowed uncontrollably. The trouble with weeping was that once begun it became almost impossible to stop. For I had not had sufficient space to mourn for my boys, or for the ruin of the life I had imagined for myself, mothering them both to manhood.

My face was wet and my shoulders shaking, but I tried to make the tea anyway. I lifted the kettle from the hob and stood, frozen, unable to remember what I needed next to do. I was standing there still when Elinor came. She took the kettle from my hand, sat me down, stroked my hair and held me. As my sobs subsided, she began to whisper.

'Tell me,' said Elinor, and so I did. The whole of it. All his brutalities; all the neglect and ill-use of my lost and lonely childhood.

Somehow, the telling of all this rinsed my mind clean and left me able to think clearly once more. By gathering my own feelings so, I was able to fashion a scale on which I could weigh my father's nature and find a balance between my disgust for him and an understanding of him; my guilt in the matter of his death against the debt he owed me for the manner of my life. At the finish of it, I felt free of him.

Elinor sat quietly for a time. 'I always wondered,' she said at last, 'why your father bound himself by the Sunday Oath. For it seemed to me that he was the type of man who would flee and spare himself.'

'I believe he felt himself protected,' I said. I told her of Aphra's strange behaviour during the laying of my father's corpse to rest. 'Aphra has ever been superstitious. I believe she convinced my father

245

that she had obtained charms or somesuch to preserve them from the Plague's infections.'

'If that is so,' she said, 'they are not alone in embracing such beliefs.' She went to her whisket and brought out a piece of stained, frayed cloth. She showed it to me, then let it flutter onto the hearth and watched the fabric burn. The marks on the cloth were clumsy, as if the hand that had made them was not used to forming letters. As best I could make it out before the flame tongued them black, the words were a nonsense foursome: AAB, ILLA, HYRS, GIBELLA.

'I had this from Margaret Livesedge, who lost her baby daughter yesterday. A "witch" gave it her. The ghost, she said, of Anys Gowdie. The ghost told her the words were Chaldee—a powerful spell from sorcerers who worshipped Satan at each full moon. She had her twine the cloth round the child's neck where the Plague sore was. As the moon waned, the Plague sore was supposed to diminish.'

I told her then of finding Kate Talbot's ABRACADABRA on that snowy day when we'd met each other unexpectedly at the Gowdie cottage.

'We must tell Mr Mompellion of these things,' she said. 'He must warn people not to fall into these superstitions.'

The rector was out, writing a will for the miner Richard Sopes, but presently we heard Anteros blowing and snorting in the stableyard. Elinor went to greet him while I prepared some broth and oatcake, and when I carried it into the library, the two of them were deep in conference. Elinor turned to me.

'Mr Mompellion, too, has come upon these talismans. It seems the madness is spreading as fast as the disease amongst us.'

'Indeed,' he said, 'I am come back here to fetch one of you to the Mowbray croft, for the infant there needs your herb-knowledge.'

'Then it isn't Plague, Rector?' I asked.

'No, no; it is not the Plague, not yet at least. I found the babe's fool parents out in the Riley field, passing the poor naked child back and forth through the bramble hedge. By the time I got up to them his tender little body was all scratched, with the fools saying that they've protected him so from Plague seeds.' He sighed. 'They told me they'd had the instructions from the ghost of Anys Gowdie. I wrapped the child in my cloak and made them carry him home, where I said I would send one of you directly with a salve for his scrapes.'

I told Elinor that I would go, since I needed some useful occupation to divert my mind. I made the salve as quickly as I could. The bramble leaf itself has that in it to soothe its own thorns' pricks, so I compounded some with silverweed, comfrey and mint and bound the result with almond oil. It was a sweet-smelling ointment, and its scent lingered on my hands. But the stench as I neared the door of the Mowbray croft drove the fragrance from my nose.

Lottie Mowbray was holding the baby aloft and steering the thin stream of his piss into a cooking pot that had just been lifted off the fire. They clearly had been boiling this pot of piss for some time, for the stink of it filled the croft. She looked up blankly as I entered.

'Lottie Mowbray, what new foolishness is this?' I demanded, lifting the whimpering infant from her hands. This was the boy I had midwifed just after Shrovetide and I had wondered, even then, how someone like Lottie, herself in many ways a child, would care for him. The father, Tom, a gentle-seeming soul, was little better than simple himself, scraping a living as ploughboy or mine-hand.

'The witch told us we should boil the babe's hair in his piss and this would keep off the Plague,' Tom said. 'Since the rector was vexed with us over the bramble charms, I thought to try this in its stead.'

I had brought a lambskin from my cottage and I spread this before the fire. I gently laid the little one down upon it and unwrapped the dirty cloths that Lottie had swaddled him in. He began to give a thin cry, for in places the cloth had stuck to the bleeding scratches.

'And how much,' I asked, trying to keep my voice calm, 'did the woman take from you for this advice?'

'Thruppence for the first, and tuppence the second,' Lottie replied.

I happened to know, because Tom had sometimes worked for Sam, that even in good times five pence was his whole sennight's wage. I did my best to contain my anger, for one could not blame simpletons like the Mowbrays for falling prey to such superstitions. But my wrists were limp with rage at this predatory woman, whoever she be.

I washed the baby's scrapes and dressed them with my salve, then wrapped him in the piece of clean linen that Elinor had given me, and tucked him up, with the lambskin, in the hollowed-out log the Mowbrays used for a cradle. Then I took the stinking piss pot to the door and flung its contents far out into the yard. Lottie cried out at this, so I took her by the shoulders and gave her a gentle shake.

'Here,' I said, holding out the salve. 'This costs you nothing. In the morning, if the room is warm enough, leave him bare awhile so the air can work upon his cuts. Then dress them, as you just saw me do it, with the salve. Feed him as well as you are able, and stay clear of any you know to be sick. That is all we can do against this Plague. That, and pray to God for deliverance.' I sighed then, for her blank gaze told me I was wasting my breath. 'See that you scour that pot well before you cook in it again,' I said. 'Put water in it and boil it on the fire this night. Do you understand?'

At that she nodded dumbly. Potscrubbing, at least, was something she could grasp.

As I walked away from the croft, I caught my toe on a stone and stumbled, grazing the hand I flung out to break my fall. As I sucked at the injured place, a question began to press upon me. Why did we, all of us, both the rector in his pulpit and simple Lottie in her croft, seek to put the Plague in unseen hands? Why should this thing be either a test of faith sent by God, or the work of the Devil? Perhaps the Plague was neither of God nor the Devil, but simply a thing in Nature, as the stone on which we stub a toe.

It came to me then that if we balanced the time we spent contemplating God, and why He afflicted us, with more thought as to how the Plague spread and poisoned our blood, we might come nearer to saving our lives. And if we could be allowed to see the Plague as a thing in Nature merely, we could work upon it as a farmer might toil to rid his field of unwanted tare, knowing that when we found the tools and the method and the resolve, we would free ourselves, no matter if we were a village full of sinners or a host of saints.

9

We greeted our Maying with a mixture of hope and fear: the hope, I suppose, that comes naturally into the human heart at the end of any hard winter; the fear that the gentler weather would bring with it an increase in disease. The season eased in with an accustomed steadiness, as if the skies knew we could not cope, this year, with the sudden reversals that are more typical here.

But the warm weather brought death more than we had thought possible. Even Cucklett Delf, beautiful as it was now, all decked with tumbles of hawthorn blossom, had become unable to conceal from us our diminishment. Every Sunday the spaces between us grew greater and the distance from the rector's rocky pulpit to the last row of worshippers grew less.

By the second Sunday of June we had reached a sorry marker: as many of us were now in the ground as walked above it. The dead roll now stood at one hundred and four score souls. Sometimes, if I walked the main street of the village in the evening, I felt the press of their ghosts. I found that I had begun to carry myself hunched, keeping my arms at my sides and my elbows tucked, as if to leave room for them. I wondered then whether I was drifting into madness. There had been fear here, since the beginning, but where it had been veiled, now it was naked. Those of us who were left feared each other and the hidden contagion we each might carry. People scurried, stealthy as mice, trying to go and come without meeting another soul.

It became impossible for me to look into the face of a neighbour and not imagine him dead. My mind would turn over how we would manage without his skill at the plough or the loom. We were sorely depleted already in trades of all kinds. We were without farrier and mason, carpenter and weaver, thatcher and tailor. Fields lay covered in clods, neither harrowed nor sown. Houses stood empty, entire families gone, and names known here for centuries gone with them.

Fear took each of us differently. Andrew Merrick, the maltster, went off to live alone, save for his cockerel, in a hut he built for himself near the summit of Sir William Hill. He would steal down to Mompellion's Well in the night to leave word of his needs. Since he did not know his letters, he would leave a cup containing a sample of the thing he needed—a few grains of oats, the bones of a herring.

Some slaked their dread in drink and their loneliness in wanton caresses. But it was John Gordon's fear that led him upon the queerest path. Gordon, who had beaten his wife the night of Anys Gowdie's murder, had ever been a solitary and difficult soul, so no one was much surprised when, in early spring, he and his wife stopped coming to Sunday services at Cucklett Delf. As they lived at the far edge of the village, I had not seen John for many weeks. Urith I had seen and had some short speech with, so I knew that their absence from the Delf was not caused by illness. I had noticed that Urith looked thinner than usual, but the same could be said for most of us.

Yet John Gordon's altered appearance was another business. I had gone late to the well one evening to fetch a sack of salt bespoke for the rectory kitchen. The light was fading, and it took me a long time before I recognised the stooped figure making a halting way up the steep track through the trees. Although the evening was chill, the man was naked to the waist, with only a piece of sacking bound round his loins. He was spare as a corpse, his bones pressing almost through his flesh. He carried a staff in his left hand, on which he leaned heavily. His right hand held a scourge of plaited leather, into the ends of which had been driven short nails. As John Gordon moved up the path, I perceived that he stopped, every five paces or so, and raised the scourge to strike himself. One of the spikes was bent like a fish-hook, so that where it connected with the skin it caught and tore away a tiny piece of flesh.

I dropped the salt sack and ran towards him then, crying out. Close to, I could see that he was a mass of scabs and bruises, with fresh blood trickling into the dried tracks of earlier injuries.

'Please,' I cried, 'cease this! Do not punish yourself so! Rather, come with me and let me lay a salve upon your wounds!'

Gordon only stared at me and went on murmuring. '*Te Deum laudamus, te judice . . . te Deum laudamus, te judice . . .*' He applied the lash to himself in rhythm with his prayer. Then he pushed past me as if I were not there, and went on in the direction of the Edge.

I picked up the salt and hurried on to the rectory. Mr Mompellion was in his library, working on a sermon, but when I told Elinor what I had seen, she insisted that the news could not wait. He stood up at once at our knock and looked at us with grave attention, knowing we would not interrupt him for a small matter. When I told him what I had witnessed, he pounded his fist upon the table.

'Flagellants! I feared it.'

'But how should this arise here,' said Elinor, 'far from the cities?'

He shrugged. 'Who can say? Gordon is a lettered man. It seems that dangerous ideas may spread on the very wind and seek us out near or far, as easily as the seeds of disease have done.'

I did not know what they were speaking about. Elinor, sensing my confusion, turned to me. 'Flagellants have ever been the spectre that stalks with the Plague, Anna,' she said. 'At the time of the Black Death they gathered, sometimes in great numbers, passing from town to town, drawing the souls of the troubled to them. Their belief is that by self-punishment they can allay God's wrath. They see Plague as His discipline for human sin. They are poor souls—'

'Poor souls, yet dangerous,' Mr Mompellion interjected. 'Most often, they damage only themselves, but there have been times when, in mobs, they have laid blame for the Plague on the sins of others. We lost the Gowdies to a like madness. I will *not* lose another soul.'

He stopped his pacing then. 'Anna, kindly pack some oatcakes and some of your salves and tonics. For I believe we must visit the Gordons this night. I will not have this creed spread here.'

I filled a whisket as he bade me, adding in some sausage and the remains of a large custard I had made for that day's dinner. Outside, he handed me up onto Anteros, and we rode off in silence.

When we reached the Gordons' farm, Urith, at first, refused to open the door to us. 'My husband will not have me receive any man when he is not within,' she said in a quavering voice.

'Do not be concerned, for Anna Frith is with me. There can be no impropriety, surely, in receiving your minister and his servant? We have brought some victuals.' At that, the door opened a crack. Urith peered out, saw me and my whisket, and licked her lips hungrily. Trembling, she opened the door. She was clad in a rough blanket, belted with a rope at the waist.

'In truth,' she said, 'I am clemmed. For my husband has fasted me a fortnight on naught but a cup of broth and a heel of bread a day.'

I gasped when I entered the cottage, for all its furnishings had been removed. The interior had been decked out with crosses of rough-hewn wood. Some were large, standing up against the wall; other, smaller ones made of sticks, hung from the rafters by strings.

Urith saw me staring. 'This is how he does pass his time now, not in farming but fashioning crosses.'

The air inside the cottage was colder than that out of doors, for it seemed that no fire had burned in the hearth for some time. I laid out the oatcakes, the sausage and the custard upon the cloths I had wrapped them in, and Urith knelt on the floor and devoured them. Since there was no stool to sit upon, we stood and watched her eat. I beat my hands against my sides to try to get warm.

When she had done she scrambled to her feet and looked at us with fear. 'I beg you not to tell my husband of this. He is already aggrieved at me because I will not go about half naked as he does. It is the first time I have defied him in anything, and I have been sorely punished for it. If he knows I have disobeyed him in the matter of the fast . . .' Her words trailed off, but her meaning was plain.

I gathered up the cloths, scanning the floor for crumbs so as not to betray her secret, while Mr Mompellion questioned Urith gently about how her husband had come upon the teachings of the Flagellants.

'I do not know how,' she said. 'But some time in the midwinter he obtained a tract from London, and after became very strange. He said you do wrong, Rector, in encouraging people to see the Plague as anything other than God's wrath made manifest. He said you should be leading us in public confessions of our sins, so we might root out the transgression that has brought down God's wrath. It is not enough, he says, to search our soul, but we must scourge our flesh also. He began a fast, and it has become increasingly severe. Then he burned all our bedstraw and insisted we sleep on the bare stones.'

Gordon had ceased to do any farmwork and railed at her when she went herself to push the plough. 'Then, a sennight past, he hauled out the table and benches and burned them in a bonfire, throwing both his suits of clothes upon it.' He had ordered her to do likewise, but she had refused, saying his manner of dress was indecent.

'He cursed me then, and stripped me and burned my clothes.' He proclaimed that her weakness would force them to mortify their flesh all the more severely. That is when he had made the leather strop and driven the nails into it. He beat her first and then himself. He had continued his scourgings every day since. 'You may try to talk to him, Rector, but I doubt he has ears to hear you.'

'Where do you think I might find him this night?'

'In truth, I do not know,' she said. 'But it has become his habit to deprive himself even of sleep, when he can. Sometimes, he does this by walking the moors until he drops. Other times he lies himself down on a rock upon the Edge, where he says the fear of falling if he gives way to sleep helps him to stay wakeful until dawn-break.'

'He was heading towards the Edge when I saw him,' I murmured.

'Was he so?' said the rector. 'Well then, I must go that way also.'

Mr Mompellion rose then and laid a hand on Urith's shoulder. 'Try to rest, and I will do my best to calm your husband's torments.'

'Thank you,' she whispered. And so we left her, in that bleak, bare cottage, I to go to my own warm hearth and the rector to his search. As to how Urith Gordon could find any rest lying down upon those bare gritstones, I did not rightly know.

MR MOMPELLION did not find John Gordon that night, though he walked Anteros back and forth along the Edge until moonset. No sign could be found of the man on the following day, nor the one after. It was a full week before Brand Rigney, out searching for a missing lamb from the Merrills' flock, spotted the corpse, splayed amongst the rocks at the foot of the Edge's sheerest face. There was no way to retrieve the shattered body, or even to cover it, without accessing a track that ran out of Stoney Middleton. That meant passing through the town, which we were oathbound not to do. So John Gordon's flesh was left to the untender mercies of Nature.

The rector preached a memorial for John Gordon at the Delf the following Sunday. It was a sermon full of love and understanding, saying that Gordon had sought to please God, even as he embraced conduct unpleasing to God. Urith was there, dressed in clothing that other villagers had sent her when they learned of her plight. She looked a little better, despite her loss, for in the days since her husband's death she had been able to eat decently again. Villagers had sent her food and bedding.

But her respite was brief, for the Plague felled her the following week. While I wondered whether Plague seeds had been carried to her home with the good intentions of people who had gifted her bedstraw and clothing, others drew a different conclusion: that perchance John Gordon had walked a true path, and so kept the Plague from his door. Most dismissed such talking. But within a sennight, Martin Miller had girt his family in sackcloth and fashioned himself a scourge. Randoll Daniel did likewise, though he did not ask it of his wife and babe. Together, Randoll and the Millers went about exhorting others to join them in their bloody self-chastisement.

At the rectory, Mr Mompellion wavered between rage and self-reproach. When I went to clean the library I would find many pages from his hand, close-written and scratched over and written again. Every week he seemed to find it more difficult to gather up words for sermons that would keep us all in heart. It was during this time that he began meeting with his old friend Mr Holbroke, the rector of Hathersage. He would walk up to the land above Mompellion's Well and wait there for his colleague. Mr Holbroke would draw as near as he dared and the two would converse, shouting across the gulf between them. If Mr Mompellion wanted to send a letter to the earl, or to his patron, Elinor's father, he would dictate it to Mr Holbroke, so that the letter's recipient would not be alarmed by receiving a paper from a hand that had touched the hands of Plague victims.

Sometimes, Mr Mompellion would return from these encounters a little lifted in spirits. On other occasions, the contact with the outside world seemed rather to press upon his mind, and as I came and went about my tasks, I would hear Elinor reassuring him in her low, soothing voice, telling him that he was the author of great good for all of us, no matter how dark the present days might seem.

One such afternoon, I had stood outside the door with a tray of refreshment, heard their quiet voices and crept away so as not to disturb them. Returning a little later with the tray and hearing nothing, I had eased open the door and peeked inside. Elinor had fallen asleep in her chair. Michael Mompellion stood behind her, leaning over her a little. His hand hovered in the air, just above her head.

He will not chance her rest, even to caress her, I thought. I wondered if any couple had ever dealt so tenderly together. Thank you, God, I thought, for sparing them for each other. And then, as I stood there, spying upon their intimacy, a baser feeling swept over me. Why should they have each other, when I had no one? I was jealous of both of them. Of him, because Elinor loved him, and I hungered for a greater share of her love than I could hope for. And yet I was jealous of her, too; jealous that she was loved by a man as a woman is meant to be loved.

IT WAS ONE of those summer days as soft as the blow-ball fluff drifting on the honeysuckle breeze. We were walking back to the rectory in the bright evening, having visited, for once, the well rather than the ill. Elinor had wanted to call upon the eight elderly who had survived the Plague even as their vigorous sons and daughters had fallen to it.

We had found all but one faring well. James Mallion, a toothless, bent old soul, we had found sitting in the dark, spare from lack of nourishment and glum in spirits. Together we had lifted him out to take the warm air and fed him a good dinner, which I took the trouble to mash as fine as for an infant. As I spooned the soft food into his mouth, he had grabbed my arm and in a quavering voice asked, 'Why should one like me, who is weary of his life, be spared, when all the young ones are plucked unripe?' I patted his hand and shook my head, unable to command my voice to reply to him.

Elinor and I spoke of this as we walked back to the rectory, for we had come no nearer to fathoming why the Plague felled some and not others. Those few, like Andrew Merrick, who had taken themselves off to live away from others in caves or rude huts, certainly had escaped infection. So much we knew: proximity to the ill begat illness. What remained a puzzlement was why some lived who dwelt all together in one house, sharing with the ailing their food and bedding and even the very air they breathed. I said that Mr Stanley held that the choice seemed random because it rested entirely with God.

'I know it,' Elinor replied. 'Mr Stanley has ever believed that God bestows suffering on those whom He would spare from torments after death. It is not a view I can embrace.'

We fell silent then and I tried to rest my mind from such imponderables, watching the lazy wheeling of the kestrels and listening to the raw calls of the corncrakes. When Elinor coughed, I told myself it was a crake. A few minutes later, she coughed again. She stopped as the spasm racked her, pressing a piece of lace to her mouth. I placed an arm round her shoulders to support her. My face must have shown the depth of my feeling, for she tried to smile at me through the coughing. When it subsided, she pushed me playfully away saying, 'Now, Anna, don't bury me on the basis of a cough!'

I felt her face with my hand, but since the evening was warm and we had walked quite far, I could not tell whether the heat of her brow meant fever or no. 'Sit here,' I said, pointing to a large stone under a rowan shade, 'and I will run ahead and fetch Mr Mompellion.'

'Anna!' she said. 'You shall do no such thing! I perceive I am perhaps coming down with a slight cold, and I will not have you fuss and panic me so! If I am truly ill, you will be the first person I shall confide in. Until then, do not you dare to trouble Mr Mompellion with this.'

She walked on, briskly. I followed, caught up with her, and reached for her arm. She let me take it, and as we walked my eyes misted and overflowed with tears that ran unchecked down my face.

Elinor stopped and looked at me, a slight smile upon her lips. She raised the hand that clutched her small lace handkin and was about to wipe my tears with it. But then she stopped, crumpled the white square, and plunged it deep into her whisket.

That told me all. I wept then in earnest, standing right there in the middle of the field.

ELINOR'S FEVER ROSE. Michael Mompellion and I tried to bring her comfort, as we had tried to bring comfort to so many others. I was by her side as much as tact and duty would allow. It was her Michael who had first call upon her last hours, and my role was to keep as much of his own work from him as I myself was capable to do. But some things I could not do, and from time to time he was called away to fulfil obligations at other deathbeds. And so I found myself alone with my Elinor.

To me, she had become so many things. So many things a servant has no right to imagine that the person they serve will be. Because of her, I had known the warmth of a motherly concern—the concern that my own mother had not lived to show me. Because of her, I had had a teacher and was not ignorant and unlettered still. When we worked together on our herbs, I forgot she was my mistress; at times I even directed her in this or that knack of identification or decoction. She never reminded me of my place. In my heart I could whisper it: she was my friend, and I loved her.

Every time Michael Mompellion came to sit by her, I would leave her room seething over his greater claim to the place at her side. At first, when he dismissed me, I withdrew myself just outside her door and sat there, to be as close to her as possible. When Mr Mompellion found me there, he told me in clear terms that I was not to hover so, and that it would be better if I retired to my cottage until he sent for me.

It would have taken more than his word to keep me long away from her. The next evening, as I placed the cooling cloths upon her brow, it was as if she read my thoughts. She sighed and gave a faint smile. 'That feels so good,' she whispered. Her hand fluttered weakly on mine. 'I am a fortunate woman, to have been loved so . . . to have been given a husband such as Michael and a friend as dear as you, Anna. I wonder if you know how you have changed. It is the one good, perhaps, to come out of this terrible year. Oh, the spark was clear in you when first you came to me—but you covered your light as if afraid of what would happen if anybody saw it. You were like a flame blown by the wind until it is almost extinguished. All I had to do was put the glass round you. And now, how you shine!'

She closed her eyes, and after a time her breathing slowed, so that I thought she had fallen into sleep. But as I rose she spoke again, her eyes still closed. 'I hope you will find it in your heart to be a friend to Mr Mompellion, Anna . . . For my Michael will have need of a friend.' The sob rising in my throat would not let me answer. But she did not seem to need an answer, for she turned her face to the pillow then and fell truly into sleep.

I could not have been gone for more than ten minutes, but when I returned I could see at once that her condition had worsened and her face was even more flushed. I lay the cool cloths upon her, but she tossed under my hand. She began speaking then, in a strange, high, girlish voice, and I understood that she was delirious.

'Charles!' she called. She was giggling, a light, lilting laughter that belied her grave state. Her breathing was fast, as if she were running. 'Charles?' She cried out the name in a pitch still high and childish, but distressed, agitated, keening.

I was glad it was I, and not the rector, who was witness to this. She was moaning now. I clasped her hand and called to her, but she was somewhere beyond my reach. And then her face changed, and her voice became her familiar adult voice, but speaking in a whisper so intimate it made me blush. 'Michael . . . Michael, how much longer? Please, my love? Please . . .'

He had opened the door and entered the room without my hearing him, and when he spoke I jumped. 'That will do, Anna,' he said, his voice strangely cold. 'I will call you if she needs anything.'

'Rector, she is much worsened. She is delirious . . .'

'I can see that for myself,' he snapped, distraught. 'You may go.'

Reluctantly, I rose and withdrew to the kitchen. Sitting, waiting, exhausted with worrying, I must have fallen asleep, for when I awoke it was to birdsong and sunshine streamed through the high casement windows. I crept upstairs and stood listening outside her bedchamber.

All was silent. Gently, I eased the door open. Elinor lay sunken into her pillows, the flush all gone from her face. Michael Mompellion lay sprawled across the foot of her bed, his hands outstretched towards where she lay, as if he reached to catch her fleeting soul.

The cry that I had been fighting back for three days escaped me then, a groan of grief and loneliness. Michael Mompellion did not stir, but Elinor opened her eyes and smiled at me.

'The fever is broken,' she whispered, 'and I have been lying here awake this hour, parched for a posset. I could not call for you because I did not want to bestir my poor, tired Michael.'

I flew down the stairs to make that posset. As I heated milk I felt like singing. Elinor rose from her bed briefly that day. I sat her in a chair by the window. The next day, she said she felt well enough to take a turn in her garden. Mr Mompellion gazed at her, as if he beheld a vision. He seemed a man reborn that day and those that followed. To be convinced, as he had been, that Elinor was lost to Plague, and then to find her recovered from an ordinary fever . . . I did not have to imagine the wonder he felt, for I felt it also. His step was buoyant as a boy's, and he approached his grim duties with a renewed energy.

Elinor was taking some air on a bench in the south corner of the garden. I had brought her a cup of broth and she had kept me by her, talking, as she had not done in an age, about pleasant trivialities such as whether the iris clumps could do with dividing.

Mr Mompellion saw us there and came striding from the stable-yard. He had ridden from the Gordon farm. The Gordons were tenant farmers, and since John Gordon had destroyed all his chattel, there was little to trouble about in terms of an estate. But neighbours had felt uneasy about all the crosses Gordon had fashioned and had not known how to deal with them. The rector had deemed that they should be burned, prayerfully and with respect, and had gone himself to see to it. It was from this task that he had returned.

The day was warm, and as the rector settled beside her on the bench, Elinor waved her hands playfully. 'Husband, you reek of smoke and horse sweat! Let Anna warm some water for your toilet!'

'Very well,' he said, jumping to his feet again and smiling. I turned to do as she bade me. As I withdrew into the rectory, I heard him speaking to Elinor in a most animated voice. Presently, when I carried out a basin and some cloths, he was gesticulating broadly.

'I don't know why it did not come to me before this,' he said. 'But as I stood there, offering a prayer over those fiery crosses, I saw it so clearly, as if God Himself had placed the truth of it into my heart!'

'Let us pray that it is so,' said Elinor, her face ardent.

She rose then, and the two of them walked off along the path, leaving me standing there, forgotten. After a moment, I went back inside to my tasks. Whatever engrossed them so, I thought, flinging a washclout into a pail, I would learn of it when they saw fit to tell me.

THE NEXT DAY was Sunday, and I learned along with everyone else in the village what Michael Mompellion believed God had shown him.

'To save our lives, my friends, I believe we must undertake a great burning. We must shed ourselves of our worldly goods—all that we can of what our hands have touched and our bodies worn. Let us gather these things and bring them here, and then scour our houses as the Hebrews are commanded to do to mark the feast of their deliverance from Pharaoh. After, let us gather here this night and offer up our goods with our prayers to God for our own deliverance.'

I saw heads shaking around the Delf, for people had already lost so much that further sacrifice sat ill with them. I thought of young George Viccars on his deathbed croaking 'Burn it all!' If I had burned all those half-sewn garments made from the cloth sent here from London, I wondered how many of us might have been spared.

This thought racked me so that I did not concentrate on Mr Mompellion's words, and cannot recount how he brought the villagers to a reluctant agreement. I know he spoke about the cleansing power of fire. I know that he spoke, as always, with eloquence and force. Yet we were, all of us, weary of words.

As the afternoon wore on, the pile for the burning grew but slowly. The rector and Elinor set the example, carrying out many of their possessions. But Elinor quailed when it came to the library, and declared that she could not burn the books, 'For though there may be Plague seeds within them, yet also may there be the knowledge to rid us of Plague that we have not yet the wit to read rightly.'

I gathered up my own scant stuff to consign to the flames. But there was one thing with which I could not part: the tiny jerkin I had made for Jamie in his first winter and had been saving for Tom when he grew big enough to wear it. This I hid away.

It seemed odd, to be scrubbing and sweeping on the Lord's Day, but the rector had spoken with such conviction that even the ordinary business of cleaning house seemed sacramental. I boiled cauldron after cauldron, first at the rectory and then at my cottage, and scalded tables, chairs, every board and stone of those dwellings.

I was exhausted when we gathered at the Delf at dusk. I gazed at the sad pile of belongings—the sum of such meagre lives. We had been stripped bare indeed. At the base of the pyre stood the crib—hewn with love and joyful expectation—that the Livesedge child had died in. There were hose lying limp that had held the muscled calves of strong young miners. There was much bedding, straw-filled pallets that once had provided sweet rest. All these humble things spoke to me of the other losses: the daily gestures of tenderness between man and wife; the peace in a mother's heart at the sight of her sleeping babe; the private memories of all the dead.

Michael Mompellion stood near the rock that was his pulpit. He held a flaming brand high in his right hand. The pile of belongings rose before him, and we stood below it. 'Lord God Almighty,' he cried, 'as it once pleased You to accept burnt offerings from Your children in Israel, so may it please You to accept these things from us, Your suffering flock. Use this fire to cleanse our hearts as well as our homes, and deliver us at last from the wrath of the disease that assaults us.'

He plunged the brand into the straw spilling from a mattress, and the flames licked upwards. It was a clear, windless night, and the fire poured aloft in a twisting column of red and gold, hot sparks leaping wildly as if to join the stars. The heat seared my face, drying the tears on my cheeks. We sang then, against the roar of the burning, the Psalm that we had sung countless times since the Plague began:

> 'Thou shalt not be afraid of the terror by night,
> nor for the arrow that flieth by day,
> nor for the pestilence that walketh in darkness . . .'

Between the singing and the crackling of the fire, we did not hear the woman's cries until she was amongst us. There was a stir behind me, and I turned to see young Brand Rigney and the Merrills' nearest neighbour, Robert Snee, dragging a struggling figure up to the edge of the blaze. The woman was clad all in black, with a black veil falling over her face. The singing stopped abruptly, as the two young men flung her onto the ground in front of Michael Mompellion. Brand reached down then and pulled back the veil. It was Aphra.

'What is the meaning of this?' demanded the rector, as Elinor reached down to assist Aphra to her feet.

Aphra peered around wildly, as if she were searching for a bolt-hole through the crowd, but Brand lay a hand hard on her shoulder.

'Here is the "ghost" whose visitations have been chousing us!' Brand cried. 'I caught her, clad in these black weeds, in the woods near the Boundary Stone, trying to frighten my sister, Charity, into parting with a shilling for a charm to fend the Plague away from young Seth.' He held up a strip of fabric scrawled with foreign words, then dropped it, grinding it into the dirt with his boot.

'Shame!' yelled a woman's voice. I saw that it was Kate Talbot, her face awash with grief. 'Thief!' cried Tom Mowbray. The whole congregation erupted then, hurling insults at Aphra, who dropped to her knees and hid her face as the spittle and clods of earth began to fly. 'Dunk her!' someone called. 'To the stocks!' yelled another voice.

We were like wounded animals, our hurts so raw that we would lash out at anyone, especially one who had acted as evilly as Aphra. I was filled with anger and felt the urge myself to hurl spittle upon her. Then I saw at the edge of the crowd the tiny, tear-streaked figure of Aphra's daughter, Faith. I turned my back on the jeering faces and ran to the child and gathered her into my arms. Whatever was going to happen at the Delf, I did not want that little girl, my half-sister and only surviving blood-kin, to witness it. The child was too shocked to struggle as I carried her away.

We were halfway up the hill to the path when the rector's voice rose over the clamour of the crowd. 'Silence! Do not desecrate this sacred place—this, our church—with such unholy cursing!'

To my surprise, they did fall silent, and I turned to hear what next he would say.

'The charges against this woman are grave, indeed, and they will be heard, and she will answer them. But not here, not now. That is tomorrow's business. Go now to your homes, and pray to God to hear our prayer for His divine mercy.'

There was much muttering, but the people, accustomed to obeying, did as he said. I took Faith to my cottage, where she tossed and whimpered through the night. For myself, I snatched at threads of sleep, and when I awoke, it was to the smell of smouldering ashes.

Who am I to blame Michael Mompellion for what happened that night? No one man, no matter how wise or well-intentioned, can ever judge perfectly in all matters. That night, he erred grievously, and grievously indeed did he pay for it.

Since Brand and Robert had uncovered Aphra's crime, the rector charged them with confining her until her hearing the next day. He did not think to tell them how she should be confined, nor to admonish them against taking her punishment into their own hands. But the young men's wrath was so hot that the idea, when it occurred to Robert, seemed to them in their bitterness an apt one.

Robert Snee was a good farmer and had contrived many clever methods to raise his yields. One of his practices was to muck out the slops and droppings of the pig pens together with the spent straw of the stableyard into a deep cavern in the limestone—a natural cistern set conveniently into the side of the hill. He had fashioned a gutter in the low side of the cavern from which he could spud the well-rotted manure into his barrow for spreading.

It was into this stinking pit that Brand and Robert threw Aphra. Later, when I saw the place, I could not imagine how she survived the night there. The stench was caustic, the brown muck lapped high against the limestone—high enough, as I judged, that Aphra would have had to tilt her head to keep the slops from splashing into her mouth at the slightest movement. Yet it was impossible to be still, for to keep from sinking into the manure meant constant scrambling for handholds in the slimy rock wall. Aphra must have used every shred of her will to keep from fainting, for had she succumbed she would have smothered and drowned.

The woman they dragged out of that pit and brought to the village green the next morning was a gibbering, broken thing. The two young men had tried to clean her, pouring bucket after bucket of icy well water over her, so that she was wet through and shivering but still she stank. Her skin was all broken out in blebs. Too weak to stand, she lay on the grass, curled up and whimpering like a newborn.

Elinor wept when she beheld her. Michael Mompellion balled his hand into a fist and advanced on Brand and Robert Snee, so that I thought he would strike them. Brand was pale as a ghost and ill with guilt at what he had done. Even Robert Snee, a harder sort of man, looked at the ground and would meet no one's eyes.

Some dozen had gathered on the green to see to Aphra's punishment. Margaret Livesedge's widower, David, was there, no doubt recalling his wife's dashed hopes for the 'Chaldee charm'. There, too, was Kate Talbot, whose abracadabra had not saved her husband. The Merrill children and the Mowbrays had come; simple folk seeking simple justice. There were others, also, but if they had been deceived out of their coppers by the so-called ghost, not all were of a mind to admit to it.

I think that these accusers had gathered ready to mete out a harsh punishment. But when Brand and Robert brought Aphra, so abject and miserable, they seemed to lose the appetite for it, and one by one they melted away. The rector crouched near to Aphra and spoke quietly, asking her to make restitution of the money she had choused, and gave her a penance. I could not tell whether she understood. The rector asked for a cart to carry her home, and Elinor and I rode with her. We had to hold her up, so weak was she. Because she cried out for the child Faith, we stopped at my cottage to fetch her. All the rest of the way, the silent child cowered by her mother, clinging to her thigh.

Inside Aphra's croft we heated water and tried to bathe her, salving her weeping sores. She submitted to our tending for a short while, but as her wits began to return to her, so, too, came her temper, and she began muttering fierce insults upon us and ordering us to go away.

I did not want to leave her so, nor leave Faith with her. 'Stepmother,' I said quietly, 'I pray you, let me take the child for a day or two until you are recovered in your strength.'

'Oh, no, you sly doxy!' she shrieked, clutching at the frightened little girl. 'Pox take you and your schemes! You think I don't know?' She dropped her voice and stared at me. 'I can see through you. You're not my stepdaughter now. Oh, no. You're too fine for the likes o' me. You're *her* creature.' She pointed a trembling finger at Elinor. 'That barren scarecrow would steal my last babe.'

Elinor flinched, and grasped at a chair-back as if she felt faint.

Aphra's voice was rising again. 'That's what you're after, I know it. I know how it'll be. I'll not have you blacken me to m'own daughter. I'll not have your lies poured into her ears.'

It was clear that Aphra's agitation was only causing Faith further upset. I signalled to Elinor, and we went from there, although our attempts at a kind leave-taking did not stop the curses flying after us.

I worried all morning about the child. In the afternoon I walked back to the croft with a whisket of food and more ointment for Aphra's sores. She refused to open the door to me and cursed me foully, until finally I left the food on the step and went away. It was a like story the next day, and the next. Each day, Faith would stand at the window regarding me, her eyes wide and grave. But on the third day, I did not see the child. And when I asked Aphra where Faith was, her answer was a high-pitched, keening chant in words I could not fathom.

The next day, I again caught no sight of her, nor the next, so on the evening of that day I sat up late and made my way up to the croft in darkness. I hoped that the surprise to Aphra of being woken from her sleep might give me a few moments when her guard was down, in which time I might gain some sense of how Faith fared.

But Aphra was not asleep. From far off I could see that the croft was lit from within by a blaze at the hearth. When I drew closer, I could see darting shadows through the window, and as I came closer still I saw that Aphra was dancing before her fire. She had sheared off her hair almost to her scalp and stood in a filthy shift that showed a fleshless body beneath. Plunging and leaping, she barked out a chant that rose in pitch to a piercing cry: 'Arataly, rataly, ataly, taly, aly, ly . . . eeeeeeeee!' She reached up her arms as if in supplication, then seemed to draw something down to her from the rafters, but what it was I could not at first say. She held the dark thing in her hands, but as her back was towards me I could not make it out, only that it seemed to move and be alive.

I will own it: I became afraid then. I do not believe in witchcraft, but I do believe in evil thoughts—and in madness. And as the snake slithered out of Aphra's hands and wound itself round her waist, my impulse was to run away as swiftly and as silently as I could.

And yet I stood rooted there, desperate to get Faith away from the lunatic that her mother had become. I flung myself against the door. It gave way and left me standing there, confronting Aphra and her snake.

She screamed when she saw me, and I might have screamed, too, had my breath not been stolen away by the stench. I knew without looking at the corpse that the child was long dead. In the corner, Aphra had Faith's body strung up like a puppet, suspended by the wrists and ankles from the rafters. Aphra had tried to mask the dead, black Plague flesh with some kind of chalky paste.

'For pity's sake, Aphra, cut her down and let her lie in peace!'

'Pity?' she shrieked. 'Who has pity? And where, pray tell me, may peace be found?' She hissed then and flew at me with the serpent in her hand. I am not, as a rule, afraid of snakes, but as the firelight blazed red in those two shining eyes and the forked tongue flicked at me, I quailed. There was nothing I could do for Faith, or for Aphra, so I fled from that place as fast as my legs would propel me.

THE RECTOR WENT to the croft that night, and again, with Elinor, the next morning. But Aphra had the door barred by then, and the window covered. She no longer paused in her frenzied chanting to hurl abuse but danced on as if they were not there. The rector stood outside and said prayers for Faith's soul.

At the rectory, there was discussion of bringing a party of men to break the door and bring the child's body out, but the rector decided against it, for the risk to the men from Aphra in her distemper and the corpse in its decay he deemed too great. 'It is not as if we can do aught for the child but bury her,' he said. 'And that we can do in due time, when Aphra's frenzy has exhausted her.'

There was another concern he did not speak, but Elinor confided it to me. Michael Mompellion did not trust the men he might take to the croft to understand Aphra's behaviour as a lunatic malady, and he did not want to unleash the fear and rumour that encounters with a witch and her snake familiar might bring to the surface.

I DID NOT GO to Aphra's croft again. My heart whispered that I should not abandon Aphra to her madness, but I did not listen to it. For the truth is, I did not feel that my grip upon my own reason was strong enough to withstand the horrors of that house. I have had many days and nights in which to blame myself for my decision.

Within a very little time, I had schooled my mind to avoid the matter entirely. I was helped in this by having much else to reflect upon. For during the fortnight that followed the great burning, something happened in the village. At first, none of us marked it. Then, none of us spoke of it. Hope, disbelief, superstition—all these made pact with our old friend, fear, and prevented us from doing so.

I said that something happened. But what I began to take note of was the lack of certain happenings. For after the last Sunday in July, we heard no word of new fevers or Plague sores. For the first sen-night I did not, as I said, mark this, for I was still concerned with a number who were already some days ill and approaching death. But by the next Sunday, when we gathered at the Delf, I did my habitual count of persons and was surprised to find that all who had been there when last we gathered for worship were there again. For the first time in almost a year, there was not one newly missing face.

THE NEXT MORNING, I went out to my yard to search for an egg and found a strange cock discomposing my hens. He was a bold fellow and did not budge when I shooed at him but stepped towards me, tilting his fine red comb and regarding me with a sideways eye.

'Well, odd's fish! You're Andrew Merrick's cockerel, if I'm not mistaken!' As I spoke, he fluttered up onto the well windlass and let forth a mighty peal. 'And what might you be doing here, my feathery friend, when your master bides on yonder lonely peak?' He made me no answer but flew off towards Merrick's long-abandoned cottage.

How did the bird know it was safe to return to his old roost? It will ever be a mystery. But later that day Andrew Merrick too came home, his beard grown long and bushy. He came, he said, because he trusted in the judgment of his bird.

Shall I say we rejoiced as the conviction grew in man and beast that the Plague was truly gone from us? No, we did not rejoice. For the losses were too many and the damage to our spirits too profound. For every one of us who still walked upon the Earth, two of us lay under it. We were all of us also exhausted, for each person who lived had, in the course of the year, taken up the duties and tasks of two or three of the dead.

But that is not to say there was no lightening in even the heaviest heart, as it came to us, one by one, that at last our losses were stanched and that we ourselves were spared. For life is not nothing, even to the grieving. Surely humankind has been fashioned so, otherwise how would we go on?

AT THE RECTORY, there arose a difference between Michael Mompellion and Elinor, the first I had ever marked. She believed he should hold a service of Thanksgiving for our deliverance; he held that the time was yet not ripe.

'For what will be the effect if I am wrong?' I overheard him say to her as I was passing by the parlour. 'If we have done anything at all here, we have succeeded in confining this agony amongst us. For there has been no case of Plague in all of Derbyshire that can be traced to our village. Why risk all we have sacrificed for in the haste of a sennight or two?'

'But, my love,' Elinor replied, her voice soft but insistent. 'Why, when I know you believe the Plague is gone, must you prolong it? There are people here who have seen every member of their families into their graves. They should not have to bide here for one day longer than needs be. They should be free to go to their kin, so that they may find what love and comfort and new life they can.'

'Do you not think that I consider them?' His voice had a bitter edge. 'Despair is a cavern beneath our feet, and we teeter on its brink. If I speak, and the Plague is with us still, would you have me plunge these people into depths from which I cannot fetch them back?'

I heard the rustle of her dress as she turned and moved towards the door. 'As you judge best, husband. But do not make these people wait for ever. Not everyone is made as firm of purpose as you.'

As she passed through the doorway, I withdrew into the library. She did not see me as she swept by, but I saw her, her lovely face twisted, struggling to hold back tears.

I DO NOT KNOW how it was finally decided, but only a matter of days after I overheard that conversation, Elinor whispered to me that the rector had fixed upon the second Sunday in August, provided no new cases blighted us beforehand. There wasn't any formal announcement, but word passed swiftly through the village. When the nominated day arrived, we gathered in the Delf's stippled sunshine for what we hoped would be the last time. People approached one another without fear, shook hands and chatted easily as they waited for the rector.

He came at last, wearing a white surplice edged in fine lace. Elinor, by his side, was also clad in white: a simple gown of summer cotton embroidered with white silk figures. Her arms were laden with blossoms that she'd gathered from her garden and from the hedges along the path from the rectory. There were delicate pink mallow flowers and dark blue larkspur, deep-throated lilies and sprays of fragrant roses. As the rector began to speak, she beamed at him, her face all lit, and in the dappled sunlight her bright, pale hair glowed around her face like a coronet. 'She looks like a bride,' I thought.

'Let us give thanks—' That was all Michael Mompellion had time to say. The shriek that answered him was a raw, ragged sound that pierced the air and echoed round the Delf. Only after it stopped could I perceive words, English words, embedded in the noise.

'For whaaaaat?' she shrieked again.

Mompellion's head had gone up sharply at the first cry, and now we all turned to look in the direction of his gaze.

Any one of us could have stopped Aphra. The ravages of her madness had thinned her down to a wisp. To be sure, in her right hand she had a knife, and as she swept by me, waving it in wide, erratic curves, I recognised it as the miner's knife she had pulled from my father's hands. Her other arm was clutching her daughter's corpse, so to come at her from the left should have been a simple matter. But instead of falling upon her, we all of us fell back, stumbling in our haste.

'Mom-pell-ion!' she screamed, from some deep place within her.

He, alone, did not back away, but stepped down from his rocky pediment, and walked towards her as one would walk to greet a lover. His arms, as he raised them, lifted the lace of his surplice in a wide arc. Aphra ran, the knife raised above her head.

He stepped right into the path of it, his arms locking round her. Though I could see the strain in her forearm, his strength was such that she had no chance of breaking his grip. Elinor ran towards both of them, dropping her blossoms and opening her own arms wide.

Mompellion was speaking to Aphra, his voice a low and soothing hum. I could not hear the words, but slowly the tension seemed to go out of her body, and as he eased his grip, I could see her shoulders heave with sobbing. Elinor was stroking Aphra's face with her left hand, while with her right she reached up to take the knife.

It might have been all right; it might have ended there. But the rector's arms, so tight upon Aphra, also encircled the remains of Faith's corpse. The pressure of that grip proved too much for the fragile bones. I heard the snap: a dry sound like a chicken's wishbone breaking. The little skull popped free of the spine and fell to the grass, where it rolled back and forth, the empty eyeholes staring.

I turned away in revulsion, and so I never saw exactly how it was that Aphra, wild in her new frenzy, landed her blows as she did. I know that it was an instant's work, merely. An instant's work, to take two lives and leave another ruined.

The wound on Elinor's neck was a wide, curved thing. For a second it was just a thin red line, upturned like a smile. But then the blood began spurting in bright bursts, streaking her white dress red. She crumpled to the ground, where the scattered flowers she had carried received her like a bier.

Aphra had turned the knife on herself and sunk it to the hilt, deep into her chest. Yet somehow she staggered to where her baby's skull lay, then dropped to her knees, reached down, and with exquisite tenderness, gathered it up in her hands and pressed it to her lips.

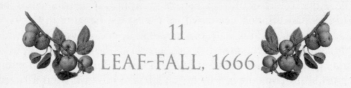

11
LEAF-FALL, 1666

They buried Faith in the garth of my father's croft, beside the place where her brothers lay. I begged the men to lay Aphra there as well. But none wanted her body to lie within the village precincts. In the end, young Brand came to my aid. Together we took her corpse up to the moors and Brand toiled to dig her a grave in the rocky earth beside my father's cairn.

Elinor we buried in the churchyard. Since the Plague was past, there was no reason not to do so. Young Micha Milne, the son of our dead mason, graved the stone.

It was Mr Stanley who prayed at the graveside, for Michael Mompellion was not capable to do it. He had expended the last of his strength in the Delf, fighting those who led him away from Elinor's body. He had clung to her till nightfall and nothing anyone could say would budge him from the spot. In the end, Mr Stanley commanded the men to remove him by force, so that Elinor's body could be decently tended.

That, I did. Afterwards, I continued to serve her as best I could. *Be a friend to . . . my Michael*, she had said, when she lay sick with what we had taken for the Plague. How could she have thought he would let me be so? I did, instead, what was in my power to do. I served him. But I might as well have been a shade, for all he noticed me.

Attending upon Mr Mompellion's grief, at least, gave me a way of managing my own. Walking each day where Elinor had walked, and disciplining my mind to think, at every hour, what it was that she might do or say, was an exercise that brought me a measure of mental peace. As long as I could fill my days in emulation of Elinor, I did not have to consider my own state closely, or my own bleak future.

The day after her death he left the rectory, and I followed him, fearing that in his dark state he might mean to throw himself off the Edge. Instead, he walked up to the moors above Mompellion's Well, where his friend Mr Holbroke was waiting, by what prior arrangement I do not know. There, he dictated the last of his letters of the Plague year. The first was to tell the earl that he believed the pestilence was fled and to beg that the roads to the village be reopened. The second was to Elinor's father, bearing the news of her death. Afterwards, he returned to the rectory.

When I arrived for my work the next day I did not find him in his room. There was no sign that he had slept there. I searched for him in the library and the parlour and then in the stable. It was midmorning before I found him. He was standing in Elinor's bedchamber, peering at the place where her head had rested, as if some impression of its shape lingered there. He did not move when I opened the door. His legs were trembling, perhaps from the effort of standing so long immobile. There were beads of sweat upon his brow. I came quietly to his side, took his elbow, and steered him back to his own room. He gave a great sigh as he sank into his chair. I fetched a ewer of steaming water and bathed his face.

The rector had not shaved since the day of Elinor's death. Hesitantly, I asked if he would have me do it for him. He made no answer. So I fetched the things and set to work. I stood behind his chair and bent over him, my fingertips, slippery in the creamy lather, sliding gently over his skin. I wiped my hands, and set to work with the blade. My face was just inches from his. As I worked, a long strand of my hair came loose and fell from my cap. It brushed the side of his throat. He opened his eyes and returned my gaze. I drew back. I felt the prickling of a blush steal over me, and knew I could not continue. I handed him the blade and brought a glass so that he could finish the job, then I backed out of the room, saying something about fetching a dish of broth. It took me some time to become composed enough to bring it to him.

After that, he ceased to move around the house at all, keeping to his room day and night. I fetched Mr Stanley at the end of the first sennight, hoping to do some good by it. The old man left the rector's room much agitated. As I brought him his hat, he turned to me and, hesitatingly, began to probe me on the rector's mental state.

I did not feel it was my place to betray Mr Mompellion's private behaviours, even to well-meaning Mr Stanley.

'I am sure I cannot judge, sir.'

'I think grief has quite undone him,' the old man muttered. 'Why else would he laugh when I advised him to accept God's will?'

Mr Stanley returned the next day, but Mr Mompellion would not have me admit him. When he came a third time, I went up to bring the news to the rector. The lines about his mouth deepened in annoyance.

'I would have you take a message to Mr Stanley, if you are capable.

269

Repeat this, please, Anna: *Falsus in uno, falsus in omnibus.*'

I repeated the Latin, and as I did so, it fell into my heart that I could grasp the meaning. Before I could school my tongue, I blurted it aloud: 'Untrue in one thing, untrue in everything.'

Mr Mompellion looked up sharply, his brows raised. '*How* can you possibly know that?'

'If you please, Rector, I have gathered a little Latin, a very little, from the great study we made here this past year . . . the medical books, you see, are mostly Latin, and we, that is . . .'

He stopped me then, not wanting me to speak her name. 'I see, I see. Then you may give Mr Stanley the message and beg him to be so kind as to call upon me no more.'

It is one thing to know the meanings of words; it is another to grasp their intent. I had no idea of what it was that Mr Mompellion was trying to convey to the old man. But when I passed on the message, Mr Stanley's face turned stern. He left directly—and did not come back.

I HAD MUCH TO DO, outside my hours at the rectory. As well as caring for my sheep, the villagers looked to me still for tonics and small remedies, and for this I had to keep the Gowdies' garden, cutting the summer's herbs and hanging them to dry whenever I had a spare moment to attend to it.

The village did not spring suddenly back to life with the opening of the roads. Some few fled the place as soon as they might, but most stayed. And hardly any persons from outside had the courage to make the reverse journey. At summer's end, some few relatives of the dead ventured here to claim their inheritances, but for most, the fear that the Plague might yet lurk within our village proved too great.

Mr Holbroke was one of the first to come. I hoped the presence of such an old friend would ease Mr Mompellion's melancholy. But the rector would not see him. Day after day, he sat in his chair, rising only to pace the floor. The weeks of his grieving turned to months, and finally, as summer faded into leaf-fall, a season.

For many weeks, I searched for ways to rouse him. I tried to bring scraps of good news. The handfasting of my widowed neighbour, Mary Hadfield, to a well-liked farrier in Stoney Middleton. The sisterly friendship that had begun to blossom between the optimistic little Quaker, Merry Wickford, and the grim Jane Martin. But none of this touched him at all.

I begged him to think about his horse, fretting in his stall for want of exercise. I suggested that this person or that one might welcome a word from him, of counsel or of prayer. In truth, requests for the rector's attentions arrived seldom. At first I thought this was a natural reticence born of respect for his own suffering. But then it came to me that many people in the village did not love him for what he had done here during our ordeal. Some went so far as to whisper blame upon him for their losses. The unfairness of this pained me, and helped me to deal with him tenderly.

And so we went on, until at last I believed that I was just biding my time, bound by Elinor's wishes, until Mr Mompellion wasted away in his room with myself as the only witness.

AND THEN, AT APPLE-PICKING time, the Bradfords returned. I have already set down how it was I encountered Elizabeth Bradford and how her demand that Mr Mompellion attend her ailing mother rekindled all the rage he had felt when that family fled from here, abandoning their duty. I have set down, too, my botched attempt to bring him comfort and his flinging of the Bible to the floor.

I can tell you further that I was hard put to it not to run, after I closed the door to his room. There was a vivid red mark on my forearm where he had seized me, and I rubbed at it, angry myself, but also much confused. I left the rectory by the kitchen door and headed without thinking towards the stable.

Before he let fall the Bible, he had almost hissed the words of that beautiful Psalm:

'Thy wife shall be as a fruitful vine by the sides of thine house;
thy children like olive plants round about thy table . . .'

His wife had been hacked down in front of him. My olive plants had been blighted. *Why?* His unasked question roared in my head. Just such a *why* had nagged at my unquiet mind through many sleepless nights. But that he, too, should be asking it . . . Could he have come to believe that all our sacrifice, our pain and misery, had been for nothing?

I needed solitude, but I could not bear the weight of my own confusion. I opened the door to Anteros's stall and slid inside, my back to the wall. The horse reared once, then stood, blowing and snorting, regarding me sidelong with one large, brown eye. We stayed that way for many minutes. When I judged that he meant me no harm, I eased myself slowly down upon the straw.

'Well, Anteros, he is lost, at last,' I said. 'His reason has left him entirely.' That was it, surely. He was mad. There could be no other explanation.

'It's no good waiting for him any more, my friend,' I said. 'You and I will have to accept that he has given himself up to his darkness.' I sat there, breathing the sweet rich scent of horse and hay. Anteros dropped his massive head to my neck and nuzzled me. Slowly, I lifted my hand and ran it down his long nose. 'Here we are, alive,' I said, 'and you and I will have to make of it what we can.'

He did not shy at my touch but pushed against my hand as if asking for more caresses. Then he raised his head, as if trying to catch the scent of the outside air. 'Let's go then,' I whispered. 'Let's go and live, since we have no choice in it.' I stood up, slowly, and fetched the bridle from its hook. He did not flinch when he saw it, but lowered his head, and I slid it on, gentle as I could. I kept a good hold on him as I lifted the bar to the stable door, though I knew that if he wanted to bolt I would have scant chance to keep him.

Out in the courtyard, I mounted him bareback, as I had learned to ride as a child. I was ready for anything, thinking that I would cling on just as long as I was able. Instead, he danced a little as he felt my weight upon him, but waited for my signal. When I clicked my tongue, we were off in a smooth surge. He leapt the wall as neatly as a cat. I barely felt the landing.

I turned his head for the moors and we galloped. The wind rushed by, blowing off my cap and freeing my hair so that it blew out like a banner behind me. The big hoofs beat the ground as the blood throbbed in my head. *We live, we live, we live,* said the hoofbeats, and the drumming of my pulse answered them. I was alive, and I was young, and I would go on until I found some reason for it. As I rode that morning, I understood that where Michael Mompellion had been broken by our ordeal, I had been tempered and made strong.

I rode for the sake of the movement, not caring where. After a while I found myself in the field of the Boundary Stone. The path that had been so well-trodden was already overgrown. The stone itself was invisible among the high grasses. I brought Anteros to a halt and looked down the hill to Stoney Middleton. I recalled how I had longed to run down there and escape. Now there was no oath holding me. We galloped down the slope, barely slowing through the village, galloping fast again into the fields beyond. I am sure that the good citizens of Stoney Middleton did not know what to make of us. The sun was high before I turned Anteros's head for the climb back up to our village. As we neared the Boundary Stone we slowed, that powerful horse easing into a soft trot. He was stepping sedately when we reached the rectory yard.

Michael Mompellion strode out of the door in his shirtsleeves, anger and incredulity upon his face. He ran towards us and grasped the horse's bridle. His grey eyes scanned me, and I became aware that I was barely decent, riding astride with my skirt tugged up above my placket, my hair loose to my waist, my cap lost upon the moors.

'Have you,' he said, 'taken leave of your senses?'

I looked down at him from Anteros's broad back. For once, I did not flinch from his stare. 'Have *you*?' was my reply.

The rector stared up at me, his eyes blank as slates. Abruptly, he looked away and let go of the horse, raising his hands to his face and pressing the heels of his palms into his eyes.

'Yes,' he said at last. 'Yes, truly, I think my senses have left me.' At that, he dropped to his knees in that filthy courtyard.

I swear, it was Elinor I thought of as I watched him: how the sight of him, so abject, would break her heart. Before I knew what I was about, I was off the horse and taking him in my arms, as Elinor surely would. He buried his head in my shoulder, and as I clung to him I could feel the hard muscles of his back through the flimsy stuff of his shirt. I had not held a man so in more than two years. It happened then: a sharp pang of desire pierced me and I moaned. He drew back at that and looked at me. His fingers brushed my face and travelled into my wild hair. He buried his hands in the tangles. His grip tightened, and he drew my mouth to his.

And that is how we were when the stableboy found us. He had been cowering in the tack room, fearing to be blamed for my wild ride. Now he stood, his eyes wide. We jumped up and flew apart, putting Anteros's bulk between us. But he had seen what he had seen.

Somehow I mastered my voice enough to speak. 'So there you are, Master Richard. Kindly see to Anteros. He will want water, and he is calm, I think, sufficient to tolerate a brushing after all this time.'

My hands shook as I handed him the reins, and I walked to the kitchen not daring to look behind me. Presently I heard the door open and close and the tread of footsteps going up the stairs. I pressed my hands to my temples, trying to calm my breathing. Then I gathered my unruly hair and knotted it up as best I could. I was peering into the shiny surface of a hanging pan to see what kind of a job I'd made of it when I saw his reflection as he moved behind me.

'Anna.'

I had not heard him come back downstairs, but he stood now in the kitchen doorway. I stepped towards him but he put his hands out and grasped me by the wrists—gently, this time—and held me at bay. He spoke so softly I could barely hear him. 'I don't know how to explain my behaviour there in the courtyard. But I apologise for it—'

'No!' I interrupted, but he let go of one wrist and placed a finger on my lips. 'I am not myself. As you know, better than anyone. You have seen how I am, these last months. I cannot think clearly—indeed, much of the time I cannot think at all. There is only a weight in my heart, a formless dread that shapes itself into pain . . .'

I barely heard his words. I know he did not want me to do what next I did. But desire was so strong within me that I did not care. I raised my hand to his hand, where it still lay on my lips, and then I opened my mouth and brushed my tongue lightly against the tip of his finger. He groaned, and pulled me to him with the hand that was still upon my wrist. We fell together then upon the gritstone floor, and nothing, I think, could have stopped us. The pain as the rough flags grazed my flesh seemed to match the pain that was in my heart.

I do not know how we got upstairs, but later we lay together on the lavender-scented bed. We were tender then, taking exquisite care for each other. Afterwards, as rain rapped lightly on the windows, we spoke softly of the things that we had loved in our lives before the ravages of the past year. Of the Plague year itself we did not speak.

In the late afternoon, when he seemed to have fallen into a light doze, I crept from the bed, dressed, and went to feed my sheep. The rain had stopped and a light wind whispered in the wet weeds. I was forking hay from the stook, when he approached me.

'Let me do that,' he said. He took the fork and then, pausing, reached down and dusted the straw from my dress. He bucked the hay with the economical motion of a practised hand. At my direction, he hauled the load out into the field and up to where the flock grazed in the shelter of a copse of rowans. Together, we made short work of spreading it. He broke open a dense clump of hay, releasing a sudden scent of white clover. He lifted it and breathed deeply. When he raised his face, it was lit with a smile the like of which I hadn't seen there in more than a year.

'It smells like the summers of my boyhood,' he said. 'I should have been a farmer, you know. Perhaps now I will be.'

We walked back down the hill in the low light, and as we neared my cottage, he took me by the hand. 'Anna, may I lie in your bed this night?'

I nodded, and we went in, he ducking his head to pass under the low lintel. I started to build up the fire, but he stopped me. 'Tonight, I mean to serve you,' he said. He led me to the chair and draped my shawl round my shoulders. He bent to the hearth, and when he had the fire crackling, he pieced together a simple plate of cheese and apples, oatcake and ale. We ate it with our hands, off the same board. We said little to each other as we watched the fire burn, but the quiet was a companionable one. When we climbed up to my bed, we lay gazing at each other, and it seemed that we did not even blink until the warm rush of our pleasure pierced us both. When we finally separated, I fell into an exhausted, dreamless sleep from which, for once, I did not waken until morning.

Light spilled through the diamond windowpanes and fell onto his long, still body. I propped myself on an elbow and gazed at him, tracing the bright angles on his chest with a fingertip. He awoke then but did not move, only watched me, his eyes crinkling with pleasure. As I looked at my hand on his chest, at its ruddied, work-rough skin, I thought of Elinor's fine, pale fingers.

He reached for my hand and kissed it. I pulled it back, embarrassed by its condition, and blurted out the thought that filled my mind.

'When you lie with me,' I whispered, 'do you think of Elinor?'

'No,' he said. 'I have no such memories. I never lay with Elinor.'

I pushed myself up and stared at him. His grey eyes regarded me, inscrutable as pieces of smoky glass. I grasped a corner of the sheet to cover my nakedness. 'How can you say such a thing? You—you were three years married. You loved each other . . .'

'Yes, I loved Elinor,' he said softly. 'And that is why I never lay with her.' He sighed, and the truth of it flew into my mind: in all the time I had spent near them, I had never seen a touch pass between them.

I drew my legs up under me and pulled the sheet all round my body. He did not look at me but stared up at the rafters. His tone was patient, the tone one would use to explain something to a child. 'Anna, understand: Elinor had greater needs than those of her body. Elinor had a troubled soul. She had need of expiation, and I had to help her. Elinor, as a girl, committed a great sin, of which you could not know—'

'But I do know,' I interrupted. 'She told me of it.'

'Did she so?' he said. He turned to look at me now, his brows creasing and the grey eyes darkening. 'It seems there was much between the two of you—much that I was unaware of. More, I should say perhaps, than was fitting.'

I thought, fleetingly, that he, lying naked upon my bed, was barely in a position to comment on the fitness of my friendship with his wife. But my mind was too much troubled to linger there.

'Elinor told me of her sin. But she repented. Surely—'

'Anna. There is a great difference between repentance and atonement.' He sat up, his back against the rough wood wall. We faced each other now upon the pallet. 'Elinor's lust caused the loss of the life of her unborn child. What could she give in atonement for the life that, because of her actions, never could be lived? Because lust caused the sin, I deemed that she should atone by living some part of her life with her lusts unrequited. I *had* to be assured that my Elinor was cleansed, or else risk the loss of her for eternity.'

'And you?' I said in a small, strangled voice.

'Me?' He laughed. 'For myself, I took a page from the papists. Do you know how the papists teach their celibates to master their desire? When they want a woman, they school themselves to turn their thoughts to all the vile emissions of her body. I did not allow myself to look at Elinor and see her fair face or to breathe the fresh scent of her. No! I looked at that lovely creature and made myself think of her bile and her pus. I dwelt on the reek of the stuff in her nightjar . . .'

'Enough!' I cried, covering my ears. I felt ill.

His body is strong, but I fear the strength of his will far exceeds it. It can drive him to do what any normal man cannot do, for better and for worse. Believe me, I have seen this. Elinor had said this to me, many months ago. Now I knew what had been in her mind.

He was kneeling now upon the bed. His voice had gained the ringing timbre of the pulpit. 'Know you not that I, the husband, am the image of God in the kingdom of the home? Was it not I who drove the whore from Eden? I turned my lust into holy fire! I burned with passion for God!' And then he laughed, a mirthless laugh, and fell back upon the pallet. He closed his eyes and a spasm racked his face, as if he felt a sudden pain. His voice dropped to a hoarse whisper.

'And now it seems that there is no God, and I was wrong. In what I asked of Elinor. In what I asked of myself. For I did love her and desire her. Wrong in doing that, and wrong, shockingly wrong, in what I asked of this village. Because of me, many are dead who might have saved themselves. Who was I to lead them to their doom? I thought I spoke for God. Fool. My whole life, all I have done, all I have said, all I have felt, has been based upon a lie. Untrue in everything. So now,' he said, 'I have learned at last to do as I please!'

He reached for me then, but I slid away from under his hand and rolled off the pallet. I grabbed what I could of my scattered garments and fled the room, shrugging my smock over my head as I stumbled down the stairs. My only thought was to get away.

I reeled blindly towards the churchyard. I wanted Elinor. I wanted to hold her and tell her that I was sorry he had used her so. My beautiful friend, full of affection, made for love. In lying with him, I had sought to bring her closer to me. Instead, in taking my pleasure from his body, I had stolen from her—stolen what should have been hers, her wedding night. I went to her tombstone and lay down upon it, sobbing until the stone was slick with tears.

I was lying there, prone on her gravestone, when I heard him calling me. I did not want to see him. The face that had moved me so, the body I had desired—suddenly his whole person was repulsive to me. I slid down off the stone and ran across the lumpy grass towards the church doorway. I had not been inside since the Sunday in March when the rector had closed it to all of us. I pushed the door open and slipped inside, easing it gently closed behind me.

The air inside seemed stale. I slid forward, muffling my footfalls out of the habit of reverence so long ingrained in me. I ran my hands round the old stone font, remembering the two joyful mornings when I brought the babies to have their heads wet here. Sam had beamed so that it seemed his face might split.

Simple Sam. Sometimes I had been ashamed of the plain feelings written on his face. How I had envied Elinor! The delicacy of her husband's manner, the subtlety of his mind. How could I have understood so little? And yet how could *anyone* understand such things: that delicacy masked a most unnatural coldness; that subtle thought had twisted itself into perversion.

Wax scents, damp stone, empty pews. I pictured the faces that had filled each one. We had sat here and listened to him, and believed in him, just as Elinor had done. Trusted him to tell us what was right. Now two-thirds of those faces were gone. I stood there, willing a prayer to form for them. But nothing came. I tried the old, rote words on my tongue. 'I believe in God, the Father Almighty, Creator of Heaven and Earth . . .' My echo whispered and died amidst the dry scratching of scurrying mice.

'Do you, Anna? Do you still believe in God?'

The voice came from the Bradford pew. Elizabeth Bradford rose from where she had been kneeling, hidden from my sight by the high oaken backrest. 'My mother does. It is on her request that I am come here, although I doubt it will do her much good. She has been in labour since late yesterday, a full month before her time, and the surgeon gives her up; he says a woman of her age flirts with death by getting with child, and that she cannot be delivered. And as soon as he had pronounced himself of this grim prognostic, he mounted his horse for home.'

She sank down into the pew and her voice turned to a whisper. 'The blood, Anna. Never have I seen so much blood.' She buried her face in her hands for a long moment, then I saw her back straighten. 'Well,' she said, 'I have done as she begged me and said her prayers for her in this so-sacred church, sanctified by all of you, the brave beloved of God. And now I must return and listen to her screaming.'

'I will come with you,' I said. I had seen so much death that I would try to save a life if I could. 'I have had some small experience attending at childbirths; perhaps I can help her.'

Something flickered in her face, an instant of hopefulness. Then the face set again into its prideful sneer. 'So the housemaid knows more than the surgeon? I think not. But come if you like. She will die in any case. And it may gratify you to bring word to Mompellion of how God has fulfilled his prophecies regarding my family.'

I followed behind Elizabeth Bradford, trying to tamp down the anger rising within me. At the church door I looked around for the rector. There was no sign of him, so I followed Miss Bradford to where her mare was tethered and clambered up behind her.

We rode up the hill in silence. At the Hall, Miss Bradford dismounted and handed me the reins, assuming that I would stable the mare. I handed them back to her and turned towards the front door. She made a sound that was half hiss, half sigh, and walked the mare to the stables. Even from outside I could hear the screams within the Hall. When Miss Bradford returned, we entered, passing the shrouded furniture and mounting the stairs to her mother's chamber.

She had not exaggerated about the blood. The floor was slick with it, and wads of muck-wet linen lay all about. The girl who tended Mrs Bradford was a stranger to me. Her eyes were wide as chargers as she groped for a fresh towel to stanch the flood. Quickly, I barked out a list of my needs. 'Bring me whatever you have of broth or jellies, a little good wine, and some warm toast to sop in it, for she is in need of strengthening if she is to survive the loss of so much blood. Bring me also a kettle of boiling water and a basin.' The girl rushed from the room as if she could not quit it fast enough.

Mrs Bradford had stopped her screaming as soon as we had entered. She reached out weakly for her daughter, and Elizabeth ran to her and kissed her tenderly. Whatever low opinion she had of my skills, she obviously wanted to calm her mother's terrors, for she spoke in a soothing voice of how she had heard high praise of my midwifery and how all would now be well. I looked at her across the body of her mother and gave a slight shake of my head, for I did not want to mislead anyone about how desperately the matter stood. Elizabeth held my eye and nodded, implying that she knew my meaning very well.

Once I had the scalding water, I washed my hands and drew away the saturated towel between Mrs Bradford's legs. I worked quickly, not wanting to lose her before I saved the child. I let my hands search out the baby's lie and found it a simple breech. Why, I wondered, had the surgeon abandoned this case as hopeless? Had he persevered here he could easily have done what I was about to attempt. It came to me then that he must have arrived here under instruction to be negligent.

The baby, being before its time, was small, and I was able to turn it with little difficulty. The mother was too weak to do much pushing, and for a while I feared we would fail because of it. But somehow she summoned up the small bit of strength we needed, and a perfect, precious little girl eased out, alive, into my hands.

I looked into her deep blue eyes and saw reflected there the dawn of my own new life. To have saved this small, singular one—this alone seemed reason enough that I lived. I knew then that this was how I was meant to go on: away from death and towards life, from birth to birth, from seed to blossom, living my life amongst wonders.

No sooner was the cord cut and tied than Mrs Bradford's bleeding slowed to a trickle. The afterbirth came away without strain, and she was able to sip some broth. Silently, I cursed the surgeon for abandoning this woman. Had he delivered her hours since, she would not have lain here bleeding. Now Mrs Bradford would need a miracle to survive the loss of such a prodigious amount of blood. Still, I meant to fight for her. I told Elizabeth Bradford to ride in haste to my cottage and instructed her where she might find a flask of nettle tonic, which I deemed might strengthen her mother.

'Nettle?' She pronounced the word as if it tasted ill in her mouth. 'I'm sure I cannot find such a thing.' She placed a hand upon her mother's brow, and her eyes softened as she looked at her face. 'I would she have what you deem her to need, but you must go yourself, for I fear to leave my mother lest she pass away while I am gone.'

I could see the reason in that, so I consented, instructing the maid to clean the babe and settle her at her mother's breast as soon as may be. I was halfway to the stable when I noticed I was chilled right to the bone. I was still wearing nothing but the thin serge smock I'd grabbed up that morning when I'd fled Michael Mompellion. I turned, thinking to borrow Elizabeth's cloak. The kitchen door was the one closest to me, so I made for it in haste and barged inside.

Elizabeth Bradford had her back to me, but it took less than an instant for me to grasp what she was about. A bucket filled with water stood on the bench before her and her forearms were sunk into it, her muscles tensed with the slight effort of holding the baby under. I crossed the distance between us in a stride and pushed her aside with more force than I knew I possessed. She lost her grasp on the slippery babe and fell sideways. I plunged my arms into the bucket and drew that tiny body out and hugged her to me. The baby was cold from the water, so I rubbed her, hard, as I would rub the life into a new lamb born on a cold night. She sputtered, blinked, and let forth a cry of outrage. She was, thank God, unharmed.

Elizabeth Bradford had scrambled to her feet. 'It is a bastard, born of adultery. My father will not suffer it near him.'

'That may be, but you have no right to take her life from her!'

'Do you not see?' she said, her voice plaintive. 'An end to this business is my mother's only chance for a new beginning. Her life is over, otherwise. Do you think I want to kill it? My mother's child, who shares my blood? I do it to save my mother from my father's wrath.'

'Give the baby to me,' I said, 'and I will raise her with love.'

She stood there, pondering, and then she shook her head. 'No. We cannot have our family's shame flaunted in this village for all to stare at and whisper over.'

'Well, then,' I said, cooler now and as calculating as she. 'Give me the means, and I will take her far from here, and you will have my promise never to hear a word from either of us again.'

Elizabeth Bradford raised her eyebrows at this and drew her lips tight together, considering. My eyes searched her face for a trace of the compassion that she showed to her mother. But there was only cold reckoning. I looked down, at the baby, and tried to form a prayer for her. A single word formed in my mind. *Please.*

As hard as I willed it, I could not draw up anything to follow: no formal supplication, no Bible verse, no scrap of liturgy. All of the texts and Psalms I had by rote were gone from me. After so many unanswered prayers, I had lost the means to pray.

'Yes,' Elizabeth Bradford said at last. 'Yes, that might do very well.'

I swaddled the baby warmly, and we sat then, at Maggie Cantwell's beloved kitchen table, and haggled over the details. It did not take us long, for I was firm, and Elizabeth Bradford anxious to be rid of me.

When we had agreed terms, I climbed the stairs to her mother's chamber. She had drunk the broth and managed a piece of sopped bread. When she saw the baby, tears brightened her swollen, blood-shot eyes. 'She yet lives!' she quavered in an exhausted voice.

'So she does, and so she shall.' I told her then what Elizabeth and I had agreed upon.

She struggled up from her pillows and grabbed my forearm with her limp fingers. I thought she was going to protest, but instead she kissed my hand. 'Oh, thank you! Bless you.' But then her eyes widened and her whispering became urgent. 'You must go, quickly, this day, before my son or his father learn that the child lives.'

She pointed then towards a coffer at the foot of her bed. Inside, in a hidden drawer, an emerald ring and necklace gleamed against dark velvet. 'Take them. Use them for her if you have the need, or give them to her when she is grown. Tell her that her mother would have loved her, if she had been allowed . . .'

I hurried to fashion a warm sling from one of her woollen shawls and nestled the baby inside it, tight against my body. I knelt then beside her bed, took her white hand, and laid it on the child's silken head. 'Know, always, that she will be cherished.'

I descended the stairs and went outside to where Elizabeth Bradford waited with the horse. The three of us rode to my cottage. Once there, I handed Elizabeth a flask of nettle tonic, with instructions on how best to dose her mother. In exchange, I took from her a purse containing more gold pieces than I had ever thought to see.

THE COW EYED ME reproachfully when I entered her byre with my bucket. 'I'm sorry I made you wait,' I said, 'but I've good use for your milk this day.' In the cottage, I skimmed off the cow's rich cream and thinned what remained with a little water. I held the babe in the crook of my arm. Her mouth was wide now, uttering the weak cries of the newborn. I stroked her cheek until she turned towards my finger, then dribbled liquid down into her mouth for as long as she would take it. She stopped crying and presently became drowsy. I laid her on some straw by the hearth and busied myself gathering the few possessions I would take with me. There was so little left. The winter jerkin I had made for Jamie and saved from the great burning; a medical book of Elinor's that she and I had pored over until our eyes ached. These I took for the memories.

And then I put the thoughts of the past year away from me and tried to think of the future. I determined to give my land and cottage to the Quaker child, Merry Wickford, so that she would have a home more certain than a tenant's croft. The flock I would give to Mary Hadfield in exchange for her older mule, which would do to convey us from the village—to where, I did not know.

I still had the piece of slate on which Elinor had taught me my letters. I drew it out and was scratching down the directions for these dispositions when the door to the cottage opened. He had not knocked, and in the sudden glare, I could not make out his face. I jumped up from my stool and put the table between us.

'Anna, don't flinch from me. I am sorry for what passed between us, sorry for everything. More than you can know. But I have not come here for that, for I know that you cannot yet be ready to hear me on these matters. I am come now only to help you go from here.'

I must have looked surprised at that, for he rushed on. 'I know what happened this morning at Bradford Hall—*all* of what happened there.' He raised a hand as I was about to interrupt him. 'Mrs Bradford lives, and gains in strength. I am just come from her. I have looked hard into my heart this day. You, Anna, have recalled to me what my duties are. I do not propose to go on as I have been, feeding on my own grief. For you grieve, and yet you live, and are useful, and bring life to others. One does not have to believe, after all, to bring comfort to those who yet do. I think you have saved more than two lives this day.' He took a step, as if he meant to come round to where I stood across the table. But the look upon my face stayed him.

'Anna, I am not come here to tell you these things. I am come because you are in grave danger. Soon, it will occur to Elizabeth Bradford that you are the one person who can bear witness that she attempted a murder this day. Her father already wants the baby dead: it will be a small matter to such a man to add your life to the due-bill. I want you to take Anteros'—his eyes creased in the merest hint of amusement—'for we both know you can handle him.'

I stuttered a few words of protest, but once again he hushed me. 'You are in need of speed. By chance I am just met with Ralf Pulfer, an ore merchant from Bakewell. He leaves this day for Liverpool port with a load of lead pigs from the Peak mines. He has agreed that if you come to Bakewell before his departure, he will escort you to Elinor's father, my patron, whose estate lies close to Pulfer's route. I have written a letter of introduction, setting down your situation. He is a fine man, and it is a large estate. Somewhere—in the village or the farms, if not in his household service—I am sure he will find a place for you. The Bradfords will not think to seek you there. They will look for you on the London road rather. But you must go now.'

And so I left my home with barely the time for a last look at the rooms that had held the sum of my life's joys, and most of its grieving. The baby did not wake when I lifted the sling again and secured her to me. There was a moment of awkwardness in the garth, when Michael Mompellion reached out to help me up onto Anteros. I turned from him and mounted unassisted, preferring an ungraceful scramble to the touch of his hand.

I was halfway down the road, and going at a canter, when I realised that I could not let it end so. I turned then in the saddle and saw him standing there, his grey eyes fixed upon me. I raised my hand to him. He lifted his in return. And then Anteros reached the bend that leads to the Bakewell road, and I had to turn away and give all my attention to the downhill gallop.

12

EPILOGUE

This house is large and very fine, set into the wall of the citadel, high on the mount that rises sharply behind the wide arc of the gulf.

I have my own room here, where I may do my work in quiet, away from the chattering and children's noise in the women's quarters. My room is circular, with a window that overlooks the garden, and beyond to the hivelike roofs of the lower town, and finally to the sea. I can see the boats from Venice and Marseilles, and more distant ports, unloading their glass and tin wares and tapestries and taking on their return freight of gold dust, ostrich feathers, ivory and, sometimes, that saddest of cargoes—the chained lines of tall Africans, destined to be slaves. I pity them their terrible journey.

For myself, I do not expect to travel anywhere ever again. But if I do, I am determined that it shall not be by sea. The waves that carried me away from England were jagged crags from the landscape of a nightmare. As the timbers groaned and the mariners cursed at rending sails and fraying halyards, I breathed the stink of tar and vomit and fully expected to die. Indeed, I was so ill that very often I wished to do so. It was only the thought of the child that gave me the will to continue.

But I do not mean to dwell on the difficulties through which we got hither. Only to say, in short, that Anteros carried me easily to Bakewell, where I hired a wet nurse and we left with Mr Pulfer and his load of ore. But when we came to the turn that would have led us to Elinor's childhood home, I told Mr Pulfer that I would not trouble him to escort us there after all but would carry on with him instead for the port. I do not know, even now, what made me so headstrong in this, but it seemed good to sever every tie that bound me to my old life. It was time to seek a place where the child and I together might make something entirely new.

I bespoke a room at a portside inn, and in the following days there were many times that I rued my rashness, for it proved no simple matter to decide what course to follow. In the end, I did not make the choice so much as have it made for me. The innkeeper, who seemed a decent man, came pounding on my door one morning just before dawn. He was in a state of agitation, saying that a young gentleman had been asking my whereabouts all over the town. ''E's noising it all about that you've stolen jewels from 'is family—I didn't credit it, mind; as if you'd be 'ere wearin' your own name if you was a thief. And another odd thing: it was your baby he kept on and on about. 'E seemed much keener on that than the matter of the jewels. I don't like to mind my guest's business, Mistress, but 'e's an unpleasant piece o' work, and if you known your'n, you'll be taking yer chances on the next ship, whatever it be and wherever it be bound.'

As it happened, a carrack loaded with Peak-mines pigs was the only ship sailing on that morning's tide, bound for the great glassmakers of Venice. So I paid out some of the Bradfords' gold for a cabin and more to quiet the wet nurse, who wailed that she had not bargained on a sea voyage. And thus I travelled away from my home atop a hold brimming with the very ore my feet had trodden over all my lifetime. I soon lost count of the days and nights as the babe and I rocked together in our bed, and I thought that our story would end there, with the glassy green water cracking through the timbers and carrying us down into the deep.

And then one morning I awoke to a smooth sea and spiced warm air. I gathered up the baby and went on deck. I will never forget the dazzle of the sunlight, glinting off white walls and golden domes, or the way the city spilled down the mountain and embraced its wide blue harbour. I asked the captain what the place was, and he told me we were come to the port of Oran, home of the Andalus Arabs.

I had Elinor's book in my luggage, one of the few belongings I had brought with me. It was her precious final volume from Avicenna's *Canon of Medicine*. I had packed it, despite its weight, as a memento of her and the work we'd tried to accomplish together. One day, I thought, I will learn everything that great book contains. Elinor and I had marvelled that an infidel of long ago should have owned such a wonderful amount of knowledge. I thought then of all that the Mussulman doctors might have discovered since it was written, and suddenly it seemed to me that I had been brought to this sunlit city so that I might learn more of the craft that had become my vocation. I paid off the nurse, providing for her return passage, reasoning that I could find another in so large a city.

The ship's captain tried to dissuade me from disembarking, but when he saw I was fixed in my purpose, he kindly assisted me. The captain knew of Ahmed Bey, which was not strange, since his writings have made him the most famous doctor in Barbary. What was astonishing, to me at least, given my circumstances and condition, was the speed with which the Bey reached his decision to take me in. Later, when we knew each other better, he told me that he had just come from noon prayer, at which he had called on Allah to take pity on a tired old man and send him some assistance. Then, he had entered the women's quarters and found me, sipping coffee with his wives.

I am one of his wives now, in name if not in flesh. It was the only way he could bring me into his household that would win acceptance here. Since it was obvious that I was not a virgin, the mullah needed no male guardian to give consent for me, so the rite was simply accomplished. We have spoken much since then about faith: the adamantine one by which the doctor measures every moment of his day, and that flimsy, tattered thing that is the remnant of my own belief. I have told Ahmed Bey that I cannot say that I have faith any more. Hope, perhaps. We have agreed that it will do, for now.

I think that the Bey is the wisest man I have ever known. Certainly he is the gentlest. His medicine does not rely upon tearing the body with sharp probes and blistering cups like the barber-surgeons at home. His way is to strengthen and nourish, all the time studying the workings of the well body and the nature of disease: how it spreads, and to whom, and how its course runs in this person and in that.

I think that by the time I arrived here he had reached a point of despair, for the Mussulmans' wives are strictly kept, and he had anguished for many years over the numbers whose husbands would see them die rather than send for his assistance. And so I think he would have taken any woman of normal intelligence who was willing to learn. I have repaid his trust by bringing many safely through their labours and showing them ways to preserve their health and that of their children. As I continue to study and learn, I hope to accomplish a worthy life's work here. I am reading Avicenna now, or Ibn Sīnā, as I have learned to call him. I am reading his writings in Arabic.

It is sunset now, and the summons of prayer callers ring from scores of high minarets. The hour after the sunset prayer is my favourite time to walk in the city, for the air begins to cool. Many of the women know me now and greet me as I go about the streets. As is the way of their culture, they know me by the name of my firstborn, and so here I am Anna Frith no longer, but *Umm Jam-ee*—mother of Jamie. It pleases me to have my little boy remembered so.

It took me a long time to name the Bradfords' baby. I did not call her anything during that terrible sea voyage, I think because I was sure we would not survive it. When we came here, Ahmed Bey suggested Aisha, which is his word for 'life'. Later, I learned that the women in the market also use it as their word for bread. It is an apt name, for she sustained me.

She is waiting for me in the women's courtyard, her white *haik* dragging in the dust as she skips towards me, straight through the small garden where Maryam, Ahmed Bey's eldest wife, cultivates herbs to flavour her tea. Maryam unleashes a torrent of scolding, but her tattooed face is crinkled with gentle amusement. I smile at the old woman and salaam, reaching for my own veil where it hangs, limp and ready, on a peg by the street door.

I look round then for the other one. She is hiding behind the blue-tiled fountain. Maryam inclines her head to show me where. I pretend I have not seen her and walk right past, calling her name. I turn swiftly and snatch her up into my arms. She gurgles with delight, her small hands patting my cheeks as she plants her wet kisses on my face.

I birthed her here, in the harem. Ahmed Bey helped in her delivery, but I did not need his assistance in her naming. When I toss the little *haik* over her head, she pulls it expertly into place so that all I can see are her wide grey eyes. She has her father's eyes.

We wave goodbye to Maryam and push open the heavy teak door. The warm air catches our veils and sends them billowing behind us. Aisha grabs one hand. Elinor clasps the other, and together we plunge into the jostling swarm of our city.

GERALDINE BROOKS

'I first became interested in Eyam when I was working as a foreign correspondent for the *Wall Street Journal* and based in London,' says Geraldine Brooks. 'In between Middle Eastern assignments I used to love to go rambling in the countryside. My husband and I were in the Peak District, wandering around the Bakewell area, when I saw an intriguing signpost saying "Plague Village" and I just had to visit. We went to see an exhibition in the church that tells the story of the villagers' extraordinary decision to isolate themselves in order to contain the disease.'

Although the story lodged itself in her mind, it wasn't until nearly nine years later that she started to write the novel. By then she had written two nonfiction books, the second of which, *Foreign Correspondence,* had won her an award and a financial prize. This gave the author both the confidence and the means to focus on her novel. Further motivation came from wanting to change her life after the birth of her son, Nathaniel, now aged six. 'I want to be around while he is growing up,' she says, 'and this would have been impossible if I had continued as a foreign correspondent.'

Geraldine Brooks clearly loves her new career and particularly enjoys writing historical fiction. 'The journalist in me likes having a skeleton of facts to work with. There was no written record of what the ordinary people in Eyam felt about the events of that time, and, in a way, that was an invitation for me to imagine what it was like and to bring those people to life.' She cites the example of Anna, the central character in the book, who was inspired by a half-line reference in one of the rector of Eyam's letters. 'Three letters from that time survive, and in one the rector writes: "Fortunately my maid continued in good health, which was a blessing, for had she quailed I would have been ill-set." I tried to find out more about her but I couldn't, not even her name. So I was free to imagine her,' the author says.

The combination of fact and imaginative storytelling in *Year of Wonders* has made it an instant publishing success, and Geraldine Brooks is already at work on another historical novel.

the analyst
John Katzenbach

'Happy fifty-third birthday, Doctor.
Welcome to the first day of your death.
You ruined my life.
And now I fully intend to ruin yours.'

ONE

In the year he fully expected to die, he spent the majority of his fifty-third birthday as he did most other days, listening to people complain about their mothers. Thoughtless mothers, cruel mothers, sexually provocative mothers. Dead mothers who remained alive in their children's minds. Living mothers, whom their children wanted to kill. Mr Bishop, in particular, along with Miss Levy, and the genuinely unlucky Roger Zimmerman, who shared his Upper West Side apartment and, it seemed, all of his waking life and his vivid dreams with a hypochondriac, manipulative, shrewish woman dedicated to ruining her only child's every meagre effort at independence—all of them used the entirety of their hours that day to effuse bitter vitriol about the women who had brought them into this world.

He listened quietly to great surges of hatred, all the time wishing that just one of his patients would step back from their rage for an instant and see it for what it truly was: fury with themselves. He knew that eventually, after years of talking in the oddly detached world of the analyst's office, all of them—even poor, desperate Roger Zimmerman—would reach that understanding themselves.

Still, the occasion of his birthday, which reminded him most directly of his own mortality, made him wonder whether he would have enough time remaining to see any of them through to that moment of acceptance that is the analyst's eureka. His own father had died shortly after he reached his fifty-third year, heart weakened through years of chain-smoking and stress, a fact that he knew lurked subtly and malevolently beneath his consciousness. So as the unpleasant Roger Zimmerman whined his way through the final few minutes of the last session of the day, he was not paying the complete attention he should have been when he heard the faint triple buzz of the bell he'd installed in his waiting room.

The bell was his standard signal that a patient had arrived. Upon entry every client would produce two short rings followed by a third, longer peal. This was to differentiate the ring from any tradesman, meter reader or delivery service that might have arrived at his door.

Without shifting position, he glanced over at his daybook, next to the clock he kept on the small table behind the patient's head, out of sight. The 6.00pm entry was blank. The clock face read twelve minutes to six, and Roger Zimmerman seemed to stiffen on the couch. 'I thought I was the last every day.'

He did not respond.

'No one has ever come in after me, not once.'

Again he did not reply.

'I don't like the idea that someone comes after me,' Zimmerman said decisively. 'I want to be last.'

'Try to bring that thought with you tomorrow,' he said. 'We could begin there. I'm afraid our time is up for today.'

Zimmerman hesitated before rising. 'Tomorrow? Correct me if I'm mistaken, but tomorrow is the last day before you disappear for your damn stupid August vacation. What good will that do me?'

He remained silent, letting the query float in the space above the patient's head.

Zimmerman snorted loudly and swung his feet off the couch. 'I don't like it when something is different,' he said sharply. 'I don't like it at all.' He tossed a quick, pointed glare at the doctor as he rose. 'It's supposed to always be the same. I come in, lie down, start talking. Last patient every day. That's the way it's supposed to be.' Zimmerman pivoted abruptly and strode purposely across the small office and out of the exit door without once looking back.

For a moment he remained in his armchair, listening for the faint sound of the angry man's footsteps resounding down the exterior hallway. Then he rose and made his way to the entrance, a second door that led to his modest reception area. In some respects the room that served as his office, with its unique design, had been the sole reason he'd rented the apartment in the year after his residency and the reason he'd stayed there more than a quarter of a century.

The office had three doors: one leading to the vestibule, which he'd reinvented as a tiny waiting room; a second leading out to the apartment building corridor; and a third that took him to the kitchen, living area and bedroom of the remainder of the apartment. His office was a sort of personal island, with portals to these other worlds.

He had no idea which of his patients had returned without an appointment. He opened the door to the waiting room and stared ahead. The room was empty.

He was confused. 'Hello?' he said, although there was clearly no one there. He could sense his forehead knitting with surprise, and he adjusted the wire-rimmed glasses perched on his nose. 'Curious,' he said out loud. And then he noticed an envelope on the seat of the chair he provided for patients waiting for their appointments.

He stepped over and picked up the envelope. His name was typed on the outside. He tore it open and withdrew two sheets of paper filled with typing. He read only the first line: *Happy 53rd birthday, Doctor. Welcome to the first day of your death.*

Dr Frederick Starks breathed in sharply. The stale air of the apartment seemed to make him dizzy, and he reached out for the wall to steady himself. He walked over to his small antique maple desk, a gift from his wife. It had been three years since her slow and painful death, and when he sat down at the desk it seemed he could still hear her voice. He spread the letter out in front of him on the blotter. He thought to himself that it had been a decade since he'd actually been afraid of something, and what he'd been afraid of then was the diagnosis delivered by the oncologist to his wife.

He took a second to try to calm the rapid beating of his heart, acutely aware of his loneliness at that moment, hating the vulnerability that solitude created within him.

Ricky Starks—he rarely let anyone know how much he preferred the informal abbreviation to the more sonorous Frederick—was a man of order, devoted to regularity. Imposing reason on his life, he thought, was the only safe way to make sense of the chaos his patients brought to him. He was a slight man physically, just short of six feet, with a thin, ascetic body helped by a daily lunchtime course of brisk walking and a steadfast refusal to indulge in sweets.

He took pride in the fact that his hair, though thinned, still rode upright on his scalp like wheat on a prairie. He no longer smoked, and he took only a rare glass of wine. He felt far younger than his years most days, but he was acutely aware that the year he was entering was the year that his father had failed to live past. And yet, he thought, I am not yet ready to die. He read on slowly.

I exist somewhere in your past. You ruined my life. You may not know how, or why, or even when, but you did. Brought disaster and sadness to my every second. You ruined my life. And now I fully intend to ruin yours.

At first I thought I should simply kill you to settle the score. Then I realised that was too easy. You are a pathetically facile target, Doctor. You do not lock your doors during the day. You take the same walk on the same route Monday through Friday. On Sunday mornings you pick up the Times, *an onion bagel and a hazelnut coffee, two sugars, no milk, at the coffee bar two blocks to your south. Far too easy. Stalking and killing you wouldn't deliver the necessary satisfaction.*

I've decided I would prefer you to kill yourself.

Ricky Starks shifted uncomfortably in his seat. He could feel heat rippling up from the words in front of him, like fire catching in a wood stove. His lips were dry.

Kill yourself, Doctor. Jump from a bridge. Blow your brains out with a handgun. Step in front of a midtown bus. The method you choose is entirely up to you. But it is your best chance. Your suicide will be far more appropriate, given the precise circumstances of our relationship. And certainly a far more satisfying method for you to pay off your debt to me. So here is the game we are going to play. You have exactly one fortnight, starting tomorrow morning at 6.00am, to discover who I am. If you succeed, you must purchase one of those tiny one-column ads that run along the bottom of the New York Times *front page, and print my name there. That's all. Just print my name.*

If you do not, then . . . well, this is the fun part. You will take note that the second sheet of this letter contains the names of fifty-two of your relatives. They range in age from a newborn, barely six months old, the child of your great-niece, to your cousin, the Wall Street investor, who is as dried up and dull as you. If you are unable to purchase the ad as described, then you have this choice: kill yourself immediately or I will destroy one of these innocent people.

Destroy. What an intriguing word. It could mean financial ruin. It could mean psychological rape.

It could also mean murder. That's for you to wonder about.

All I promise is that it will be the sort of event that they—or their loved ones—will never recover from, no matter how many years they might spend in psychoanalysis. And whatever it is, you will live every remaining second of every minute you have left on this earth with the knowledge that you alone caused it.

Unless, of course, you take the more honourable approach and kill yourself first. There's your choice: my name or your obituary. In the same paper, of course.

As proof of the length of my reach, I have this day contacted one of the names on the list with a most modest little message. I would urge you to spend the remainder of this evening ferreting out who was touched, and how. Then you can begin on the true task before you without delay in the morning.

I do not, of course, truly expect you to be able to guess my identity. So to demonstrate that I am a sporting type, I've decided that from time to time over these fifteen days I will provide you with a clue. Here is a preview.

> *In the past, life was fun and wild,*
> *Mother, father and young child.*
> *But all the good times went astray,*
> *When my father sailed away.*
> *Poetry is not my strong suit.*
> *Hatred is.*

You may ask three questions. Yes or no answers, please. Use the same method, the front-page ads in the New York Times. *I will reply in my own style within twenty-four hours.*

Good luck. You might also try to find time now to make your funeral arrangements. I don't think it would be a smart idea to contact the police. They would probably mock you, which I suspect your conceit would have difficulty handling. And it would likely enrage me more, and right now you must be a little uncertain as to how unstable I actually am. I might respond erratically, in any number of quite evil ways.

But of one thing you can be absolutely certain: my anger knows no limits.

The letter was signed in all-capital letters:

RUMPLESTILTSKIN

Ricky Starks sat back hard in his chair, as if the fury emanating from the words on the page in front of him had been able to strike him in the face like a fist. He pushed himself to his feet, walked over to the window and cracked it open, allowing the city sounds to burst into the quiet of the small room, carried by an unexpected late July breeze. He took two deep breaths, then closed the window.

He turned back to the letter. A significant part of him insisted that he ignore the document. Simply refuse to play what didn't sound like much of a game to him. He shook his head. That wouldn't work. For a moment he had a shot of admiration for the writer's sophistication. The threat was oblique. Someone else was slated to suffer if he did nothing. Someone innocent and in all likelihood someone young, because the young are far more vulnerable. Ricky swallowed hard.

I would blame myself, he thought, and I would live out my remaining time in true agony. Of that the writer was absolutely correct.

Or else kill myself. Suicide would be the antithesis of everything he'd stood for his entire life. He suspected the person who signed his name Rumplestiltskin knew that.

'I should call the police,' he said out loud. Then he stopped. And say what—that he'd received a threatening letter? And then listen to some dull and unimaginative desk sergeant tell him, So what? The idea crossed his mind to call an attorney, but the situation posed by Rumplestiltskin's letter wasn't legal. He had been approached on the playing field that he knew. The game suggested was one of intuition and psychology, emotions and fears. He shook his head and told himself: I can play in that arena.

'What do you know already?' he asked himself in the empty room.

Someone knows my routine, when I break for lunch, what I do on the weekends. Was clever enough to ferret out a list of relatives. Knows my birthday. Someone has been watching me.

'What did I do to make someone hate me so?' he asked.

This question was like a quick punch in the stomach. Ricky knew he enjoyed the arrogance of many care-givers, thinking he had delivered good to his small corner of the world. The idea that he'd created some monstrous infection of hatred in someone was extremely unsettling. 'Who are you?' he demanded of the letter.

It must be some former patient, one who cut his analysis short and plunged into depression. One who has harboured a near-psychotic fixation for a number of years. Ricky thought about the fairy-tale character whose name the letter writer had signed. Rumplestiltskin. Cruel, he told himself. A magical gnome with a black heart who isn't outfoxed but loses his contest through sheer bad luck. This observation did not make Ricky feel any better.

He pushed the letter to one side, reached into the top right-hand drawer of his desk and removed an old leather-bound address book.

For starters, he told himself, I can find the relative who has been contacted by this person. He opened up the address book, searching for the number for the first person on the list of fifty-two. Grimacing a little, he started to punch the numbers onto the telephone keypad. In the past decade he had had little contact with any of his relatives, and he suspected none of them would be very eager to hear from him. Especially given the nature of the call.

TWO

As he dialled number after number, Ricky Starks thought himself singularly ill-suited to prising information from relatives surprised to hear his voice. It was already approaching 10.00pm, and he still had more than two dozen names on the list. So far he had been unable to discern anything enough out of the ordinary in any of the lives he'd checked to warrant further investigation.

The twenty-first name seemed only vaguely familiar. His older sister, who'd passed away a decade before, had two sons, and this was the elder of the two. There was an address in Deerfield, Massachusetts, in the 413 area code. A burst of memory flooded him. The son was a history teacher at the private school located in that town. Ricky sighed and, equipped at least with a small parcel of information, reached for the telephone.

He dialled the number and listened while the phone rang half a dozen times before being answered by a voice that had the unmistakable tone of youth.

'Hello,' Ricky said. 'I'm trying to reach Timothy Graham. This is his uncle Frederick. Dr Frederick Starks.'

'This is Tim junior.'

Ricky hesitated, then continued. 'Hello there, Tim junior. I don't suppose we've ever met—'

'Yes, we did. Actually. One time. I remember. At Grandmother's funeral. You want to speak with my dad?'

'Yes. If possible.'

'Why?' The question had a slightly protective air to it.

'Well, it's something a little strange,' Ricky said.

'It's been a strange day here,' the teenager responded. 'My dad's tied up right now. The cops are still here.'

Ricky inhaled swiftly. 'The police? Is something wrong?'

The teenager ignored this question to pose one of his own. 'Why are you calling?'

Ricky launched into his set speech. 'A former patient of mine may try to contact some of my relatives. And I wanted to alert people. That's why I'm calling. I think I ought to speak about this with your dad. Why is he speaking with the police?'

'It has to do with my sister. Someone followed—' The teenager started, then stopped. 'I think I'll get my father,' he said briskly. Ricky heard the phone clatter to a tabletop.

In a moment the phone was picked up. 'Uncle Frederick?'

'Hello, Tim. I apologise for barging in like this.'

'That's all right. Tim junior said you had a warning.'

'In a way. I received a cryptic letter from what might be a former patient today. It indicated that the letter writer might contact one of my relatives. I have been calling around the family to alert people and to determine if anyone has already been approached.'

There was a long, cold silence on the phone. Then Tim senior asked sharply, 'What sort of patient? Is this someone dangerous?'

'I don't know who it is exactly. The letter wasn't signed. I'm only presuming it is an ex-patient.'

'Have you spoken with the police?'

'No. Sending me a letter doesn't seem to break the law, does it?'

'That's exactly what the bastards just told me.'

'I beg your pardon?' Ricky said.

'The cops. I called the cops, and then they came all the way over here to tell me they couldn't do anything.'

'Why did you call the police?'

Timothy Graham took in a long breath of air. 'It was disgusting. Some sick bastard. I'll kill him if I ever get my hands on him. On her birthday, if you can believe it. Her fourteenth birthday, of all days.'

Ricky stiffened. A memory burst behind his eyes. He realised he should have seen the connection right away. Of all his relatives, only one shared his birthday. He berated himself: *This should have been your first phone call.* 'What happened?' he asked bluntly.

'Someone left a birthday card for Mindy inside her locker at school. You know, one of those oversized, tritely sentimental cards that you buy at the mall. I still can't figure out how the bastard got in there and got the locker opened without being seen by someone. I mean, where the hell was security? Unbelievable. Anyway, when Mindy got to school, she found the card, figured it was from one of her friends, and opened it. Guess what? The card was stuffed with disgusting pornography. Pictures of women tied up in chains. Real hard-core, triple-X stuff. And the person wrote on the card, "This is what I intend to do to you as soon as I can catch you alone."'

Ricky shifted about in his seat. Rumplestiltskin, he thought. But what he asked was, 'And the police? What did they tell you?'

'The local police,' his nephew said briskly, 'are complete idiots. They blithely tell me that unless there exists substantial and credible evidence that Mindy is actively being stalked by someone, there's nothing they can do. They want some sort of overt act. In other words, she has to actually be attacked first. Idiots. They believe that it's a practical joke. It's just awful. You try so hard to protect your children from how sick and evil the world really is, then let your guard down for a second, and blam! It hits you.' And with that, the history teacher hung up the telephone.

Ricky Starks leaned back at his desk. He felt an unruly despair within him. Rumplestiltskin had attacked his great-niece at a moment of childish vulnerability. He had taken a day of joy and awakening— her fourteenth birthday—and rendered it ugly and frightening. Ricky glanced over at Rumplestiltskin's letter. *Ruin*. He'd used that word, right alongside *destroy*.

IT WAS NOW just midnight, and Ricky felt stupid and utterly alone. His office was strewn with manila folders, stenographer's notebooks, sheets of foolscap and minicassette tapes. As he stood in the centre of the growing mess, he felt like a man emerging from an underground shelter after a tornado has swept overhead. Already he suspected that trying to sort through decades of patients and hundreds of therapies was hopeless. Rumplestiltskin wasn't there.

If the person who'd written the letter had ever graced his couch for any measurable length of treatment, Ricky would have recognised him. Tone. Style of writing. These elements would have been as distinctive to him as a fingerprint to a detective. No patient would return years later so changed that they could hide their identity from him. They might be angry, feeling that they had wasted years in talk. There were bound to be therapies that were less victorious than others. There had to be people he hadn't helped. Or people who had lapsed, who were in despair again.

But Rumplestiltskin presented a very different portrait. The tone of his letter and the message relayed to a fourteen-year-old girl showed a calculating, aggressive and perversely confident person. A psychopath, Ricky thought. Over the decades of his career he had treated individuals with psychopathic tendencies, but none who had ever displayed the depth of hatred and fixation that Rumplestiltskin did. Yet someone whom he'd treated less than successfully was connected to the letter writer.

The trick, he realised, was determining who these ex-patients were and then tracing them to Rumplestiltskin. Now that he had thought about it for a few hours, that was clearly where the connection rested. The person who wanted him to kill himself was someone's child, spouse or lover.

He manoeuvred back to his desk amid the mess he'd created, and picked up the letter: *I exist somewhere in your past.*

Ricky sighed. Had he made some mistake as a hospital resident more than twenty-five years earlier that was now returning to haunt him? Could he even remember those first patients? While he was undergoing his own analytic training, he had been engaged in a study of paranoid schizophrenics who had committed serious crimes. It had been the closest he'd ever come to forensic psychiatry, and he hadn't liked it much. When the study was finished, he'd immediately retreated into the far safer world of Freud and his followers.

Exhausted, Ricky stumbled out of his office and into his small bedroom. It was a simple, monastic room with a bedside table, a chest of drawers and a bed. He slid out of his clothes, taking time to fold his slacks carefully and hang up his blue blazer. Then he plopped down on the edge of the bed in his underwear. In the bedside drawer he kept a vial of sleeping tablets. He swallowed one, hoping it would quickly deliver a deep and dreamless sleep.

HIS FIRST PATIENT on this final day before his projected month-long August vacation arrived promptly at 7.00am, signalling her arrival with the three distinctive peals of the waiting-room buzzer. The session went well, he thought. Some steady progress. When he coughed slightly, shifted in his seat, and said, 'Well, I'm afraid that's all the time we have for today,' the young woman, who had been describing a new boyfriend of questionable potential, sighed. 'Well, we'll see if he's still around a month from now . . .'—which made Ricky smile.

The patient swung her feet off the couch and said, 'Have a nice vacation, Doctor. I'll see you after Labor Day.' Then she gathered her bags and briskly exited the treatment room.

The entire day seemed to fall together in routine normalcy.

He went out at noon, walking the same path as always. But more than once he had to fight the urge to pivot quickly and see if he was being trailed. When he returned to his apartment, he was breathing heavily with relief.

The afternoon patients followed the same pattern as the morning group. A few had some bitterness towards the upcoming vacation; this was as he expected. Some expressed more than a little anxiety.

When he heard the three peals of the buzzer at 5.00pm, Ricky pushed himself to his feet and walked to the door. Mr Zimmerman did not like to wait in the anteroom. He showed up seconds before the session was to begin and expected to be admitted instantly. Ricky swung the door open at exactly five o'clock every weekday so that the angry man could barrel into the treatment room, toss himself onto the couch and launch immediately into sarcasm and fury over all the wrongs that had been perpetrated on him that day.

Ricky took a deep breath as he opened his door and adopted his best poker face. 'Good afternoon,' he started, his standard greeting.

But it was not Roger Zimmerman in the waiting room.

Instead, Ricky was suddenly eye to eye with a striking and statuesque woman. She wore a black belted raincoat, and dark sunglasses, which she removed quickly, revealing penetrating, vibrant green eyes. He would have guessed her age at just on the better side of thirty. A woman whose looks were at their peak.

'I'm sorry,' Ricky said hesitantly. 'But—'

'Oh,' the young woman replied airily, shaking shoulder-length blonde hair. 'Zimmerman won't be here today. I came instead.'

'But he—'

'He won't be needing you any longer,' she continued. 'He decided to conclude his treatment at two thirty-seven this afternoon. Curiously enough, he was at the Ninety-second Street subway station when he reached this decision after the briefest of conversations with Mr R.'

And then she pushed past the startled doctor into his office.

Ricky wordlessly trailed her into the small room, and watched as she surveyed it. She walked over and inspected the books he had on the shelves. Then she approached the cream-coloured wall where he'd hung his diplomas and an oak-framed portrait of the great man himself: Freud. She tapped the glass over the portrait with a long finger tipped with a nail painted fire-engine red.

'Isn't it interesting how every profession seems to have some icon hanging on the wall. I mean, every two-bit politician puts up a picture of Lincoln or Washington. And a psychoanalyst like you, Ricky, needs the picture of Saint Sigmund. It gives you a tiny bit of legitimacy that might otherwise be called into question, I suppose.'

Ricky Starks silently picked up an armchair and moved it to the space in front of his desk. Then he manoeuvred to the opposite side and gestured to the young woman to take a seat.

'What?' she asked. 'I don't get to use the famous couch?'

'That would be premature,' he replied coldly.

The young woman swept her green eyes over the room again, as if trying to memorise everything, then sat down in the armchair. She slumped in the seat languidly, simultaneously reaching into a pocket of the black raincoat and removing a packet of cigarettes. She took one, stuck it between her lips, ignited a flame from a clear butane lighter, but stopped the fire just inches away from the cigarette tip.

'Ah, how rude of me. Would you care for a smoke, Ricky?'

He shook his head.

'Of course not. When was it you quit? Actually, I think it was 1977, if Mr R informs me correctly. A brave time to stop smoking. It was ever so popular a habit back then.'

The young woman lit the cigarette, took a single long puff, and blew smoke out into the room. 'An ashtray?' she asked.

Ricky reached into a desk drawer and removed the one he kept hidden there. He put it on the edge of the desktop.

The young woman immediately stubbed the cigarette out. 'There,' she said. 'Just enough of a pungent, smoky smell to remind us of that time.'

Ricky waited a moment before asking, 'Why is it important to remember that time?'

She rolled her eyes, tossed her head back and let loose with a long, blaring laugh. The harsh sound was out of place, like a guffaw in a church. When her laugh faded, she fixed Ricky with a penetrating glare. 'Everything is important to remember. Isn't that true for every patient? You don't know what it is they'll say that will open up their world to you, do you? So you must always be ready. Always vigilant. Isn't that a fair assessment of the process?'

He nodded in reply.

'Good,' she said brusquely. 'Why would you think that this visit today is any different from any other? Even though it obviously is.'

He remained quiet for a while, hoping to unsettle her. But she seemed oddly cold-blooded and even-tempered. Finally he spoke quietly. 'I am at a disadvantage. You seem to know much about me, and I don't even know your name. I would like to know what you mean when you say Mr Zimmerman has ended his treatment, and I would like to know what your connection is to the individual you call Mr R, whom I presume is the same person who sent me the threatening letter, signing it Rumplestiltskin. Please respond to my questions promptly. Otherwise I will turn all this over to the police and let them sort it out.'

She smiled, unflustered. 'No sense of sport, Ricky? No interest in playing the game?'

'I fail to see what sort of game is involved with sending disgusting, threatening pornography to an impressionable girl. Nor do I see the game in demanding that I kill myself.' He put his hand on the receiver.

'But, Ricky,' the woman said, 'wouldn't that be the biggest game of all? Outplaying death?'

This made him pause.

The woman grinned. 'It's a game you can win, Ricky. But not if you pick up that telephone. Then someone, somewhere, will lose. Trust me. Mr R is, if nothing else, a man of his word. And when that someone loses, you lose, too. This is only Day One, Ricky. To give up now would be like conceding defeat after the opening kickoff.'

He pulled his hand back. 'Your name?' he asked.

'Call me Virgil. Every poet needs a guide.'

'And your connection to Rumplestiltskin?'

'He's my employer. He's extremely wealthy and able to hire any kind of assistance he wants, to achieve whatever ends he envisions. Currently he is preoccupied with you.'

'So presumably, as an employee, you have his name and address, which you could simply pass on to me and end this foolishness.'

Virgil shook her head. 'Alas, no, Ricky. Mr R is not so naive as to fail to insulate his identity from mere factotums such as myself. And even if I could help you, I wouldn't. Hardly be sporting. Imagine if the old poet Dante and his guide, Virgil, had looked up at the sign that said "All hope abandon, ye who enter here!" and Virgil had shrugged and said, "You don't want to go in there." That would have ruined the poem. Can't write an epic about turning away at the gates of Hell, can you, Ricky? Nope. Got to walk through that doorway.'

'Why, then, are you here?'

'He thought you might doubt his sincerity—though that young lady up in Deerfield who had her teenage emotions rearranged so easily should have been message enough for you. But doubts sow hesitation, and you only have two weeks to play. Hence he sent a bona fide guide to get you jump-started. Me.'

'You keep talking about this game,' Ricky said. 'Well, it is not a game to Mr Zimmerman. His treatment is at an important stage. Your mysterious Mr R can screw around with me—that's one thing. But when you involve my patients, that crosses a boundary.'

The young woman who called herself Virgil held up her hand. 'Ricky, try not to sound so pompous. Zimmerman elected to become part of the game. Not so eagerly at first, I'm told, but with an odd sort of enthusiasm after a short time. But I wasn't a participant in that particular conversation. I'll tell you who did get involved, however. A middle-aged, somewhat disadvantaged woman called LuAnne. I think you'd be wise to have a talk with LuAnne. Who knows what you might learn?'

Ricky was about to demand clarification when Virgil stood up.

'Ricky,' she said curtly, 'the session has ended for today. I've given you lots of information, and now it's up to you to act. That's not something you do well, is it? What you do is listen. And then nothing. Well, those times have ended. Now you'll have to get out into the world and do something. Otherwise . . . well, let's not think of the otherwise.' She strode quickly towards the exit door.

'Wait,' he said impulsively. 'Will you be back?'

'Who knows?' Virgil replied with a small grin. 'Maybe. We'll see how you do.' Then she tugged the door open and exited.

He listened for a moment to the click-clack of her heels in the corridor. Then he jumped up and raced over to the door. He pulled it open, but Virgil had disappeared from the hallway. He retreated into his office and thrust himself up to the windowpane, staring out just in time to see the young woman emerge from the front of the apartment building. As he watched, a long black limousine slithered to the front, and Virgil stepped from the kerb into the vehicle. The car slid away down the street, moving too suddenly for Ricky to observe the licence plate even if he had thought of it.

He tried to grip hard on his emotions and took a deep breath. Then he seized his appointment book and found Zimmerman's number. He dialled rapidly, only to be greeted by empty ringing. No Zimmerman. No overprotective mother. No answering machine. Just a steady, frustrating ringing.

He slammed the telephone down and seized his coat. Within seconds he was outside. The city streets were still filled with sunlight, though it was well into the dinner hour. Instead of hailing a cab, Ricky set off to cross Central Park on foot. He thought the time and exertion would help him to get a grip on what was happening to him.

The day's heat lingered on into the early evening. Within a few

hundred yards he felt sticky sweat gathering under his arms. He loosened his tie and removed his blazer, slinging it over his back, giving
him a jaunty appearance that contradicted how he felt. The park was
filled with joggers and people walking their dogs.

It took him another fifteen minutes of brisk walking to reach the
block where Zimmerman's apartment building was. He hesitated on
the corner. He took two or three steps down the block, then stopped.
He shook his head. 'What did Virgil say?' he whispered to himself.

Zimmerman decided to end his treatment at 2.37pm in a nearby
subway stop. This made no sense.

He strode over to a telephone kiosk and stuck a quarter in the payphone, rapidly punching in Zimmerman's number. Again the phone
rang a dozen times, unanswered. This time, however, Ricky felt
relieved. The absence of a response seemed to absolve him of the
need to knock on the man's door.

He hung up and stepped back. He told himself, You've got to take
control of this situation. His eyes caught the entrance to the 92nd
Street subway station. He moved in that direction, paused at the
head of the stairs, then stepped down. A distant train groaned
through a tunnel. There were few people in the station at that
moment, and he spotted a woman working in the token kiosk. He
bent towards the round metal speaking filter in the Plexiglas window.

'Excuse me,' he said.

'You want change? Directions? Map's on the wall over there.'

'No,' he said, shaking his head. 'I wonder . . . well, I was wondering, did something happen down here today? This afternoon?'

'You gotta talk to the cops about that,' she said briskly.

'But what—'

'Happened before my shift. I didn't see nothing.'

'But what happened?'

'Guy jumped in front of a train. Or fell, I dunno. Cops been here
and gone by the time my shift begun.'

'What cops?'

'Transit. Ninety-sixth and Broadway.'

Ricky stepped back, his stomach clenched. He needed air. A train
approached, filling the station with a steady screeching noise that
flooded over him, pummelling him like fists.

'You OK, mister?' the woman in the booth shouted above the
racket. 'You look kinda sick.'

He nodded and whispered a reply. 'I'm fine,' he said, but this was
clearly a lie.

EVERYTHING ABOUT THE WORLD Ricky entered that evening was alien to him. The sights, sounds, and smells of the Transit AuthorityPpolice station at 96th and Broadway represented a city he was only vaguely aware of. There was a faint aroma of urine fighting the harsher odour of strong disinfectant. A man was shouting unintelligible word concoctions from some hidden holding area. There was an angry woman holding a crying child in front of the sergeant's thick wooden reception desk, spilling out imprecations in rapid-fire Spanish. A telephone rang somewhere, unanswered.

Ricky swayed inside the door, assaulted by all he heard and saw, unsure what to do. The woman at the sergeant's desk let burst with a final cascade of words and, giving the child a shake, turned away scowling, pushing past Ricky as if he were as insignificant as a cockroach. Ricky stumbled ahead and approached the officer behind the desk.

'I'm sorry—' he started, only to be interrupted.

'Nobody's ever really sorry, fella. It's just what they say. Never really mean it. But what is it you think you're sorry about?'

'No, you misunderstand me. What I mean is—'

'No one ever says what they mean either. Important lesson in life. It would be helpful if more people learn it.' The policeman was in his early forties and wore an insouciant smile that seemed to indicate he'd seen just about everything in life worth seeing.

'Let me start over,' Ricky finally stated sharply. 'Earlier today there was an incident at the Ninety-second Street station. A man fell—'

'Jumped, I heard. You a witness?'

'No. But I knew the man, I believe. I was his doctor. I need some information.'

'Doctor, huh? What sort of doctor?'

'He was in psychoanalytic treatment with me for the past year.'

'You're a shrink?'

Ricky nodded.

'Interesting job, that,' the officer said. 'You use a couch?'

'That's correct.'

'Cool. Well, one guy ain't gonna be needing a couch no more. You better speak to the detective. Riggins caught the case. Or what there was of it after the Eighth Avenue express came through the Ninety-second Street station at about sixty miles per.'

The policeman gestured in the direction of a pair of doors marked DETECTIVE BUREAU. Ricky walked over and pushed through, entering a small office warren of grimy grey steel desks.

A detective wearing a white shirt and red tie, sitting at the closest desk, looked up at him. 'Help you?'

'Detective Riggins?'

The detective shook his head. 'Not me. She's over in the back, talking to people who got some kinda look at the jumper today.'

Ricky looked across the room and spotted a woman just shy of middle age, wearing a man's pale blue button-down shirt and striped silk tie, grey slacks, and a contradictory pair of white running shoes with a Day-Glo orange stripe down the side. Her dirty-blonde hair was pulled back sharply from her face in a ponytail, which made her seem a little older than the mid-thirties that Ricky might have guessed. The detective was speaking with a pair of black teenage boys, each wearing baseball caps cocked at odd angles.

The detective sitting in front of him asked, 'You here on that jumper today at Ninety-second Street?'

Ricky nodded. The detective picked up his phone. He gestured to half a dozen wooden chairs lined up against one wall. Only one chair was occupied—by a bedraggled, dirt-strewn woman of indistinct age who appeared to be speaking to herself. The woman wore a thread-bare overcoat that she kept hugging increasingly tighter to her body, and she rocked a little in the seat. Homeless and schizophrenic, Ricky diagnosed.

'Just have a seat over there next to LuAnne,' the detective said. 'I'll let Riggins know she's got another live one to talk with.'

Ricky stiffened when he heard the woman's name. He took a deep breath and walked over towards the row of chairs.

'May I sit here?' he asked, pointing to a seat next to the woman.

She looked up at him, astonished. 'He wants to know if he can sit here. What am I? The queen of chairs? He can sit where he likes.'

Ricky sat in the seat next to her. He shifted about, as if trying to make himself comfortable, then asked, 'So, LuAnne, you were in the subway station when the man fell on the tracks?'

LuAnne looked up into the fluorescent lighting. She gave a little shudder with her shoulders, then replied, 'So he wants to know was I there when the man went in front of the train. I should tell him what I saw, all blood and people screaming, awful it was. Then the police came.' She turned towards Ricky. 'I saw,' she said.

'Tell me, LuAnne, what did you see?'

She coughed, as if trying to clear her throat. 'He wants to know what I saw,' she said. 'He wants to know about the man who died and the pretty woman who came up to me and spoke to me very softly, saying, "Did you see that, LuAnne? Did you see how that man stepped right over to the edge as the express train was coming through and how he just jumped down!" She says to me, "LuAnne, no one pushed the man," she says. "Be absolutely sure of that, LuAnne. No one pushed him." And then there's a man right next to her, and he says, "LuAnne, you must tell the police what you saw." And then the beautiful woman gives me ten dollars. Did she give you ten dollars, too?'

'No,' Ricky said slowly, 'she didn't give me ten dollars.'

'Oh, too bad,' LuAnne replied, shaking her head.

Ricky looked up and saw Detective Riggins crossing the room towards them. 'Hello,' she said. 'I gather you're here about Mr Zimmerman?' But before he could reply, she turned towards LuAnne. 'LuAnne, I'm going to have an officer drive you over to the One hundred and second Street shelter for the night. Thank you for coming in. You were very helpful. Stay at the shelter, LuAnne, OK? In case I need to talk to you again.'

LuAnne rose, shaking her head. 'She says stay at the shelter.'

'The car ride will be fun, LuAnne. If you like, I'll ask them to put on their lights and siren.'

This made LuAnne smile. She nodded her head with childlike enthusiasm. The detective gestured towards a pair of uniformed cops and said, 'Guys, give our witness here the red-carpet treatment. Lights and action all the way, OK?'

Ricky watched as the deranged woman shuffled off towards the exit with the policemen. Detective Riggins was watching her departure as well. The policewoman sighed. 'She's not nearly as bad off as some,' she said. 'I wonder who she really is. You think, Doctor, maybe there's someone somewhere worrying about her? Maybe she's an heiress to some oil fortune, or a lottery winner. That would be kinda neat, huh? Wonder what happened to her to have her end up like this. All those crazy chemicals in the brain just bubbling out of control. But that's more your territory, not mine.'

'I'm not really big on medications,' Ricky said. 'What I do probably wouldn't help LuAnne all that much.'

Detective Riggins motioned him towards her desk, which had a chair pulled up beside it. They walked across the room together. 'You're into talking, huh?' she said as they sat down. 'You were Mr Zimmerman's therapist, correct?' She pulled out a pad and pencil.

'Yes. He'd been in analysis during the past year. But—'

'Any suicidal tendencies in the last couple of weeks?'

'No. Absolutely not,' Ricky said with determination.

The detective raised her eyebrows. 'Really? Was he getting better?'

Ricky hesitated. 'I would say that he was still struggling deeply with the issues that plagued his life. But he didn't present with any of the classic symptomology. Had he, I would have taken steps—'

'Have you ever lost a patient to suicide in the past?'

'Yes. Unfortunately. But in that case the signs were clear-cut. My efforts, however, weren't adequate for the depth of that patient's depression.'

'That failure stick with you for a while, Doc?'

'Yes,' Ricky replied coldly.

'It would be bad for business if another of your patients decided to take on the Eighth Avenue express one on one, wouldn't it?'

Ricky rocked back in the chair, scowling. 'I don't appreciate the implication in your question, Detective.'

Riggins smiled, shaking her head slightly. 'Well, let's move on, then. If you don't think he killed himself, the alternative is that someone pushed him. Did Mr Zimmerman ever speak about anyone who hated him or bore a grudge? A business partner? Estranged lover?'

Ricky hesitated. He realised this was his opportunity to unburden himself of everything, tell the police about the letter, the visit from Virgil, the game he was being asked to play. All he had to do was say that a crime had been committed and that Zimmerman was a victim of an act that had nothing to do with him except his death. But he had no idea how dangerous this might be. All the events that surrounded him were hazy, elusive and impossible to decipher.

He shook his head. 'Mr Zimmerman never mentioned anyone who would fit the categories you suggest. But I have sincere doubts that he would kill himself. His condition most definitely didn't seem that severe. Write that down and put it in your report.'

Detective Riggins shrugged. 'Doctor, your opinion is noted.' She smiled again. 'Dollars to doughnuts, I'll find a note in his personal belongings somewhere. Or maybe you'll get a letter in the mail this week. If you do, make a copy for my report, will ya, Doc?' She reached into a box on her desk and removed a card, which she handed over with a small flourish.

Without glancing at it, Ricky put it in his pocket and rose to leave. He crossed the detective bureau rapidly, looking back only as he passed through the door, catching a single glimpse of Detective Riggins hunched over an old-fashioned typewriter, starting to peck out the words of her report on the ordinary and seemingly inconsequential death of Roger Zimmerman.

THREE

Zimmerman's ghost seemed to be laughing at him.

It was the morning after a fitful night. Ricky had not slept much, but when he had, he dreamt vividly of his dead wife sitting by his side in a red two-seater sports car. They were parked in deep sand by the edge of the ocean, near their vacation cottage in Wellfleet on Cape Cod. It had seemed to Ricky in the dream that the grey-green Atlantic waters—the colour they took on in anticipation of a storm—were sweeping ever closer, threatening to overtake the car in a flood tide, and he struggled madly to open the door. But when he tried to work the handle, he had seen a bloodstained and grinning Zimmerman standing outside, holding the door closed, and he'd been trapped inside. The car would not start. In the dream, his dead wife had seemed calm, beckoning, and he'd had little trouble interpreting all this as he stood in the shower.

Ricky dressed in an old blue shirt and faded khaki trousers that showed all the signs of years of wear and tear during his summer vacation, the only time he wore them. For years he had woken on August 1 and gleefully put on the battered clothes that signalled he was stepping away from the carefully constructed and regimented character of Upper East Side Manhattan psychoanalyst—a man of accomplishments dressing down for the beginning of vacation. Vacation was a time to get his hands dirty in the garden up in Wellfleet, to get sand between his toes on long walks down the beach, and to read popular mystery novels. This vacation promised no such return to routine.

He shook his head and dragged himself into the small kitchen. For breakfast he made himself a slice of dry toast and some black coffee. He chewed the toast with indifference and carried the coffee into his office, where he put Rumplestiltskin's letter on the desk in front of him. He sat at the desk and stared at the words. For a moment he felt a dizziness mingled with a flash of heat.

'What is happening?' he demanded of himself out loud.

The idea that Zimmerman was pushed in front of a subway train to send Ricky a message was horrifying. He envisioned himself walking back into Detective Riggins's overbright office and claiming that some strangers had deliberately murdered a person they didn't know in order to force him into playing some sort of death game.

But then, he realised, the man who called himself Rumplestiltskin and the woman who went by the name of Virgil understood that there was no hard evidence whatsoever that might connect them to this random crime. Even if Detective Riggins didn't laugh Ricky out of her office, what incentive did she have to pursue a wild story from a physician who would prefer some crazy mystery-novel explanation rather than the obvious suicide that reflected so poorly on him?

Sitting back hard in his chair, Ricky knew he was at a critical moment. In the hours since the letter had appeared in his waiting room, he'd been caught up in a series of actions that he had absolutely no perspective on. Analysis is about patience, and he'd had none. It is about time, and there was little available. The fourteen days remaining seemed impossibly brief. For a second he thought of a death-row prisoner, told that the governor had signed his death warrant, specifying the date and time of execution. This was a crushing image. It is the greatest luxury of our existence, he thought, that we don't know our allotted span of days.

He seized Rumplestiltskin's letter and examined the small rhyme. It's a clue, he said to himself. A clue from a psychopath. '*Mother, father and young child.*' Well, Ricky thought, it's interesting that the letter writer uses the word *child*, because that doesn't specify gender. '*When my father sailed away.*'

The father left. *Sail* could be either literal or symbolic, but in either case, the father left the family. Whatever the causes of the abandonment, Rumplestiltskin must have harboured his resentment for years. It had to be further fuelled by the mother, who was left behind. Ricky had played some part in the creation of a rage that had taken years to turn murderous. But which part? Rumplestiltskin, Ricky believed in that moment, was the child of a patient.

How long, he wondered, does it take to create a murderer? Ten years? Twenty years? A single instant?

He did not know, but he suspected he could learn.

RICKY WAS BACK at the creation of a list. He was taking a period of ten years—from 1975, when he began his residency, to 1985—and writing down the name of everyone he'd seen in treatment during that time. It was relatively easy, as he went year by year, to come up with the names of the long-term patients, but he doubted that anyone who'd had a long course of treatment had created the person now threatening him. Rumplestiltskin would be the child of someone whose connection had been more tenuous. Someone who left treatment abruptly. Remembering those patients was far more difficult.

Ricky sat at his desk, a pad of paper in front of him, wishing he'd kept more organised records.

It was near noon when the buzzer on his door rang. He rose and crossed his office, stepped into the waiting room and cautiously approached the door. There was a peephole in the middle of the oaken slab, and he put his eye to the circle as the buzzer sounded a second time. On the other side was a young man wearing a sweat-stained blue Federal Express shirt, clutching an envelope. Ricky loosened the dead bolts, leaving the chain fastened.

'Yes?' he asked.

'I have a letter here for a Dr Starks.'

Ricky hesitated. 'Do you have some identification?'

'What?' the young man asked with a grin. 'The uniform isn't enough?' He sighed and twisted his body to show a plastic-encased picture identification that was clipped to his shirt. 'Can you read that?' he asked. 'All I'm looking for is a signature.'

Ricky reluctantly opened the door. 'Where do I sign?'

The delivery man offered him the clipboard. 'Right there,' he said. Ricky signed. The young man checked the signature, then handed him the small cardboard express envelope. 'Have a nice day,' he said.

Ricky paused in the doorway, staring down at the label on the envelope. The return address was for the New York Psychoanalytic Society. He stepped back into his waiting room, locking the door behind him. He found the tab and pulled open the cardboard envelope. Inside there was a regular letter-size envelope. He opened it and withdrew two sheets of paper. The first bore the masthead of the society. He saw immediately that the letter was from the organisation's president, a physician he knew only vaguely. He read swiftly:

Dear Dr Starks,

    It is my unfortunate duty to inform you that the Psychoanalytic Society is in receipt of a significant complaint concerning your relationship with a former patient. I have enclosed a copy of the complaining letter.

    As per the society's bylaws, I have turned the entire matter over to the state's board of medical ethics investigators. You should be hearing from personnel in that office in the very near future.

Ricky barely glanced at the signature as he turned to the second sheet of paper. This was a letter addressed to the society's president, with copies to the vice-president, ethics committee chairman and each doctor on the six-person ethics committee. It read:

Dear Sir,

More than six years ago I entered into a course of psychoanalytic treatment with Dr Frederick Starks, a member of your organisation. Some three months into a four-times-weekly series of sessions, he began to ask me questions about my sexual relations with the various partners I had had, leading up to and including a failed marriage. I assumed that these enquiries were a part of the analytic process. However, as the sessions continued, these questions became increasingly pornographic. I complained, but he countered that the root of my depression resided in my failure to fully give myself in sexual encounters. It was shortly after that suggestion that he raped me. He told me that unless I submitted, I would never feel better about myself.

It has taken me several years to recover from my relationship with Dr Starks. During this time I have been hospitalised three times. I bear the scars of two suicide attempts. It is only with the constant help of a caring therapist that I have begun the process of healing. This letter to your organisation is part of that process.

For the time being, I feel I must remain anonymous, although Dr Starks will know who I am. If you decide to pursue this matter, please direct your investigation to my attorney and/or my therapist.

The letter was unsigned but contained the name of a lawyer with a midtown address and a psychiatrist with a suburban Boston listing. Ricky's hands shook. He was dizzy.

There was not a single word of truth in the letter. He wondered whether that would make even the slightest bit of difference.

HE PACED BACK and forth across his office for a few moments. Finally he flung himself down into his old leather chair behind the head of the couch. He had no doubt who had concocted the complaint against him. The false anonymity of the phoney victim guaranteed that. The more important question was determining why.

Ricky kept a telephone on the floor next to his chair, and he reached down and seized it. Within seconds he acquired the office number for the head of the Psychoanalytic Society and furiously punched the numbers into the receiver.

The call was picked up by an answering service. 'Hello,' a woman's voice responded wearily. 'This is Dr Roth's service.'

'I need to get the doctor a message,' Ricky said briskly.

'The doctor is on vacation. In an emergency you should call Dr Albert Michaels at—'

Ricky interrupted. 'It's not that sort of emergency, and it's not that sort of message. He will want to hear this.'

'I don't know,' the woman repeated. 'We have a procedure.'

'Everyone has a procedure,' Ricky said bluntly. 'People with small minds fill them with procedures. People of character know when to ignore protocol. Are you that sort of person, miss?'

The woman hesitated. 'What's the message?'

'Tell Dr Roth that Dr Frederick Starks . . . You had better write this down because I want you to quote me precisely.'

'I am writing it down,' the woman said sharply.

'That Dr Starks received his letter and wishes to inform him that there is not a single word of truth in the complaint. It is total fantasy.'

'Not a single word of truth. OK. Fantasy. Got that. You want me to call him with that message? He's on vacation.'

'We're all on vacation,' Ricky said bluntly. Then he hung up.

He leaned back in his seat. He couldn't recall being that rude in years. It was against his nature. But then he recognised that he was likely to have to go against his nature in many ways over the next few days. He returned to the cover letter from Dr Roth and then read through the anonymous complaint a second time.

It was far more subtle than one would first think. The writer cried rape but placed the time frame just distant enough to be beyond any legal statute of limitations. No police need be involved. Instead, it would trigger a slow, cumbersome inquiry by the board of ethics. This would be unlikely to get in the way of the game clock running.

'He wants me alone,' Ricky blurted out. 'He doesn't want me to get help.' He almost smiled at the diabolical nature of what Rumplestiltskin had done. The man knew that Ricky would be internally buffeted by questions surrounding Zimmerman's death and panicky at the rapid-fire series of events that had taken place. And where would Ricky turn for help? He would have turned to another analyst, a friend who could function as a sounding board.

But that wouldn't happen now. An allegation that he'd used his position as therapist for sexual favours was the psychoanalytic equivalent of the plague. He inhaled sharply, as if the air in his office had grown cold. I am all alone, he thought. Isolated. Adrift. That was what Rumplestiltskin wanted.

Again Ricky looked at the two letters. In the fake complaint the anonymous writer had included the names of a Manhattan lawyer and a Boston therapist. Ricky couldn't help himself from shuddering. Those names were installed for me, he thought. That's the route I'm supposed to travel.

HE WASTED THE REMAINDER of that day examining every detail of Rumplestiltskin's first letter, trying to dissect the rhymed clue further. But the following morning, after he had dressed in a suit and tie and then had taken the time to draw an X through another day on his calendar, he once again started to feel the pressure of time. It was important to at least come up with his first question and to call the *Times* to place the question in an ad.

Outside, the morning heat seemed to mock him. He assumed he was being followed, but once again refused to turn and look. Everyone on the street was suspicious. The man on the corner delivering items to a deli, the businessman pacing down the sidewalk, the homeless man in the alcove. Anyone could be watching him.

Ricky shrugged and hailed a cab at the corner. The cabbie was listening to an odd Middle Eastern music station. He grunted when Ricky gave him the address, and sped off into traffic.

A large white removal van blocked most of the side street where the lawyer's office was located. Three or four burly men were moving in and out of the front doors of the building, carrying boxes, desk chairs and the like up a ramp into the van. A man in a blue blazer with a security badge stood to the side, keeping watch on the progress.

Ricky got out of the cab and approached the man. 'I'm looking for the office of an attorney, Mr Merlin. He's—'

'Sixth floor, all the way to the top,' the blazer man said. 'You got an appointment? Pretty busy up there with the move and all.'

'He's moving?'

'Breaking into the big time,' the blazer man said. 'Big money, from what I hear. You can go on up, but don't get in the way.'

The elevator hummed, but thankfully no Muzak played. When the doors opened on the sixth floor, Ricky immediately saw the lawyer's office. A door was propped open, and two men were struggling with a desk, lifting and angling it through the doorway as a middle-aged woman in jeans, running shoes and a designer T-shirt watched them carefully. 'That's my desk, and I know every scratch on it. You put a new one there and you'll be buying me another one.'

The two men scowled, and the desk slid through the door with millimetres to spare. Ricky walked up quickly.

'I'm looking for Mr Merlin,' he said. 'Is he around?'

The woman turned quickly. 'Are you a client? We don't have any appointments scheduled for today. Moving day.'

'My name is Dr Frederick Starks, and I believe it safe to say that Mr Merlin and I have something to discuss. Is he here?'

The woman briefly looked surprised, then smiled unpleasantly, nodding her head. 'That's a name I recognise. But I don't believe Mr Merlin was expecting a visit quite so quickly.'

'Really?' Ricky said. 'I would have guessed the exact opposite.'

It seemed to Ricky that the woman was about to dismiss him, when a man in his early thirties, slightly overweight and slightly balding, wearing pressed khaki slacks and an expensive designer sports shirt, emerged from the back of the office.

'I'm Merlin,' the man said, removing a folded linen handkerchief from his pocket and wiping his hands. 'If you will forgive the chaotic nature of our surroundings, we could perhaps speak for a few moments in the conference room. Most of the furniture is still there, although for how much longer is an open question.'

Ricky was ushered into a room dominated by a long cherry-wood table and chairs. There was an end table at the rear of the room, with a coffee machine. The attorney pointed towards a seat, then went and inspected the machine. Shrugging, he turned to Ricky.

'I'm sorry, Doctor,' Merlin said. 'No coffee left.'

'That's all right. I didn't come here because I was thirsty.'

This response made the lawyer smile. 'No. Of course not,' he said. 'But I'm not sure how I can help—'

'Merlin is an unusual name,' Ricky interrupted. 'One wonders whether you're a conjurer of sorts.'

Again the lawyer grinned. 'In my profession we are frequently asked by clients to pull the proverbial rabbit out of a top hat.'

'And can you do this?' Ricky asked.

'Alas, no. I have no magic wand. I rely less on magical powers than on a torrent of papers and a blizzard of demands.'

'And you are moving?'

The attorney passed a business card across the table to Ricky. 'The new digs,' he said, not unpleasantly.

Ricky looked at the card. It had a downtown address. 'And am I to be another pelt on your wall?'

Merlin nodded. 'Probably,' he said.

'Who is your client?' Ricky demanded abruptly.

The lawyer shook his head. 'I am not at liberty to divulge her name. She is in the process of recovery and—'

'None of this ever happened.' Ricky sliced through the lawyer's words. 'It is all a fantasy. Your real client is someone else, true?'

The attorney paused. 'I can assure you my client is real,' he said. 'As are her complaints. Miss X is a very distraught young woman.'

'Why not call her Miss R?' Ricky asked. 'R as in Rumplestiltskin. Wouldn't that be more appropriate?'

Merlin looked a bit confused. 'I don't know that I follow your thinking. X, R, whatever. That's not really the point, is it? Dr Starks, you are in real trouble. And trust me, you want this problem to disappear just as quickly as humanly possible. If I have to file suit, well, then the damage will be done. Pandora's box, Doctor. All the evil things will just come flying out. Everything will become a part of some public record.'

'At no time have I ever abused a patient's trust.'

'Well, Doc, that's dandy. I hope you're right about that. Because'— as he spoke, the lawyer's voice gained a razor-sharp edge—'by the time I get through interviewing every patient you've had for the past decade or so and talking with every colleague you've ever had a dispute with, whether or not my client exists is not going to be relevant, because you will have absolutely no reputation left. None.'

Ricky wanted to respond, but did not.

'Do you have any enemies, Doctor? How about jealous colleagues? Have any of your patients over the years been less than pleased with their treatment? Have you ever kicked a dog? Maybe failed to brake when a squirrel ran out in front of your car up there at your vacation house on Cape Cod?' Merlin smiled. 'I already know about that place. A nice farmhouse in a lovely field with just a little bit of ocean view. Twelve acres. Purchased back in 1984. Do you have any idea how the value of that property has increased? I'm sure you do. Let me suggest to you, Dr Starks, one thing and one thing only. I'm going to own that property before this is finished. And I'm going to own your apartment and your bank account at Chase and the modest stock portfolio you keep with Dean Witter.'

'How do you know—?' Ricky started lamely.

Merlin cut him off. 'I make it my business to know. If you didn't have something I wanted, I wouldn't be bothering. But you do, and trust me on this, Doc, the fight isn't worth it.'

The lawyer's words were battering Ricky like so many punches in a mismatched prize fight. He took a deep breath, thinking he was stupid to have come, and the smart course was to get out rapidly.

He was about to rise when Merlin added, 'Hell can take many forms, Dr Starks. Think of me as merely one of them.'

'Come again?' Ricky said. He recalled what Virgil had said when she told him that she was to be his guide to Hell.

The lawyer smiled. 'In Arthurian times Hell was very real in the minds of all sorts of folks. They truly believed in demons, devils, possession by evil spirits. Today things are more complicated. We don't really think we're going to suffer eternal damnation in some fiery pit. So what do we have instead? Lawyers. And trust me, Doc, I can quite easily turn your life into something resembling a medieval picture etched by one of those nightmare artists.'

The door to the conference room swung open just then, and two of the removals men hesitated before entering. 'We'd like to get this stuff now,' one man said. 'It's pretty much all that's left.'

Merlin rose. 'No problem. Dr Starks was just getting ready to leave.'

Ricky, too, stood up. 'Yes. I am.' He looked down at the lawyer's card. 'This is where my attorney should contact you?'

'Yes.'

Ricky nodded, then turned and exited the office.

RICKY SLID INTO A CAB and told the driver to take him to the Plaza Hotel. For what he had in mind, it seemed the best selection. He sat back as they raced through midtown, thinking how hard it is sometimes to get a cab in Manhattan, and wasn't it intriguing that one was so readily available as he emerged, shaken, from the attorney's office? Just as if it had been waiting for him.

The cab driver pulled sharply to the kerb outside the hotel's entrance. Ricky pushed some money through the Plexiglas partition and got out of the cab. He jumped up the stairs and through the revolving hotel doors. The lobby was milling with guests, and he rapidly threaded his way through them. He went directly to the Central Park South exit of the hotel and stepped back onto the street.

There was a doorman flagging cabs for guests. Ricky stepped past one family gathered at the kerb. 'Do you mind?' he said to a middle-aged father in a Hawaiian print shirt who was riding herd on three rowdy children. A mousy wife stood to the side. 'I have a bit of an emergency. I don't mean to be rude, but . . .' He gestured to the cab waiting for them, jumped in, slamming the door behind him as he heard the wife say, 'That was ours.'

This cab driver, Ricky thought, at least wasn't someone hired by Rumplestiltskin. He gave the driver the address on the attorney's card. It took a quarter of an hour to battle through traffic. The new office was near Wall Street. It reeked of prestige.

The driver pulled to the side just shy of the building. Ricky paid and dragged himself from the tight confines of the rear seat. There was no sign of a removal van outside the building. He checked the address on the card, then stepped into the building and approached an office directory printed on the wall. He found no listing for Merlin. Ricky walked over to the uniformed guard at the security desk just inside the front door. The guard looked up as he came forward.

'I seem to be confused,' Ricky said. 'I have this lawyer's card, but I can't seem to find his listing.'

The guard checked the card. 'That's the right address,' he said, 'but we've got nobody by that name.'

'Maybe an empty office? He's moving in today.'

'There aren't any vacancies. Haven't been for years.'

'Well, that's strange,' Ricky said. 'Must be a printer's mistake.'

The guard handed back the card. 'Could be,' he said.

Ricky pocketed the card, thinking that he'd just won his first skirmish with the man stalking him.

RICKY WAS STILL feeling slightly smug as he arrived at his own building. He was unsure whom he'd met in the attorney's office. Was the man who called himself Merlin really Rumplestiltskin? This was a distinct possibility.

'What do you know about psychopaths?' he asked himself as he walked up the steps to the brownstone that housed his home/office and five other apartments. 'Not much,' he answered quietly to himself. What he knew about were neuroses. He knew about the lies well-to-do people told themselves to justify their behaviour.

He saw that the mail had been delivered, and he opened his box. One long, thin envelope bore an official seal in the upper left-hand corner from the Transit Authority. He opened this first.

There was a small piece of paper clipped to a larger photocopied sheet. He read the small letter first.

Dear Dr Starks,

Our investigation uncovered the enclosed among Mr Zimmerman's personal effects. Because it mentions you, I send it along. Our file on this death, incidentally, is now closed.

Sincerely,

Detective J. Riggins

Ricky flipped the cover letter back and read the photocopy. It was brief, typed and it filled him with a distant dread.

To whom it may concern:
I talk and talk, but never get better. No one helps me. No one listens to the real me. I have made arrangements for my mother. These can be found along with my will in my desk at work. Apologies to all involved, except Dr Starks.
Roger Zimmerman

Even the name had been typed, not signed by hand. Ricky stared at the suicide note, feeling his emotions simply drain through him.

FOUR

Zimmerman's note, Ricky thought, could not be real. Internally, he remained adamant. Zimmerman was no more likely to take his own life than Ricky was. He showed no signs of suicidal ideation, no inclinations to self-destruction. Ricky looked down at the suicide letter and realised he was the only person named.

Any elation he felt at outmanoeuvring the attorney that morning dissipated and was replaced with a queasiness bordering on nausea. He rode the elevator to his apartment with a sensation of weight dragging at his heels. By the time Ricky reached his office, he felt exhausted. He threw himself down behind his desk and seized the letter from the Psychoanalytic Society. The name of the Boston-based therapist his alleged victim was seeing was included in the letter. That was undoubtedly meant to be his next call.

Still feeling sick to his stomach, Ricky reached out and dialled the therapist's number. It rang once, then he got an answering machine: 'This is Dr Martin Soloman. I cannot take your call at this moment . . .' At least, Ricky thought, he hasn't left for vacation yet.

'Dr Soloman,' Ricky said briskly to the machine, 'this is Dr Frederick Starks in Manhattan. I have been accused by a patient of yours of serious misconduct. I would like to inform you that these allegations are totally false. They are fantasy, without any basis in substance or reality. Thank you.'

Then he hung up. He looked at his watch. Five minutes, he thought. Ten at the most, before he calls back.

About this he was correct. At the seven-minute mark, the telephone rang.

He answered with a solid, deep, 'Dr Starks speaking.'

The man at the other end of the line seemed to inhale sharply before saying, 'Doctor, this is Martin Soloman. I received your brief message and thought it wise if I got right back to you.'

Ricky waited for a moment before continuing, 'Who is your patient? Who has accused me of this reprehensible behaviour?'

He was greeted with an equal space of quiet before Soloman said, 'I don't know that I'm at liberty yet to divulge her name. She has told me that when investigators from the proper medical ethics authorities contact this office, she will make herself available. Surely you know who your patients were such a short time ago. And claims such as hers, with the detail she has provided me over the past six months, certainly lend credence to what she's said.'

'Detail?' Ricky asked. 'What sort of detail? I don't believe for a second that this person exists.'

'I can assure you she is completely real. She has described you, physically and intimately. She has described your office.'

'Impossible,' Ricky blurted.

Dr Soloman paused again, then asked, 'Tell me, Doctor, on the wall in your office next to the portrait of Freud, is there a small blue-and-yellow woodcut of a Cape Cod sunset?'

Ricky almost choked. The picture had been a present to him from his wife. He paused before asking, 'How long has this patient been seeing you?'

'I have been in therapy with her now for six months. Two sessions each week. She has been utterly consistent. Nothing she has said up to this point would make me doubt her in the slightest.'

'And where is she now?'

'She is on vacation until the third week in August.'

'Did she happen to give you a phone number where she could be reached during August?'

'No. I don't believe so. We merely made an appointment for shortly before Labor Day and left it at that.'

Ricky thought hard, then asked another question. 'And does she have striking, extraordinary, penetrating green eyes?'

Soloman paused. When he spoke, it was with an icy reserve. 'So you do know her, then?'

'No,' Ricky said. 'I was just guessing.'

Then he hung up the phone. 'Virgil,' he said to himself.

RICKY FOUND HIMSELF staring across his office towards the picture on the wall that had figured so prominently in the false recollections of the phoney patient. They were here, Ricky thought, long before the other day. His eyes cruised around the office. Nothing was safe.

Rage like a blow to the stomach staggered him, and his first response was to rise, stride across the office and seize the woodcut, ripping it from its hook on the wall. He dashed it into the waste basket by his desk, cracking the frame and shattering the glass. The sound was like a gunshot echoing in the small office space.

As quickly as it arrived, the anger fled, replaced by another wave of nausea. He felt dizzy. Ricky stumbled to the chair behind his desk and saw that the red light on his answering machine was blinking steadily. He reached down and pressed the switch to listen to the first of the messages. He immediately recognised the voice of a patient, a late-middle-aged journalist at the *New York Times*.

'Dr Starks,' the man said slowly, 'I apologise for leaving a message on your machine during your vacation, but this morning's mail brought a very disturbing letter.'

Ricky inhaled sharply.

'The letter was a copy of a complaint filed against you with the state medical ethics board. I recognise that the anonymous nature of the allegation makes it extremely hard to counter.' The patient hesitated. 'I have been placed in a substantial conflict of interest. There is little doubt in my mind that the complaint is a worthy news story and should be turned over to our city reporting staff. On the other hand, this act would obviously compromise our relationship. I am troubled deeply by the allegations, which I presume you deny.' The patient seemed to catch his breath, then added with a touch of bitter anger, 'Everyone always denies wrongdoing. Presidents. Government officials. Businessmen. Doctors . . .'

The patient paused, then hung up the phone.

Ricky's hand shook as he again pressed the PLAY button on the machine. The next message was merely a woman sobbing. He recognised another long-time patient. She, too, he guessed, had received a copy of the letter. Two remaining messages were also from patients.

Ricky didn't return any of the phone calls from his patients, and, by evening, all had called. Hours that totalled weeks that turned into years with each of the patients had been savaged by a single well-constructed lie. He didn't know how to respond or whether to respond at all. For the first time in his professional life, Ricky didn't know what to say.

IN THE MORNING he crossed another day off his calendar and composed the following enquiry:

> Searching high and looking fast,
> Inspecting all from twenty past.
> Is this year right or wrong?
> (Because of time, I have not long.)
> And although it seems like such a bother,
> Am I hunting for R's mother?

Ricky realised that he was stretching Rumplestiltskin's rules, first by asking two questions instead of one, and not exactly framing them for a simple yes or no response. But he guessed that by using the same nursery-school rhyme scheme that his tormentor had used, he might prompt Rumplestiltskin to ignore the violation of the rules and answer with slightly more detail.

The lady at the *Times* who took the order for the single-column front-page ad seemed intrigued by the rhyme. 'This is unusual,' she said lightly. 'Usually these are just Happy Fiftieth Anniversary ads, or come-ons for some new product. What's the occasion?'

Ricky, trying to be polite, replied with an efficient lie. 'It's part of an elaborate scavenger hunt. Just a summertime diversion for a couple of us who enjoy puzzles and word games.'

'Sounds like fun,' the woman replied. She read the rhyme back to him to check the wording, then took down his credit card details. 'Well, that's it, then. The ad will run tomorrow. Good luck with your game,' she added. 'I hope you win.'

'So do I,' he said. He thanked her and hung up the phone. He turned back to the piles of notes and records.

Narrow and eliminate, he thought. Be systematic and careful. Rule out men or rule out women. Rule out the old and focus on the young. Find the right time sequence. Find the right relationship. That will get a name. One name will lead to another.

Ricky breathed hard. He had spent his life trying to help people isolate blame and render it into something manageable. An analyst thinks of revenge as a crippling neurosis and tries to help patients find a way past that anger so that they can get on with their lives unencumbered by the need to get even. Getting even, in his world, was a weakness. Perhaps even a sickness.

As Ricky, his head spinning, tried to sort through what he knew and how to apply it, the telephone on the desk rang. It startled him. He reached for the phone, wondering whether it would be Virgil.

It was not. It was the ad lady at the *Times*.

'I'm sorry to call you back, Dr Starks, but we had a little problem. The Visa card number you gave me came back cancelled.'

'Cancelled? That's impossible,' he said indignantly.

'Well, maybe I got the number wrong.'

He reached for his wallet and pulled out the card, reading off the sequence of numbers again, slowly.

The woman paused. 'No. That's the number I submitted.'

'I don't understand,' Ricky said. 'I didn't cancel anything. And I pay off the entire balance every month.'

'The card companies make more mistakes than you'd think,' the woman said apologetically. 'Have you got another card? Or maybe you'd prefer to pay by cheque?'

Ricky started to remove another card from his wallet, then stopped abruptly. He swallowed. 'I'm sorry for the inconvenience,' he said slowly, working hard to stay under control. 'I'll have to contact the credit card company. In the meantime, please just send me the bill.'

The woman mumbled an agreement, double-checking his address, then adding, 'It happens all the time. Did you lose your wallet? You better call the issuing company and get it straightened out. They'll probably overnight you a new card.'

'I'm sure,' Ricky said. He hung up the phone.

Slowly he extracted each of the credit cards from his wallet. They're all useless, he told himself. They have all been cancelled. He didn't know how, but he knew by whom.

STILL, HE STARTED the tedious process of calling to discover what he already knew to be true. The customer service clerks at each credit card company were friendly but not very helpful. When he tried to explain that he hadn't actually cancelled his cards, he was informed that he indeed had. That's what their computers showed. The request had been made electronically, through their websites. He told each company he would get back to them. Then he took some scissors and cut each of the useless pieces of plastic in half.

Ricky did not know how far into his finances Rumplestiltskin had managed to penetrate. A visit to his bank was in order, he thought. He also placed a telephone call to the man who handled his modest investment portfolio, leaving a message with a secretary, asking that the broker call him back promptly. Then he sat for a moment, trying to imagine how Rumplestiltskin had entered this part of his life.

Ricky was a computer idiot. His knowledge of the Internet, chat rooms, websites and cyberspace was limited to a vague familiarity with the words but not the reality. If he had to compose a letter, he used an antique electric typewriter. His wife had purchased a computer a year before her death. He had been aware that she used the machine to contact support groups and speak with other cancer victims. Shortly after she'd died, he'd packed it away in the basement storage rooms of his building. He decided to recover it.

Ricky locked his front door behind him and took the elevator to the basement. It had been months since he'd been down there. Each of the building's six apartments had a storage area delineated by chicken wire nailed to cheap wooden frames. It was a place of broken chairs, rusty bicycles, boxes and trunks. Ricky approached his own cubicle with the padlock key in hand.

But the lock was already open.

He looked more closely and saw that it had been sliced open with bolt cutters. Ricky's first instinct was to turn and run, but instead he walked slowly forward to the chicken wire. What he saw immediately was that his wife's computer was missing. He moved inside the storage area and saw that another box was absent. This was a large plastic file container that held copies of his completed tax returns.

Staggered by an overwhelming sense of defeat, Ricky turned and headed back to the elevator. His stomach churned. No wonder Merlin knew so much about his assets. A tax return is like a road map. From Social Security number to charitable donations, it displays all the well-travelled routes of one's existence.

The missing computer frightened Ricky just as much. He had no idea what remained on the hard drive, but he knew that his wife had spent hours on the machine before the disease robbed her even of the strength to type. How much of her pain, memories and insights were there, he had no idea. He assumed that Rumplestiltskin had the ability to extract from the machine whatever he wanted.

RICKY'S DREAMS that night were filled with dark, violent images of being cut by knives. In one dream he saw himself trying to manoeuvre through a poorly lit room, knowing that if he stumbled he would fall through the blackness into oblivion. He awoke in the pitch-darkness of his bedroom, filled with panic, sweat staining his nightshirt. For a moment he was unsure whether he'd left the nightmare behind. He dropped his head back onto his pillow, desperate for rest, knowing none was readily available.

The ad ran in the *Times* that morning on the front page at the bottom, as specified by Rumplestiltskin. Ricky read it over and felt a momentary surge of success, as if he had taken a step forward.

By the end of the morning he had created two separate working lists. Still confining himself to the period from 1975 to 1985, he identified seventy-three people he had seen in courses of treatment that ranged from three months to seven years. The majority were traditional Freudian-based analyses, four or five times a week.

There were also a number of patients, perhaps two dozen over that ten-year period, who had started treatments and then interrupted them. Some hadn't the money to cover his fees. Others had relocated. A few had simply decided that they weren't being helped enough, or were too angry with the world to continue. They comprised his second list. This was, he realised, the far more dangerous list. They were the people who might have transformed their rage into an obsession with Ricky and then passed that obsession on.

He placed both lists on the desk in front of him and thought he should start the process of tracking down the names.

All morning he had been expecting the telephone to ring, with a reply from his account executive. He dialled the number again.

The secretary seemed flustered when she heard his voice. 'Oh, Dr Starks, Mr Williams was about to call you back. There's been some confusion over your account.'

Ricky's stomach clenched. 'Confusion?' he asked. 'How—?'

'I'm going to connect you with Mr Williams.'

'Dr Starks?' The executive came on the line, brusque and speaking swiftly. 'I'm sorry to have kept you waiting, but we're trying to figure out a problem here. Did you open up a personal trading account with one of the new online brokers?'

'No, I haven't. In fact, I hardly know what you're talking about.'

'Well, that's the confusing part. It appears that there's been significant day-trading in your account.'

'What's day-trading?' Ricky asked.

'Trading stocks rapidly, trying to stay ahead of market fluctuations.'

'OK. I understand. But I don't do this. Where is my money?'

The broker hesitated. 'I can't say precisely. We have our internal auditors going over the account now. All I can say is that there has been significant activity.'

'What do you mean activity? The money's just been sitting there.'

'Well, not exactly. There are dozens, maybe even hundreds, of trades, transfers, sales, investments . . .'

'Where is it now?'

The broker continued. 'A truly extraordinary trail of extremely complicated and aggressive financial transactions—'

'You're not answering my question,' Ricky said, exasperation filling his voice. 'My funds. My retirement account . . .'

'We're searching,' the executive said slowly, 'but right now there is no money. At least, none that we can find.'

'That's not possible.'

'Our investigators will track the transactions,' the man continued. 'We'll get to the bottom of this. It's just going to take time.'

'How much time?'

'I'd guess no more than a couple of weeks. At the most.'

Ricky hung up the phone. He did not have a couple of weeks.

By the end of the day he was able to determine that the only account that he owned that hadn't been raided was the small current account he kept at First Cape Bank up in Wellfleet. There was barely $10,000 in the account—money he used to pay bills at the local fish market and grocery, money to make his vacation run smoothly.

He was a little surprised that Rumplestiltskin had not assaulted these funds as well. He called the manager of the First Cape Bank and told him that he was going to close the account and wanted the balance in cash. The manager informed him that he would have to be present for that transaction. Ricky wished the other institutions handling his money had had the same policy. The manager offered to have the funds written into a cashier's cheque, which he would keep for Ricky's arrival. The problem was how to get the money.

Ignored in his desk was an open plane ticket from La Guardia to Provincetown. He wondered whether the reservation was still intact. He opened his wallet and counted out $300. In the top drawer of his bedroom dresser he had another $1,500 in traveller's cheques.

He could get to the Cape. And get back as well, he thought. It would take at least twenty-four hours. But in the same moment he was overcome with a sudden sense of lethargy. He felt dull, stupid. A black exhaustion flowed through his body. He recognised the warning signs of a clinical depression and held out his hands in front of him, looking for some quiver or palsy. They were steady.

How much longer? he wondered.

RICKY HAD DIFFICULTY sleeping that night, so when he heard the faint thump of the delivery service dropping the *Times* outside his apartment, he was alert. Within seconds he had seized the paper and brought it inside. He flung it open on the kitchen table. His eyes dropped to the small ads on the bottom of the front page, only to see an anniversary greeting, a come-on for a computer dating service, and a single-column box ad: SPECIALISED OPPORTUNITIES, SEE PAGE B-16.

Ricky threw the paper across the small kitchen in frustration. He had expected a rhyme at the bottom of the front page. 'How do you expect me to beat your damn deadline when you don't reply in timely fashion?' he almost shouted.

He noticed that his hands were shaking slightly as he made himself some coffee. The hot liquid did little to calm him. He sat at his table, outwardly immobile, inwardly churning, unable to imagine his next step. He needed to make plans, decisions, to take action, but not getting a reply when he expected one had crippled him.

Ricky did not have any idea how long he sat like that before lifting his eyes just slightly and fixing on the *Times* lying in a fluttered heap where he had flung it. He noticed a small streak of bright red just ducking out from underneath the pile. He picked himself up out of his chair and crossed the room. He bent over the mess of newspaper, reached for the splash of colour and pulled it towards him.

It was page B-16, the obituary page. But written in dramatic, glowing fluorescent red ink across the death notices was:

> *You're on the right track,*
> *As you travel back.*
> *Twenty certainly covers the base.*
> *And my mother is the right case.*
> *But her name will be hard to find,*
> *Unless I give you a clue in kind.*
> *So I will tell you this,*
> *You would have known her as a miss.*
> *You promised much, but delivered none.*
> *That's why revenge is left to her son.*
> *Father left, mother dead:*
> *That is why I want your head.*

Beneath the poem was a large red R, and beneath that, this time in black ink, the man had drawn a rectangle round an obituary, with a large arrow pointing at a picture of the dead man's face. Beside the arrow were the words: *You will fit perfectly right here.*

Ricky stared at the poem and the message it contained for close to an hour. As the day began to flee from beneath him, he realised that he now knew much more about the man stalking him. Rumplestiltskin's clues in the poem had been curiously generous, especially from someone who had first insisted that questions be answerable with a yes or a no. Twenty years, give or take a couple, put him into a range from 1978 through 1983. And his patient had been a single woman. Now he had a framework that he could function with.

As was Ricky's training and habit, he sat, trying to focus, trying to remember. Who was I twenty years ago? he asked himself. And who was I treating? There is a tenet to psychoanalysis that helps form the foundation of the therapy: everyone remembers everything. One might not remember it with journalistic accuracy; perceptions and responses may be coloured by all sorts of emotional forces. But when it is finally sorted through, everyone remembers everything. Hurts and fears can lurk deeply concealed under layers of stress, but they are there and can be found, no matter how powerful the psychological forces of denial can be.

So, alone in his office, he began to plumb his own memory. Occasionally he would glance over the shreds of notes and jotted images that constituted his record-keeping, angry with himself for not being more precise. He concentrated hard, a note pad on his lap, reconstructing his past. One after another, images of people took form. Names came slowly.

When he looked up, he saw that his office had filled with shadows. The day had drifted away from him. On the sheets of paper in front of him he had come up with twelve separate recollections. At least eighteen women had been in some sort of therapy with him between 1978 and 1983. This was a manageable number, but he was troubled that there were others that he was unable to recall. Of those he recollected, he had produced names for only half. And these were the long-term patients. He had an unsettling sensation that Rumplestiltskin's mother was someone he'd seen only briefly.

He rose from his chair, feeling stiffness in his knees and shoulders from sitting far too long in the same position. He stretched slowly and realised he had not eaten. He knew there was little for him to fix in his kitchen, and he turned and looked out of the window at the fast-crawling night gliding across the city, realising he would have to go out and purchase something. The thought of emerging from his apartment almost stifled his hunger. He had a curious response: the simple act of exiting his home made him pause. But he determined to head two blocks south. There was a little bar where he could get a sandwich. He did not know whether he would be watched.

On the sidewalk, he marched like a soldier, eyes front. The place he was looking for was in the middle of the block, with half a dozen small tables set outside for the summer. Inside it was narrow and dark, with a bar against one wall and another ten tables packed into the space. Ricky stepped inside.

A middle-aged waitress spotted him. 'All alone?' she asked.

'Right.'

The waitress pivoted, spotted an empty table at the rear. 'Follow me,' she said. She gestured towards a chair and opened a menu in front of him. 'Something from the bar?' she asked.

'A glass of wine. Red, please,' he said.

'Be right back. Special tonight is linguine with salmon. It's not bad.'

Ricky watched her depart for the bar. The menu was large. He propped it up against the water jug in front of him. After a moment he set the menu down, expecting to see the waitress with his wine.

Instead, Virgil stood opposite him.

In her hands were two glasses, each filled with red wine. She wore faded jeans and a purple sports shirt, and she had an expensive mahogany-coloured leather portfolio pinned under one arm. She set the drinks down on the table, then pulled a seat up and plopped herself down across from him, placing her portfolio on the floor. She reached out and took the menu from Ricky's hands. 'I already ordered each of us the special,' she said with a small, seductive grin. 'The waitress is one hundred per cent correct. It's not all that bad.'

Ricky stared hard across the table at the young woman as she took a slow sip of wine.

'Really should be drinking white with fish,' she said. 'But drinking red suggests a kind of devil-may-care attitude—a bit of adventure and lawlessness, playing outside the rules. Don't you think, Ricky?'

'I think that the rules are constantly changing,' he replied.

Virgil shook her head, causing her mane of blonde hair to bounce seductively. She threw her head back slightly to laugh, revealing a long, attractive throat. 'Of course, Ricky. You're right about that.'

The waitress brought them a basket filled with rolls. When she moved away, Virgil reached for one. 'I'm famished,' she said.

'So ruining my life burns calories?' Ricky posed.

Again Virgil laughed. 'It seems to,' she said. 'I like that. I really do. What shall we call it, Doc? How about the Ruination Diet?'

'Why are you here?' Ricky demanded. 'You and your employer seem to have my ruin all planned out. Step by step. Are you here to mock me? Perhaps add a bit of torment to his game?'

'No one has ever described my company as a torment,' Virgil said, adopting a look of false surprise.

Ricky's stomach had clenched into a ball, and the taste in the back of his mouth was acid. 'My life—' he started.

'Your life has changed. And will continue to change. At least for a few more days. And then . . . Well, that's the rub, isn't it?'

'You enjoy this, then?' Ricky asked suddenly. 'Watching me suffer. It's odd, because I wouldn't have taken you for a dedicated sadist. I don't see you as possessing the necessary psychopathology. But of course, I could be wrong about that. And that's what this is all about, right? When I was wrong about something?'

Ricky poured some water into a glass and sipped from it, hoping he'd baited the young woman into revealing something. He saw the start of anger crease the corners of her eyes. But then she recovered.

'You misunderstand my role here, Ricky.'

'Better explain it again.'

'Everyone needs a guide on the road to Hell. Someone to steer them through the hidden shoals of the underworld.'

'And you're that someone.' He took the wineglass in his hand, raised it to his lips, but spoke instead of drinking. 'Are you happy, Virgil? Happy with your criminality?'

'What makes you think I've committed a crime, Doctor?'

'Everything you and your employer have done, everything you have planned, is criminal. So far you've committed a number of felonies—including the possible murder of Roger Zimmerman . . .'

'His death has been ruled a suicide by the police.'

'You managed to make a murder appear to be a suicide. Of that I am persuaded.'

'I thought keeping an open mind was a hallmark of your profession.'

Ricky ignored this dig and persisted. 'Also robbery and fraud. Not to mention libel, with the bogus letters to the Psychoanalytic Society. That was you, wasn't it? Leading on that idiot in Boston with such an elaborate fiction?'

Virgil leaned back slightly in her seat. 'Isn't it remarkable how much a person will believe when they want to believe . . .?'

'I will get my reputation back,' Ricky said fiercely.

Virgil grinned. 'You need to be alive for that.'

Ricky looked up and saw the waitress approach with their dinners. She set them down and asked if there was anything else she could bring to the table. Virgil wanted a second glass of wine, but Ricky shook his head.

'That's good,' Virgil said as the waitress left. 'Keep a clear head.'

Ricky poked for an instant at the plate of food steaming in front of him. 'Why,' he asked abruptly, 'are you helping this man? Why don't you drop all this pretence and come with me to the police? I'd see to it that you regained some semblance of normal life. No criminal charges. I could do that.'

Virgil kept her eyes on her plate as well. When she lifted her gaze to meet his, her eyes barely concealed anger. 'You'll see that I return to a normal life? Are you a magician? And anyway, what makes you think there's anything so wonderful about a normal life?'

He ignored this question. 'If you're not a criminal, why are you helping one?'

Virgil continued to stare at him. All the breezy eccentricity and liveliness in her manner had dissipated, replaced by a sudden frosty harshness. 'Perhaps because I'm well paid. Many people are willing to do anything for money. Could you believe that of me?'

'Only with difficulty,' Ricky replied cautiously.

'Well, what other motives could there be? C'mon, Ricky, we've had two sessions together. If it's not money, what motivates me?'

Ricky stared hard at the young woman. 'I don't know enough about you,' he started lamely.

She put down her knife and fork with stiff deliberateness. 'Do better, Ricky. For my sake. After all, I'm here to guide you. Without me you'll get no closer to an answer, which will kill either you—or someone close to you who is in a state of complete ignorance. And dying blindly is stupid, Ricky. In its own way worse than a crime. So now, answer my question: what other motives might I have?'

'Love,' Ricky said abruptly.

Virgil smiled. 'Love?'

'You're in love with this man Rumplestiltskin.'

'That's an intriguing idea. Especially when I told you I don't know who he is. Never met the fellow.'

'Yes, I recall you said that. I just don't believe it.'

'Love. Money. Are these the only motives you can come up with?'

Ricky paused. 'Perhaps fear as well.'

Virgil nodded. 'Fear is good, Ricky. Perhaps Mr R has some sort of threatening hold over me. Do I behave like a person being asked to perform tasks against my will?'

'No,' Ricky replied.

'Well, OK then. On to business. You got the reply to your questions in your paper this morning?'

Ricky paused, then answered, 'Yes.'

'Good. That's why he sent me here this evening. To double-check.

Wouldn't be fair, he thought, if you didn't get the answers you were searching for. Pick your next questions wisely, Ricky, if you want to win. As of tomorrow morning, you have only a single week left. Seven days and two remaining questions.' Virgil bent down and lifted the small leather portfolio that she'd been carrying when she arrived. She opened it, removed a manila envelope and handed it across the table to him. 'Open it up,' she said.

He undid the clasp. Inside were half a dozen eight-by-ten black and white photographs. He removed these and examined them. The first shots were of a young woman, perhaps sixteen or seventeen years old, wearing blue jeans and a T-shirt. The next two photographs were of a girl, perhaps twelve years old, seated in the bow of a canoe, paddling across a lake. Then there was a third set of a teenage boy with longish hair and an insouciant smile, gesturing with a street vendor in what appeared to be a street in Paris. All six pictures seemed to be taken without the knowledge of the subjects.

'Recognise anyone?' Virgil asked coldly.

Ricky shook his head.

'Those are pictures of some of your distant relatives, Ricky. Each one of those children is on the list of names Mr R sent you.'

He looked again at the pictures.

'Do you think it was hard to take these photographs? Could one replace a camera with a high-powered rifle?' She reached across the table to take the pictures from his hands. 'I think all that we need to leave you with are the mental portraits, Ricky. Put the smiles those children wear into your head. Will you rob the future from one of them—or someone like them—by obstinately clinging to your own pathetically few years remaining?'

Virgil paused. Then she grabbed the photographs and returned them to her portfolio. She pushed back from the table and stood up, simultaneously dropping a single $100 bill on top of her half-eaten plate of food. 'You've stolen my appetite,' she said. 'But I know your financial situation has deteriorated, so I'll pay for dinner.'

She turned towards the waitress, who was hovering at a nearby table. 'Do you have some chocolate cake?' she asked.

'A chocolate cheesecake,' the woman replied.

Virgil nodded. 'Bring a piece for my friend here,' she said. 'His life has suddenly turned bitter, and he needs some sweetness to get him through the next few days.'

Then she walked out, leaving Ricky alone. He reached for a glass of water and noticed that his hand shook, rattling the ice in the glass.

HE WALKED HOME in the growing city darkness, his isolation nearly complete. In a curious way, Ricky realised, he was almost transparent. His face, his appearance, his very being did not mean anything to anyone except the man stalking him. His death, on the other hand, was of critical importance to some anonymous relative.

As he fixed the faces of the three young people in the photographs in his memory, his stride lengthened. He began to hurry. He could hear his shoes slapping against the sidewalk. He looked down and saw that he was running. He gave in to a sensation he didn't recognise, but to anyone stepping aside on the pavement to let him pass, must have looked like a full-blown panic.

Ricky ran one block, then another, not stopping until he was within sight of his home. He heaved to a stop, bending over, gasping for breath. He remained like that, regaining his wind, for several minutes. When he did lift his eyes, he thought: I am not alone.

He pivoted sharply, trying to spot whoever was watching him. His eyes raced from candidates strolling down the street to empty windows in nearby buildings. He spun about and stared at his own building. He was overcome with the thought that someone had been in his apartment while he was out bantering with Virgil. He told himself to be calm, centred. He took a long, deep breath. For the first time, he thought: I must find a safe spot. Not having any idea where, Ricky trudged up the steps.

To his astonishment, there were no obvious signs of disruption. The door wasn't ajar. The lights functioned normally. He closed and locked the apartment door behind him, feeling a momentary surge of relief. Still, his heart continued to race.

'You need a good night's sleep,' he told himself, speaking out loud, recognising the tones that he might use for a patient.

As he tried to focus his thoughts, his eyes travelled to his desktop. He noticed that the list of relatives Rumplestiltskin had sent him was prominently placed in the centre of his blotter, and Ricky did not recall leaving it there. He reached out slowly, then pulled the sheet of paper towards him. A dizzying sensation of doubt and confusion slid through him. He started to look about, his eyes darting back and forth. He picked up notes, paper pads and other debris from his desk, searching. But in the same instant he knew that what he wanted was gone: Rumplestiltskin's first letter, describing the game and containing the first clue, had been removed from his desk. The physical evidence of the threat to Ricky had disappeared. All that remained was the reality.

FIVE

The next morning, he drew another X through a day on his calendar and then wrote down two telephone numbers on a pad in front of him. The first number was for Detective Riggins of the New York City Transit Authority Police. The second was a number he had not used in years. It was for Dr William Lewis. Twenty-three years earlier Dr Lewis had been his training analyst, the physician who undertook Ricky's own analysis while Ricky was obtaining his certificate. It is a curious facet of psychoanalysis that everyone who wants to practise the treatment must undergo the treatment.

The two phone numbers, he thought, represented polar opposites of help. He was unsure whether either would actually be able to provide any, but he needed to talk to someone.

The detective answered her phone on the second ring simply by brusquely speaking her last name: 'Riggins.'

'Detective, this is Dr Frederick Starks. You will recall we spoke last week about the death of one of my patients.'

'Sure, Doctor. I sent you a copy of the suicide note we uncovered the other day. I thought that made things pretty clear-cut. What's bothering you now?'

'I wonder if I might speak with you about some of the circumstances surrounding Mr Zimmerman's death.'

'What sort of circumstances?'

'I'd prefer not to speak on the phone.'

'That sounds terribly melodramatic, Doctor. But sure. Want to come here? We have a nasty little interview room where we extract confessions from criminal suspects. More or less the same thing you do in your office—just a little less civilised and a lot more rapid.'

RICKY FLAGGED A CAB on the corner. He had the taxi take him north ten blocks and drop him at the corner of Madison and 96th Street. He walked into the first store he could see, a women's shoe store, and spent exactly ninety seconds examining the shoes. Then he exited, walked across the street and flagged down another cab. He instructed this driver to head south to Grand Central Terminal.

At Grand Central, Ricky entered the stream of people that flowed through the cavernous interior towards commuter trains or subway connections. He took the first subway heading west, rode it one stop, then bounded from the train, rising from the stifling underground into the superheated air of the street, and again flagged the first cab he could spot. He scrunched down in the seat and rode in silence to the Transit Authority Police station at 96th and Broadway.

Riggins stood up as he walked through the door to the detective bureau. She offered her hand in a firm shake. 'Doc, glad to see you, although I must say, this is a bit unexpected.' She seemed to assess his appearance. 'You look lousy, Doc. Maybe you're taking Zimmerman's confrontation with a subway train a little hard.'

He shook his head, smiling. 'Not sleeping much.'

Riggins gestured towards the interview area she'd mentioned.

The room was bleak, a narrow space devoid of adornment, with a single metal table in the centre and three steel folding chairs. A fluorescent overhead light filled the room with glare.

Riggins must have noticed the way he was assessing the room, and she said, 'The city's decorating budget is very lean this year. We had to give up all the Picassos on the walls.' She gestured at one of the seats. 'Pull up a chair. Tell me what's bothering you.'

Ricky took a deep breath before replying. 'A relative of a former patient has been threatening me and my family members with some unspecified harm. To this end, they have taken some steps to disrupt my life. These steps include bogus charges against my professional integrity, electronic assaults on my financial status, break-ins at my home, invasions of my personal life, and the suggestion that I take my own life. I have reason to believe that Zimmerman's death was part of this system of harassment that I have been undergoing in the past week. I don't believe it was a suicide.'

Riggins's eyebrows had shot up. 'Dr Starks, sounds like you're in some sort of mess. A former patient?'

'No. The child of one. I don't know which one quite yet.'

'And you think this person who has it in for you persuaded Zimmerman to jump in front of the train?'

'Not persuaded. Perhaps he was pushed.'

'It was crowded, and no one saw a push. No one whatsoever.'

'The lack of an eyewitness doesn't preclude it happening.'

'Of course not, Doctor. But here we have LuAnne, who says he jumped, and even if she's not terribly reliable, she's something. And we have a suicide note and a depressed, angry, unhappy man.' Riggins fixed Ricky with a long stare before continuing. 'Doctor, it seems to me you should take this to someone who can help you.'

'And who might that be?' he asked. 'You're a police detective. I've told you about crimes. Or what might be crimes. Shouldn't you make a report of some sort?'

'Do you want to make a formal complaint?'

Ricky looked hard at Riggins. 'Should I? What happens then?'

'I present it to my supervisor, who's going to think it's crazy, and then I channel it through police bureaucracy, and in a couple of days you'll get a call from some other detective who's going to be even more sceptical than I am. Sounds to me like you need to be talking to someone in the extortion and fraud bureaus of the NYPD. And if it were me, I'd be looking to hire a private detective—and a damn good lawyer.'

'You don't think that you should look into these things? As a follow-up on the Zimmerman case?'

This question made Riggins pause. She had not taken any notes. 'I might,' she said carefully. 'I need to think about it. It's hard to reopen a case once it has received a closed status.'

'But not impossible.'

'Difficult. But not impossible.'

'Can you get authority from your superior—?' Ricky started.

'I don't think I want to open that door quite yet,' the detective said. 'As soon as I tell my boss there's an official problem, then all sorts of bureaucratic stuff has to occur. I think I'll just poke around myself. Maybe. Tell you what, Doctor. Why don't I look at a few things, then get back to you.'

'I'll expect your call at your earliest convenience,' Ricky said.

Then he rose, feeling as if he'd just struck a blow for himself. Not a victorious sensation, but at least one that made him feel a little less alone in the world.

RICKY TOOK A CAB to Lincoln Center. The Metropolitan Opera House was empty except for a few tourists and some security guards. There was a bank of payphones he was familiar with. The advantage was that he could make a call while keeping an eye on anyone who might follow him into the opera house.

The number he had for Dr Lewis had been changed, as he'd expected. But he was connected to a second number with a different area code. The receiver rang eight times before being answered.

'Yes?'

'Dr Lewis, please.'

'This is Dr Lewis.'

It was a voice Ricky had not heard in many years, yet it filled him with a rush of emotion that surprised him. A torrent of hates, fears, loves and frustrations was loosed within him. He struggled to maintain composure. 'This is Dr Frederick Starks.'

'Well, I'll be darned. It is nice to hear from you, Ricky, after so many years. I am quite taken aback.'

'Doctor, I didn't know where else to turn.'

There was a brief silence. 'You are troubled, Ricky?'

'Yes. I was hoping you might lend me some time to talk.'

'I do not really see patients any more,' Lewis said. 'Age. Infirmity. All sorts of things simply sliding away.'

'Will you see me?'

The old man paused. 'You would have to come out here, I'm afraid. No more midtown office.'

'Where's here?' Ricky asked.

'Rhinebeck,' Dr Lewis said, adding an address on River Road. 'You can get a train from Pennsylvania Station.'

'If I get there this afternoon—'

'I will see you whenever you arrive. That's one of the advantages to retirement—a distinct lack of pressing appointments. Take a cab from the station, and I will be expecting you around dinner time.'

THE TRAIN TRAVELLED north, following the course of the Hudson River. Only a small group of people got off in Rhinebeck, and Ricky lingered on the platform inspecting each one, still worried that somebody had managed to follow him. No one even glanced in his direction, except a little boy who paused and made a face. Ricky waited until the train had departed, then climbed the long flight of stairs leading away from the tracks. Outside the station he saw only a single bedraggled white taxi with a large dent in the front.

The driver spotted Ricky and sharply pulled to the kerb. 'You need a ride, fella?' he asked.

'Yes,' Ricky answered. He gave the man Dr Lewis's address.

The road to the old analyst's house was meandering and narrow. Stately oaks created a canopy of shade above the road. Ricky could see clusters of horses standing in fields and, in the distance, large, imposing mansions.

Dr Lewis's home was a reconditioned farmhouse, painted a vibrant, glowing white, with a placard that read 1791. A hammock and some garden chairs stood to the side, and a ten-year-old blue Volvo station wagon was parked in front of a stable.

The cab pulled away behind him, and Ricky paused on the edge of the gravel drive. He breathed in sharply, feeling a rush of conflicting emotions that turned his feet leaden and accelerated his heart rate. The relationship between analyst and analysand is in many ways like that between an authority figure and a child. The doctor knows virtually every emotional intimacy of the patient, who, in turn, knows next to nothing about the therapist.

Ricky was halfway to the front steps when the door swung open. He heard the voice before he saw the man: 'Slightly uncomfortable, I will wager.'

Ricky replied, 'You read my mind,' which was something of an analyst joke.

He was ushered into a study right off the hallway. White walls. Books on a shelf. Tiffany lampshade. Oriental carpet. He could smell a faint odour of lilac.

Dr Lewis was a slight man, bent a little at the shoulders, bald, with aggressive tufts of hair bursting from his ears. He wore glasses perched far down on his nose, so that he rarely seemed to actually look through them. He moved slowly, limping slightly, and finally settled into a large red leather wing chair, gesturing to Ricky to sit in an armchair a few feet away. Ricky sank down into the cushions.

'I am delighted to see you, Ricky, even after so many years. How long has it been?'

'More than a decade, certainly. You're looking well, Doctor.'

Dr Lewis grinned and shook his head. 'Probably should not start this out with such an obvious lie, although at my age one appreciates lies. The truths are always so inconvenient. I need a new hip, two new eyes and ears, and some new teeth. I could use a new car and the house could use new plumbing. Come to think of it, so could I. The roof is fine, though.' He tapped his forehead. 'Mine too. But I am sure you did not track me down to find out about me. You will join me, of course, for dinner, and I have had the guest bedroom made up for you. And now I should keep my mouth shut and have you tell me why you are here.'

Ricky paused, uncertain where to begin. He stared across at the old man and felt his control sliding away. What he said was choked out past lips that quivered. 'I believe I have only a week left to live.'

Dr Lewis's eyebrows arched upwards. 'You are ill, Ricky?'

Ricky shook his head. 'I think I must murder myself.'

The old analyst leaned forward. 'That is a problem,' he said.

Ricky spoke nonstop for more than an hour. He told of receiving the first letter, the poetry and threats, the stakes of the game. He described Virgil and Merlin. He tried to leave out nothing—from the electronic assaults on his bank and brokerage accounts to the two visits to Detective Riggins. He spoke about Zimmerman and the false accusation of sexual impropriety. He ended by talking about the impact of the photographs of the three young people shown to him by Virgil. Then he leaned back and grew silent.

'Most intriguing,' Dr Lewis finally said, emitting a long sigh. 'I suppose the central question here, Ricky, is the one Rumplestiltskin has posed: will you kill yourself to save another?'

Ricky was taken aback. 'I'm not sure,' he stammered. 'I don't think I've really considered that alternative.'

Dr Lewis shifted in his seat. 'It is not all that unreasonable a question,' he said. 'Your choice, it seems to me, is simple. Can you win? Can you determine the identity of the man called Rumplestiltskin in the few days you have remaining? If not, will you kill yourself to save another? Can you make that sacrifice?'

'I can't believe . . .' Ricky started. Then he stopped.

Dr Lewis looked at him and lifted his shoulders. 'I am sorry. Of course you have not considered this consciously. But I wonder if you have not asked yourself these same questions in your unconscious, which is what prompted you to find me.'

'I came for help,' Ricky said. 'I need to probe the era in my past where Rumplestiltskin's mother was my patient. I believe that I was seeing her at the time when you were my training analyst. I must have mentioned her to you during our sessions. So what I need is a sounding board. Someone to bounce those old memories off.'

Dr Lewis nodded. 'Not an unreasonable request, and clearly an intelligent approach. The analyst's approach. Talk, not action. Do I sound cruel, Ricky? I guess I have become irascible in old age. Of course I will help. But it seems to me it would be wise to look at the present as well. Perhaps, too, your future. To win, you must plan further ahead than your opponent.'

'How do I—?'

Dr Lewis rose. 'That is what we should figure out over a modest dinner and the remainder of the evening.' He smiled. 'Of course, you are assuming one great factor.'

'What is that?' Ricky asked.

'Well, it seems quite obvious that this fellow Rumplestiltskin has spent months, probably years, planning his revenge.'

'Yes.'

'I wonder, then,' Dr Lewis said slowly, 'why you assume that he has not already enlisted me, perhaps through threats or outside pressure of some sort, to help him. Maybe he paid me off. Why, Ricky, do you presume I am on your side?' And with a sweeping gesture for Ricky to accompany him instead of answering the question, the old analyst led the way into the kitchen.

Two places had been set at an antique table in the centre of the kitchen. A jug of iced water graced the table.

Dr Lewis lifted a casserole from the oven, placed it on a trivet, then took a salad out of the refrigerator. 'Have a seat, Ricky. The concoction that stands before us is chicken. Please help yourself.'

Ricky hesitated. He reached out and poured a tall glass of water, then gulped at it like a man who has just crossed some desert. 'Has he?' he demanded abruptly.

'Has he what?'

'Has Rumplestiltskin approached you? Are you a part of this?'

Dr Lewis sat down and helped himself to a generous portion of casserole and salad before replying. 'Let me ask you this, Ricky,' he said slowly. 'What difference would it make?'

'I need to know that you are on my side.'

The old man shook his head slowly. 'No, you do not, Ricky. You need to know only that I am willing to help you. My motives are irrelevant. Perhaps Rumplestiltskin has something on me. Perhaps he does not. Now eat some dinner. I anticipate a long night ahead.'

They ate their meal in relative silence. The casserole was excellent and was followed by a homemade apple pie that had a touch of cinnamon in it. There was black coffee as well.

Dr Lewis removed the plates to the sink. He refilled his coffee cup, then gestured for Ricky to return to the study. They went back to the seats they had occupied earlier, facing across from each other.

'So, Ricky, where would you like to begin?'

Ricky fought his anger at the older physician's oblique and elusive character. 'Twenty-three years ago. When I first came to you.'

'I recall you were filled with theory and enthusiasm.'

'I believed I had the ability to save the world from despair and madness, single-handed.'

'And did it work out that way?'

'No. You know that. It never does.'

'But you saved some?'

Ricky wanted to stifle his first reply, but was unable. 'I couldn't save the person I cared the most for.'

The old analyst's eyebrows arched slightly. 'I presume we are speaking of your wife?'

'Yes. We met. We fell in love. We were inseparable for years. She grew ill. She died. End of tale. She isn't connected to this.'

'Of course not,' Dr Lewis said. 'But you and she met when?'

'Our courtship took place while I was in analysis with you. You should recall that.'

'I do. And what was her profession?'

'She was an attorney. At the time we met, she had just joined the Manhattan office of the public defender.'

'I see. She was involved in defending criminals. And now you seem involved with someone who fits the category of criminal, but you think there can be absolutely no possible link?'

Ricky stopped, mouth open to reply. This thought chilled him. 'Rumplestiltskin has not mentioned—'

'I merely wonder,' Dr Lewis said, waving a hand in the air.

Silence grew around the two men. Ricky began to picture himself as a young man, filled with energy, at a moment when the world was opening for him. 'During the course of my treatment with you, Dr Lewis, I saw patients in three venues: at the outpatient clinic at Columbia Presbyterian Hospital, a brief stint with the severely compromised at Bellevue—'

'Yes,' Dr Lewis nodded. 'A clinical study. I recall you did not particularly enjoy treating the truly mentally ill.'

Dr Lewis's statement had a provocative quality to it, a bait Ricky didn't rise to. 'And then, perhaps twelve to eighteen patients in therapies that became my first analyses. Those were the cases you heard about while I was in therapy with you.'

'Yes. Yes. These are figures I would agree with.'

Ricky leaned back. 'Rule out the people I saw at Bellevue, because they were far too crippled to produce someone this evil. That leaves my private practice and the people I treated in the clinic.'

'The clinic, then, first.'

Ricky closed his eyes for a moment, as if this might help him picture the past. The outpatient clinic at Columbia Presbyterian was a warren of small offices on the ground floor of the immense hospital. The majority of the clientele travelled up from Harlem or down from the South Bronx. They were mostly poor working-class folks who occupied the no-man's-land of mental health, between the middle class and the homeless. Their problems were real; he saw drug abuse, sexual abuse, physical abuse. He saw many more than one mother abandoned by some husband, with cold-eyed and hardened children whose career goals appeared to be limited to joining a street gang.

'The people I saw at the clinic were all disadvantaged,' Ricky said. 'People on the fringes of society. I would guess that the person I'm seeking is among the first patients I had in analysis. Not these others. And Rumplestiltskin has already told me that it is his mother. But she went by her maiden name—"a miss", he said.'

'Interesting,' Dr Lewis said. His eyes seemed to flicker with intrigue. 'So of all those patients, how many were single women?'

Ricky thought hard, picturing a handful of faces. 'Seven.'

Seven women. They ranged in age from their early twenties to early thirties. All were what used to be called career women in that they were brokers, executive secretaries, lawyers or businesswomen.

Slowly, voices returned, words spoken in his office. Specific moments, breakthroughs, understandings—all forced themselves back into his consciousness, prodded by the questioning of the old doctor perched crowlike on the edge of his chair. The night swept around the two physicians, closing off everything save the small room and Ricky's recollections. He wasn't sure how much time had passed, but he knew the hour was late. He paused suddenly in mid-recall. Dr Lewis's eyes gleamed with an otherworldly energy.

'She is not there, is she Ricky?' he suddenly asked.

'These were the women in treatment,' he replied.

'And all treated more or less successfully. Can you not recall any failures, Ricky? Because that is where you must find your link to Rumplestiltskin. Not in successes.'

'I'm sure that's possible, but how would I—?'

'This group of patients at the clinic were somehow lesser in your mind, were they not? Less affluent? Less educated? Perhaps they did not register quite as firmly on young Dr Starks's radar screen.'

Ricky bit back any answer, because he could see both truth and prejudice in what the old physician was saying.

'Who came but stopped coming, Ricky?'

'I don't know.'

'Who did you see for fifteen sessions?'

'Fifteen? Why fifteen?'

'How long did Rumplestiltskin give you to uncover his identity?'

'Fifteen days.'

'You might have been more sensitive to the number, because there is the connection. And what is it he wants you to do?'

'Kill myself.'

'So, Ricky, who saw you for fifteen sessions, then killed herself?'

Ricky reeled, his head suddenly aching. I should have seen it, he thought. I should have seen it because it is so obvious.

'I don't know,' he stammered again.

'You do know,' the old analyst said, a little anger in his voice. 'You just don't want to know.' He rose then. 'It is late, and I am disappointed. I have had the guest bedroom made up for you. Up the stairs and to the right. Perhaps in the morning, after you have done some additional reflection, we can make some legitimate progress.'

'I think I need more help,' Ricky said weakly.

'You have been helped,' Dr Lewis replied.

THE BEDROOM WAS TIDY, well appointed, with a sterile hotel-room quality to it that made Ricky think it was infrequently used. No magazines stacked by the bed, no pictures of family on the walls.

Ricky stripped to his underwear and threw himself into the bed, after a single glance at his watch showed him that it was well past midnight. He was exhausted, but sleep eluded him. The sounds of crickets and the occasional moth bumping up against the window screen were twice the racket that the city created. He slowly filtered these noises away and could just make out the distant sound of Dr Lewis's voice. Ricky tried to concentrate. The old analyst was angry about something, his tone raised in tempo and tenor. Ricky strained to make out the words but was unable. Then he heard the unmistakable clattering of the phone being slammed into its cradle.

He was not aware when he plunged into sleep, but he awoke to shafts of bright sunlight striking his face. The summer morning might have seemed perfect, but Ricky dragged with the weight of disappointment. He had hoped that the old physician would be able to steer him to a name. If Dr Lewis's observation was accurate, what remained hidden, Ricky realised, was the context that the woman existed in. He told himself that he had far too quickly dismissed the less well-heeled women he'd seen in the psychiatric clinic.

He pulled on his clothes, dashed water on his face, grabbed his jacket and headed downstairs, energised by the idea that, with Dr Lewis's help, he could assault these memories like a World War II dam buster—that he could simply lob a big enough explosion at the concrete of repressed history and it would all burst through.

He poked his head into the study area, searching for his host, but saw the room was empty. He walked towards the kitchen, where he could smell the aroma of coffee. Dr Lewis wasn't there.

A fresh pot of coffee was warming on a hot plate, and a single cup had been left out for him. A folded piece of paper was propped up with his name written on the outside. Ricky opened the note.

Ricky,

I have been called away unexpectedly and do not anticipate a return within your time frame. I believe you should examine the arena you left for the critical person, not the arena you entered. I wonder, as well, whether by winning the game you will not lose, or conversely, by losing, you can win. Consider strongly the alternatives that you have. Please never contact me again for any reason.

W. Lewis, MD

Ricky reeled back sharply, as if he'd been slapped in the face. For a second he gripped the edges of the counter, trying to steady himself. In that moment he heard the sound of a car coming up the gravel driveway. His first thought was that it was Dr Lewis returning with an explanation, so he half ran to the front door. But what he saw instead surprised him.

Pulling to the front was the same cab driver who had picked him up the day before at the train station. The driver gave him a little wave and rolled down his window as the taxi stopped.

'Hey, Doc, how you doing? We better get a move on if you're gonna catch your train. The next one isn't until late this afternoon.'

'How did you know to pick me up?' Ricky asked. 'I didn't call.'

'Well, someone did. I got a message on my beeper says get right over here and pick up Dr Starks pronto and make certain you make the nine fifteen. So I burn rubber, and here I am, but if you don't toss yourself in the back there, you ain't making that train.'

Ricky hesitated, then grabbed the door handle and thrust himself into the back seat. He felt a momentary pang of guilt for leaving the house wide open, but dismissed this. 'OK,' he said. 'Let's go.'

The driver accelerated sharply, kicking up some gravel and dust.

Within a few minutes the cab reached the intersection where the access road to the Kingston-Rhinebeck Bridge, which crosses the Hudson, cuts across River Road. A New York State trooper was standing in the centre of the roadway, waving traffic to the left. The cab driver rolled his window down and shouted to the trooper, 'Hey, Officer! Can't I get through? Gotta make the train!'

The trooper shook his head. 'No way. Road's blocked about a half-mile down. You need to drive around. Some old guy lost it on one of the turns. Wrapped himself around a tree.'

'He dead?' the cab driver asked.

The trooper shook his head as if to signify that he wasn't sure. 'Rescue's there now.'

Ricky sat forward sharply. 'What kind of car?' he asked.

'Old blue Volvo,' the trooper said as he waved the cabbie to get moving. The driver accelerated.

'I've got to see!' Ricky said. 'The car—'

'We stop to sightsee, ain't gonna make the train.'

'But that car . . . Dr Lewis drove an old blue Volvo.'

'Hell, there's dozens of those cars around here.'

'No, it can't—'

'The cops won't let you down there. And even if they would, what you gonna do?'

Ricky didn't have an answer. He slumped back in the seat.

'You get back to the city, then call the Rhinebeck state trooper barracks. They'll fill you in. Unless you want to go to the hospital, but I wouldn't advise it. You'd just sit around the ER waiting and still not know much more than you do right now. Haven't you got someplace important to be?'

'Yes,' Ricky said, although he was unsure of this.

'The guy with the car—he a good friend?'

'No,' Ricky replied. 'Not a friend at all. Just someone I knew. I thought I knew.'

'Well,' the driver said, 'there you have it.' He accelerated again, pushing the cab through a yellow light. Ricky leaned back in the seat, just once glancing over his shoulder through the rear window, where the accident remained hidden. He strained to see flashing lights and tried to hear sirens, but they all eluded him.

He MADE THE TRAIN with a minute or two to spare. There were only a handful of people waiting for the midweek, midmorning trip back to New York City. The carriage was almost empty. Ricky went to the rear and scrunched himself into a corner, immediately turning his head to the window, where he could inspect the Hudson River.

He felt like a buoy cut loose from its mooring, adrift and vulnerable. There was some mental block between him and the right memory. The right patient, the right relationship seemed to be just out of his reach, no matter how hard he stretched for it.

Of one thing he was sure. All that he had become in his life was irrelevant. The mistake he had made, which lay at the core of Rumplestiltskin's anger, came from his initial foray into the world of psychiatry. It came from the moment he had turned his back on the difficult and frustrating business of treating the disadvantaged and headed into the stimulating business of treating the neurotic rich.

This observation enraged him. Young men make mistakes. This is inevitable in any profession. Now he was no longer young, and he wouldn't have made the same error, whatever it was. He was being held accountable for something he had done more than twenty years earlier. That seemed unfair and unreasonable. Had Ricky not been so battered by all that had happened, he might have seen that his entire profession was more or less based on the concept that time only exacerbates the injuries done to the psyche. It never heals them.

He continued to stare through the window throughout the trip. At the various stops, he barely looked up and hardly shifted in his seat. The last stop before the city was Croton-on-Hudson, perhaps fifty minutes from Pennsylvania Station. The carriage was still ninety per cent empty, with dozens of vacant seats, so Ricky was startled when another passenger came up from behind and slipped in beside him, dropping into the seat with a heavy thud.

Ricky turned sharply, astonished.

'Hello, Doctor,' the attorney Merlin said. 'Is this seat taken?'

SIX

Merlin's breathing seemed a little laboured and his face flushed, like a man who'd run fifty yards to catch the train. A line of perspiration marked his forehead, and he reached inside the breast pocket of his jacket and removed a white handkerchief, which he dabbed at his face. 'Almost missed the train,' he said. 'I need to do more exercise.'

Ricky took a deep breath before asking, 'Why are you here?'

The attorney folded the handkerchief and returned it to his breast pocket. Then he stowed his briefcase and a waterproof gym bag in the area at his feet. He cleared his throat and replied, 'Why, to encourage you, Dr Starks. Encourage you.'

'You lied to me before. I went to your new address. They hadn't heard of you. So who are you?'

The attorney looked bemused. 'You went to the new offices?'

'Yes. I didn't believe you were who you said you were, and when I arrived at the location printed on your business card—'

'I gave you a card?' Merlin shook his head. 'On moving day? That explains much. The first batch of business cards I ordered from the printer came back with the wrong address, and I'm afraid we didn't notice right away. The new offices are a single block over.'

'I don't believe you,' Ricky said. 'And you know what, Mr Merlin? There are plenty of seats on this train.' Ricky gestured at the nearly empty car. 'Take one of those, and leave me alone.'

Merlin did not budge. 'That would not be wise,' he said slowly.

'Perhaps I'm tired of behaving wisely,' Ricky said. 'Maybe I should behave rashly.'

The attorney smiled. 'Ah, Dr Starks, I detect some desperation in your voice.'

'Deliver your message, why don't you?' Ricky said bitterly. 'That's what you are, after all, right? A message boy. So get on with it.'

'Urgency, Doctor. Pace. Speed.'

'How so?'

'You need to ask your second question in tomorrow's paper. You've got to get a move on, Doctor. Time is flitting past.'

Merlin reached down and lifted his briefcase up to his lap. He opened it. Ricky saw that it contained a laptop computer, several manila file folders and a portable telephone. It also contained a steel-blue semiautomatic pistol. The attorney pushed the weapon to the side and seized the phone. He flipped it open and turned to Ricky. 'Isn't there a question left over from this morning on your mind?'

Ricky continued to eye the pistol. 'What do you mean?'

'What did you see this morning on the way to the train?'

Ricky's face was set, his voice steely. 'An accident.'

'Are you certain about that, Doctor?' Merlin punched a series of numbers on the phone's keypad, then handed Ricky the cellphone. 'Ask your question. Press "send" to make it work.'

Ricky hesitated, then took the phone and did as suggested. The line rang once and a voice came on. 'State police, Rhinebeck. Trooper Johnson. How can I help you?'

'Hello. This is Dr Frederick Starks calling. As I was heading to the train station this morning on River Road, there was an accident. I'm concerned that it involved someone I knew.'

The trooper's reply was curious but brisk. 'This morning?'

'Yes,' Ricky said. 'Not more than two hours ago.'

'I'm sorry, Doctor, but we have no reports of any accidents this morning.'

Ricky sat back hard. 'But I saw . . . involving a blue Volvo? The victim's name was Dr William Lewis. He lives on River Road.'

'Not today. I've been on dispatch duty since six this morning, so any calls would come through me. Are you sure about what you saw?'

Ricky took a deep breath. 'I must have been mistaken. Thank you.'

'No problem,' the man said, disconnecting the line.

Ricky's head whirled dizzily. 'But I saw a trooper. He was waving traffic around, and he said—'

'"He said." What a great phrase. So he said something, and you took it for the truth. You saw a man dressed like a state trooper, and you assumed he was one. Did you see an ambulance? A fire truck? Did you hear sirens?'

Ricky was forced to shake his head. 'No.'

'So you took one man's word that there was an accident, but you didn't check further? You felt that whatever you had to do was more important than ascertaining whether someone needed help.' Merlin smiled with the irritating appearance of someone in utter control. 'Perhaps you should try to telephone the person you went to visit. Make certain they are OK.'

Ricky quickly punched in Dr Lewis's telephone number. The phone rang repeatedly, but there was no answer.

Before he could say anything, the lawyer was speaking again.

'What makes you so sure that that house truly was Dr Lewis's place of residence?' Merlin asked. 'What did you see that connected the good doctor directly to that place?'

Ricky concentrated. The study where they'd sat most of the night was a typical study. Books on the walls. Chairs. Lamps. Carpets. Nothing unique stood out in his recollection. The kitchen was simply a kitchen. The guest room was noticeably sterile.

He remained silent.

Merlin took a deep breath. 'Let me summarise briefly, Doctor. The only thing that you can be sure of is that you spent some hours in the presence of a physician you knew years ago. You don't know whether that was indeed his home or not, or whether he has been in an accident. You don't know for certain that your one-time analyst is alive or not, do you?'

Ricky started to reply, then stopped.

Merlin continued. 'Ricky, was there a car accident this morning?'

'No.'

'You're sure?'

'I just spoke to the state police. That guy said—'

'How do you know it was the state police? I dialled the number and handed you the phone, right? Maybe your friend Dr Lewis is on a slab in the Dutchess County Morgue right now.'

'But—'

'You're missing the point, Ricky.'

'All right,' Ricky said, snapping sharply. 'What is the point?'

The attorney's eyes narrowed slightly. He indicated the gym bag at his feet. 'Maybe he wasn't in an accident at all, Doctor, but instead, in that bag right now I've got his severed head. Is that possible, Ricky?'

Ricky recoiled sharply in surprise.

'Is it possible, Ricky?' the lawyer probed, his voice now hissing.

Ricky's eyes fell to the bag. It was a simple duffle shape, it was big enough to carry a person's head, and it was waterproof, so that it would be without stains or leakage.

He raised his eyes towards Merlin. 'It's possible,' he whispered.

'It is important that you understand that anything is possible, Ricky. An automobile accident can be faked; bank accounts can be eviscerated; relatives can be murdered. You need to act!'

There was a quaver in Ricky's next question. 'Don't you have any limits?'

Merlin shook his head. 'None whatsoever.'

Ricky shifted in his seat. 'Suppose,' he said hoarsely, 'I were to walk away right now. Leave you sitting with whatever is in that bag . . .'

Again Merlin smiled. He reached down and turned the bag slightly, revealing the letters F.A.S. embossed on the top. Ricky stared at his initials. 'Don't you think that there's something in that bag alongside the head that links you to it, Ricky? Don't you think that the bag was purchased with one of your credit cards before they were cancelled? Of course, I can always take the bag with me.'

'How—?'

'Ask your second question, Ricky. Call the *Times* right now.'

'I don't know that I—'

'Now, Ricky.' Merlin started to dial the cellphone. 'There,' he said, with brisk efficiency. 'I've dialled the *Times* classified for you. Ask the question, Ricky!'

Ricky took the phone. In a moment he was connected to the same woman who'd taken his call the prior week.

'This is Dr Starks,' he said slowly. 'I'd like to place another front-page ad.' His mind churned swiftly, trying to formulate words.

'Of course, Doctor. How's the scavenger hunt game going?' the woman asked.

'I'm losing,' Ricky replied. Then he said, 'This is what I want the ad to say.' He paused and took a breath.

> *'Twenty years, it was no joke,*
> *At a hospital I treated poor folk.*
> *For a better job, some people I left.*
> *Is that why you are bereft?*
> *Because I went to treat some other,*
> *Did that cause the death of your mother?'*

The ad lady repeated the words to Ricky and said, 'That seems like a pretty unusual clue for a scavenger hunt.'

Ricky answered, 'It's an unusual game.' He gave her his billing address again and disconnected the line.

Merlin was nodding his head. 'Very good,' he said. 'Most clever, considering the stress you're under. You can be a very cool character, Dr Starks. Probably much more so than you even realise.'

The train abruptly descended beneath the surface of the earth, leaving midday behind, lurching towards the station. Merlin rose as it pulled to a stop.

'Do you ever read the *New York Daily News*, Ricky? No, I suspect you're not the type for a tabloid. But I think you would be well served by reading the *News* today, because there is a story there that you will find most intriguing. I would suggest absolutely essential.' He gave a little wave of the hand. 'This has been the most interesting ride, don't you think? The miles have simply flown past.' He pointed at the bag. 'That's for you, Doctor. A present.'

Then Merlin turned, leaving Ricky alone in the carriage.

Ricky's heart and hands seemed to quiver. He bent over and lifted the bag from the floor, feeling dizzy. Something inside shifted position. He seized the zipper on the top and opened it slowly. He pulled back the opening and stared inside.

In the centre of the bag was a large cantaloupe.

Relief filled him, and the world seemed to return to focus.

He zipped the bag back up and rose. The train was empty now.

Throwing the bag over his shoulder, Ricky proceeded down the platform. The core of Pennsylvania Station was ahead, and he moved steadily towards the glow of the station lights. As he marched, his eye picked out one of the porters sitting on a hand truck, engrossed in the *Daily News*. In that single second the man opened the paper, so that Ricky could see the screaming headline on the front page. He read TRANSIT COP IN HIT-RUN COMA.

RICKY SAT on a hard wooden bench in the middle of Pennsylvania Station with the *News* on his lap. Every word he read seemed to skid across his imagination like a car out of control, careening inevitably towards a crash.

Joanne Riggins, a thirty-four-year-old detective with the New York Transit Authority Police, had been the victim of a hit-and-run driver the night before, struck less than half a block from her home as she crossed the street. The detective remained on life-support systems in a coma at Brooklyn Medical Center after emergency surgery. Prognosis questionable. Witnesses had seen a red Pontiac Firebird fleeing the site of the accident. One such vehicle was owned by the detective's estranged former husband, who was being questioned by police. He was claiming that his car had been stolen the night before the accident. The paper also reported that the ex-husband had publicly threatened his wife during the final year of their marriage. It was a tabloid dream story, filled with out-of-control passion that resulted in violence.

Ricky also knew that it was fundamentally untrue.

The driver of the car wasn't the man the police were interviewing. Ricky crumpled the *News* in anger, tossing the pages aside. He considered telephoning the detectives working the case. He considered calling Riggins's boss at the Transit Police. He shook his head in growing despair. There was no chance whatsoever, he thought, that anyone would hear what he had to say. Not one word.

He rose and, like a wounded man, started to make his way out of the station, heading towards the cab stand. There was a homeless man begging by the station entrance. Ricky stopped and dropped all his loose change into the man's empty Styrofoam coffee cup.

'Thank you, sir. Thank you,' the man said. 'Bless you.'

Ricky stared at the man for a moment, taking note of the sores on his hands, the lesions, partially hidden by a scraggly beard, that marked his face. Dirt, grime and tatters. Ravaged by the streets and mental illness. The man could have been anywhere between forty and sixty years old.

'Are you OK?' Ricky asked.

'Yes, sir. Yes, sir. God bless you, generous sir. God bless you.'

'Where are you from?' Ricky asked.

The homeless man stared at him, filled with a sudden distrust. 'Here,' he said carefully, indicating his spot on the sidewalk.

'Where's home?' Ricky asked.

The man pointed at his forehead. This made sense to Ricky.

'Well then,' Ricky said, 'have a nice day.'

'Yes, sir. Yes, sir. God bless you, sir.'

Ricky stepped away, abruptly trying to decide whether he had cost the man his life merely by speaking with him. He walked towards the taxi stand wondering if every person that he came in contact with would be targeted like the detective had, like Dr Lewis might have been. Like Zimmerman. One injured, one missing, one dead. He realised: Whoever I touch is vulnerable.

Poison, he thought. I've become poison.

It was nearly sixty blocks to his apartment, and he walked them all, barely aware that he even took a breath of air on the trip.

Ricky locked himself in his apartment and slumped down into the armchair in his office. That was where he spent the remainder of that day and the entirety of the night, afraid to go out, afraid to stay still, afraid to remember, afraid to leave his mind blank, afraid to stay awake, afraid to sleep.

HE MUST HAVE nodded off sometime towards morning, because when he awoke the day was already blistering outside. His neck was stiff and every joint in his body creaked with the strain of spending the night in a chair. He rose gingerly and went to the bathroom, where he brushed his teeth and splashed water on his face, pausing to stare at himself in the mirror. Tension seemed to have made inroads in every line and angle he presented to the world. Not since his wife's final days had he appeared so close to despair.

The *Times* was outside his door, and he picked it up and saw his question at the bottom of the front page, next to an ad seeking men for impotency studies. He quickly flipped through the newspaper, half hoping that the reply was somewhere within, because, after all, Merlin had heard the question and presumably passed it on to his boss. But Ricky could find no evidence that Rumplestiltskin had toyed with his paper a second time.

The idea that he would have to wait twenty-four hours for an answer was impossible. Ricky knew that he had to make progress even without assistance. The only avenue he thought viable was to try the clinic where he had worked so briefly twenty years earlier. He dressed quickly and headed to the front door of his apartment. But once standing there, his hand on the doorknob, he stopped. He felt a sudden wave of anxiety sweep over him and send his heart rate pitching high. Internally, a massive warning screamed, insisting that he not go out, that he was unsafe outside the doors to his apartment.

He recognised what was happening to him. He'd treated many patients with similar anxiety attacks. He bit down on his lip, understanding that it is one thing to treat, another to experience. A black wind seemed to envelop him, and he thought that if he stepped outside he would surely die.

It took every iota of power he had within him to open the door. It was painful to take a step forward. By the time he reached the street, he was stained with sweat. He stepped to the kerb, his hand raised. In that second a yellow taxi miraculously pulled up directly in front of him to disgorge a passenger. Ricky reached for the door to hold it open for whoever was inside and, in that time-honoured city way, to claim the cab for himself.

It was Virgil who stepped out.

'Thanks, Ricky,' the woman said. She adjusted dark sunglasses on her face. 'I left the paper for you to read,' she added.

Without another word she spun away, walking quickly down the street. Within seconds she had turned a corner and disappeared.

'Come on, buddy, you want a ride?' the driver demanded. Ricky looked inside the cab, saw a copy of that day's *Times* folded on the back seat, and, without thinking further, threw himself in.

'Columbia Presbyterian Hospital,' he said. 'The outpatient clinic.'

The driver pushed down the meter flag and accelerated into the midmorning traffic.

Ricky reached for the newspaper. He found what he was looking for on page A-13, written in red pen in large letters across an ad from Lord & Taylor's department store.

> *Ricky narrows the track,*
> *Getting closer, heading back.*
> *Ambition, change, clouded your head,*
> *So you ignored all the woman said.*
> *Left her adrift, in a sea of strife,*
> *So abandoned it cost her life.*
> *Now the child, who saw the mistake,*
> *Seeks revenge for his mother's sake.*
> *Who once was poor, but now is rich,*
> *Can fill his wishes without a twitch.*
> *You may find her in the records of all the sick,*
> *But is it enough to do the trick?*
> *Because, poor Ricky, at the end of the day,*
> *There's only seventy-two hours left to play.*

The simple rhyme, like before, seemed mocking, cynical in its childlike pattern, like the singsong taunts and insults of the kindergarten playground. There was nothing childish about the results that Rumplestiltskin had in mind, however. Ricky tore out the single page from the *Times*, folded it up, and slid it into his trouser pocket.

The cab dropped him on the sidewalk outside the huge hospital complex. He could see an emergency entrance down the block, with a large red-lettered sign and an ambulance in front. Ricky felt a chill sweep down his back despite the oppressive midsummer heat.

THE PAUNCHY, MIDDLE-AGED clerk at the records storage bank counter looked at Ricky with bemused astonishment when he explained his request. 'You want *what* from twenty years ago?'

'All the outpatient psychiatric clinic records from the six-month period I worked there,' Ricky said.

'This will take some time, Doctor,' the clerk said. 'And I've got lots of other requests.'

There was $250 in Ricky's wallet. He removed $200, placing it on the counter. 'Perhaps this will help put me at the head of the line.'

The clerk glanced around, saw that no one else was watching, and scooped up the money from the countertop. 'Doctor,' he said with a small grin, 'my expertise is all yours.' He pocketed the cash.

The clerk showed Ricky to a small steel table off to the side of the records office. There was a stiff-backed wooden chair, where Ricky took up his position while the clerk checked the computer records and started to bring files to him. It took the remainder of the morning to collect all the relevant files—for 279 people. The clerk stacked them on the floor next to Ricky and provided him with a yellow legal pad and a ballpoint pen.

Hours fled. Reading the files was a little like standing in a waterfall of despair. Each contained a patient's name, address, next of kin, and insurance information, if there was any. Then there would be some typed notes on a diagnosis sheet. Meagre words were unable to hide the bitter truths that lay behind each person's arrival at the clinic: sexual abuse, beatings, drug addictions, schizophrenia. When he first joined the clinic staff, Ricky had been filled with idealism, determined to bring analytic techniques to the desperate urban poor. His altruism had lasted about a week.

In his first five days, Ricky had his desk rifled by one patient seeking drug samples, he'd been assaulted by a wild man hearing voices, and he'd been forced to send a pre-teen girl to the emergency room with cigarette burns on her arms. The girl would not tell Ricky who had put them there. He remembered her well enough; she was Puerto Rican and had soft, beautiful black eyes and no insurance. He saw her five times, which was all the state would allow.

He picked up another file and briefly wondered how he'd even managed to last six months. The entirety of his time here he'd spent feeling utterly helpless. Ricky spotted his handwritten notes. He pulled these out and tried to connect the name on the file with the words he had scrawled down.

A few feet away, the records office clerk dropped a pencil from his desk and with a small cursed obscenity reached down for it.

Ricky eyed him as he bent back to the computer screen glowing in front of him. The man was hunched over slightly, nervously drumming the pencil against the desktop. In that second Ricky understood something, something he should have seen in the way the man's hand had clawed up the money he offered him. Ricky quietly pushed away from the table and stepped over behind the clerk.

'Where is it?' Ricky demanded in a low voice. As he spoke, he reached out and gripped the man's collarbone tightly.

'What the hell?'

'Where is it?' Ricky repeated sharply.

'What are you talking about? Let me loose!'

'Not until you tell me where it is.' By now Ricky had seized the clerk's throat. 'Where is it?'

'They took it!'

'All right. Who took it?'

'A man and a woman. Just about two weeks ago. What the hell's this all about?'

Ricky released him. 'How much did they pay you?'

'More than you did. A whole lot more. I didn't think it was so damned important, you know. It was just one file that nobody'd even looked at for two decades. I mean, I didn't see the problem.'

'Especially when he handed you some cash.'

The clerk shrugged. 'Fifteen hundred. In hundreds.'

The coincidence of the amount was not lost on Ricky. Fifteen days' worth of hundreds. He glanced over at the stack of files and despaired at the hours he'd wasted. 'So they took the file and paid you off, but you're not that stupid, are you?'

The clerk twitched slightly. 'What do you mean?'

'I mean, you haven't worked in a records office for all these years without learning a little bit about covering your tail, right? You didn't give up that file without copying it, did you?'

'Yeah, I copied it,' the man said slowly.

'Hand it over,' Ricky said.

The clerk paused. 'You gonna pay me?'

'Consider the payment the fact that I don't call your boss.'

The clerk bent down and opened a drawer. He reached in and produced an envelope that he handed to Ricky. 'There,' he said. 'Now leave me alone.'

Ricky glanced inside. 'This is it?' he asked.

The clerk plucked another, smaller envelope from the drawer. 'Here,' he said. 'This was attached to the outside of the file—you know, clipped on. I didn't give it to the guy. I don't know why.'

'What is it?'

'A police report and a death certificate.'

Ricky breathed in sharply.

'What's so important about some poor woman who showed up at the hospital twenty years ago?' the man asked abruptly.

'Someone made a mistake,' Ricky answered.

'So now someone's got to pay?'

Ricky gathered himself to leave. 'It would seem so.'

RICKY WALKED OUT of the hospital building feeling a tingling in his hands. He was unable to recall a previous moment in his life when he'd used force to accomplish something. He felt that he'd crossed some sort of barrier. He'd been a man of words—until he received the letter from Rumplestiltskin.

He walked towards the Hudson River, heading through the huge hospital complex. There was a small courtyard not far from the front of the Harkness Pavilion, a branch of the hospital that catered to the wealthy. It was a quiet place where one could sit on a bench and allow the city noises to fade away.

It did not take him long to spot a bench, and within moments he was seated, the file and envelope on his lap. Ricky paused, then reached into the folder.

The name of the woman patient he'd seen twenty years ago was Claire Tyson.

He stared at the letters of her name. It meant nothing to him. No face sprang into his recollection. No voice echoed in his ear. His inability to recall a single detail filled him with ice.

Ricky read quickly through the intake form. The woman had come to the clinic in a state of acute depression coupled with panic-like anxiety. She had been referred to the clinic by the emergency room, where she'd gone for treatment of contusions and lacerations. There was evidence of an abusive relationship with a man who was not the father of her three children. Their ages were given as twelve, ten and eight, but no names were included. She'd had no health insurance and had been working part-time in a grocery store. Her Social Security number was the only other completed item on the form.

He turned to a second sheet and saw his own handwriting. The words filled him with dread. They were clipped, curt, to the point.

Miss Tyson presents as a twenty-nine-year-old mother of three young children in a possibly physically difficult relationship with a man not their father. She states that the children's father abandoned her several years ago to take a job working on oil rigs in the Southwest. She is able to work only part-time, as she has no funds to hire adequate childcare. She receives state assistance from welfare, and federal AFDC, food stamps and a housing subsidy. She further states that she is unable to return to her native Florida, having been estranged from her parents by her relationship with the children's father.

Miss Tyson appears to be a woman of above-average intelligence who cares deeply about her children and their welfare. She has a high-school diploma and two years of college, having dropped out when she became pregnant with her first child. She appears significantly undernourished and admits to spontaneous eruptions of tears of despair. She says she remains alive only for the children, but denies any other suicidal ideation. She denies drug dependency or addiction, but a toxicology screen is warranted.

Initial diagnosis: Acute persistent depression caused by poverty. Personality disorder. Possible drug use.

Recommendation: Outpatient treatment to state-mandated limit of five sessions.

There was a second sheet, showing that Claire Tyson had come back to see him four times and had failed to appear for her fifth and last authorised session. So Dr Lewis had been wrong about the number of sessions. But then another thought occurred to Ricky. He flipped open the copy of the death certificate and compared that date to the initial treatment date on his clinic form: fifteen days.

He sat back hard on the bench. The woman had come to him, and half a month later she was dead.

The death certificate seemed to glow in his hand, and Ricky quickly scanned the form. Claire Tyson had hanged herself in the bathroom of her apartment using a leather belt looped over an exposed pipe. The autopsy revealed she had been beaten shortly before her death and that she was three months pregnant. A police report clipped to the death certificate said that a man named Rafael Johnson had been questioned about the beating but not arrested. The children had been handed over to the department of youth services.

And there it was, Ricky thought. In the whirlpool of life that trapped young Claire Tyson, there had been only one thing that gave her meaning: the three children.

And now one of them was out to get him.

The oldest, Ricky thought. She must have told the oldest that she was going to the hospital to see him and to get help.

Find that child, and you find Rumplestiltskin.

He rose from the bench, thinking he had much to do, pleased in an odd way that the pressures of time and deadlines were so pressing, because otherwise he would have been forced actually to consider what he had done—or not done—twenty years earlier.

RICKY SPENT THE REMAINDER of the day in New York City bureaucratic hell. Armed only with a twenty-year-old name and address, he was shunted between offices and clerks throughout the state department of youth services in downtown Manhattan, trying to determine what happened to the three children of Claire Tyson.

He was standing across from a large, pleasant Hispanic woman in the records division of juvenile court. She had a massive flow of raven-black hair that she pulled back sharply from her face. 'Doctor,' she said, 'this is not much to go on.'

'It is all I have,' he replied.

'If these three children were adopted, the records were likely sealed. They can be opened, but only with a court order.'

'A court order would take days.'

'That's right. You get a little more information about these people, get one of those fancy search programs on your computer— maybe you'll come up with the info.'

'I don't really use computers much.'

'You ought to try,' the clerk said. 'Big help if you got a Social Security number, or something like that.'

Ricky looked down at the sheets of paper he'd received at the hospital records office. The officers who had questioned Rafael Johnson, the dead woman's abusive boyfriend, had taken down his

Social Security number. 'Hey,' Ricky said suddenly, 'if I give you a name and a Social Security number, will that computer of yours find someone for me?'

'It might. What's the name?'

Ricky showed the woman the name and number from the police report. She looked round quickly, to see if anyone in the office was watching her. 'Not really supposed to do something like this,' she muttered. 'But you being a doctor, well, we'll see.'

The clerk clicked red-painted fingernails across the keyboard. The computer whirred. Ricky saw an entry come up on the screen, and simultaneously, the woman's eyebrows rose in surprise.

'This be some bad boy, Doctor. He got a robbery, another robbery, an assault, did six in Sing Sing for aggravated assault. Man, some kind of very nasty record.' The woman read further, then said, 'He isn't going to be any help to you, Doctor. He's dead. Just six months ago. Looks like a good riddance, to me. There's a report with the entry. Seems like somebody beat Rafael Johnson to death. Oh, nasty, real nasty. Seems like after they beat him, somebody strung him up over a pipe, using his own belt.'

Ricky reeled back. It wasn't hard for him to guess who'd found Rafael Johnson. And why.

FROM A PAYPHONE in the lobby of the courthouse building, Ricky dialled the number for the *New York Times* advertising department to ask his final question. The clerk seemed annoyed that Ricky had just managed to beat the 6.00pm deadline for the ad. Her voice was curt. 'All right, Doctor. What do you want the ad to say?'

Ricky thought, then said:

> *'Is the man I seek, one of the three?*
> *Orphaned young, but now no fool,*
> *Seeking those who were so cruel?'*

The clerk read the lines back to him without making a single comment, and Ricky was thankful for that.

He walked out to the street and started to lift his hand to flag down a cab, then thought he would rather ride the subway. A steady stream of people was descending into the bowels of Manhattan to ride the trains home. He joined them, finding an odd sanctuary in the press of humanity. The subway was packed, so he rode north hanging from a metal rail, jostled by the rhythm of the train. It was almost luxurious to be gripped by so much anonymity.

He tried not to think that in the morning he would have less than seventy-two remaining hours.

The subway stop was two blocks from Ricky's home, and he rose up through the station, grateful to be out in the open again, and set off rapidly down the street. He turned the corner to his block and stopped abruptly in his tracks.

In front of his brownstone there were three police cars, lights flashing, one red city fire truck and two yellow public works vehicles. Ricky could see several policemen standing about by his front steps, talking with workers wearing hard hats. With a deep engine roar and a siren's harsh blare, the fire truck headed off down the street.

Ricky hurried forward. When he arrived in front of his building, he was out of breath. One of the policemen turned and faced him.

'Hey, slow down, fella,' the officer said.

'This is my home,' Ricky replied anxiously. 'What happened?'

'You live here? Oh, man. You better go talk to the suit over there.'

Ricky looked towards another group of men. He saw one of his neighbours, a stockbroker who headed the building association, arguing with a department of public works man wearing a yellow hard hat. Two other men stood nearby. Ricky recognised one of them as the building supervisor and another as the man in charge of building maintenance.

The DPW man was speaking loudly. Ricky approached and heard him say, 'I'm the guy who decides occupancy, and I'm saying no way!'

The stockbroker turned away in frustration, pivoting in Ricky's direction. He gave a small wave and stepped towards Ricky, leaving the other men arguing.

'What is going on?' Ricky asked him.

'It's a mess. One huge mess. Apparently there was some sort of massive plumbing failure on the third floor. Several pipes burst wide open simultaneously, because of some kind of pressure build-up. Gallons and gallons of water have flooded the first two floors, and the other floors have no utilities at all. Now this idiot wants the entire building cleared.'

'But my things—'

'One of the DPW guys will escort you in to get what you need. They're saying the whole place is dangerously compromised.'

'But how?'

'They don't know. The guy said it was like the plumbing simply exploded. And apparently the apartment where it all started was right above yours, so I hope you know a good general contractor.'

Ricky stepped back, staring up at his home of a quarter of a century. It was a little like being told of a death. He gestured at the building maintenance man. 'Take me in,' he demanded. 'Show me.'

The man nodded unhappily. 'You ain't gonna like it,' he said, handing Ricky a hard hat.

There was still water dripping through the ceiling and leaking down the walls of the lobby as Ricky entered the building. The atmosphere inside was moist, humid and musty, like a jungle. There was a faint odour of human waste in the air.

They took the stairs up slowly, avoiding the standing water as much as possible, although Ricky's shoes had already begun to make squishing sounds, and he could feel wetness seeping through the leather. On the second floor he saw a large bulge in the ceiling, like a gigantic boil about to burst.

The door to his apartment was open wide. He took a single step inside and stopped in his tracks.

It was as if some kind of hurricane had swept through his home. Brown-tinged noxious water was pooled up an inch deep. Huge portions of the ceiling were bowed and buckled; others had burst open, spreading white, snowlike plaster dust around. As he stepped farther in, the smell of waste increased, almost overwhelming him.

He cautiously entered his office, standing in the doorway. A huge slab of plaster had fallen onto the couch. There were at least three different holes in the ceiling, and exposed pipes hung down like stalactites in a cave. Water covered the floor. The artwork, his diplomas, and the picture of Freud had fallen.

When Ricky stepped forward, the maintenance man reached out. 'Not in there,' he said. 'I don't think the floor is safe. And I ain't trusting what's left of that ceiling to stay put.'

'My things . . .'

'Things are just things, Doc. Not worth risking injury. We need to get out of here and let the experts take over. They gonna have to gut this place top to bottom.'

That was what Ricky felt in that second. Gutted from top to bottom. He turned and followed the man out. A small piece of ceiling fell behind him as if to underscore what the man had said.

Back out on the sidewalk, the stockbroker, accompanied by the man from DPW, approached him.

'Bad?' the broker said. 'Ever seen worse?'

Ricky shook his head.

The broker handed Ricky his business card. 'Look, call me in a couple of days. In the meantime, have you got a place to go?'

Ricky nodded, pocketing the man's card. He had just one untouched place left in his life, but he did not have much hope that it would remain that way.

SEVEN

The last of the night clothed him like an ill-fitting suit, tight and uncomfortable. He pressed his cheek up against the glass of the Bonanza bus window, listening to the diesel drone of the engine. After a stop in Providence, the bus had finally reached Route 6 on the Cape and was making its slow and determined progression up the highway, discharging passengers in Falmouth, Hyannis, Eastham.

The bus was by now only about one-third filled. Sitting alone in the back, Ricky measured what he was heading to, a modest inventory that did more to depress than encourage. A house dusty with memories. A dented and scratched ten-year-old Honda Accord used solely during summer vacations. Some weathered khakis, polo shirts, and sweaters with frayed collars. A cashier's cheque for $10,000 awaiting him at the bank. A life in utter disarray.

And about sixty hours before Rumplestiltskin's deadline.

For the first time in days he fixated on the choice facing him: the name or his own obituary. Otherwise someone innocent would face a punishment that Ricky could only begin to imagine. He had no doubt any longer of Rumplestiltskin's sincerity. Nor of his reach.

Ricky glanced at his wristwatch. He would arrive in Wellfleet around dawn.

PERHAPS THE MOST wondrous thing about starting his vacation, year in, year out, had been the greeting of routine. Every year on August 1 he took the same flight from La Guardia to the small airport in Provincetown, where the same cab company picked him up. The process of opening the house remained the same, from tossing the windows open to the clear Cape air, to folding the threadbare sheets that had covered the wicker furniture.

This year everything was different. The bus unceremoniously deposited him in the parking lot at the Lobster Shanty Restaurant.

He trudged off down the highway. It took just under an hour to reach the dirt track that led to his house, which was barely a quarter of a mile from the road but hidden from roadside view. Built over a hundred years earlier, the house had been a small farm, so it was set at the edge of fields that had once grown corn.

He stood on the front step, relieved that he'd found the spare key beneath the loose grey flagstone, as expected. He unlocked the door and stepped inside. The musty smell of stale air was almost a relief. But as Ricky recognised the tasks that awaited him—tidying up, sweeping out—a dizzying exhaustion filled him. He walked up the narrow flight of stairs to the bedroom and tossed himself onto the creaky double bed where he'd slept alone for the past three summers, dropping almost immediately into a deep but unsettled sleep.

RICKY COULD SENSE that the sun had scoured the day when he opened his eyes to the early afternoon. For a moment he was disorientated, but then, as he awoke fully, the world around him jumped into focus.

He moved swiftly to the ordinary chores of summertime. A trip to the barn to pull the car cover off the old Honda and plug in the electric battery charger that he kept in storage. Then, as the car was being re-energised, he went back to the house to strip the furniture covers off and run a few quick broom swipes along the floors.

He breathed a long sigh of relief when a short time later the Honda started up. He pumped the brakes, and they seemed to work as well. He backed the car out gingerly.

The First Cape Bank was a small building with shingle siding, like many of the older homes in the area. But the inside was modern. The manager, a short, outgoing fellow, shook Ricky's hand vigorously.

'Well, we've been expecting you, Dr Starks. Yesterday a courier delivered a package here addressed to you, care of the bank.'

'A package?'

The manager handed him an overnight mail envelope. It had Ricky's name and the bank manager's name. It had been sent from New York. In the box for a return, there was a post office box number and the name R. S. Skin. Ricky took it but did not open it.

'Thank you,' he said. 'I apologise for the irregularities.'

The bank manager produced a smaller envelope from his desk drawer. 'Cashier's cheque,' he said. 'In the amount of ten thousand, seven hundred and seventy-two dollars.'

Ricky stared at the cheque. 'I wonder, if it's not too inconvenient, could I have the amount in cash?'

The manager rolled his eyes slightly. 'It might be dangerous to carry that much cash around, Doctor. Perhaps traveller's cheques?'

'No, thank you, but you are kind to be concerned. Cash is better.'

The manager nodded. 'Be right back. Hundreds?'

'That would be fine.'

Ricky sat alone until the manager returned and handed him another envelope containing the cash.

'Would you care to count it?'

'No. I trust you,' Ricky said, pocketing the money.

'Please, Dr Starks, if we can ever be of service, here's my card.'

Ricky took this as well. Muttering his thanks, he turned and exited into the last of the day—his last day but one.

THE WEIGHTLESS DARK of early evening had descended by the time Ricky returned to the farmhouse. He had half expected Merlin or Virgil to be waiting for him inside, but the interior was silent and empty. He made himself a cup of coffee, then sat at the wooden table, where he'd shared so many meals with his wife, and opened the package he'd received at the bank. Inside was a single envelope with his name printed on the outside. Ricky tore it open and removed a folded sheet of paper.

Dear Dr Starks,

Regarding your recent enquiry to this office, we are pleased to inform you that our operatives have confirmed that your assumptions are correct. We are unable, however, to provide any further details about the individuals in question. We understand that you are operating under significant time constraints.

Bill for services to follow within twenty-four hours.

Very truly yours,

R. S. Skin, President

R. S. Skin Private Investigations

Ricky read through the letter three times before setting it down on the table. It was, he thought, a truly remarkable document. He shook his head, almost in admiration. The letter told him what he needed to know, but in such a manner that if someone else were to come upon it, it wouldn't attract attention. And it would directly lead anyone who might be curious to an impenetrable brick wall.

What good would it do to circle the name R. S. Skin in red ink and leave it behind for some detective with the note: *This is the man who made me kill myself*?

The man did not exist. At least not in a place where some local policeman in Wellfleet, Massachusetts, would be capable of finding him. Instead, what anyone looking at Ricky's life would discover almost instantly was that his wife had passed away, his career was in tatters, his finances were a mess and his home had been accidentally destroyed. A fertile groundwork for a suicidal depression.

His death at his own hand would be an absolute textbook case. No one would think it unusual.

For an instant Ricky felt a surge of anger directed at himself: You made yourself into such an easy target. He clenched his hands into fists and placed them hard on the tabletop in front of him.

Ricky took a deep breath and spoke out loud: 'Do you want to live?' The room around him was silent. He listened, as if half expecting some ghostly response.

'Can you live if it costs someone else their life?' he demanded.

He breathed in again, then answered his own question by shaking his head. 'Do you have a choice?'

Again silence answered him.

Ricky understood one thing with crystal clarity: within twenty-four hours Dr Frederick Starks had to die.

THE FINAL DAY of Ricky's life was spent in fevered preparations.

At the Harbor Marine Supply store he purchased a nautical flare pistol and two five-gallon outboard-motor fuel tanks. He picked out the cheapest possible pair after rudely asking assistance from a teenage boy who was working in the store. When the boy asked why he needed two, Ricky made a point of saying that just one wouldn't do for what he had in mind.

His next stop was a drugstore. He went to the back of the store and introduced himself to the pharmacist. 'I need a scrip filled,' he said. He gave the man his DEA authorisation number. 'Elavil. A thirty-day supply of thirty-milligram tablets. Nine thousand milligrams total.'

The pharmacist shook his head in surprise. 'I haven't filled that much in a long time, Dr Starks. And there are newer mood elevators on the market that are more effective, with fewer side effects. Are you certain that Elavil is what you want?'

'Absolutely,' Ricky answered.

From the drugstore, Ricky drove down Route 6 towards Provincetown. This town, at the end of the Cape, catered to a young, hip crowd, the polar opposites of the conservative doctors, lawyers and writers who were drawn to Wellfleet. It was a place where there was little chance that Ricky would see anyone who knew him. Consequently, it was the ideal spot for him to acquire his next items.

At a sporting goods store he bought a small black backpack and a pair of running shoes. At a large chain drugstore he acquired some Grecian 5 5-Minute Haircolor in black, a pair of cheap sunglasses, and a set of adjustable aluminium crutches.

He had one other stop in Provincetown, at the Bonanza bus terminal. He waited outside, wearing the sunglasses, until a bus arrived and deposited a flock of weekend visitors. He then walked in and made his purchase rapidly.

In his Honda, heading towards his home, he thought he barely had enough time left that day. Sunlight filled the windshield; heat poured in through the open side windows. It was the point of the summer afternoon when people gathered themselves off the sand, collected towels and food coolers and began the slightly uncomfortable trek back to their vehicles—a moment of transition.

He pulled into a Texaco petrol station and stopped at the row of pumps. He took the pair of gas tanks out of the trunk, and proceeded to fill them to the brim with regular fuel. A teenage boy working at the full-serve section saw him and called out, 'Hey, mister, you want to leave enough room for oil if those are going into an outboard. Some take a mix of fifty to one, others a hundred to one, but you gotta put it right in the tank.'

Ricky shook his head. 'Not for an outboard, thanks.'

The teenager persisted. 'They're outboard tanks.'

'Yeah,' Ricky said. 'But I don't own an outboard.' He paid, placed the tanks in the trunk of the car, and set out for his home.

HE SET THE TWO gasoline canisters down temporarily in the living room and went into the kitchen. He felt parched, and in the refrigerator he found a bottle of spring water, which he gulped at rapidly. His heart seemed to have picked up pace as the hours of this last day dwindled, and he told himself to remain calm.

He went to the phone and called the *Times* advertising department as he had on three other occasions. This time, however, his ad was different. No rhymes, no questions.

Mr R: You win. Check the Cape Cod Times.

Once that was accomplished, Ricky sat at the kitchen table with a writing pad in hand. He chewed on the end of his pen for a moment, then wrote rapidly.

To whom it may concern:

I did this because I was alone and hate the emptiness in my life. I could not tolerate causing any further harm to any other person.

All property and funds remaining in my estate should be sold and the proceeds turned over to the Nature Conservancy and the American Cancer Society. What is left of my home here in Wellfleet should become conservation land.

To my friends, if any, I hope you will forgive me.

To my patients, I hope you will understand.

And Mr R, who helped to bring me to this stage, I hope you will find your own way to Hell soon enough, because I will be waiting there for you.

He signed this letter with a flourish, sealed it in an envelope, and addressed it to the Wellfleet Police Department.

Taking the hair colouring and his backpack in hand, he went to the upstairs shower and emerged minutes later with jet-black hair. He stole a quick glance at his appearance in the mirror, thought it mildly foolish, then towelled himself dry. From his chest of drawers he selected some of the old summer clothes and stuffed them, along with a frayed windcheater, into the backpack. He kept an additional change of clothes out, folded carefully on top of the pack. Then he dressed again in the clothes he had worn that day.

He took the backpack, the change of clothes and the crutches out to his car, leaving them on the passenger's seat next to his sunglasses and running shoes. Then he returned inside and sat quietly in the kitchen for the remaining hours of the evening.

Ricky did not know who he might be saving, but knew it was someone. Think about that, he told himself.

Shortly after midnight he rose. He allowed himself one final tour of the house. Each corner and creak in the floorboards was beloved.

His hand shook slightly as he took the first canister of gasoline upstairs, where he spread it liberally about on the floor. The second canister was used on the ground floor. In the kitchen, Ricky blew out the pilot lights on the old gas stove. Then he opened every jet, so that the room filled immediately with the distinctive odour of rotten eggs.

Seizing the marine flare pistol, Ricky walked outside to a spot opposite the living-room windows. He took a deep breath, tried not to dwell on what he was doing, took careful aim and fired a flare through the centre window. A muffled thud was followed by an immediate crackle and glow. Within a few seconds he saw the first licks of fire dancing about the floor and beginning to spread.

Ricky turned and ran to the Honda. As he slipped the car in gear, he heard an explosion. The flames had hit the gas in the kitchen. He decided not to look back, but accelerated into the deepening night.

He drove carefully and steadily to Hawthorne Beach. There were several beaches in the Wellfleet area that would have suited his purposes, but this was the most isolated, a wide expanse of flat sand resting at the base of a fifty-foot bluff, with some of the strongest surf on the Cape. At the end of the parking lot there was a warning sign: STRONG CURRENTS AND DANGEROUS UNDERTOW. DO NOT SWIM.

Ricky parked by the sign and placed the envelope addressed to the Wellfleet police in the centre of the steering wheel.

Seizing the crutches, the backpack, running shoes and change of clothes, he stepped away from the car. These he placed at the top of the bluff, a few feet away from a wooden barrier that marked the narrow path down to the sand.

A full moon spread wan light across the beach, making his slippery, stumbling trip down to the water's edge considerably easier. As a chill breath of wind struck him in the chest, he breathed in deeply.

Then Ricky removed everything he wore and folded them into a neat pile, which he placed on the sand well above the high-water mark. He took the vial of pills he'd acquired that morning and emptied it into his hand, sticking the plastic container with the clothes.

The last thing he did was raise his head and look out at the immense expanse of black ocean before him and the stars dotting the sky above. It is, he told himself, a nice enough night to die.

Then, naked as the morning that was only hours away, he walked down slowly towards the fury of waves.

EIGHT

Two weeks after the night he died, Ricky sat on the edge of a lumpy bed that creaked whenever he shifted position. He was listening to the sound of traffic filter through the thin walls of a shabby motel room on the outskirts of Durham, New Hampshire, a place he had selected because it was a college town. By now the black hair dye was fading, and Ricky was beginning to regain his normal appearance. He thought this slightly ironic, for even if he once again looked like the man he was, he would never actually be that person.

On the table at his side were copies of the *Cape Cod Times* and the *New York Times* for the days following his death. The paper on the Cape had stripped the story across the bottom of their front page: PROMINENT PHYSICIAN AN APPARENT SUICIDE; LANDMARK FARM-HOUSE DESTROYED IN BLAZE. The reporter had managed to discover that there had been recent 'allegations of impropriety' against Ricky, as well as 'financial reversals'.

Both stories stated that his death was apparently by drowning and that Coast Guard units were searching Cape waters for Ricky's body. The *Cape Cod Times*, though, to Ricky's relief, quoted the local commander as saying that body recovery was extremely unlikely, given the strong tides in the area of Hawthorne Beach.

When he reflected upon it, Ricky thought it was as good a death as he could come up with on such short notice.

He'd walked down to the edge of the water, carefully leaving footprints in the newly scoured sand. Waves licking at his toes, he'd thrown the handful of pills into the ocean, then walked through the wash a hundred yards, distant enough so that the new set of footprints when he emerged from the cold water would not be noticed by anyone inspecting the scene.

The hours that had followed seemed to Ricky, alone now in the motel room, like the remembered details of a dream. He could see himself dressing on the bluff in the extra set of clothes, pulling on the running shoes. He'd strapped the crutches to his backpack, then run six miles to the parking lot of the Lobster Shanty. He had to get there before anyone else taking the 6.00am express to Boston arrived.

It was there that he'd unstrapped the crutches from the backpack and slung them on his arms. When the bus arrived two minutes late, Ricky had crutched out into the line to board. Two young men stood aside, letting him struggle up the steps, where he had handed the driver his ticket, purchased the day before.

In Boston, there had been an hour delay before the bus to Durham. In that time he'd walked away from the South Street bus terminal until he'd found a Dumpster outside an office building. He'd thrown the crutches into the Dumpster. Then he had returned to the station and boarded another bus.

Durham, he thought, had other advantages: he had never been there and had absolutely no connection with the city. He also liked the New Hampshire licence plate, with the motto: LIVE FREE OR DIE.

Ricky went to the motel window and stared out into the darkness. There is much to do, he told himself. Dr Frederick Starks no longer exists. He understood that his first priority was to create a new identity for himself.

He walked over to the wall, where he flicked the light switch, dropping the room into darkness. An occasional sweep of headlights from outside sliced across the walls. He lay down on the bed.

Once, he reminded himself, I studied hard to learn to save lives.

Now I must educate myself in how to take one.

RICKY WOULD NOT ALLOW himself to fantasise that he could ever go back to his home in New York. That wasn't the point, he understood. The point was to make the man who'd ruined his life pay for his fun. Ricky knew he needed to outplay Rumplestiltskin at his own game. He had to invent a new persona without creating any telltale sign that Dr Frederick Starks still existed.

In this country, Ricky realised, what we are first and foremost are numbers. Social Security numbers. Bank account and credit card numbers. Driver's licence numbers. Creating these was the first order of business. And then he needed to find a job.

He went to the public library on Jones Street. The library had a long table with four computers set up. Ricky wandered into the aisles of books and within moments spotted one entitled *Getting Started in Home Computing*. He dumped himself into a leather armchair. After reading for an hour, he approached the computers, clicked on one of the machines and drew himself up to it. On the wall were instructions on how to access the Internet. He followed the directions, and the computer screen leaped to life. He then opened up a search engine and typed in the phrase *false identity*.

By the end of the day Ricky had learned that the business of creating identities was a thriving one. There were dozens of companies that would provide him with virtually every sort of false documentation, sold under the disclaimer FOR NOVELTY PURPOSES ONLY. He made lists of places and documents. He knew what he needed, but he realised swiftly that obtaining it was a bit of a problem. People seeking fake identities already were someone. He was not.

The cash he had was useless. They wanted credit card numbers. He had none. They wanted an email address. He had none. They wanted a home to deliver the material to. He had none.

Ricky pushed himself away from the computer and walked outside the library. The sun was shining brightly, and the air was still filled with the heat of summer. He continued walking until he found himself in a residential area filled with modest two-storey houses. In the front window of one house he saw a small hand-lettered sign: ROOM TO RENT. ENQUIRE WITHIN.

Ricky began to step forward. That's what I need, he said to himself. Then, as abruptly, he stopped. I have no name. No references.

He made a mental note of the location of the house and walked on, thinking: I need to be someone. I need to be someone who can't be traced. Ricky's problem was different from the criminals, the men seeking to run away from alimony payments, the women hiding from abusive husbands.

He needed to become both dead and alive.

He thought about this contradiction, then smiled.

He knew exactly what to do.

IT DID NOT TAKE Ricky long to find a Salvation Army clothing store. It was located in an undistinguished shopping mall on the main bus route. The store was painted a flat, reflective white that glowed in the afternoon sun. Inside, it was like a small warehouse, with electrical appliances for sale and rows of donated clothing hanging from racks.

Everything was cheap, but he selected the cheapest of the offerings: a long, ripped woollen winter overcoat that reached to his ankles, a threadbare sweater, and trousers two sizes too large for him.

The cashier was an elderly volunteer who wore thick glasses and an incongruously red shirt that stood out in this bleak world of donated clothing. The man lifted the overcoat to his nose and sniffed. 'You sure you want this one, fella?'

'That's the one,' Ricky replied.

'Smells like it's been somewhere nasty,' the man continued. 'There's much nicer stuff, you look a little harder.'

Ricky shook his head. 'It's exactly what I need. It's for a theatre production,' he lied. He paid and left the store.

In the morning he packed the new old articles of clothing in a brown paper bag. Everything else—the few documents he had about Rumplestiltskin, the newspapers, his other items of clothing—went into his backpack. He settled his bill with the clerk at the motel and took a midmorning Trailways bus to Boston.

In a toilet stall at the South Street bus terminal, Ricky stripped off the reasonable clothing he had been wearing, replacing it with the items purchased at the Salvation Army. He packed his clothes into his backpack along with everything else he had, including all his cash, with the exception of a hundred dollars in twenties, which he slid into a tear in the overcoat. Emerging from the stall, he stared at himself in a mirror above the sink. He had not shaved in a couple of days, and that helped, he thought.

He stuffed his backpack into a metal storage locker, put two quarters into the lock and turned the key. He then pocketed the key and walked away fast from the bus station, pausing only once, when he believed no one was watching, to scoop some dirt from the sidewalk and rub it into his hair and face. By the time he'd walked two blocks, sweat had begun to rise beneath his arms and on his forehead, and he wiped it away with the sleeve of the overcoat.

Before he'd reached the third block, he thought: Now I look to be what I am. Homeless.

HIS FIRST NIGHT was spent alone beneath the curved brick of a Charles River bridge. He wrapped himself in his overcoat and thrust himself against a wall, struggling to steal a few hours away from the night, waking shortly after dawn with a crick in his neck. He rose, stretching carefully, trying to remember the last occasion he'd slept outdoors and thinking it was not since his childhood.

He spent the day going from shelter to shelter throughout the city, searching. It was deep in the afternoon, with the sun still pounding down, that Ricky spotted a possibility.

The man was rooting through a garbage can on the edge of a park not far from the river. He was about Ricky's height and weight, with thinning streaks of dirty brown hair. He wore a knitted cap and a woollen overcoat that reached down to one brown shoe and one black. The man was muttering to himself, intent on the contents of the garbage can, coughing repeatedly as he worked. Ricky moved close enough to see lesions on the man's face. He saw the man pull a discarded soda can from the garbage and toss it into an old steel shopping cart. A second can had some problem, and the man threw it to the ground, kicking it into a nearby bush.

Bipolar, Ricky thought. And schizophrenic. Hears voices, prone to sudden bursts of manic energy. The lesions could be Kaposi's sarcoma. AIDS was a distinct possibility. So was tuberculosis or lung cancer, given the man's racking cough.

After a few minutes the man determined that he'd taken everything of value from the trash, and he headed off, pulling his cart behind him. Ricky trailed after him.

It did not take long to reach a street in Charlestown that was filled with low-slung and grimy stores. Ricky watched as the man headed straight to a faded yellow building with a prominent sign on the front: AL'S DISCOUNT SODA AND LIQUORS. Beneath that was a second sign: REDEMPTION CENTRE. This sign had an arrow pointing to the rear. The man, towing the cart filled with cans, marched directly around the corner of the building. Ricky followed.

At the back of the store was a half-door with a sign above the lintel: REDEEM HERE. There was a small doorbell button to the side, which the man rang. Within a few seconds a teenager appeared. The transaction itself took only a few minutes. The man handed in the collection of cans; the teenager counted them and then peeled off a couple of bills from a wad he pulled from his pocket. The man took the money, reached into the overcoat and pulled out a fat old leather wallet. He put a couple of the bills into the wallet and handed one back to the teenager. The kid disappeared, then returned moments later with a bottle, which he handed to the man.

Ricky slunk down, sitting on the alley concrete, waiting while the man walked past him. Ricky hung his head for a few seconds, then rose and continued to follow him.

They covered dozens of city blocks, winding in and out of traffic. The neighbourhood they travelled through grew seedier with every stride. He saw the man hesitate midblock and turn round. Ricky dipped against a building, concealing himself. Out of the corner of his eye he saw the man abruptly lurch down an alleyway between two brick buildings. Ricky followed.

He came up to the entrance to the alleyway and peered round the edge. It was dark and closed in. Ricky could just make out a collection of abandoned cardboard boxes and a green Dumpster at the far end. He heard a faint sound, a voice singing softly and out of key.

Ricky moved cautiously towards the noise. He stumbled once or twice, his feet getting tangled in unrecognisable debris. He sensed he was almost on top of the man when the singing stopped.

'Who's there?'

'Just me,' Ricky replied.

'This is my alley,' came the reply. 'Get out.'

'Now it's my alley, too,' Ricky said. He took a deep breath and launched himself into the realm he'd known he would have to find in order to communicate with the man. Welcome madness. Ricky said, 'He told me we're supposed to speak together. That's what he told me. "Find the man in the alley and ask him his name."'

The man hesitated. 'Who told you?'

'Who do you think?' Ricky answered. 'I'm not allowed to say his name, not out loud or someone might hear me. Shhhh! But he says that you will know why I've come, if you're the right one. Are you?'

'I don't know,' was the reply. The man seemed to be trying to absorb all this. 'I can't think straight. My head is hurting.'

'Tell me who you are!' Ricky half whispered.

The man sobbed. 'I didn't do anything. What do you want?'

'Your name. I want your name.'

'I don't want to say,' he said. 'I'm scared. Do you mean to kill me?'

'I will not harm you if you prove to me who you are.'

The man paused. 'I have a wallet,' he said slowly.

'Give it here!' Ricky demanded.

The man reached inside his coat. In the darkness Ricky could barely see him holding something out in front of him. Ricky grabbed it and thrust it into his own pocket.

The man started to cry then.

Ricky softened his voice. 'You don't have to worry any more. I will leave you alone now.'

'Please,' said the man. 'Just go away.'

Ricky grasped a twenty-dollar bill from the lining of his coat. He thrust it at the man. 'Here,' he said. Then he turned and picked his way gingerly down the alleyway, thinking that he had not exactly stolen what he needed, nor had he purchased it. What he'd done was what was necessary and was well within the rules of the game. He moved steadily back through the darkness towards the weak light of the city street just ahead.

RICKY DID NOT OPEN the man's wallet until after he'd reached the bus station and retrieved his clothes from the locker. In the men's room he managed to get partially cleaned up, scrubbing some of the dirt and grime from his face and neck and hands. He dumped his filthy clothes into the nearest waste basket and climbed into the acceptable khakis and sports shirt that he'd kept in the backpack.

He exited the men's room and purchased a ticket for a bus back to Durham. He had nearly an hour's wait, so he repaired to a corner of the station and opened up the wallet.

The first thing he saw brought a smile to his face: a tattered and faded, but legible, Social Security card.

The name had been typed: RICHARD S. LIVELY. Ricky liked this. Lively was what, for the first time in weeks, he felt. And he wouldn't have to learn to accommodate a new first name, the common nickname of Richard and his own Frederick being the same. Rebirth in a bus station, he thought. He supposed there were worse places.

In addition there was an expired Illinois driver's licence with a slightly out-of-focus picture of Richard Lively, and a hospital clinic identification card from a Chicago facility that was marked with a red asterisk in one corner. AIDS, Ricky thought. HIV-positive. He'd been right about the sores on the man's face. There were also two yellowed newspaper clippings, which Ricky unfolded carefully and read. The first was an obituary for a seventy-three-year-old woman; the other was an article about workforce layoffs in an automobile plant. The first, he guessed, was Richard Lively's mother, and the second was the job the man had had before launching into the world of the homeless. Ricky read through the two clippings swiftly, committing the details to memory. He stuffed the clippings back inside the wallet, then tossed it into a nearby waste basket.

I know enough, he thought.

The announcement for his bus came over the loudspeaker. Ricky rose, swinging his backpack over his shoulder. Putting Dr Starks deep within, he took his first step forward as Richard Lively.

HIS LIFE BEGAN to take shape rapidly. Within a week he had rented the room in the house not far from the public library and acquired two part-time jobs. The first was manning a register at a local Dairy Mart for five hours a day in the evening; the second was stocking shelves in a Stop & Shop grocery store for five hours in the morning.

He used Richard Lively's Social Security number to open a bank account, where he deposited the remainder of his cash. Once that was accomplished, Ricky found that sorties into the world of bureaucracy were relatively easy. He'd been issued a replacement Social Security card by filling out a form, one that he signed himself. A clerk at the Department of Motor Vehicles hadn't even glanced at the picture on the Illinois licence when Ricky turned it in and obtained a New Hampshire driver's licence, this time with his own picture and signature. He joined a video rental club and the YMCA. Anything that provided another card in his new name.

An important coup came in mid-October, when he spotted an ad for part-time help on the janitorial staff at the University of New Hampshire. He quit his job at the Dairy Mart and started sweeping and mopping in the science labs for four hours a day. He approached this task with a singleness of purpose that impressed his supervisor. But more critically, this provided Ricky with a university identification card, which in turn gave him access to the computer system.

He gave himself an electronic name: Odysseus. This gave rise to an electronic mail address and access to all the Internet had to offer. He opened various accounts, using a post office box as a home address. Gradually he became more adept at the computer.

He made two different electronic searches for his own family tree, discovering how easy it had been for Rumplestiltskin to acquire the list of relatives that had been the fulcrum of his initial threat. The fifty-odd members of Dr Frederick Starks's family emerged in only a couple of hours' worth of enquiries.

When his own name came up—and the second of the family tree programs that he was employing showed him as recently deceased— he stiffened in his chair, surprised, though he shouldn't have been.

He then took a second step—to create an entirely new person. Someone who had never existed but who had a modest credit history and the sort of past that is easily documented. Some of this was simple, such as obtaining false identification in a new name. He once again marvelled that there were so many companies on the Internet that would provide fake 'novelty' IDs. He started ordering driver's licences and college IDs. He obtained a diploma from the University of Iowa, class of 1970, and a birth certificate from a non-existent hospital in Des Moines. He invented a phoney Social Security number for himself. Armed with this pile of new material, he opened a small bank account in a second name. This name he chose with some thought: Frederick Lazarus.

He had the simplest of ideas: Richard Lively would be real and would have a safe and secure existence. He would be home. Frederick Lazarus was a fiction. He had no substance other than phoney numbers. He could be dangerous. He could be criminal. He could be a man of risks.

NINE

R icky let weeks slide into months, let the New Hampshire winter envelop him. He let his life as Richard Lively grow daily while he continued to add details to his secondary persona, Frederick Lazarus.

Richard Lively went to college basketball games on his evenings off and occasionally baby-sat for his landlady. Two nights a week he volunteered at a suicide-prevention hot line, working the 10.00pm to 2.00am shift—a small way, he thought, to do penance for his lack of attention years earlier, when Claire Tyson had come to him.

Frederick Lazarus was someone different. Frederick Lazarus was a member of a health club, where he pounded out solitary miles on a treadmill, followed by attacking the free weights. His waistline shrank. His shoulders broadened. He worked out alone and in silence, save for an occasional grunt and the pounding of his feet against the mechanised tread. He took to combing his sandy hair back from his forehead, slicked aggressively.

And on a Saturday afternoon in late January, he spent a pleasant hour discussing the merits of various weapons with a clerk at a sporting goods store. The store had a shooting range in the basement, where the clerk eagerly showed Ricky, who had never fired a weapon in his life, how to sight down the barrel and how to stand, two hands on the weapon, holding it out in such a way that the world narrowed and only the target mattered. Ricky fired off dozens of rounds, ranging from a small .22 automatic, through the .357 magnum and 9mm favoured by law enforcement, up to the .45, which sent a jolt into his shoulder and chest when he fired it.

He settled on something in between, a .380 Ruger semiautomatic with a fifteen-shot clip—the same weapon he'd seen in Merlin's briefcase on the train to Manhattan.

He filled out the permit forms using a fake Social Security number that he'd created almost precisely for this purpose.

'Takes a couple of days,' the clerk said. 'Although we're a helluva lot easier than Massachusetts. How're you paying for it?'

'Cash,' Ricky said. 'Plastic just complicates your life.'

'A Ruger .380 simplifies it.'

Ricky nodded. 'That's more or less the point, isn't it?'

LATE ONE SPRING night nine months after his death, Ricky spent three hours on the telephone with a distraught, deeply depressed young woman who called the suicide prevention line in despair, a bottle of sleeping pills on the table in front of her. He spoke to her of what her life had become and what it could become. He wove hope into every thread of what he said, and when the two of them greeted the first dawn light, she had put aside the threatened overdose and made an appointment with a clinic physician.

When he walked out that morning, feeling more energised than exhausted, he decided that it was time to make his first enquiry.

Later that day, when he had finished his shift in the maintenance department at the university, he used his electronic pass card to enter the computer sciences department's study room. This was a square space cut up into study carrels, each with a computer linked to the university's main system. He booted one up, entered his password, and slid into the system. In a folder by his left hand he had a small amount of information that he'd obtained in his former life about the woman he had ignored.

This is what he knew: twenty years earlier a woman died in New York City, and her three children were turned over to the state for adoption. Ricky's first computer sorties, chasing Claire Tyson's name, came up curiously empty. The family tree programs, which had displayed his own stack of relatives so rapidly, proved to be significantly less effective at tracing her.

Next he searched electronic telephone directories for the north of Florida. That was where she had come from. The death certificate listed a Pensacola address for her next of kin, but when he cross-checked the address against the name, he discovered that someone different was living at that location.

Ricky decided to start there anyway.

He made a flight reservation and arranged with his bosses to switch round some workdays and hours to give himself a block of time. Then he stopped in at a secondhand clothing store and purchased a cheap summer-weight black suit. More or less, he thought, what a mortician would wear, which, he believed, was appropriate for his circumstances. Late in the evening of the day before he was to depart, wearing his janitor's uniform, he let himself into the theatre department at the university. One of his passkeys opened the storage area where costumes for various college productions were kept. It did not take him long to find what he needed.

THERE WAS A HEAVY dampness hidden like a veiled threat in the heat of the Gulf Coast weather. Ricky's first breaths of air, as he walked from the air-conditioned chill of the airport lobby out to the rental car waiting area, seemed to hold an oily, oppressive warmth far removed from even the hottest days up on Cape Cod, or even in New York City during an August heat wave.

His plan was simple: he was going to check in to a cheap motel, then go to the address written on Claire Tyson's death certificate. He would knock on some doors, ask around, see if anyone knew of her family's whereabouts.

Ricky found a Motel 6 located on a wide boulevard dedicated to fast-food restaurants and discount shopping outlets. He could taste the ocean nearby, the scent was in the air, but the vista was one of endless commerce and garish signs.

He checked in under the name Frederick Lazarus, left his bag and walked through the parking lot to a convenience store. There he was able to purchase a detailed map for the Pensacola area.

THE HOUSING near the sprawling naval base had a certain uniformity: rows of freshly painted cinder-block houses with splotches of well-mown grass steaming beneath the sun. But as Ricky drove farther from the ocean, the houses gained a worn appearance.

He found the street where Claire Tyson's family lived, and he looked for number thirteen, which was in the middle of the block. He pulled up and parked outside. It was a small single-storey house, painted a faded pink. A large yellow dog chained to a steel fence started to bark as he walked up the driveway. He touched the front doorbell and heard it sound inside. A baby was crying, but quieted almost instantly as a voice responded, 'I'm coming, I'm coming . . .'

The door opened, and a young black woman, toddler on her hip, stood before him. She did not open the screen door. 'What you want?' she demanded. 'You here for the TV? The washer? Maybe the baby's bottle? What you gonna take this time?'

'I'm not here to take anything,' he said.

'You with the electric company?'

'No. I'm a man with a couple of questions,' Ricky said. He smiled. 'And if you have some answers, maybe some money.'

The woman continued to eye him suspiciously, but now with some curiosity as well. 'What sort of questions?' she asked.

'Questions about someone who lived here once. A while ago. Family named Tyson.'

'He be the man got evicted before we move in.'

Ricky took out his wallet and removed a twenty-dollar bill. He held it up, and the woman opened the screen door.

'You a cop?' she asked. 'Some sort of detective?'

'I'm not a policeman,' Ricky said, 'but I might be some sort of detective.' He stepped inside the house.

He blinked for a moment, his eyes taking a few seconds to adjust to the darkness. It was stifling in the small entrance, and he followed the woman into the living room. The windows were open but the built-up heat still made the narrow room seem like a prison cell. There was a chair, a couch, a television and a red and blue playpen, where the child was deposited. The walls were empty save for a single stiffly posed wedding photo of the woman and a young black man in a naval uniform. Ricky looked at the picture and asked, 'Is that your husband? Where's he now?'

'He shipped out,' the woman said. 'He's in the Gulf of Arabia somewhere. Got another two months 'fore he gets home.'

'What's your name?'

'Charlene,' she replied. 'Now, what about those questions that's gonna make me some money? Navy pay don't go too far.'

Ricky moved over and sat on the single chair, and Charlene took up a spot on the couch. 'Tell me what you know about the Tyson family,' he said. 'They lived here before you moved in?'

'That's right,' she said. 'But all I know about is the old fella. He was here all alone. Why you interested in that old man?'

'He may have come into a small amount of money in a will,' Ricky lied. 'I was sent by the family to try to locate him.'

'I don't know he gonna need any money where he be.'

'Where's that?'

'Over at the VA nursing home on Midway. If he's still breathing.'

'And his wife?'

'She dead. More'n a couple of years.'

'Did you ever meet him?'

Charlene shook her head. 'Only story I know is what I was told by the neighbours.'

'Then tell me that story.'

'Well, I heard they had a daughter, but she'd died a long time ago. They were living on Social Security cheques. Old woman, she got sick with her heart. Got no insurance, just the Medicare. They suddenly got bills, same as me. Old woman, she up and dies, leaving the old man with more bills. One day the old man finds out that it ain't the bank he thinks that owns the mortgage any more. Someone bought the note. He misses a payment, maybe one more, the sheriff's deputies come with an eviction notice. They put the old guy out onna street. Next I hear, he's in the VA.'

'You came in after the eviction?' Ricky asked.

'That's right.' Charlene sighed and shook her head. 'I heard the old man's story from folks across the street. They gone now. Probably all the folks who knew that old man be gone now. But it didn't seem like he had too many friends.'

Ricky thought for a moment, then asked, 'Do you have the name, maybe the address, of the guy you pay rent to?'

Charlene looked a bit surprised but nodded. 'Sure. I make the cheque out to a lawyer downtown, send it to another guy at the bank. When I got the money. But the landlord be cool. Some lawyer called and told me to pay when I could.' She took a piece of crayon from the floor and wrote down a name and address on the back of an envelope. 'I hope this helps you out some.'

Ricky pulled two twenty-dollar bills from his wallet and handed them to the woman. She nodded her thanks. He hesitated, then pulled a third out. 'For the baby,' he said.

'That's nice of you, mister.'

He shielded his eyes from the sun as he walked back out onto the street. The sky above was a wide expanse of blue, and the heat had increased. He looked towards where his rental car was parked by the kerb, and he tried to imagine an old man sitting amid his meagre possessions by the side of the street. Cast out and friendless. Ricky knew who had evicted the old man. He wondered, however, if the old man had sat in the heat and despair of that moment and understood that the man who had cast him out was the child of his child, who so many years earlier he'd turned his back upon.

THERE WAS A LARGE, sprawling high school less than seven blocks from the house that Claire Tyson had fled from. Ricky pulled into the parking area and stared up at the building. It was a huge concrete structure, with a football field behind a ten-foot-high fence.

There was a security checkpoint just inside the main entrance, where a school guard gave Ricky directions to the administrative offices.

A secretary at a desk inside the door marked ADMINISTRATION steered him to the principal's office after he explained his reason for visiting the school. He waited outside while the secretary had a brief conversation, then appeared in the doorway to usher him in. He stepped inside and saw a middle-aged woman look up from where she worked at a computer screen. She gestured towards a chair while she swung round and sat behind a desk cluttered with papers. 'How can I help you?' the principal asked briskly.

Ricky nodded. 'I'm searching for information,' he said. 'I need to enquire about a young woman who attended school here in the late sixties. Her name was Claire Tyson—'

'School records are confidential,' the principal interrupted. 'But I remember the young woman.'

'You've been here a while?'

'My whole career,' the woman said. 'But short of letting you see the class of 1967 yearbook, I don't know if I can be of much help.'

'Well, I don't really need her school records,' Ricky said, removing a letter from his pocket and handing it to her. 'I'm searching for anyone who might know of a relative.'

The letter was from a fictional cancer-treatment centre, requesting assistance in tracing family members of a Hodgkin's disease patient in need of a bone-marrow match. The woman read it swiftly. Her face softened. 'Oh,' she said apologetically. 'I'm so sorry. I didn't realise.'

'That's OK,' Ricky said. 'This is kind of a long shot. But when you have a niece this sick, you're willing to take any long shot there is.'

'Of course,' the woman said rapidly. 'But I don't think there are any Tysons related to Claire left around here.'

'I'm surprised you remember Claire,' Ricky said.

'She made an impression. In more ways than one. Back then I was her guidance counsellor.' The woman rose, went to a bookcase against a rear wall, and returned with a yearbook from the class of 1967. She passed it across to Ricky.

Ricky flipped through page after page until he came to Claire Tyson. He had trouble reconciling the woman he'd seen a decade later with the fresh-faced, well-scrubbed almost-adult in the yearbook. He read the entry adjacent to her portrait. It listed her clubs—French, science and the drama society. It also listed her academic honours, which included a National Merit Scholarship commendation. There was a quote, played for humour, but which to Ricky had a slightly ominous tone: 'Do unto others before they have a chance to do unto you.' A prediction: 'Wants to live in the fast lane. In ten years she will be: on Broadway or under it.'

The principal was looking over Ricky's shoulder. 'She had no chance,' she said.

'I'm sorry?' Ricky replied, the words forming a question.

'She was the only child of a . . . uh, difficult couple. Living on the edge of poverty. The father was a tyrant. Perhaps worse.'

'You mean . . .?'

'She displayed many of the classic signs of abuse. I spoke with her often when she would have uncontrollable fits of depression. Crying. Hysterical. Then calm, cold, almost removed, as if she were somewhere else, even though she was sitting in the room with me. I would have called the police if I'd had the slightest bit of concrete evidence.'

'Of course.'

'I knew she would flee first chance. That boy—'

'Boyfriend?'

'Yes. I'm certain she was pregnant when she graduated that spring.'

'His name? I wonder if any child might still be . . . It would be critical, you know.'

'There was a baby. But I don't know what happened. They didn't put down roots here, that's for sure. The boy was heading to the navy, although I don't know for certain that he got there, and she went off to college. I don't think they actually ever married.'

'The boy?'

'Daniel Collins. Good-looking. A ladies' man. Football and baseball, but never a star. Smart enough, but didn't apply himself in the classroom. The sort of kid who always knew where the party was.'

'You didn't like him much?'

'What was there to like? He was a bit of a predator. More than a bit. Had all the girls he wanted on a string. Especially Claire.'

'Do you have his family's local address?'

The principal rose, went over to a computer, and typed in a name. Then she took a pencil and copied down a number onto a piece of scrap paper, which she handed over to Ricky.

'So you think he left her?' Ricky asked.

'Sure. After he used her up. That was what he was good at: using people, then discarding them. Whether that took one year or ten, I don't know. You stick in my line of work, you get pretty good at predicting what will happen to all these kids. Some might surprise you, one way or the other. But not all that many.'

BEFORE HEADING to the VA hospital, Ricky stopped at his motel and changed into the black suit. He also took the clerical collar that he'd borrowed from the property room of the university theatre department, and fitted it round his neck.

The hospital building was two storeys of whitewashed brick. There were a few green bushes planted by the entrance, and a few old men in wheelchairs sat unattended in the afternoon sun. Ricky walked inside. He saw a receptionist behind a desk, and he approached her.

'Good morning, Father,' she said brightly. 'How can I help you?'

'Good morning,' Ricky replied, fingering his collar. 'A hot day to be wearing the Lord's chosen outfit,' he said.

The receptionist laughed.

'I am here to see a patient. His name would be Tyson.'

'Are you a relative, Father?'

'No, but I was asked by his daughter to look him up.'

This answer seemed to pass muster. The woman checked through some computer records. She grimaced as the name came up on her screen. 'I'm afraid Mr Tyson is in the hospice section,' she said.

'He is . . .'

'Terminal.'

'Then perhaps my timing is better than I hoped. Perhaps I can give him some comfort in his final days.'

The receptionist nodded. She pointed to a schematic drawing of the hospital. 'This is where you want to go,' she said.

RICKY'S CLERICAL COLLAR and suit did their job impeccably. No one asked him for identification; no one seemed to think he was out of place. As he entered the hospice unit, the nurse on duty looked up and said, 'Ah, Father, they called and told me you were coming down. Room three hundred for Mr Tyson.'

'Thank you,' Ricky said. 'I wonder if you could tell me what he's suffering from.'

The nurse dutifully handed Ricky a medical chart. Lung cancer.

Calvin Tyson was emaciated. He wore an oxygen mask that hung from his neck, occasionally lifting it to help him to breathe. His scrawny, naked legs were stretched out on the bed like sticks knocked from a tree by a storm. The man in the bed next to him was much the same, and the two men wheezed in a duet of agony. Tyson turned, just shifting his head as Ricky entered.

'I want to be left alone,' Tyson said. 'Don't need no religion.'

'And I'm not going to try any,' Ricky replied. 'At least not like what you think.' He paused, making certain that the door was shut behind him. He walked around the end of the bed and stared at Tyson's room-mate. Ricky pointed at a set of headphones by his bed. 'You want to put those on so I can speak with your neighbour privately?'

The man shrugged and slipped them onto his ears.

'Good,' Ricky said, then moved in close, bending over the dying man. 'You know who sent me?' he asked.

'No idea,' Tyson croaked. 'Ain't nobody left that cares about me.'

'You're wrong about that,' Ricky answered. 'Your daughter—'

'My daughter's dead. She was no good. Never was.'

'You think you maybe had something to do with that?'

Calvin Tyson shook his head. 'You don't know nothing. Nobody know nothing. Whatever happened be history. Ancient history.'

Ricky stared into the man's eyes. He saw them hardening. 'Your daughter, Claire, had three children—'

'She was a whore, ran away with that boy. Then on up to New York City. That's what killed her. Not me.'

'When she died,' he continued, 'you were contacted. You were her closest living relative. Someone in New York City called you up and wanted to know if you would take her children.'

'What did I want with those bastards? She never married. I didn't want them.'

Ricky stared at Calvin Tyson. 'So you signed some papers giving them up for adoption, right?'

'Yes. Why you want to know this?'

'Because I need to find them.'

'Why?'

Ricky looked around. He made a small gesture at the hospital room. 'Do you know who foreclosed on your house and tossed you out so that you ended up here, dying all by yourself?'

Tyson shook his head. 'Somebody bought the note from the mortgage company. Didn't give me no chance to make good. Just bang! Out I went.'

'What happened to you then?'

The man's eyes grew rheumy, suddenly filling with tears. 'I was out on the street. Got sick. Got beat. Now I'm fixing to die.'

'The man who put you here is your daughter's child,' Ricky said.

Calvin Tyson's eyes widened. 'How that be?'

'He bought the note. He evicted you because you turned your back on him and on his mother. So he repaid you in kind. He probably arranged to have you beaten as well.'

The man sobbed once. 'All the bad that happened to me—'

Ricky finished for him, 'Comes from one man. That's the man I'm trying to find. So, I'll ask you again. You signed some papers to give the children up for adoption, right?'

Tyson nodded.

'Did you get some money, too?'

Again the old man nodded. 'Couple thousand.'

'What was the name of the people who adopted the children?'

'I got a paper.'

'Where?'

'In a box in the closet.' He pointed at a scarred metal locker.

Ricky opened the door and saw some threadbare clothes hanging from hooks. On the floor was a padlocked box. The clasp had been broken. Ricky opened it and shuffled through some old papers until he found several folded together, with a rubber band around them. He saw a seal from the state of New York. He thrust the papers into his jacket pocket. 'You won't need them,' he told the old man.

'What you going to do?' Tyson asked. His voice was a shocked whisper, filled with gasps and wheezes.

'Find those children.'

'Why you want to do that?'

'Because one of them killed me, too,' Ricky said, turning to leave.

IT WAS JUST BEFORE the dinner hour when Ricky knocked on the door of a trim two-bedroom ranch house on a quiet street. He was still wearing his priest's regalia, which gave him an extra bit of confidence. He heard shuffling inside, and then the door cracked open and an elderly woman peered round the edge. 'Yes?' she asked.

'Hello,' Ricky replied cheerily. 'I wonder if you might help me. I'm trying to trace the whereabouts of Daniel Collins.'

The woman gasped and lifted a hand to her mouth. Ricky watched as she struggled to recapture her composure.

'He is lost to us,' she said.

'I'm sorry,' Ricky said. 'I don't understand what you mean.'

The woman shook her head, not replying directly. 'Father, why are you looking for my son?'

He pulled out the phoney cancer letter, guessing that the woman wouldn't read it carefully enough to find questions in it.

'You see, Mrs . . . Collins, correct? My parish is trying to reach out to anyone who might be a marrow donor for a youngster who is related to you distantly. I'd ask you to take the blood screening test, but I suspect you're beyond the age where marrow can be donated. You're over sixty, correct?' Ricky had no idea whether bone marrow ceased being viable at any age. 'Perhaps we could sit down?'

The woman nodded reluctantly and held the door open for him. He stepped into a house that seemed as fragile as the old woman who lived there. It was filled with small china objects and figurines, and had a musty, aged smell. The sofa made a squeak as he sat down.

'Your son . . . is he available? You see, he might be a match—'

'He's dead,' the woman said coldly. 'Dead to all of us. Dead to me, now. Dead and worthless, nothing but pain, Father. I'm sorry.'

'How did he . . .?'

She shook her head. 'Not yet. But soon enough.'

The woman reached down and removed a scrapbook from a shelf beneath a coffee table. She opened it, flipped through several pages, then handed it across to him.

Centred on a single sheet of the scrapbook was a story from the *Tampa Tribune*. The headline was MAN ARRESTED AFTER BARROOM

DEATH. On the adjacent page another headline: STATE TO SEEK DEATH IN BAR FIGHT SLAYING. Ricky scanned the clipping. Daniel Collins had been arrested at the scene, unconscious, drunk, a bloody knife near his hand, the victim spread-eagled a few feet away. The victim had been eviscerated in a particularly cruel fashion.

When Ricky looked up, the old woman was shaking her head. 'My lovely boy,' she said. 'Lost him first to that bitch, now to death row.'

'Have they set a date?' Ricky asked.

'No. His lawyer says they've got appeals. I don't really understand too well. All I know is that my boy says he didn't do it.'

'He says he's innocent?'

'That's right. Says he's got no memory of the fight at all. Says he woke up all covered in blood with that knife by his side when the policemen shoved him with their sticks. I guess having no recollection isn't much of a defence.'

She rose, and Ricky rose with her.

'Talking about this makes my heart feel filled with sickness, Father. And there ain't no comfort.'

'I think, my child, that you should open your heart to the goodness that you remember.'

'The goodness stopped with that girl, Father. When she got pregnant that first time, why, any chance my boy had just went right away. All the trouble he had, I blame it on her.' The woman's voice was cold, clipped and utterly committed to the idea that her darling boy had nothing to do with creating any of the trouble that befell him.

'Do you know what happened to the three children? Your grandchildren?' Ricky asked.

The woman shook her head. 'They was give up, I heard. Danny signed some paper when he was in jail in Texas.'

'Did you even know their names?' he asked.

Again the woman shook her head. The cruelty in that gesture almost struck him like a fist, and he understood where young Daniel Collins had found his own selfishness.

When the last of the day's sunshine hit Ricky's head, he stood dizzily on the sidewalk for a moment, wondering if Rumplestiltskin's reach was so far that it had put Daniel Collins on death row. He guessed that it was. He just wasn't precisely certain how.

UPON HIS RETURN to New Hampshire, Ricky took up the simple routines of his life in Durham with unbridled enthusiasm. He lost himself in the steadiness of getting up each morning and going to work, of swabbing floors, cleaning bathrooms and polishing hallways. He discovered he didn't miss his life as an analyst. In a curious way, Richard Lively was closer to the person Ricky had wanted to be, closer to the person who'd found himself in summers on the Cape than the Dr Starks who treated the rich and neurotic.

But for every second that he forced himself to grow comfortable with who he was, the revenge persona of Frederick Lazarus shouted contradictory commands. He renewed his physical fitness training and spent hours perfecting marksmanship skills on the pistol range.

Late at night, sitting in his rented room, he asked himself whether he could simply turn his back on everything that had happened, abandon any emotional connection to his past and live paycheque to paycheque. It seemed to him that he had reached the moment where he had to make a choice. One thing was abundantly clear: if Rumplestiltskin learned that he'd escaped, he would be on Ricky's trail instantly with evil intentions. Ricky doubted that he would have the opportunity to play any game the second time around.

A part of him insisted he could be happy as Richard Lively. Another part of him saw things differently. Dr Frederick Starks did not deserve to die. There was no denying he could have done better for Claire Tyson. Rumplestiltskin was right about that.

'But I didn't kill her,' he said out loud.

Next to him, spread out on the bed, were the documents that he'd taken from old man Tyson. In the papers were the names of the adoptive parents who had taken the three children in twenty years ago. That, he knew, was his next step.

Alone in his room, Ricky reached for the papers.

'All right,' he said quietly to himself, 'the game starts up again.'

RICKY SWIFTLY LEARNED that Social Services in New York City had placed the three children in a succession of foster homes for the first six months after their mother died, until they were adopted by Howard and Martha Jackson, who lived in West Windsor, New Jersey. A social worker's report stated that the children had been difficult placements; that except for their last and unidentified foster home, they had proved to be disruptive, angry and abusive. The social worker had recommended therapy, especially for the oldest.

The children were listed as male child Luke, twelve years; male child Matthew, eleven years; and female child Joanna, nine years.

He made several computer sorties but drew blanks. He checked the electronic white pages, found many Jacksons in central New

Jersey, but no name that dovetailed with those he had on the meagre sheaf of papers. What he did have was an old address. Which meant that again there was a door he could knock on.

Ricky ceased shaving, rapidly growing a patchy beard. Another late-night inspection of the drama department's wardrobe room provided him with a fake stomach—a strap-on pillow that made him appear perhaps forty pounds heavier—and a brown suit that accommodated the extra girth. He slipped the items into a green garbage bag and took it home with him. When he got to his room, he added his semiautomatic pistol and two fully loaded clips to the bag.

He rented a car from the local Rent-A-Wreck, which generally provided for students. The clerk dutifully took down the information from the phoney California driver's licence Ricky provided, and the following Friday evening, when he'd finished his shift in the maintenance department, he started driving south towards New Jersey.

It was well past midnight when he skirted Manhattan, stealing a glance back over his shoulder as he cruised across the George Washington Bridge. Even in the dead of night the city seemed to glow. A curious blend of emotions slapped him as he swept past the tolls and arrived in New Jersey. New York seemed to be all about who he was, the car that rattled as he steered it over the highway represented what he'd become and the darkness ahead what he might be.

A vacancy sign at an Econo Lodge on Route 1 beckoned him, and he stopped for the night. In the morning he strapped the fake stomach beneath his T-shirt, dressed in the cheap suit and stuck his pistol in one pocket, along with the back-up clip of bullets.

The area he drove through had once been rural but now carried the burden of upmarket development. He passed numerous housing complexes, ranging from the decidedly middle-class to far more luxurious mock mansions with pools and three-car garages.

He found a mailbox by the side of a back road in the midst of some remaining farmland, and the number corresponded to the address he had. He hesitated. There was a sign by the driveway. SAFETY FIRST KENNELS: BOARDING, GROOMING, TRAINING, BREEDERS OF 'ALL NATURAL' SECURITY SYSTEMS. Next to this was a picture of a Rottweiler. Ricky drove down the driveway between some trees that formed a canopy above him.

When he came out from under the trees, he pulled up to a 1950s ranch house with a brick façade. The house had been added on to, in several phases, with white clapboard construction that connected to a warren of chain-link enclosures. As soon as he got out of his car, he was greeted by a cacophony of barking dogs. He saw a sign that said OFFICE. In the kennel closest to him a large Rottweiler, weighing over a hundred pounds, rose up on its hind legs, baring teeth.

Ricky stepped inside the office and saw a middle-aged man sitting behind an old steel desk, punching numbers onto a calculator. He was lean, bald, rangy, with thick forearms. The man rose and came towards him. 'How can I help you?' he said.

Ricky pulled out a private investigator's identification card he'd acquired from the novelty outlet over the Internet.

The man stared at it for a moment, then said, 'So, Mr Lazarus, I guess you're not here looking for a puppy.'

'No.'

'Well, what can I do for you?'

'Some years ago a couple lived here. Howard and Martha Jackson.'

When Ricky spoke the names, the man stiffened. The welcoming appearance he displayed disappeared instantly.

'What makes you interested in them?'

'I'm interested in their three children.'

The man hesitated, as if considering what Ricky had asked. 'They didn't have no children. Died childless. Just a brother lived some ways away. He's the one sold me the place. I fixed it up real good. Made their business into something. But no kids. Never.'

'No. You're mistaken,' Ricky said. 'They did. They adopted three orphans from New York City in May 1980.'

'Mister, I don't know where you got your information, but you're wrong. Dead wrong. There weren't any children. Adopted or otherwise. So what's your real interest?'

'I have a client. One who's interested in the three children. He's got some questions. The rest is confidential,' Ricky said.

The man's eyes narrowed. 'Somebody paying you to come around here and ask questions? Well, you got a card? A number where I can reach you if maybe I remember something?'

'I'm from out of town.'

The breeder continued to eye Ricky. 'Telephone lines go state to state, fella. How can I reach you if I need to?'

'What is it that you think you can remember later that you can't remember now?' Ricky demanded.

Now the man was measuring, assessing, as if trying to imprint every detail of Ricky's face and physique. Everything about him screamed warnings to Ricky. He realised that he was suddenly close to something dangerous.

Ricky took a step back towards the door. 'Tell you what. I'll give you a couple of hours to think this over; then I'll call you.'

He quickly manoeuvred out of the office and took several strides towards the rental car. The breeder was a few steps behind, but then he turned to the side and within a second had reached the kennel containing the big Rottweiler. The man unlatched the gate, and the dog, mouth agape, sprang immediately to his side. The breeder gave a small open-palm signal, and the dog instantly froze, eyes locked on Ricky, waiting for the next command.

'I don't think coming round here and asking questions is a real good idea,' said the breeder. 'Not with Brutus here.'

Ricky took the last few steps to the car backing up slowly. As he reached into his pocket for the car keys, the dog emitted a low growl.

The breeder put his hand on the dog's collar, restraining it. 'New Hampshire plates,' he said after a moment. 'With the motto "Live Free or Die". Very memorable. Now get out of here.'

Ricky did not hesitate to slip into the car and slam the door shut. Within seconds he was pulling away, but he saw the breeder in his rearview mirror, the dog still at his side, watching him depart.

RICKY WAS OVERCOME with the sense that he was on the edge of something larger than what he'd expected. He told himself that he needed to get back to the safety of New Hampshire. He halted the car outside the office of the Econo Lodge and stepped inside.

'I'm going to check out,' he said to the clerk. 'Mr Lazarus. In room two thirty-two.'

The clerk pulled up a bill on the computer and said, 'You're all set. Except there were a couple of phone messages for you.'

Ricky hesitated, then asked, 'Phone messages?'

The clerk nodded. 'Guy from some dog kennel called, asking if you were staying here. Wanted to leave a message on your room phone. Then, just before you came in, there was another message. Just pick up the phone over there and punch in your room number. You can hear the messages that way.'

Ricky did as instructed.

The first message was from the kennel owner: 'I thought you'd be staying someplace cheap and close. Wasn't too hard to figure out where. I been thinking about your questions. Call me. I think maybe I've got some information that might help you out. But you better get out your chequebook. Gonna cost you.'

The next message played automatically. The voice was clipped and cool and astonishing, almost like finding a piece of ice on a hot side-walk on a summer day: 'Mr Lazarus, I have just been informed of your curiosity concerning the late Mr and Mrs Jackson, and believe I might have some information that might assist you in your enquiries. Please telephone me at 212-555-1717 at your earliest possible convenience, and we can arrange a meeting.'

The caller did not provide a name. That was unnecessary. Ricky recognised the voice. It was Virgil.

TEN

Ricky fled. Bag hurriedly packed, tyres squealing, he raced away from the motel in New Jersey and the familiar voice on the phone.

He did not know what the connection was between the man at the kennel and Rumplestiltskin, but it surely existed, and the ease with which the man had found the motel where Ricky had been staying was daunting.

Ricky drove hard and fast, heading back to New Hampshire, trying to assess how compromised his existence truly was. He had just passed the WELCOME TO MASSACHUSETTS sign on the roadway when an idea came to him. He saw an exit up ahead and just beyond that the common American landscape marker: a shopping mall. He steered the rental car into the mall's parking lot.

It did not take him long to find a gathering of telephones near the food court. He remembered the number easily.

'*New York Times* classified.'

'Yes,' Ricky said pleasantly. 'I'd like to purchase one of those small one-column ads for the front page.'

In rapid order he read off a credit card number. The clerk took the information, then asked, 'OK, Mr Lazarus, what's the message?'

Ricky hesitated, then said, 'Mr R. Game on. A new Voice.'

The clerk read it back. 'That's it?' he asked.

'That's it. Make sure you uppercase the word *Voice*, OK?'

The clerk acknowledged the request, and Ricky disconnected the line. He then walked over to a fast-food outlet, purchased a cup of coffee and grabbed a handful of napkins. He found a table and settled in with a pen in his hand. He shut out the noise and the activity

and concentrated on what he was about to write. Finally, after a few
fits and starts, he came up with the following:

> *You know who I was, not who I am.*
> *That is why you're in a jam.*
> *Ricky's gone, he's very dead.*
> *I am here, in his stead.*
> *Lazarus rose, and so have I,*
> *And now it's time for someone else to die.*
> *A new game, in an old place,*
> *Will eventually bring us face to face.*
> *Then we'll see who draws the last breath,*
> *Because, Mr R, even bad poets love death.*

Ricky admired his work for a moment, then returned to the bank
of telephones. Within a few minutes he'd connected with the classified department at the *Village Voice*. 'I'd like to place an ad in the
personal section,' he said.

'No problemo,' the clerk said. 'What sort of heading?'

'Heading?' Ricky asked.

'You know, like WM for white male, SM for sadomasochism.'

Ricky thought a moment, then said, 'It should read, "WM, 50s,
seeks Mr Right for special fun and games."'

The clerk repeated this. 'OK,' he said. 'Something else?'

'Oh, yes, indeed,' Ricky said. He then read off the poem.

'Well,' the clerk said when he'd finished reading it over, 'that's different. Way different. This will bring all the crazies out of the wood-
work. Now, we give you a box number, and you can access the replies
by phone.' Ricky heard the clerk clicking on a computer keyboard.
'All right,' he said. 'You're box 1313. Hope you're not superstitious.'

'Not in the slightest,' Ricky said. He wrote the number for accessing the answers on his napkin and hung up the phone.

For a moment he considered calling the number he had for Virgil.
But he resisted this temptation. He had a few things to arrange first.

IN *THE ART OF WAR*, Sun Tzu discusses the importance of the general choosing his battleground, occupying a position of mystery,
seizing a location of superiority. Ricky thought these lessons applied
to him as well. He realised it would not take long for someone to
arrive in Durham searching for him. The licence plate number
noticed by the dog kennel owner fairly guaranteed that.

When he reached Durham, he returned the rental car, stopped

briefly at his room and then went directly to his volunteer job at the crisis hot line. He did not know how much time he had purchased for himself with the ads, but there would be a little. The *Times* ad would run the following morning, the *Voice* at the end of the week. There was a reasonable likelihood that Rumplestiltskin would not act until he'd seen both. All the man knew so far was that an overweight private investigator named Frederick Lazarus had arrived at a dog kennel in New Jersey asking questions about the couple who, records showed, had adopted him and his siblings years earlier. But Ricky did not delude himself that Rumplestiltskin wouldn't find other signs of Ricky's existence rapidly. The advantage Ricky had, he thought, was that there would be no clear-cut link between Frederick Lazarus and either Dr Frederick Starks or Richard Lively. One was presumed dead. The other still clung to anonymity.

If Richard Lively was to survive the upcoming confrontation, Ricky would have to lead Rumplestiltskin away from Durham.

He whispered to himself, 'Back to New York.'

HE BEGAN MAKING arrangements the next morning. He paid his rent for the following month but told his landlady that he was likely to be out of town on business. He had put a plant in his room, and he made certain she agreed to water it regularly. It was, he thought, the simplest way of playing on the psychology of the woman; no man who wants his plant watered was likely to run out. His supervisor at the university gave him permission to take some accumulated overtime. At the local bank where Frederick Lazarus had his account, Ricky made a wire transfer to an account he opened electronically at a Manhattan bank.

He also made a series of hotel reservations around the city, for successive days. He guaranteed each reservation with Frederick Lazarus's credit cards, except for the last hotel he selected. The final two hotels were located on West 22nd Street, more or less directly across from each other. At one he simply reserved a two-night stay for Frederick Lazarus. At the other he reserved a two-week block using Richard Lively's Visa card.

He closed Frederick Lazarus's post office box, leaving a forwarding address of the second-to-last hotel.

Finally, he packed his weapon and several changes of clothing into a bag, returned to Rent-A-Wreck and rented another car. But on this occasion he was careful to leave a trail. On the rental agreement Ricky wrote the name and telephone number of the first of the hotels where he'd made a reservation for Frederick Lazarus.

'One other thing,' he said to the clerk. 'I left a message with my friend to rent a car here as well. So if he should come in here in the next couple of days, you be sure to give him a good deal, OK?'

The clerk nodded.

'And if he asks about me, tell him I took off on business. In New York City.'

The clerk shrugged. 'No problem. Does he have a name?'

Ricky smiled. 'Sure. R. S. Skin. Easy to remember. Mr R. Skin.'

On the drive down Route 95 towards New York City, Ricky stopped at three shopping malls and acquired five cellphones and a laptop computer.

It was early evening when he arrived at the first of his hotels, in Chinatown. As he checked in, the desk clerk looked surprised when the credit card in Frederick Lazarus's name actually worked. He also looked surprised at the word *reservation*. Ricky thought it wasn't a place that got many reservations. It was as seedy as he'd guessed it would be, the type of place where the fact that he checked in with no bags and then walked out again fifteen minutes later wouldn't gather much attention.

He took the subway over to the last of the hotels on his list, where he became Richard Lively. He went out once that night to a deli for some sandwiches and a couple of sodas. The rest of the night he spent in quiet planning, except for a single sortie out at midnight.

A passing shower had left the street glistening. Yellow streetlights threw arcs of wan light across the black road. Ricky crossed town, walking rapidly until he found an isolated payphone. A siren creased the night air. Ricky waited until the racket faded. Then he dialled the number at the *Village Voice* and accessed the replies to his personal ad at box 1313. There were nearly three dozen.

The majority were sexual come-ons that mentioned Ricky's 'special fun and games'. The thirtieth was different. The voice was cold, with a metallic, tinny sound to it. Ricky guessed the speaker was using an electronic masking device. But there was no concealing the psychological thrust of the reply.

> '*Ricky's clever, Ricky's smart.*
> *But here's a rhyme he should take to heart:*
> *He thinks he's safe, he wants to play,*
> *But where he hid, is where he should stay.*

He escaped once, impressive, no doubt.
But this success, he shouldn't flout.
A second chance, another game,
Will likely just end up the same.
Only this time the debt owed me,
Will be paid in full, I guarantee.'

Ricky listened to the response three times. There was something recognisable in the voice that seeped past the hollowness of the masking device. The thought pierced him that this was Rumplestiltskin, and he shuddered.

Immediately following the poem, Ricky heard Virgil's voice.

'Ricky, how nice to hear from you. How truly special. And genuinely surprising, too, I might add. I warned them, you know. I told them, "Ricky's a clever sort. Intuitive and fast-thinking," but they didn't want to believe me. They thought you would be as careless as all the others. And now look where it has landed us.'

She sighed deeply, then continued. 'Well, personally, I can't imagine why you want to go another round with Mr R. I'd have guessed you'd stay under whatever rock you found to hide yourself. Because my suspicion is that Mr R will need better proof of victory this time around. He's a very thorough individual. Or so I'm told.'

Virgil's voice disappeared, as if she'd hung up her telephone abruptly. Ricky listened to an electronic hissing noise, then accessed the subsequent telephone message. It was Virgil for a second time.

'So, Ricky, I'd hate to see you have to repeat the outcome of the first game, but if a new game is what it's going to take, well, the choice is yours. We await the opening move.'

IN THE MORNING Ricky took the subway uptown to the first of the hotels where he'd checked in but not stayed. He returned the room key to a disinterested clerk reading a pornographic magazine behind the counter. The man took the key with hardly a word.

'Hey,' Ricky said, getting the barest response from the clerk. 'Hey, there's a chance a man might come looking for me.'

The clerk nodded, still not particularly focused.

Ricky glanced around, determining that they were alone in the drab lobby, then reached into his jacket pocket and, keeping his hands below the counter front, removed his pistol and chambered a round, making a distinctive sound.

The clerk abruptly looked up, his eyes widening slightly.

Ricky grinned nastily. 'Perhaps I have your attention now?'

'I'm listening,' the man replied.

'So let me try again,' Ricky said. 'A man comes asking for me, you're gonna give him this number: 212-555-2798. That's where he can reach me. Got it?'

'I've got it.'

'Make him give you a fifty. Maybe a hundred. It's worth it.'

The man looked sullen, but nodded. 'What if I ain't here? Suppose the night guy is here?'

'You want the hundred, you be here,' Ricky answered.

'OK. I got it.'

'Good,' Ricky said, returning the weapon to his pocket. He smiled at the clerk and pointed at the porn magazine. 'Don't let me keep you from advancing your education,' he said as he turned to leave.

HE HEADED ACROSS TOWN to check in at the next of his hotels.

In decor this one was much the same as the first—depressing and threadbare. In the hallway he passed two women—short skirts, glossy make-up, spiked heels, unmistakable in their profession—who had eyed him with financial eagerness as he cruised past. He shook his head when one of them offered an inviting glance his way. He heard the other remark, 'Cop,' and that surprised him. He thought he was doing a good job of accommodating the world he'd descended into. But perhaps, Ricky thought, it is harder to shed where you've been in your life than you realise.

He lay on the bed, feeling the springs sag beneath him. He stared up at the bare light bulb, listening to the unmistakable rhythms of sex in the next room. The milieu was precisely what he wanted. He needed Rumplestiltskin to think that Ricky had somehow become familiar with the nether world, just as Mr R was.

THAT AFTERNOON Ricky found an army and navy surplus store, where he purchased a few items he thought he might need for the next stage of his game. These included a small crowbar, an inexpensive bicycle lock, some surgical gloves, a mini-flashlight, a roll of duct tape and the cheapest pair of binoculars that they had.

He returned to his room and packed these items, along with his pistol and two of his newly acquired cellphones, into a small backpack. He used the third cellphone to call the next hotel on his list, the one he had not checked into yet. There he left an urgent message for Frederick Lazarus to return the call as soon as he checked in. He gave the cellphone number to a clerk, then thrust that phone into an outside pocket of the knapsack, after carefully marking it with a pen. When he reached his rental car, parked in an outdoor lot, he took out the phone and gruffly called the hotel a second time, leaving yet another urgent message for himself. He did this three more times as he headed towards New Jersey, each time growing more strident and more insistent that Mr Lazarus get back to him instantly, as he had important information to pass on.

After the last message on that cellphone he pulled into a rest stop on the Jersey Turnpike. He went into the men's room, washed his hands and left the telephone on the edge of the sink. He noted that several teenagers passed him on his way out, heading to the men's room. He thought there was the likelihood that they would grab the phone and start using it pretty quickly, which was what he wanted.

It was on the edge of evening when he arrived in West Windsor. He found a diner along Route 1, where he stopped and killed a bit of time eating a cheeseburger and fries. When he emerged, there was still some time before darkness settled in. He drove over to the local cemetery. He was fortunate that the entrance wasn't locked, so he pulled the rental car over behind a small white clapboard storage shack and left it there, more or less concealed from the roadway and appearing innocuous enough to anyone who might spot it.

The daylight was beginning to fade, turning the New Jersey sky a sickly grey-brown. Ricky threw the backpack over his shoulder and, with a glance down the deserted rural road, started jogging towards the kennel, where he knew the information he needed was waiting.

He turned off the roadway and ducked beneath the canopy of trees, sliding past the kennel sign and the picture of the Rottweiler. Then he stepped off the driveway, into the shrub brush and greenery that hid the kennel from the highway and carefully picked his way closer to the house and the pens. Still hidden by the foliage, Ricky removed the binoculars from the backpack and used them to survey the exterior.

His eyes went first to the pen beside the main entrance, where he spotted Brutus pacing back and forth nervously. Ricky wasn't yet close enough to be considered a threat. Sweeping the glasses in an arc, Ricky saw the unmistakable wan glow of a television set in a room near the front of the main house. The kennel office, a little way to his left, remained dark and, he guessed, locked. Some of the other dogs in their pens were now moving around, sniffing the air.

Ricky took a deep breath. Lifting his eyes to the sky, he saw that the day's last light had finally slid away. He removed the crowbar and the bicycle lock and gripped them in his right hand. Then he burst from the bushes, sprinting hard for the front of the building.

A bedlam of yelps, howls, barks and growls pierced the air. Ricky was aware of the animals racing about in their small enclosures. Within seconds he'd reached the front of Brutus's kennel. The huge dog leapt across the pen, threw itself against the chain-link fencing, then fell back, frothing with rage. Ricky moved quickly, rapidly threading the bicycle lock round the twin posts of the kennel door. He then secured the combination lock. The dog immediately tore at the rubber-encased steel of the chain.

Ricky ran to the front of the kennel office. He thrust the crowbar into the doorjamb and snapped out the lock. The door came open, and Ricky stepped inside. He swung his backpack round to his front, stuffed the crowbar inside and removed his pistol.

Inside was an opera of dog anxiety. Clicking on his flashlight, he raced down the foul-smelling corridor where all the dogs were penned, stopping to open each cage as he ran past. Within seconds he was surrounded by a leaping, barking tangle of breeds. He returned to the kennel office, waving his arms, shooing the animals along like some wildly impatient Moses at the edge of the Red Sea.

He saw a floodlight click on outside and heard a door slamming. The kennel owner, he thought. Ricky counted to ten, then heard a second noise above the roused dogs: The man was trying to open the Rottweiler's cage. It was at that moment that Ricky threw open the front door to the kennel office.

'OK, guys, you're free,' he said. Nearly three dozen dogs bolted through the door, heading towards the warm New Jersey night, their voices raised in a confused song of joyous freedom.

As Ricky stepped out, staying at the edge of the spotlight's arc, he heard the kennel owner swearing wildly as he was bowled over by the rush of animals. The man scrambled up, partially regaining his feet, searching for his balance. When he finally looked up, what he saw was Ricky's pistol levelled at his face.

'Are you alone?' Ricky asked.

'Huh?' The man rocked back in surprise.

'Are you alone? Is there anyone else in the house?'

The kennel owner shook his head. 'No. Just me.'

Ricky thrust the pistol closer to the man, close enough for the pungent odour of steel and oil and maybe death to fill his nostrils.

'Good. Now we can have a conversation.'

'Who are you?' the man asked. It took a second for Ricky to

remember that he'd been wearing a disguise on his first visit.

'I'm someone you would probably rather not know,' he said, gesturing at the man's face with his weapon.

It took a few seconds for him to get the kennel owner where he wanted him, which was seated on the ground with his back up against the gate to Brutus's pen, hands out on his knees where Ricky could see them. By now some of the dogs had disappeared into the darkness, others had collected near the owner's feet, and still others were jumping about, playing on the gravel driveway.

'I still don't know who you are,' the man said. 'I don't keep any cash here, and—'

'This isn't a robbery. Right now all you need to know is that I'm a man with a gun who would like some questions answered.'

The kennel owner nodded.

'I want to know about the couple who died and the three kids they adopted that you said they didn't. And I would like to know about the phone call you made after my friend Lazarus came to visit you the other day. Who did you call?'

The man shook his head. 'I'll tell you this: I got paid to make that call.'

'By whom?'

The man shook his head again. 'My business, mister tough guy.'

Ricky levelled the pistol at the man's face.

The kennel owner grinned. 'I've seen guys who will use that thing, and fella, I'm betting you ain't one of 'em.'

'You know,' Ricky said slowly, 'you're one hundred per cent right. I haven't really been in this position all that much. So maybe I should practise some.' As he said this, he lifted the pistol and sighted down the barrel at the Rottweiler.

'Just hang on for a second!' the kennel owner spat out.

'You have something to say?' Ricky asked.

'That dog is worth thousands,' the man said. 'I've spent half my damn life training him. And you're gonna shoot him?'

'Well, you see,' Ricky replied, 'now you've got something to think about. Is withholding information worth the dog's life?'

'I don't know who they are,' the man started, causing Ricky to take aim at Brutus again. This time the man held up both hands. 'OK. I'll tell you what I know.'

'That would be wise.'

'I don't know much,' the kennel owner said.

'Bad start,' Ricky said. He immediately fired a shot in the direction of the Rottweiler. This shot cracked into the dog's wooden hut in the rear of the pen. Brutus howled in insult and rage.

'Stop! I'll tell you. You're right about the old couple. I don't know exactly, but they adopted those three kids on paper only. The kids were never here. I don't know who they fronted for, because I came in after the couple was killed. Both of them in a car accident. I'd tried to buy this place from them a year before they died, and after they smashed up that car, I got a call from a man who said he was the executor of their estate, asking me if I wanted the place and the business. The price, too, was unbelievable. Bargain basement. We signed papers right quick.'

'Who did you deal with? Some lawyer?'

'Yeah, a local guy.'

'Do you know who sold the property?'

'I only saw the name once. The lawyer said it was the old couple's next of kin. A cousin. Pretty distant. I don't remember the name, except that it was a doctor something or other.'

'A doctor?'

'That's right. And I was told if anyone ever came asking about the old couple or the three children, I was supposed to call a number.'

'Did they give you a name?'

'No, just a number in Manhattan. And then about six, seven years later a man calls me one day out of the blue and tells me that the number has changed. Gives me another New York City number. Then, maybe a few years after that, same guy calls up, gives me another number, only this time it's in upstate New York. He asks me if anyone has ever come visiting. I tell him no. It never happened until the other day when this guy Lazarus shows up. Asks his questions, and I run him out. Then I call the number. Man picks up the phone. Old man now. You can hear it in his voice. Says thank you for the information. Maybe two minutes later I get another call. This time it's some young woman. She says she's sending me some cash, like a grand, and that if I can find Lazarus, there's another grand. I tell her he's probably staying at one of maybe three or four motels. And that's it, until you show up.'

'The number you called—what is it?'

The man rattled off all ten numbers rapidly.

'Thank you,' Ricky said coldly. He didn't need to write it down. It was a number he knew. He gestured with the pistol for the man to roll over. 'Place your hands behind your back,' he instructed. 'I need to restrict your activity for a few minutes, just long enough to depart before you find some bolt cutters and let Brutus there loose. I'm thinking that perhaps he'd like to have a moment or two alone with me in the dark.'

This made the kennel owner grin. 'He's the only dog I ever known that carries a grudge. OK. Do what you got to.'

Ricky secured the man's hands with duct tape. Then he stood up. 'You'll call them, won't you?'

The man nodded. 'If I said I wouldn't, you'd know I was lying.'

Ricky smiled. 'Quite correct.' He paused, considering precisely what he wanted to say. 'All right, here's what you need to tell them:

> *'The game's afoot, and closing in.*
> *Lazarus believes he's going to win.*
> *It may no longer be your choice,*
> *But better check this week's* Voice.*'*

'Sounds like a poem,' the man said.

'A kind of poem. Now, repeat it for me.'

It took several efforts for the kennel owner to get it straight.

'Close enough,' Ricky said. 'Can I give you one piece of advice?'

'What's that?'

'Make the call. Recite the poem. Go out and collect the dogs that ran away. Then forget any of this ever happened. Go back to the life you have for yourself, and don't think about all this ever again.'

Leaving the man on the ground behind him, Ricky started to jog down the driveway and then out towards the cemetery, where he'd parked his car. He had miles to travel that night. Highway miles and heart miles. Both leading into his past and pointing the way to his future. He hurried, like a marathon racer who senses the finish line ahead, just beyond his sight.

A LITTLE AFTER MIDNIGHT he reached the tolbooth on the western side of the Hudson River, just to the north of Kingston, New York. He paid his toll, the only car crossing the bridge at that late hour. On the Rhinebeck side he found a place to pull over. Using one of his cellphones, he dialled the front desk number at the last hotel where Frederick Lazarus was scheduled to be staying.

'Excelsior Hotel. How can I help you?'

'My name is Frederick Lazarus,' Ricky said. 'I had a reservation for tonight. But I won't make it until tomorrow. Can you check to see if anyone left any messages for me?'

'Hang on,' the man said. Ricky could hear the telephone being placed on the counter. The man came on in a moment and said, 'You must be a popular guy. There's at least three or four.'

'Read them to me,' Ricky said. 'And I'll take care of you when I get there.'

The man read off the messages Ricky had left for himself, but no others. This made him pause.

'Has anyone been there looking for me?'

The night clerk hesitated.

In that hesitation Ricky learned what he needed. Before the clerk could lie by saying no, Ricky said, 'She's gorgeous, isn't she?'

The clerk coughed.

'Is she there now?' Ricky demanded.

'No,' the clerk whispered. 'She left. A little less than an hour ago, right after she got a call on her cellphone. Took off real quick. And so did the guy she was with. They've been in and out of here all evening asking for you.'

'The guy she's with?' Ricky asked. 'Kinda round and pasty?'

'You got it,' the clerk said. He laughed. 'That's the guy.'

Hello, Merlin, Ricky thought. 'They leave a number?'

'No. Just said they'd come back. And they didn't want me to let on that they'd been here. What's this all about?'

'Just a business arrangement. Tell you what, if they show, you give them this number.' He read off the last of his cellphone numbers. 'But make them slip you some cash in return. They're loaded.'

He disconnected the call and sat back in his seat. By now the kennel owner would have got free from the duct tape handcuffs and made the phone call, so Ricky expected at least one light to be on at the house where he was headed.

AS HE HAD EARLIER that night, Ricky left the rental car parked off a side road, out of sight. He was a good mile from his destination, but he thought he could use the time on foot to consider his plan. As he ran, he asked himself: Are you willing to kill someone tonight?

He pulled up short when he reached the drive to the house. As he'd expected, he saw a single light in the study.

He knows I'm coming, Ricky thought. And Virgil and Merlin, who might have helped him, are still in New York. Even if they'd driven hard after he'd called, they were still a good hour away.

He put the pistol in his right hand and chambered a round. He clicked the safety off and then walked nonchalantly up to the front door. He didn't knock; he simply turned the handle. As he'd guessed, the door was open. He walked in. A voice came from the study to his right. 'In here, Ricky.'

He took a single stride forward, raising the pistol in front of him. Then he stepped into the light that flowed through the doorway. 'Hello, Dr Lewis.'

The old man was standing behind his desk, his hands flat on the surface, leaning expectantly forward. 'Did you really come all this way just to murder me?' he asked.

'Yes,' Ricky said, though this was a lie.

'Then go ahead.' The old doctor eyed him intensely.

'Rumplestiltskin,' Ricky said. 'All along it was you.'

Dr Lewis shook his head. 'No, you are wrong. But I am the man who created him. At least in part.'

Ricky moved sideways, coming deeper into the office, keeping his back to the wall. The same bookcases lined the walls. It was a cold place. Nothing on the walls or the desk said anything about the man who occupied the office. You don't need a diploma on the wall to certify being evil, Ricky thought darkly. He wondered how he had missed seeing it before. He gestured with his weapon for the old man to take a seat in the leather desk chair.

Dr Lewis slumped down, sighing.

'Please keep your hands where I can see them,' Ricky said.

The old man lifted his hands up. Then he pointed at his forehead, tapping it with an index finger. 'It is never what is in our hands that is truly dangerous, Ricky. Ultimately it is what is in our heads.'

'I might have agreed with you once, Doctor, but now I have a clear-cut reliance on this device, which is a Ruger semiautomatic pistol. There are fifteen shots in the clip, any one of which will remove a goodly portion of your skull.'

Dr Lewis paused, eyeing the gun. After a moment he smiled. 'Ricky, you were on my couch four times a week for four years. I know the inner you. I know you are not a killer.'

Ricky shook his head. 'The man you knew as Dr Frederick Starks was on your couch. But he's dead, and you don't know me. Not the new me. Not in the slightest.' Then he fired the pistol.

The bullet tore through the air above Dr Lewis's head, slapping into a bookcase directly behind him. Ricky saw a thick medical tome suddenly shred as it absorbed the shot.

Dr Lewis paled. 'My God,' he blurted out. He rotated slightly in his seat and inspected the location where the bullet had landed. He burst out a half laugh, half gasp, then shook his head. 'Quite a shot,

Ricky. A remarkable shot. Closer to the truth than my head.'

Ricky arranged an armchair in front of the old physician. 'If not you,' he asked coldly, 'then who is Rumplestiltskin?'

'The eldest child of the woman you failed to help.'

'That I discovered on my own. Keep going.'

Dr Lewis shrugged. 'My adopted child.'

'This I learned earlier tonight. And the two others?'

'His younger brother and sister. You know them as Merlin and Virgil.'

'Adopted as well?'

'Yes. We took all three in. First as foster-children, through the state of New York. Then I arranged for cousins in New Jersey to front for us.'

'So they carry your name?'

'No.' The old man shook his head. 'Not so fortunate, Ricky. They are not in any phone book listing under Lewis. They were reinvented completely. Different names for each. Different identities. Different education and different treatment. But brothers and sister at heart.'

'Why? Why the elaborate scheme to cover up their past?'

'My wife was ill, and we were beyond the age guidelines for the state. My cousins were convenient. And for a fee, willing to help. Help and forget.'

'Sure,' Ricky replied sarcastically. 'And their little accident? They died in a car crash.'

Dr Lewis shook his head. 'A coincidence,' he said.

'Why them? Why those three children?'

The old psychoanalyst shrugged again. 'Arrogance. Egotism.'

'They are just words, Doctor.'

'Yes, but they explain much. Tell me, Ricky. A killer—a truly remorseless, murderous psychopath—is this someone created by his environment? Or is he born to it? Which is it, Ricky?'

'Environment. The genetics guys might disagree. But we are a product of where we come from, psychologically.'

'And I would agree. So I took in a child who was a laboratory rat for evil. Abandoned by birth father. Rejected by relatives. Beaten by a series of his mother's sociopathic boyfriends. He eventually saw his own mother kill herself in poverty and despair. A formula for evil, would you not agree?'

'Yes.'

'And I thought I could take that child—and his two siblings—and reverse all that weight of wrong. I thought I could turn him into a productive member of society. That was my arrogance, Ricky.'

'And you couldn't?'

'No. But I did engender loyalty, and an odd sort of affection. It is a terrible and yet truly fascinating thing, Ricky, to be loved by a man devoted to death. And that is what you have in Rumplestiltskin. He is a professional. A consummate killer. One equipped with as fine an education as I could provide. Exeter. Harvard. Columbia Law. You know what the curious aspect of all this is, Ricky?'

'Tell me.'

'His job is not that different from ours. People come to him with problems. They pay him well for solutions.'

Ricky found himself breathing hard.

'And you know what else, Ricky—other than being extremely wealthy—do you know what other quality he has? He is relentless.' The old psychoanalyst sighed and added, 'But perhaps you have seen that already. How he waited years, preparing himself, and then singled out and destroyed everyone who ever did his mother harm.'

'But why me?' Ricky blurted. 'I didn't—'

'Of course you did. She went to you desperate for help, and you were too wrapped up in your own career to assist her.'

After a moment Ricky asked, 'When did you learn—?'

'Of your connection to my adopted experiment? Near the end of your own analysis. I simply decided to see how it would play out over the years.'

'And when he came after me? You could have warned me.'

'Betray my adopted child in favour of my one-time patient? And not even my favourite patient, at that.'

These words stung Ricky. He could see the old man was every bit as evil as the child he'd adopted. Perhaps even worse.

'And the other two?' he asked.

'The man you know as Merlin is indeed an attorney, and a capable one. The woman you know as Virgil is an actress with quite a career ahead of her. Especially now that they have almost completed tying up all the loose ends of their lives. The other thing you should know, Ricky, is that they both believe it was their older brother, the man you know as Rumplestiltskin, who saved their lives. Not I, really, though I contributed to their salvation. No, it was he who kept them together. So if nothing else, Ricky, understand this: they are devoted—utterly loyal to the man who will kill you.'

'Who is he?' Ricky demanded.

'You want his name? His address? His place of business?'

'Yes. I want all their names.'

The old analyst shook his head. 'Ricky, here we are, alone in this house. But for how much longer? Knowing as I did that you were heading this way, do you not think I took the precaution of summoning help? How long before it arrives?'

'Long enough.'

'Ah, there is a wager I'm not sure I would be so confident about.' Dr Lewis smiled. 'But perhaps we should make it slightly more complicated. Suppose I were to tell you that somewhere here in this room is the information you seek. Could you find it in time? Before help arrives to rescue me?'

'I'm tired of playing games.'

'It is in plain sight. And you have already come closer to it than even I guessed you might. There. Enough clues.'

'I won't play.'

'Well, I think you are going to have to play a bit longer, Ricky, because this game has not concluded.' The old analyst held both his hands up abruptly and then said, 'Ricky, I need to remove something from the top drawer of this desk. It is something that you will want to see. May I do that?'

Ricky aimed the pistol at Dr Lewis's forehead and nodded.

The doctor smiled again, a nasty, cold smile. He removed an envelope from the drawer and placed it on the desk.

'Hand it to me.'

'As you wish.' Dr Lewis thrust the envelope across the desktop, and Ricky grabbed it. He took his eyes off the old physician for an instant. This was a mistake. Ricky lifted his eyes and saw that the old man now had a .38-calibre revolver in his right hand.

The two men were facing across the desktop, weapons aimed squarely at each other.

'This,' Dr Lewis whispered, 'is an analytic fantasy, is it not? In the system of transference, do we not want to kill the analyst, just as we want to kill our mother or our father or everyone who has come to symbolise all that is wrong with our lives? And the analyst, does he not have a murderous passion at much the same time?'

Ricky didn't reply at first. Finally he muttered, 'The child may have been a laboratory rat for evil, like you say, but he could have been turned around. You could have done it, but it was more intriguing to see what would happen if you left him adrift, wasn't it?'

Dr Lewis paled slightly.

'You knew, didn't you,' Ricky continued, 'that you were as much of the psychopath as he was? You wanted a killer, and so you found one, because that was what you always wanted to be: a killer.'

The old man scowled. 'You always were astute, Ricky. Think of what you could have made of your life had you been a bit more ambitious. A little more subtle.'

'Put the weapon down, Doctor. You're not going to shoot me.'

Dr Lewis kept the revolver trained on Ricky's face, but nodded. 'I do not really have to, do I?' he said. 'The man who killed you once will do it again.'

'Not if I have anything to say about it. Perhaps I'll just disappear again. I succeeded once, and I can evaporate a second time.'

'I think you are wrong, Ricky.' Dr Lewis shrugged his shoulders. 'But our time is up for the evening. One last session. I have a question for you to take away from this. If Rumplestiltskin was so devoted to seeing you kill yourself after you failed his mother, what will he do when he believes you have killed me?'

'What do you mean?' Ricky asked.

But the old physician didn't reply. Instead, in a sweeping gesture, he lifted the revolver to his temple and fired a single shot.

ELEVEN

Ricky half shouted, half screamed in surprise and shock. His voice seemed to blend with the echo of the revolver's report.

By the time the reverberation had faded into the night air, he was on his feet, standing at the edge of the desk, staring down at the man he'd once trusted so implicitly. Dr Lewis had slammed backwards, twisted slightly by the force of death delivered to his temple. His eyes had remained open, and now they stared out with macabre intensity. A scarlet mist had painted the bookcase, and deep maroon blood was seeping down across the physician's face. Ricky gasped as the old man's body twitched with muscles coming into tune with death.

Ricky tried to organise his thoughts. He gripped the desk to steady himself. 'What have you done to me, old man?' he said out loud.

And then he realised the answer to his own question: He's tried to kill me. The old physician's death was likely to be taken hard by three people who had no restrictions on how they would respond. What the old man wanted was to endow all the people playing out the murderous game with a moral depravity that equalled his own. That was far more important than simply killing Ricky and himself. All along, Ricky thought, this hasn't only been about death. It's been about the process. It's been about how death is reached.

An appropriate game for a psychoanalyst to invent.

Rumplestiltskin may have been the agent of revenge and the instigator, as well, Ricky thought, but the design of the game came from the man dead before him. Of that he was certain.

It took Ricky a second or two to realise that he still clutched the envelope his one-time mentor had handed him. He tore open the flap and pulled out a single sheet of paper. He read rapidly:

> Ricky: The wages of evil are death. Think of this last moment as a tax I have paid on all I have done wrong. The information you seek is in front of you, but are you clever enough to see what you need to see? I doubt it. I think it is far more likely that you will die tonight in more or less the same fashion that I have. Only your death is likely to be far more painful, because your guilt is far less than my own.

The letter wasn't signed.

Ricky sucked in a new panic with his next breath. He tried to do the travel maths: when did the old man call and tell Merlin and Virgil and perhaps Rumplestiltskin that Ricky was on his way? From the city to the country home was two hours. Maybe a little less. Did he have seconds? Minutes? A quarter of an hour?

Right in front, he thought. Sliding gingerly round the desk, he put his hand on the top drawer and pulled it open. It was empty. The other drawers, too, were barren. Ricky bent down and searched under the desk surface but saw nothing.

Then he turned his attention to the dead man. Breathing in sharply, he let his fingers travel inside the man's pockets. Nothing.

Again Ricky swept his eyes over the office. He wanted to bellow in rage. It's here, he insisted.

He took another deep breath. Perhaps it isn't, he thought, and all the old man wanted me to do was to be here when his murderous adopted offspring arrive. No, that would be a simple lie, and Dr Lewis's lies were far more complex. There is something here.

Ricky turned to the bookcase. Rows of psychiatric texts. Books on depression, anxiety, dreams. Dozens of books, including the one that housed Ricky's bullet. He looked at the title on the spine: *The Encyclopedia of Abnormal Psychology*. Only the *ology* of the last word had been shredded by his shot.

He stopped, staring forward. Why did a psychoanalyst need a text on abnormal psychology? Their profession dealt with the modestly displaced emotions, not the truly twisted ones.

Dr Lewis had turned and seen the place the bullet landed, and laughed. Ricky pulled the text from the shelf. He opened it to the title page. Written in thick red ink right across the title were the words: *Good choice, Ricky. Now can you find the right entries?*

He looked up and heard the clock ticking. He did not have time to answer that question. He took a final glance at the old analyst's body. He thought he should say or feel something, but he no longer was sure what that could be. Instead, he ran.

Settling into a comfortable jog, Ricky headed back to his car. He had covered only half the distance when he heard the sound of a vehicle moving fast, heading in his direction. Without hesitating, he scrambled behind a stand of trees. He ducked down but lifted his head as a large black Mercedes roared past.

IT WAS DEEP into the pre-dawn morning when Ricky reached the city. He returned to his rented room, where he fought the urge to throw himself onto the bed and devour sleep. Answers, he told himself. He clutched answers in the book on abnormal psychology. He just needed to read them. The question was, where? The encyclopedia was organised alphabetically and contained 779 pages of text. Short of examining every page, he was unsure what to do.

He flipped through the pages, trying to think through the problem in front of him. He passed the few pages devoted to the letter V. Almost by luck his eyes caught a mark on the initial page of the section. In the upper corner, written in the same pen Dr Lewis had used for his greeting on the title page, was the fraction 1/3. That was all.

Ricky turned to the entries under M. In a similar location was another pair of numbers: 1/4. On the opening page of the letter R, he found 2/5. There was no doubt in Ricky's mind that these were keys. Now he had to uncover the locks. He bent forward slightly as he concentrated on the problem in front of him. It was a conundrum of personality as complex as any he'd experienced in his years as an analyst. He asked himself: What do I really know?

Portraits began to form in his imagination, starting with Virgil. Dr Lewis said she was an actress. She had been a child of poverty, the youngest of the three. Lurking in her unconscious would be issues of identity, of who she truly was. Hence the decision to enter a profession that constantly called for redesigning one's self.

Ricky shifted in his seat. Make a guess, he told himself. An educated guess. Narcissistic personality disorder.

He turned to the encyclopedia entry for that diagnosis. His pulse quickened. He saw that Dr Lewis had touched several letters in the midst of words with a yellow highlighter pen. Ricky grabbed a sheet of paper and wrote down the letters. Then he sat back sharply, staring at gobbledegook. It made no sense. He went back to the encyclopedia definition and recalled the '1/3' key. This time he wrote down letters three spaces away from the marked ones. Again, useless.

He considered the dilemma once again. Then he looked at letters three words away. But before writing these down, he thought: One *over* three. So he went instead to letters three lines below.

By doing this, the first three dots produced a word: *The*.

He continued rapidly, producing a second word: *Jones*.

There were six more dots, and they translated to: *Agency*.

Ricky stood and walked to the bedside table, where there was a New York City telephone book. He looked up the section for theatrical talent and found a small advertisement for 'The Jones Agency—a theatrical agency catering to the up-and-coming stars of tomorrow'.

One down. Now Merlin, the attorney.

He pictured the man: hair carefully combed, suits without wrinkles, manicured. A middle child, who wanted everything to be in order, who couldn't tolerate the messiness of the life he'd come from. This diagnosis came easily: obsessive-compulsive disorder.

Ricky turned rapidly to that section of the encyclopedia and saw the same series of highlighted letters. Using the key provided, he swiftly came up with a word that surprised him: *Arneson*. It wasn't exactly a jumble of letters, nor was it something he recognised.

He persisted and found the next letter was *v*. The remaining letters spelled out the word *Fortier*. A court case. A clerk with a computer and access to current dockets would probably turn it up.

Returning to the encyclopedia, Ricky thought of the man at the core of everything that had happened: Rumplestiltskin. He turned to the section under P that dealt with psychopaths. There was a subsection for homicidal psychopaths.

And there were the series of dots that he'd come to expect.

Ricky quickly deciphered the letters, writing them down on the sheet of paper. When he finished, he sat up straight, sighing deeply. Then he clenched the paper in his hand, crumpling it into a ball, and angrily threw it towards the waste basket.

The message he'd come up with had been: *Not this one*.

RICKY HAD NOT HAD much sleep, but adrenaline energised him. He showered, shaved and dressed himself in a jacket and tie. A lunch-hour trip to a court clerk's office and some modest cajoling provided him with some information about *Arneson* v. *Fortier*. It was a civil dispute over a real-estate transaction, scheduled for a pre-trial hearing in superior court the following morning.

The court docket gave him the names of all the parties. None stood out, but one was the man he was seeking. He left the clerk's office with a plan already forming in his head.

He took a cab first to Times Square, where he entered one of the many novelty stores and had half a dozen phoney business cards made up. Then he flagged another cab, which bore him to a glass-and-steel office building on the East Side. There was a guard at the entrance who made him sign in, which he did with a flourish, signing *Frederick Lazarus*, and listing his occupation as *Producer*. The guard issued him with a plastic clip-on badge, which designated the floor he was travelling to. The man didn't even glance at the sign-in sheet after Ricky handed it back to him.

An attractive receptionist greeted him when he entered the office of the Jones Agency. 'How can I help you?' she asked.

'I spoke with someone earlier,' Ricky lied, 'about a commercial shoot we've got coming up. We're looking for some fresh faces and checking out some of the new talent available. I was going to have a look through your portfolio.'

The receptionist smiled. 'No problem,' she said. She reached beneath the desk and came up with a large leather binder. 'These are the current clients. If you see anyone, then I can direct you to the agent who handles their bookings.' She gestured towards a leather couch in the corner of the room. Ricky took the portfolio over and started flipping through it.

Virgil was the seventh photo in the book. 'Hello,' Ricky said under his breath as he flipped the page and saw her real name, address and phone number, along with a list of off-Broadway and advertising credits. He wrote all this down on a pad of paper. Then he did precisely the same for two other actresses. He handed the portfolio back to the receptionist, checking his wristwatch as he did so.

'Look, I'm in a terrible bind with time,' he said. 'Perhaps you could call these three and set up meetings for me? Let's see, this one at lunch tomorrow at noon at Vincent's over on East Eighty-second. Then the other two, say at two and four, same place? I would appreciate it. We're a little under the gun here, if you know what I mean.'

The receptionist looked discomfited. 'Usually the agents have to set up every meeting,' she said reluctantly. 'Mr—'

'I understand,' he said. 'But I'm only in town until tomorrow, then back to Los Angeles. Sorry to be so rushed on all this.'

'I'll see what I can do . . . but your name?'

'It's Ulysses,' Ricky said. 'Mr Richard Ulysses. And I can be reached at this number.' He pulled out one of the fake business cards listing his last remaining cellphone number. 'See what you can do,' he said. 'If there's some problem, call me at that number.' With that, he turned and exited.

BEFORE RICKY LEFT his rented room the following morning for the courthouse, he confirmed with Virgil's agent the luncheon appointment, as well as the subsequent meetings with the two other actress-models that Ricky had no intention of attending.

He reluctantly left his handgun behind, knowing that he couldn't risk setting off a metal detector at the courthouse. He had dressed nicely, in blazer and tie, dress shirt and slacks. As he stared at himself in the bathroom mirror, he recalled one of the first lectures he'd ever heard on psychiatry. The physician had explained that no matter how much was known about behaviour and no matter how confident one was in diagnosis, ultimately one could never predict with total certainty how any one individual would react.

Ricky wondered whether he'd guessed right on this occasion. If he had, he would be free. If not, he would be dead.

His thoughts crept over to the three people who had stalked him. The children of his failure. Raised to hate everyone who'd failed to help. 'I know you now,' he said out loud, picturing Virgil in his mind. 'And you, I'm about to know,' he continued, conjuring up a portrait of Merlin. But Rumplestiltskin remained elusive, a shadow.

RICKY BREEZED into the courtroom where the man he knew as Merlin was arguing a motion. As he suspected, the room itself was only sparsely filled. He slipped quietly through the door and into a seat, where he slid down, making himself as unobtrusive as possible.

Half a dozen lawyers and plaintiffs were inside the bar, seated at sturdy oak tables in front of the judge's bench. They were all men, and they were intent upon the reactions of the judge to what they had to say. There was no jury in this preliminary stage, which meant that everything they said was directed forward.

A surge of excitement raced through Ricky when Merlin stood.

'You have an objection, Mr Thomas?' the judge demanded.

'Indeed, I do,' Merlin replied smugly.

Ricky looked down at the list he'd made of all the lawyers involved in the case. Mark Thomas, Esquire. He had a name.

It was Ricky's cue to exit, which he did quietly.

He took up a position next to the emergency stairwell across from a bank of elevators. He waited until the group of lawyers left the courtroom, then he ducked into the stairwell. He had lingered just long enough to see that Merlin was carrying two briefcases stuffed to overflowing with documents and court papers. Too heavy to carry beyond the closest elevator, Ricky knew.

He took the stairs two at a time, emerging on the second floor. There were several people waiting by the elevators. Ricky joined them, his hand in his pocket, where he'd placed a children's toy that he'd bought from a drugstore on the way to the courthouse. He stared up at the device that shows the location of the car and saw that the elevator had stopped on the floor above. Then it began to descend. Ricky knew one thing: Merlin wasn't the type to move to the back and make room for anyone else. The elevator stopped, and the doors swung open.

Merlin was in the direct centre. He lifted his eyes, and Ricky stared right into them. There was a flash of recognition, and Ricky saw a momentary panic slide onto the attorney's face.

'Hello, Merlin,' Ricky said quietly.

In the same instant he lifted the child's toy from his pocket and brought it to bear on the attorney's chest. It was a water pistol in the shape of a World War II German Luger. He squeezed the trigger, and a stream of black ink shot out, striking Merlin in the chest.

Before anyone could react, the doors slid shut.

THE RESTAURANT he had chosen for luncheon with Virgil had a large plate-glass window that separated the sidewalk from the diners. Ricky waited until a group of tourists reached the front of the restaurant. He simply tagged along. As the tourists cruised past, he quickly turned and saw Virgil sitting, as he'd expected, in a corner of the restaurant, waiting eagerly. And alone.

He stepped past the window and took a single deep breath.

The call will come any second now, Ricky thought. Merlin would have cleaned himself up, made his apologies to the other attorneys. When he finally made his first call, it would have been to the older brother, a substantial conversation recounting what had happened, trying to assess the implications. In line for a second phone call would be Virgil, but Ricky had beaten that call. He smiled, turned round sharply, and headed through the restaurant's front door. A hostess at the front began to ask the inevitable question, but he waved her off, saying, 'My date is already here,' and striding across the restaurant.

Virgil was turned away, then shifted when she sensed movement.

'Hello,' Ricky said. 'Remember me?'

Surprise struck her face.

'Because,' Ricky said, sliding into his seat, 'I remember you.'

Virgil rocked back in surprise. She had placed a portfolio of pictures and a résumé on the table. Now, slowly, she took it and slipped it to the floor. 'I guess I won't be needing that,' she said.

Before Ricky responded, a buzzing sound went off in her bag. A cellphone. Ricky shook his head. 'That would be your middle brother, the lawyer, calling to warn you that I appeared in his life this morning. And there will be another call, soon enough, from the older brother, who kills for a living. Because he, too, will want to protect you. Don't answer it.'

Her hand stopped. 'Or what?'

'Well, you should be asking yourself, How desperate is Ricky? and then the obvious follow-up: What might he do?'

Virgil ignored the phone, which stopped buzzing.

'What might Ricky do?' she asked.

He smiled at her. 'Ricky might do anything.'

Virgil shifted uncomfortably. 'True, but he's not going to shoot me in this restaurant in front of all these people. I don't think so.'

Ricky shrugged. 'I don't need to shoot you here, Virgil. I can shoot you any number of places. Because now I know who you are. I know your name. Your address. More important, I know who you want to become, your ambition. You're as trapped as Ricky was. And so is Merlin. You played the game with me once, and now I will play a game with you. It's called How Do I Stay Alive? It's a game about revenge. I think you already know some of the rules.'

Virgil had paled. She reached for a glass of iced water, took a long sip, staring at Ricky. 'He'll find you,' she whispered. 'He'll find you and kill you and protect me—because he always has.'

Ricky leaned forward. 'Like any older brother? Well, he can try. But you see, now he knows next to nothing of who I have become. The three of you have been chasing around after Mr Lazarus and thinking you had him cornered. But guess what? Poof! He's about to disappear. Because he's used up every little bit of usefulness.' Ricky rose, pushing the chair back quickly. 'Goodbye, Virgil,' he said. 'I think you will never want to see my face again, because then it might be the last thing you will ever see.'

Without waiting for her response, Ricky turned and walked briskly out of the restaurant. He cut through the throngs of people like a skater on a crowded rink, but his mind was elsewhere. He was trying to picture the man who'd once stalked him. How, Ricky wondered, will the psychopath react when the only two people left on this earth he truly holds dear have been threatened to their core?

Ricky pushed forward on the sidewalk, and thought, He will want to move fast. He will not prepare or plan. He will let cold rage overcome all his instincts and all his training.

But most important, he will make a mistake.

COLLECTING HIS THOUGHTS in his cheap New York room, Ricky knew, as much as he'd ever known anything, that he had to best Rumplestiltskin in this final phase. He thought he knew how to accomplish this. The first elements of his scheme had already been put in place. He could imagine the conversation between brothers and sister that was happening even as he sat in the rented room. It wouldn't be a phone conversation. They would have to meet. Voices would be raised. There would be tears, anger, harsh words. Everything had gone smoothly for them, wreaking murderous revenge on all the obvious targets of their past. Only one had come a cropper. He could hear the phrase 'You got us into this!' shouted at the shadowy figure who had meant so much to them over so many years.

Even with their compulsion to go along with him, the younger brother and younger sister still had aspirations of lives in the mainstream: a life in court and a life on the stage, playing by certain rules. Rumplestiltskin, alone of the three, was willing to live outside normal boundaries. But the two others were not, and that was how they became vulnerable.

Ricky found some paper and worked for a few moments on a rhyme. Once again he called the *Village Voice* classified section, but this time he was careful to ask the clerk several key questions and deliver some critical information.

'If I'm out of town, can I still call in and get the responses?'

'Sure,' said the clerk. 'Just dial the access code.'

'Great,' Ricky replied. 'You see, I have some business up on the Cape this weekend, and I still want to get the responses.'

'It won't be a problem,' the clerk said.

'I hope the weather is good. You ever go up to Cape Cod?'

'Been to Provincetown,' the clerk said. 'It's pretty wild up there after the Fourth of July weekend.'

'No kidding,' Ricky said. 'My place is in Wellfleet. Or at least it used to be. Had to sell it. A fire sale. Going up just to settle a few left-over matters, then back to the city and back to the grind.'

'I hear you,' the clerk said. 'I wish I had a place on the Cape.'

'Maybe someday,' Ricky said. He cleared his throat to deliver the message for the classifieds. He had it run under the modest headline: SEEKING MR R.

> *'Ricky's here. Ricky's there.*
> *Ricky could be anywhere.*
> *Someplace old, someplace new,*
> *Ricky will always elude you.*
> *Mr R can search high and low,*
> *Still he will never know,*
> *When Ricky might return again,*
> *As an adversary, not a friend,*
> *Carrying evil, toting death,*
> *Ready to steal someone's last breath.'*

The ad was scheduled for the following Friday, but the paper actually hit the newsstands the evening before, and that would be when all three of them would read the message. Merlin would call the ad supervisor and work his way down through the paper's hierarchy until he found the clerk who took the poem over the telephone. And the clerk would recall the conversation about the Cape. Then the three of them would argue once again. The two younger ones would say they wanted to join Mr R on his hunt, but the older brother would have none of it. This is a killing he wants to handle alone.

And so, Ricky thought, alone is how he will proceed.

Alone he will hurry towards another death.

RICKY CHECKED OUT of the cheap room and drove north to Durham. He returned the rental car and spent the next morning killing off Frederick Lazarus. Every membership, credit card and phone account was cancelled or closed. Frederick Lazarus evaporated.

Richard Lively was a little more difficult because Richard Lively needed to live. But he also needed to fade away from his life in New Hampshire with a minimum of fanfare. He had to leave it all behind, but not appear to be doing so—on the offchance that someone someday might come asking questions and connect the disappearance with that particular weekend.

Richard Lively's bank account was left intact, with only a minimum deposit. He told his supervisor at the university maintenance department that family trouble on the West Coast was going to require his presence for a few weeks. He had a similar conversation with his landlady and paid an extra month's rent in advance.

As he walked down the street, he felt a momentary pang of regret. He had developed an ease and a familiarity with this small world, and it saddened him to walk away.

He caught a midday Trailways bus to Boston and then the Friday afternoon Bonanza bus to the Cape. They have read the poem by now, he thought. And Merlin has questioned the ad clerk. Ricky glanced at his wristwatch and thought, He will take off soon. He will be driving hard.

Just outside Provincetown, there was a motel that hadn't already blinked on its NO VACANCY sign, probably a result of the desultory weather. Ricky paid cash for the weekend, then walked into town to a camping goods store and purchased a powerful flashlight and an oversize olive-drab poncho. He also bought a wide-brimmed camouflage hat that had one critical feature. The brim was a shroud of mosquito netting, which could drop over the head. The forecast for the weekend helped: humid, thunderstorms, grey skies and warm temperatures. A sickly sort of weekend.

Ricky walked back outside and saw the first of a line of huge thunderheads building up in the west. He surveyed the greying skies above him, which seemed to usher the arrival of evening, and then he hurried to make his preparations.

By the time he reached the road that led to his old house, the sky had taken on a brownish hue. The bus that travelled Route 6 had dropped him a couple of miles away, and he had jogged the distance easily. His backpack, crammed with his purchases and his weapon, rode comfortably on his back.

Ricky was lucky. The road was deserted. He turned into the driveway, slowing his pace to a walk, and was immediately concealed by a stand of trees. When he came out from beneath the trees, he saw what he'd hoped for: the still charred remains of his home. Even after a year, the earth was blackened for yards around the gaunt skeleton of the old farmhouse.

Ricky walked up to where the front door had once stood. He stepped inside, moving slowly amid the ruins. The spot he'd hoped to find was waiting for him, directly to the side of the chimney breast where the living-room fireplace had been. A slab of ceiling and thick wooden beams had tumbled to the side, making a sort of decrepit lean-to, almost a cave. Ricky donned the poncho, seated the bug hat on his head, and removed the flashlight and his semiautomatic pistol from his backpack. Then he crawled into the darkness of the wreckage, concealed himself and waited for night, the approaching thunderstorm and a killer.

THE RAIN CAME in spurts throughout the first part of the night, falling heavily, with cracks of thunder and lightning strikes out over the ocean, before tapering off into a steady, irritating drizzle. Ricky remained hidden, like a hunter in a blind, waiting for the quarry to come into sight. He moved only occasionally, and then just to stretch his muscles. From where he was concealed, he could still see across the open field leading to his home, especially when the sky was streaked with bolts of electricity.

By 10.00pm the world around him had funnelled itself into a damp, musty arena of blackness. He found his senses heightened, his mind alert to all the nuances of the night. Once, he was startled by a bat swooping through the air above him; another time a pair of deer emerged briefly from the woods, then bounded away.

Ricky continued to wait. The assassin was probably a man accustomed to the night and comfortable in it, Ricky told himself. Daytime compromises much for a killer. I know you, Mr R, he thought. You will want to end all this in the dark. You will be here soon enough.

Some thirty minutes after the last car's headlights had swooped past in the distance, Ricky spotted another car, this one travelling a little slower, with just the slightest element of indecision. The glow paused near the entrance to his property, then sped up and disappeared. Someone found what they were searching for, he thought.

Twenty minutes passed in utter darkness. Ricky could feel adrenaline pumping wildly through his veins. His pulse was racing.

The drizzle had finally stopped. A little bit of moonlight slid into a hole carved by the passing of a cloud, dropping like a shaft through the night. Ricky moved his eyes from right to left and saw a shape step away from the trees.

Ricky froze. Amid the charred slabs of wood and piles of burnt rubble he would appear as just another shape of twisted wreckage.

The dark figure crossed Ricky's field of vision. It moved slowly, cautiously, slightly crouched, an experienced predator. The shape reached the one-time garden. Ricky watched the man hesitate, then step forward more aggressively to stand in what was once the doorway, searching the ruin.

He knows I should be here, Ricky thought.

The man moved forward, stumbling slightly on a chunk of roof beam. He stopped and kicked at the detritus.

'Dr Starks,' the man whispered, 'I know you're here. Come on out, Doctor. It's time for an ending.'

Ricky did not move.

'Where are you, Doctor?' the man continued, turning right and left. When he spoke again, it was loudly, with resignation. 'Just where the hell are you?'

The man turned his back to Ricky. And as he turned, Ricky took the semiautomatic pistol from beneath the poncho, lifting it up as he'd been taught at the gun store in New Hampshire, holding it with both hands and bringing the barrel sight squarely in line with the middle of Rumplestiltskin's back.

'I'm behind you,' Ricky said quietly.

NOW TIME SEEMED to lose its grip on the world around him. Seconds that would ordinarily have collected themselves in an orderly progression of minutes seemed to scatter like flower petals caught in a strong breeze. He remained frozen in position, weapon bearing directly on the killer's back, his breathing shallow and laboured.

The man in front of him stood immobile.

'I have a gun,' Ricky croaked, voice raw with tension. 'It is pointing at your back. It is a .380-calibre semiautomatic, and if you move even in the slightest, I will fire. I will get off two, maybe three shots before you can turn and bring your own weapon to bear.'

If Rumplestiltskin was surprised, it was not readily apparent. He laughed out loud. 'To think that I waltzed right into your aim. Ah, you have played well, Dr Starks, far better than I ever expected, and you have displayed resources I didn't think you possessed.' He paused, then said, 'But I think you would be wise to shoot me now. In the back. You currently have the advantage. But every few seconds that pass, your position weakens. As a professional having dealt with these sorts of situations before, I would strongly recommend that you not waste the opportunity.'

Ricky did not reply.

The man laughed. 'Come on, Doctor. Channel that anger. Focus your rage. Do it now, Doctor.'

Ricky aimed ahead, but did not fire. An unsettled sensation crept into his heart. 'I know you,' he said. 'I know your voice.'

'Yes, you do,' Rumplestiltskin replied with a slight mocking tone. 'You've heard it often enough.'

Ricky felt suddenly as if he were standing on a sheet of slippery ice. Unsteadiness crept into his voice. 'Turn around,' he said.

Rumplestiltskin shook his head. 'You don't want to ask me to do that. Because once I turn around, almost every advantage you have will be erased. I will see your precise position, and trust me, Doctor, once I have you located, it will only be a short time before I kill you.'

'I know you,' Ricky repeated, whispering.

'Is it that hard? The voice is the same,' Rumplestiltskin said. 'After all, we were in more or less the same physical relationship five times each week for nearly a year.'

Ricky's throat was completely dry, but he still choked out the name. 'Zimmerman?'

Rumplestiltskin laughed again. 'Zimmerman is very dead.'

'But you're—'

'I'm the man you knew as Roger Zimmerman. With the invalid mother, and the job that went nowhere, and all the anger that never seemed to get resolved despite all the yakety-yak that filled up your office. That's the Zimmerman you knew.'

Ricky felt dizzy. 'But the subway . . .'

'That is indeed where Zimmerman—the real Zimmerman, who was indeed quite suicidal—died. Nudged to his demise.'

'But I don't . . .'

Rumplestiltskin shrugged. 'Doctor, a man comes to your office and says he is Roger Zimmerman and presents himself as a proper patient for analysis and has the financial wherewithal to pay your bills. Did you ever check to be certain that the man was, in truth, the man he said he was?'

Ricky was silent.

'I didn't think so. Had you done so, you would have found that the real Zimmerman was more or less as I presented him to you. The only difference was that he wasn't the person coming to see you. I was. I simply borrowed his life and death. Because, Doctor, I had to know you. I had to see you and study you. It took some time, but I learned what I needed.'

'Who are you?' Ricky asked.

'You will never know,' the man replied. 'And then again, you already know. You know of my past. You know of my brother and sister. You know much about me, Doctor. But you will never know who I truly am.'

'Why did you do this to me?' Ricky asked.

Rumplestiltskin shook his head. 'You already know the answer. Is it so unreasonable to think that a child would see so much evil delivered to someone he loved, see them thrown into a despair so profound that they had to murder themselves to find salvation, and when this child reached a position where he could exact a measure of revenge from all the people who failed to help out—yourself included, Doctor—that he wouldn't seize that chance?'

'Revenge solves nothing,' Ricky said.

'Spoken like a man who never indulged.'

Ricky could sense a smile on the man's face. It would be a soul-dead, cold smile.

'I think, Dr Starks, as interesting as this last session has been, it is now time for someone to die. The odds are it is about to be you.'

Ricky sighted down the pistol. He was wedged against the rubble, unable to move either to the right or to the left, his route behind him blocked. In a world of options he had none remaining.

'You forget something,' he said slowly. Coldly. 'Dr Starks has already died.' Then he fired.

It was as if the man responded to the slightest change in the inflection in Ricky's voice, so that his actions were incisive and immediate. As Ricky pulled the trigger, Rumplestiltskin dropped obliquely, spinning as he did, so that Ricky's first shot, aimed at the centre of his back, instead tore savagely through the killer's shoulder blade. The second shot sliced through the muscles of his right arm.

Ricky fired a third time, but this time wildly, the bullet disappearing into the darkness.

Rumplestiltskin twisted around, gasping with pain, trying to lift his own weapon with his mangled arm. He grasped at the weapon with his left hand, trying to steady it as he staggered back, his balance precarious. Ricky froze, watching the barrel of the pistol rise like a cobra's head, darting back and forth.

A shot cracked the air, and he could feel the hot wind of the bullet pass through the shapeless form of the poncho hanging from his shoulders. He sucked in air, tasting the cordite and smoke, and again sighted down the barrel of his gun. As he brought the barrel to bear on Rumplestiltskin's face, the killer crumpled to the earth in front of him. His weapon slid to the ground. He lifted his good hand to his face as if to deflect the coming blow.

Adrenaline, anger, hatred, fear, the sum of all that had happened to Ricky came together right then in that single instant, demanding that he watch the man die.

He did not.

Rumplestiltskin had paled, his face white. Blood that seemed like streaks of black ink was coursing down his arm and chest. He tried once more, feebly, to grasp his weapon, but was unable.

Ricky struggled to his feet and jumped forward. He kicked the pistol away from the killer's hand, then slipped his own into his backpack. Then, as Rumplestiltskin mumbled something, battling unconsciousness, Ricky reached down and grasped his adversary round the chest. Struggling against the weight, Ricky lifted the killer up and threw him over his own shoulder in a fireman's lift. He straightened slowly, adjusting himself against the weight, and staggered forward through the wreckage, carrying the man who wanted him dead out of the rubble of the farmhouse.

Sweat stung his eyes, and he struggled with each stride. He could feel Rumplestiltskin lose consciousness. Ricky stopped at the edge of the road and dropped Rumplestiltskin to the ground. He then ran his hands over the man's clothing. To his relief he found what he'd expected: a cellphone.

Rumplestiltskin's breath was coming in shallow, pained spurts. Ricky stanched the man's wounds as best he could, then called the number long remembered for Wellfleet fire and rescue.

'Cape Emergency,' came a clipped, efficient voice.

'Listen very carefully,' Ricky said slowly. 'There has been a shooting accident. The victim is located on Old Beach Road at the entrance to the late Dr Starks's vacation home, the place that burned down last summer. He's right on the driveway. The victim has multiple gunshot wounds and is in shock. He will die rapidly if you are not here within minutes. Do you understand what I've just told you?'

'Yes. I'm dispatching rescue now. Old Beach Road. Who is this?'

'Are you familiar with the location I've given you?'

'Yes. But I need to know: who is this?'

Ricky thought a moment, then answered, 'No one who is anyone any more.'

He disconnected the phone. He took his own weapon out and ejected the remaining bullets from the clip. These he tossed into the woods, then he dropped the pistol onto the ground. He removed his flashlight from the backpack, switched it on and placed it on the unconscious killer's chest. Ricky could hear a distant siren. He looked down at the man one more time and could not tell whether he would live through the next few hours. He might. He might not. For the first time, perhaps, in his entire life, Ricky enjoyed uncertainty.

He turned and started to jog away, slowly for the first few steps but then gathering pace rapidly until he was flat-out sprinting forward, feet pounding against the road surface with a steady rhythm, letting the darkness swallow him.

Like a newly inspired ghost, Ricky disappeared.

OUTSIDE PORT-AU-PRINCE

It was about an hour past dawn, and Ricky was watching a small lime-green gecko dart about on the wall, defying gravity with every step. The tiny animal moved in spurts, occasionally pausing to extend its orange throat sac before dashing forward a few strides. Ricky envied the wondrous simplicity of its day-to-day world: find something to eat and avoid being eaten.

Ricky shifted his legs, swinging them out of bed. He stretched, ran a hand through his thinning hair, grasped the pair of khaki hiking shorts that hung from the bedstead, and searched for his glasses.

The room Ricky occupied was nearly square and more or less undecorated, with faded white stucco walls. He had few possessions: a radio, some clothes, a laptop computer. Two shelves against the wall were crammed with medical texts.

He went to the window and stared out at the hills, a lush and enthusiastic green rising high above the city, and he thought to himself that Haiti was truly one of the most intriguing countries on the planet. It was the poorest spot he'd ever seen, but in some ways the richest as well. He knew that when he walked down the street, he would be the only white face for miles. This might have unsettled him once, but no longer. He revelled in being different.

He descended from his room, stopped at a small grocery for some coffee and freshly baked bread, and stepped briskly towards the clinic. People crowded around the entrance, obscuring the hand-written sign that read in large, black, uneven letters DOCTOR DUMONDAIS EXCELLENT MEDICAL CLINIC. HOURS 7 TO 7 AND BY APPOINTMENT. Ricky recognised some of the more regular customers and smiled greetings in their direction. Faces flashed replies, and he heard more than one whisper, *'Bonjour, monsieur le docteur.'* He shook hands with one old man, a tailor named Dupont, who had made him a tan linen suit after Ricky had obtained some Vioxx for the arthritis that afflicted his fingers. As he'd suspected, the drug had done wonders.

As he entered the clinic door, he saw Dr Dumondais's nurse, an imposing woman who possessed a voluminous knowledge of folk remedies and voodoo cures.

'*Bonjour, Hélène,*' Ricky said. '*Tout le monde est arrivé.*'

'Ah, yes, Doctor. We will be busy all day.'

Ricky shook his head. He practised his island French on her, and she in return practised her English on him. '*Non, Hélène, pas docteur. C'est* Monsieur *Lively. Je ne suis pas un docteur . . .*'

'Yes, yes, *Mister* Lively.' She smiled widely, as if she didn't quite understand but still wanted to join in with the great joke that Ricky played—to bring so much medical knowledge to the clinic and yet not want to be called a doctor.

Ricky knocked on a wooden door and stepped into an examination room. Auguste Dumondais, a wispy, small man who wore bifocals and had a shaved head, was pulling on a white coat.

'Ah, Ricky, we shall be busy today, no?'

'*Oui,*' Ricky replied. '*Bien sûr.*'

'But is not this day the day you are leaving us?'

'Only for a brief visit home. Less than a week.'

The doctor nodded. Ricky could see lingering doubt in his eyes. Auguste Dumondais had not asked many questions when Ricky had arrived at the clinic door six months earlier, offering his services for the most modest salary. Now he was afraid that the serendipity that had delivered Ricky to his door was going to steal him away.

'A week at the most. I promise you.'

The day went by so rapidly that Ricky almost missed his Caribe Air flight to Miami. A middle-aged businessman named Richard Lively—travelling on a recently issued American passport with only a few stamps from various Caribbean nations—was waved through US customs without much delay. Ricky was booked on the 8.00am plane north to La Guardia, so he spent the night in the airport Holiday Inn. He took a lengthy hot shower—true luxury after the spartan accommodations he was accustomed to. But he slept fitfully. The sheets seemed too soft and the mattress too springy. In the quiet, he remembered the last call he'd made to Virgil, nearly nine months earlier.

IT WAS MIDNIGHT when he'd finally covered the distance to the motel room on the outskirts of Provincetown. He had slumped down on the bed and dialled the number of Virgil's apartment in Manhattan.

When Virgil picked up on the first ring, she said only, 'Yes?'

'This isn't the voice you expected,' he replied.

She fell instantly quiet.

'Your brother, the attorney, is there, isn't he?'

'Yes.'

'Then have him pick up the extension and listen in.'

Within a few seconds Merlin was on the line.

'Now be quiet and listen to me. Your brother is currently in the Mid Cape Medical Center. Should he survive his wounds, he will need the support of the sister and brother he loves. The police will have questions. I think your first task is to deal with his situation.'

Both remained silent.

'And there are a few other matters that need to be dealt with.'

'What sort of matters?' Virgil asked, her voice flat, trying to not betray any emotion.

'First, the truly mundane: the money you stole from my retirement and other investment accounts. You will replace that sum into Credit Suisse account number 01-00976-2. Write that down. You will do this promptly.'

'What else?' Virgil asked.

'We have a new game,' Ricky said. 'It's called the game of staying alive. It's designed for all of us to play. Simultaneously.'

Neither brother nor sister responded.

'The rules are simple,' Ricky said.

'What are they?' Virgil asked softly.

'I was charging patients between seventy-five and one hundred and twenty-five dollars per hour for analysis. On average I saw each patient four, sometimes five times each week, generally forty-eight weeks each year. You can do the maths yourselves.'

'Yes,' she said.

'Great,' Ricky said briskly. 'So this is the way the game of staying alive works: everyone who wants to keep breathing enters therapy. With me. You pay, you live. As soon as the money stops, I will be forced to start hunting you.' Ricky paused, then added, 'Or someone close to you. A wife. A child. A lover. A partner.'

Again they were quiet.

'It is,' Ricky continued, 'more or less the same choice you once gave me. Only this time it is about balance.' Then he hung up.

IT TOOK about ninety minutes to get from La Guardia to Greenwich, Connecticut. Ricky stopped in the centre of town and purchased an expensive bottle of wine at a gourmet shop. Then he drove out to a home on a street that was—by the inflated standards of one of the nation's richest communities—fairly modest.

He parked outside a fake Tudor-style home. There was a swimming pool at the back and a large oak tree in the front.

With the bottle of wine in his hand, he rang the doorbell and waited in the mid-March sun.

It did not take long for a young woman, no older than her early thirties, to answer. She wore jeans and a black turtleneck sweater and had sandy hair that was swept back from her face. Before he could say anything, she said, 'Shhhh, please. I've just gotten the twins down for a nap.'

Ricky smiled back. 'They must be a handful,' he said pleasantly.

'You have no idea,' the young woman replied. She kept her voice very low. 'Now, how can I help you?'

Ricky held out the wine. 'Your husband is owed this,' he said. 'We had some business together a year or so ago, and I just wanted to thank him and remind him of the successful outcome of the case.'

She took the bottle, a little nonplussed. 'Well, thank you, ah, Mr—'

'Ricky,' he said. 'He'll remember.'

Then he turned and walked back down the drive to his rental car. He had learned all he'd needed. It was a nice life that Merlin had. But this evening, at least, he would have a sleepless night.

He thought of visiting Virgil as well, but instead merely had a florist deliver a dozen lilies to the film set where she had acquired a modest role in a big-budget Hollywood production. White lilies were perfect. One usually sent them to a funeral. He suspected Virgil would know that. He had the flowers wrapped with a black satin bow, and he enclosed a card that read simply:

Still thinking of you.
  Dr S.

He had, he thought, become a man of far fewer words.

JOHN KATZENBACH

For a man who has written eight successful novels since 1979, and been twice-nominated for the prestigious mystery-writers' Edgar Award (*In the Heat of the Summer* and *The Shadow Man*), John Katzenbach makes his decision to become a writer sound rather hit and miss. 'It seemed to me that the world had plenty of lawyers, doctors, cooks and accountants . . . I had to do something.' After college, what he chose to do first was to become a journalist, a career which began in 1973 and would include a stint as a criminal court reporter in Miami, before he decided to focus on writing books and screenplays.

Everything Katzenbach learned during his years as a crime reporter helped to fuel his first thriller, *In the Heat of the Summer* (1982), hailed by P. D. James as 'one of the most impressive crime-writing debuts of recent years'. Since then, three of Katzenbach's books have become Hollywood films—the most recent, *Hart's War*, starred Bruce Willis and was based, to an extent, on listening to his father's reflections on life as a prisoner of war during the Second World War.

Katzenbach's latest best seller, *The Analyst*, was also the result of a conversation, this time with his mother, a Manhattan psychoanalyst. He began to think about what would happen if an analyst made a mistake that came back to haunt him years later, and built the book around that possibility.

In contrast to the psychological tensions generated in the pages of *The Analyst*, Katzenbach claims that he leads a quiet, routine life in picturesque Amherst, Massachusetts, where he lives with his wife, the Pulitzer Prize-winning writer, Madeleine Blais, and their two children. But there's nothing routine about John Katzenbach's writing, so what does he see as the key to his success? 'I simply like to write books that I think people will enjoy and find exciting and might also stimulate them to think about the way things are . . . or were . . . or might be. There's a mystery about who did what to whom, but I try to find a mystery of the heart as well.'

Major Phil Ashby
UNSCATHED
Escape from Sierra Leone

Sierra Leone. May 2000.

He was a Royal Marines
commando.

He was on a peacekeeping
mission in a war zone.

Unarmed, outnumbered
and surrounded.
Under attack . . .

PROLOGUE

My thirtieth birthday was memorable for all the wrong reasons. I spent the morning lying under a tree, feverish with malaria, my head feeling like someone had parked a bus on it. In the afternoon, I inadvertently kicked off a civil war.

A week later, malaria was the least of my problems—the war had caught up with me. Five hundred of my United Nations colleagues had been killed or captured by rebels, who were now baying for my blood. I was trapped, with three other colleagues, in a small compound surrounded by a mass of rebel soldiers. Rescue attempts had failed. Diplomacy had failed. We were on our own.

All my life I had sought out challenges, the more extreme the better. And somehow—luck, military training or a combination of both—I had always come through. Now, as I looked out on the rebel cordon, I could only wonder if my luck would stay with me, if my years of training would be enough. We were hungry, dehydrated and unarmed: the odds of getting out alive seemed stacked against us. But we all knew it was better to be shot while trying to escape than to be captured and tortured. We had seen what these rebels would do to a man—and I was their number-one hate figure.

We would have to go over the wall. The longer we delayed, the weaker we would become. The decision had to be made. So I made it.

1   LANDING ON MY FEET

If you're going to face the harshest conditions the world can throw at you, then you'd do well to grow up on the west coast of Scotland. If you can navigate in a snowstorm in the Cairngorm Mountains, when you can't even see your hand in front of your face, you can navigate anywhere. And after Scottish midges, it's easy to cope with tropical mosquitoes or biting soldier ants in the jungle.

What's more, if you're going to be a commando and ultimately a Mountain Leader—able to get through the most demanding physical and mental training—it helps to love the outdoor life and have a good head for heights. I started young in both respects, with a fun childhood that took me camping, sailing, swimming in the freezing River Clyde every New Year's Day and—particularly exciting—water-skiing on my father's shoulders on Loch Lomond. When I wasn't immersed in the cold and wet, I'd be climbing trees: an early indication of a love affair with heights.

It must have been in the genes. My father, a nuclear engineer on Royal Navy submarines, was always a tough, outdoor type. Born in New Zealand and brought up in Canada, he was a firm believer in 'character-building' activities for all the family. It was only in later life that I realised not all fathers took their kids on long-distance, overnight hill walks. I remember asking on one occasion why everyone else at the Glen Coe ski centre was allowed to take the chair lift but we had to walk up carrying our skis. My dad said he didn't like queuing and we'd only get cold if we stood around waiting, which seemed reasonable enough.

My mother, on the other hand, was a bit of a worrier, but like most boys I refused to be mollycoddled, and her attempts to stem my adventurous impulses were in vain. She eventually resigned herself to letting me learn by my own mistakes.

My parents sent me to boarding school. I won a scholarship to Glenalmond College in rural Perthshire. This was one of those Scottish schools in the middle of nowhere, where boys' energies were directed into outdoor activities and sport—if only because there was scant opportunity for anything less wholesome. Glenalmond was not the social centre of the world but the teaching was excellent and, more importantly to me, the climbing was great. I don't know of many schools that offer ice-climbing as an alternative to football on winter Wednesday afternoons.

I began to develop a reputation for getting through scrapes in one piece, while others around me came a cropper. Bored at the back of a geography class one day, I was staring out of the window, watching a truck dump a load of coal against the school wall. I reckoned it would be possible to leap from the classroom window on the second floor and land on the pile of coal without injury. When I told my friends this, they thought I was mad. So I determined to prove my theory. I crept back to the classroom after dark, opened the window, climbed onto the windowsill, aimed for the coal and jumped. It felt like landing in a sand dune and I emerged jubilant and covered in coal dust. Word got around of this 'feat' and another would-be dare-devil tried the same stunt the following night. Egged on by his mates, he jumped, plummeted and hit the ground where he lay screaming in pain and indignation. He had failed to notice that workmen had come along that afternoon and shifted the pile of coal elsewhere.

I may have a bit of a reckless tendency—but I do know to look before I leap.

I LEFT SCHOOL with good enough exam results to get a place at Cambridge University. I had won a couple of academic prizes but was much prouder of holding the unofficial school record in the pole vault and being able to swim four lengths of the pool under water. I had also been concussed a few times on the rugby pitch and almost expelled for (accidentally) setting my next-door neighbour's bed on fire.

I was seventeen when I left school and I wanted to do some grow-ing up before going to university. I thought about joining the army, but you had to be eighteen. And anyway, I was put off by the crusty old army colonel who gave me an interview, then sent me a regimen-tal Christmas card featuring pictures of castles and bagpipes. I was much more impressed by the Royal Marines careers officer who came to visit our school. He led a group of us on a long run, made us swim across a river and then took us to the pub. This was much more my kind of thing. Plus you only had to be seventeen and a half to join the Marines. So, at seventeen and a half and three days, I joined the Royal Marines as a second lieutenant on a 'gap year' commis-sion. This made me the youngest officer in HM Armed Forces.

The highlight of that year was arctic warfare training in northern Norway during the winter with 42 Commando. Our instructors were

Royal Marines Mountain Leaders from the elite Mountain and Arctic Warfare Cadre, and I aspired to join their branch. Back in Britain, I passed an arduous commando course, earned my Green Beret a few days after my eighteenth birthday and made some friends for life. I knew that if I were to join the Marines full-time, I would have to go through this course all over again—and more.

When the Marines offered to sponsor me through Pembroke College, Cambridge, I signed up for a longer commission and spent three very enjoyable years as an engineering student. The academic side was challenging enough, without the numerous distractions on offer . . . and I was very easily distracted.

What I didn't realise until I got to Cambridge was how good the climbing would be. Ironically for such a flat place, it has the second-oldest climbing club in the world. What Cambridge lacks in mountains it makes up for with long holidays (trips to Scotland and the Alps), and architecture that is inspiring, not only to look at, but especially to climb on.

Climbing buildings is something of a cult activity in Cambridge and whole guidebooks have been published on it. The pastime has long been outlawed by the university authorities, for the good reason that student climbers periodically fall off and kill themselves. At the time, this meant that die-hard climbers like me could practise our sport only at night. The climbing was unique: generally unroped and in the dark, It made for some memorable nights. We ticked off all the 'classic' routes and added a few 'first ascents' of our own.

Continuing my love of all things watery, we also made a first descent that nearly went badly wrong. After weeks of rain, the River Cam was flooded and my friend Pete and I decided it was deep enough to jump six storeys from the roof of St John's College into the river. After a quick recce to check for submerged shopping trolleys, we climbed the conveniently ornate Bridge of Sighs, then up onto the roof to our take-off point. Once up there, we rapidly realised this was a stupid idea and agreed that if we both chickened out there'd be no face lost.

Unfortunately, at this point we were spotted by a concerned resident. 'Don't jump! It can't be that bad. The porters are coming, they'll help you down . . .'

We didn't think the college porters would be quite as sympathetic. Reversing our previous decision not to jump, we landed in three feet of water and some soft mud. We had intended to keep a low profile during this outing, but had inadvertently become a public spectacle.

Someone had called the police, who were now forcing their way through the crowd that had formed on the river bank. In all the commotion, we let the current sweep us downstream for about half a mile, before climbing out and walking across town back to my flat.

The grounding I had had at home and at school had made me a competent and experienced mountaineer for my age. Furthermore, six months of holiday every university year, and financial independence thanks to my Marines sponsorship, gave me ample opportunity to broaden my experience further afield. Mountaineering highlights included trips to Greece, Spain, Kurdistan and Iceland, and numerous expeditions in the Alps.

Another Cambridge night, memorable for more romantic reasons, was Valentine's Day 1991, when I met Anna for the first time. A pretty Scottish girl studying French and Arabic, she immediately shared my sense of fun and adventure. We quickly became inseparable and have been in love ever since.

As THE END of my university days loomed, I felt I had to pack in as much as possible before joining the Marines again. So, two weeks before my final exams in May 1991, the lure of a good weather forecast and a great piss-up was more than enough to overcome my guilty conscience for not revising. With three mates, I drove up to the Peak District late on a Friday night and dossed down in a pub car park.

We climbed all the next day on gritstone outcrops and I was feeling confident enough to solo an E5 rock climb. In climbing terminology, 'E' stands for 'extremely severe'. The extreme category is subdivided from one to nine, so there were only a few harder climbs around. From the ground, it looked desperate—sixty feet of smooth, sheer rock with tiny holds for your fingertips and relying only on friction for your feet. This was as hard a route as I'd done and, standing at the bottom of it, I felt extremely nervous. As soon as I left the ground, though, I felt calm and focused.

A steady nerve is useful in most walks of life, but in climbing it is essential. I have seen climbers lose their nerve, start to tremble uncontrollably and literally shake themselves off the rock face. For me, though, fear has often been a positive force—there is no better way of concentrating the mind. In fact, one of the reasons I love climbing is because it relieves stress. Overcoming physical danger puts the less immediate stresses of everyday life into perspective. Deadlines and workloads have no relevance when you're 300 feet off the ground and a small mistake could mean falling to your death.

Of course, there is an adrenaline buzz to be had from rock-climbing. After a while, being off the ground becomes more exhilarating than frightening, and intensive physical exertion just adds to the experience. But climbing is more than that. Most people can appreciate the rugged beauty of mountains. As a climber, this sensation is heightened by being intimately involved with those awe-inspiring surroundings.

For me, rock-climbing combines the mental challenge of problem-solving with the physical challenge of a good workout. The best climbers have brains and brawn, as well as flexibility, balance and a cool head. I find it enormously satisfying to know that I can stay in complete control in a potentially dangerous situation where a moment of panic could be disastrous. This has obvious military applications, as I was later to discover. Meanwhile, though, I was simply enjoying my climbing—convinced, as many young men are, that accidents only happened to other people. And if they did happen to me, I seemed to bounce. This rather cavalier attitude had been only slightly dented by an experience in July 1990, which brought me very close to death.

I had been climbing with a friend called Mark in the French Alps. Mark, a skinhead with bulging neck muscles and scars all over his face (the result of too many Rugby League matches), looked more like a bouncer than the Latin teacher he actually was. I trusted Mark with my life and we made a strong, if inelegant, climbing team.

One of the most impressive mountains near Chamonix is the Aiguille des Drus, or 'Druids' Needle', a 13,000-foot-high spire of granite that soars above a glacier called the Mer de Glace, or 'Sea of Ice'. Mark and I had climbed its southwest face the previous summer. We now wanted to attempt its north face. The north face of the Drus is one of the six classics in the Alps and is a long, steep, exposed route on rock that is usually sound, at least according to the guidebook . . .

The climb takes two days, and there are some excellent bivvy ledges halfway up the route. (A bivvy ledge is a ledge on a steep cliff where there is just enough room to sit or lie down to spend the night.) After 2,000 feet of climbing on the first day, Mark and I reached the bivvy ledges suggested in the guidebook as the best place to spend the night. However, we still had a couple of hours until last light so, on the spur of the moment, we decided to continue climbing a few more pitches, even though we knew it would mean spending an uncomfortable night on a smaller ledge higher up. We had chosen not to carry sleeping-bags, to save weight on a difficult climb, but had a small gas cooker and enough warm clothing not to freeze. The night was long and cold, but very atmospheric as we sat on our ledge, several thousand feet above the lights of Chamonix. We spent the time chatting and drinking tea, before eventually dozing off, still firmly anchored to the rock face in case we rolled off the ledge during the night. Every few minutes, I'd wake up shivering, move around for a bit to warm up and go back to sleep. Mark, on the other hand, is one of those people who seem able to sleep, uninterrupted, anywhere—as his loud snoring constantly reminded me.

An hour before first light, we were too cold to enjoy a lie-in. We got up and made breakfast by chipping chunks of ice from a niche in the rock and melting them on our cooker to make porridge. We had the kind of conversation that everyone has at breakfast: Mark was rude about my cooking and I grumbled about his snoring. We concluded that the food and bedding in our accommodation were not up to much, but the amazing view at sunrise more than made up for it. We peered back down the face and could make out the head-torches of other groups of climbers on ledges further down.

The first pitch of the day's climb was a steep, overhanging crack, made even more awkward by the fact that there was still ice lurking in the back of it. It was my turn to lead so I set off, shouting down to Mark to keep a close eye on me as I made the 'crux' move—the hardest part of the climb.

Just at that moment, we heard a rumble nearby. A massive rock-fall had started somewhere above us and was crashing down the steep rock face towards us. My stomach lurched as I realised there was absolutely nothing I could do to get out of the way. If the flying rocks were heading in my direction, then my time was up. If the rocks missed me, I still had to avoid falling off my climb. Resisting the urge to panic, I concentrated hard on the immediate necessity of hanging on, regardless of the rock-fall.

Huge boulders came crashing down just to our left and continued on down the face. The whole mountain shook with the impact of falling rocks, each one triggering yet more rock-fall. We could feel the rush of displaced air on our faces and smelt the sulphurous smoke produced as huge rocks crashed into each other at hundreds of miles an hour.

In fact, we were lucky and the rocks fell straight past us. But we watched in horror as, seemingly in slow motion, rocks swept over the ledge where we had previously intended to spend the night. Five climbers were killed: some buried under boulders, others ripped off the rock face, falling thousands of feet to the glacier below. Had we stuck to our original plan, that would have been us.

We wondered whether we should go back down but, realistically, with a rock-fall like that, the other climbers' chances of survival were minimal. In any case, rescue helicopters were on the scene within a few minutes and we didn't want to add to their problems by getting into difficulties ourselves.

We carried on to the top of the route, the safest way off the mountain. As we climbed we could see that the very shape of the mountain had changed. High-altitude Alouette rescue helicopters buzzed around beneath us looking for survivors. We arrived at the summit, relieved to be off the north face and in the sunshine again. Sitting on the summit, Mark the 'hard, northern rugby player' and Phil the 'tough Marine' admitted we could both do with a hug. For a few minutes, I thought I would be quite happy if I never did another dangerous climb in my life. This feeling later subsided but had left me with a more acute sense of my own mortality. I love adventure but I also love life and, unlike some mountaineers, I don't have a death wish—despite what some of my friends might say.

When we eventually reached Chamonix that evening after a long, difficult descent, we reported to the local gendarmerie and told them what we had witnessed. They were surprised to see us as they hadn't believed anyone on the north face could have survived. I couldn't help wondering: why had we survived? Not for the last time, I felt my guardian angel had been looking out for me.

I KNEW I SHOULD make the most of the summer holidays immediately after graduation—such long breaks would not come round again very often once I was in the world of work. There were still countless mountains left to climb but, when a mate suggested an 'ocean-rowing expedition in the Arctic', I was intrigued. Pete, an intrepid geology student who had also spent time in the Marines, invited me to join him in an attempt to circumnavigate the island of Spitsbergen in a small, wooden rowing boat.

I had scarcely heard of Spitsbergen before, but a bit of research and a few alcohol-fuelled nights with Pete poring over maps soon whetted my appetite. Spitsbergen lies 600 miles south of the North Pole, is about the same size as Scotland and almost totally covered in ice. It has more polar bears living on it than humans. The ocean around it is just about navigable because the Gulf Stream melts the pack ice for a couple of months during the short polar summer, but no one had ever successfully rowed round Spitsbergen before.

Pete was an experienced offshore sailor and I had also done a fair amount of inshore sailing, as well as being used to very cold weather conditions. We reckoned we were as well qualified as we could reasonably be.

The day after graduation, Anna saw us off at the airport. We flew to Norway then on to Longyearbyen, Spitsbergen's capital. After a delay of ten days waiting for the weather, we set off from our start point, Kapp Linné. It was to take us six weeks to cover the thousand miles, half of them through pack ice, heading clockwise round the island back to our start point.

Our wooden rowing boat, seventeen feet long and with an open top, was already out there waiting for us. Named *Kotick* (after Kotick the white seal in Rudyard Kipling's *Jungle Book*), she was a fine boat but very leaky and we had cold, wet feet for all of the six weeks.

Fully laden with our food and equipment, the boat weighed in at nearly half a tonne. The difficulty of beaching and launching meant that we came ashore as little as possible. If the weather and sea were calm, we preferred to sleep, cook and eat in the boat. This far north, we had the advantage of twenty-four-hour daylight and soon found that our bodies adjusted to a thirty-six-hour cycle. Throughout the trip, thirty-six hours became our standard 'day'.

The rowing itself was physically very hard work but, after the first few days, our bodies adjusted to the prolonged effort. By the time we got home, we were lean, mean . . . and sunburnt. This close to the North Pole, the ozone layer has been partially destroyed, so the ultraviolet radiation from the sun is intense and any exposed flesh soon becomes burnt to a crisp. The irony did not escape me that my toes, at one end of my body, were going down with frostbite while, at the other end, my face was being badly burnt.

We had arranged for a Dutch survey ship to pre-position six food and fuel caches at strategic points around the island. Each cache was supposed to contain cooker fuel and ten days' food in an airtight, waterproof barrel (to keep out both the weather and marauding polar bears). I had prepared all six barrels in my room in Cambridge, stuffing them with freeze-dried rations and huge quantities of chocolate. The barrels may have been polar-bear-proof, but unfortunately they weren't protected against students with the munchies. Cold and hungry when we finally reached one of the food caches, Pete and I were a tad disappointed to find empty Mars bar wrappers among the rations. Some of my friends had at least left amusing IOU notes: *Hello Phil, it's 2am, I'm trashed and you're not in. Hope you don't mind if I borrow a Mars bar or two. I'll buy you one later. Love, Andy.* We had to laugh.

The first time I saw a polar bear, it was six inches from my face when it woke me up. We were sleeping in a derelict trapper's hut, and I felt something nudge me. I assumed it was Pete until I smelt its breath. Not even Pete's breath smelt that bad, so I peered out of my sleeping-bag to investigate and saw a bear looking back at me. Luckily it seemed more curious than hungry, otherwise it would have gone straight for us. Polar bears are fierce predators and they are particularly hungry in the summer, when it's harder to catch seals. That's why polar explorers always carry powerful rifles—just in case.

I kicked Pete to wake him up, and we sat there with our rifle and camera, arguing with our eyes over whether to shoot at the bear or take his picture. This bear weighed nearly half a tonne but we didn't want to shoot him—he had done us a big favour by not eating us as we slept and he was not attacking us. Eventually, we fired a signal flare over his head and he ambled off.

Something terrifying happened nearly every day on that expedition. We capsized once and, on more than one occasion, found ourselves being swept downwind away from land faster than we could row towards it. The nearest land in this direction was Siberia, 3,000 miles away and we were starting to feel very alone.

In among the pack ice, the ice floes acted as breakwaters and kept the water calm. Here, at least, the rowing was easier, but sometimes the ice was so thick that the channels would completely close up. We discovered we could make progress by pushing giant lumps of ice apart using one of our oars. Sometimes it would take an hour of pushing to create enough momentum to make a channel wide enough for *Kotick* between floating lumps of ice, some of which weighed several thousand tonnes. In places, though, the ice just closed in completely. Then we were forced to winch the boat out of the water and pull it like a sledge across the frozen sea.

Despite the hardship—in fact partly because of the hardship—it was a privilege to be in places normally only visited by icebreakers, nuclear submarines, polar bears and itinerant whales. We witnessed some of nature's most savage and beautiful terrain, weather and wildlife. It became easier to ignore blistered hands and aching muscles as we rowed past stunning ice sculptures, watched new icebergs calving off the ends of glaciers and saw whales, rare birds, walruses, arctic foxes and reindeer. For me, though, the polar bears were hard to beat.

On the rare occasion that the sea was totally calm, we allowed ourselves the luxury of setting up our Walkman and a small pair of loudspeakers in the boat. To save weight, we had taken only a couple of tapes with us—*Sunshine on Leith* by The Proclaimers, and the soundtrack from *Grease*. A pretty random choice by any standards.

At one stage, Pete was asleep in the front of the boat and I was rowing on my own, chilling out, listening to *Grease* for the hundredth time. Every few strokes, I checked over my shoulder in case we were heading for a 'growler' (small icebergs that can damage a boat if you hit them). As we were over ten miles from the nearest land or any ice floes, I did not expect to see a polar bear. Suddenly, though, I noticed that the lump of ice a few yards ahead was covered in fur and swimming towards us. I turned the boat round and started rowing for my life.

Our rifle was lashed in a waterproof barrel at the bottom of the boat. If the bear caught up with us, it could easily tip us into the water before we could get the rifle out. I shouted at Pete to wake up, but he thought this was just a ruse to get him out of his sleeping-bag.

The bear was gaining on us while, in the background, John Travolta and Olivia Newton-John were singing 'You're the One That I Want'. I got ready to use an oar as a weapon. Pete now realised this was no joke, scrambled out of his sleeping-bag and hurriedly started rowing. With the two of us pulling together, we were able to shake off our pursuer. I still get butterflies in my stomach when I hear that song.

Although I'd been scared before, it had never been for such a prolonged period of time: six weeks of being continually frightened was emotionally draining, and I did a lot of growing up very quickly. I didn't stop taking risks after this, but it did make me think harder about things. And in terms of physical and mental effort, it was to make commando training seem almost tame in comparison.

I RETURNED FROM SPITSBERGEN with just enough time to spend a few days with Anna before reporting to the Commando Training Centre Royal Marines in Lympstone, Devon.

Thirty-five individuals started officer training on September 4, 1991. All of us had been through a rigorous selection process just to be there. Fifteen months later, twenty-six older and wiser individuals passed out as Royal Marines officers, fully prepared to lead thirty experienced commandos in any operational environment.

Unlike any other service in the British Armed Forces, Royal Marines officers are trained alongside the other ranks, and the award of a Green Beret is an absolute standard that all have to meet. This really does help build mutual respect and a bond between all commando soldiers. You are a commando first; the rank comes second.

The hardest part of officer training is the commando course, which you have to pass to earn your Green Beret. For me it was second time around. Four weeks long, it consists of a combination of demanding field exercises, which wear you down both physically and mentally, ending with the commando tests. These tests, derived from the experience of battle-hardened men in the Second World War, comprise a series of load carries, forced marches and assault courses. Then there's the appropriately named endurance course, which involves running and crawling six and a half miles while carrying an assault rifle and twenty-two pounds of ammunition over hills and through water and tunnels. You've got to be careful to keep your weapon clean and dry, as the final part of the endurance course is on the rifle range, where you have to hit seven out of ten targets. If your weapon fails, or you're too tired to shoot straight, then you fail the test. The final commando test is a thirty-mile forced march across Dartmoor carrying weapons and equipment. Officers must complete this final test in seven hours, other ranks in eight.

Training was hard work but a great laugh at the same time. By the end, we calculated we had run or 'yomped' 2,500 miles; done 40,000 press-ups and 60,000 sit-ups; and had climbed 7,500 feet of rope.

Weekends were valued for catching up on sleep and painstaking preparation of kit. I was desperate to keep things going with Anna and we saw each other whenever possible. Particularly hard were the long, sleepy car journeys back to Devon from Cambridge, where Anna was still a student. I remember driving 270 miles with all the car windows down in the middle of winter, slapping my face to stay awake, all too aware that I would have only two hours in bed before the first parade in the morning.

MY REPUTATION for landing on my feet followed me into the Marines. On one occasion, we were woken in the middle of the night and given a current affairs test with some near-impossible questions. The more questions we got wrong, the further away from camp we would be dropped off before having to run back. So, as none of us managed to guess the name of the President of Ecuador or on what day of the week Saddam Hussein had invaded Kuwait, we psyched ourselves for a long run.

A truck drove us to our drop-off point and, as it stopped, I managed to clamber on top of its canvas canopy. I stayed where I was and the truck drove me back to camp. Here I jumped down, fetched my car and started ferrying my colleagues back to base.

AT THE END of officer training, I was surprised and proud to be awarded the Commando Medal for 'Leadership, Unselfishness, Cheerfulness in Adversity, Determination and Courage'. I was posted to 45 Commando, based in Arbroath, Scotland, which was due to go on a six-month operational tour to Belize in Central America. In that former British colony, the presence of a small British force helps maintain stability in a volatile part of the world. In preparation, I was sent on a ten-week jungle warfare instructors' course, in Brunei in Southeast Asia, to gain first-hand experience of the skills we would be teaching to the rest of the unit in Belize. Those skills would prove invaluable to me in Africa several years later.

In the jungle, hi-tech gadgetry doesn't work very well as the trees get in the way, so you rely on basic soldiering skills such as patrolling, ambushing and good camouflage and concealment. Although patrolling in the jungle is hard, at least you get lots of sleep, as the total darkness beneath the jungle canopy makes it impossible to move at night. If you're well away from the enemy, you can afford to put your hammock and mosquito net up and get a good night's sleep.

Life becomes a lot less comfortable if you're on 'hard routine'. This means you're too close to the enemy to risk putting up a hammock, cooking, or even taking your shirt off to wash. You sleep on the ground, your weapon by your side, using your webbing as a pillow.

In April 1993, we deployed to Belize, where I spent most of my six months as an instructor helping to run a jungle warfare training camp. While I was away, Anna was having adventures of her own studying Arabic in Yemen and Syria. Communications weren't easy. One Valentine's card I sent took over four months to reach her via assorted mailrooms. Being apart was hard enough, but the next time we were together was to prove even harder, though for very different reasons.

ANNA AND I were both back in the UK for Christmas 1993. We had invited a group of friends to Edinburgh for New Year, including Alistair, my oldest climbing partner from school and university. We had a great Hogmanay and crashed out late, so I was not popular when I bullied the others into getting up early on New Year's Day. The fine weather forecast was too good to ignore and I was unable to resist the lure of fresh snow in the Highlands.

Alistair, Anna and I set off north, intent on climbing a group of six Munros (Scottish mountains over 3,000 feet) in the Fisherfield and Letterewe Wilderness, north of Inverness. These hills are too far from a road to climb in a single day. So, having parked the car and with the winter sun setting behind the hills of Skye to our west, we walked the twelve miles or so through fresh snow to a bothy (mountain refuge) called Sheneval. There we cooked by candlelight and caught up on the sleep we should have had the night before.

The next day turned out more overcast but still fine enough for a ridge walk. We started out soon after first light and headed up the east ridge of our first Munro of the day. This was Beinn a' Chlaidheimh, a beautiful, craggy peak, whose name is Gaelic for 'Mountain of the Sword'.

As we gained height, the snow deepened, but conditions seemed excellent. We had stopped to dig a snow pit, examining the layers of snow to check for avalanche danger. Everything seemed fine, but, as we were soon to discover, the safe snow conditions low down the mountain were not replicated higher up. After two hours we had climbed the steepest part of the hill and were making our way up the now easy-angled slope towards the summit. Knowing that it would be uncomfortable and windy on the very top, Anna and I stopped a few yards beneath the summit, to admire the view. Alistair, fed up with playing gooseberry, continued on over the other side of the ridge. After a quick kiss, Anna and I followed.

Suddenly, I was aware of a dull thud and felt the slope beneath my feet give way. We had triggered an avalanche. A huge chunk of snow started sliding down the hill—with us on top of it. I was slightly higher up than Anna and contemplated jumping to the side and jabbing my ice axe into something solid to stop myself. Then I heard Anna scream and decided to stick with her. I dived down the slope, grabbed her and we fell, clinging on to each other for dear life.

For the first few seconds, we rode on top of the large slab of snow and the slope was not too steep. But then we went over a cliff. I felt us fall through the air and muttered a silent prayer. Anna displayed a less spiritual approach and was swearing like a trooper.

I tensed up, anticipating a violent impact . . .

Whoomph! We hit the ground with a thud and for a brief moment I thought it was over. The snow slab carrying us had cushioned the blow and we seemed all right. But the giant slab, about fifty metres square, had now broken into smaller chunks and was travelling on downwards, sweeping us along with it. We were tumbling wildly and I did my best to protect Anna by cocooning her in my arms, while frantically trying to dig my feet into something solid. We were being thrown around like rag dolls and buffeted by falling chunks of snow and ice. Everything around us was white. Disorientated, I struggled to dig my feet into firm ground.

Eventually, more through luck than judgment, my feet caught behind a large boulder and we lurched to a sudden halt. I was lying on my back with my feet facing downhill and Anna was more or less sitting on my lap. For a split second, I thought we had made it intact. But now the remnants of the avalanche swept over us and we were being crushed. It seemed as if thousands of tonnes of snow were landing on our heads and I dreaded being buried. By a quirk of fate, though, we had stopped so suddenly that nearly all the snow swept past us, and we ended up near the surface of the avalanche debris.

'Anna, are you OK?'

She could only moan a weak reply: 'My back.'

There had been no time to feel frightened as we fell. But now I could feel fear rising in my throat and had to concentrate on staying calm. I was pinned underneath Anna, who was clearly in a lot of pain. Looking down the hill, I saw we had come to a halt on a steep slope, just above another large cliff. Without the cushioning effect of a large slab of snow, we would not have survived this next drop. Looking back up, I was shocked to see how far we'd fallen—well over 300 feet. I checked my body for broken bits, in case I was injured and the adrenaline had numbed the pain. Everything seemed normal. In fact, the only thing broken was my watch strap. Perhaps I had been partly protected by my rigid-framed rucksack. Anna, however, had not been so lucky and was badly crushed.

'Sweetheart, I need you to try to move off me.' We were wedged, precariously, on a steep slope above a large drop, and I had to stop us falling further. She tried to lift herself up but screamed in agony and couldn't move. 'Can you wiggle your toes?' She could—a good sign. 'OK, take a deep breath and try standing again.' Another yelp. I could only imagine how much pain she was in. I could do nothing more than dig my feet in, hold on to her and hope that Alistair had not been caught in the avalanche.

After what seemed an eternity, he emerged above us on the ridge. Considerate as ever, he had assumed we were still canoodling and had not wanted to invade our privacy. Eventually, though, he retraced his steps to see what was happening.

'What are you doing down there?' he shouted down to us.

'We enjoyed the walk so much, we wanted to do this bit again! What the hell do you think we're doing?'

'Oh, right. Hang on. I'm on my way.'

He made his way back down towards us, gingerly in case he dislodged more snow. By the time Alistair reached us, we had been wedged behind our boulder for twenty minutes. Anna had stopped moaning: a bad sign. Shock and cold were making her start to lose consciousness. Alistair and I had a quick 'team talk'. We needed to move Anna somewhere flatter and safer, where we could put extra clothes on her and get her inside the sleeping-bag and bivvy bag I had in my rucksack.

I suspected Anna had broken her back. I knew moving her would cause her terrible pain and possibly further injury, even paralysis. But if we did nothing, she might well die, either by falling further from this precarious position, or from cold. Raising the alarm would take hours (mobile phone technology had not yet reached this part of the Highlands) and rescue, especially if the weather deteriorated, could take days. It was a hard decision to make.

'Sweetheart, we're going to have to move you. I'm sorry. It's going to hurt.'

Ignoring her groans, we lifted her up. We did our best to keep her in the same hunched position she had landed in, to minimise further damage to her spine, and carried her across the slope towards a decent-sized ledge.

As gently as possible, we tried to brush the snow from her clothes, then manoeuvred her into my sleeping-bag and bivvy bag. Once again, we had to ignore her screams. Although I had some painkillers with me, I couldn't risk giving them to her, as they would have reduced her level of consciousness and made her even more susceptible to exposure. Far better to endure pain than die of cold.

Another team talk. I would look after Anna and Alistair would go for help. It was now just after midday, and we had about four hours till nightfall. Alistair set off back down the hill to raise the alarm. Although risky for him, he decided to travel light, leaving us with most of his clothes.

For Anna and me, it was a long, cold wait. I made her as comfortable as I could, then set about doing everything possible to improve our chances of survival. The snow was too loose to make an igloo, but I managed to make a windbreak, and used rocks to make a large cross on the hillside, to improve our chances of being seen from the air. As I worked, we chatted to keep our spirits up. Although I felt quite calm at the time, with hindsight I was perhaps acting a little oddly. Apparently this can happen after a traumatic incident. At one point I asked Anna if she would mind if I went back up the hill to bag the peak. A string of colourful expletives suggested this was not such a good idea.

It was well below freezing and Anna was lying motionless in a damp sleeping-bag. She had been shivering violently all afternoon, but now she had stopped—and not because she was warming up. As a hypothermia victim's body starts to close down, the shivering stops. The next stages are coma and death. This was now happening to the love of my life and I was beginning to get seriously worried. I lay on the snow next to Anna and tried to hug her to let her share my body heat. I cajoled her into talking and stroked her face. Anything to keep her conscious.

As the light faded so did my morale. I felt helpless, realising that Anna could die there in my arms. I decided that if Anna lost consciousness, I would have to drag her off the mountain, whatever the damage. I started psyching myself for the descent and wandered a few yards from the ledge, looking for the easiest way down. Below, in the gloom, I saw a lone figure coming towards us. My best friend Alistair was back.

Alistair had run and slid back down the mountain. Having left us with his warm clothes, he needed to move fast to keep warm. To his relief, another group of walkers had just reached the bothy. They must have thought it odd to see a scantily clad, manic stranger come bounding across the snow. Nevertheless, one of this group volunteered to go for help. To this day I have no idea who the Good Samaritan was. I suspect he was a fell-runner as he covered the twelve miles back to the road in three hours, a remarkable feat given the deep snow. We heard later that when he reached the road he attempted to flag down passing motorists, but the first few drove past him. He was about to break into and hot-wire a vehicle (mine, I hope), when a passing car finally stopped. The nearest telephone was several miles away in a village called Dundonnell. There, he dialled 999. By a stroke of luck, an RAF mountain rescue Sea King helicopter was on a training exercise on Ben Nevis, just forty minutes' flying time away. After touching down briefly in Dundonnell to refuel and pick up the local mountain rescue team, it would be on its way to search for us.

Back up on the mountain, Alistair's arrival was timely. With the extra gear he had carried back up, we were able to start rewarming Anna. Almost as importantly, our morale picked up. We fed Anna some hot chicken soup (vegetarian for ten years, she temporarily waived her principles) and began settling down for the night. Anna was still in pain but now seemed quite cheerful.

A couple of hours later, we heard the distinctive throb of rotor blades, then saw the flashing taillights of a Sea King helicopter flying up out of the glen. We flashed our torches to show where we were.

The rescue team placed Anna on a spinal stretcher and she was winched carefully up into the helicopter and flown to Raigmore Hospital in Inverness. In Accident and Emergency, showing traditional Scottish priorities, Anna wouldn't let the doctors use scissors to cut her out of my expensive sleeping-bag. 'Fair enough,' they shrugged. Advising her to take a deep breath, they simply whipped the sleeping-bag off her, like a trick with a tablecloth.

X-rays showed that one of her vertebrae had shattered, with shards of bone now lingering 'literally a hair's-breadth away' from her spinal cord. She had only just escaped permanent paralysis.

I had to steel myself to call Anna's parents. Her father, himself an experienced mountain man, received the news with characteristic calm and generosity, but I felt horrible. I might have saved his daughter's life in one sense, but she wouldn't have been on the mountain in the first place, were it not for me. Nearly losing Anna was a defining moment in my life and made our relationship even stronger. We had never taken each other for granted before and we never will.

Anna spent a month immobile in hospital on a special spinal bed and many months in a plaster 'jacket', then a back brace. After a few months convalescing at her parents' home, she was suffering 'cabin fever' and wanted to get out of the house. She couldn't walk very far and couldn't sit up for more than a few minutes, so she travelled in the boot of my car lying on an old mattress. On a couple of occasions, she even braved train journeys to see me. She would lie across two seats or in the guard's van—apparently, British Rail gin and tonics were the best form of pain relief available. After an extra year out of university, Anna gradually got herself back to full fitness. As a bonus, she has since got into rock-climbing, which has turned out to be great therapy for keeping her back strong and supple—and great for me! I am really lucky to have a soul mate who is also such a close partner on the rock face. We both know—from real experience—that we can catch each other's fall.

2 TRAINING FOR SURVIVAL

'Remember, men, you're all volunteers,' 'Snowy' Snowden, the Mountain Leader course sergeant major reminded us at the beginning. But when you're freezing cold, wet and knackered, being reminded that you're going through all this of your own volition and you can quit at any time is not what you want to hear. Dead on my feet, I tried to remember why I had chosen to try to become a Royal Marines Mountain Leader.

One of the tasks of the Royal Marines is to provide an extreme cold weather warfare capability, spearheaded by instructors known as Mountain Leaders. To become a Mountain Leader (ML) involves passing the longest, and arguably the hardest, specialist infantry training course in the world. This qualifies you for membership of the Mountain and Arctic Warfare Cadre. Within the Royal Marines, Mountain Leaders have a reputation second to none and I was keen to join their number. For me, one of the highlights of commando training had been a day we had spent on Dartmoor, learning cliff assault techniques with the MLs—a physically hard day but immensely satisfying. The MLs were the embodiment of what I thought all commandos would strive to be: highly trained, well-motivated, professional soldiers, working in small teams behind enemy lines in the harshest climatic conditions. The Mountain and Arctic Warfare Cadre may not have achieved the cult status of other specialist units such as the Special Boat Service (SBS) or the Special Air Service (SAS) but, in our field of expertise, our reputation is unrivalled.

As well as being a volunteer, you must also be an officer or a non-commissioned officer with a specific written recommendation from your commanding officer. In other words, you've got to be good even to apply. Only two or three officers and about twelve corporals are accepted each year, so the competition is stiff. Occasionally members of the army are allowed to apply, but normally only Royal Marines are accepted.

First, though, you must pass the innocuously named 'Acquaint'. On paper, the Acquaint sounds reasonable, especially as it is only a week long. What the brochure doesn't say is that squeezed into the one-week Acquaint is about a year's worth of physical activity and mental tests, including difficult night navigation and a climbing aptitude test. On some Acquaints, not a single candidate passes (six out of twenty passed on mine). ML training is extremely demanding, both physically and mentally, and the Acquaint filters out those who lack the requisite strength and determination.

EACH YEAR, fifteen to twenty men who have passed the Acquaint begin the eleven-month ML course. I felt privileged even to be starting it.

We assembled for the first time at Stonehouse Barracks, Plymouth, in August 1995. I knew some of my fellow course members from the Acquaint, but most were strangers. There was one other Royal Marines officer and fifteen corporals. Ranks don't matter on a course like this, and we were all to become close friends over the next year, bonding through shared experiences and hardship.

The first week was spent learning about the theory of climbing, with six periods of teaching or practicals every day and two periods of physical fitness training, intended to build up the stamina we would need throughout the course. This is known in Royal Marines slang as 'being beasted'.

The course then moved to Cornwall. For the next month we learned the basics of military climbing on the sea cliffs around Land's End. We learned skills such as 'steep earth climbing', which involves using ice-climbing equipment to climb up rock or earth too loose for normal rock-climbing techniques. We erected aerial cableways to hoist heavy equipment up a cliff or casualties down it, and used grappling hooks to scale completely smooth cliff faces. We learned how to set up abseil ropes and how to dispatch a group of Marines from the cliff top. Later on the course, we would all qualify as helicopter abseil instructors.

One particular afternoon's climbing training involved a circuit up and down the cliff face at a place called Sennen Cove. As each of us waited at the bottom of the cliff for the man in front to reach the top, an instructor would quiz us to check we had been taking in the lectures. Each wrong answer was worth fifty press-ups. 'What is the breaking strain of eleven-millimetre nylon rope?' *Easy enough*. 'Name three climbing areas in Snowdonia.' *Still easy*. But the questions got harder. One of the instructors had just returned from six months on the Antarctic island of South Georgia and had an obscure line of questioning that even the climbing know-it-alls couldn't answer. 'How deep can the leopard seal dive?' *Ummm . . .* 'Name seven types of penguin.' *Emperor, king, chinstrap. Shit, that's only three . . .* At least the press-ups were making us stronger.

As a relatively experienced climber, I thoroughly enjoyed this phase, but not everybody could hack it and our numbers soon dwindled. Despite stringent safety measures, two members of the course had to drop out after breaking their ankles. Others just gave up because of the incessant physical 'beastings'. Every day started with a long run along the cliff tops ('to warm up') and ended with an even longer one along the cliff tops ('to warm down'). To keep us on our toes during the day, any minor misdemeanour would be punished, in traditional military fashion, with press-ups. The consequences of cocking up for real while climbing can be fatal and, as future instructors, it would not be just our own lives at risk. So, until they knew we were proficient, our instructors kept us under constant, close supervision. This kept us alive, but did make for an awful lot of press-ups. In the end, it didn't really matter how few genuine mistakes you made—the press-ups never eased up. We realised they were there to test our will to hang in there and to build us up, physically and mentally, for the rigours of the course ahead. In a moment of madness I queried the training value of press-ups to the course sergeant major, Snowy Snowden. I thought pull-ups, for example, seemed a more relevant exercise for budding mountaineers.

'Well, sir, if I make you do pull-ups before you go climbing, you'll run out of energy and fall off.' (This seemed reasonable to me.) 'But since you've asked, give me ten pull-ups and fifty press-ups.'

I didn't query his logic again.

As well as the practical climbing training, we received lectures every evening on such diverse topics as geology and navigation using the stars. And as a test of nerve and confidence, we had to pass a series of 'bottle-tests'. One of these was the 'Land's End Long Jump', which involved jumping across a twelve-foot gap between two rock pinnacles, 200 feet above the sea. Just when you were pleased with yourself for making it, though, they made you come back a few days later and do it again in the dark.

By the end of the Cornwall phase, we were down to twelve students. The course now moved to North Wales for four weeks of climbing in Snowdonia; longer, harder rock climbs and a progression of ever more demanding mountain marches: first by day and then by night, carrying heavier and heavier equipment. We honed our navigation skills using map and compass, counting paces to work out exactly how far we'd walked. As a Mountain Leader, you have to be able to navigate confidently even under the harshest conditions and it takes a lot of practice. I got a buzz from being in the mountains, but the heavy packs and often miserable weather did not always make it much fun.

There were many other technical skills to master, first in the classroom and then in the field: advanced rope-work, aid-climbing and fixing lines for less experienced troops to follow over difficult terrain. We also practised mountain river crossings. They were the sort of rivers normally tackled by white-water canoeists—but we had to go across them, not down them. We'd learned the theory in the classroom, but it had been raining solidly for two or three days before the practical, and the water was surging down out of the hills. We arrived at the river bank, distinctly unenthusiastic. Snowy Snowden could sense our gloom—none of us was keen to jump into the cold, dark waters.

'OK, men, when you teach Marines river crossing, they're so nervous about getting in the water that they don't listen to anything you've got to say. As I'm sure you'll agree, the reality of being cold and wet is never as bad as the anticipation of being cold and wet. So, get them used to it straight away.'

And with that, he ran into the water. We followed. We all now shared a vested interest in getting the job done as quickly as possible, and nobody pussyfooted around trying to stay dry.

Every morning we dragged ourselves out of bed for an hour of PT in the dark before breakfast. Most of these sessions ended with a bracing swim in a nearby river. On one occasion, our instructor, Sergeant Al Willis, led us onto an old bridge over the River Llugwy. It was still dark and we could hear the water flowing forty feet below. Sergeant Willis stood on the parapet and told us to peer over the edge. I looked down towards the river. It was too dark to tell the difference between the rocks below us and the water, but I could see two luminous markers directly below where Sergeant Willis was standing.

'Right, men. As an ML, you must learn to trust your fellow Mountain Leaders without hesitation. Down there, you can see two lights. Each one is on a rock two yards apart. But between them, the water is deep enough for you to jump into. Follow me.'

And with that, he jumped. I clambered onto the parapet and made the leap of faith, my colleagues close behind. We all missed the rocks.

The Welsh phase of the course culminated in a twenty-four-hour forced march across North Wales's highest peaks. Our training was paying off and we all made it.

So FAR SO GOOD: we had learned a lot about mountaincraft. But now we had to learn the practicalities of mountain warfare. Mountain Leaders must be able to operate in small reconnaissance teams, acting as the eyes and ears of the commander of 3 Commando Brigade. So we now learned how to operate in teams of four to six men, behind enemy lines, going in by helicopter or on foot.

We were taught how to establish covert observation posts inside bushes or dug underground on a hillside; we learned how to conduct a close-target recce, which involves using fieldcraft skills to sneak right up to an enemy position.

As recce teams, you try to avoid contact with the enemy, but when things go wrong you have to be able to fight your way out. We learned how to use special lightweight weapons such as the M16 assault rifle and its shortened version, the Colt Commando. It takes a long time to become a good shot; first in the classroom and then on the rifle range. Everyone has a slightly different way of holding and firing a weapon, so it's a matter of trial and error, overseen by an experienced coach, to work out exactly where you have to aim to hit a particular target. In fact, as I was to find out a couple of years later in Sierra Leone, troops with no previous formal training are often very bad shots, even if they are battle-hardened. Firing a burst of automatic rifle fire from the hip may look good in the movies or on TV, but you don't actually hit anything useful.

Finally we learned E & E (escape and evasion) techniques—which were to come in very useful later on in Sierra Leone. We practised all these skills for four weeks on Dartmoor, before moving to the colder, less forgiving mountains of Scotland in mid-November. We knew this would be the toughest part of the training and arrived in Kinlochleven, near Glen Coe, with a feeling of trepidation.

The first few days were easy enough—nontactical mountain marches on hills that I knew and loved, including Ben Nevis. Then we travelled to a remote estate in the Western Highlands, near Glen Shiel, to learn the rudiments of survival. We slept in a tepee made out of an old parachute and huddled together at night to keep warm. Extra clothing, waterproofs and sleeping-bags were all banned, but at least we were issued with that little-known publication, *Beginners' Guide to Edible Fungi*.

For three days we practised skills such as shelter-building, fire-lighting and trapping wild animals. We even received a lecture on how to find water in a desert—someone's idea of a bad joke as we sat there in the pouring rain.

In a nearby fishing village we were shown how to collect shellfish and cook seaweed. Seaweed can be highly nutritious, but you have to boil it for four hours first to make it easier to digest. In a survival situation, you can expend more energy collecting the firewood needed to boil water for this long than you gain from actually eating the seaweed. The water in this part of Scotland is so clean that you can consume shellfish raw. We ate mussels, limpets and even periwinkles straight from their shells.

We had been told to prepare waterproof sketch maps of the area on silk that could be sewn into our uniforms as 'escape maps'. As part of our survival kits we were allowed a miniature button compass each and we tested our 'escape maps' on a short night navigation exercise. The final checkpoint was a pub in the middle of nowhere. The barmaid was not allowed to sell us any food but we were able to boost our intake of calories with beer! We slept well that night, back in our tepee. But this three-day package had just been the 'teaching phase' of our survival training. The 'test phase' was still to come. At least we now knew the sorts of things to keep in our survival kits. Each of us carried a waterproof metal tin in the chest pockets of our shirts, containing stuff such as fire-lighting kit (waterproof matches, magnesium powder, potassium permanganate and some cotton wool as kindling), wire snares, fish-hooks, scalpel blades, chlorine tablets to purify water for drinking or washing wounds, strong painkillers, a couple of sugar lumps and a cigarette, for when it got really bad.

We returned to Kinlochleven to prepare for our next tactical field exercise and spent two days studying maps, planning routes, packing and repacking our bergens. As well as weapons, ammunition, spare clothing, a week's supply of food, radios (with a week's worth of batteries), thermal-imaging equipment, long-range telescopes and medical kit, we also had to carry mountaineering kit, including ropes, helmets, ice axes and crampons. Each bergen was so heavy— mine weighed nearly 120 pounds—that it was near impossible to put it on single-handedly. Now I realised why we had done so many press-ups back down in Cornwall: to build up the muscle bulk on our backs and shoulders. We made a group decision not to take any tents, as they were simply too heavy. Lightweight ponchos would have to suffice. In hindsight, this was the wrong decision.

At last light on a wet and windy mid-November night, we clambered into a Sea King helicopter and deployed onto Exercise Gaelic Venture. We would not be sleeping in a bed again for nearly a month.

We split into two groups and each moved independently from different start points. Our orders were to go in by helicopter to a remote landing site behind notional enemy lines, then move across mountainous terrain to locate an enemy position three nights' march away.

We landed near Loch Arkaig on the remote Knoydart Peninsula. I stepped off the helicopter straight into knee-deep mud. I struggled to put on my bergen and sank in even deeper. We set off on a compass bearing, heading slowly towards our target. It was raining hard and the going underfoot was truly horrendous. We struggled in complete darkness through peat bogs and across steep, waterlogged hillsides where every minor stream had become a raging torrent of white water. We repeatedly cursed the cripplingly heavy packs on our backs. If you fell over, you couldn't get up again without assistance. At first light we lay up under our ponchos. The ground was waterlogged and after a few hours our sleeping-bags were soaking wet. It was hard to think of much else apart from the cold, the wet and my aching shoulders.

Even the sheep had come down off the hills because the weather was so miserable—we were the only living things up there. I knew we were not the first people to have such a low opinion of this place, since the hill had been named 'Gulvain'—'Hill of Shite' in Gaelic.

The rain got harder throughout the day, and by the time we set off again we were walking into a storm.

During the midnight radio schedule, we could hear that the other team was having difficulties. Their radio signal was weak, but we distinctly heard the word 'casualty' being repeated over and over. Our headquarters told us they would send a team out to investigate and we were ordered not to get involved. As instructed, we continued on.

As we crossed the West Highland railway line near Loch Shiel we sheltered for a few minutes underneath a bridge. Taking advantage of the only dry ground for miles, we spread some of our kit out on the railway. We joked about a train coming but, on the West Highland line, at this time of night in November, it seemed highly unlikely. We sat on our packs and got our cookers out to make a hot drink. A few seconds later, the shrill whistle of an Intercity sleeper cut through the wind and rain. *Shit!* In a frenzy as the train approached, we threw our kit off the railway . . . and straight into a large puddle. Cooking on a railway track is definitely not recommended.

As my team struggled on, we were unaware of the tragedy that was unfolding nearby. One of the other team had fallen into a ravine and broken his arm. Without a tent to shelter in, they were now trying to evacuate him. To improve communications, Snowy Snowden had driven out from Kinlochleven in a Land Rover nearer to the exercise area with a signaller and a powerful, vehicle-mounted radio.

The signaller, Corporal Chris Brett-Iversen, had been sitting in the back of the Land Rover, tuning the radio while Snowy erected the radio mast. In the darkness, both were unaware that their vehicle was parked near power lines. While Snowy was erecting the antenna, a 20,000-volt electric shock arced through the wet night air and flowed down through the antenna that was connected to the radio. The Fibreglass mast that Snowy was holding did not conduct electricity, and he was unharmed. Corporal Brett-Iversen, however, bore the full brunt of a massive electric shock and was killed instantly.

Two days later, we reached our first target, but morale was low following this tragic accident and the exercise was beginning to feel pointlessly difficult. As we lay in our observation posts high on the hillside above the 'enemy' position, the weather turned really cold and our wet clothing and equipment began to freeze.

In the morning, several members of the course were suffering from hypothermia so the patrol commander took the decision to retreat to a mountain bothy, where we could light a fire and dry our kit.

We expected little sympathy from our training team but they too realised how difficult conditions were and respected the patrol commander's decision to retreat. In order to salvage the training benefit of the exercise, the training team called in a Sea King helicopter to fly us closer to our next target. Relieved, we climbed aboard.

We should have known not to relax too much. The training team was never going to let us off that lightly. This was dislocation of expectation. Only a few minutes into the flight, the helicopter landed abruptly in a nearby glen. We were unceremoniously kicked off the helicopter to fend for ourselves again, but at least we were now twenty miles closer to our next target. As the last man disembarked, he was handed an envelope containing a set of written instructions, informing us the helicopter had been shot down by an enemy missile. We were the only survivors (*what a surprise*) and had to escape and evade to an emergency rendezvous fifty miles away, where we would be picked up by boat in a week's time.

Wearily, we slung our packs on our backs and trudged on over the hills. The weather slowly improved and we successfully evaded capture as we made our way to 'safety'.

This 'helicopter crash' gave me a philosophy that I have tried to stick to ever since: 'Hope for the best but plan for the worst.'

Planning only for the best is living very dangerously.

A week later, we were picked up by boat from a remote, desolate beach near the end of the Ardgour Peninsula and were all looking forward to being warm and dry again. We were expecting our instructors to pat us on the back, say well done and give us a nice cup of tea. Instead, there was a distinctly unfriendly atmosphere. It now dawned on us, once again, that the exercise was far from over.

3   MOUNTAIN LEADER

Our kit was taken off us, along with our clothes, watches, everything we had, and we were left standing naked except for our underpants and boots. We were then strip-searched and told to put on new uniforms provided for us. Mine was far too small and all the buttons had been ripped off. Our survival kits (in small tobacco tins) were taken off us, searched for contraband such as money or credit cards and returned to us.

After a few hours of shivering, the chief instructor of the Mountain and Arctic Warfare Cadre, Colour Sergeant Brent Hushon, came up on deck to tell us what would happen next.

'Gentlemen, welcome to Exercise BLUE—the test phase of your survival training. We will shortly reach the Isle of Islay. You will be taken to an exercise area, where you will remain until further notice. If you are caught cheating, you will be thrown off the course. The rules are these:

One: Do not build survival shelters less than one kilometre from any forests, roads, or houses.

Two: Do not speak to any locals.

Three: Do not leave your shelters during the hours of darkness.

Four: Do not enter buildings.

Five: Do not kill any farm animals or domestic pets. Good luck.'

When we reached Islay, the Hebridean island famous for its whisky and foul weather, we were all cold, wet and seasick. We still only had the clothes we stood in—all our other kit had been confiscated. We were split into groups of four, blindfolded with sandbags over our heads, led ashore and manhandled onto the back of a truck. An hour later, we were dragged off again, and forced face first into the cold, wet mud. The truck drove off. I took the blindfold off my head, turned it into a hat and put it back on again. I looked around me, disorientated and shivering uncontrollably. The wind was whipping across the barren moorland, but at least it had stopped raining. With my three teammates, I set to work. We had two hours before last light. Our first priority was shelter.

For the next ten days, we lived off the land as best we could. This was real survival as opposed to 'playing at survival', which you normally do on exercise. I doubted the training team would let us die of cold, but they'd let us get halfway there before rescuing us. Ending up in hospital would mean we had failed the exercise and would be chucked off the course.

We built a small but sturdy shelter (or 'hooch') out of logs, scraps of corrugated iron and turf. With a fire at the entrance to the hooch, we stayed warm but smoky. We caught brown trout from a nearby lochan. They were not much bigger than goldfish but they added variety to our diet of cattle feed and seaweed. Our traps were less successful but we enjoyed the road-kill we scraped off nearby roads.

To stay warm at night, we heated rocks in our fire then wrapped them in sacking and used them as hot-water bottles. We also made a 'duvet' out of agricultural sacks stuffed with bracken. We scavenged for food and collected firewood all day, dressed like scarecrows with 'waterproofs' made out of plastic bags.

On the tenth night, I woke in the middle of the night when I felt something land by my feet at the entrance to the hooch. Half asleep, I wondered what it was.

Bang! My head ringing, I realise it's a stun grenade.

Someone is ripping the roof off our hooch and I can hear men shouting '*Get the fuckers!*'

Dazed and confused, we are dragged out by a group of about thirty soldiers in balaclavas. We struggle but, outnumbered and weak through lack of food, we get a good kicking. We're blindfolded, thrown into a frozen pond, then led at gunpoint to a road. We're shoved onto the back of a truck and are well and truly suffering the 'shock of capture': fear, confusion and extreme discomfort.

WE MORE OR LESS know what to expect: this is the 'conduct after capture' phase of the course. UK service personnel who are deemed 'prone to capture', including all Special Forces, MLs and front-line aircrew, have to undergo conduct after capture training. You cannot be taught how to resist torture but, by introducing you to the mind games that interrogators will use against you, you at least know what to expect. You must try to remain the 'grey man' to avoid unwanted attention, and hold out for long enough not to jeopardise the lives of any of your colleagues who might have evaded capture.

We spend the rest of the night in stress positions in an aircraft hangar at Islay's airport. Stress positions involve kneeling or standing in contorted positions for hours on end, such that your joints seize up and your muscles cramp. They are exceptionally painful and are an effective way of wearing down a prisoner without actually torturing him. If we move we are kicked in the small of the back. Given that it is impossible not to move at all after a while, we get kicked a lot. Not too painful to start with, but we are always kicked in exactly the same spot, and the pain of being struck on already bruised flesh is excruciating. Most of us take it stoically, but some can't help screaming and moaning.

By now it is the second week in December and very cold. As the thin cotton uniform I'm wearing is too small, my midriff, ankles and forearms are all exposed to the bitterly cold wind. We have been out in the field for nearly a month, the last ten days of which we've effectively not eaten, so we are all run-down already.

If we collapse through cold or exhaustion, we are dragged into a warm room for a few minutes and sat in front of a heater until we stop shivering. Then we are dragged back out into the cold again. Going in and out of the cold is far worse than just staying in the cold. At one stage, I am given a pair of socks and told to put them on. This seems too good to be true. And it is. As I struggle, blindfolded, trying to undo my bootlaces with numb fingers, the socks are taken off me again—a cruel ploy.

In the morning, still blindfolded, we are led onto an aircraft, and fly for about an hour, still in stress positions. I later hear that we had been led past astonished passengers at the airport (who thought we were being kidnapped).

On landing, we are bundled into another truck and driven to what feels like an old stone fortress and thrown into a dungeon. For the next thirty hours we are kept in stress positions. The monotony and discomfort are alleviated every six hours when we are fed half a slice of bread each and a sip of water. Despite the blindfold I'm aware of day turning to night. As I stand there all night with my hands in the air, I begin to hallucinate from lack of sleep and sensory deprivation. We are being conditioned for interrogation.

The next day our blindfolds are briefly removed and we are spoken to by a doctor. We are told that we will not be physically harmed and that, if we choose to give up, our request will be respected. Only when we see this same doctor will the exercise be over. Until then, anything else that happens is just a ploy by our interrogators and we must not be taken in.

We are led to a holding centre. The sensory deprivation is total. White noise (like a badly tuned TV) blares out from loudspeakers around us and, blindfolded for days on end, we lose all sense of what is happening. We don't know where we are, who we are with or what the time is.

It's difficult to explain the effect this has on you. Time seems to creep by and, more than anything else, it starts to make you lose your grip on reality. I try counting an hour's worth of seconds but it's too depressing as it seems to go on for ever and I never get beyond 100. We also have no idea of how many guards there are around us. They have a policy of never talking to each other in our presence. All we know is that if we move or make a noise, someone is there immediately to slap us in the face or push us around.

For the interrogations we are taken into a brightly lit room, and suddenly have our blindfolds removed, so we are completely disorientated. At first the interrogators shout at us in different languages: Russian, Arabic, Spanish—and I'm sure one of them is speaking Welsh. Although we know they aren't going to do us any serious physical damage, they make a good show of breaking up the furniture around us and we are slapped around a bit.

The physical stuff doesn't bother me so much: the real problems are in my head. I am pretty close to flipping out at times. I have a mental strategy of saying to myself, 'OK, whatever you want to do now, just wait for five minutes and see how you feel then.' I have to do my 'five-minute plan' over and over again until something changes, either mentally or physically, and it seems to do the trick. It's hard to describe just how grim it all is.

For the next twenty hours, we are subjected to a series of interrogations: some aggressive, some friendly and some downright boring. We are not allowed to give away any more information than our name, rank, number and date of birth. During one session I am stripped naked and subjected to an extended, internal body-cavity search in front of a scathing group of female interrogators.

After the search, I am led outside and left spread-eagled, stark

naked, against a wall. It's a cold, frosty night and in my weakened
state I grow dangerously cold very quickly. For ninety minutes I
stand there, literally freezing. As I feel myself slipping into hypothermia, I think maybe the exercise has gone wrong or that someone's
cocked up. In fact, I am being monitored via a hidden camera and,
on the point of collapse, I am brought back inside to a warm room,
given a blanket and a cup of tea and spoken to gently by a kind lady.
She tries to coax me into speaking freely, offering me more tea and
some biscuits if only I tell her where I am from. I refuse and am led
back to the holding area.

One of my hooch mates from Islay finally cracks. He is taken into
a cell and his blindfold removed. He is joined by another 'prisoner'
he does not recognise and they are left alone. The 'prisoner' is really
an interrogator, but my mate doesn't realise this and chats openly to
his cellmate. He tells the interrogator who we are, everything we've
been doing and that there's an officer in his group called Phil. I'm
dragged into the cell, my blindfold's removed and I see my friend and
the other 'prisoner'. I twig what's going on and tell him to shut up,
but the damage has been done. My friend's gone a bit mad. I have
time to give him a reassuring squeeze on the arm, and tell him to
hang in there, before I'm dragged out again.

My next interrogation lasts for three and a half hours, during
which I am asked the same question over and over again.

'What is your regimental number?'

'N034354T.'

'Number?'

'N034354T.'

And so it goes on, over and over again.

For the first half-hour this is easy and I wonder what the point of
the interrogation is. But as I get sleepier, it becomes harder to concentrate. My mind starts to play tricks on me. I picture my regimen-
tal number in my mind's eye and try to read it out loud each time I
am asked. It's like I'm reading off an autocue. While the autocue
gives me the right answers most of the time, every now and then an
inappropriate word or number appears and it's difficult not to blurt
it out. It's as if the coordination between your brain and your mouth
has stopped working.

'Number?'

'N034354T.'

'Number?'

'N034354T.'

'Number?'

'I'll have the chocolate cake, please.'

After asking the same question over 1,000 times, the interrogators start to slip in different ones.

'Number?'

'N034354T.'

'What unit are you from?'

In my mind-numbed state, it's hard not to answer. I can see how false confessions could easily be dragged out of prisoners.

After what seems an eternity, our blindfolds are removed for the final time and we see the doctor. We have successfully resisted interrogation. All except my old hooch mate, who is thrown off the course. We sympathise, but this is no game.

A few years later, I ended up sharing an office with an experienced Joint Service interrogator who admitted that the trainee Mountain Leaders were his favourite subjects as, after everything we had been through, we most closely resembled captured POWs.

AFTER AN ALL-TOO-BRIEF Christmas leave, we deployed to a village called Haugastol on the edge of the Hardangervidda National Park in the mountains of western Norway. For the next three months, we underwent the extreme cold weather warfare phase of the course. Haugastol is 3,000 feet above sea level, and the Hardangervidda is the wilderness area where the Norwegian resistance fighters of the Second World War, including the 'Heroes of Telemark', hid from the occupying German Army for years. A memorial in the nearby settlement of Finse is dedicated to Scott of the Antarctic, as it was here he did his training before setting off for his infamous expedition to the South Pole. More recently, the snowy scenes from *The Empire Strikes Back* were also filmed here.

All of us were already trained in arctic warfare from previous deployments to Norway with regular Royal Marines units. Now we were being trained to be instructors and would have to do more than just fend for ourselves. In the future, we would all need to have the 'spare capacity' to look after our subordinates and students in the most demanding of conditions.

Among the many and various things we learned was how to teach 'ice-breaking' drills—what to do if you fall through the ice into a freezing lake or river. As long as you don't panic, it's relatively straightforward. You know the ice behind you is strong enough to take your weight, as you've just been standing on it. But the problem is climbing out with all your equipment before your body weakens with the cold. If you abandon your equipment, even if you don't drown, you will probably freeze to death. All your dry clothing, your sleeping-bag, tent and cooker are in a waterproof bag inside your bergen, so you need to hang on to it.

The drill goes like this. If you have to cross a stretch of thin ice, you first loosen your ski-bindings and sling your weapon and bergen over one shoulder (to make them easier to take off if you fall through the ice). If the ice breaks and you fall into the water, the cold around your chest makes it hard to breathe but, if you don't panic, you soon get used to it. As an adult male, you can expect to stay conscious for about eight minutes in water at 0°C (longer if you're a woman or if you're wearing thick clothes), which is plenty of time to sort yourself out. To prove the point, in a lecture to a course I was running in Norway a couple of years ago, I gave the whole of the 'ice-breaking' lecture standing in freezing water.

Your skis and bergen (which has air trapped inside it) float, so you can worry about them later. First, you turn round to face the point at which you fell in. Then, as you tread water, you pass your weapon out onto the ice, then your skis, then your bergen. Next comes the tricky bit. Holding your ski-poles at the bottom, and using the sharpened tips as daggers to grip on the ice, you haul yourself back out, keeping your body spread flat to minimise the pressure. You drag yourself back towards the thicker ice, then roll in the snow to absorb much of the water on your body and clothes before it has time to freeze. Snow has the unusual property of absorbing water like a sponge, and the colder the snow, the more effective it is. It's then a race against time to put up a tent, or get in a vehicle before you freeze to death. The coldest still air temperature in which I have ever done this drill was –27°C, so cold that any water on your body freezes almost instantly—including the water on your eyeballs. You must work quickly but not rush around like a madman. If you do and your heart rate goes up too much, the blood that has cooled down in your extremities will not have time to rewarm before entering your heart—and the shock can make your heart stop.

As a Mountain Leader, you have to demonstrate this technique to worried novices. It's crucial to do it confidently to show them it's no big deal (as well as being a matter of personal pride). So any of us showing distress while carrying out the drill had to practise it again and again until they could do it 'properly'. Luckily, most of us sussed it first time, but a couple of the lads had to repeat it four or five times during the same afternoon. They were given only twenty minutes between each dunking to warm up. I was not jealous.

By March, we could see light at the end of the tunnel. Although we had months of training still to go, we were 'badged' at the end of the Norway phase. This meant having the ML badge sewn onto our parade dress uniform and, just as importantly, receiving specialist ML pay for the first time.

Back in the UK, we had a whole series of technical qualifications to acquire, including helicopter abseil instructor training, parachute training and, for the officers, a Special Forces operations planning course, but we had now finally earned the respect of our instructors, which meant no more press-ups.

The course ended in July, with a month's alpine climbing in the Bernese Oberland in Switzerland. I was being paid extra money to do what I loved doing and I made the most of it. A highlight was a quick ascent of the Eiger with a fellow ML officer called Kev. We summited in a storm, but after some of the conditions we had endured during the course, this seemed almost tame.

AFTER ALL THIS TRAINING, I was looking forward to getting a job putting everything I'd learned into practice. My appointer told me there was a job going for an ML officer with the Parachute Regiment, whose 3rd Battalion had a cold weather warfare role as part of a NATO reaction force. This opportunity was too good to miss and I enjoyed two years working with some of the best of the British Army. There is considerable rivalry—and mutual respect—between the Paras and the Marines. As the only Bootneck (slang for Royal Marine) among several hundred Paras, I received my fair share of stick, learned a lot, taught a lot, and thoroughly enjoyed myself.

During this time, I spent nearly four months each winter back out in Norway, planning and running arctic warfare training courses.

Anna came out to Norway for a long weekend in January 1997. After a whisky-fuelled Burns' Night dinner we were walking down an icy slope on the way to my accommodation. We slipped and landed in a snowdrift and lay there giggling with snow up our kilts, looking at the stars. On the spur of the moment, I asked Anna to marry me. She said yes, but, with horrendous hangovers, we had to double-check in the morning that we both remembered what had happened.

We were married on July 26, 1997 in Abden House at the foot of a hill called Arthur's Seat in Edinburgh. It pissed with rain, babies cried, I sang badly but not as badly as my father, and my best man, Alistair, who had been with us in the avalanche, tried to snog some of the bridesmaids—which he enjoyed but his girlfriend didn't. Our wedding cake was a snow-covered mountain, with two miniature climbers at the bottom. My head fell off as we cut the cake. Not one to worry too much about symbolism, Anna popped it in her mouth and ate it.

After an all-night ceilidh Anna and I decided to walk back to our hotel. As we wandered through the deserted streets of Edinburgh's Old Town, I felt I had married the loveliest girl in the world. She was wearing a backless dress that just failed to cover the small bump where she had broken her back and when I caught a glimpse of it, I had to pretend not to have a tear in my eye. This had definitely been the best day of my life.

We went to Venice for our honeymoon—well, we spent the first two days of our honeymoon in Venice. The Dolomites were only two hours' drive away, so we spent the rest of the holiday walking and climbing in the mountains. We started out in a five-star hotel, downgraded through four-, three-, two- and one-star hotels, then a mountain hut, and ended up in the cosy surroundings of my two-man tent. Even the best hotels would struggle to compete with the view you can enjoy from a tent pitched halfway up a remote mountainside. Still, we avoided bivvying out in the open—this was our honeymoon, after all.

Newly married, Anna and I managed to juggle our professional lives enough to be in the same place at the same time for a while. In 1998 I passed my promotion exams, earning myself the rank of major and a desk job in London. Although this was an interesting enough posting, it wasn't the most exciting. I went to work in a suit, struggled with IT systems, processed mountains of paperwork and only put on my uniform for special occasions. I ran a few marathons to keep myself fit and was fortunate when my boss allowed me a month away from my desk to take part in an expedition to climb Mount McKinley in Alaska.

In January 2000, I took up the opportunity of working for six months as a Military Observer attached to the United Nations in tropical West Africa. Like all British officers before they work with the UN, I attended a week-long briefing package to find out what I needed to know about my destination, Sierra Leone. Little did I know just how much I was going to depend on the specialist skills I had acquired as a Mountain Leader.

1. After rowing 1,500 miles in a 5.5 metre open-top boat, Pete and I were burnt, blistered and frozen-footed, but it was worth it to be in one of the most beautiful places in the world. 2. Spitsbergen, 1991. Stuck in pack ice at 81° North. 3. January 1994. Approaching Beinn a' Chlaidheimh in the Scottish Highlands. The last photo before the avalanche. 4. Officer training. On a 'collective punishment' mud run with fellow officers in the River Exe estuary. 5. July 27, 1997. Getting

married at the foot of Arthur's Seat in Edinburgh was the happiest day of my life. **6.** Ice-breaking drills in Norway. On one occasion I gave my five- minute lecture on self-rescue whilst treading water. I'm told that a man lasts eight minutes without losing consciousness in these conditions. **7.** Resistance to Interrogation training. We were given a small sip of water every six hours. Only troops designated prone to capture, such as aircrew, MLs, SAS and SBS, receive this training. **8.** On our honeymoon in the Italian Alps, 1,200 feet up a 2,000-feet rock climb. We stayed in hotels, a mountain hut and a tent but we weren't forced to bivouac—this was our honeymoon, after all!

4   PEACEKEEPING IN SIERRA LEONE

Just outside Freetown, Sierra Leone's capital, there is a beach called River Number Two, where miles of gleaming white sand stretch out under palm trees. It looks so idyllic that the original 'Bounty' chocolate bar ads were filmed here, with the slogan, 'A Taste of Paradise'. Yet now, only twenty yards away, there is a rehabilitation centre for former child soldiers. These children bear terrible physical scars—apart from war wounds, most have been branded like cattle by their commanders. Their emotional scars can only be guessed at.

On the Atlantic coast, unspoilt sandy beaches and mangrove swamps stretch for hundreds of miles, broken only by the natural harbour of the Sierra Leone River, the second-biggest natural harbour in the world after Sydney. Freetown lies on the south side of the river estuary. The town was once known as the 'Athens of West Africa' and, despite the years of fighting, is still a beautiful place—at least from a distance. The lush, rolling hills around it are scattered with impressive white villas. In colonial days, Graham Greene sat on his verandah in one of these and wrote *The Heart of the Matter*. Sadly, the only Sierra Leoneans rich enough to live in places like this fifty years later are rebel commanders who have made a fortune through diamond smuggling and extortion.

The country is small by African standards, about the size of Ireland. It's surrounded by Guinea to the north and east and war-torn Liberia to the south. It got its name—which means 'Lion Mountains'—from early Portuguese explorers, who heard the roar of tropical thunderstorms booming out of the coastal hills on the Freetown peninsula. But Sierra Leone is not especially mountainous and its lions have long since been driven out by years of civil war.

Before deploying from the UK, I had attended a week of briefings that concentrated mainly on the risks of living and working in Sierra Leone. On the face of it, Sierra Leoneans should be well off by African standards. They don't suffer from Mozambique's floods, Ethiopia's droughts, Algeria's religious conflict, Rwanda's ethnic hatred or Angola's legacy of unexploded land mines. In fact, until 1990, Sierra Leone was a stable, tolerant and prosperous country, a net exporter of food and blessed with rich mineral resources. After that, it plummeted to the bottom of the UN's Human Development Index. When I was there, it was officially the poorest country in the world, vying for this dubious honour with Afghanistan. In the year 2000, the average annual wage was less than $100 per person, and in territory controlled by the Revolutionary United Front (RUF), male life expectancy was as low as twenty-six. Half the population of about four million are effectively refugees or slaves. Most soldiers in the region have contracted HIV but expect to die young in fighting anyway, so don't much care. Here, malaria kills many more people than HIV/AIDS, and so AIDS is just one more deadly hazard.

How did this disaster happen? The main reason: the fight for diamonds. Sierra Leone has some of the world's biggest diamond reserves, mostly found in the eastern part of the country. These reserves have fuelled and financed a brutal civil war that has destroyed the infrastructure and quality of life for all but the most ruthless. When the RUF started the civil war in 1991, they might have had genuine grievances, but the war soon degenerated into a bloody scrap for control of the diamond mines.

The basic conflict has been between a succession of governments based in Freetown and the rebels of the RUF with a power base in the east of the country, armed and financed by Liberia in return for diamonds. What has complicated matters has been the on/off involvement of other parties, including the Sierra Leone Army— sometimes with the government or as the government, sometimes with the RUF and sometimes on both sides at once.

A Civilian Defence Force (CDF) soon emerged to counter the savagery of the RUF and the ineptitude of the Sierra Leone Army. The CDF are mostly Kamajors (indigenous hunters), who make up for a lack of decent weapons or formal training with a generous dose of black magic. These Kamajors are, by local standards, the good guys, though some of their habits are a little unusual. Some believe, for example, that you become a stronger warrior from eating the heart of a respected enemy killed in battle, or that wearing jewellery made from the pubic hair of virgins can keep you healthy. However strange their habits may have seemed, I was later to be immensely glad of their support when they risked their lives to help me.

Sierra Leone's West African neighbours were also drawn into the civil war: the Nigerian-dominated forces of the Economic Community Monitoring Organisation (ECOMOG) on the government side, Liberia with the RUF. ECOMOG is the military wing of the Economic Community of West African States (ECOWAS)—West

Africa's version of the European Union. As mercenaries, nationalities from further afield have become involved, including the British, though the UK-based organisations don't use the word 'mercenaries' these days, preferring to be known as 'private military companies'.

Sierra Leone's civil war has been bloody, even by African standards. In January 1999, the President, Tejan Kabbah, was up for re-election. His campaign slogan was 'The future is in your hands'. Tragically, the RUF chose a macabre, literal interpretation of this slogan and countered it by systematically hacking off the hands of many thousands of people, both adults and children.

On January 6, 1999, the rebels smuggled weapons into Freetown, then infiltrated the city, hiding in the crowds of people who had come to vote. A charity, Human Rights Watch, compiled evidence of the ensuing butchery.

> Civilians were gunned down . . . thrown from the upper floors of buildings, used as human shields, and burned alive in cars and houses. They had their limbs hacked off with machetes, eyes gouged out with knives, hands smashed with hammers, and bodies burned with boiling water. Women and girls were systematically sexually abused, and children and young people abducted by the hundreds.

Having looted the capital, the rebels were forced out of Freetown by Nigerian peacekeepers and Kamajor militiamen.

In the aftermath of these atrocities, the people of Sierra Leone decided that enough was enough. At Lomé, the capital of Togo, West Africa, in July 1999, a peace accord was signed between the government and the RUF. A blanket amnesty was given to all combatants and the UN was invited to oversee the peace process and a process of Disarmament, Demobilisation and Reintegration (DDR).

When I arrived, in January 2000, there had been—more or less—a six-month cease-fire. After everything I had heard and read about the place, I was half expecting to step off the aircraft straight into scenes of strife and violence. The reality was a little more mundane.

I SPENT MY FIRST WEEK completing a tortuous 'joining routine' with the UN Mission in Sierra Leone, known as UNAMSIL. Never have I filled in so much paperwork for so little tangible benefit, but at least it gave me a week to discover the joys of Freetown and adjust to the rhythms of UN life.

As the ex-colonial power (granting independence in 1961), Britain is popular, if not universally loved, and you can see signs of its residual influence everywhere. English is the official language. The university, the Fourah Bay College in Freetown, was originally part of Durham University, and all the kids seem to support English football teams. Where they got them from I don't know, but several rebels wore Manchester United football shirts. As a Chelsea fan, this did not endear them to me any more than their subsequent attempts to take me hostage or kill me!

A few days before arriving in Sierra Leone I'd been ice-climbing in Scotland, so I really noticed the heat and humidity. During the day the temperature went as high as 100°F (38°C), and even at night it didn't drop very much below 83°F (28°C). It felt like being stuck on a crowded train in the London underground on a hot summer's day while wearing thick winter clothes. The other thing that struck me was the smell—a pungent mixture of stale sweat, rotting fruit, fish and meat. Sierra Leone is a hot and sticky place but there is no running water, so bathing is a weekly, not daily, luxury, and when I was there its civil infrastructure was almost non-existent. Discarded food remained where it was dropped: scraps lay by the side of the road until eaten by packs of disease-ridden dogs, rats or vultures. In comparison to 'developed' countries there was very little man-made litter—anything like strips of paper or polythene bags had salvage value. When I bought some oranges from a street vendor, I was amazed to discover that the polythene bag I bought to carry them in cost more than the oranges. No wonder people don't drop litter.

Every one of UNAMSIL's numerous different nationalities seemed to have its own idea of working hours. The European nations preferred to take Sundays off while the Muslim nations took Fridays off. Every nation had the right to celebrate an annual national day but many seemed to have adopted a monthly one. And a surprising number of nationalities claimed that a siesta was an integral part of their culture.

The highlight of the first week was my UN driving test. The roads had almost no traffic on them, but my instructor, a Jamaican guy called Trevor, still advised extreme caution: 'If there are people about, never drive faster than walking speed.' I asked why. He explained that after a local resident had been knocked down by a UN jeep and awarded $100 in compensation, half the population seemed to be trying to cash in. Locals had developed the unnerving habit of throwing themselves or their elderly relatives in front of UN vehicles, hoping to collect their bounty. Life in Sierra Leone is cheap.

Freetown was chaotic but friendly, its people optimistic that the UN would bring them prolonged peace and prosperity. The streets bustled with traders, and the schools were full of smartly dressed pupils. But the relative normality of Freetown was only surface deep, hiding the grim reality of life in the interior of the country, especially in territory controlled by the RUF.

The rebels still controlled two-thirds of the country. Their military headquarters were in Makeni, a market town and the provincial capital of the mainly Muslim Northern Province. I was assigned to a team of UN Military Observers (UNMOs) based in Makeni itself. As observers we were not allowed to bear arms and, in fact, our unarmed status was in many respects our best means of self-defence as nobody felt threatened by us. I lost count of the number of times I was searched at gunpoint by the RUF. If I'd carried a weapon openly, I'd have been treated as an enemy. If they had discovered a hidden weapon, I'd have been treated as a spy. I took all the British badges off my uniform—the commando daggers and parachute wings were only likely to draw unwanted attention from the RUF.

I deployed to Makeni on the weekly UN resupply flight, an hour's journey in an ancient Russian MI-8 helicopter. We landed on an old football pitch in the next-door town of Magburaka, where I was met by my new UNMO team. Here, inland, the heat was far more oppressive. When I got off the helicopter I felt a blast of hot air. I initially thought it was the heat of the exhaust, then realised this was the normal air temperature here. Just the strain of carrying my bags off the helicopter was enough to drench my clothes with sweat. I jumped into a 4x4 Toyota jeep with Mustafa, an Egyptian officer, for the twenty-minute trip to Makeni. He wound the windows up, turned the air conditioning on, put Madonna's *Like a Virgin* on the car stereo and lit a cigarette. A group of kids had gathered at the helicopter landing site to watch the weekly arrival. I was surprised when Mustafa simply accelerated towards them, sounding his horn loudly and forcing all the children to dive out of his way.

The main road between Magburaka and Makeni was surprisingly good quality tarmac. Built in the 1950s, it had not seen enough traffic over the years to do it much damage. Despite the occasional pothole, we zoomed along the narrow road at over seventy miles per hour, narrowly missing locals carrying large loads on foot or bicycle. It struck me as arrogant to show such little regard for the local people, especially when Mustafa started beeping his horn as we overtook. In a crowded village, locals started running for cover.

Pretending to be carsick, I asked him to slow down a bit.

'Does everyone drive this fast?' I asked.

'No. The others are much faster, but I am getting better.'

From then on, I resolved that when I was in charge of a vehicle I would drive slowly with the windows down and say hello to people as I went by.

We passed several roadblocks manned by bored-looking rebels but were waved straight through. At the last checkpoint before Makeni, I thought my eyes were deceiving me.

'Did I just see a chimpanzee manning that checkpoint?'

'Yes,' replied Mustafa.

'And was he holding an AK 47?'

'Yes.'

'Can he fire it?'

'I don't know—there's a cease-fire, remember,' Mustafa answered, with no hint of sarcasm.

A few days later, I paid a visit to the checkpoint and, sure enough, there was the chimpanzee. This time he was not holding a weapon. He had put it down to smoke a cigarette. When he saw me approaching, he picked up his rifle and started snarling at me.

'The sergeant major doesn't like you,' the checkpoint commander shouted over to me. 'He has no bullets but he might try to stab you.' The chimp's AK 47 had a bayonet attached to it. I decided this was a good point to turn back.

The next time I saw the chimp he was smoking a joint. I never did find out whether he knew how to shoot.

THE TEAM SITE was in a walled compound on the outskirts of Makeni. On one side of the compound, there was a long, single-storey breeze-block house overlooking the main road, and there were two smaller buildings on the other side of the compound. The UN jeeps were parked in between the buildings out of sight of prying eyes. On the far side of the main road outside the compound was a well. This was the dry season and we had to top the well up once a week by water tanker.

I met my new colleagues. Our team of fourteen observers had ten nationalities, eight languages, six religions and, for a while, a pet monkey called Oscar. The team leader was a British Parachute Regiment colonel, Jim Skuse. We had an area of responsibility about the size of Northern Ireland and two main tasks: assessing the security situation and overseeing the disarmament process.

Major Igor Kotov, a tough-looking Russian, showed me to my digs in one of the shacks on the far side of the compound. It had breeze-block walls, bars over the windows, a corrugated-iron roof and a sturdy metal door that could be locked only from the outside. I asked Igor if this had been a storeroom.

'No. RUF prison. You sleep here. Very safe.' The previous occupant of our house had been Dennis Mingo, a.k.a 'Superman', an RUF commander with a feared and brutal reputation even by rebel standards. I subsequently discovered that Mingo had earned his nickname as a result of his preferred method of killing—throwing his victims off tall buildings and telling them to 'fly like Superman'.

The room was filthy. I scrubbed the walls but was unable to remove some ominous dark red stains. A fresh lick of paint soon put the evidence of Superman's torture victims out of sight, if not out of mind.

The corrugated-iron roof kept out the rain but meant the room stayed as hot as an oven, even at night. I was determined to acclimatise properly and didn't give in to the temptation to install a fan. Even though this meant that for the first few days I was continuously drenched in sweat and too hot to sleep properly, it was a price worth paying. Once you're acclimatised, everyday life is much more comfortable. Although some of my colleagues thought my attitude a little strange, when things did go wrong being properly acclimatised was to prove a lifesaver.

My room was right next to the generator, which throbbed loudly, though after a day or two I no longer minded the noise. Actually, it was easier to get to sleep with the generator running. When it was switched off, I could hear the scurrying and scratching of the rats that lived in the roof space above me, which drove me to distraction. I tried rat poison, which did kill one of the creatures, but I never found the carcass. Believe me, the only thing worse than sharing your bedroom with a live rat is sharing a room with a dead, rotting one.

I came to know the habits of my rodent room-mates quite well. Every three days they would clean out their nest, kicking droppings down onto my mosquito net. Scraping off the rat shit became a regular chore. Disturbingly, a British aid worker based nearby died a few weeks later from Lassa fever. This is a disease that humans catch from breathing in the droplets of rat's urine that drip down from roof cavities. This prompted me to try an assortment of rat-catching techniques—smoking them out (no effect on the rats but my room reeked of smoke for weeks), and ripping the roof apart to look for them (the rats scurried away before I could catch them and thereafter the roof leaked). I even tried to buy a cat, but the only one I saw in Makeni was a scrawny, disease-ridden moggy, not much bigger than the rats themselves, and I didn't rate its chances.

I was initially appointed as the team's Military Information Officer. 'Military information' is UN-speak for 'intelligence', a word that has too many Cold War connotations and suggests that everybody is spying on each other. As the new man on the ground, I did not know very much about the intelligence situation, but the role was given to me because with English as my first language it would be easier for me to compile our daily situation reports.

There were some almost irreconcilable differences within the team. The African guys tended to go womanising every afternoon. Unfortunately, the devout Muslims in the team just could not come to terms with this and refused to share a house with them. A compromise was reached—the Africans hired the house next door as a love shack and a notice was erected in the operations room: NO SMOKING OR WHORING IN THE OPS ROOM.

All members of the team had their own strengths and weaknesses, but the bottom line was this: we all wore the same UN beret. Our diversity was our strength, despite the occasional misunderstanding.

The team was assisted by a battalion of 500 lightly armed Kenyan infantry. It was considered unlikely that the rebels would choose to disarm unless we had some means of protecting them—their fear of retribution from the local population was real and justified. The Kenyans were spread thinly, with never more than 100 men in any one location. However, they were usually in smaller groups and we had just six men guarding our compound.

My standard routine involved getting up early to make the most of the coolest part of the day. I enjoyed my early-morning runs which, as well as keeping me fit, were the best way to explore the local area. Sometimes accompanied by our landlord, Musa, I explored the back-streets and footpaths of Makeni and the surrounding fields and villages. Musa introduced me to the commanders of the numerous checkpoints on the roads and paths. He still enjoyed the patronage and protection of Superman, so I felt reasonably safe. Local kids would shout friendly abuse at us in the local language, Mende, as we ran. One group always shouted the same message. Musa translated for me: 'Look how elegantly the white man runs!' This seemed too good to be true. And it was. I asked a neighbour for an accurate translation: 'Good morning, chicken legs!'

After my daily run, I'd take a shower—hanging a water-filled plastic bag with holes in it off a tree branch—and shave out of a mess tin while listening to the World Service.

After breakfast, the day's work began. We tried to get the bulk done in the morning while the rebels were still subdued. By early afternoon, most would be too fired up on drink or drugs to make much sense, and even more unpredictable and dangerous than usual.

Our first major task was assessing the security situation. This involved patrolling on foot or by jeep and speaking to as many rebels and civilians as possible, to find out what was going on. We also tried to 'sensitise' the local rebels by explaining why the UN was there and why disarmament would benefit them. As part of the Lomé Peace Accord, to which the rebels had signed up, the UN was supposed to have freedom of movement throughout the country. Despite this, most checkpoint commanders expected anybody who wanted safe passage through their position to bribe them. I refused to hand over money as this would have set a precedent. Each time I returned to the same checkpoint, the rebels would have expected more of the same, so instead I dished out Royal Marines paraphernalia such as pens and pencils that I'd brought out from the UK.

One of the hardest patrols we undertook was when we tried to reach the diamond mining town of Kono, 150 miles further east. As part of the Lomé Peace Accord, there was supposed to be a moratorium on the illegal mining and export of diamonds, so the RUF were unwilling to let the UN go there to discover what was really happening. Kono was, technically, in another team's area of responsibility. But they had repeatedly found excuses not to go.

Exasperated, the UN HQ asked our team to go instead. Colonel Jim led the patrol and I volunteered to accompany him in the lead vehicle. George, a Zambian, and Rizvi, a Pakistani, brought up the rear, and we took an armed escort of Kenyans along.

To ensure a smooth passage through the numerous rebel roadblocks, Colonel Jim and I took two moderate RUF commanders along with us, Lieutenant-Colonel Alfred Jimmy and Colonel Sherif. Both were well-educated, pragmatic men who saw the benefits of the peace process, if only because they saw themselves as budding politicians. But Jimmy and Sherif had earned their ranks through fighting, not politics. As we advanced towards Kono, we passed through the sites of several battles where they had been in command. They made grim scenes. Many of the victims of these battles still lay where they had died, stripped of their uniforms by their killers, their skeletons picked clean by vultures. Many of them were headless, with the skulls displayed on nearby stakes. I asked Sherif whether the heads were severed before or after their owners died.

'Whichever,' he replied, then continued, 'See that log? We put that across the road to stop the lead armoured car. And when the Nigerian soldiers got out to move it out of the way, we fired an RPG [rocket-propelled grenade] from here, then machine-gunned the crew from behind that bush. You can see their heads in a pile over there!'

My conversation with Sherif moved on to cannibalism. He explained that many fighters believed that if you ate the heart of a strong man you would acquire his strength. Sherif did admit that he was not totally taken in by this philosophy but that eating the heart of your enemy was good for bonding and group morale.

I asked as nonchalantly as I could, 'So, Sherif, have you ever eaten anyone?'

'Yeah.'

'Is it true the meat tastes like pork?'

'I wouldn't know,' he replied with implacable logic. 'I'm a Muslim.'

I asked Sherif how he had become a rebel. After leaving school with A levels in English, History and Politics in 1987 (the same year I left school), he'd started a law degree in Freetown. However, in 1990, he witnessed a terrible event. His father, a policeman, was on duty during an attempted coup. Sherif watched as mutinous soldiers gouged out his father's eyes then poured battery acid into the empty sockets. Sherif joined the RUF soon afterwards. I could see how hard it would be to break the cycle of violence.

Sherif had become a cruel thug but was still capable of displays of kindness—on one occasion, I saw him give his lunch to a hungry beggar. I found him easy enough to get along with and wondered how I would have turned out if I had had his life.

5   DISARMING THE REBELS

For the first fifty miles or so of our patrol, the rebels manning checkpoints recognised Sherif and Jimmy and progress was straightforward enough. Once outside their home turf, though, Sherif and Jimmy were no longer automatically recognised or respected, and they became a lot more twitchy. It took longer and longer to negotiate our way through each checkpoint.

With just five miles to go to Kono, we were stopped again. The checkpoint commander here was called Major Psycho, aged all of fifteen. He was nothing more—and nothing less—than a dangerous nutter. I remember his distinctive red beret, with a bullet hole through each temple. The Kenyan escort was forced to stay at the checkpoint while Jim and I were 'invited' to drive to a nearby village. We were told it would be impossible to continue to Kono that day and that we could spend the night with them there. Given the increasingly hostile atmosphere, this was the last place in the world I wanted to spend the night. Jim agreed with me but Psycho was now refusing to let us leave. Even Sherif and Jimmy were frightened.

Back at the checkpoint, the Kenyans were having more success with their negotiations. They had convinced the rebels that 'the two white men don't know what they're doing but they're harmless' (I guess they had a point), and asked to come down to the village to sort things out. Their arrival helped, but it took another three hours of delicate negotiations to extract ourselves.

Jim and I both agreed we had pushed it too far. We drove through the night back to Makeni and never did make it to Kono. Before we were able to try again, the cease-fire had ended.

OUR SECOND MAJOR TASK was overseeing the disarmament process when, or rather if, it started. The RUF were blatantly stalling for time, more or less observing the cease-fire so that aid agencies would operate in their territory, and yet refusing to hand in any weapons. Some slow progress, however, was being made. A team from the UK Department for International Development (DfID) had persuaded the RUF commanders to let them start building a number of disarmament camps in the rebel heartlands. Our nearest one was ten miles to the south of Makeni. The plan was that RUF fighters would live in these camps once they had disarmed. They would be fed, given medical attention, and receive $300 and some basic training in skills such as farming or building. By the beginning of April, construction of the first Disarmament, Demobilisation and Reintegration (DDR) camps in RUF territory was almost complete.

The DDR process was going well in other parts of the country, so we were able to visit some UNMO teams to see what the practical difficulties were. There were many. One of the major problems was determining exactly who was a combatant. To be considered an ex-combatant, you had to hand in a weapon, but not any old weapon. For example, the UN did not consider you a combatant if you tried to disarm with just a hand grenade. This was because you could buy a hand grenade on the black market for $10, then receive $300 for handing it in. One local woman who tried this ploy met a sticky end. When she was told she would not receive $300, she pulled the pin.

There were about 2,000 rebel fighters in the vicinity of Makeni and maybe 10,000 in our whole area of responsibility. We had been warned to expect to encounter child soldiers, but it was still a shock to witness in reality. I reckoned the average age of an RUF soldier in Makeni was twelve or thirteen years old. Some were much younger.

Interacting with child soldiers was problematic, both morally and practically. On the one hand, you realised they were children and that their wrongdoings were not really their fault. On the other hand, their very ignorance of normal morality made them particularly dangerous, and rebel commanders were quick to exploit this. RUF recruitment was brutal but effective. A typical method was simply to attack a village, kill or maim the adults and abduct the children. To ensure loyalty, the RUF would then force their new recruits to take drugs and carry out an atrocity against their own family or community. Once they were orphaned, the RUF would then become the children's surrogate family.

After a while, it became hard to view rebel child soldiers as anything but savage little hooligans with no sense of right or wrong or value for life (other people's or their own). Yet they were armed with high velocity rifles and normally high as kites on cannabis, cocaine or palm wine—often all three.

After my first month with the team, I sent an email home. Not wanting to worry my loved ones, I tried to concentrate on the lighter side of life among the RUF.

Feb 20, 00

All goes well in a hot and hanging-around-waiting-for-things-to-start-happening sort of way. I am deployed as a UN Military Observer in a place called Makeni, 150 km NE of Freetown. As always, the dangers of a particular country or environment are exaggerated in the pre-deployment briefings. That said, there are a lot of people around here with fewer limbs than is traditional and this area is openly controlled by the RUF (Revolutionary United Front). Their leaders are more or less going along with the peace process, but this message does not necessarily filter down to the 'troops' on the ground.

The average age of the RUF is mid-teenager. It's all a bit

Lord-of-the-Flies-like. Promotion is a result of successful rebel action (killing)—I've yet to meet anyone who's less than a self-promoted captain. Generally, as long as you are firm with them you can do what/go where you want, but (sorry for sounding middle-aged) they're so drugged up/generally mental that they don't often know their own names, let alone that there's a peace process. The RUF are slaves to fashion. Sunglasses and flat-tops, fair enough, but I'm not so sure about their clothes—'Leonardo di Caprio' T-shirts seem to be their current favourite.

There is supposed to be a Disarmament, Demobilisation and Reintegration (DDR) process going on. It has yet to start in this area. The RUF leadership claims to back DDR, but does not match its words with actions. This is frustrating as there seems to be a feeling of optimism and genuine desire for peace at grass-roots level—expectations are high, and every day that goes by with no DDR is one step closer to a recurrence of widespread violence. The RUF foot soldiers receive no pay. Their only remuneration comes from the spoils of war, so we are, perhaps, living on borrowed time. As there is no DDR to oversee, we busy ourselves with patrolling and interacting with the local community—my Frisbee-throwing skills go from strength to strength. I am now known as Mr 'Are you ready?' by the local horde of kids who come round to watch every evening. They are experts at fetching dropped Frisbees. Every so often, I throw the Frisbee into the seething mass of kids ('Are you ready, kids?'—hence the nickname). It normally ends in a mass stampede with some children being trampled underfoot, but they seem to love it, especially when the Frisbee hits someone in the face.

My fellow UNMOs range from excellent, through nice but ineffectual, to lazy, useless, money-grabbing bastards whose only reason for being here is financial. The UN gives us a generous 'mission subsistence allowance' (= money). That said, the guys from the poorest nations get more money every day from the UN than they do from their own government in a month, so you can't blame them. English is the official UN language here, but more importantly, the only common language with the rebels. Most of my colleagues speak reasonable English, but the combination of poor quality radio communications and bureaucratic levels of report writing mean that as a Brit you are much in demand.

Food is repetitive but healthy enough, and there is ample

opportunity for entertainment. This afternoon we are going to the local 'discotheque' to watch a football match (the final of the Africa Cup of Nations) on a satellite TV as guests of an RUF brigadier (he's a Liberian mercenary with a soft spot for George Weah, who plays for Chelsea, so I stick to talking football, not politics). He looted the TV and generator from Freetown last year. The RUF are supporting Nigeria. Bizarrely, many of the rebels wear the uniforms of Nigerian soldiers they have killed during the civil war, but they don't seem bothered by the double standards . . .

We also have a monkey called Oscar, whose freedom we bought from some local kids. We expected he'd do a runner, but he now lives in a tree by the house and visits regularly.

Communications here are not good—contact with the outside world is via satellite phone at the cheeky rate of $6 per minute. Hopefully someone will have forwarded this to you, but send me an email and I should be able to read it at some stage.

Regards, Phil

Unfortunately, Oscar was not to last much longer. Monkey meat is popular in Sierra Leone (I only tried it once, with salad and pitta bread. Served as a kebab, it was delicious). Some local hunters had shot Oscar's parents, but Oscar had been too small to eat and a group of kids had kept him as a pet. They kept him chained up and used to taunt him cruelly, so the animal-loving Europeans in my team decided to buy his freedom.

Oscar, perhaps lacking a monkey's normal fear of humans, was too friendly for his own good. We found his antics amusing—running into the house, stealing bananas, chasing chickens and the neighbours' kids—but our neighbours didn't and this was to have serious consequences. Eventually, Oscar went too far when he started ripping palm leaves off our neighbours' roof. They threw stones to stop him and he scampered back to his tree. But Oscar had become addicted to damaging the neighbours' roof and, when the stoning stopped, he attacked it with renewed vigour. That evening, he disappeared.

I tasked one of our houseboys, Ibrahim, to do some detective work. The next day he brought grim news. Oscar had paid the ultimate price for vandalism and ended up in the cooking pot. It wasn't worth falling out with the neighbours so we said nothing. For obvious reasons, animal welfare is fairly low down most people's priorities in rebel-held Makeni.

I ALSO HELD the position of chairman of a Cease-fire Monitoring Committee (CMC) in a town called Kabala, two hours' drive north of Makeni. Kabala was still held by the Sierra Leone Army and there was a weekly meeting in which alleged cease-fire violations could be discussed. Each warring faction sent a representative to the meeting: the RUF, the Sierra Leone Army, the Kamajors and the Armed Forces Revolutionary Council (AFRC). Meetings had a tendency to deteriorate into shouting matches, but the deal was, if there was no physical violence during the meeting I'd buy everyone lunch afterwards. This seemed to have the desired effect.

One of the issues that arose concerned the Savage Group, a splinter group of the AFRC commanded by the self-styled 'Colonel Savage', which had been allied to both the Sierra Leone Army and the RUF at various stages. It had now managed to fall out with both, and they were using my meeting to hatch a plot to make the Savage problem 'go away'.

I pointed out that, as the chairman of the CMC, I could not condone a cease-fire violation, at which point the RUF rep, genuinely trying to be helpful, suggested that the problem could be solved without firing a shot. I asked him to elaborate. 'Well, we could club them all to death.'

The RUF, however, were still keen to take matters into their own hands, and over the next few days we started receiving unconfirmed reports of Savage Group attacks against their positions. Whether true or not, it was obvious the reports would give the RUF the justification to counterattack without being seen as the aggressors.

To prevent a massacre, I deployed with Colonel Jim and six other UNMOs to Kabala. We hoped that if we could disarm the Savage Group, we would be allowed to escort them to a demobilisation camp in a safer part of the country. We sent a message to Savage pointing out that if he cooperated with us we could arrange safe passage for him and his followers. If he refused, the RUF would kill him. His group of fighters were now stuck in a village near Kabala between the Sierra Leone Army, who refused to help them, and the RUF. They had nowhere else to run to, but, for two days, Savage and his men fought on.

We sent a series of teams to negotiate, but Savage still refused to cooperate. On the third day it was my turn, and I drove as far as the last Sierra Leone Army checkpoint, then walked across no-man's-land into the village. The Savage Group had been living in the bush for nearly two years and looked like a medieval army. The dishevelled fighters were accompanied by an assortment of camp followers: young women they had abducted as sex slaves, older women as cooks, and children forced to carry ammunition or forage for food.

I was taken to Savage himself, a striking individual with a goatee beard and wraparound sunglasses. He was directing the battle from an armchair, surrounded by bodyguards and a powerful hi-fi system blaring out American rap music. I told him bluntly that I was his last chance. I was prepared to stay for an hour but, once I left, that would be it. Feigning nonchalance, I put my own sunglasses on, took off my shirt and lay down to sunbathe.

We continued this pretence for some minutes. The stalemate was broken when an RPG exploded nearby. The timing was perfect and Savage immediately told me his men would disarm.

We worked late into the night to disarm about 350 combatants. For each weapon handed in, there were also two or three camp followers. These pitiful hangers-on were not entitled to be treated as ex-combatants, but we couldn't just abandon them to their fate, so we agreed to offer them safe passage out of the area as well.

Now that the Savage Group had disarmed, the Sierra Leone Army was prepared to let them enter the relative safety of Kabala. The nearest demobilisation camp was 300 miles away across RUF territory. So a convoy of Indian and Kenyan trucks with an armed escort was dispatched from Freetown to provide the transport we needed, taking nearly three days to reach us.

I enjoyed my enforced sojourn in Kabala as we waited for the trucks to arrive. This town had never fallen to the RUF so we got an inkling of what the country must have been like before the civil war. It was a bustling market town surrounded by stunning hills—impressive granite spires that rose sharply out of the jungle. I decided to lead a small group of ex-combatants on an ascent up one of these peaks. My main motivation was the aesthetic appeal of climbing a beautiful mountain, and as a bonus I found it satisfying to show the lads that there was more to life than fighting.

The last hundred feet beneath the summit involved easy rock-climbing, and I was pleasantly surprised to see that my motley crew of fellow climbers seemed to be enjoying themselves as much as I was. For a few moments we were on the same wavelength, united by the bond of a shared challenge. On the one technical move to overcome a small overhang, I lowered my belt for the others to use as a handhold. As I helped them up the rock face, they were just a group of kids enjoying an adventure. Sadly, they reverted to type when we got back down to Kabala, where they got their fun from banditry.

I asked them to suggest a name for our new peak.

'Savage Mountain,' they proposed after some discussion.

'You can call it that if you like, but the second-highest mountain in the world, K2, is already known as the Savage Mountain,' I told them.

More deliberation.

'OK, then. How about Virgin Blood Ripper Peak?'

I had to concede that it was unlikely another mountain would already have this name.

When the trucks arrived, half the population of Kabala were now claiming to be ex-combatants, wanting to cadge a free lift to Freetown. Men, women, children, goats, chickens and even a small cow squeezed themselves onto the trucks.

The UN had agreed to send a helicopter for Savage and his immediate family as we didn't believe the RUF would have resisted the temptation to do them in, had we taken them through their territory by road. If we'd failed to give Savage the safe passage we had promised him, the message would then have gone around that the UN couldn't protect anybody and it would have become impossible to persuade other rebel commanders to disarm. We gave Savage and his wife a lift to the helicopter landing site in our car and the ungrateful bastard stole my sunglasses off the back seat. In the end, it amused me to think that such an image-conscious individual coveted my £2.99 Woolworths' specs. Finally, we were able to start the truck journey back through RUF territory with our human cargo.

At every town or village along the 300-mile trip, we had to pass through a series of RUF checkpoints. One was commanded by a twelve-year-old rebel called Regimental Sergeant Major Killer. He had been told by his commanders to cooperate, but he was not at all happy with the arrangements. I persuaded him to lower the rope that acted as the barrier at the roadblock and the first couple of trucks drove by unchallenged. Then Killer recognised an old adversary on one of the trucks and started shouting wildly, 'That man, he attack my men!' He ordered his men to pull the rope back across the road, but it was too late for the next truck to stop. The rope caught on the front of the truck, which drove on. Killer's checkpoint was torn to pieces. He went berserk, his anger now directed at me. He unslung his AK 47. I considered grabbing it, then realised there were another ten weapons pointing at me. In the distance I could see some armed Kenyans deploying from one of their trucks.

I tried to speak calmly but with authority in my voice. 'RSM, two days ago the Savage Group were your enemies. I have disarmed them. I am not your enemy. Put your gun down, and we can all live to fight another day.'

Killer did not look totally convinced, but I had introduced an element of doubt. To my relief, the Kenyans slung their rifles over their shoulders and continued approaching us, armed only with broad grins. The moment of danger had passed and yet as I climbed back into my jeep I could feel myself shaking. It had been too close for comfort and it was a relief to finally off-load our human cargo in a demobilisation camp at Lungi, near the international airport.

I had no reason to suspect I would see any of the Savage Group again. Some of them, however, decided to join another militia, the West Side Boys. It was this group of bandits that took some British soldiers hostage a few months later, in September 2000, after I had finished my tour of Sierra Leone. I didn't know any of the British hostages but I did know several of the hostage-takers. I felt no regret when I heard that not all of Savage's men had survived the battle with British Special Forces when the hostages were rescued. I wonder who's wearing my sunglasses now . . .

THE NEXT WEEK I was due some leave, so jumped on a plane to nearby Gambia for a week of pampering with Anna in a five-star hotel. It felt strange being in such luxury, less than two hours' travel from Sierra Leone. I've never been a great one for lying by a pool but this time, for the first time in my life, I was happy to do little else apart from eating, drinking and just being together. Anna had brought my wedding ring out with her from the UK, as taking expensive jewellery to Sierra Leone would not have been sensible, and it felt every bit as special putting it on as it did the day we were wed. Our week flashed by, and before I knew it I was taking my ring off again and saying farewell to Anna.

With only a couple of weeks until my thirtieth birthday, Anna had given me a few presents. Working on the theory that I should only take stuff I was prepared to lose, these included a new pair of Woolworths' sunglasses, several music tapes, a *Father Ted* video and a small can of Heinz baked beans.

Seeing Anna had made me miss her even more than usual, but I felt reinvigorated and was looking forward to pitting my wits against the hard-core RUF once again. So far, our achievements in Makeni had included disarming the Savage Group and 350 child soldiers. But we had not yet disarmed a single mainstream rebel.

By April 2000, nearly 25,000 ex-combatants (from all warring factions except the RUF) had entered the DDR process. But in the RUF strongholds, disarmament had yet to start. Colonel Jim now appointed me as the team's disarmament officer and I felt honoured to be given the responsibility. Makeni was seen as the key to UN success. If the RUF in Makeni could be persuaded to disarm, the rest of their number would follow. Or so we hoped.

6 HOW TO START A CIVIL WAR

During the last days of April, things started to go wrong. After months of painfully slow negotiation—and stalling by the RUF—we had at last finished the construction of a Disarmament, Demobilisation and Reintegration camp, ten miles south of Makeni. We had also persuaded the rebels to allow us to establish a number of temporary reception centres where combatants wanting to disarm would hand over their weapons.

The process was this: a combatant would turn up at a reception centre, hand over his weapon, and be issued with a set of identity papers. From there, they would be taken to a DDR camp for medical screening and rehabilitation. The reception centres had to be separate from the DDR camps, to pre-empt the problems of rival factions fighting each other when some were armed and others weren't.

Our DDR camp and the first reception centre formally opened on April 20, and we dutifully started manning the sites even though, at this stage, there were no ex-combatants to use them. As the team's disarmament officer, it was my job to oversee the reception centre in Makeni itself and to issue documentation to any combatants choosing to disarm. On the first day the DDR camp opened, I helped the Kenyans set up the reception centre. We arranged tents, tables, chairs, sandbags, signposts and a sheltered waiting area where any disarming rebels could enjoy a cup of tea and a biscuit before being transported, minus weapons, to the DDR camp itself.

For a week, we set up our desks every day and waited for our first customers. None came. After all our efforts to build the camp it was an anticlimax that nobody was using it. But I had been feeling rough for a few days and was glad to have some enforced inactivity.

Dealing with the RUF was hard work both physically and mentally,

UNSCATHED

and we were supposed to take a few days off every month to recharge our batteries. I had certainly needed my time away from it all in Gambia. But my team leader, Colonel Jim, had not had a day off since January and looked drained, so we persuaded him to take some long-overdue leave. When he finally took a break, he joked as he left, 'Don't start any civil wars until I get back.' With hindsight, this looked decidedly like tempting fate.

Certain rebel commanders, particularly Colonel Augustine Bao, the RUF's Chief of Security, had started to direct veiled threats at Jim and me, accusing us of being personally responsible for assorted British 'crimes' against the RUF. Our alleged crimes included colonialism, exploitation and tacit support for mercenary organisations, including the British company, Sandline International and a South African set-up, Executive Outcomes. Both organisations had either directly or indirectly been involved in successful military action against the RUF. In RUF eyes, this meant the British had taken sides against them and this was reflected in their attitudes to us personally.

Bao reserved a special loathing for Britain. He had lived for a while in both London and Glasgow and never lost an opportunity to tell us about the abuse he had suffered there. This may have been the case but, when I asked him for examples, the best he could come up with was the 'crime against humanity' committed when he was asked to turn his music down while driving through Peckham in south London. Hardly worth going to war over, I thought.

Colonel Jim appointed Major Ganase, a Malaysian, as his deputy while he was away and asked me to help keep things on track. It would have been one conspiracy theory too far to have put me in charge.

On the day Jim left, however, I had another preoccupation. What had started as a dull headache and general lethargy was getting progressively worse. After a few days, the pain became so intense it was hard to think about anything else. Someone suggested I might have malaria, but I had been taking my weekly Larium antimalarial pills religiously and thought I probably just had bad flu. Larium, however, is only 95 per cent effective and I was destined to be one of the unlucky 5 per cent. I struggled on for a couple of days and went through the motions of going to work, but my headache felt like every hangover I'd ever had rolled into one. The racking pain made me feel sick and I was finding it hard to eat. A colleague took me to the Kenyan Battalion HQ to see their medical officer, who did some tests before confirming I had malaria. He pumped me full of drugs, and cheerfully told me I had the sort of malaria that either goes away quickly—and stays away—or kills you. 'So just take it easy for a couple of days,' he suggested.

I asked whether I should come back and see him again. 'Not much point,' he observed, with typical Kenyan pragmatism.

I spent the rest of the day being violently sick (a side effect of the medicine) but then started to feel much better. Clearly the medicine was having an effect, but also I had found a colleague who was even worse off than me. Andy Samsonoff, another British UNMO who had recently joined the Magburaka team down the road, had just been released from hospital after a bout of typhoid. We compared medical notes and, as Andy drily pointed out, at least I was only losing bodily fluids from one end of my body. It's always reassuring when there's someone feeling rougher than you.

ON SEVERAL OCCASIONS, small groups of rebels had come either to the reception centre or our team house to find out more about the DDR process. Initially, however, I suggested they go away and wait until they received formal orders from their commanders to start disarming. Considering the low opinion that rebel commanders such as Bao already had of me, I was not keen to add 'incitement to mutiny' to their list of grievances. In any case, the government of Sierra Leone was planning to open six new DDR camps simultaneously across the country on May 1: two for the RUF, two for the CDF and two for former Sierra Leone Army soldiers. On the same day the Sierra Leone Army itself would also return its weapons to its armouries in a show of solidarity. We guessed the RUF at large would be unlikely to disarm before then.

On April 29, my thirtieth birthday, ten rebels approached me and asked to disarm. I hoped they would set a precedent for others to follow, but still thought it unwise to proceed until the local commanders gave their approval. I was not the only one with such concerns. These were shared by the Kenyan commanding officer, the next-door Magburaka UNMO team and Fergus, the leader of the DfID team, who knew the rebels better than anyone. Fergus was the site manager for construction of the DDR camp. He was a big, red-haired Irishman who could out-talk, out-smoke and out-drink almost anyone. A canny operator, he could play the anti-British card to great effect with the rebel commanders, and they had a soft spot for him.

The UN headquarters, however, did not see things as we did. They considered it a risk worth taking to start disarming people in Makeni. I suspected we in Makeni better understood the likely reaction of the local RUF commanders, and our formal written report that day was blunt: 'If we proceed as instructed, we risk provoking a violent reaction from the RUF without the military capacity to contain it.'

Our protestations were overridden and that afternoon I dutifully disarmed the ten rebels and issued them with their new ID papers. They were apprehensive, and understandably so. Most of them had had to smuggle their weapons past RUF checkpoints and would have been executed had they been caught.

We knew the local commanders would be upset, but hoped their anger would not turn violent. As I manned my desk in the reception centre that day, I noted in a letter home that 'if this leads to large-scale RUF disarmament, it'll be a pretty cool birthday present'. I never had the chance to post this letter—it was soon stolen by the rebels along with all my other belongings.

During the morning of April 30, the Kenyans took the ten ex-combatants by truck to the DDR camp for registration and medical screening. We had tried to keep the disarmament low key—there was no point in publicly humiliating the local commanders. But that afternoon, Colonel Bao, another hard-liner called Colonel Kallon and several hundred rebels turned up at the DDR camp. They quickly surrounded the camp and the Kenyan platoon guarding it.

I had been on duty at the DDR camp during the morning, and a few minutes before the rebel mob arrived, I had returned to the team house in Makeni for lunch. For me, this mundane fact turned out to be a lifesaving twist of fate. I had actually passed Colonel Bao as I left the DDR camp and waved cheerily to him as I drove past. He scowled and shouted at me, but as he did this every time he saw me, I thought nothing of it. Little did I know, as I nonchalantly ate pasta with my teammates from the morning shift, that the afternoon shift was being taken hostage.

There was an armed stand-off. Then, as negotiations broke down, the rebels seized Major Ganase, our Malaysian acting team leader, and a number of Kenyans. Bao was incensed that his men had disobeyed his orders by disarming. Unable to punish the ten 'deserters', who had unsurprisingly legged it into the bush, he had decided to take brutal revenge on his UN tormentors instead.

At the DDR camp, the remaining Kenyans and another UNMO (a Bangladeshi called Salah Uddin) spent the night on a knife-edge, surrounded and heavily outnumbered. Back in Makeni, we knew things were going wrong from the initial situation reports sent on the radio. These ended abruptly, though, when the rebels seized the UN vehicles that were fitted with radios. In an attempt to find out what was going on, an increasingly worried UN HQ in Freetown ordered us to send another negotiating team to meet the rebel commanders. I was about to drive down to the rebels' HQ when a message came through from the ops room that I was wanted on the telephone. So my place was taken by a Norwegian officer. He was accompanied by a Gambian lieutenant-colonel. Neither man returned.

As the Norwegian was being snatched, he managed to press TRANSMIT on a radio he had hidden in his daysack. We listened in horror as he and his companion were badly beaten up, stripped naked, trussed up with wire and sexually assaulted. When the rebels found the hidden radio they went mad and the two men's screams became even more desperate as they begged for mercy. The screaming ended with a burst of automatic fire and we assumed the worst, but we later discovered the rebels had been playing mind games. Our colleagues had been 'lucky': they were not killed, but were to endure three weeks of hell. The Norwegian officer, a white man, was staked out naked in the sun for twelve hours a day and was badly burnt. The Gambian lost a leg. They were eventually released in a deal brokered by Liberia.

The Kenyans, bravely, also sent parties to negotiate with the rebels. They too did not return.

I felt particularly vulnerable—the RUF saw Britain as the root of all evils in Sierra Leone. Moreover, as a commando, my slaying would be good for rebel street cred. To cap it all, it was my signature on the rebels' disarmament forms.

Of our team of fourteen, four were now missing, including Ganase, the acting team leader. Four others were on leave or back in Freetown, including Colonel Jim and Igor. Six of us remained.

That night, the rebels reinforced their positions on the routes out of the town and closed the roads. We were now effectively trapped. Reports from other parts of the country made depressing listening. Hostages had been taken in numerous locations, including British Army Major Andy Harrison, who coincidentally was my next-door neighbour back in London. Meanwhile, Foday Sankoh, the RUF leader, was cranking up the propaganda machine, claiming the UN had attacked his men and forced them to disarm.

More and more rebels were now arriving in the town from nearby villages, and their excitement was tangible. We could hear intermittent gunfire from the town centre (an indication of high spirits) as well as chanting and singing. Groups of rebels on foot or in pick-up trucks continually patrolled past our house, firing occasional bursts of gunfire to test our reaction. We bolted the doors and windows and I prepared a 'grab bag' of emergency gear—food, water and a satellite phone—in case we had to make a run for it.

No one in the UN HQ in Freetown seemed to be taking our deteriorating security situation seriously. It was exasperating, to put it mildly, to be told over the radio that 'everything was calm' and we should stop making a fuss. Bizarrely, even some of the five UNMOs still with me were refusing to acknowledge that we were in serious trouble. One of them asked me whether we would go on patrol the following morning as he wanted to buy some cigarettes in town!

I didn't want to escalate the situation, and told the six Kenyan armed guards to keep a low profile. They should return fire only if we actually came under 'effective enemy fire' (that is, if one of us was struck by a bullet or clearly about to be shot). The RUF could easily have brought a lynch mob of heavily armed rebels to storm our house, and I didn't want to provoke them or give them the excuse that we had 'attacked' them. I hoped that everything would calm down in the morning. But the omens were not looking good.

The thirty-strong platoon of Kenyans back at the DDR camp had managed to assemble a working radio. They were still surrounded and the rebels were repeating their threats to attack if the ten 'deserters' were not handed over. Morally and legally, the UN had a duty to protect all ex-combatants who had disarmed in good faith, but these ex-combatants had long gone.

A surreal interlude occurred when RUF Colonel Sherif and his deputy, Lieutenant-Colonel Alfred Jimmy, came to the house and asked to speak to me. I had come to know these guys quite well from the Cease-fire Monitoring Committee. I trusted them enough to let them come in for a chat.

Sherif was looking worried. He told me there had been 'a terrible mistake and misunderstanding'. He told me that Bao and Kallon had become loose cannons and that it was not RUF policy to take UN personnel hostage. To protect himself, Bao had told the RUF leader Foday Sankoh that the UN had attacked his men and forced them to disarm at gunpoint.

Sherif thought he might be able to persuade Sankoh that Bao and Kallon had been lying to him, so I let him use our satphone to call his leader. Sherif spoke to Sankoh himself, but his protestations were in vain. Sankoh preferred to believe what the hard-liners were telling him. Even if Sherif and Jimmy had been sidelined by the other rebel commanders, I still thought it worthwhile staying in their good books, so I offered them a beer. I was too preoccupied to make small talk, so suggested we watch a video. Unfortunately the only videos the team had were violent war movies—*Rambo I, II* and *III* and *Terminator*. This did not seem the ideal moment to glamorise violence, especially with trigger-happy bodyguards trying to peer in through the windows. So instead, I dug out the *Father Ted* video that Anna had given me as a birthday present. I don't think my RUF companions got many of the jokes but it seemed to help calm things down a bit. Before Sherif left, he warned us that we should leave the town. I asked him how. He shrugged his shoulders. Did he know of any plans to attack us? 'Tomorrow, I think. Watch out for Bao. He has special plans for you.'

'You mean he's going to look after me as an honoured guest?'

'No, I mean he's going to eat you.'

Ah. As conversation stoppers go, this was hard to beat. Sherif wished me good luck and left, and I spent a long, nervous night on radio watch, unable to think of much apart from being Bao's lunch.

The next day, May 1, the cease-fire came to a spectacular end at the DDR camp. Shortly after first light, a huge mob of rebels forced their way in on the pretext of 'liberating' their ten colleagues who had been 'forced' to disarm. While searching the camp, they looted everything and set the buildings on fire. Within minutes they had destroyed what had taken four months to build. The Kenyan platoon and Salah Uddin, the Bangladeshi, took up a hasty defensive position among their trucks. Colonel Bao now demanded that the Kenyans hand over Salah Uddin. They refused, and the rebels attacked. The Kenyan platoon, by now outnumbered by about twenty to one, stood little chance. We heard the fire-fight, then the Kenyan radio operator's final message: 'We are being overrun.'

Then silence, and we assumed the worst.

Friendly civilians now came to warn us that we were to be next.

We had just six armed men guarding our house. The nearest Kenyan company position (normally 100 strong), 'A' Company, was only 800 yards from our house.

We needed to reach 'A' Company but the house was being watched and it would be hard to slip out undetected. We had to create a diversion, and quickly. It wouldn't take long for Colonel Bao and his lynch mob to reach us from the DDR camp.

An idea struck me. A Canadian park ranger once told me how to survive a grizzly bear attack: just take off your backpack and calmly walk away. The bear will be more interested in eating your sandwiches than in eating you. I'd never had the chance to try it with a grizzly bear, but reckoned the same principle might apply to the rebels. So, leaving some expensive-looking kit unguarded at the front of the house, we slipped out the back. To my relief it worked, as the rebels who should have intercepted us were too busy stealing our belongings to bother giving chase. We lost our TV, video and fridge, but not our lives. Adrenaline pumping, we legged it towards the Kenyan company position. Ten minutes after we abandoned the house, the rest of the rampaging RUF mob arrived, fired up from their victory at the DDR camp. We had moved just in time.

7   SURROUNDED

It was a great relief to make it into the Kenyans' defended compound and, for a moment, we felt safe. But our new predicament was only marginally better than our last one. 'A' Company's position was a small compound, 100 by 150 yards, surrounded by a six-foot mudbrick wall. The seventy Kenyan soldiers there were armed with powerful rifles but had only 100 rounds of ammunition each. Their company commander was missing, along with thirty men—the platoon that had been on duty at the DDR camp.

The compound was an old Catholic mission, consisting of a small chapel and three derelict buildings. Apart from the chapel, which was still in a good state of repair, the roofs of all the buildings had either collapsed or been burnt. The soldiers were spread thinly around the perimeter wall in two-man trenches, with machine guns at three of the four corners.

The company second-in-command, Captain Moses Korir, had taken over and was coping admirably. I offered what assistance I could—moral support and technical advice—and we did as much as possible to improve the position. Our resources were limited, though. We had very little food, water or medical supplies, no barbed wire or sandbags, and almost non-existent fields of fire (the areas our weapons could cover). The mudbrick wall was a mixed blessing. Although it made it harder for the rebels to see in, it also made it near impossible to see out. Initially, the Kenyans were reduced to sticking their heads up over the wall. With their helmets painted bright blue (the UN colour) this made them ideal targets. From the rebel perspective, shooting Kenyans must have felt like playing an arcade game. So we cut some holes in the wall, enabling the Kenyan soldiers to stay in the relative safety of their trenches.

Furthermore, the compound was completely surrounded by houses and trees, making it very easy for rebels to approach right up to the perimeter. Ironically, the UN HQ itself had earlier refused the Kenyans permission to improve their own defences, as barbed wire and sandbags were considered 'too aggressive'.

As far as I was concerned, our unarmed observer status was now academic. Some of my colleagues, however, thought otherwise and still considered their best means of self-preservation was to dissociate themselves from the armed Kenyans. In any event, I threw my lot in with the soldiers and helped them improve their defences. We managed to site their three machine guns more effectively, and clear some vegetation to improve the fields of fire.

On the bright side, from my point of view, the Magburaka team of UNMOs was also seeking refuge in the compound, including some other Brits: Lieutenant-Commander Paul Rowland, Major Dave Lingard and Major Andy Samsonoff (my recent fellow invalid).

Paul Rowland was one of the most highly trained officers in the Royal Navy. Unfortunately, his speciality was nuclear engineering . . . He was also a talented orienteer and very fit. Like me, he was tall and skinny and all the locals were convinced we were brothers. They saw him as mildly eccentric, as he had a policy of walking everywhere with a large black umbrella. It kept the rain off him in the wet season, the sun off him in the dry season and ensured he looked faintly ridiculous in all seasons.

Dave Lingard was only an honorary Brit (a dubious honour in the circumstances), as he was really a New Zealand army signals officer. Unfortunately for him, though, the rebels didn't appreciate that New Zealand was separate from the United Kingdom. He had soon realised that playing the 'non-aligned Kiwi' card would not work with the RUF, so had little option but to join us.

Andy Samsanoff, a light infantry officer, was normally a fit, strong guy, but he was still run-down from the aftereffects of his illness. He had not been in the Makeni area for long. For the previous three months he had been working in Moyamba, a relatively safe, pro-government part of the country. Thoroughly bored, he had hassled our boss to send him to a more 'interesting' area. We now congratulated him on his timing.

Sitting in the compound, the four of us had a quick confab and all reached the same conclusion: it would be better to do something positive than simply do nothing and wait for the worst to happen. Some of the other UNMOs had now become fatalistic and were suffering from terror-induced lethargy. They were just sitting around, staring into space, waiting for the end.

As a Royal Marines commando, I was fortunate to enjoy considerable respect from the Kenyans. Most of them had trained alongside British soldiers on exercise in Kenya, where the British Army maintains a training base near Nairobi. Lightheartedly, I suggested that now was a good time to demonstrate their renowned bravery and I would be 'right behind them' if they chose to take on the RUF. They returned the compliment but said that as a commando I should lead from the front and they would be right behind me. We compromised and sensibly stayed exactly where we were.

Military historians and psychologists have repeatedly noted that well-trained and well-led soldiers are often more scared of letting down their colleagues than of injury and death. I'd always been rather sceptical and wondered whether it would really work that way in practice, but I began to see what they meant. None of us, either Kenyans or Brits, really considered the UN mission important enough to die for, but it would have been inconceivable to let each other down by going to pieces or giving up.

As night fell, the rebels started to attack. Under cover of darkness, they first encircled our position, then began rhythmic drumming and chanting. I crawled up to the wall and everywhere I looked there appeared to be a solid mass of rebels. I tried not to think too hard about Sherif's final words to me, warning me about Bao's special plans. The rebels were trying to terrorise us, and they succeeded. I did my best to stay calm outwardly, but inwardly I was terrified. I wondered what it would feel like to die and hoped it would be swift. I hoped I could keep my dignity if it was not. I cannot describe the impotence I felt without a weapon in my hands.

I found myself a stand-to position in the front Kenyan trench and hoped that if any of my trenchmates was killed I could pick up his rifle and keep shooting. The Brit UNMOs did likewise, while the others huddled together in the chapel, trying to convince themselves they could simply declare their unarmed observer status when the rebels overran the position. I didn't share their optimism. In the dark the rebels would, at the very least, shoot first and ask questions later. Andy, Paul, Dave and I agreed to stick together, whatever happened.

I had no idea how many rebels were attacking us—most likely several hundred, but in the darkness it seemed like thousands. The distinctive crack and thump of incoming rifle fire is disconcerting, but we could hear the noise of bullets cutting at supersonic speed through the air above our heads, so we knew that the rebels were aiming high. I guessed they must have been shooting over the wall so, as long as we kept our heads down, we were relatively safe. The Kenyans kept their nerve and, in contrast to their poorly trained adversaries, proved to be good shots. As the rebels started to sustain casualties, they seemed less keen to put themselves in the danger zone and the attack began to peter out.

The rebels then appeared to choose the easier option of starving us out. A sporadic gunfight continued throughout the night and on and off for the next four days. With the proximity of the rebels and incoming fire, sleep and rest were impossible. I tried lying down on the concrete floor of the chapel, shutting my eyes and trying to nod off, but I soon realised I wasn't really resting and would be better off keeping myself busy. So I spent my time walking or crawling round the position, encouraging the Kenyan soldiers and trying to ascertain the rebels' positions, numbers and tactics.

I was crouching in an isolated trench with two Kenyans, shortly before first light, when I heard something landing in the bushes nearby. A hand grenade? Ten seconds and no explosion. I crawled over to investigate. I couldn't initially see what it was in the darkness so I picked it up. It was a freshly severed human hand. I decided not to tell the others, but confided in the Kenyan sergeant major. He told me that I was not the only one to come across severed body parts that night, but he had told his men to keep it to themselves so as not to create panic.

For that first night, I kept my Kevlar body armour and combat helmet on as I crawled around, but discarded them in the morning when I realised how much they were making me sweat. Water was going to be scarce, and I knew that dehydration would be as big a threat as gunfire. Makeni is the hottest part of Sierra Leone and May is the hottest month of the year. With the dry season coming to an end, the combination of heat and humidity was crippling. Under the midday sun, the temperature was well over a hundred degrees and even at night rarely dropped beneath ninety. I was glad I had stubbornly refused the luxury of air conditioning in the preceding months.

There was a well in one corner of the compound but, like the well outside our house, it needed filling once a week by water tanker. We estimated how much water was left in the well and started rationing straight away. Each man would drink no more than one litre per day—much less than we would need in the extreme heat but better than nothing, and it would keep us going for three or four days. We hoped this would be enough time for someone to come and help us. I remembered the recommended intake of fluid as laid out in the *Staff Officer's Handbook* for tropical conditions: eight to nine litres a day.

Just after first light, a Kenyan soldier carrying a badly injured colleague ran through the rebel cordon and into the compound. The rebels were clearly expecting the cordon to prevent people leaving the compound, not entering it. The man, Sergeant Stephen Nyamohanga, and his colleague, were from the platoon attacked at the DDR camp. The platoon commander had ordered his men to attempt a fighting withdrawal into the jungle. Sergeant Nyamohanga didn't know how far they had got. But as their position in the DDR was being overrun, he bravely chose to stay behind with an injured corporal. The corporal had been shot through the thigh and had had his right arm almost ripped off by an RPG. Nyamohanga somehow managed to stop the man bleeding to death and to hide from the rebels until dusk. Overnight, he carried his mate nearly fifteen miles through rebel-held territory to reach Makeni, before breaking in through the cordon.

Both men survived. After witnessing an act of heroism like this, nobody in our compound was going to give up without a fight.

FOR THE FIRST TWO DAYS of the siege, the surrounding town was in anarchy, with rebels running riot, looting, raping and pillaging. Hearing this was bad enough, but being powerless to stop it was far worse. The rebels started using acts of atrocity as bait, to try to lure us out of the relative safety of the compound. Their first ploy was rape. The screams of their victims normally went on all night, but sometimes ended abruptly with a gunshot. Some of the Kenyans had struck up relationships with local girls and they must have found it even harder to listen to the distressed—and distressing—cries.

I thought the surrounding anarchy might offer the distraction needed to attempt to escape. I asked the UN HQ for permission to attempt to lead a break-out, but was refused. My immediate boss in the UN was coincidentally another Royal Marine, Colonel Peter Babbington, MC. A tough, no-nonsense individual, he had won his Military Cross as a company commander in the Falklands War. I knew he wouldn't be put off making tough decisions if needed, and he was a source of immense strength. On one occasion, I was talking to him on the satphone as an attack started and it was looking like the rebels were about to break into the compound. In desperation, I asked him what to do.

'Stand and fight!' was his firm response.

'But, sir, we don't have any weapons,' I whined.

'Don't fuck about, man. Stand and fight anyway!' he commanded.

If the colonel was telling us to stay where we were, I knew it would be for a good reason. A massive diplomatic effort was under way. President Kabbah, other West African heads of state and even UN Secretary General Kofi Annan were lobbying Foday Sankoh hard to order his men to stop. Incredibly, though, Sankoh was still denying that the RUF had done anything wrong, and dismissing reports of UN casualties and hostage-takings as government propaganda. It was exasperating to listen to his denials being broadcast on the World Service, but there was nothing we could do about it.

While the diplomats were trying to defuse the situation, a battalion of Zambian UN troops was tasked to relieve our siege. Their orders had been ridiculously vague and they were poorly equipped. I had a horrible feeling that sending them in would just escalate the situation but, once again, our advice on the ground was ignored. So the Zambians started towards Makeni, with 500 soldiers and twenty-five armoured cars. On paper, this was a strong and well-armed unit. But in years of civil war, the RUF had learned how to ambush armoured columns. The road to Makeni, though tarmac, was narrow with jungle on both sides, so only the front vehicle in the column could engage targets ahead. In effect, the firepower of twenty-five armoured cars was reduced to one. To confuse things further, the Zambians had terrible communications.

We listened to the Zambians' progress on the UN command net. This was an insecure radio net, meaning anybody who had a suitable radio could listen in, including the RUF. The Zambians' advance started well enough. When they entered RUF territory and reached the first checkpoints, they were waved straight through. I knew it would not be that easy. My suspicions grew when the Kenyan 'D' Company, on the north side of Makeni, reported that they had seen several trucks of armed rebels moving west on a road parallel to the main Lunsar–Makeni road. From there it would be easy to swing south to reach the main road. If I had been planning to ambush the Zambians, this would have been my route.

Finally, the Zambians were stopped at a village called Makoth,

just twelve miles west of Makeni, and reported that they were negotiating with the checkpoint commander. Eventually, a 'compromise'
was reached. The rebels were claiming that it had all been 'a terrible
misunderstanding' and invited the Zambian commanding officer
and his entourage to drive into Makeni to discuss 'arrangements'
with the local commanders. The rebels politely asked the Zambians
to send only a small group, 'so as not to scare the locals'. We heard
the Zambian vehicles driving past our position and tried to shout a
warning to them, but they couldn't hear us over the noise of their
vehicles. We tried to raise them on the radio but they could use their
radios only when their vehicles were stationary.

Weeks later, we found out what had happened. The Zambian commanding officer and his three armoured cars drove right into the
rebel HQ and the gates were shut behind them. Suddenly, a huge
mob rushed out of the surrounding buildings. The Zambians were
pulled from their vehicles, stripped and tied up.

Back at the main convoy, after three hours had passed, the
Zambian second-in-command decided to lead another recce party to
Makeni. As before, the rebels were cooperative so long as the
Zambians only sent a small group. We heard the sound of more
armoured cars approaching on the main road and we made a snap
decision to try to warn them. We grabbed a group of Kenyans and
ran out of the compound towards the road. I was about to flag down
the approaching convoy when I noticed that the lead vehicle was
swarming with rebels. The Zambians were nowhere to be seen. We
only just made it back into the compound before the rebels cut us off.

The main Zambian column had no idea what was going on. They
had lost their CO and second-in-command and all their radios, so
stayed where they were. The RUF now forced the Zambian CO to sign
a letter ordering his men to advance towards Makeni in small groups.
He initially refused, even when tortured. The rebels then took one of
the Zambian soldiers and skinned him alive. The CO now signed.

The rebels delivered the letter to the main body of the Zambians,
who were relieved to receive formal orders. So, yet again, the column
split into smaller groups and headed for Makeni. And yet again they
were systematically ambushed and taken prisoner.

Back in our compound, we watched, incredulous but helpless, as
truckload after truckload of Zambian prisoners was driven past our
position. I felt I was trapped in a farce—if it wasn't so serious, it
would have been funny. Morale sank. We were now on our own.

Sadly, the RUF were then able to deceive some UN troops.

Dressed as Zambians, and driving in Zambian vehicles, they advanced towards Freetown. Having driven unopposed up to a UN checkpoint, it was easy for them to surprise and overpower the UN troops and take them prisoner or execute them. With poor communications, not all outposts were warned off in time and the Nigerian units to our west lost several positions in this way.

OVER THE NEXT three days we held out, with a constant feeling that we were only seconds from a violent death. Being constantly frightened is physically very tiring, as the adrenaline makes your heart beat quickly so you use considerable nervous energy even if you're just sitting around.

Of course, there were moments of humour. On the third day, for example, the Kenyans decided to cook their remaining food. When the cry went up that dinner was served, the Kenyans, almost to a man, rushed to the mess tent. I started shouting at them not to leave their posts at the same time, but their sergeant major took me aside and calmed me down. 'Don't worry,' he said, 'this is Africa. The rebels will be eating too and won't attack until later.' Luckily, he was right.

Fergus and his colleagues from DfID had also taken refuge in the same compound. They had an alternative coping strategy—huge quantities of marijuana. I was more than a little jealous as they sat in their jeep, stoned out of their heads, giggling maniacally as the bullets flew overhead.

On the third day of the siege, we received more bad news on the satphone: Foday Sankoh's bodyguards had shot twenty-five unarmed civilians at a rally in Freetown. In the ensuing chaos, Sankoh himself had escaped into the bush. Diplomacy had failed.

On the same day, General Issah, the RUF military field commander who lived in Makeni, personally tightened up the rebel cordon around our compound and imposed a curfew on civilian and rebel movement at night. This would make any attempt to escape considerably harder. Ironically, the advice now came through from Colonel Babbington: 'Attempt to escape.'

I felt bitter that we had been refused permission to attempt an escape earlier, yet were now being encouraged to do just that when the circumstances were less favourable.

I didn't rate our chances too highly of making it out alive if we tried to break out through the cordon, and told Colonel Babbington so.

'Sir, if I told you I thought we had a twenty per cent chance of making it through the cordon, what would your advice be?'

'Go for it!'

The inferred message was sobering. Shit, I thought. He thinks we're all going to be butchered. Colonel Bao knew by this stage that the UK was considering a military response to help out the UN. The RUF's anti-British persecution complex was bad enough already. If British troops started arriving in Sierra Leone and fighting against the rebels, any pretence at British neutrality would disappear. The rebels would not be able to do much about that, but they could direct their anger at us. Although the UK might be able to save UNAMSIL from collapsing, we were likely to be the sacrificial lambs. And like many retreating armies in war, the RUF's worst atrocities had always occurred when they were about to lose militarily.

Tensions continued to rise the following day when a rebel 'delegation' sent a message to the Kenyans that their safety would be guaranteed if they handed over the British UNMOs. 'Brother Africans, we have no fight with you. Hand over the white men and you can go free. Refuse, and we will kill you all.'

The Kenyan sergeant major took me to one side and quietly told me the bad news. Again, I decided not to tell the others. The Kenyans had already proved that they were prepared to fight and die to protect Military Observers, but I felt that, morally, this put unreasonable pressure on them. I knew that we, as British officers, would have to escape or die trying. I also knew that once the food and water were gone, our reserves of strength would rapidly diminish. It would have to be tonight or never. The Kenyans reckoned they could go a few more days on iron rations. Half of them were Masai tribesmen, for whom drought and famine were almost a way of life, but I doubted that we Europeans could hold out much longer. By making a break for it now, we would be maximising what little chance we had.

I had repeatedly asked the Kenyans for a rifle but there were not enough to go round, even for Kenyan soldiers, so my requests were turned down. Our UK bosses would have backed us if we'd chosen to steal weapons from the Kenyans. It would have been easy enough to steal Captain Korir's pistol from him when I saw him sleeping at his desk in the ops room, but I could not do it. And it would have been easier still to have stolen a rifle off one of the badly injured Kenyans in the sickbay. But, again, I couldn't bring myself to do this. At least we would have some chance of running away, but the wounded would have none.

We decided not to tell the Kenyans officially what we intended to do, as I thought they would try to stop us. I suspect the sergeant major knew what our intentions were, but he kept his silence.

I prayed for rain but nature was not on our side. In the distance I could see thunderclouds and sometimes even lightning, but Makeni was enjoying perfect weather. The clouds stayed agonisingly far away and I felt the full moon and stars were mocking us.

Our escape plan was simple. I had identified a possible blind spot at the northwest corner of the compound. We would climb over the wall at this point, attempt to run through the cordon, make our way out of the town and into the jungle, then head for Mile 91, the nearest UN-held town. Mile 91 was about fifty miles away as the crow flies, most of this distance in rebel-held territory. The jungle in this part of Sierra Leone had been cleared in places for agriculture, and there were numerous small villages and farms and lots of people. Many would be civilians, but the RUF would have personnel in most of the settlements. This meant that it would be impossible to move during the day if we wanted to remain undetected. We would move only at night and lie low during daylight.

It would be like walking from London to Brighton in total darkness, with almost no food or drink, through thick vegetation in what would feel like a sauna, doing our best to avoid the locals. Fifty miles as the crow flies could easily become 150 miles on the ground. I reckoned it might take us a week.

I confided in Fergus and felt guilty that we were abandoning him. As Fergus candidly observed, though, we were more of the problem than the solution. He had decided he would risk his luck the following day with the rebels and try to talk or bribe his way out. I asked if his group would prefer to try their luck with us. He didn't think they would be strong enough physically to cope, so turned down the offer. We wished each other luck.

Having already abandoned most of our kit, we would take:

- one litre of water each (saved for the occasion)
- a few scraps of bread and my small tin of baked beans
- 1:500,000 map—one-tenth of the scale of a standard UK Ordnance Survey map (1 cm on the map represented 5 km on the ground)
- a compass
- Andy's handheld GPS (Global Positioning System)
- a small first-aid kit
- handheld water filters, plus iodine and purifying tablets

PAUL WAS ADAMANT he would take his camera. This was not as frivolous as it might appear. The rebels loved posing and showing off. On more than one occasion, the simple act of getting the camera out was enough to turn potentially hostile villagers into our best friends.

I would carry the satphone. Satphones are about the same size and shape as a laptop computer. Like a laptop, they are not very tough and the batteries tend to run out at inopportune moments.

I used the satphone to pass details of our intended escape and evasion route to Colonel Jim, our absent team leader, who was stuck in Freetown. Jim told me that he thought Freetown might be about to fall to the RUF, who were advancing rapidly towards the capital.

As the sun set, I made three calls back to the UK. First, I spoke to my dad, and thanked him for being such a great father. I wanted to speak to my mother but didn't, so as not to worry her. My father told me he loved me and wished me luck and I briefly went to pieces.

Next I phoned Dan Bailey—an old mate from commando training. I told him my preferred funeral arrangements. I didn't mind where I was buried, but asked for some rousing hymns and a happy send-off. I also asked him to make sure Anna was OK if we didn't make it. Dan pointed out I had started speaking like a corny Hollywood war movie, so we went on to discuss the football scores.

Lastly, a fifteen-minute conversation with Anna. I tried to sound upbeat but had to admit that it might be goodbye. I couldn't think of enough ways to tell her how much I loved her and it was hard to hang up. Our final message to each other was the same: 'Take care of yourself. I love you.'

I felt relieved to have spoken to her. I don't know what it feels like to die but it would have been unbearable not to have said farewell.

8 ON THE RUN

If you stay up all night (without chemical assistance, that is) you feel at your lowest ebb at about four o'clock in the morning. We had to take advantage of this. Adrenaline was making us feel wide awake, despite our own lack of sleep, but I hoped many of the rebels surrounding us would be groggy enough to give us a chance of sneaking past them. If we waited until four o'clock, though, we would have less than two hours before daybreak to make it out of the town and into the relative safety of the jungle. This would not give us enough time. Three o'clock would have to do.

With half an hour to go, we checked our kit and talked through our escape plan one final time. I made everyone jump up and down to check their kit didn't rattle. We then used charcoal from a fire to blacken our faces. Dave had recently been paid and had $1,000 in cash. We split this between us in case we were separated. Finally, we ripped the UN badges off our uniforms. These bright blue badges are a symbol of UN neutrality and are supposed to guarantee the safety of the person who wears them, but all they were going to do for us was to make us show up more easily in the dark. As we removed the badges, we were abandoning our last symbol of neutrality. We would no longer be observers. From now on, despite being unarmed, we were combatants.

Dave and I shared a last cigarette, to calm our nerves, and then another one. With possible life expectancy down to thirty minutes, I didn't worry too much about the long-term health implications.

At 2.45, we had no more preparations to make and there seemed little point in waiting any longer. I suggested we go early and the others agreed. As quietly as possible, we crept over to the northwest corner of the compound. I propped a chair against the wall, to make it easier to climb over. We had agreed not to tell Captain Korir what we were up to. He might have stopped us. So, instead, I briefed the corporal whose men would cover us. He objected, and told us not to go anywhere until he had checked with his boss.

I did my best to sound confident: 'Corporal, I have been ordered by my government to attempt to escape. As you are Kenyan, I cannot order you to help. So I'm asking you as a brother-in-arms. We're going to try to make it through the cordon. If you see any movement from the rebel positions, please tell your men to give us covering fire.'

He said nothing, but I decided to interpret this as tacit agreement.

I whispered a few final words to the others. 'Good luck, guys. Stay close behind me.' Then I climbed over the wall into no-man's-land.

Things started to go wrong straight away. I dropped off the wall, waited . . . and waited. Suddenly, one of the Kenyans, perhaps half-asleep, cocked his weapon and started shouting. Maybe he thought we were RUF. Clearly this was not the low-profile start we were after. I could see some rebels moving. I hoped they couldn't see me.

I thought about climbing back over the wall. Maybe escape wasn't such a good idea—or we could just try later? But, in my heart, I knew it was now or never. As I crouched there in front of the wall, I felt horribly exposed. I willed the others to hurry up. But they were having problems of their own. On the 'safe' side of the wall, one of the Kenyans had pointed his rifle in Andy's face, and had threatened to shoot him if he climbed over the wall. I then recognised the voice of the sentry I had sat next to for three hours earlier that night, and heard him put in a good word for us. It seemed to make the difference, and the others eventually managed to calm the soldier down.

Paul was next. Despite being frightened, I couldn't help smiling as he managed to snag his webbing belt on top of the wall. For a few seconds he dangled inelegantly with his legs kicking in the air before freeing himself. Dave and Andy then clambered over as quietly as they could. In the still night air, though, even the slightest noise would signal our presence.

We were now irreversibly committed.

'Everyone OK? Right, follow me.'

From early-morning runs during the previous few months, I knew the backstreets and footpaths of Makeni well. I had created a map in my head and now I had to follow it.

We had decided a fast walking pace would offer the best compromise of speed and stealth, but it was difficult to resist the temptation to run. I regretted this as I rounded the first building and ran face first into a barbed-wire fence, cutting my eye and mouth. Out of the corner of my eye, I could make out someone moving at the nearest rebel position. I tensed up, expecting incoming fire.

None came. Perhaps they thought we were a rebel patrol, or just chose 'not to see us' in case we won the ensuing fire-fight. For a split second, I looked into the nearest rebel's eyes, then glanced away and kept going. My guardian angel must have been having a late night.

At every corner and behind every building as we wove through the town, I expected to run into a rebel ambush. Several times we saw rebel patrols but shied away from them before they could work out who we were. Everything seemed eerily quiet—the loudest noise was our own breathing. I could even hear my own heart beating. All my senses felt highly tuned and, with every step, my fear seemed to turn to exhilaration. I felt more alive than I ever had before and enjoyed a surge of primeval strength. Now totally committed, I was surprised to feel strangely calm. For a few moments, I felt almost invincible, both physically and psychologically. If a rebel tried to stop me now, I was sure I would kill him with my bare hands, even if he shot me.

I used an old radio mast on the outskirts of town to orientate myself in the darkness. Once we had passed it, I used a star in the night sky as a marker. We passed near to our old house. I wondered whether Superman had moved back in. Best not to hang around and find out. We pressed on, heading for agricultural land. For just over a mile we headed northwest on a deception bearing (deliberately heading in the wrong direction), then swung south onto the correct bearing. I hoped this would be enough to confuse any RUF follow-up or search.

The next major obstacle was the main road we had to cross. We had heard rebel patrols driving up and down the road throughout the night and had planned to stake it out before crossing. In the event, I literally stumbled onto it. One minute I was forcing my way through thick vegetation, the next I had fallen down a bank and on-to the tarmac. I picked myself up, glanced both ways then legged it across, with the others close behind.

For the next hour, we scrambled around the side of a steep hill. By following difficult terrain we hoped to avoid any people, friendly or otherwise. But it was hard going underfoot and we kept falling over. Fortunately, we saw rebel checkpoints before they saw us. Usually, they gave themselves away by smoking, and we could see the glow of their cigarettes in the dark.

We nearly came a cropper when we inadvertently wandered straight into a village. I could make out the shape of hills far away, and as they were in the right direction I started walking towards them. Suddenly, a dog started barking and men started shouting. My eyesight had fooled me—the hills were actually huts, and they were only yards, not miles, in front of me. We turned and ran.

After an hour or so we stopped for a map check and I made a quick assessment. Paul and I were feeling strong, but Andy and Dave were moving too slowly. We took a drink from a communal water bottle. I told everyone to drink as much as they thought they needed. I only took a sip. I begrudged not drinking my fair share of the water, but our speed as a group was limited by the slowest man. So if I could help that man by giving him some of my share of the water, it would be doing us all a favour.

We reached the point at which I had always turned back on my morning runs. Now we were no longer on familiar ground, we would have to follow a compass bearing. With every step I knew we were getting further from the worst of the danger, and for a while I was actually enjoying myself. My mind started to wander, anticipating how good it would feel to be back in civilisation. *Beer, sleep, a soft bed* . . . A dull thud and a moan behind me brought me back to reality.

Dave had fallen. He got back up, but was now starting to struggle badly. His rapid, shallow breathing was a sure sign of heat exhaustion. I remembered my first-aid training: 'Cover the casualty with a cool, wet cloth and administer fluid.' Simple—if we'd only had any to spare. The best we could do was to take off our shirts and use them as fans to try to cool Dave down.

I thought of something else to try.

'Dave, have you got a sweat rag?' I whispered.

'Sure, mate, what for?'

'Give it here—I'll piss on it for you, and you can use it to cool your face.' He suddenly claimed to be feeling much better. We pressed on.

With only thirty minutes before daybreak, I started looking out for a good spot to lie up. We pushed on for another mile or so, along the side of some ploughed fields. This was relatively easy going but risky, as our tracks would be simple to follow, so I took advantage of some rockier ground to make another abrupt change of direction. We forced our way into the thickest clump of bushes we could find, pulling the branches back together behind us as we squeezed in. We managed to find a gap in some thorn bushes with enough room for the four of us to lie down. This was a good lie-up position. As long as we kept still and quiet, no one would be able to see or hear us and there were some overhanging branches to give us a bit of shade. We psyched ourselves for a long, hot wait.

I lost count of the number of insects that bit me as I lay there. We did have insect repellent with us but couldn't risk putting it on. Anybody walking nearby would be able to smell it. Despite the discomfort, all was going according to plan, and it was a good feeling. Kind of brazenly, Paul even took a photo. I began to feel more confident we might actually make it.

Inevitably, perhaps, pride was to come before a fall. Our carefully chosen lie-up position turned out to be right next to a village. We listened as the villagers started their daily routine. We were so close that we could hear the noise of water sloshing about in buckets from the well, and we could also hear rebel soldiers. We were in dire need of water, yet the well could have been on the other side of the world.

It was a long, hot day. There was not much shade, so we had to take turns sitting in it. We were almost on the equator and this was the hottest time of year. With the humidity, it felt as if we were in a sauna. We still had one more litre of water between us, but I'd given strict instructions not to touch it until the next night.

I'd been chewing a small piece of chewing gum for several days. It had long since lost any flavour. I offered pieces of it to my companions but it was too small to split, so we passed the gum round, taking it in turns to chew it for an hour or so each.

With my little short-wave radio pressed against my ear, I was able to monitor some of the frequencies being used by the UN and by the RUF, so I had a fair idea what was going on around the country.

Even in our bush, there was some light relief. It was a Saturday afternoon, when the BBC World Service broadcasts live football from the English Premiership. Today's featured match was Arsenal *v.* Chelsea and, as a dedicated Chelsea fan, I couldn't resist the temptation to listen in. (The others thought I was dutifully monitoring UN radio transmissions and I didn't put them right.) It was a close match but, with fifteen minutes to go, Arsenal scored the winning goal . . . I almost swore out loud.

The hours dragged by. We were all desperately craving water, but nobody complained and we kept these thoughts to ourselves.

By six o'clock in the evening, we'd been lying in the fierce tropical heat for over twelve hours without drinking. I took stock of our situation. As the crow flies, we were now just under four miles from Makeni, but had used considerable energy and most of our water to get there. Without water, we would not get much further. Dehydration had become as much the enemy as the RUF. Ideally, we would not leave our lie-up position until after midnight, when the locals would most likely be asleep. But with every hour that passed we would grow weaker and weaker. I suggested to the others that we drink our final water bottle now and move as soon as it was dark. I hoped that drinking our remaining water in one go would give us the physical and psychological boost we needed to reach a fresh water source. Everybody agreed.

Our map showed a dotted blue line meaning 'river—seasonal' about five miles away. Although it was still the dry season, we hoped there would be some water in the river. The deal was this: if we pushed ourselves hard, we would make it to the river. If the river turned out to be dry, then we were screwed.

As soon as it was dark, we skirted round the village. We continued on a bearing towards the river but soon found ourselves in almost impenetrable vegetation, which blotted out the moonlight. In the pitch darkness, I was literally fighting my way forwards, flailing with both arms to rip holes through the dense foliage and using my head and shoulders to burrow through the almost solid wall of trees and shrubs. I asked the others to take turns in front but they lacked the energy to break trail, so I crashed on, digging deep into my last reserves of strength. I was too knackered to feel much pain but was aware of trickles of blood running down my arms from numerous cuts and scrapes, and my uniform was getting slowly shredded. Our progress slowed to 100 yards an hour. The river we were aiming for was beginning to seem impossibly far away, let alone the safe haven, which was still over fifty miles away.

We reached a slight clearing, and collapsed in a heap. I could feel the group's negative vibes. I promised the others there would be water in the river, and that our strength would return once we drank. 'Just a few more miles. We can do it.'

Nature seemed against us, but luck was ultimately on our side and we stumbled across a path that had been cut through the vegetation. I couldn't worry too much about the risk, so just turned onto the path and kept going.

As point man, I felt dangerously exposed and, for the umpteenth time, wished I had a weapon. Physically, it was a relief to be on easier terrain, but we were now in greater danger. In the event the gamble paid off. After about a mile on the path, we reached an area where the jungle had been slashed and burnt. I left the path, not wanting to tempt fate any more than I had to. The terrain now consisted of knee- and groin-high stubble and stakes, strewn with fallen tree trunks and branches. It was hard going underfoot but at least we could see where we were headed. We could now make out probable RUF positions and were able to detour round them unseen. Thank God the RUF were not better soldiers—all their sentries seemed to be sitting by fires or smoking cigarettes, so we could see them before they saw us.

My memory goes a bit hazy at this point. I realised that I had stopped sweating, but not because I had cooled down. There was just no more liquid left in me to sweat out. Our mental faculties were going awry as, unable to regulate our body temperature by sweating, our brains were literally starting to stew.

Andy began to collapse. He kept begging, 'Just ten minutes. I need to rest.' I couldn't let him. I suspect that if he had lain down, he would never have got up again, and I told him so.

'Get up! If you stay here, you're dead. You're not staying here on your own, so that means we're dead as well, and I have no intention of dying so let's keep going.'

We staggered on, but then Andy toppled over again and seemed oblivious to our attempts to rouse him. Paul knelt down beside him then suddenly leapt back up again, saying, 'Andy, there's a large snake by your head.' Paul might have been bluffing, but if he was it was a moment of genius. Andy was up again, quick as a flash.

It took us four hours to cover the five miles to where we hoped the river would be. Every step was a huge effort, and all I could think about was water.

We reached a large ditch, banked by trees. We had arrived at the river. It was dry. We slumped back onto the ground, and sat there in silence, each man dealing with the disappointment as best he could. I lay back and looked at the stars above, perhaps searching for diving inspiration.

And then we heard a noise. Quietly at first, then louder and louder. Frogs!

'Where there's frogs there's got to be water!' I took a compass bearing on the frogs, and we headed towards them. Once we started moving, though, the frogs could hear us again and immediately stopped croaking. If we'd not stopped and sat there staring into space, we'd never have known they were there. I trusted my compass bearing, and, sure enough, we almost walked right into the large muddy pool that was their home.

Even in the moonlight, I could make out a scum of insect larvae and algae on the surface of the water, and there was a powerful stench of mud and rotting vegetation. But, in my uncritical state, I reasoned that if it was good enough for frogs, it was good enough for us.

Paul and I had handheld water filters with us, and we scraped the pond's surface scum aside and started pumping water into our bottles. The water was so full of silt that my pump soon broke. As well as filtering the water, we added drops of iodine and triple the normal dose of chlorine-based purifying tablets to kill anything harmful. The resulting water tasted more like something you'd use to clean the sink than a refreshing drink, but it did the trick. In our dehydrated state, if we drank too much too quickly, we could make ourselves ill, so we sat there for nearly two hours, drinking slowly, but forcing water down our throats until our stomachs felt bloated. I dreaded to think what might now be living in my guts and hoped any side effects would wait until we reached safety. We were also able to wash down the few scraps of bread we had with us. As we rehydrated, so our strength returned.

Feeling a little better, we continued on as best we could. Frustratingly, it clouded over. When we had prayed for total darkness in Makeni, we had got bright moonlight. Now we got the opposite. In the gloom it was impossible to progress without falling over. Every two or three paces I tripped over some obstacle hidden in the darkness, and seemed to use as much energy getting back on my feet as I did actually walking.

I walked with the compass in my hand, stopping every five paces to ensure I was still on the correct bearing. There were no visual points of reference such as the moon or stars or landmarks, so without a compass we'd have been walking round in circles.

I enforced a strict regime. One hour walking, five minutes' rest. One hour walking, five minutes' rest. Over and over. The going was relentless. Yomping was not pleasant that night.

Dehydration was now not such a problem, but fatigue was. By this stage, I hadn't slept for a week, and my mind was playing all sorts of tricks. It was getting harder and harder to tell the difference between what was real and what was not. My hallucinations became more and more extreme. I had to have several reality checks with my companions. If all four of us could see the same thing, then it was real. If only one or two of us could see it, then we ignored it.

Before first light, we took another bearing on some croaking frogs and made our way back to the 'river', looking for a lie-up position close to water but hidden in a forested area. A map check revealed we were now about nine miles from Makeni, still less than a quarter of the distance we needed to travel. The water here was even more disgusting than before and I wondered whether drinking it would do us more harm than good. We drank anyway. This seemed like a good moment to produce the treat that I had been saving for a special occasion: the can of baked beans that Anna had given me for my birthday. We enjoyed our one mouthful of beans each and as a bonus used the can to scoop up water, avoiding as many of the insect larvae swimming in the fetid pond as possible.

We needed to reassess our options. I reckoned we were now far enough from known rebel positions to make helicopter pick-up feasible. We agreed on this, and at first light set the satphone up.

I pressed the ON/OFF button. Nothing happened. I tried again. Still nothing. *Shit. It must be the battery. How to tell the others?*

I guessed that the phone had switched itself on as I had struggled through the bush, and the battery had drained.

Without the satphone working, we could not call for extraction by helicopter. Psychologically, we had all made the mistake of convincing ourselves we'd made it. Now we knew we had not, morale hit rock bottom. Two nights' forced march had taken us less than a quarter of the distance we needed to cover. Seizing the moment, Paul took a photo. We couldn't even force a grin for the camera. We just lay there, too tired to think, feeling nothing.

We must have fallen asleep, as the next thing I remember, two hours had passed and I was waking up with gentle rain falling on my face. I felt a little more human again. I woke the others up and we had another team talk. They thought that progress at night was too hard and we should consider moving by day. I conceded the point when it occurred to me that, if we took too long, there was a danger that our intended 'safe haven' might have fallen to the rebels. Reports on the World Service indicated that the RUF were still advancing relentlessly towards Freetown.

If we started moving by day, our tactics would have to change. We agreed we should gamble and attempt to enlist the help of friendly civilians. It would be impossible to avoid the local population during daylight, so why not find a guide who would know the jungle paths and be able to steer us clear of known RUF-controlled villages? This seemed a reasonable plan, and with nothing to gain by staying where we were, we continued on.

We soon came to the edge of the forested area and stopped again to study the agricultural land in front of us. We could see a couple of mud huts and an old man lying by a fire. We watched for a few minutes. There was no one else around. We could see the man was a farmer, and he looked too old to be a rebel.

We put on our UN baseball caps and approached the local farmer. He was very friendly but my sign language seemed to go over his head. I swapped a cigarette I was carrying for some water and a handful of nuts and we moved on to the next farm.

The farmer here had a wife and kids. A few more cigarettes changed hands, and I tried my sign language again. I read out some place names from the map. With each name, if I knew the place was controlled by the RUF I gave a 'thumbs down' sign and frowned. If I knew the place was not controlled by the RUF, then I gave a 'thumbs up' sign and smiled. They soon caught on. I read out the names of local villages and they gave me thumbs up or thumbs down. The nearest rebel-free village was called Yela, four or five miles away. One of the farmer's kids took us there and it was obvious that this village hated the RUF—several villagers were missing limbs thanks to the rebels. The chief talked to us through a fourteen-year-old interpreter called Alusayne, and told us his village had suffered terribly at the hands of the RUF. We explained that we had come to Sierra Leone to help the Sierra Leonean people, but the RUF had turned on us and killed our colleagues. He told us that hospitality to visitors was an integral part of Sierra Leonean culture, and was dismayed and upset by the RUF's behaviour. I asked the chief if there was a guide who could take us to Mile 91, and Alusayne, the interpreter, volunteered.

Alusayne was as hard as nails. He was suffering an attack of malaria and had an open wound on his abdomen which was dressed with a poultice of leaves and bark. He dismissed the injury as 'a gift from the RUF', but didn't elaborate further. And, for some reason, he never stopped smiling. He had never seen a map before and his only concept of distance was how long it took to walk somewhere ('fourteen hours to Mile 91 if we go fast'). This was not a good place to hang around as rebel patrols 'visited' regularly to gather food, so we filled our water bottles, ate a couple of the most delicious mangoes I've ever tasted, then set off again. We still had a forty-mile walk through RUF-held jungle to crack.

Even in his flip-flops, Alusayne had only one pace (fast) and he didn't like stopping. He pointed out that news of four white soldiers in the area would spread quickly and was keen to travel faster than the rumours. Every time we stopped for a drink, Alusayne rolled himself a small joint of cannabis. No wonder he smiled so much. He clearly knew all the bush paths like the back of his hand, and which routes the rebels tended to use. We still tried to avoid all habitation but, when this was impossible, we lay low while Alusayne scouted ahead.

If we had to go through a village that was clear of rebels, at least we were able to fill our water bottles from the well. We also made sure we paid our respects to each village chief, leaving generous tips, knowing that other UN escapees might be following in our footsteps.

I was impressed by the many locals who helped us, especially Alusayne. I asked him why he was prepared to risk his life to help us. He took a drag on his cigarette and replied wistfully, 'Well, I had nothing else to do today.'

It got hotter and hotter as the day went on, but we stuck to a good fast pace, spurred on by the thought that every step was a step closer to safety. We passed through vast forests and lush agricultural land. The scenery and the people were beautiful. I was almost beginning to enjoy myself again. For me, the tired legs, blistered feet and fear of death or capture made our surroundings even more absorbing. All my senses were primed to identify potential threats to my safety. So, as a bonus, I found I picked up all kinds of detail I would normally miss, like the noise of birds singing in the distance and the sight of monkeys playing in the trees. Never had mangoes tasted so divine or water been so refreshing, but by two o'clock that afternoon, we had been walking virtually nonstop for twenty hours, and our feet were in bits. I ordered a halt, to avoid exerting ourselves during the hottest part of the day, and we lay for two hours in the shade of a tree.

Our change of tactics was paying off. Moving by night we could have stumbled around for weeks. But with the benefits of daylight and a guide, we covered nearly twenty-five miles before dusk, arriving just north of a Kamajor village called Mbenti.

Mbenti lay on the south bank of the Rokel River which, here, marked the historical boundary between RUF and the Civilian Defence Force (CDF). But with the RUF advancing towards Freetown, we were not sure whether Mbenti would be friendly or not.

While we hid, Alusayne asked some local farmers, who assured him that Mbenti was still in CDF hands. On the map, the Rokel River looked a formidable obstacle. But Alusayne knew a spot where we were able to wade across. The river was about 200 yards wide at this point, but never more than waist deep, and was wonderfully refreshing to our tired legs.

As the sun was setting, we wandered into Mbenti. It had been a long day. I suggested to Alusayne that he stay the night with us in Mbenti, but he didn't want to hang around. I paid him generously—enough, I hoped, to pay for an operation for his wound and some extra for his village. I thanked him one final time. Still smiling, he headed off into the darkness, seemingly unperturbed at the thought of walking another twenty-five miles that night back to his own village.

Mbenti's chief was away but the Kamajor commander, Ibrahim, promised to protect us. Ironically, his fighters had disarmed to the UN just two weeks before, leaving him with only an ancient hunting rifle, machetes, and black magic to protect his village from the rebels. The nearest RUF position was less than a mile away, on the far bank of the river. Ibrahim asked his wife to slaughter a chicken for us to eat, then we were invited to sleep, surrounded by machete-wielding Kamajor hunters, who were quite happy to take on rebels armed with AK 47s or machine guns.

BACK HOME, the UK government had acted to prevent the collapse of UNAMSIL and pre-empt the mayhem that would ensue if the RUF captured Freetown. As we dined on chicken and rice with the Kamajors that evening, the advance elements of Britain's Joint Rapid Deployment Force were beginning to arrive in Sierra Leone.

They included the 1st Battalion of the Parachute Regiment and 42 Commando Royal Marines. The force's initial task was to secure the airport and evacuate foreign nationals before the rebels reached Freetown. Their secondary task was to bolster UN resolve and to provide a small body of highly trained professional soldiers who were not afraid to stand up to the RUF.

At one stage, the rebels had reached as close as twelve miles from Freetown and panic had set in. As the UN had disarmed many of the pro-government militias such as the CDF, there was no one else to counter the rebels, who were advancing almost unopposed.

It was now two days since we had last established communications with the outside world and, back in the UK, our next of kin had been told we were Missing in Action. Anna was calm and collected, but she was under no illusion about the dangers we had already escaped and how precarious our situation must now have been.

WE WERE STILL fifteen miles from Mile 91. We hoped the town was still occupied by a company of Guinean UN troops. Our feet were not in good condition, especially Dave's. He had lost most of the skin on the soles of his feet during our long hike the previous day. At hobbling pace, it was going to take at least another day to cover the remaining distance, so we sent the village messenger forward with a letter and my ID card, asking for a UN patrol to pick us up.

While we waited for him to return we ate, drank and tried to improvise a battery for the satphone. We scrounged as many torch batteries off the locals as we could lay our hands on. Paul wired them up in series and attached them to the phone. The batteries were not enough to power the satphone on their own, but at least, in Paul, we had a genuine expert on the matter. (His speciality was actually charging submarine batteries using nuclear reactors, but the theory must be the same.) Paul suggested we try leaving the torch batteries connected to the satphone to 'trickle charge' for an hour or so.

We waited impatiently and tried again. I hit the ON/OFF button. The light came on and the display powered up. *Welcome to Inmarsat . . . Please enter your PIN code . . .* I tapped the code in furiously. *Searching for satellite . . . Connecting with satellite . . . Please dial number now . . .* I started dialling. *Battery low . . . Battery empty.* And with that, the phone switched off.

'Shit.'

Paul was optimistic. 'Well, the principle's right. Let's try again but leave it even longer this time.'

1. Sierra Leone. A beautiful and fertile place, but in 2000 it was officially the poorest country in the world and in some areas male life expectancy was only twenty-six. 2. One of my tasks in Sierra Leone was disarming child soldiers. The average age of the rebel combatant was twelve. 3. On patrol, telling local rebels about the disarmament process. Pointing a camera at unfriendly rebels was often the best way to win them over. 4. Kamajor militiamen and Sierra Leone Army soldiers—in Sierra Leonean terms these were the good guys. 5. Andy Samsanoff (left) and me on the run. I hadn't slept for over a week and had been

allucinating badly all night. **6.** My fellow escapees (l to r), Lieutenant Commander Paul owland, Major David Lingard, me and Major Andy Samsonoff, on day one of the siege— efore the water ran out **7.** Foday Sankoh, leader of the RUF, at a disarmament centre. efore the ceasefire ended 25,000 weapons were handed in. **8.** Relaxing with Anna after scaping from Sierra Leone. Topically, we chose a climbing trip to East Africa. **9.** I'd just had y thirtieth birthday and was feeling fitter and stronger then ever. But three weeks after is photo was taken I was rushed to hospital paralysed from the waist down.

Before we had time to try the phone again, the messenger returned with good news. The Guineans still occupied Mile 91 and had promised to send out a patrol to escort us back to their position. We rewarded the villagers with our remaining cash and I gave Ibrahim my penknife. In due course, a Guinean patrol arrived, and we jumped into one of their pick-up trucks and stormed off towards Mile 91.

As we bumped along in the truck, I asked the patrol commander in my pidgin French what was happening in their area. His reply was understated: they were having some 'slight problems of their own with the rebels'.

Mile 91 was now an isolated pocket, as the surrounding area had fallen to the RUF. Remobilising Sierra Leone soldiers were piling into Mile 91, along with an assortment of pro-government militias, including the infamous West Side Boys. There was a danger that these militiamen would swap sides if they thought the RUF were winning. The Guinean commander expected imminent attack and tensions were high. To complicate matters, thousands of civilians were beginning to seek refuge in the area, some of whom would have been RUF infiltrators. He explained that ambushes were common on this section of track. I asked him what his anti-ambush drills were.

'*Rouler plus vite*' ('Driving faster').

We passed several groups of armed militiamen. Either they were pro-government or the Guinean commander's rally-driving anti-ambush technique worked well, and we made it to Mile 91 without having to stop.

The Guinean position at Mile 91 did not inspire confidence. They had a couple of machine guns overlooking the road they expected the rebels to approach down, but that was about it. No trenches, no lookouts, and no contingency plans. The Guinean soldiers had only twenty rounds of ammunition each. Their company commander explained that if they were issued any more than this, they tended to sell it on the black market to the rebels.

We now managed to improvise a power supply for the satphone using a car battery, and it partially recharged. The battery display indicated one minute twenty seconds of talk time. I phoned the UN HQ in Freetown. No one answered. I let the phone ring for thirty seconds. Now I had only fifty seconds of battery life left.

Our spirits sank. We surmised (wrongly) that Freetown had fallen to the rebels. *Who to phone next?* One of the last things I had done leaving the compound in Makeni was to wipe the satphone's memory. If you think you might be captured you 'sanitise' your kit.

This means making sure you have no marked maps, address books, jewellery, love letters or photos on you. If you are caught with any of these things, your interrogators can use them against you. Stupidly, I had committed to memory only Jim's number in Freetown. Forty seconds of battery life. *Who do I trust to pass on a message? Who'll answer the phone quickly enough? Hurry up! Think!*

I phoned Anna and she answered immediately.

'Hi. We're safe.' No time for what I really wanted to say to her. I told her where we were and what we were up to and trusted her to pass on the necessary information.

Andy and Dave borrowed a Guinean radio and managed to speak to the UN HQ in Freetown. The UN had evacuated from their normal headquarters, but only as far as the Mammy Yoko Hotel, a hotel complex on the very western tip of the Freetown peninsula. The Mammy Yoko was a considerably better position to defend than their original HQ in the city centre. Colonel Jim had relocated there and, to our amazement, he told us a British RAF helicopter was on its way to pick us up and would be there in fifteen minutes.

This seemed too good to be true, as the nearest airstrip was forty-five minutes' flying time away, but it turned out our previous abortive phone call back in Mbenti had been partially successful. We hadn't known it at the time, but the phone had connected briefly with the satellite, and UK electronic warfare 'assets' had managed to gain a fix on our position. This warranted putting a British helicopter on standby, ready to come and investigate.

In preparation for the helicopter pick-up, we used Andy's GPS to give an exact latitude and longitude of where we were standing and a suggested direction of approach for the helicopter. Finally, I spent a frenzied quarter of an hour before the helicopter arrived, cajoling and bribing with cigarettes as many trigger-happy factions as possible not to shoot at the helicopter. The local militiamen were used to UN helicopters, which were painted white, but a British one would be green, and might be regarded as hostile.

With thirty seconds to go, there was nothing to indicate the imminent arrival of our pick-up and an element of doubt crept in. But with fifteen seconds to go, we heard the deep throb of a Chinook helicopter approaching. It arrived exactly on cue.

'D'you think they'll let me on as a Kiwi?' Dave asked, only half in jest.

The downwash from the Chinook's powerful rotor blades sent debris flying everywhere, including the helmets of several Guinean soldiers who had not bothered to fasten their chin straps. Some of the local militiamen looked as if they were witnessing a UFO landing. Within an hour we were landing at the international airport near Freetown, where the newly arriving British forces were a welcome sight.

9   AFTERMATH

Before we could relax or even wash, we had to undergo a 'hot debrief' straight away. Who were the rebel leaders? Where did they live? What were their intentions? Where were the hostages being held? Did they have antiaircraft weapons?

The questions went on and on but it was immensely satisfying no longer to be constrained by being an unarmed observer. Sure, I was not actively going into battle against the RUF, but inside information can be as powerful a weapon as military might. After four months living among the RUF, I knew them inside out. Did I feel guilty dishing the dirt on them? Absolutely not. I had worked hard to try to help the RUF break the cycle of violence in which they seemed to be stuck. If the RUF were not willing to give peace a chance under the generous terms they had been offered, I had no sympathy. The RUF had violated my neutrality and trust and had murdered my UN colleagues in cold blood, so I had no moral qualms about taking sides against them now. I hoped that information I gave to the British debriefing teams would find its way to the pilot of the Sierra Leone Army's only helicopter gunship, which would soon be paying a visit to some of the rebel commanders' homes in Makeni.

Hot debrief over, I washed the dirt out of the cuts on my arms and legs and went for a stroll round the airport. The first unit to arrive in Sierra Leone was the 1st Battalion, the Parachute Regiment. From the two years I had spent working with the Paras, I knew many of the officers and NCOs, and it was surreal to keep bumping into old friends. It felt good now to be part of an organisation that was able to bring some order to the chaos in Sierra Leone. The UK had certainly not deployed a major task force just to save Andy, Paul and me. But I had known throughout my time in Sierra Leone that my actions would be backed by my country and this had given me the confidence to make difficult decisions. The timely arrival of the

British forces was the best back-up I could have hoped for.

We scrounged some rations off the Paras, then tried to rest. I was still too wired to sleep properly and spent most of the night observing the build-up of the British troops or watching CNN in the airport VIP lounge. Against the busy backdrop of a major military build-up, Paul, Andy, Dave and I sat on the balcony of the airport lounge and chatted long into the night. We all agreed that we were mildly pissed off to have had everything stolen from us by a bunch of thugs. Paul was sad to have lost his umbrella and I minded losing my yellow Frisbee, my address book and some tapes that friends had compiled for me. We laughed at the fact that doubtless there were now rebels dressed as Royal Marines commandos, sleeping on my camp bed and listening to my dubious music collection.

In the morning, I visited the field hospital to have my feet dressed properly, then jumped on board a Chinook with a company of Paras for the short flight across the estuary to Freetown itself. The Paras had established their HQ in the Mammy Yoko Hotel, alongside the UN HQ, and I was keen to track down Colonel Jim to thank him for the tireless vigil he had kept for us. While the rest of the UN had been evacuating, Jim and another Brit called Mike had set up their communications kit in a shack by the hotel swimming pool and maintained a twenty-four-hour watch, awaiting our call.

I finally found Jim's new office, hidden in a quiet corner of the hotel. Since he was simultaneously my boss, my teammate and my friend, I wasn't sure whether to salute, shake his hand or give him a hug. In the end, I did a bit of all three (unfortunately for Jim, as I'd been wearing the same clothes for over a week in the sweatiest place in the world).

Jim's office had an en suite bathroom and shower. He lent me a towel and razor and I immediately made the most of the facilities. What I didn't realise was that Jim had convened a meeting in the adjoining room, so I was a little surprised to wander out of the shower stark naked only to bump straight into a senior Iranian UN diplomat and a pair of British police hostage negotiators. But not as surprised as they were.

Afterwards, I was keen to find out what was happening to my UN colleagues and asked Jim what was going on. He explained that the RUF was still holding over 500 UN personnel hostage, including Parachute Regiment Major Andy Harrison, my next-door neighbour from London. I was relieved that we had managed to escape but there was not much cause for celebration while others were still missing.

BACK IN FREETOWN, the priority was stopping the RUF advance towards the capital. I tagged along with a patrol of Paras and we drove into the town centre to find out what was going on. Freetown was eerily quiet. There wasn't a civilian to be seen. The normally bustling markets were deserted and the shops were boarded up to prevent looting. The local population seemed terrified of what might be about to happen. Everyone had vivid memories of the mayhem and butchery that had taken place last time the rebels hit Freetown back in January 1999.

The only locals on the streets were groups of remobilising soldiers and Kamajors. No one asked too many questions about where they were getting their weapons from. Freetown was supposed to be a UN-controlled demilitarised zone, but guns just seemed to be an integral part of the local infrastructure.

The arriving British soldiers were finding it hard to distinguish between rebels and friendly militias, none of whom wore official uniforms or badges. After months in the country, I was a little more streetwise and was asked to brief various groups of Brits, based on my local knowledge.

I explained the telltale features of different factions, some of which were easy to spot, others less so. For example:

Weapons:	The RUF preferred AK 47s; pro-government militias tended to use British-made SLRs.
Hair:	The current RUF fashion was for flat-tops; the Kamajors went for the scraggy 'bushman' look.
Clothes:	The RUF in Freetown dressed like would-be members of an American rap band; the Kamajors stayed with the wild 'bushman' look.
Intoxication:	The Kamajors were normally stoned, which made them a bit deranged and incomprehensible; the RUF were normally stoned and drunk, which made them even more deranged and aggressive. It also gave them permanently bloodshot eyes.
Attitude:	The RUF strutted around like they owned the place; the Kamajors wandered around in a daze.

If the men were really aggressive—and wore uniforms—they were probably Nigerian peacekeepers. Some of the Nigerians, who had been 'peacekeeping' in Sierra Leone for four or five years, now resented the high-profile British presence and took it out on any British soldier they came across. It never got beyond a lot of shouting and posturing, but it took some delicate negotiations to remind everyone that we were all on the same side.

I also explained to the newly arrived British troops about the groups of kids that would inevitably crowd round their positions. Although some of these children might have been RUF spies, if you were nice to them they became an excellent early-warning system, as they knew exactly who everyone was. We weren't too bothered if, in turn, they passed on what they saw to the RUF—it was pretty obvious to everyone who the white soldiers with the guns were. Anyway, short of rounding up all these crowds of kids, beating them off with sticks (the traditional local method of crowd control), or shooting at them, it was impossible to make them go away. So it was as well to have them on your side.

The Paras had set up a roadblock on the main road that ran parallel to the beach. I wandered down to their position and, having got the briefing out of the way, asked them to keep a look-out while I went for a quick dip in the ocean. Despite the bank of armed men pointing their guns in my general direction as I swam, this was the best relaxation I'd had for weeks.

Once they had secured the airport, 1 Para established a secure cordon around the UN headquarters and began evacuating any foreign (that is, non-Sierra Leonean) nationals who wanted to leave the country. Within forty-eight hours, the British operation to evacuate noncombatants had been completed. Almost immediately, there was pressure from the UK for the British forces to withdraw promptly from Sierra Leone and avoid 'mission creep'—getting sucked into somebody else's civil war as one of the warring factions. However, the UK forces could not abandon UNAMSIL until it had regained some kind of control. So far, a timely show of British force had been enough to persuade the RUF to halt their advance without physically coming to blows. The UK military presence, though not strong in numerical terms (never more than 1,000 troops on the ground in comparison to the UN's 12,000), did a lot to reassure both the UN and the people of Sierra Leone that the RUF would not be able to capture Freetown. Not only were there 600 Paras guarding Sierra Leone's 'vital ground' (the airport, seaport and Freetown itself), but it was public knowledge that up to 1,000 Royal Marine commandos would be arriving in Sierra Leone in a couple of days. If this wasn't enough, RAF and Royal Navy Harrier jump jets made regular sorties from HMS *Illustrious*, one of Britain's two aircraft carriers, which was loitering just over the horizon. These air-presence sorties, overflying rebel strongholds and troop concentrations, showed the RUF what they would be up against if they took on the British forces or the UN troops they were there to support.

Two weeks after he fled into the bush, Foday Sankoh turned up in Freetown. With a group of bodyguards, he had tried to link up with his RUF fighters as they advanced towards the city. This was one of the reasons why the RUF had been so keen to reach the capital. Sankoh, however, never made it off the Freetown peninsula, as the arrival of the UK forces had effectively stopped the RUF in their tracks. On May 17, he was captured. He had re-entered Freetown, disguised as a woman, intending to bribe some Nigerians to smuggle him out of the country. Some locals saw through his disguise. He was handed over to an angry mob who beat him severely and shot him in the leg. They were about to rip him to pieces when a British patrol drove past and saved him from the lynch mob. Ironic, given the RUF's hatred of all things British. At the time of writing, Sankoh is still in prison, a fallen man awaiting trial for treason.

THE PARACHUTE REGIMENT'S ethos is to get in and out of an operation as quickly as possible, and they had reacted to this crisis with impressive speed. Having arrived, though, with only the kit they could carry on their backs, they lacked the logistical support for a prolonged stay. So 500 Marines from 42 Commando were now arriving to take over from the Paras. They travelled on board the helicopter carrier HMS *Ocean*. Thanks to HMS *Ocean*, the Marines had the self-sufficiency to stay as long as it took for the situation to stabilise.

I spent a couple of days showing an advance party of Marines around Freetown. Having spent so long as the unarmed underdog, I enjoyed being a part of what now felt like the strongest gang in town. I made a point of sewing my commando flashes back onto my uniform. I also took up an invitation to spend a couple of days on board HMS *Ocean* having a small but welcome fix of Britain—a roast dinner, warm beer and the football highlights as Chelsea beat Aston Villa 1–0 to win the FA Cup. Plus I was able to draw some clothes from the quartermaster to replace the kit stolen from me by the rebels in Makeni.

After a few days sleeping on someone's office floor in the UN HQ, Andy, Paul and I moved back into a rented house we had once shared with the other Brits working for the UN in Freetown. This was a little risky, as our night watchman was very good at sleeping but not very good at watching. What's more, the rebels knew exactly where we lived. Just to be safe, we invited several heavily armed Royal Marines from 42 Commando to come and live with us. With British soldiers now occupying their country, the RUF saw any British serviceman as a legitimate target. I'd learned my lesson the hard way and, given Sierra Leone's gun culture, reasoned: 'If you can't beat them, join them.' So I bought myself a Chinese-made AK 47 for ten dollars and felt a little safer.

I was worried to see RUF sympathisers hanging around outside the UN headquarters. Being in the RUF was not a crime in itself as the peace process was technically still ongoing. Some Sierra Leonean friends of mine offered to make these rebels 'go away' for a small fee (five dollars). I thanked them for the offer but decided that sponsoring extrajudicial assassinations might be deemed inappropriate and not the best career move. Instead, I paid them five dollars to help me find a guard dog. This was not easy as most Sierra Leonean dogs seem to have had all the aggression beaten out of them and we couldn't find many suitable candidates. We cruised the backstreets of Freetown and eventually tracked down a dog that at least had the guts to bark loudly at strangers. I suggested we gave it a macho-sounding name, like Ripper or Fangs. Unfortunately she would only answer to her existing name: Topsy. When we brought her into our compound for the first time, the change of environment completely freaked her out to the extent that she wet herself whenever she saw a stranger. With a little loving care and training, though, she soon regained her nerve and became a passable burglar alarm.

Andy, Paul and I were asked if we wanted to return to the UK to recuperate. We all declined the offer. We had an important role to play here, liaising between the UN and the newly arrived British forces. The military situation was still finely balanced: hundreds of UN soldiers were still being held hostage, including my friend and London neighbour Andy Harrison, and we were all keen to do what we could to help.

There was another, less positive reason for not returning home straight away: we needed to cool down emotionally and psychologically. I don't think I'd have been good company if I'd returned home immediately. Going straight from the madness of Makeni to the creature comforts of home was tempting, but I think it would have screwed me up mentally. I spoke to Anna at length and she agreed with me. I was longing to see her again, but not until I had calmed down a bit. Every kid I saw still looked like a rebel, and I didn't want this to happen at home. The best form of therapy after our experiences was to keep busy and stay involved with what was going on.

A week after the British forces arrived, the UN started to find its feet again and, as UN Military Observers, we still had a job to do. We received reports about the West Side Boys militia who, at this stage, were cooperating with the UN and UK forces. The West Side Boys had managed to recapture the town of Rogberi Junction from the RUF. Rogberi Junction was no more than a collection of mud huts, but it was strategically important as Sierra Leone's two main highways met there. This was the place where the RUF had previously used 'Trojan horse' tactics to overcome the Nigerian peacekeepers stationed there. The RUF had donned the uniforms of captured Zambian soldiers and forced their drivers to take them in Zambian armoured cars through UN checkpoints. The Nigerian soldiers had not realised what was happening and several of them had paid for this deception with their lives. The West Side Boys now claimed to have discovered the bodies of executed UN soldiers in Rogberi Junction, and Andy Samsonoff and I were given the task of going to investigate. We were accompanied by a heavily armed patrol of Nigerians, who had temporarily abandoned all their UN insignia and readopted their Nigerian Army colours.

We headed for Rogberi Junction in the Nigerian armoured cars, driving at breakneck speed through bandit country. When we reached our destination, the town had been burnt to the ground as a final spiteful gesture by the RUF before they retreated.

The West Side Boys took us to the edge of the town, a couple of hundred yards behind the front line. The stench of rotting flesh made us gag, made worse by the knowledge that this was human flesh. The bodies had been lying in the hot tropical sun for nearly two weeks and there was not much left of them. You didn't have to be a forensic scientist to work out what had happened here. Some of the bodies were dressed in Nigerian uniforms and were still propped up in their trenches where they had been shot. At least these guys had died fighting. Other bodies found nearby, in Zambian battle dress, had been tied to trees and dismembered. This is what the RUF had done to the Zambian drivers after they no longer needed them.

I picked up a torso and, fighting the urge to vomit, I searched the dead man's pockets and found his passport and ID card. We moved quickly from body to body and extracted whatever documentation we could. It was not a healthy place to hang around for long and we had no idea how long the lull in the battle would last. I asked a few local militiamen to help Andy and me collect the human remains and bury them in one of the abandoned trenches. We made a sketch map of where the mass grave was, so that the bodies could be disinterred and repatriated when the security situation allowed. As I left, I caught sight of two bored-looking combatants playing football with a skull.

This made me angry and I shouted over to them, 'What the hell d'you think you're doing? Show some respect!'

The man with the 'ball' misunderstood me, maybe thinking I was asking to join in their kick-about, and he neatly flicked the skull in my direction. I resisted the urge to kick it back, instead picking it up and placing it in the temporary grave. The sad fact was, it was easier to get hold of a human skull than a football. This was just another sorry example of how cheap life had become in Sierra Leone.

Less than a week later, on May 24, 2000, two Western journalists, Kurt Schork of Reuters and a cameraman called Miguel Gil Moreno de Mora, had made their way to Rogberi Junction, looking for a story—and they found one. They wandered into an RUF ambush and were hacked to death.

I HAD FULLY EXPECTED never to see the armed Kenyans from Makeni again. On the day we reached Freetown, the Kenyans had sent a radio message to the UN HQ reporting that they would attempt to fight their way out of Makeni. We knew some of them had had virtually nothing to eat or drink for over a week and they were on their last legs. We waited anxiously for news.

We later heard the full story. With no formal direction from UN HQ, the Kenyan commanding officer had ordered his exhausted men to attempt to fight their way out. Under cover of the first decent rainstorm of the wet season, 'A' Company were able to bulldoze their way out of the compound, driving straight through the mudbrick wall to fool the waiting rebels. They burst out, all guns firing, and drove in a convoy through the backstreets of Makeni to link up with 'D' Company and their Battalion HQ on the north side of town. As a column, they then fought their way north to Kabala, which was still being held by the Sierra Leone Army. They were ambushed a total of eleven times and took heavy casualties. The survivors were then stuck in Kabala for another three weeks before being airlifted out by a combination of UN helicopters and British Chinooks.

I had an emotional reunion with my Kenyan colleagues, all the more so as several of their number hadn't made it. Some of their accounts were heart-rending. Like the Kenyan who'd been badly injured during the RUF attack on the DDR camp. His colleagues thought he was dead but friendly civilians had rescued him and were nursing him in their house. The injured Kenyan had sent a messenger with a letter to his comrades, asking them to come and find him or at least give the messenger money or medicine to pass to him. The Kenyans gave the messenger some money and asked him to bring their injured colleague to the camp. The brave messenger later returned with the injured Kenyan lashed to the back of a motorbike. But word of this had leaked to the rebels and, as the motorbike 'ambulance' tried to enter the compound, both messenger and casualty were gunned down. For good measure, the rebels also slaughtered all the members of the messenger's immediate family.

After everything the Kenyan soldiers had been through, the UN system unbelievably did not allow the survivors a free phone call home. And even a short call on a satellite phone cost more than their monthly wages. So Jim and I let them use our British Army-issue phone instead. Some of their families back in Kenya had been wrongly informed that their loved ones were dead, and it was moving to hear these battle-hardened Masai warriors telling their shocked and happy wives that they weren't widows after all.

As for Fergus, he and his colleagues from DfID had also escaped from Makeni by the skin of their teeth. At first light on the same day that we had made a break for it, Fergus walked boldly and calmly out of the compound into the hands of the waiting rebels. Showing astonishing nerve, Fergus somehow persuaded Colonel Kallon to let him and his fellow aid workers go. Everyone else who had tried appealing to the rebels had either been killed or was still being held captive. I don't know exactly what Fergus said, but his charm—and several thousand dollars—obviously did the trick. Escorted by Kallon, Fergus and his team then drove out of rebel territory.

I received a message from a Nigerian sentry in Freetown that a man called Usman Kamara had turned up at the checkpoint outside the Mammy Yoko Hotel and was asking to see me. Usman was a teacher who had helped me to organise a football tournament among some teams of schoolkids in Makeni back in February. I had given Usman a pair of shoes to say thank you and we had become good friends. We went for a drink together and he told me what had happened to him and his family, who had been forced to flee their home.

Like most Sierra Leoneans, Usman knew from bitter experience that it was always civilians who suffered the most during fighting. He had chosen, not for the first time in his life, to take his wife and family into a squalid refugee camp rather than live under the RUF. As soon as the civil war had started up again, the RUF had begun 'recruiting' in Makeni. Both Usman and his six-year-old son Mohammed were in the right age bracket for recruitment. Rather than join them, Usman had joined a 10,000-strong column of refugees from Makeni and walked with his family to safety, carrying what possessions they could. Usman's wife, Mariatu, had given birth to a baby boy halfway through their four-day trek. Gobsmacked by this, I asked if there was anything I could do to help. He thanked me but said no. Before I left for the UK I gave him some money to set himself up with a small business—as a teacher, he had not earned a penny for three years.

What of Andy Harrison, the Parachute Regiment major captured by the rebels? I had been following developments closely and his full story now came out. He had been working in an UNMO team in Kailahun, a desolate town in the southeast corner of the country. Just as I had done in Makeni, he had enjoyed relatively cordial relations with the local RUF commanders until the day I disarmed the rebels in Makeni. That day, Andy was invited to the house of the commanding officer of the RUF Kailahun Battalion with his UN team leader and some Indian peacekeepers. The meeting started amicably enough but, halfway through, the RUF commander announced there would be a 'peaceful protest' and that all the UN personnel present would be detained. At this point, around fifty armed rebels stormed the room and overpowered the Indian peacekeepers, Andy and his team leader. The RUF stated that the UN personnel would be held in retaliation for the alleged UN detention of the ten RUF 'deserters' in Makeni. These were the ten rebels we had disarmed in good faith.

Andy and his colleagues were dragged from the room and driven to a rebel stronghold in the village of Geima, on the Sierra Leone/Liberia border. The volatile atmosphere came to a head when guards severely beat one of their colleagues for stealing a watch from one of Andy's group. The rebel soldier was taken away and executed. Andy found it worrying that the rebels were prepared to kill one of their own over such a trivial issue. This did not bode well for his own safety.

That afternoon, Andy was told he was going to be released but, as he drove back towards Kailahun, escorted by the rebels, he was suddenly ordered back to Geima at gunpoint. He was thrown into a shed on the outskirts of the village. That evening, Andy was joined by other UN hostages, including a Russian naval officer called Andre, who was to become Andy's closest friend for the next two months.

As the security situation across the country deteriorated and we had started fighting for our lives in Makeni, so the atmosphere in Geima worsened. Andy and Andre, the two white officers, received the brunt of the harsh treatment. Andy was told on several occasions that he was about to be executed in retaliation for the deaths of the RUF soldiers killed by my Kenyan colleagues, and he was beaten repeatedly. On one occasion, a rifle was held to his head and he was told to 'kneel down and prepare to die'. Andy refused, saying if they were going to shoot him, they would have to shoot him standing up. This act of defiance earned him a savage beating, but ultimately his bravery impressed even his captors and he was given a stay of execution.

Nationwide, frantic efforts were being made behind the scenes to split the RUF leadership. Britain and the UN were conducting PsyOps—psychological operations or military spin doctoring— to convince Andy's RUF captors that the rebels in Makeni were acting against the wishes of the overall RUF leadership. A wedge was being driven between the RUF in the Northern Province (Makeni) and the RUF in the Eastern Province (Kailahun and Geima). The Revolutionary United Front turned out not to be par- ticularly 'united'. This PsyOps campaign, together with Andy's cool- headedness, was to save his life.

The rebels made it clear that if any of the UN personnel escaped, the remainder would be executed. Andy's team agreed that if they were to attempt an escape, then it would only be if they could all get out together. If any one of the team was shot, then escaping would become an individual decision.

The news that 1 Para had landed in Freetown was not good news for Andy. If the Paras came to blows with the RUF in Freetown, their Kailahun counterparts would surely not miss the chance to exact personal revenge on the British paratrooper in their clutches. Andy passed a message to the rest of his captured team, telling them that if 1 Para inflicted any casualties on the RUF, he would have to attempt to escape. He spent the next few days straining to hear each BBC World Service news report on the guards' radio.

In Kailahun, the rest of Andy's team had also been overpowered, beaten and held in their own house until May 9, when they too were moved to Geima. As had happened to the Kenyans and us in Makeni, the two companies of armed Indian peacekeepers in Kailahun were surrounded in their camps. Andy's team tried repeatedly to persuade their captors to let them return to their house in Kailahun.

After eleven days in captivity, a groundswell of local opinion demanded that the RUF move Andy and his fellow captives back to the house in Kailahun. Here, their conditions improved slightly but they were still hostages.

With the British troops in Freetown becoming more active, Andy knew that to stay isolated in town was becoming increasingly dangerous. With two colleagues, he decided he had to try to reach the Indian peacekeepers' defended location. In the end, the three of them simply told their guards that they had been summoned to see the RUF commanding officer, then walked boldly out of the house and into town. As they strode off, resisting the overriding urge to look back, they realised that their bluff had worked.

The other two made their way to the Indian peacekeepers, but Andy actually did go and speak to the RUF commanding officer in an attempt to secure the release of those left in the house. Amazingly, he persuaded the rebel warlord to allow the whole team to visit the Indians' position 'to wash'. Andy shepherded his somewhat confused colleagues into the Indian compound. Once in, they were not going to leave. Not surprisingly, the RUF were furious and repeatedly attempted to force them out. But the Indian troops, all Gurkhas, were well armed and had a strong defensive position which the rebels failed to overrun. Two days later, the Pathfinder Platoon (the Paras' specialist reconnaissance unit) killed a number of rebels near Freetown. Andy had removed himself from the rebels' clutches just in time.

Andy and the Indians were besieged in their new location for another two months. The RUF did occasionally let resupply convoys into the town, and we had managed to smuggle a satphone in to him, hidden in a container of cooking oil. From then on, Andy could at least speak to the outside world. He was adamant that there should be no attempt to rescue him that might in any way jeopardise any other UN personnel.

Eventually—when the RUF refused to allow in any more convoys—the UN, with British support, mounted an operation to extract all the UN soldiers in Kailahun, including Andy. The operation was codenamed Op Kukri (the name of the Gurkhas' fighting knife). At dawn on Friday, July 14, 2000, in a driving rainstorm, two British Chinooks extracted Andy's team and nineteen injured

Indians. With helicopter gunship and artillery support, the remaining Indians broke out and linked up with the rest of their battalion in the nearby town of Daru.

Andy was subsequently awarded an MBE for his exemplary conduct throughout these episodes.

OVER A YEAR LATER, the RUF has been brought back into the peace process. While Sankoh remains in prison, awaiting trial for treason, other RUF commanders have fared a little better. Colonel Bao is still the RUF's Chief of Security. Colonel Kallon, the RUF commander who led the attack on the UN and killed my Kenyan colleagues, was recently promoted to brigadier.

Major General Jetley, the Indian officer in charge of UNAMSIL, was short-toured as the overall military commander. He was replaced by Lieutenant-General Daniel Opande who—perhaps coincidentally—is a Kenyan officer.

As of September 2001, UNAMSIL and the disarmament process appear to be back on track. UNAMSIL's strength has increased from 12,000 to nearly 17,000. As I write, it is still the biggest UN mission in the world. The RUF still controls two-thirds of Sierra Leone but they have now allowed UNAMSIL back into their territory and some have even disarmed. Why the apparent change in attitude? When the main body of British troops withdrew in June 2000, a British Military and Advisory Training Team (BMATT) stayed behind in Sierra Leone. Several hundred strong, it has provided the backbone needed to shore up the previously ramshackle Sierra Leone Army. The BMATT has trained several thousand soldiers since then and has helped reorganise the command infrastructure of the Sierra Leonean Ministry of Defence. For the first time in over a decade, the Sierra Leone Army is once again a credible force and the RUF realise that ultimately they're not going to win the war. Faced with a choice of either military defeat at the hands of the Sierra Leone Army or cooperation with UNAMSIL, it's not surprising that the rebels are at least going through the motions of re-entering the peace process.

One thing is sure, though: the RUF still hold the diamond mines and they are unlikely to give them up without a fight.

MY SIX-MONTH TOUR in Sierra Leone was over at the end of June. On the morning I was to leave Freetown, I awoke in a feverish sweat with a headache from hell. For a moment, I feared another malarial attack—until I noticed I was still fully dressed, and remembered I had been trying to have a drink the night before with every different nationality involved with UNAMSIL. That meant a lot of beer. Then I noticed I was wearing a Chinese Red Army uniform. Andy brought me a coffee and explained that I'd swapped clothes with a Red Army major called 'Harry the Spy' halfway through the evening . . . I stuck to mineral water and orange juice on the flight home.

After everything I'd been through, I was happy to finish my tour with nothing worse than a bad hangover. I had survived essentially unscathed the threat of armed and hostile rebels, and the punishing rigours of heat and thirst. I was now looking forward to going home. But a tiny part of Sierra Leone had got through my defences. It was invisible and, for now, lying low.

A FINAL TEST OF NERVE

Our tours in Sierra Leone over, we all took up other posts. Dave is back with his regiment in New Zealand. Paul is an instructor at Britannia Royal Naval Academy, teaching new entry naval officers. Andy has completed a six-month tour in Kosovo and is currently back out in Sierra Leone with his regiment, training new recruits in the Sierra Leone Army. Looking back, I realise the four of us were an assortment of servicemen with totally different areas of experience and expertise thrown together in an extraordinary situation. And I couldn't have asked for a braver group of men to break out with. Had one of us dithered as we climbed over that mud wall, I don't believe that any of us would have made it.

I meet up with Andy and Paul from time to time, to catch up over a beer. We've always got plenty to talk about—it's easier to get stuff off your chest with someone who has been through the same things as you. Even if this means joking about events that would seem taboo or shocking in normal conversation—you get some odd looks in the pub when you are casually discussing cannibalism.

THE FIRST THING I did when I got back from Sierra Leone was to have a belated thirtieth-birthday party (three different people gave me Frisbees). Then I returned to Africa for my summer holidays, on a climbing trip to Kenya with Anna. We trekked up Kilimanjaro to acclimatise, then attempted a technical, multi-day rock climb on the north face of Mount Kenya. We were forced to retreat after it snowed heavily while we were bivvying on a small ledge, but summited by another, easier route. From the friends I had made in Sierra Leone, I was able to do some handy name-dropping among Kenyan soldiers at the numerous army checkpoints near Nairobi. The Kenyan battalion I had been with had, deservedly, been hailed as heroes in their home country, and I enjoyed being associated with them. After Sierra Leone, I was well acclimatised and climbing strongly. I was feeling stronger, fitter and tougher than ever before. Unfortunately for me, however, this was not to last.

At the beginning of September 2000, I began my next posting—as a staff officer in the Directorate of Naval Manning in Portsmouth. Three weeks in, the intricacies of 'strategic manpower planning' were just starting to make some sense. After a particularly mind-bending Thursday morning I had gone for a run at lunchtime to clear my mind. It was a wet and windy day and I remember deliberately jumping in all the puddles as I ran around the dockyard. I felt a slight pain between my shoulder blades, but thought nothing of it. I had a shower and went back to the office. An hour later, I was sitting behind my desk, staring at a computer screen full of numbers, when I felt my left leg go numb. I assumed it was just the way I was sitting so got up off my seat, strolled around the office and sat back down. Then my right leg went to sleep. Then the numbness began spreading up my body and my vision started going funny.

By the time I was rushed to hospital later that night, I was effectively paralysed from the waist down, with shooting pains in my back and head. In Accident and Emergency, I was initially told I had broken my back. I thought this unlikely as I'd been sitting at my desk when it happened, and an X-ray soon confirmed my scepticism. Next my legs went into spasm. There was something pressing on my spinal cord that was affecting my nervous system. If it was a tumour, they would have to operate that night. This sounded serious. For the second time in a couple of months, I phoned my father and asked him to tell my mother a little white lie so as not to worry her unduly. Anna, no stranger to spinal injuries herself, did her best to reassure me.

I lay awake on my hospital bed all night, worried but grimly amused that my luck appeared to have run out in this way. I entertained myself with thoughts of Sierra Leonean witch doctors pushing pins into my effigy.

The next morning, British doctors were pushing pins into my body for real. They were checking for loss of sensation and I couldn't feel a thing below my waist. I had one of the country's top neurologists looking after me, but it seemed the most sophisticated method of checking for nerve damage was to stick a needle in my arse and watch to see if I flinched. I didn't.

The doctors carried out dozens of tests over the next few weeks: more X-rays, brain scans, blood tests, lumbar punctures and general proddings. Samples of my blood and spinal fluid were sent to laboratories around the country, including the School of Tropical Medicine and even Porton Down, Britain's research establishment for biological warfare. One by one, the doctors eliminated possible causes of the symptoms: spinal fracture, meningitis, tuberculosis, cancerous tumours on my brain and spine, Guillain-Barré syndrome, multiple sclerosis and AIDS.

They eventually concluded that I had carried back an unwanted memento of Sierra Leone in the form of a tropical virus, which was now living in my spine. The resulting swelling in my spinal cord was causing nerve damage—a condition called virally induced acute transverse myelitis. Whether this was from something I had eaten, drunk, been bitten by, or caught from my rodent room-mates back in Makeni, I shall probably never know.

After a few days, the spasms had worn off sufficiently for Anna to be able to push me around in a wheelchair, but more than anything I wanted to get out of hospital and go home. The doctors told me they would let me go when I could make my own way to the toilet, twenty feet away. After a week of practising with sticks I could manage it, but those twenty feet felt as difficult as fifty miles through the jungle in Sierra Leone. In the end, my body fought off the virus on its own, but I have been left with significant neurological damage.

A year later, it's like recovering from a stroke. My left leg is especially weak and I have almost no feeling in either leg from the knee down. Every morning when I wake up it feels like my feet have been in a bucket of ice-cold water. Sometimes they tingle, sometimes they ache and sometimes they feel nothing at all. On occasions my legs shake uncontrollably. I am told that these symptoms may continue to wear off slowly but some of the damage will be permanent. The physical part I can cope with, but tests have shown that the virus also attacked my brain. When I was told I had minor brain damage, it at least helped explain the short-term memory loss, poor concentration span and insomnia I have been suffering. None of these made an ideal starting point for the master's degree I've just embarked upon! I feel like I have a permanent hangover. It is all very frustrating.

Despite my condition, I can think of nothing more demoralising than complete inactivity, so I've been 'back on the rock'—an interesting experience with numb feet and wobbly legs. Scary for me, but worse for Anna on the other end of the rope, faced with the prospect of fifteen stone of damaged Royal Marine landing on her head! Still, I have been determined to continue life as normal as much as possible.

The novelty of sick leave soon wore off and I found that work was the best therapy, and kept me sane, despite not firing on all cylinders. The Marines have been immensely supportive, especially my last boss, Joss, who not only did my job for me when I was off work, but had the patience to bear with me when I went back to work and spent the best part of six months asking him stupid questions.

In some ways, I would rather have had a concrete, visible injury that I could point to and come to terms with—even a missing limb. Not knowing exactly what is wrong with you, or how bad or good it is going to get, is mentally as well as physically debilitating. It sounds bigheaded, but I was used to being one of the best at whatever I set out to do, and the thought of not being able to work hard and play hard is a pretty desperate prospect.

I still consider myself lucky, though; West Africans with 'wobbly leg syndrome' don't even have access to a doctor, let alone the safety net that I have had to catch me and look after me, and I try to look on the bright side. I know that when you go climbing, you can get a buzz from performing near your limits, regardless of what those limits are. I hope this applies to other walks of life.

I like to think that in a couple of years I'll be able to look back on the whole setback and see it as another life-enriching experience. Anna has been a great role model in this respect; she has shown nothing but determination and optimism in overcoming her own physical trauma. I'm inspired by her zest for life following the accident, which threw things into perspective for both of us. And whatever else happens, we know we'll always have each other.

I may not be climbing many physical mountains right now, but I will do my best to scale the other peaks ahead of me. As far as I'm concerned, there are plenty more adventures to come.

MAJOR PHIL ASHBY

Despite the ordeals described in *Unscathed*, Phil Ashby is still positive about his time in Sierra Leone. 'For every devil I met there I met five angels. It's wonderful to see how people can make the most out of a really, really bad time—that was something I found incredibly life-enriching. Things in Sierra Leone are still not perfect, but are basically looking good. There are some loose ends to tie, and a war-crimes tribunal has been set up. I've been involved in that and have been asked to give evidence, which, in turn, is helping me to close that chapter in my own life.'

Thankfully, Ashby's health has improved since he wrote the book. 'My fitness is now back to ninety per cent strength, and although it's that extra ten per cent that makes the difference between being a commando and working behind a desk, I feel that once again I've been incredibly lucky. Estimations vary, but one doctor told me the disease I had has a fifty-per-cent mortality rate, and those who do survive often spend the rest of their lives in a wheelchair, so it could have been a lot worse.'

Although he has the occasional 'wobble' and has no sensation in his legs from the knee down, Ashby is still planning adventures. 'I'm hoping to be part of a team that's entering a ski race to the North Pole. I'm not sure if I'll be fit enough, but I'm hoping that even if I'm firing on only three out of four cylinders, I'll still be stronger than some of the other guys. I'll be skiing on the flat so it's not far to fall if my legs do give out, and a perk of not being able to feel my feet is that I won't mind the blisters!'

Ashby will soon be swapping life in the forces for a new life as a civilian, although he's not sure yet where he will be based. His wife Anna works for the Foreign Office and he plans to go with her if she is offered a foreign posting.

'I've had a fantastic time in the Marines, but I'd rather quit while I'm ahead. My dream job now would be to become an adventurer, to go off, come back to tell people about it and write it up, before heading off somewhere else. I can see a lot of attractions to that. Life's a big adventure, and I want to see what else is out there.'

ACKNOWLEDGMENTS AND PICTURE CREDITS: *Hornet Flight*: pages 6–8: Neil Gower; page 151 © Barbara Follett. *Year of Wonders*: pages 152–154: The Bridgeman Art Library/John Sherrin; page 287 © Gerrit Fokkemar. *The Analyst*: pages 288–290: Gettyone Stone; page 429 © Jerry Bauer. *Unscathed*: Pages 430–431: © Royal Marines; page 432: Richard Rochester; pages 468–469: photographs as numbered: 1, 2: Pete Webb; 4: Matthew Ford; 5: Studio 16 Photography, Edinburgh; 6, 7: Royal Marines; pages 518–519: photographs as numbered: 1, 2, 3, 4, 7: Richard Rochester; 5, 6: Paul Rowland; 9: Huan Davies; page 539 © Michael Trevillion; all other photographs: Major Phil Ashby.

DUSTJACKET CREDITS: Spine from top: Neil Gower; The Bridgeman Art Library/John Sherrin; Gettyone Stone; © Royal Marines.

Printed by Maury Imprimeur SA, Malesherbes, France
Bound by Reliures Brun SA, Malesherbes, France